MOGHUL

Other books by Alan Savage:

OTTOMAN

MOGHUL

Alan Savage

Macdonald

A Macdonald Book

First published in Great Britain in 1991 by
Macdonald & Co (Publishers) Ltd, London & Sydney

Typeset by Leaper & Gard Limited, Great Britain
Printed and bound in Great Britain by
BPCC Hazell Books
Aylesbury, Bucks, England
Member of BPCC Ltd.

British Library Cataloguing in Publication Data
Savage, Alan
Moghul.
I. Title
823.914 [F]
ISBN 0 356 19700 X

Macdonald & Co (Publishers) Ltd
165 Great Dover Street,
London SE1 4YA

A member of Maxwell Macmillan Pergamon Publishing Corporation

'A *savage place! as holy and enchanted*
As e're beneath a waning moon was haunted
By woman wailing for her demon-lover!
And from this chasm, with ceaseless turmoil seething,
As if this earth in fast thick pants were breathing,
A mighty fountain momently was forced.'

Kubla Khan
Samuel Taylor Coleridge

CONTENTS

BOOK THE FIRST — THE MEN FROM THE NORTH

Chapter 1 The Envoy
Chapter 2 The Land of the Peacock
Chapter 3 The Lion
Chapter 4 The Moghul
Chapter 5 The Empire

BOOK THE SECOND — THE PHOENIX

Chapter 6 The Fugitive
Chapter 7 The Traveller
Chapter 8 The Homecoming
Chapter 9 The Return of the Moghul
Chapter 10 Akbar

BOOK THE THIRD — THE EMPEROR

Chapter 11 Shah of Shahs
Chapter 12 The Bride
Chapter 13 The Rebel
Chapter 14 The Parricide
Chapter 15 The Executioner

BOOK THE FOURTH — THE GREAT MOGHUL

Chapter 16 The Prodigal
Chapter 17 The Princess
Chapter 18 The Avenger
Chapter 19 The Couple
Chapter 20 Return of the Moghul

BOOK THE FIFTH THE COMPANY

Chapter 21 The Tyrant
Chapter 22 The Betrothal
Chapter 23 The Outrage
Chapter 24 The Fury
Chapter 25 The Flight

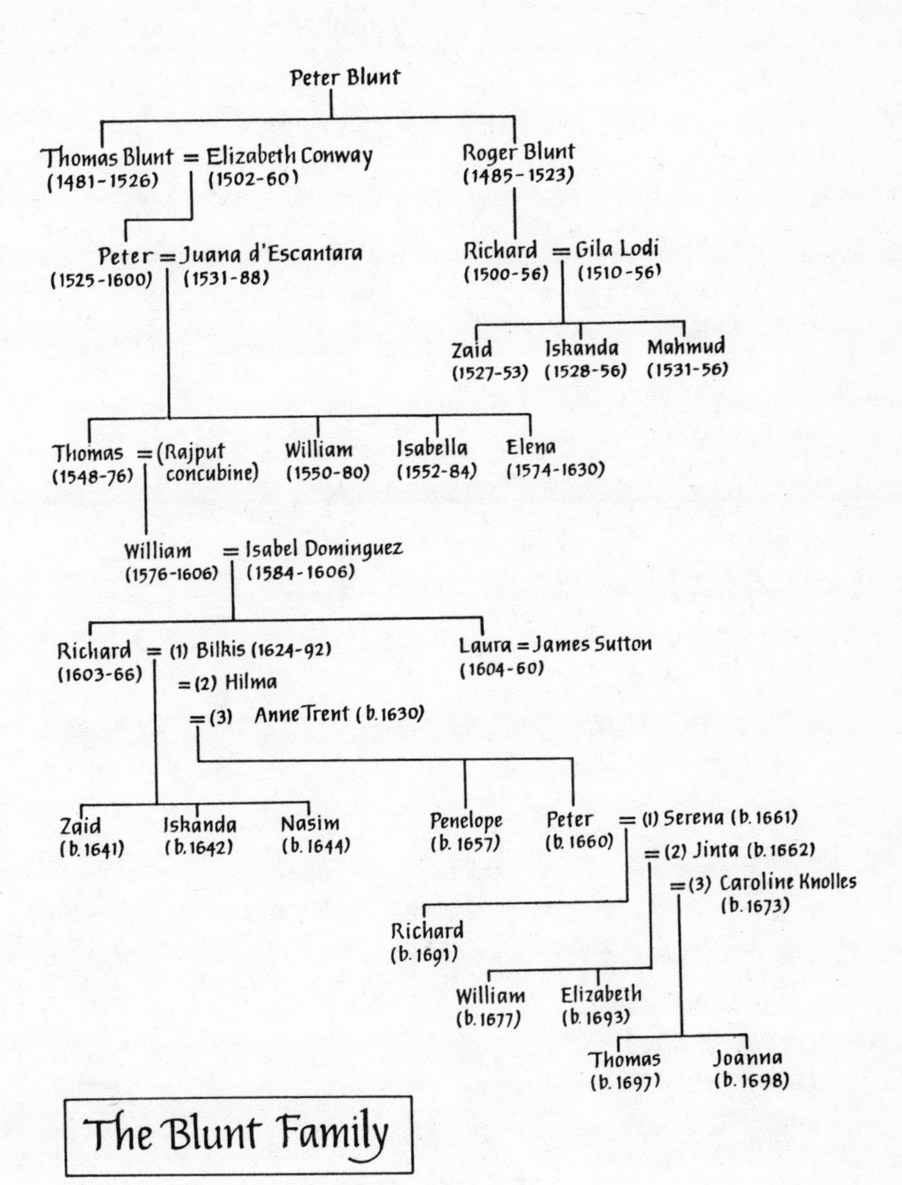
Peter Blunt
Thomas Blunt = Elizabeth Conway
(1481-1526) (1502-60)
Roger Blunt
(1485-1523)
Peter = Juana d'Escantara
(1525-1600) (1531-88)
Richard = Gila Lodi
(1500-56) (1510-56)
Zaid
(1527-53)
Iskanda
(1528-56)
Mahmud
(1531-56)
Thomas = (Rajput concubine)
(1548-76)
William
(1550-80)
Isabella
(1552-84)
Elena
(1574-1630)
William = Isabel Dominguez
(1576-1606) (1584-1606)
Richard = (1) Bilkis (1624-92)
(1603-66)
= (2) Hilma
= (3) Anne Trent (b. 1630)
Laura = James Sutton
(1604-60)
Zaid
(b. 1641)
Iskanda
(b. 1642)
Nasim
(b. 1644)
Penelope
(b. 1657)
Peter = (1) Serena (b. 1661)
(b. 1660)
= (2) Jinta (b. 1662)
= (3) Caroline Knolles
(b. 1673)
Richard
(b. 1691)
William
(b. 1677)
Elizabeth
(b. 1693)
Thomas
(b. 1697)
Joanna
(b. 1698)
The Blunt Family

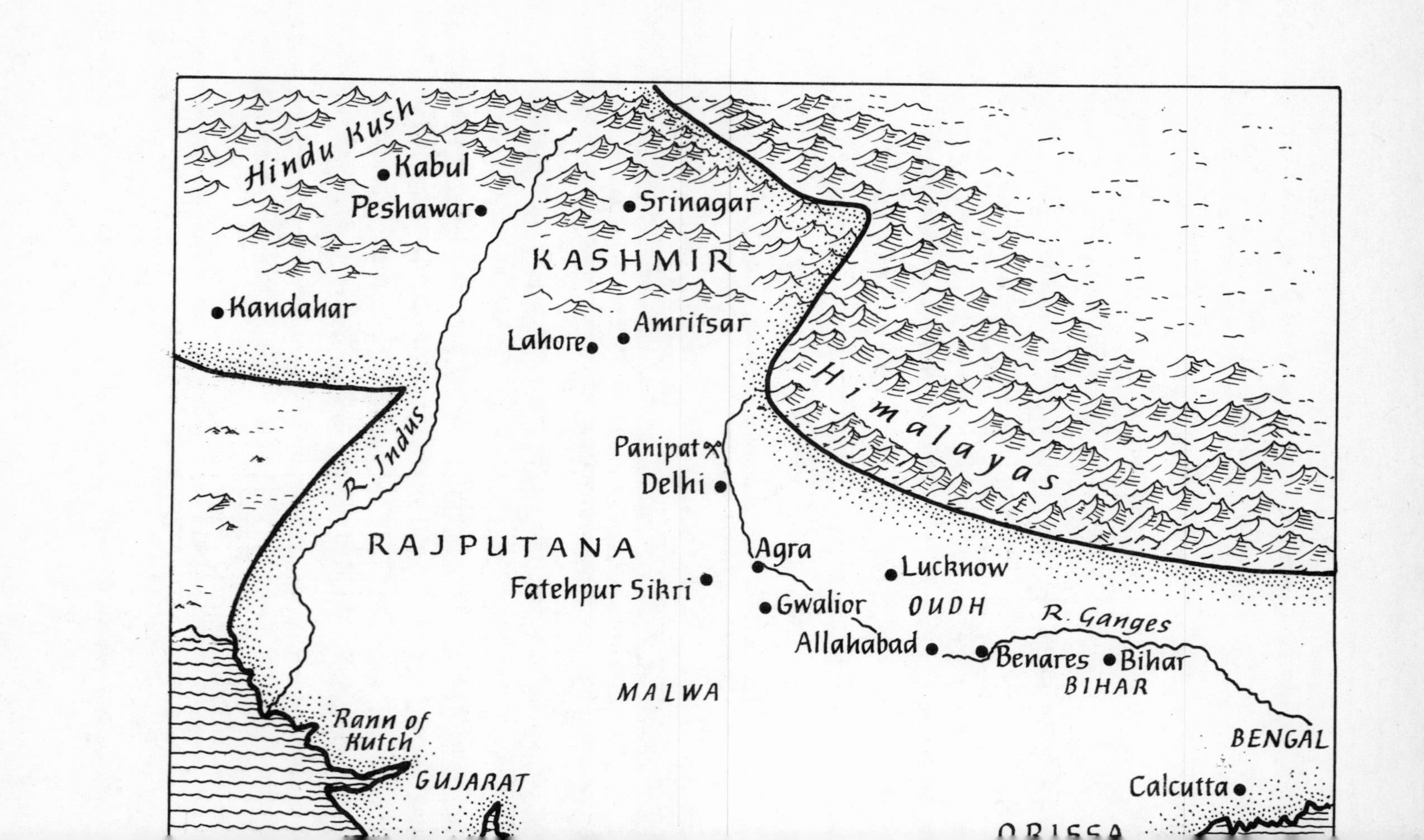
Hindu Kush
Kabul
Peshawar
Kandahar
Srinagar
KASHMIR
Amritsar
Lahore
R. Indus
Himalayas
Panipat
Delhi
RAJPUTANA
Agra
Fatehpur Sikri
Gwalior
Lucknow
OUDH
R. Ganges
Allahabad
Benares
Bihar
BIHAR
MALWA
Rann of Kutch
GUJARAT
BENGAL
Calcutta

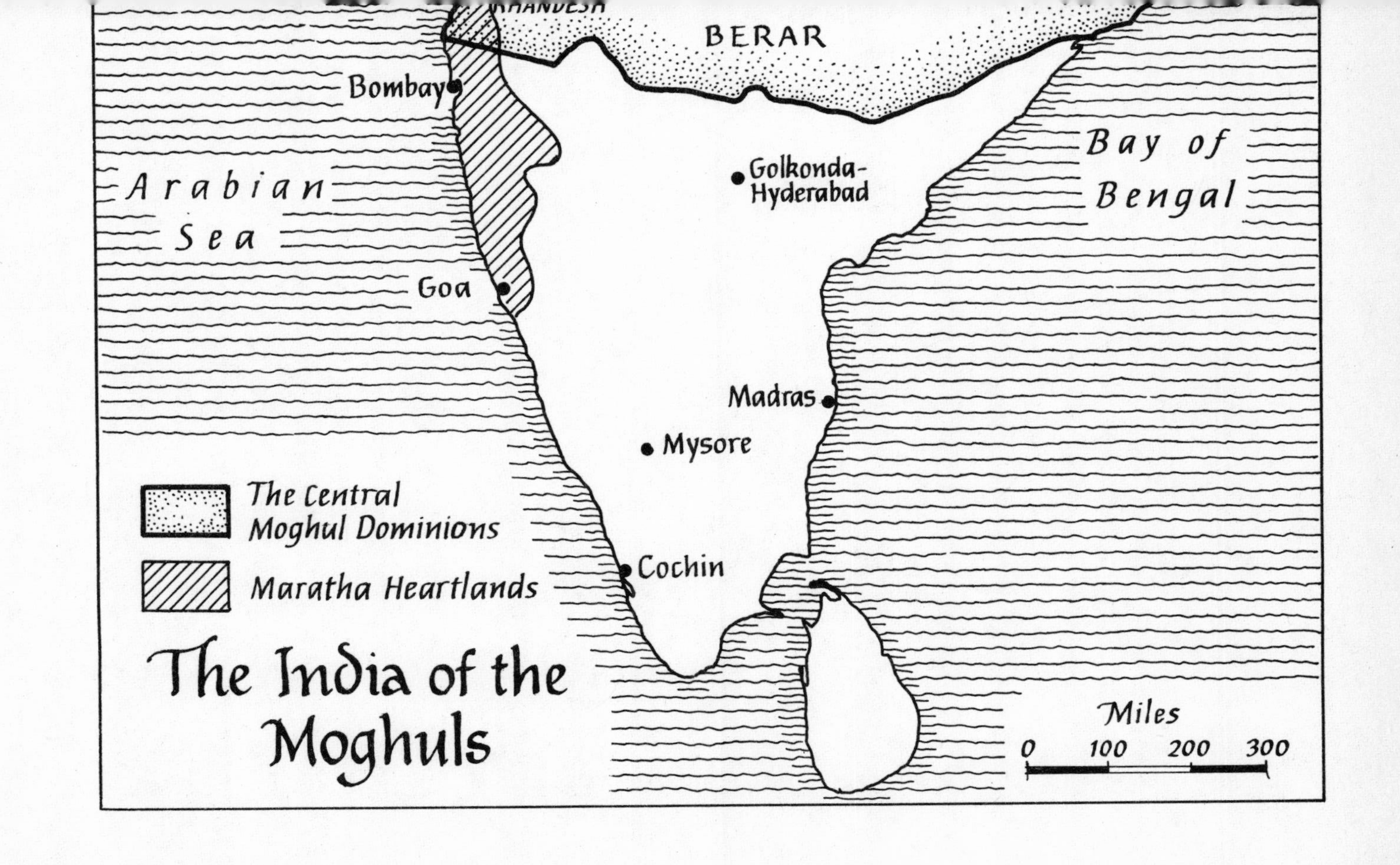

The India of the Moghuls

BOOK THE FIRST
The Men from the North

'Oh, wherefore come ye forth in triumph from the north,
With your hands, and your feet, and your raiment all red?
And wherefore doth your rout send forth a joyous shout?
And whence be the grapes of the wine-press which ye tread?'

Thomas Babington, Baron Macaulay
The Battle of Naseby

1

THE ENVOY

Master Bottomley climbed into the rigging of the carrack, to see better. Several of his men followed his example, and so did Richard Blunt, for all the grunting of alarm from his cousin. But during the long, weary months at sea, Richard had become as professional a seaman as any member of the crew.

They stared across a burnished ocean, the blue turning almost white beneath the tropical sun; there was no cloud and only just sufficient breeze to give the carrack steerage way.

'Five of them,' Master Bottomley muttered.

'Will they be pirates, do you suppose?' Richard asked, staring at the distant shapes creeping across the sea, considerably smaller than the *Bonaventure*, and with a completely different rig. Despite the absence of wind, the dhows were approaching quite quickly.

'They will be Muslims, which amounts to the same thing,' Bottomley said. 'But to them, we are the pirates, venturing into their seas.'

He sighed, as he looked down at the deck of his ship. All things considered, it had been a very successful voyage, up to this last month. When he had first been told the purpose for which his ship was being chartered, he had been appalled. A journey to the other side of the world, where no English vessel had ever been before . . . to search for Prester John?

There was a forlorn hope.

But the charter had been at the expense of the King himself, and if Young King Hal was undoubtedly the most popular monarch ever to sit on the throne of England, he was still not a man to be crossed.

Thus the *Bonaventure* had left Plymouth harbour and made south, following the route of the great Portuguese navigators, da Gama and Diaz, equipped indeed with Portuguese charts and letters to the Governor of Goa, for was not King Henry married to the aunt of Charles, King of Spain, and did not that young man just happen to be the Holy Roman Emperor as well? All Christendom, save for the scurvy French, bowed before that immense power.

The voyage had been a pleasant one, southerly. They had stopped for water and fresh food in more than one sheltered African bay, and seen the strangest sights, from men whose skin was black as night to monkeys as big as men. They had rounded the Cape of Storms in fine weather. They had gazed in horror at the enormous waves beyond, and gratefully put into the huge island called Madagascar for shelter and provisioning.

In Madagascar things had begun to go wrong. They had been attacked by the natives, and two men had died. They had hurriedly put to sea again, and in their haste had run the ship onto a reef. She had been refloated without too much difficulty, but several timbers had been strained, and she was making water, not dangerously, but remorselessly; it had been necessary to keep the pumps working day and night.

Returning to Madagascar was out of the question. But now at last the end had seemed in sight. According to Master Bottomley's Portuguese charts, they were in the Arabian Sea, with India ahead of them, at no great distance.

What would happen then was not his concern. He would have delivered his passengers, and would hopefully be able to careen his ship and refasten the sprung planks, and make her capable of withstanding the voyage home.

Just as what was to happen now, while very much his concern as he was in no hurry to die or spend the rest of his life as a Muslim slave, must be decided by Sir Thomas Blunt, standing foursquare on the quarterdeck beneath him.

'They mean to have us, if they can, Sir Thomas,' he announced.

Tom Blunt pulled his nose. At forty, he looked what he was, a courtier who was yet a soldier, and above all, a man of the King. Even after a year at sea his hose was clean and only darned in one or two places, and his doublet very slightly tarnished. He wore a feather in his cap, and even that still suggested life. His face was burned nut-brown by the sun, and his shoulders had a breadth to match the sturdy legs.

From his baldric there hung a very serviceable sword.

Tom Blunt had been no less appalled than Master Bottomley at having been thus despatched to the far side of the globe. It had happened so suddenly. He had been playing at tennis with the King, and Henry had suddenly thrown down his racket and said, 'Prester John. Let us find Prester John, Thomas. That will make them think.'

By 'them', of course, King Henry meant the crowned heads of Europe, amongst whom he was always seeking to prove himself the best – although he ruled the smallest realm. He had in fact taken his rivalry so far as to engage in a wrestling match with King Francis of France, only five years previously at that famous tournament called the Field of the Cloth of Gold, held outside Calais in 1520.

He had won that encounter ... and made an enemy of the proud Frenchman. But the man Henry truly sought to emulate was his nephew-in-law, the Emperor Charles V. The two men were the best of friends, as Henry was devoted to his wife Katherine of Aragon, Charles's aunt, but Henry could never forget that, as a result of several suitable marriages and lucky explorations, his nephew was not only Holy Roman Emperor but, as King of Spain into the bargain, laid claim to the entire new continent discovered by Christopher Columbus.

How could the king of a small island hope to match such splendour? Only by accomplishing something entirely out of the ordinary – by discovering a treasure trove of his own.

But Prester John?

The name Prester was a corruption of 'Presbyter', and the name John was supposed to represent a direct descendant of 'John the Elder', a somewhat shadowy disciple of Jesus. The legend that he had fled into central Asia and there created a vast Christian kingdom had first been heard in the twelfth century. By that time it had become apparent that the Crusades to win back Jerusalem and the Holy Land had failed, that the Crusader States in Palestine were themselves existing on borrowed time, as the Saracens grew ever more powerful. Christendom had badly needed a tonic, and some imaginative monks had told of this enormous Christian power which, if it could be summoned, would sweep the Muslims from the world and establish the rule of the True Church from the Atlantic to the Great Wall of China.

If it could be summoned. Many had tried. Famous men like Giovanni da Pian del Carpini, Giovanni de Montecorvina, and Marco Polo, had searched. The Pope had sent an embassy which was never heard of again.

Strangely, when, in the thirteenth century, Asia and the Middle East had been overrun by the Mongols of Genghis Khan, the legend had merely strengthened, as it was suggested that even Genghis Khan was fleeing to the west because of a clash with the mighty Christian king.

Marco Polo should have learned better, as he had travelled the length of Asia to take service with the grandson of Genghis, Kubla Khan. Yet even Marco Polo had refused entirely to dismiss the possibility of the kingdom being there, somewhere in the vastnesses that lay beyond the Gobi Desert.

In recent years, there had been a more rational approach to the subject. As the search in Asia had proved fruitless, and as no one was prepared to doubt that Prester John actually existed, it had been determined that he must reign in Africa. There was undoubtedly a Christian Kingdom in Africa, situated south of Egypt, and ruled by a monarch known as a 'negus'. The Portuguese had come into contact with these people, whom they called Abyssinians. But they had reported them to be little better than savages, however Christian.

Still ... 'You intend to send an embassy to Gondar, Your Grace?' Blunt had asked.

Henry had given a great guffaw. 'He'll not be found there, Thomas. I believe in Asia. That's where you'll find Prester John.'

Thomas had gulped: 'Me?'

'Who else could I trust with such a project?'

'Your Grace, may I remind you that I but recently took a wife, and that my lady is with child ...'

'Oh, come now, Thomas. You're not some lovesick youth. Bess is your third wife, and whatever she brings forth will but add to your multitude of children. For God's sake, man, as she is big and will then be feeding you cannot lie with her this coming twelve-month. How better could you be employed than on such a business, knowing that when you return she will be waiting for you, again slender and beautiful? And who else can

I send? Is it not true that you speak both Arabic and Persian, as well as Turkish, better than any man in the kingdom?'

Thomas had wanted to curse that weakness for accumulating knowledge. But with the Ottomans the dominating political force in the world, and himself hoping, now that his military days were drawing to a close, to obtain an appointment as an ambassador, learning the Muslims' fiendish tongues had seemed a sensible thing to do.

'So you see, Thomas,' Henry said. 'There is really no one else.'

When King Henry VIII got the bit between his teeth, there was no stopping him. And in fact, the need for Christendom to find an ally in Central Asia was far more pressing in the sixteenth than in the twelfth century. For across the future of Christian Europe there lay that immense shadow of the Ottoman Empire.

The Ottoman Turks had been expanding from their Anatolian homeland for generations. It was more than two hundred years since they had crossed the Dardanelles and rooted themselves in the Balkans. Yet as long as the great city of Constantinople was held for the West, they had appeared as transient as Genghis Khan's Mongols who had once raided into Hungary . . . and then gone away again.

But in 1453 Constantinople had fallen to the artillery and the Janissaries of the Sultan Mahomet II. And since then the Ottoman advance had been remorseless.

'Can we outrun those fellows, Master Bottomley?' Thomas demanded, watching the approaching dhows.

'With no wind, weeds twelve feet long trailing from our hull, and half the ocean trying to get in? Not a chance, Sir Thomas.'

Thomas looked at Richard.

'We must fight our way through, cousin,' Richard said. 'There is no other way.'

It was the boy's solution to every problem. Indeed, he was no longer a boy, nor had been for several years. Soldiering had been Richard Blunt's only pastime since the age of sixteen, and he was now twenty-five. England being at peace, he had taken his sword to Spain, had fought for the Emperor against the Communeros of Avila and in the resulting war with France.

Wounded on the walls of Pampeluna, he had returned to England to recuperate, with the reputation of being already one of the finest swordsmen in Europe.

Thomas had never seen his young cousin in action, but he conceded that the boy looked the part. Richard Blunt was two inches over six feet in height and had the broad shoulders and powerful legs of his family. His somewhat craggy features were now glowing with the thought of a fight, and his trusty Spanish rapier, fashioned from Toledo steel, hung at his side.

But he had brains as well as brawn. If King Henry had chosen Thomas Blunt as his envoy to Asia because he spoke the heathen tongues, Thomas had used the long, weary days at sea to pass on his knowledge to the younger man. He had found Richard an apt pupil, and more, a most companionable fellow.

Without Richard, the voyage would have been a dreary one. Lacking his support, the departure from England would have been impossible.

Elizabeth Blunt, younger even than Richard, recently embarked upon marriage with a man nearly twice her age, and now just beginning to swell into the bargain, had been predictably distraught at the thought of at best a year's separation. Her family and Thomas's own, while acknowledging the impossibility of refusing the King, had yet obviously felt they were saying goodbye to him for the last time.

Only Richard, now fully recovered from his wound and about to take his departure back to Spain, had given one of his tremendous shouts of laughter.

'Shall I come with you, Cousin Tom, and bring you safe home again? I grow tired of señoritas.'

'It is our only chance,' Thomas agreed.

Master Bottomley looked doubtful. His ship carried but six cannon, and two swivel pieces – called murderers – which could be loaded with nails or bullets for close work.

'Have you never fought a ship at sea, man?' Richard demanded.

'That I have not, Sir. Save for exchanging shots with a French pirate a few years back, off the Channel Islands.'

'Well, then, we are tyros together. So we must use our heads.' Richard considered for a moment. Then he said, 'Break out all your spare cordage, and rig it, to starboard and larboard, from stem to stern in long lines. Make it fast loosely so that when drawn tight, it will rise three feet and more above your bulwarks.'

'But ... would it not be best to string it above the bulwarks now, as a resistance to boarding?' the master asked.

'No, no,' Richard said. 'We want the rascals to board. If they do not, we cannot defeat them.'

Bottomley scratched his head.

'Next, bring all your men on deck, save for those manning the pumps, and secure all of your hatches, so that no one, be he ours or theirs, can get below.'

Bottomley nodded. That made sense.

'Next, accumulate all your firepieces on your castles fore and aft. Let there be not a single firearm, or any other weapon in the waist.'

'But with what will my people fight, when the pirates come aboard?' Bottomley demanded.

'They will not fight, Master Bottomley. They will run away. And as they cannot run away below decks, why, they will have to run fore and aft, to the castles. It were best they do this as evenly as possibly, so both ends are equally defended.'

Bottomley was looking more confused than ever.

'And finally,' Richard said. 'Have your four largest empty casks filled with soapy seawater, and place two forward, just before the forecastle, and two aft here, just below us. Haste, man, haste. Carry out my instructions. There is no time to be lost.'

Master Bottomley hesitated, and then hurried off. Instantly the carrack became a hive of activity.

'Are you sure you know what you are about, Richard?' Thomas inquired.

Richard grinned. 'No. But I have an idea of how the coming battle may go, and I cannot offer you anything better than that.'

The dhows crept inexorably nearer, their lateen sails allowing them to point closer to the wind than the carrack. Now Richard's keen eyesight could make out the dark-visaged, heavily bearded and moustached faces crouching by the gunwales. At least they possessed no artillery.

He stroked his chin; it was his fashion to remain clean-shaven, a habit he had found best in the heat of Spain, and even more so in the greatly increased heat of these equatorial seas.

'I would say they are within range, Master Bottomley,' he remarked. 'See if you can fetch them with some round shot.'

Master Bottomley, who had now entirely abdicated command, gave the orders, and the cannon exploded. But the balls plunged harmlessly into the sea, raising spouts of water and shouts of derision from the pirates ... as they would undoubtedly have fought against the Portuguese, they would have had experience of guns before.

And learned not to be afraid of so inaccurate a weapon.

'Now reload with small shot,' Richard commanded. 'And have your matches lit.'

For the lateen sails were being dropped with admirable precision, and the oars were out, to propel the dhows the last hundred yards.

The seamen, stripped to the waist and gleaming sweat, worked desperately to complete the reloading. Even so it took them some twenty minutes, and by then the Arabs were very close.

The smallshot did some damage, the hail of bullets and nails and pieces of iron sending several of the pirates tumbling over as it raged around the masts before splashing into the sea beyond. The dhows were not the least checked, however, and a moment later their crews were swarming up the sides of the carrack.

By then, Richard had all the slow matches for the arquebuses lit; long pieces of tallow-soaked cord, called serpentines, they would smoulder for hours; fitted into the breech of the cumbersome firepiece the cord would move forward when the trigger was pulled, and hopefully ignite the powder lying beneath it.

Now he waited for the first faces to appear above the gunwales, then shouted, 'Harden the ropes!'

Men hauled on the rope ends, and the strands, three to each side, rose above the gunwales and tightened. The Arabs, hurling themselves over the side, were struck in the face and on the body, and went tumbling backwards, howling their discomfort as they splashed into the sea.

The dhows fell behind as the carrack forged steadily ahead.

'Reload!' Richard shouted. 'Reload while there is time. Round shot.'

There was time, just, before the dhows, having picked up their people, again caught them up.

'Prepare to scatter,' Richard called, leaving the guns unfired.

The Arabs came up the topsides again. Knowing what to expect now, they swung their scimitars to cut the ropes, and leapt down on to the decks, well over a hundred of them, uttering the most bloodcurdling cries.

'Retreat,' Richard bawled.

The seamen ran fore and aft, and not too many of them were acting, Richard considered.

'Now the water,' he yelled, and himself put his shoulders to the first cask. Over it went, followed by the other three, and the soapy water cascaded along the main deck.

The Arabs, for a moment disconcerted by the refusal of the Christians to stand and fight, were undecided whether to attack the castles or raid the hold. Several of them tried to lift the main hatch but could not. And now the water was swirling around their ankles. They gave another yell, and divided, half charging forward and the other half aft.

But the soap had made the decks as slippery as ice, and the Muslims tumbled over each other with shrieks of dismay. This gave time for the staves to be placed, on which the heavy arquebus barrels were rested, to enable the English crew, lining the rail of quarterdeck and forecastle, to pour lead into the heaving mass beneath them. At that range and with targets which, if squirming, were stationary, the bullets could not miss. Blood mingled with the water as the Arabs were shot to pieces.

Richard added to the chaos by depressing the nearest murderer and firing this also, at point blank range, into the heaving mass.

There was a bump from astern, and fresh yells. The fifth dhow had come up unobserved and attached itself to the poop. But with the windows of the aftercabin boarded up, the Arabs could not force an entry below, and so came clambering over the bulwark,to be met by Richard himself, sword and dagger in hand, as well as Thomas and half a dozen men.

Richard gave a shout of glee, swung his rapier to send the first man tumbling back into the sea, checked a blow with the dagger in his left hand and ran a second man through, and had his sword withdrawn and ready to parry a scimitar blow from the third before despatching him as well.

Thus inspired, the Englishmen beside him fought like demons, and Thomas also sent a few of the enemy overboard.

The Saracens had had enough. One or two of the bolder spirits who had survived on deck charged at the forecastle, but were cut down by the halberds of the sailors. The rest scrambled over the side as quickly as they could. The ship astern also cut loose and fell away. Richard seized his opportunity to discharge the remaining murderer into the starboard dhow, hitting several more men with the flying pieces of metal, then the *Bonaventure* proceeded quietly on her way, while her crew cheered themselves hoarse.

'That was well done, Richard,' Thomas said.

'Indeed, Sir Thomas,' Master Bottomley cried. 'We'd not have done it without the lad. Will they come again, Sir?'

Richard gazed at the dhows. They were shipping their oars and re-hoisting their sails, but showing no signs of resuming the chase.

'I doubt it, but we could send a few shots after them just to make sure.'

Bottomley recalled his men, and treading carefully on the still slippery decks, they discharged the guns. Again none of the iron balls struck home, but the Arabs had now definitely given up the chase.

'Beaten the rascals,' Bottomley cried in glee. 'Well, now, Sir Thomas, what next?'

'Why, heave these carrion over the side, and then lay your course for Goa, Master Bottomley,' Thomas said. 'Let us announce our arrival to Senhor Alvarado.'

Dom Jaime Alvarado looked thoughtful as he regarded the English ship, at anchor in the harbour of Goa, and watched the thin streams of water pouring unceasingly over her side from the clacking pumps.

Dom Jaime was a short, stout man, with a pointed beard and bristling hair, presently concealed beneath the broad-brimmed straw hat which hardly matched the trunk hose and doublet he had hastily donned on hearing that a strange vessel was entering his port.

Now he stood in the shadow of the two large Englishmen.

'Arabs, eh? Yes, they have been thirsting for our blood ever since we destroyed their navy, oh ... fifteen years ago. You'll want to beach your ship, before she sinks.'

'The sooner the better,' Thomas agreed.

'I will make arrangements for her to be careened, immediately. Five of them, you say, and you fought them off. Splendid. You must dine with me, *senhors*, and tell me of this fight.'

'What do you think?' Richard asked.

'Of the settlement?' Thomas looked at the muddy beach, the protective reef, the cluster of houses, dominated by the church, but even the church was made of wood. Goa had been acquired by the Portuguese as their chief trading station in India some fifteen years earlier, and from the number of warehouses was already doing a brisk trade in the precious spices from the east as well as those gleaned from India itself. But it was as yet still nothing more than a staging post for the carracks from Lisbon. There was only one large building, set somewhat apart from the rest; this was clearly the Governor's residence. Behind was nothing but green jungle, for as far as the eye could see. 'A mean, uninteresting place, to be sure. And uncommonly hot.' He was fanning himself with his hat as he spoke.

'I meant the Governor.'

'He seemed friendly enough.'

'Did you notice how he never looked either of us in the eye while speaking?'

'Some men have that uncertainty.'

'It is usually a sign of deceitfulness, in my experience,' Richard said.

'Well, then, we will just have to be careful,' Thomas agreed. And grinned. 'But we are here, and our ship is under repair, and he may have news of Prester John. We will at least sample his hospitality. After all, it is but two days to Christmas.'

'Prester John,' mused Dom Jaime. 'Of course I have heard of him. We have all heard of him.'

He sat at the head of his dining table, which was laden with very good fare, both food and wine, even if much of the food, vegetables called strange names such as yams and okras, was unknown to the visitors.

Accompanying Thomas and Richard was Master Bottomley, like them dressed in his sadly tarnished best, and Dom Jaime was also entertaining his garrison commander, Captain Goncalves, while to the Englishmen's agreeable surprise, the other three places were taken by women. Dom Jaime's wife was fat and sweaty; a servant stood behind her chair and fanned her throughout the meal, while every time she breathed the huge gold crucifix resting on her amply displayed breasts caught the candlelight and sent it flickering across the room.

It was a sad thought, Richard reflected, that in time her two daughters would probably look just like that. For the moment however, they were the most charming visions he had seen in many a long day. Maria, the younger, was only fifteen, but Elena, the elder, was, he gathered, seventeen, and very much a young lady, with a dècolletage to match her mother's, although hardly as yet the breasts to support it. Neither girl was the least pretty, but to a man who had just spent eleven woman-less months on a small ship, even their somewhat sallow complexions and slight figures were worth looking at.

'As to how far away from here are his domains,' Dom Jaime was saying, 'that is a difficult question to answer. Know you anything of Indian politics, Senhor Blunt?'

'Almost nothing.'

'Well, they are not less tangled than those of Europe, to be sure. Our little holding here, on the west coast of the peninsula, is subject to the Kingdom of Bijapur. Around us are the kingdoms of Ahmadnagar, Bidar, and Kandesh. North of Kandesh lies Gujarat. We have another factory there, at a place called Diu. Gujarat is by far the most powerful of the states in our immediate neighbourhood, and exercises a kind of loose sovereignty over the others I have mentioned.'

Richard crumbled a piece of home-made bread, and found his fingers touching those of Elena. They did not move away.

'But beyond these immediate states,' Dom Jaime continued, 'there are more powerful nations. The southern end of the peninsula is occupied by Vijayanagar. North of Vijayanagar lie Golconda and Berar, Gondwana, Orissa and Malwa. Far to the east is Bengal. All of these are sizable countries. From what I have been able to gather, they are all larger than Portugal . . . or England.'

Everyone seemed to be looking at the Governor. Richard did so also, but allowed his fingers to move another inch to his right, so that they actually rested on the moist flesh. Now Elena's hand did move, and he thought she was withdrawing it to safety – but she merely turned it over, so that his fingers rested on her palm.

Instantly he knew the thrill of the chase. It was not one he had ever been able to resist; that he had not yet got himself coerced into marriage by a swelling belly was sheer good fortune.

'But all of these powerful sovereign states,' Dom Jaime went on, 'live in fear of those still further to the north. The Rajput Confederacy is a nation of warriors. And the Kingdom of Delhi, which stretches all the way across north India, from the Hindu Kush to the borders of Bengal, is the most powerful of all. Delhi is called the Land of the Peacock, because of the abundance of those strange birds to be found there. The land abounds in precious stones, and it is said that the Sultan possesses one known as the Koh-i-noor, "the Mountain of Light". Men who have seen it say it is the biggest diamond in the world.'

Thomas Blunt drank some wine, sceptically.

'It is to the north even of Delhi,' Alvarado went on, 'beyond the high mountains of Afghanistan, that you must seek Prester John.'

Gently Richard stroked his finger across the soft flesh of the palm exposed to him. He doubted the girl knew the gesture meant he wanted to bed her; if she did, she showed no embarrassment.

Well, he would very much like to bed her, if it could be done. He had been so long without a woman he thought he might even bed her mother, given the opportunity.

'How may a ship pass all of these states?' Thomas asked.

Don Jaime gave a brief laugh. 'Why, Sir Thomas, a ship may not. Delhi is several hundred miles inland from the sea. The nearest port to it would be Diu itself, some days sail up the coast. But that might be a sensible move for you to make. If you could obtain passports from the Sultan of Gujarat to the Sultan of Delhi, you would find your journey much eased.'

'Hm,' Thomas said. 'Hm. How soon can we make sail again, Master Bottomley.'

'I am afraid not for some time, sir. It will take me several weeks to have that bottom made secure.'

'And then how long, man?'

'Well, sir, to refit the ship in the sorry state she is now in . . . four months.'

'Four months?' Thomas cried.

Even Richard was sufficiently disturbed to press down a little too hard on Elena's hand. Her fingers curled up, and the hand was withdrawn.

Damnation, he thought. But . . . four months?

On the other hand, four months sitting in Goa might lead to a very interesting situation with Elena.

'That is impossible,' Thomas was declaring. 'Four months is too long.'

'My ship is no longer seaworthy, sir,' Master Bottomley said, stubbornly.

'I agree it seems a long delay,' Dom Jaime said soothingly. 'But I have a suggestion. As your ship is bound to remain here for four months, Sir Thomas, why do you not travel overland to Gujarat. I would lend you a ship if I had one, of course, but unfortunately I do not, and my next flotilla is not due for several months. But overland . . .'

'Is it practical?'

'Oh, indeed. I have told you that the states immediately to the north of us acknowledge Gujarat as their master. Letters, which I will give you, stating that you are ambassadors from a great European king to the Sultan, will ensure your safety. Nor is the journey a difficult one.'

Richard became aware of a movement beside him, and glanced at the girl. Elena was staring at her father with an expression of the utmost dismay.

'How long will such a journey take?' Thomas asked.

'At this time of the year, before the monsoon arrives, why . . . you will be in Gujarat in four weeks. Then say another four weeks on to Delhi . . . I cannot say how far you will have to travel after that, but you will know, when you return, that your ship will be waiting for you here for your voyage back to Europe. I will attend to that myself.'

Elena made a peculiar little hissing noise, but it was heard only by Richard.

'Well, that certainly seems the most sensible solution to our problem,' Thomas said. 'What do you think, Richard?'

'I am entirely at your disposal, Sir Thomas,' Richard said.

'How soon could such a journey be undertaken, Dom Jaime?' Thomas asked.

'I will arrange for your guides and bearers. You will be able to leave in three days time.'

'Capital,' Thomas declared. 'Oh, capital. By God, sir, I feel a much happier man now than I did twelve hours ago.'

After the meal they sat on the verandah to drink Oporto wine; to Richard's surprise but delight the ladies sat with them. There were a great many insects about, some which buzzed loudly but appeared harmless, and others which made no sound at all but gave painful little stings or bites wherever they landed. The Englishmen followed the Portuguese's example and slapped and scratched without ever interrupting the flow of conversation.

Dom Jaime was at his most urbane and discursive. He talked about Indian wars, and Indian customs . . . all of which Richard was sure he would have found very interesting had not Elena, seated some distance away from him, kept trying to catch his eye.

At last he could resist no longer, finished his port, and rose to his feet.

'I wonder, Dom Jaime, if I might be permitted to take Senhorita Elena for a walk in your garden. It is such a pleasant night.'

'Why, of course you may,' Dom Jaime agreed. 'Magdelena!' he shouted.

The duenna bustled from inside the house. Elena was already out of her chair, although she looked more serious than Richard had hoped. He glanced at Thomas, who merely raised his eyebrows, then followed the two women down the stairs. Within a minute they were beyond the range of the lanterns, following a path through a grove of low trees of a sort Richard had never seen before.

'It is very good of you to bring me for a walk, Senhor,' Elena said.

'It is my pleasure, senhorita.'

'Magdalena, here is your favourite bench,' Elena said. 'Why do you not sit down? Senhor Blunt and I will just walk to the end of the grove and back.'

'Mind you stay in sight,' Magdalena said.

'Of course,' Elena assured her. But she tucked her arm through Richard's for the rest of the walk. 'Listen,' she said. 'You must not take my father's advice.'

'Not take his advice? How else will we get to this place, Gujarat?'

'You should not go to Gujarat, either,' she said. 'The Sultan of Gujarat is no friend to Europeans. He tolerates the factory in Diu because of the strength of our fleet; he fought a war against us a few years ago and was defeated. Thus he signed a treaty of peace with Portugal. But he really hates us. And even if he was prepared to honour my father's credentials, there are many, many dangers between here and Surat.'

'But ... your father said it was an easy journey. Why should he lie to us?'

'Because he wants you out of Goa. And preferably, never able to return to Europe. He is under orders to turn away all interlopers. This is Portugal's trading area, nobody else's. He is not telling the truth when he says the journey is an easy one. It is very difficult, and dangerous.'

They had reached the end of the grove, and Richard glanced back along the path; he could just make out the seated figure of Magdalena.

'He has greeted us as friends.'

'You are fighting men, and have cannon on your ship. He would prefer to be rid of you by subterfuge than force.'

She had turned, as if to begin the walk back, but Richard held her hand and gently drew her into the shade of the bushes.

'This is your father you slander.'

Her features were just a blur in the darkness, but they were so close he could feel her breath on his face.

'My father has his work to do,' she said. 'His duty to perform. But I would not like you to be harmed.'

He kissed her mouth.

She gave a little gasp, then her arms went round him, her fingers tight on his shoulders.

'Oh, senhor,' she whispered, when he took his lips away.

'That is not entirely gratitude for your solicitude,' he told her, and kissed her again.

This time her lips parted, and she allowed him to bring her body against his.

'What would you have me do?' he whispered into her ear.

'Stay in Goa, and repair your ship, and then sail.'

It wasn't the answer he had been waiting for, but it was still promising.

'Sail where?'

'I do not know. Perhaps further to the east you may be able to find a way to this Prester John. Or perhaps it would be best for you to abandon the quest, and return to England.'

He kissed her again, and now she squirmed against him. His hand traced the buttons on the back of her gown, and he released several of them. She did not seem to notice.

'If I returned to England, Elena, would you come with me?'

It was a gambit he had used on a dozen occasions, always successfully.

'Oh, senhor,' she said.

Richard got his hand inside the gown and found it sliding over her shift. But only a shift. The climate was too hot for anything else, and she was too young and slender to bother about a corset, even if the climate would have allowed that, either – her mother was very obviously not wearing any.

'Will you stay?' she asked.

'To stay, and see you again, would be all I could desire,' he said.

His arm was now buried in her gown, and sliding over her buttocks.

She gave a little shiver.

'Then you will stay?' she asked again.

'I will have to speak with my cousin. He is the envoy. But I will attempt to persuade him, certainly.'

'Oh, senhor, senhor ...' she half turned her body so that his hand could not help but flop in front, against her groin. 'Oh, senhor ...'

By God, Richard thought, but I am going to have this delightful little creature here and now, and on a first acquaintance. And if her father is truly attempting to send us to our deaths, then he deserves nothing better than having his daughter debauched.

'Elena? Elena, where are you?'

They had been so concerned with each other that he had not heard the duenna's ponderous footsteps on the path. Now he hastily stepped away from the girl, while Elena reached behind her to fasten her buttons, revealing that she had not been as unnoticing as she had appeared.

'Why, we are here, Magdalena,' she said. 'We are talking politics.'

'Ha,' Magdalena commented, but it was too dark for her to see anything amiss.

Richard squeezed Elena's hand as they walked back to the house.

The *Bonaventure* having been beached and careened, emptied of her guns and stores and pinned on her side by long lines carried out to suitable trees, the Englishmen had found it necessary to use their sails to make tents for themselves – there were no lodgings to be had ashore.

Thomas and Richard naturally shared a tent, and the next night, once their servants had retired, Richard told Thomas what Elena had said.

'What nonsense,' Thomas declared.

'She would hardly speak so critically of her own father without some cause,' Richard pointed out.

'You are a devilish fellow, Dick. Now tell me straight, did you seduce the girl?'

'With that dragon standing at our elbow?'

'You must have escaped her hearing for a brief while, to have had such a conversation. Or does the duenna also traduce her employer?'

'Well ... we managed to obtain a few seconds of privacy,' Richard conceded.

'In which time you made advances.'

'Well ... I may have fondled the child. I assure you that she desired it and made not the slightest demur.'

'Richard, this weakness for women will be the death of you. I am sure she made not the slightest demur. Can you imagine the life of a young girl trapped in this place, which has got to be the most miserable in existence? She must spend her days dreaming of a handsome young sailor – he will have to be a sailor or at least possessed of a ship to reach here at all – arriving out of the ocean, sweeping her off her feet, and carrying her away, if not back to Portugal, at least back to civilisation.'

'You should be a poet.'

'I have written poetry in my time,' Thomas told him. 'But I am not so romantically blind as I cannot see when I am being made a fool of. Do you love the girl?'

'I have only just met her.'

'Do you intend to marry her?'

'Heaven forbid!'

'Well, let me tell you something. If you remain here for four months while the ship is repaired, as this young woman desires, by the end of that time you will most certainly be married to her.'

Richard could not deny, at least to himself, that Elena had revealed herself to be a very single-minded young woman.

'So, in all the circumstances, the sooner we are out of here the better,' Thomas said. 'I have already accepted Dom Jaime's kind offer of guides and porters. We leave the day after tomorrow.'

'And what if Elena is right, and her father is merely concerned with getting rid of us?'

'I do not believe that for a moment. But even if she is, well ... we shall just have to surprise him, by succeeding in our mission, and returning here to confront him. But I say again, I do not believe it for a moment. In any event, we came to carry out a mission, and this we shall do. Besides, I will admit to a certain interest in this "Mountain of Light", if it exists.'

Richard had only one other opportunity for a tête-à-tête with Elena, and this occurred the following day, Christmas Day, when Dom Jaime entertained the Englishmen to a great dinner in the middle of the afternoon. He had several of the factors and their wives as guests, and bade Master Bottomley bring his mates. There was sugar cane liquor as well as wine to drink, and in the heat of the sun everyone got very merry.

Richard found it simple to find a seat beside Elena, even if he understood there would be no possibility of taking her into the bushes before all of these watching eyes.

'I must say goodbye,' he told her. 'My cousin is determined upon making this march to Gujarat, and I must go with him.'

She only half turned her head, but her ears glowed. 'Then I will never see you again.'

'Oh, come now, we were not born yesterday. We anticipate little difficulty in reaching Surat, and then Delhi.'

'I will never see you again,' she repeated dolefully.

'I shall return within the year,' he said, and could not help adding, 'will you not wait for me?'

'If you will speak with my father.'

Definitely a young woman who knew her own mind.

'Ah ... I think I should wait to do that until I return,' Richard said. 'I would not have you tie yourself to a man whom you suppose is going to his death. I merely wish your assurance that should I return within the year you will be waiting for me.'

He wondered why he was pressing the point. He had absolutely no intention of marrying her. It was merely that irresistible challenge of having her vow her love for him.

No doubt, as Thomas had warned, his weakness would one day be the death of him.

'I shall never see you again,' Elena said a third time, and turned her attention to the man on her other side.

Clearly she had written him off.

It seemed that the entire colony turned out to see the expedition set out. Thomas and Richard were of course the leaders, and accompanying them were their four servants, Barnes and Evans, Rogers and Smith. The four servants were armed with arquebuses and a good supply of powder and shot as well as their sticks and daggers, while the Blunts also had arquebuses together with their swords and poignards.

There were six donkeys to carry their supplies, and two guides, men, Dom Jaime said proudly, whom he had picked out himself, together with six drivers for the animals.

'In four months your ship will be waiting for you, Sir Thomas,' Master Bottomley said, looking quite woebegone.

'Well, I doubt we shall make it in four,' Thomas said. 'Expect us back in six, or at least word of us.' He clasped Dom Jaime's hand. 'You have been a true friend, senhor. Whenever I can, you may believe that I will repay your hospitality.'

'It is a gift, Sir Thomas. Having you in Goa has been a great pleasure. Now I will wish you Godspeed.'

'Godspeed,' echoed Captain Goncalves.

Richard searched the crowd for a glimpse of Elena, but she was not to be seen.

Thomas took his place at the head of the little party, raised his hand, and they plodded down a well beaten and clearly marked track between the trees, the guides leading the donkeys, which were roped together.

If the going is no more difficult than this, Richard thought, it will be a simple journey.

Dom Jaime watched the little caravan out of sight, then turned to Goncalves.

'Good riddance,' he commented. 'We shall not hear of them again.'

'What of the captain and the sailors?' Goncalves asked.

'Let them get on with repairing their ship,' Dom Jaime said. 'Give them as much liquor as they can drink, and some suitable native women. Once they are drunk and diseased, we can leave them to the fever.'

2

THE LAND OF THE PEACOCK

The trail lasted for several days, and good progress was made. On the second day of the march, the travellers came upon a village, where they were welcomed by the people, fed mouth-scorching curries, stared at by wide-eyed brown children ... while the Blunts and their English servants stared in turn at the Indian girls who, well-shaped and smiling, did not seem the least concerned about concealing their breasts.

Language was a difficulty, as the Indians spoke neither Turkish nor Arabic. The head guide, Prabhankar, who also spoke Portuguese, did the interpreting, but of course anything like a private conversation was impossible.

'And a damned good thing, too,' Thomas growled. 'I swear to God, Richard, if you get entangled with one of these females you'll make the rest of the journey in manacles.'

'I wouldn't dream of it,' Richard protested.

'Well, you must admit that your Portuguese charmer was leading you up the wrong path. These people are the most friendly I have ever encountered,' Thomas said. 'Prabhankar, ask the headman if it will be like this all the way to Surat.'

Richard eyed the girls some more. He had no doubt that to have one of them wrapped about him would be an experience to remember ... but the conditions in which they lived were appalling, in his opinion. None of them possessed shoes, and he rapidly realised that their apparent lack of modesty was merely dictated by lack of clothes; yet nearly every one had at least one gold bangle on her ankle or wrist. Prabhankar said this represented her entire wealth and dowry ... and that those with any pretentions had at least several of the precious circlets. Their houses were no more than huts a few feet square, each sleeping an entire family which could amount to as many as ten people; they cooked at a communal fire, and the small flock of goats, as well as the field of corn, were also apparently communally owned.

It was not a community in which he would ever wish to become involved.

The headman told Prabhankar that most of the people between his village and Surat were friendly, although there were apparently bands of robbers to be found in the more open country further north. Tigers would be more of a danger, he suggested. But the biggest danger of all was rain, which he claimed was due any day now.

'How can that be?' Thomas demanded. 'Dom Alvarado said the monsoon would not happen for several months yet, until after we had reached Delhi.'

'The monsoon is not due for a long time, sahib,' Prabhankar agreed. 'But I think we should make haste.'

'What is so dangerous about rain?' Richard inquired.

'The rain will be very heavy, sahib. We must try to get across the river before it starts.'

Richard scratched his head, not the least convinced; the fellow had clearly never experienced an English spring downpour.

The weather was certainly very sultry, and the Englishmen poured sweat as they marched along, casting envious glances from inside their trunk hose and doublets at the dhoti-clad Indians.

'But as we are Englishmen,' Thomas reminded them, 'we will remain properly dressed.'

'Which is going to be difficult unless we can find a seamstress in Surat,' Richard confided, regarding a tear in the sleeve of his shirt where he had passed too close to a thorny bush.

Three days after leaving the friendly village they came to another, where they were again welcomed and invited to remain once the inhabitants had seen their swords and their guns. For these people were in a state of terror; the vicinity had become the haunt of tigers, and already several goats had been carried off, as well as a child. Now the villagers were hardly able to summon the courage to work their fields.

'What do you think?' Richard asked his cousin. 'Shall we seek out these beasts?'

'We did not come to India to hunt tigers,' Thomas told him. 'We are on a mission.'

So they bade farewell to the village and proceeded on their way. The trail had now dwindled virtually to nothing, although Prabhankar seemed to know where he was going, and the jungle was closing in on either side. Huge trees rose out of the bush and towered above them, so that they seldom saw the sun, and the bush itself became sufficiently thick for the Indians to have to hack a way through with their knives. Even so the undergrowth caught at their feet, and they were surrounded by seething noise, the more disturbing because the snakes and lizards and cicadas could never be seen.

Then they heard a heavier sound, accompanied by a guttural murmuring. The bearers instantly became very agitated, while the donkeys began braying, sending their cacophony ranging through the trees.

'That'll tell any enemy where we are,' Richard said.

'Oh, they know, sahib,' Prabhankar assured him.

He was trying to put a bold face on the matter, but was obviously very afraid.

'Who are they?' Thomas asked.

'It is tiger, sahib.'

Richard gave a shout of laughter. 'Seems we are going to have our tiger hunt after all, cousin ... although it will be them hunting us.'

'How many?' Thomas snapped.

'It will be just one tiger, sahib.'

'One tiger? And these fellows are scared stiff?'

'One tiger can be very dangerous,' Prabhankar assured him.

Thomas looked at Richard, who shrugged. 'He's the expert.'

When they camped that night, they brought the donkeys into the centre, and hobbled them securely. The drivers cleared a good area of ground with their knives, and Prabhankar lit a larger fire than usual. Sparks rose into the still air and settled on the trees, where they glowed for several seconds before being extinguished. It did not take much imagination to suppose the whole forest being set alight – all the wood was very dry.

But Prabhankar seemed to think the hazard of a bushfire was preferable to being attacked by a tiger.

'Now then,' Thomas said. 'Prabhankar says that this beast is a nocturnal animal, who will attack during the hours of darkness. We six white men will therefore watch in pairs, through the night. I wish the matches lit. Each pair will take three hours, and at the first sign of danger will alert the camp. Understood?'

'Barnes and I will take the middle watch,' Richard volunteered.

Thomas nodded; he had expected nothing less from his best fighting man.

After they had eaten, Richard turned in immediately, as his was the sleep to be broken. He was away in seconds; he had had to bivouac on the hard soil of Spain often enough. He did not dream, and was awakened, it seemed, a few seconds after he had laid his head on his folded blanket.

Beside him Thomas snored lustily, but the donkeys were restless, not braying now, but stamping and shuffling.

'Any sign of him?' he asked Evans, who had touched his shoulder.

'It is difficult to say, sir. There are noises we have not been able to identify. But the beasts are nervous.'

Richard nodded. Barnes was awake by now, and the two of them sat down together, each facing a different way. Richard laid his rapier across his lap, and had an arquebus at his side. Barnes had his shortsword and a firearm as well. On each of the guns the slowmatch glowed, and the stakes had already been emplaced.

'Mind you stay awake,' Richard reminded him.

'I will do that, sir,' Barnes assured him.

In fact Richard was the one who kept nodding off. The night was every bit as hot as the day had been, without a breath of air, and he was surrounded by insects, buzzing and humming. Barnes had thrown some more wood on the fire, which was blazing merrily, and the flickering flames were mesmeric, while Richard made the mistake of thinking about those dark-skinned breasts and time and again began to dream of them, too.

A nudge from Barnes had him instantly awake.

'Listen, sir.'

Richard cocked his head, and heard the rustling in the

bushes, some twenty feet away. This was too massive a movement for a snake.

Then he saw eyes, glowing in the darkness of the forest. They were huge, and red, and unblinking as they stared at him.

He leapt to his feet.

'To me!' he shouted. 'Awake! Awake!'

As he summoned the camp, there was a sudden surge towards him from the bushes. In the gloom he was not quite sure of what he saw, but it was immense – not less than seven feet long, he reckoned – and vaguely yellow and black. He threw himself to one side, as Barnes did to the other. Both men were on their feet again in an instant, thrusting their arquebuses into the forks at the top of the staves and pulling the triggers. The firepieces exploded all right, but if they hit the tiger, the lead did not disturb him. Another leap took the huge creature past the fire and into the midst of the donkeys. Two sweeps of his paw killed one and snapped the line, and then he was gone again, the dead ass held in his jaws, the bushes crackling as he disappeared into the night.

The remaining donkeys were screaming their heads off, and the men clearly felt like doing the same. The bearers babbled amongst themselves, while Richard sheathed his sword and gazed at the huge paw marks in the earth . . . and wondered at the strength of an animal which could just disappear with a full-grown donkey weighing a few hundred pounds in its jaws.

'By Christ!' Thomas stood beside him. 'Did you not see the beast?'

'I saw him,' Richard said. 'When he was already upon us.'

'And you hit him, sahib.' Prabhankar pointed at the drops of blood around the fire. 'It is good we had the donkeys, or he would have taken a man.'

'You look quite shaken,' Thomas remarked.

Richard nodded. 'I have never encountered anything quite so huge, and powerful, and quick,' he said. 'But I will know more of what to expect the next time, cousin.'

However, the tiger did not return. It was tempting to suppose that he might have bled to death, although that was unlikely. And however shaken they all were by the ferocity of the attack they had suffered, they forgot about the beast two days later when Prabhankar pointed through the trees at great black clouds, rolling up out of the south-east.

'Looks as if we may have a shower,' Richard suggested. 'If it cools the air, I'm all for that.'

'We must cross the river before the rain, sahibs,' Prabhankar insisted. 'It is not far now.'

They reached it the following afternoon, after an exhausting march. All day the clouds had been building, but there was as yet still no wind to cleanse the atmosphere.

The river was wide and looked fairly deep.

'There is a ford,' Prabhankar assured them. 'But we must look out for crocodiles.'

'Crocodiles?' Thomas demanded. 'What manner of beasts are they?'

'Dragons, sahib, with armour-plated skins. There is no weapon can kill a crocodile. We must just hope that we do not encounter one.'

Thomas looked at Richard, who shrugged. After his encounter with the tiger, he was no longer prepared to pooh-pooh any Indian talk about enormous beasts ... but he could not imagine an animal that could not be killed.

It began to rain.

'We must cross quickly,' Prabhankar said, and began waving the drivers forward.

'Should we not wait for this shower to pass over?' Thomas inquired. 'And it will be dark in an hour. I would sooner encounter these dragons of yours in daylight.'

'This rain will not stop, sahib – not for days. And within twelve hours the river will have swollen. We must cross now.'

Again Thomas looked at Richard, who looked at the sky as there was a searing flash of lightning followed by a tremendous crack of thunder. Before they had recovered from that, there was another.

The donkeys began to bray as they were driven down to the water, in which the huge raindrops made indentations like bullets.

'This is a God-forsaken country we have come to,' Thomas growled.

* * *

They did not encounter any crocodiles – Richard could not help but suppose the beasts, if they truly existed, were sheltering from the rain – and passed the river without anything worse than a soaking, as in places it was necessary to wade up to their necks. But this seemed irrelevant, as now the rain was so heavy that when they gained the northern bank they were kept just as wet as if they had remained in the water.

There was no means of lighting a fire, and they had to eat uncooked meat for supper.

'How long did you say this rain will last?' Thomas asked Prabhankar.

'Maybe twenty-four hours, maybe a week,' Prabhankar told him.

'A week?' Richard was incredulous.

'Then it will cease?' Thomas inquired.

'Oh, then it should stop, sahib. This is not the monsoon. In the monsoon it can rain for two months.'

'Could be my charmer was right after all,' Richard suggested.

'By God,' Thomas declared, 'when I get back to Goa I've a mind to wring that fellow Alvarado's neck.'

Over the next week Richard began to wonder if the operative word regarding their return to Goa might not be 'if' rather than 'when'.

The rain teemed down, sometimes slackening to a drizzle, sometimes stopping altogether, but only for an hour or two, while the lowering skies and repeated rumbles of thunder left them in no doubt of its imminent return.

Now often there was a wind as well, screaming across the jungle, causing even the largest trees to bend, occasionally uprooting them, ripping twigs and branches away and hurling them through the air with the velocity of a musket ball, sometimes strong enough to blow a man from his feet, so that they staggered along clutching each other for support.

Their clothes grew soggier and soggier, and changing them was pointless, because the rain had penetrated all their baggage. They ceased shaving and wondered why their beards sprouted when the Indians hardly had any growth at all. Their food began to spoil and they were on short rations; Thomas and Richard had anticipated being able to shoot game on the march, but their powder was as wet as everything else – and it was quite impossible to keep their matches alight.

'Can you imagine campaigning in such conditions?' Richard asked.

'It would not be possible,' Thomas agreed with him.

Yet in a sense that was what they were doing. Unlike the Indians, including Prabhankar, who stripped to their dhotis and let the water run off their bare skins, pushing through the mud with bare feet, the Englishmen in their doublets and hose and their leather shoes began to develop blisters and festering sores. Yet taking off their clothes presented a considerable challenge, especially their shoes. Richard was the first to do so, and felt an immediate relief, even if every footstep was accompanied by a surge of alarm as his toes touched twig or branch hidden in the mud.

In fact, he soon realised that apart from the danger of being hit on the head by a falling tree trunk, during a rainstorm was the safest time to pass through the jungle. If they saw more wild-life during the last fortnight of their march to Surat than at any time before, the pythons and kraits, the tigers and wild elephants, the spiders and the lizards, were all concerned, like the humans, only in finding some high ground on which to escape the flood.

But the dangers of the rain were real enough. Sometimes they found themselves knee deep in water, and streams which Prabhankar assured them would present no difficulty in dry weather, were raging torrents five or six feet deep. In crossing one of these a donkey lost its footing and was swept away, and although they found it some time later, the poor animal had drowned.

This reduced them to four pack animals, and this time some of their store of shot had gone with the dead beast.

But at last, after the longest journey in terms of discomfort that Richard had ever made, they came in sight of the minarets of Surat.

The guards on the city gate seemed thoroughly surprised to see the bedraggled band emerging from the forest, and peered at the pale complexions of the Englishmen as if supposing they might have lost their proper pigmentation in the rain – which continued to fall.

They were directed to a caravanserai, a huge walled and partly-roofed area reserved for visiting merchants, in which accommodation was free for the first three days.

'A very civilised arrangement,' Richard remarked, 'were the surroundings civilised.'

For the rain had delayed the departure of several merchants, who had thus outstayed their welcome. They were now being charged, which did not make them very welcoming to strangers. The place was packed, with men, women, children, horses, donkeys, dogs, bales and boxes, all seeking some shelter. Prabhankar had the greatest difficulty in finding a space for even their own small party, and when Richard removed the few remaining rags of his clothing in an endeavour to get dry, he found himself being stared at by half a dozen naked boys and girls.

But when he grinned at them, they grinned back.

Here at last it was possible to have a hot meal, and realise just how exhausted they were from their ordeal.

'You must have known there was a chance of rain in the jungle,' Richard said to Prabhankar. 'Yet you came with us. Why?'

'Don Alvarado is my master,' Prabhankar said. 'I must go where he sends me.'

Richard could not help but wonder how many English servants would be quite that faithful.

Not that he had anything to complain about regarding his own servants. They regained their spirits the moment they were dry, worked with a will, and although it was impossible entirely to conceal the ravages of the jungle and the wet, soon had Richard and Thomas presentable enough to make their appearance at the court of Mahmud Begarha.

Richard interested himself in his surroundings. Apart from the children, the arrival of the white men attracted the attention of several of the merchants, and Richard had by now picked up sufficient Hindustani from Prabhankar to understand that nearly all the caravans were loaded with salt.

'Salt?' he asked in amazement.

'A very precious commodity, sahib,' Prabhankar told him. 'The people of Gujarat trade salt with all the world. Because of the heat in the dry season, and the consequent evaporation, here is found the most abundant deposits of salt anywhere. It is a great source of wealth.'

Richard decided to take that ... with a pinch of salt. But he could not help being fascinated when another of the merchants unrolled a selection of glittering emeralds and rubies.

'You'll be telling me next that these are also found in abundance in Gujarat,' he remarked.

'Oh, indeed, sahib. This is a rich country.'

'Well ... maybe we should wait around here until we are sure the rain is finished, Thomas. We might do ourselves some good.'

'We'll decide after we have seen this Sultan,' Thomas said.

'The Sultan is a mighty man,' Prabhankar warned them. 'He must be treated with proper respect.'

'Why, I treat every man with respect,' Thomas said. 'Until he behaves in a disrespectful way.'

The rain continued to teem down in a sullen downpour – the wind had temporarily dropped – as they made their way through the streets towards the Sultan's palace. This lay at the head of a great square, and close by it was a large mosque in and out of which people were filing, always pausing to wash their feet at the fountain set in the courtyard – although they could just as well have held them out to the rain, Richard supposed.

The square was reached by a broad street, which apparently contained a market, although in the downpour there was very little business being done. Dogs slunk from shelter to shelter, scantily clad children peered from dark doorways at the white men, but clearly the residents of Surat shut up shop during the rain.

The city itself, for so it would have to be considered, Richard supposed, was quite large. Although situated some ten miles from the sea, as it was on the banks of a river, the Tapti, it was actually a seaport, and its waterfront was crowded with boats of every description. The river, although obviously not very wide, was swollen from the rain and threatening to burst its banks; in many places water was running ankle deep through the streets of the town, carrying with it every manner of garbage.

To Richard's practised eye, however, more interesting was

the evidence that parts of the town had been burned in the not too distant past.

'Who does the Sultan war with?' he asked Prabhankar.

'Why, sahib, with the Portuguese. The Portuguese attacked and burned the town, not a dozen years ago.'

'By God!' Richard growled. 'And you have brought us here, you rascal?'

'The Portuguese are not at war with Gujarat now,' Prabhankar pointed out. 'A peace treaty was signed after the Portuguese victory.'

'Alvarado told us of this,' Thomas reminded his cousin.

'So he did. But he did not mention that the city had been burned. And Elena told me that the Sultan hates the Portuguese, and all who deal with them.'

'He will deal fairly with us, if we deal fairly with him,' Thomas asserted confidently.

Richard could only hope he was right as they entered the palace.

Here it was at least possible to shelter from the rain beneath the roof of a large porch, while they looked at a stylised and quite beautiful inner garden, where fountains played, again somewhat incongruously in view of the weather, and various strange-looking plants drooped beneath the downpour. They were in the midst of quite a large group of men, mostly turbanned and dark-skinned, who gossiped amongst themselves and eyed the newcomers, all watched by splendidly clad guards with crimson silk capes and domed steel helmets and drawn scimitars.

No hostility was shown to them, however, and Prabhankar whispered to one of the several majordomos who came closer to inspect them before going off into a side gallery leading round the garden.

On the far side there was a large doorway, open but also heavily guarded, beyond which more people could be seen milling about. This was clearly their destination, but they had to wait for over an hour before the majordomo returned to lead them forward – and then it was to the accompaniment of ill-favoured glares from those who had been waiting even longer.

'Audiences, it seems, are the same the world over,' Thomas observed. 'What exactly is a sultan, Master Prabhankar?'

'Why, a king, sahib.'

'Ah,' Thomas said.

Richard was more interested to note that there were women in the inner room – yet this was a Muslim community. Or was it? There had been Hindu temples as well as mosques in the town, and such women as he had seen were unveiled. Here too their faces were exposed, as they clustered in a group some distance behind the throne on which sat the Sultan. The throne itself was surrounded by several men who wore the turban and flowing robes but revealed no great signs of wealth.

It was on the potentate Richard knew he had to concentrate, at least for the time being; he carried the gift arquebus forward.

The previous audience was just drawing to a close. They watched the Indian bow until his head almost touched the floor, and then perform the obeisance, the quick movement of the hand from chest to mouth to forehead, as he backed from the presence.

'Follow his example, sahibs,' Prabhankar muttered.

The majordomo was whispering in the Sultan's ear, while Richard gazed at Mahmud Begarha.

He was not impressed. Begarha was clearly short, and very fat. This was easy to see, as he was most incongruously dressed. As far as Richard could make out, for the Sultan was seated, he wore only a dhoti on the lower half of his body. One of his legs was drawn up on to his throne, the other hung down; both were entirely naked, and his feet were bare. Above the dhoti hung a loose kind of tunic. But the turban which crowned the small head was studded with emeralds, winking in the uncertain light.

The face was equally small, with tight features; the hand which half lifted as the Englishmen approached was like a claw.

'Are you mad?' he asked, when Richard and Thomas had done their bowing, speaking Arabic, to their relief. 'To travel through the rain?'

'We are on an important mission, your highness,' Thomas explained.

'You are mad. I am told you are not Portuguese. Who are you?'

'We serve a mighty king, of a place called England.'

Begarha glanced at his viziers, who shrugged and shook their heads.

'We have never heard of this place. A mighty king, you say? What business has he here?'

'He sends greetings to your highness, and commands me to present you with this fine handgun.'

On cue, Richard stepped forward, the arquebus held in both hands. One of the viziers came forward to take it from him, and show it to the Sultan. Neither man revealed any surprise at the unusual weapon, but of course they would have encountered firearms when they had fought the Portuguese.

'It is of poor workmanship,' Begarha remarked.

Richard glanced at Thomas, but Thomas had been a diplomat for years, and appeared not the least put out.

'Your highness will find that it shoots a straight bullet,' he said.

'Then shoot it for me now.'

Richard guessed that the Sultan knew all about guns, and was disposed to be disagreeable.

'I am sorry, your highness,' Thomas said. 'But it will not fire in the rain. Our powder is too damp.'

'Then it is useless,' Begarha pointed out. 'What does this king of yours wish of me?'

'Great King Henry calls for your assistance to his ambassadors in their journey to the court of Prester John.'

Thomas waited eagerly for Begarha's response, but the Sultan again glanced at his viziers, and again elicited nothing more than shrugs.

'Who is this Prester John?'

Again Thomas concealed his disappointment.

'He is a great king who reigns to the north,' he ventured.

'You speak of Ibrahim Lodi Shah,' Begarha said contemptuously, 'Sultan of Delhi.'

'I am told Prester John is far greater than the ruler of Delhi, your highness.'

'There is no ruler in India greater than Ibrahim Lodi,' Begarha told him. He smiled, his lips still tight. 'If you seek him, go to him – and do not waste my time. You come here from Goa, I know. The Portuguese are my enemies. One day I will crush them as an elephant crushes a nut. Begone. Leave my dominions. If you seek Lodi, go to him.' Again he smiled. 'Send him my felicitations.'

He waved his hand to signify that the interview was at an end, but Thomas stood his ground.

'I crave your indulgence in the matter of resting and re-equipping my people, who have suffered sorely in the jungle. I ask your assistance in the name of my illustrious master, King Henry of England.'

Begarha glared at him. 'I know of no King Henry,' he said. 'I know of no England. I know that only madmen attempt to traverse the jungle in the rain. You are madmen. Now begone. I will give you no assistance. Leave my city. Leave my domains. If you are found here the day after tomorrow, you will be impaled. I have spoken.'

Now at last Thomas was left speechless with consternation.

'We must leave, sahib,' Prabhankar whispered. 'Quickly.'

Richard grasped Thomas's arm, and bowed, virtually forcing his cousin to do the same. Then he hastily drew him from the chamber.

'This is your master's doing,' Thomas growled at Prabhankar, when they regained the caravanserai. 'The gift was not appreciated, and he did not tell us sufficient of the dispute between Portugal and Gujarat. I believe he knew we would be ill received. He is a treacherous fellow.'

'As are you, Prabhankar,' Richard agreed, refraining from adding that their affairs were turning out exactly as Elena had predicted.

'I was sent to guide you, sahibs, wherever you wished to go. I was expressly warned against giving you advice.'

Thomas glared at him. 'Well, then,' he said. 'Now you will guide us to this Lodi.'

'Sahib?'

Richard was no less surprised.

'You mean to continue with this confounded expedition? In this weather?'

'We have no choice,' Thomas pointed out. 'We must leave Gujarat, regardless of the weather. Thus we either return to Goa, or continue with our quest. If we return to Goa, we do so as penniless failures, nor am I at all sure we will be welcomed. I have more than half a feeling that Alvarado actually meant to send us to our deaths.'

He looked at Prabhankar, who hung his head.

'More than half a feeling,' he repeated. 'But if we continue, and come to this Lodi, who even Begarha says is a great king, we may yet salvage something from the wreckage of this embassy. In any event, it is a journey of no more than a few weeks.'

'According to Alvarado,' Richard pointed out.

They both looked at Prabhankar.

'I do not know how long the journey will be, sahibs,' Prabhankar said. 'I have never been to Delhi.'

'But you can guide us there?'

'I can find it for you, sahibs, undoubtedly.'

'Then that's our course. Ibrahim Lodi! He is clearly the fellow Alvarado was talking about, who possesses this Mountain of Light diamond. If he does, this Delhi must be a wealthy place, and if Lodi is a great king, he will know of Prester John.'

'And if there is no Prester John?' Richard inquired.

'That I will not accept. But should it be so, then Lodi himself may prove a worthwhile ally. I tell you, Richard, I do not intend to return to Goa unless in triumph.'

Richard had no desire to argue that point, but he could not help but feel that his cousin was taking altogether too sanguine a view of their prospects.

As it proved. They left the caravanserai, Thomas having used some of his purse of English silver coin to purchase provisions from the merchants, all of whom shook their heads at the madness of the white men in again venturing out into the rain.

This point of view now communicated itself to their drivers, who, on learning that they were not even returning to Goa, but instead making their way farther north into quite unknown country, deserted, led by the junior guide, Bhalat. Prabhankar did his best to call them back, but they would not listen.

'I wonder you do not go with them,' Richard remarked.

Prabhankar looked hurt. 'My master said I was to guide you wherever you chose to go, sahib,' he protested.

'And you are sure you can find the way to this man Lodi's dominions?'

'All roads lead to Delhi,' Prabhankar pointed out.

That seemed promising, but their immediate problem was

their caravan. The Englishmen knew nothing about driving donkeys, and the rain was relentless. It might have been amusing had their situation not been so precarious.

Remarkably, and to their great relief, they now left the coastal strip and entered upon steadily rising ground. Not only did the jungle begin to thin, but the rain also ceased.

'The weather will be good now,' Prabhankar asserted.

'Thank God for that,' Richard said. 'But do you mean you yourself have never travelled this far from Goa?'

'Never,' Prabhankar told him.

Richard looked worried, but Thomas had quite regained his spirits.

'Now there can be no doubt we made the right decision,' he said. 'How far is it to Delhi?'

Prabhankar shrugged. 'I have spoken with the men in the caravanserai. They say it is a journey of about two months from Surat.'

'Two months?' Richard cried.

'How far do you reckon we are travelling each day?' Thomas asked him.

'Ten, perhaps twelve miles. He is talking of at least six hundred miles.'

'Well,' Thomas said. 'That is no further than the south coast of England to Edinburgh ... and I have made that journey before. In a great deal less time than two months.'

'Mounted on fast horses and with reasonable weather,' Richard reminded him.

But with every day their progress improved, as did the weather. Soon they encountered blue skies, and soon after that they found it necessary to use blankets as they camped on a high plateau, looking down on river valleys to either side. Here there were extensive areas under wheat: the countryside suggesting a tremendous fertility. Equally were they surrounded by human habitation; they could see the smoke of fires, but Prabhankar felt it was safer for them to keep away from villages until their food was completely exhausted.

'I do not know how friendly these people are, sahib,' he explained.

For Richard the country through which they were now

passing was reminiscent of the Spanish plateau over which he had campaigned so often, save that in place of acre upon acre of orderly olive groves there were these endless vistas of gently waving stalks, through which the breeze set up a rustling almost like a restless sea. Such trees as were seen were huge growths with the strangest of names, such as tamarind and mango, and most were set widely apart.

Game abounded, and none of it apparently had much acquaintance with human beings, and certainly not with fire-arms. Richard was enabled to place his stake and light his match with a deer standing only fifty feet away, regarding him curiously; he could not help but feel guilty as he squeezed the trigger.

They saw several tigers, but none came close – obviously they too found hunting easy – and herds of elephants. These also Prabhankar avoided, sometimes taking a detour of several miles to the north or south of the line he was following to escape the spoor.

How he navigated Richard could not decide. But presumably he used the sun and the stars, and he knew Delhi lay to the north-east of Surat.

He was an excellent guide, however execrable his master. But for all his caution he could not keep their presence a secret from the hill folk. About a fortnight after leaving Surat they became aware that they were being followed.

Richard climbed a tall mango tree to look back whence they had come. The country undulated considerably, but when he had been watching for several minutes he caught a gleam of sunlight reflecting from some bright object, and then another. A few minutes later the gleams ceased, as the reflecting objects entered a shallow valley.

He slid down the tree.

'There is a band of armed men behind us,' he said. 'And I would say they have horses.'

'Horses,' Thomas said. 'If we could secure horses ...' he looked at Prabhankar. 'Will these people trade, do you suppose?'

'No, sahib. These are terrible people. If they are armed and mounted they must be those known as Marathas, fierce robbers who will seek to kill us and steal our weapons and mules.'

Thomas pulled his beard and looked at Richard.

'What do you propose?'

'That we continue our journey, keeping a sharp look-out. We can do nothing else. If they attack us, then we must defend ourselves as best we are able.' He grinned. 'Remembering not to shoot at the horses.'

'By God, I never met a man who relished the prospect of a fight as much as you, cousin,' Thomas growled. 'But I am glad to have your company.'

They resumed their journey, Richard lagging behind now to act as rearguard. He listened for the sound of hooves, but heard none until close to nightfall. Then he thought he heard horses galloping.

'Will they attack at night?' he asked Prabhankar.

'I think so, sahib.'

'That will be to our advantage, I would say.'

He chose to camp at a spot where three large trees grew close together, thus providing a form of protection for their rear, then placed the stakes for the arquebuses in a semicircle. The fire was lit outside the stakes, and they had their meal while one man was on watch. Then the fire was built up even more, and the men retired within the circle formed by the stakes and the trees. The arquebuses were already loaded, and the slow matches lit; this was wasteful, but Richard felt it necessary. Swords were drawn and laid on the ground beside each man.

'Do you know how these people fight?' Richard asked Prabhankar.

'I have never fought them, sahib, but I have heard that to a Maratha, his horse is everything.'

Richard nodded. 'They will not have firearms?'

'No, sahib.'

'Bows and arrows?'

'I do not think so, sahib. These people of the mountains fight with sword and spear.'

'Which should also be to our advantage,' Richard told Thomas.

As with the tiger, they watched in pairs, but this time Richard did not doze. Fighting was his profession. Yet he had gone off watch when he was awakened by his cousin.

'Listen,' Thomas said.

Richard sniffed the air, which was chill. The moon had set and it was very dark; he reckoned it might be two hours to first light.

There was also a faint breeze, coming from the west, and on it was borne the jingle of harnesses. He swallowed; his practised ear told him there were not less than twenty horses out there: he commanded seven men including himself, and he had no idea of Prabhankar's quality.

'Every man to his stake,' he commanded the servants, 'but do not fire until I give the word.'

He was relying on surprise and noise as much as bullets, here; of course his people would have no opportunity to reload, so a great deal would depend upon that first volley.

The Marathas could not see beyond the still blazing fire; the pin points of light which were the slow matches would appear to them like sparks cast from the flames, Richard was sure. He stared into the darkness, but saw nothing. Yet the clinking was coming closer, and at last he thought he could make out a gleam of steel.

'Be ready,' he told his men.

A moment later there came the clash of a cymbal, and then a huge roar, and out of the darkness, charging straight at the fire, there came not twenty, but more like forty men, Richard estimated.

'Give fire,' he shouted.

The triggers were pulled, the powder ignited, and the six arquebuses exploded virtually together. The Marathas had been charging stirrup to stirrup, and the bullets sliced into them at a range of not more than fifty yards. Two men fell, and in going down took with them several of their neighbours. The rest, uncertain what was happening, veered off to left and right, round the trees.

'With me,' Richard bellowed, and ran forward, sword in hand. Thomas was at his shoulder, the servants and Prabhankar behind. None of the fallen Marathas had been killed, but they had all been dazed by the noise and the flashing of the guns as well as the flying bullets. Now they could not match the sudden physical assault. Swords flashed and steel clanged, but four of them died. The others ran away into the darkness.

Unfortunately, the horses had also run away into the gloom.

Richard got his men back inside the stakes, and they set to work reloading as quickly as they could.

'Will they come again?' he asked Prabhankar.

The guide had killed one of the marauders with his knife. 'I think they will come again, sahib. These are very fierce men.' He grinned in the half light of the dawn as he cleaned his blade. 'But not so fierce as you.'

The Marathas did come again, but not for nearly an hour, and in that time the arquebuses were again made ready.

The Indians had learned by their experience, however, and besides, it was now growing steadily lighter; they were able to see just how few men were opposed to them.

They divided their forces, and some fifteen men came from each side. Richard saw what they were doing, and had the time to change the setting of his stakes, but it meant that each charging group was met by only three bullets instead of six; he doubted any struck home, and then the Marathas were through the fire and amongst them, slashing down with their tulwars and thrusting with their lances, uttering shrill cries. They were in the main little men, dark of skin, with hooked noses and eager expressions, and found close quarters with the husky Englishmen a dangerous business. The servants used their staves and daggers to good effect, Thomas cut and thrust with his sword, while Richard parried a lance thrust, pierced the fellow to send him tumbling from his horse, swung his sword to hit another man across the back and send him flying, and then came back to despatch a third with a stab through the groin.

The battle lasted a few furious seconds, and then the Marathas broke off the fight, galloping their mounts away to halt at a distance.

They had left seven of their number on the ground this time; four were dead, and three wounded; these Prabhankar quickly despatched with his knife, grasping them by the hair to lift their heads and cut their throats.

Richard had no time to protest at his methods; he was too concerned with his own casualties.

Smith was dead, and Evans was clearly dying; half his intestines were protruding through a gaping hole in his belly. Rogers was also wounded, although apparently not fatally, and Thomas had received a slash across the arm, which he was binding up with a kerchief. Only Barnes, Prabhankar and Richard himself were unhurt.

'You see to Rogers, cousin,' he told Thomas. 'Barnes, you and Prabhankar help me re-set these stakes and load these arquebuses.'

They soon had themselves again in a posture of defence, only to watch the Marathas riding off.

'They are robbers, not fighting men,' Prabankar said contemptuously; he had entirely changed his opinion of them.

Richard cleaned and sheathed his sword, and looked at Thomas. 'What now?'

'We continue. As soon as we are able.'

By which he meant, as soon as Evans was dead. This obviously was not going to be long delayed. Thomas knelt by him and prayed while the rest of them dug graves and buried Smith. The Marathas they left.

'The creatures of the plain will soon dispose of them,' Prabhankar assured them.

But Richard hunted through their weapons, and took a tulwar and a spear for himself to add to his rapier. Barnes and Prabhankar did likewise.

They were also fortunate enough to have secured two of the Maratha horses. These had galloped off during the fight, but now returned, seeking their dead masters. They were small, docile animals, and Richard doubted they would carry a man as large as himself very far, but they soon proved useful, especially for Rogers.

Following the death of Evans the following morning, their journey now assumed the qualities of a nightmare, as they resumed their march to the north-east. They saw no more Marathas – no doubt word was being spread of their determination to defend themselves – but their own progress was hampered by the increasing weakness of the servant. Two days after the fight his wound began to fester, and it was clear that he was also going to die.

They put him on one of the horses, and in desperation left

the high ground and descended into a valley to seek a village. Here they were received with awe; the word of how this band of strange white-skinned men had put to flight a much larger Maratha force had spread. They were given food to eat and tacitly offered their pick of the village women to bed. Not even Richard took advantage of this hospitality: the headman could do nothing for Rogers, who was now delirious. This was bad, but worse, from Richard's point of view, was the way Thomas's wound, such a little scratch, was also refusing to heal.

'It matters naught,' Thomas said. 'We cannot now turn back. We must continue, to Delhi.' He grinned. 'They will be able to cure my arm, in Delhi.'

He was revealing his stubborn streak, Richard knew. But equally was he right; there was simply no alternative, now. The four of them could never regain Surat, much less Goa.

But would Delhi provide them with succour, he wondered?

Richard found it difficult not to be angry at the dispositions of fate. Or his own stupidity in abandoning Spain, a land of friends and welcoming senoras – the senoritas were more careful in their relations with the handsome Englishman – for this forlorn and now surely doomed adventure.

Had they not been told of the countless embassies that had left the courts of Europe in search of Prester John, never to be heard of again? No doubt their bones too were bleaching beneath this pitiless sun.

They buried Rogers and marched, Thomas now mounted as he developed a fever. They had lost track of days, but Richard estimated they had travelled for at least a month since leaving Surat. A month! By Prabhankar's reckoning they were only half way. But then they fell in with a caravan bound south, where as usual they were stared at in amazement, but not hostility when Prabhankar told of their encounter with the Marathas.

'Oh, they are devils, not men,' the wagon-master told them. 'But you say you defeated them? Truly you are men amongst men.'

There was a surgeon with the caravan, and he was persuaded to inspect Thomas's arm, which was now thoroughly swollen and inflamed. He decided to lance the swelling, and did so, after Thomas had been made to chew a substance called *bhang*, gleaned from the hemp plant, which made him quite delirious. Yet the pain must have been intense, for he screamed in agony and it took several men to hold him down while vast quantities of evil-smelling pus were drawn off. Then he quietened, and the wound was bound up again.

'He should rest,' the surgeon said.

Richard bit his lip in indecision, because the caravan was bound south, and he had no doubt what Thomas's decision would be.

'Ask him how many days' march to Delhi,' he told Prabhankar.

Prabhankar had a talk with the wagon-master, and then interpreted; Richard had only been able to understand the gist of what had been said ... and hadn't liked what he'd heard.

'He says it will be a waste of time our going to Delhi, sahib. Delhi was a great city once, but many years ago it was sacked by a great Mongol conqueror, called Timur. You have heard of this man?'

Richard had actually heard of Timur, called the Lame, but very much as a legend of cruelty and destruction. He was not sure he believed in him now.

'You say that was many years ago.'

'More than a hundred, sahib. But the city has never been rebuilt. The Lodi sultans have moved the capital to a place called Agra.'

'Have you heard of this place?'

'No, sahib. I have only heard of Delhi. But now I understand that the Delhi of which I heard was the country, not the city.'

'This grows more and more into a wild goose chase with every day,' Richard growled. 'Where is Agra situated, if it exists?'

'That is good news, sahib. It is much closer than Delhi. The wagon-master says it is not more than a dozen days from here.'

'Then we will continue, as soon as Sir Thomas is strong enough.'

Prabhankar conveyed this to the wagon-master, who shrugged.

'Ask him if we will find succour in Agra,' Richard said.

The wagon-master shrugged again.

* * *

They camped for the night close by the caravan, Richard enjoying his most secure night's sleep in two months, disturbed only by Thomas's moanings and tossings.

Barnes, indeed, was so excited by this first glimpse of true civilisation for so long that he went into the main encampment to enjoy the dancing of the nautch girls, and sample the kumiss, a fermented drink made from mares' milk.

The caravan departed at dawn. Richard sat by Thomas to watch them go; Prabhankar went to mingle with the merchants one last time. The scene was colourful as the horses and mules milled about, the tents were folded, and in a vast cloud of dust the wagons went on their way.

After half an hour Prabhankar returned. But without Barnes.

'He has gone with the caravan, sahib,' Prabhankar explained.

'Gone? With the caravan?' Richard was confounded. 'How could he do that?'

'He offered the wagon-master two of the guns and a bag of powder and bullets for a safe journey to Surat, sahib.'

Richard leapt to his feet and hunted through their supplies. Two of the arquebuses were indeed gone, and half their stock of munitions.

'The rascal,' he growled. 'Unhobble that horse, Prabhankar. I'll fetch him back.'

'I would not do that, sahib.'

Richard glared at him. 'Why not? The fellow is my servant.'

'Pratap Rao, the wagon-master, is well pleased with the guns, sahib. He will not give them up. And Barnes sahib has promised to teach him their use. He will not let you take him back now. Besides ... of what use is a servant who deserts his master?'

Richard chewed his lip in indecision.

'Barnes Sahib was afraid,' Prabhankar said contemptuously.

Richard glanced at him. 'Are you not afraid, Prabhankar?'

'It is a servant's privilege to be afraid, sahib, where a master must always be courageous. But it is a servant's duty to follow his master, even into running away – should the master call upon him to do so.'

Richard scratched his head, uncertain as to the faithful fellow's true meaning.

But at least he was a faithful fellow. While Barnes ... he

watched the caravan out of sight with a growing sense of despair.

'It is my cousin's intention to reach Delhi – or as it now appears, Agra – and speak with Sultan Ibrahim Lodi,' he said. 'And then continue to the court of Prester John.'

Prabhankar inclined his head.

But those were words.

Thomas Blunt regained consciousness a few hours later, weak, but with an active brain. He too was angry when he learned of Barnes' desertion. But as Richard had estimated would be the case, he had no doubts about continuing.

'When you have regained your strength,' Richard told him. 'We have still at least twelve days to go.'

'A trifle,' Thomas said. 'After so long.'

He was determinedly confident, but within twenty-four hours his arm began to swell again, and the fever had returned.

'I think the sir sahib will die,' Prabhankar said.

'That is not possible,' Richard declared. 'We must lance the wound again.'

The wagon-master had given them some of the *bhang*.

Prabhankar looked doubtful. 'He will die,' he said again.

Richard felt like striking him. Instead he sat by Thomas and explained the situation. 'The wound will not heal,' he said. 'I am at my wits' end.'

Thomas was only intermittently lucid. But now his eyes opened, and he stared at his cousin. 'It is hard, to come to such a heathen land, and there lay down my bones. Is my child a boy or a girl, Richard, do you suppose?'

'Undoubtedly a son,' Richard said.

'And has my Lizzie survived the ordeal?'

'Undoubtedly. But you will see them again, Thomas. You are not going to die.' No matter what Prabhankar says, he thought.

'I am dying,' Thomas said. 'And you are risking your own life, staying here with me. Fetch me that wallet.'

Richard gave him the wallet, which throughout their march had hung from Thomas's belt.

'In there is my commission from King Henry,' Thomas said. 'As well as our store of coin. Strap that wallet to your own belt, and guard it with your life. Do you swear this?'

'Willingly.'

'Do you also swear to continue with this mission, to the court of Lodi Shah, and thence on to the court of Prester John?'

'We will both continue this mission, Thomas.'

'Swear!' Thomas said fiercely.

'I swear,' Richard said.

Thomas smiled. 'Then am I content.'

That night he died.

Richard and Prabhankar buried Thomas at dawn, Richard cutting some wood to make a cross while Prabhankar watched with interest, and then Richard considered the situation.

He had four donkeys left, and a horse. He had ample food, as they were only two men, and there were four arquebuses and sufficient powder and shot for at least one more action – supposing they were not again beset by forty men at one time. He also had his rapier, and Thomas's broadsword, together with the weapons he had taken from the dead Marathas.

Against these assets, his clothes were in rags, his boots long disintegrated so that he walked barefoot, as did Prabhankar; this was no great handicap – his feet had become as tough as leather, as had his skin, which was by now also burned the colour of leather, while his beard had grown again and was several inches long.

And he had the precious wallet, and a mission. Which, he was now realising, was virtually impossible of completion. How could one man, even with a faithful servant, walk right across Asia?

But perhaps Ibrahim Lodi Shah, who everyone seemed to consider the greatest King in India, would allow him to recruit from amongst his people.

It was his only hope.

Richard and Prabhankar resumed their journey. Now it was obvious that they were entering civilisation; they encountered several caravans, and a great number of people merely travelling from village to village; the villages – and some of them were small towns – were quite close together.

Everywhere great interest was shown in the white man, with his strange weapons, and while they were universally welcomed, they also proved too great a temptation to the local thieves. One night as they both slept in the supposed security of a hut given them by a village headman, Richard awoke to find his entire spare bag of clothes gone. They had been in a pretty desperate state anyway, but their disappearance still left him utterly bereft save for what he was wearing. Fortunately, he always slept with both sword and wallet clutched against his chest.

'It would be useless to protest, sahib,' Prabhankar told him. 'The headman probably sent the thieves.'

Once again they abandoned the villages and kept to the high ground wherever possible. Now it was distinctly cold at night, and they had to huddle against each other for warmth, although during the days the sun was scorchingly hot. They pressed on, down now to two donkeys and the remaining horse – the others having died or been sold, as their store of what needed carrying dwindled – two ragged scarecrows of men, putting one foot in front of the other with the grimmest determination, thinking of nothing but their goal.

Until the day that they stumbled down from a hillside where they had spent the night, into a fertile valley ... and a flock of peacocks.

3

THE LION

Situated on the banks of the Jumna River, Agra emerged out of the morning mist as something of a surprise: it was so obviously very new, and yet there was evidence that the city had been destroyed quite recently. Richard later discovered that it had been built only half a century earlier by one of Ibrahim Lodi's ancestors, who had decided that this undeniably attractive situation, in a fertile river valley some hundred miles south of Delhi, was the ideal place to create a new capital city to replace the ruined old. And that, only twenty years before, it had been wrecked by a fearsome earthquake, of which the inhabitants still spoke in whispers. In places the rebuilding was still going on.

The city was walled, and there were guards on the gates. Richard and Prabhankar had to join a huge jostle of people waiting to enter, and at Prabhankar's suggestion, Richard concealed all the European weapons, including his rapier, in the baskets borne by the donkeys. With his black hair and beard and his skin now thoroughly browned by the sun, he could very well pass for an Indian, but to make sure Prabhankar made him take off his shirt as well, and bound up his head in a form of turban. Thus adequately disguised, the two men entered the city safely enough, staring around themselves at the houses, some of considerable size, made from sun-baked brick, at the bustling, evidently prosperous people, as strangely juxtaposed as any Richard had ever seen, for here, far more than in Surat, there were mosques and Hindu temples virtually side by side, and veiled Muslim women walked the streets together with sari-clad Indians.

But he observed that the Hindus treated the Muslims with a studied deference. They were the conquered, and had been now for centuries.

Prabhankar quickly found them a caravanserai where they could wash themselves and obtain some food. Richard spent some of his precious coin to obtain Indian clothes and then Prabhankar remained to watch their animals and belongings while he made his way to the Sultan's palace.

He felt more confident than he had for a long time, not only because he had reached his destination, but because there was evidence of a considerable power here, as well as considerable wealth . . . and many people spoke either Arabic or Persian.

The inhabitants varied from the very dark complexions of southern India to skins as pale as his own, and to his relief, for all his size very little notice was taken of him as he strode along – clearly he was imagined to be a Pathan from the north.

Lodi's palace was a magnificent affair. Carved from white marble, it occupied several acres, and was, so far as Richard could make out, a place of fountains and pools connected by running water which set up an eternal rustle.

It was also a crowded place, or at least the outer porticos were, as men of every complexion and demeanour jostled together. But Richard knew the drill now, and approached one of the stately, turban-clad majordomos.

'You wish to see the Badshah?' The man looked him up and down, took in his tattered clothing and mud-stained feet. 'Begone with you, fellow.'

Richard produced a silver coin.

'I have news of great importance to the Sultan.'

The majordomo regarded the coin with contempt.

'What news can be of importance to the Badshah that he does not already possess?'

'What I have to say I will say to the Sultan alone,' Richard insisted, and produced another coin.

Two coins later he was escorted along a covered pathway surrounding a magnificent inner courtyard, in which peacocks and their hens strutted to and fro, uttering their raucous cries. The mosaic tiles which composed the floor of the yard were sadly soiled, but the birds themselves were of an exquisite beauty, the various shades of blue and green melding into each other.

At the door of the next chamber, there was another majordomo, and he also had to be supplied with silver. Richard realised this was going to be a costly business. But he had risked his life to be here, and he was not hesitating now.

He was admitted into the chamber, where there were several men standing before a table, behind which sat a most resplendent fellow, wearing a turban, and a blue silk tunic descending past his hips.

Richard had never heard of a king who sat at a table to receive his suitors, but he concealed his surprise, and took his place in turn.

After about an hour he found himself before the table.

'State your business,' the man said, in Arabic, the majordomo having whispered in his ear.

'I come from across the sea, Great King,' Richard said. 'Bearing greetings from King Henry VIII of England to your majesty. I also brought with me a large number of presents, but alas, we were beset by robbers, Marathas, and although we fought them off, most of our goods were lost.'

The seated man regarded him. 'You are a fool as well as a liar. You are a fool to imagine I would believe such a story. Just as you are a fool to imagine that the Badshah would personally receive one such as you.'

Richard shot the majordomo a glance, but was met with an impassive gaze in return.

'Robbed by Marathas, you say,' the Vizier continued. 'You are no doubt a thief and a robber yourself. I am told that wallet contains silver coin.'

'My silver coin,' Richard said. 'If you will examine a piece, you will see upon it the likeness of my king, Great Henry.'

'Give me one,' the Vizier commanded.

Richard hesitated, then handed over a groat.

The Vizier peered at it. 'Now the bag,' he said.

'This is my money,' Richard said.

The Vizier glared at him. 'It is stolen money, which I am now confiscating. Be grateful that I do not have your hand chopped off for stealing. If there is the smallest accusation made against you, that will be your punishment.' He turned to the majordomo. 'Take the wallet, and throw this fellow out.' Before Richard could properly grasp what was happening to him two men had seized his arms, and another had torn the wallet from his belt.

'Thieves and rascals!' Richard shouted, and used his strength to attempt to break free. He was certainly stronger than any two of the Indians, but now there were four men assailing him, and raining blows on his head and shoulders and arms and legs.

Borne down by sheer weight of numbers he fell to the floor, and was dragged from the chamber and along the covered walkway. If he was aware of total humiliation as well as despair, he did not seem to arouse a great deal of interest in the people looking on, and a few minutes later was hurled into the street, where a dog promptly urinated on him.

He sat up, and staggered to his feet, looking back at the gateway to the palace. The majordomo was there, speaking with the guards, who commenced staring at him in turn; he could not doubt that he would be refused admittance should he attempt to return.

He was actually too bemused to consider it, at that moment. He could only understand that after everything he had experienced, he had now been robbed and beaten up for his pains – and had lost the King's Commission.

He had failed Thomas, who had died to make this mission a success.

And now he had nowhere to turn; he did not even know if he had the means to regain Goa.

As for Prester John ... *he* remained as nebulous as ever.

Shoulders hunched, he made his way back to the caravanserai, and Prabhankar, to whom he told what had happened.

'This is very bad,' the Indian agreed. 'What will you do now, sahib?'

Richard noted that it was the first time since their expedition had begun that Prabhankar had not used the word 'we'.

'I don't rightly know,' he confessed. 'How long may we stay here without paying?'

'Three days in all, sahib. But we must still buy our food. We have very little left.'

Richard nodded.

'We will have to sell one of our animals. Can you attend to that?'

'Yes, sahib. I will see to it. The horse will fetch the best price.'

Prabhankar led the animal away, and Richard waited with the remaining two donkeys in the corner of the caravanserai they had appropriated as their own. Dejected as he felt, and exhausted and painful as he was, his brain was as active as ever – now that his initial despair was beginning to wear off he was prepared to consider his future.

He had to face the fact that the mission had turned out a complete failure. Everyone from whom Thomas had sought assistance had merely directed him to someone else who would hopefully dispose of him. As had finally happened. Sooner or later someone was going to dispose of himself, the sole survivor. Therefore he must now admit defeat, and crawl back to Goa, regain Master Bottomley and the *Bonaventure*, and commence his return to England. No doubt Dom Jaime Alvarado would be mightily amused. He wondered what Elena would say.

In any event, his entire attention must be paid to regaining the Portuguese settlement. Presumably he would obtain a good sum of money for the horse, and he was prepared to sell one of the donkeys as well; Prabhankar and himself had little enough gear to carry back. It would be a horrendous journey, he had no doubt, but they were both young and strong, he retained his weapons ... and they would just have to see to it that they did not encounter any Marathas on the way.

His decision taken, he felt much easier in his mind, and allowed himself to reflect that his failure had been no fault of his own; the expedition had been doomed from the start – if Prester John really did exist, he was not meant to be found by Europeans, that was obvious.

He even dozed from time to time, although he was very aware that the people around him were watching him, and he had no intention of sleeping and again being robbed. As the hours passed, however, he commenced to feel hungry, and began to wonder what had happened to Prabhankar.

Then it occurred to him that nothing had happened to Prabhankar ... and that Prabhankar was not coming back.

Once again he felt as if he had been kicked in the stomach. He would lead him anywhere, Prabhankar had said. Because his master had so instructed him. But had he not really only been interested in helping the Europeans as long as they possessed silver? Now that was gone, Prabhankar had started to think of himself ... and the valuable horse which he had been told to sell.

Richard realised that his position was now more disastrous than ever. He still had the two donkeys, but he spoke very little Hindustani, and were he to try to sell them he had no doubt he would be robbed blind. Yet there was nothing else he could do.

As for attempting the return journey by himself ... but once again he refused to allow himself to despair.

There was a small portion of cold curry left, and this he ate, washing it down with water sucked from the spout in the middle of the caravanserai yard. Then he decided to get some sleep, as it was now all but dark, and see if he could sell one of the donkeys the following day.

And keep his eye open for the wretched Prabhankar as well.

He slept with his sword across his lap, and the donkeys' halters looped to his wrist, but in fact no one attempted to rob him, until he awoke, just on dawn, to discover two men standing above him.

Richard leapt to his feet, sword presented, and then saw that neither man carried a weapon. He lowered his own.

'You are he who has come from across the sea?' asked one of the men, in Arabic.

'Yes,' Richard said.

'Our master would speak with you.'

'Your master?'

'Ghopal Das.'

The man obviously expected his master's name to be familiar.

'Where is this man?' Richard inquired.

'At his house. He bids you attend him there.'

'I cannot leave my goods, or my animals.'

'They will accompany you.'

Richard considered. But he reflected that he could hardly be worse off than he now was. He put away his sword, and led the donkeys behind the two men. They left the caravanserai and made their way through the just awakening streets of the city, listening to the cry of the muezzin – Richard observed that neither of his two companions obeyed the call to prayer.

Eventually they came to a high wall, and through a small gate were admitted into a courtyard which fronted a house of some size and splendour.

'This is the house of Ghopal Das,' his guides explained.

Richard was impressed.

He was even more impressed when he was taken inside the house itself, a place of soft carpets and pleasant odours. He was led along a covered gallery which enclosed one of those inner courts which he had now come to understand was the principal mark of Indian architecture; this one had a fountain in the centre in the form of a curved python, the water issuing from its mouth.

Now he encountered white-clad servants, of both sexes, who bowed to him as he passed, until he was shown into a chamber where there waited several more servants, all boys now. This room contained a huge bed as well as several ornately carved chairs, and an equally carved table. On the table there waited a nostril-tingling assortment of food, not all curries, but all evidently highly spiced, while on the bed there lay a splendid suit of clothes: a dhoti and sandals, to be topped by a white tunic embroidered with gold thread, and a white turban.

Best of all, there was a tub of steaming water in the centre of the room.

'Our master wishes his guest to be comfortable before he greets you,' his guide explained. 'These boys will see to your requirements.'

Other servants had unloaded the donkeys, and all of Richard's remaining belongings were now brought into the room. Then the door was closed behind him, and the boys immediately busied themselves. Before he could protest he was stripped of his own dirty clothing, and led to the bath. While he sat in the hot water, which felt delicious, they soaped and massaged him, discarding their own dhoties to do so, and proceeding with such enthusiasm that he realised that when the guide had said they would attend to his every requirement, he had meant just that.

It was so long since he had had sex he could not stop himself responding; but equally, it was so long since he had had the time even to think about sex he had no wish to begin with young boys.

His bath over he was invited to eat. The meal was delicious, even if it was served with nothing but water. But this was no doubt to the good; he had no idea what this Ghopal Das might want of him, and a clear head was essential. On the other hand, this was the first time since leaving Goa that he was being treated with hospitality – and what hospitality!

When the meal was completed he was dressed. The boys had by now hunted through his belongings to see if there was anything he needed, and exclaimed in wonder at the rapier and the arquebuses. They held up the weapons and offered them to him, but he shook his head. Better to remain unarmed where he could not effectively hope to defend himself.

Then at last he was taken to meet Ghopal Das.

The way led through more covered galleries, and round more inner courts. In one of these, larger than the others, some young women were playing a peculiar game; they were each armed with a carefully curved stick, with which they chased a small ball over the beaten earth with tremendous enthusiasm.

They made an entrancing sight, for they wore only dhoties, which covered from their waists to their ankles – otherwise their brown bodies, including their feet, were quite naked, and gleamed with sweat, as did their black pigtails. And they were clearly very young and very nubile.

Nor were they the slightest bit embarrassed at being passed by a group of men; although they ceased their game to stare at Richard, giggling and chattering at each other, they made no attempt to conceal their breasts from him.

Now indeed he was aware of how long he had been forced to play the monk.

The girls were left behind and he entered a large, high-ceilinged room; the walls were again worked with intricate scrolls, and there was a great deal of carved furniture. Seated very straight on one of the chairs, was a dignified looking Hindu whom Richard knew at once to be Ghopal Das. There were two other men in the room, but these stood beside the chair. One of them, from his resemblance to the seated man, was clearly a son.

All three men were dressed much as Richard himself, richly but very simply. Ghopal Das appeared to be in his fifties. He wore a moustache but no beard, and his face was full, with rounded features. His body, too, was distinctly plump.

'Welcome to my home,' he said, in Arabic.

'You are gracious to invite me, sir,' Richard replied.

Ghopal seemed pleased, and gestured him to a chair. Richard took his seat, also sitting straight. He could only wait to discover why he had been brought here – what was wanted of him.

'I am told you have come from far away. From across the sea. I have known men who have seen the sea,' Ghopal told him. 'Is it truly possible to cross it?'

'My people do so regularly,' Richard said, stretching the point a little to include the Spanish and the Portuguese as his people. 'My country is an island set in the ocean.'

'Are your people strong?'

'There are none stronger,' Richard asserted.

Ghopal Das exchanged glances with his two companions.

'How distant is this island?' he asked.

'It is a long way. We sailed for seven months to reach Goa.'

'Goa?'

'It is a place on the Indian coast. That in turn is three months journeying from Agra.'

'You have journeyed for nearly a year, to come here,' Ghopal observed. 'To see Lodi Shah? Why?'

Richard had already decided that for the time being it were best to forget Prester John. It was his business to obtain the maximum possible value from this odd, and promising, turn of events.

'My King is a mighty man, who considers it right that he should be known and respected by all the other rulers on earth.'

'Thus he sent one man?'

'The embassy was a large one, when it left Goa,' Richard explained. 'But we suffered grievous losses from illness and robbers.'

'So that you reached Agra with one servant, who has now absconded,' Ghopal observed.

Richard understood that he had been watched more closely than he had realised.

'I am sorry to say that is the case,' he agreed.

'I am told there are strange weapons in your baggage,' Ghopal remarked.

'I have my weapons,' Richard acknowledged.

'Will you show us their use?'

'If you wish.'

'Now?' asked the younger man, speaking for the first time.

'Certainly.'

Servants were despatched to fetch the weapons, and Ghopal Das escorted Richard into another inner court, this one empty of young women or servants, and faced by a blank wall. There was a form of target set against the wall, and from it protruded two eight-feet long spears, to indicate that it had recently been in use.

The spears were removed, while Richard took his rapier from the baggage roll.

'That is a strange sword,' Ghopal Das remarked. 'It has no edge.'

'But it has a point,' Richard said.

'How may a man fight with just a point?' the son inquired.

'If you will make a pass at me I will show you.'

The young man looked at his father, who nodded. A servant hurried off to return with a tulwar, one of the slightly curved blades used in Asia. It had a haft and a keen cutting edge, but was only two-thirds the length of the rapier.

'Are you ready?' the young man said.

Richard nodded, and took his stance, as if he were about to fight a duel, sword in right hand, dagger in left.

The young Indian regarded him for a moment, and then made a very quick advance, the curving blade swirling in front of him, whistling as it cut the air. Richard evaded the somewhat open attack easily enough, but he was here to display his skill, and so he engaged somewhat sooner than he would have done had he been fighting in earnest, choosing his moment to catch the tulwar on his dagger. The two blades screeched sparks as the tulwar slid along the shorter weapon to lodge against the steel finger guard. As it did so, Richard passed his rapier cleanly through the gap between the Indian's arm and body, just piercing the cloth of his tunic.

Then he leapt away.

'You are a dead man,' he said.

The young man looked down at his tunic, and then up again, his eyes gleaming with anger.

'Enough Ramdaj,' Ghopal Das said. 'That was skilfully done.'

'It can be done, sometimes to greater effect, the other way,' Richard told him. 'Catching the opposing blade with the sword, and using the poignard to finish the affair.'

'I see this.' Ghopal gestured at the arquebus. 'Is that as deadly a weapon?'

'No. But it kills at a distance.'

Richard lit his slow match, and set his stake, watched with great interest by the Indians. Clearly he was meant to shoot at the target, but he was seeking the greatest effect, and instead selected one of several large earthenware pots, presently empty, which stood against the adjacent wall.

'Am I permitted to destroy this?'

'If you imagine you can,' Ghopal agreed, clearly mystified.

Richard loaded his piece, ramming the bullet well home, then placed the barrel in the cleft stake and sighted very carefully. He pulled the trigger, and the Indians gave shouts of alarm at the explosion and the puff of smoke. And then gazed at the pot in consternation; the bullet had only just struck the side of it, but the impact had been sufficient to crack it from top to bottom.

'By the Lord Krishna,' Ramdaj commented.

'Are all of your king's soldiers armed as you?' Ghopal inquired.

'All,' Richard told him, deciding not to go into the relative uses of pikemen and arquebusiers at that moment.

'Then he must be, as you say, a formidable warrior.'

'Does he also have elephants?' Ramdaj said eagerly.

'No,' Richard said. 'Such creatures are unknown in my country.' He observed their disappointment, so added, 'but he possesses weapons of far greater value.'

'What can these be?' Ghopal asked.

'Firepieces, like this ...' he patted the arquebus. 'But much larger, which can hurl a stone ball for half a mile, say, eight hundred paces, knocking down all in its way.'

'I have heard of such things,' Ghopal said.

'But there are none in India?'

'None,' Ghopal said. 'We will talk some more, Blunt Sahib.'

That evening Richard dined with Ghopal Das' wife and two daughters, as well as Ramdaj and Ghopal himself.

As this was a Hindu household, none of the women was veiled. Ghopal Das' wife was dark-skinned and dignified, and must once have been a great beauty, Richard thought; she was adorned with a red spot in the middle of her forehead. Her daughters, who were also decorated with this spot, were certainly beautiful, with straight, slightly long noses, wide lips and white teeth, and sparkling black eyes. It was hard to estimate their ages, but he thought the elder one, whose name was Shana, might be sixteen or seventeen, and the younger one, Ghona, perhaps thirteen or fourteen. Both had been playing their ball and stick game earlier; now they had bathed and their hair had been carefully re-plaited, and like their mother they were dressed in saris, pale blue and dark green, which clung to their bodies when they moved and revealed enough hill and valley to suggest untold delights – especially to someone who had already had part of those delights displayed for him.

Unfortunately, like their mother, they spoke no Arabic, and Richard's Hindustani was not sufficient to carry on a conversation, at least with words. But he made do very well with looks and smiles, and resolved to learn the language properly as soon as possible if only to obtain some understanding of why he had been so miraculously rescued from the pit of despair. In Ghopal Das' house he was fed and clothed with the very best, treated as a member of the family . . . he even took a turn at playing stick and ball with the girls, to their great amusement.

He would have greatly enjoyed doing much more than that, but kept himself carefully in check, at least until Ghopal revealed his true intentions – Richard did not for a moment suppose his inclusion in such a household was an act of charity.

Resistance of temptation was not made easier by the statues of gods and goddesses which were to be found in every room and every courtyard, filling niches in the walls. These were invariably naked figures, the men with pronounced phalluses and women also displaying their sexual characteristics. People who worshipped such deities naturally suggested moral ethics very different to those obtained in Christianity. In fact, when he asked questions, Richard discovered that the Hindu religion and social structure was at once fascinating and entirely moral, except in relation to such things as nudity, and this was easily explained by the Indian climate, which made the wearing of clothes, except for decoration, an absurdity.

Ghopal Das and his family were vaishas: they believed themselves to be the third highest form of human life, only beneath the Brahmins, who were the only people on earth entitled to perform dharma, offer sacrifices to the universal Supreme God, Brahman, and the kshattriyas.

This religion was based on a holy book, the *Rigveda*, which was far more ancient than the Christian Bible, and by a later work, the *Upanishads*. These works told that the Brahmins were the people who had conquered India from the north, defeating the dark-skinned aboriginal inhabitants and driving them to the south or making them slaves. As slaves they had remained, the panchamas, or outcastes.

The caste system had developed slowly. When the Brahmins had conquered India it had been a golden age: all Brahmins had been noble and brave, and acceptable to the gods, all panchamas had been obedient and servile. As time went by, however, some of the Brahmins had abandoned the quest for perpetual righteousness, and thus lost their places in the elite. They had become kshattriyas, professional soldiers.

Those were still happy times, when the Brahmins and the kshattriyas ruled a prosperous and orderly world. Then came a further decline, with men seeking to make money rather than their peace with God. These men, who sank lower than the kshattriyas, were the vaishyas, or merchants. In this age men first began to know unhappiness – apart from the panchamas, of course, who had never *known* happiness.

Sadly, men had yet to decline another stage, into one where misery affected everyone because of their sloth and veniality. Those who had so sunk became the shudras, or cultivators. This was the stage in which the world was at present, the Brahmins said, and was typified by the Muslim conquest of so much of the subcontinent.

Escape from the caste system could only be achieved through death, which involved the doctrine of re-incarnation.

The ultimate aim of every man was to reach the state of moksha, when all earthly ambitions and lusts and fears were forgotten, and one lived in harmony with the gods. Once moksha was reached, there was no more rebirth. Reaching such a blissful state was however no easy task. This was the result of the concept of karma, or cause and effect, often confused with fate. One was reborn according to one's behaviour in one's previous life. Thus one might begin as a snake and wind up as a Brahmin, but even that did not guarantee moksha after death. For if the man's life, even the Brahmin's, was not virtuous, he would be reborn further down the scale, and might even become a snake again.

The gods occupied a hardly less ambivalent position. Brahman himself, regarded as the Creator, was conceived of as a trinity. This much was in line with Christian thought, but the other partners were very different to Jesus Christ and the Holy Ghost. Second of the gods was Vishnu, regarded as the preserver, the protector of the world and the god who had instituted dharma. Like all the gods, however, he was many-sided, and could manifest himself in any one of several avatars, or incarnations, the most famous being those of Rama, the hero of the epic poem *Ramayana*, and Krishna, the divine cowherd.

The images of him showed him sitting in the company of various of his consorts, or sleeping on the coils of a vast serpent, or standing, his four hands grasping different weapons.

The third member of the trinity, and far more disturbing, was Shiva, the destroyer, to complete the cosmic pattern, as often as not depicted with aroused phallus. Unlike Vishnu, here was a totally contradictory concept, for Shiva was both destroyer and restorer, a supreme ascetic and yet the epitome of sensuality.

Richard found it a strangely satisfying pantheon.

It was on the fourth day that Ghopal once again invited him into the private room.

'It seems to me that Karma has sent you to Delhi, and to me,' he remarked. 'What are your intentions, Blunt Sahib? Lodi has refused to accept your embassy, and he has stolen your credentials as well as your money.'

'Believe me, Ghopal Das, I fully understand my situation. But for you I would be destitute. As for what I must do, why, much as I honour and am grateful for your hospitality, I fear the time is coming when I must make my way back to Goa, and seek a ship for home.'

'You said it is three months' journey to Goa. You would attempt this alone?'

'I have no choice.'

'You would not survive. I have a caravan leaving for the south-west in two weeks' time. You will accompany it, and I will instruct some of my servants to continue with you to this place Goa.'

'Why should you do so much? I can never repay you.'

'I think you can,' Ghopal said. 'You have now lived under my roof for several days, and I have studied you carefully. I believe you are a man to be trusted. I will therefore speak plainly to you. I cannot believe you have anything but hatred for Lodi Shah.'

'It is difficult to hate a man I have never even seen,' Richard said. 'But I certainly can feel neither loyalty nor respect for him.'

'You may believe that he is also hateful. He is mean and cruel, as well as vicious. More, he is a Muslim, and as such is obnoxious to my people. Do you know anything of the history of this land?'

'Unfortunately, no.'

'Then listen. This has been a fertile, prosperous and famous country for many hundreds of years. Have you heard of Alexander the Great?'

'Oh, indeed.'

'He invaded this country nearly two thousand years ago, and won a mighty battle against the then king, Porus. Alexander went away again, but the land was then ruled by the Maurya, famous men. Have you heard of Ashoka?'

Richard shook his head.

'He was the greatest king who ever ruled. He conquered far to the south, and made Delhi the centre of the universe. After the Maurya, there came the Gupta, only less mighty than their predecessors. But, after the Gupta, our kings were less successful. The great empire was split up into several different states.'

'I heard something of this, in the South,' Richard said.

'Thus were we victims to Mahmud of Ghazni, the greatest warrior of his time. Fifteen times did he come down from the mountains of Afghanistan to plunder our cities and carry off our women. He was a Muslim.'

Ghopal Das brooded for several seconds, as if that was the ultimate crime.

'He left the country weak and disunited. A hundred and fifty years after Mahmud, Mohammed of Ghur invaded us, and stayed. That was three hundred and fifty years ago, Blunt Sahib. For that time, the Muslims have been our rulers. Many were the Muslim dynasties who have sat on the throne in Delhi, for the Muslims fight amongst themselves more than any other people. And they were helpless when Timur the Mongol came down from the North, a hundred and twenty-five years ago, to rout their armies and sack Delhi. He too was a Muslim.

'But Timur went away again, and the land was left desolate. It was seized by an Afghan chieftain, Buhlul Lodi, who declared himself Badshah seventy years ago. My father told me of these things. Of all the Muslims who have ruled this land, the Lodis have been the worst tyrants to my people.'

'May I ask what is meant by the word Badshah?'

'Why, acknowledged king: master of the country. The present Badshah is a descendant of this Buhlul. He reigns here by force of arms, and has so suborned some of my compatriots that the rest of us are helpless without outside assistance. And where is this to be gained? It is true Lodi has many enemies. There is one power in particular, a Tatar robber chieftain named Zahir-ud-Din Muhammad, whom they call Babur, or the Lion, of whom Lodi is very afraid. This Babur has set himself up in Kabul as a sultan, and has been raiding south of the Khyber Pass for some years now, but like Mahmud of Ghazni, he always goes away again. But as you will have gathered from his name, Babur is also a Muslim, and undoubtedly would also treat us Hindus with contempt. My people have been subjected to Muslim rule for too many generations. Now they lack spirit. Yet one day, surely, we must free ourselves from such a yoke, if we can gain but a single worthwhile ally. It occurs to me that you may be the man to help us accomplish this.'

'Me?' Richard asked uneasily.

'You, because you have the ear of this great king of yours. Were he to send an army to our aid, equipped with such swords and firing pieces as you have displayed to us, then surely Lodi would fall.'

'Ah,' Richard said. The Indian's dream was even more impossible of achievement than he had feared. He had never even spoken with King Henry – although no doubt he would be given an audience should he return from this adventure. But as for the rest . . . 'Ghopal Das, you have been straight with me, so I will be straight with you in return. My king is a great and noble man, who would like nothing better than to help you. But you are speaking of an undertaking of enormous expense, to send an army so far. To conduct such a war would strain the resources of my country beyond endurance.'

'Do you imagine,' Ghopal asked, 'that I would seek such assistance and not be prepared to pay for it. Listen to me, Blunt Sahib. You will tell your king that in the palace of Lodi Shah there is sufficient wealth to finance a hundred armies. Have you never heard of the 'Mountain of Light', the Koh-i-noor?'

'Well, I have,' Richard said. 'But I have little idea what it is.'

'Why, it is a diamond, but of enormous size; it weighs one hundred and ninety-one carats. And yet it is but a small part of the wonders to be found in Lodi's treasure house. All of these things will belong to your king when he brings Lodi down, and allows us a ruler of our own in his place.'

Richard stroked his chin. The offer was certainly tempting.

'You have the power to make such a promise?' he asked.

'Yes,' Ghopal replied. 'I speak for a considerable group of my people who think as I do. They are men who will honour my promise.'

'Then I will promise in turn to do my utmost to persuade my king to undertake such an expedition,' Richard said. 'I can do no more than that.'

'Nor can I ask more,' Ghopal agreed.

The idea was of course preposterous, Richard told himself. Or was it? Where Master Bottomley could take his ship, there could a fleet sail. And where six ill-prepared men had walked several hundred miles, and all died save one, was it not possible for a thousand men, well-armed and led, and knowing what to expect – for he would lead them himself – to reach Delhi for the loss of perhaps no more than half their number?

He did not doubt that five hundred English soldiers would be sufficient to overturn Ibrahim Lodi Shah.

And if King Henry was not interested, then could he not raise such an army of his own – with the promise of the greatest treasure on earth at the end of it?

It was certainly something to be considered.

He became impatient for the caravan to leave, even if it meant abandoning his delightful surroundings and even more delightful companions. Shana very seldom left his side now, and they laughed and winked at each other as they ate sweetmeats or played games or just sat in one of the arbours, swinging idly to and fro on the suspended settees.

She was a constant temptation, for he had no fear that she would resist him should he attempt to interfere with her. And how he wanted to cup those swelling young breasts she displayed so carelessly, or stroke the smoothly rounded buttocks against which the silk of the sari flattened itself, or investigate the curling black down he could equally discern through the thin material.

But to do that would be to betray Ghopal Das' hospitality, indeed, their new partnership. The sooner the caravan left the better.

And finally it was ready. The afternoon before his departure he played at his last game of ball and stick with the two girls and their maids, laughing as loudly as anyone when he was neatly tripped and went sprawling, one of the girls tumbling over him in a flail of hair and arms and legs. A second later he sat up straight when there was a tremendous crash from the front of the house, followed by the clash of weapons.

The girls stopped laughing and looked towards the sound, insensibly closing around the big Englishman. For a moment Richard was uncertain what to do, then the urge to arm himself became overwhelming – and his weapons were in his bedchamber.

Gently he parted the brown shoulders in front of him, and looked at Ramdaj, running along the walkway, waving and shouting incoherently. He reached the play area, and then fell to his knees and on to his face.

Shana screamed, for sticking out from between his shoulder blades was a spearhead.

Ramdaj was dead before his sisters reached him. He was the

most fortunate member of his family.

Behind him there ran armed men, wearing the distinctive blue and gold colours of Lodi Shah, with drawn and bloody swords in their hands.

The girls screamed even louder, and clung to Richard for protection. He had none to offer. The soldiers closed on them and he expected them all to be massacred. Instead the serving girls were chased away, and the two daughters, as well as Richard himself, were herded towards the front of the house, where they encountered Ghopal Das and his wife, also surrounded by armed men.

'We have been betrayed,' Ghopal gasped, and was struck across the shoulders by the flat of a sword. He fell to his knees, but was immediately dragged to his feet and pushed towards the doorway and the street.

His wife went behind him, and Richard and the two girls were herded behind them. Quite a crowd had gathered on the street, staring and chattering, but no one attempted to help them, as they were forced towards the palace.

Richard's brain was racing. As Ghopal Das had said, his plans for the overthrow of Lodi Shah must have been betrayed, and thus ... he had no idea what to expect. But he had seen enough of this land to know that just as great wealth sat cheek by jowl with great poverty, so did beauty and manners and generosity lie lightly on top of ruthless cruelty and an utter disregard for human life of whatever age or sex.

He looked at the girls. They had been given no time to dress and were holding hands and shivering as they were marched through the gates of the palace and along various covered walkways into a somewhat small chamber, the right hand wall of which consisted of a heavy curtain. Against the rear wall there was a single high-backed chair. Standing beside it was the Vizier Richard had encountered on his earlier visit.

'Kneel,' the Vizier commanded.

Ghopal Das fell to his knees, as did the women. Richard followed their example. Survival was what mattered here, however he must humiliate himself.

They waited, kneeling, scowled at by the Vizier, while their guards stood behind them. Then the curtain parted on the far wall, and Ibrahim Shah Lodi entered, accompanied by two other men, clearly of distinction for they were richly dressed.

But not so richly as the Sultan, who wore a cloth of gold tunic over blue silk pantaloons, gold-coloured shoes, and a blue turban, in which was set a huge ruby. He carried no weapon, but Richard observed that his face was rouged like that of a woman, and his fingers were covered in rings of varying designs.

His moustache was thin, and drooped beside his lips, which were equally thin; they matched his body.

One of the other men was clearly his brother.

Lodi seated himself, and stared first at Ghopal Das, and then at Richard; even kneeling, Richard rose above the Indians.

'You are the man from across the sea,' Lodi remarked in Arabic. 'Speak.'

'I am he, your excellency,' Richard acknowledged.

'You are in my land conspiring with this wretch to rebel against me.'

'I came to this land, your excellency, to bring you the greetings of my king, Henry of England. But I was prevented from seeing you, and beaten and robbed. Ghopal Das has taken me into his house and given me food and shelter. I am to leave tomorrow.'

Lodi stared at him, then looked at Ghopal.

'I wish the truth.'

'The foreigner speaks the truth, Badshah.'

'I know differently. Speak the truth. Now that this wretched Mongol has dared to cross my border, you seek to rise up against me and stab me in the back.'

'I have spoken the truth, Badshah. Until this moment I was unaware that your kingdom had been invaded.'

'You are a liar. You conspire against me, you and many others of your debased race. Give me their names, or see your family die. And then die yourself.'

Ghopal's shoulders shook. 'There is no conspiracy, Badshah.'

Lodi pointed, at Ghona, the younger of Ghopal's daughters. 'Deflower her.'

Four of the guards seized the girl and dragged her to the open space before the throne.

'Ghopal,' Richard begged, 'you cannot permit this.'

Ghopal made no reply, and the girl had already been stripped of her dhoti and stretched on the floor. Three of the guards held her down while the fourth raped her.

She seemed too shocked by what was happening to her to protest or fight them in any way; only at the entry did a thin wail of agony escape her lips.

'Tell me the names of your conspirators,' Lodi said.

'I have no conspirators,' Ghopal said. 'I swear it by our Lord Krishna.'

Lodi's lip curled. 'Have I respect for a heathen god? he asked. 'Strike off her head. And bring the second girl forward.'

A tulwar flashed, and Ghona's head rolled across the floor, an expression of frozen disbelief on her features. Her mother uttered a terrifying wail. Shana gave a shriek and clung to Richard, who rose to his feet, holding her in his arms. A blow on the head made him stagger, and before he could recover she had been torn away, while now the guards produced cords to bind him.

Thus helpless he had again to watch both the girl and her mother stripped and tormented by the guards before they cut off their heads. His blood seemed to boil as he gazed at everything he had longed to touch defiled. Shana screamed to the very moment the blade sliced into her neck, while her mother moaned and wailed, but then it was her turn to be raped and then beheaded. Ghopal watched as well, silently.

'Your family is destroyed,' Lodi pointed out. 'Now you have nothing, old man.'

Ghopal's shoulders bowed.

'Perhaps you hope to join your women in hell,' Lodi said. 'No doubt you shall, but yours will be a painful journey. Impale him.'

A large curved saddle was brought, and across this Ghopal Das was stretched. He made no effort to resist. His dhoti was torn from his body, his legs parted. Four guards held him down, one to each wrist and each ankle, while two others stood ready, one with a thin stake about four feet long in his hands, the other with a mallet.

'Commence,' Lodi said.

Ghopal's buttocks were parted and the stake thrust into his anus. The mallet swung and it was driven deeper, and then deeper. Blood flowed and even Ghopal's stoicism was broken. The old man screamed and writhed against the hands holding his limbs and shoulders.

Richard stared at the scene in utter horror. He was no stranger to death in a variety of terrible forms. He had watched a man executed for treason in England, hanged by the neck until he was all but dead, then taken down to be castrated and have his stomach slit open before his head was cut off . . . but he had never seen a man die in so humiliating a fashion. That it should be happening at all! But that it should be happening to these people, who a few hours before had seemed the happiest and most secure on earth . . . and in a few moments it would be happening to him. He felt sick, even as his body seemed to fill with air.

Ghopal's corpse was dragged away, and Richard gazed at Lodi.

'He was a fool,' the Sultan said. 'Are you a fool, stranger? How are you called?'

Richard had to swallow the saliva that filled his mouth before he could reply. 'My name is Blunt.'

'Blunt. Tell me of this conspiracy, Blunt.'

'I know of no conspiracy, your excellency.'

'Do you suppose you can lie to me? One of that carrion's servants overhead your conversation. You are to return to your country and raise an army to overthrow me. Is that not the truth?'

'If you knew so much, your excellency, why was it necessary to murder that man and his family?'

'For conspiracy. Do you wish to die?'

'No, your excellency.'

'Well, then, you will return to your country as planned, and raise your army, and bring it back here . . . to assist me in defending my empire against this Babur, this so-called Lion of the North.'

Richard replied without thinking. 'I do not wish to die, your excellency, but I would rather die than aid you in anything.'

Lodi's brows drew together.

'You are a stubborn rogue,' he said. 'Throw him into a cell, that he may reflect. When next I see him, he will do as I wish.'

* * *

Too late Richard realised that had he only temporised, and agreed to do what Lodi had required, he could have made his escape from this accursed land, and regained Goa and then, hopefully England – no doubt assisted by the Sultan.

But was it an accursed land? There was much to abhor here – but there was much to abhor in England. And there was much beauty and wealth here, more than in England, more even than in Spain, into which the riches of America were pouring year by year.

The 'Mountain of Light'; even if it weighed nearly two hundred carats, it could still fit into a man's satchel, to make him wealthy for life. How that captured his imagination.

As had the beauty of Shana. When he thought of her stretched on the floor ... he wanted to avenge her. But he also wanted to find another like her.

Most of all he wanted to be avenged on Lodi.

But before that could happen it was necessary to do some more suffering. He was thrust into a cell, half below the ground, in which there was a single small barred window. Here there were already some twenty men, and the room was not twelve feet square.

He could not really communicate with them, but they showed no hostility towards him and little curiosity. No doubt they were too weak, for the cell was stiflingly hot and they were fed and watered only once a day, nor were they allowed out for any purpose whatsoever; the stench was suffocating.

At the first opportunity Richard told the guards that he had changed his mind, and would willingly serve the Sultan. They ignored him. He tried again the next day, and the next, equally unsuccessfully, while his once fine clothes became filthy and sweat-stained, and his spirits sank with his empty belly.

He found it difficult to understand the machinations of fate, that the expedition, and himself, should be brought to the point of extinction, that he should have been so miraculously raised up again by Ghopal Das, and that he should then have been the cause of the destruction of that good man and his family, and himself once again left hovering on the brink of death. But yet, still alive.

And during this time he was gradually aware that the entire city was filled with a rustle which could best be described as apprehensive. There was a great deal of martial noise to be heard, the clip-clopping of hooves, the stamping of elephants.

Could it be that this 'Lion' of whom Lodi had spoken was actually marching on Agra?

Now he was more desperate than ever to gain another audience with the Shah, but the guards were even less co-operative than before.

'Our master has more important matters to deal with than you, barbarian,' they told Richard.

It was a week later that the doors of the cell were suddenly thrown open, and the prisoners commanded to come out. When they discovered that the entire gaol was apparently being emptied; Richard calculated that there were more than a thousand naked or half-naked dusky bodies around him.

Several mail-clad officers sat their horses before them, supported by a large body of troops; each foot soldier carried several spears.

'Our lord the Sultan is going to war,' one of the officers shouted. 'In his mercy he has decided that your sentences will be commuted to service in the army. Fall in to receive your weapons.'

The men obeyed with amazing docility, forming a long double line which stumbled slowly past the mounted officers and between the ranks of the foot soldiers, each man being presented with a spear; no other weapon was apparently considered necessary, neither were shields nor any form of protective armour offered.

Richard had no choice but to go with them. A spear was thrust into his hand, and he was marched away, out of the city, and along the road leading north, where within a few miles they came upon the rest of the Delhi army.

It made an imposing array. There were some hundred elephants, clad in huge mail blankets to protect them from arrow wounds, each bearing a howdah in which there were half a dozen men armed with bows and arrows; there was a large contingent of Rajput cavalry – allied to Lodi, although Hindus – wearing chain mail tunics and steel helmets surmounted by a short spike, and armed with both sword and lance; there was a gaudily clad contingent of foot, surrounding the brilliantly accoutered general officers – and there was a huge mass of unarmoured spearmen.

Richard's practised eye estimated there were at least thirty-five thousand men in Lodi's army. As to their quality . . . had he been general in command, he would have had little faith in the spearmen with whom he was surrounded.

The army marched north for several days, past Delhi itself, a tumbled ruin to their right, and then encamped, and apparently intended to remain so, for they did not move again. Richard, like his fellows, was exhausted by the rapid advance from Agra, and was glad of the rest, but their situation was soon as uncomfortable as in their cells. The spearmen were herded out in front of the regular troops and the elephants, and their diet was the inevitable curried rice in huge bowls – the Hindus ate with their fingers, crowding round the bowls to thrust their hands inside. There was a stream close by from which they took their drinking water, although it soon became muddied and unpalatable.

The entire area soon turned into a huge cesspool.

But the army did not move. Gallopers came and went; there were rustles of command amongst the generals, but no orders. The officers and the cavalry spent their time playing a peculiar game, rather like that of the girls in Ghopal Das's house, in that they chased a small ball with specially shaped sticks, but they did so mounted, displaying the most amazing horsemanship and a total disregard for the safety of either themselves or their ponies.

The Hindus became restless, but their sergeants, Muslims, were everywhere, armed with fearsome steel-tipped whips, which soon induced obedience and discipline. Nor was there the slightest attempt to teach the conscripts even the rudiments of drill, or the handling of their spears as a body of pikemen.

Perhaps Lodi means to overawe his enemy by sheer numbers, Richard thought.

However grateful he was to have been released from that unbearable cell, he found it difficult to believe that he had actually improved his lot. He had no doubt now that Lodi had entirely forgotten about him, and if as a professional soldier he managed always to respond quickly enough to avoid being beaten, he still had to face the fact that he was a half-naked foot conscript, armed with a single weapon, fed just enough to keep him alive, forced to sleep in the open – and soon to be required virtually to commit suicide, as he did not doubt he and his fellows would be the first to be sent into action.

And there was nothing he could do about it. The sergeants were too alert for desertion. Several men tried it, were caught, and brought back to be impaled before the entire army.

It was not a fate Richard was prepared to risk again.

The army remained in camp for a week, and they awoke to noise from the north. There was a great deal of movement amongst the officers, more gallopers went off, and the troops were stood to. Grasping his spear, Richard found himself, as he had suspected, one of several lines of foot soldiers grouped to either side of the road.

It was going to be an encounter battle, that was obvious. The road provided a good surface, and to either side the land had been cleared and was under cultivation for perhaps half a mile. But after that there was thickly wooded rising ground; there was no room for manoeuvering this essentially undisciplined force in flank marches.

The road divided close in front of their position, and that on the left led to the town of Panipat, but Lodi apparently felt that a fortified town would repel the invaders – or perhaps he was hoping they would turn aside to attack it, allowing him to move against their flank. If they did not, then their advance would necessarily have to be along this road.

Thus the Sultan's strategy was dictated. But why he had not used the week to advance and meet the invaders even further away from his capital was beyond Richard's understanding.

In any event, the moment was clearly at hand. The noise grew louder, and into sight there came a body of horsemen, mounted on surprisingly small, shaggy ponies, but wearing chain mail armour and steel helmets, and like the Rajputs, armed with sword and lance – and also with bows, slung on their shoulders.

Richard calculated there were about a thousand of them. They halted when they saw the huge force opposed to them, but without any great sign of alarm, even when the Hindu infantry were commanded by their officers to make as much noise as possible. Indeed the entire army sounded off, the men shouting, the elephants trumpeting, while the *kourrouns* – long brass bugles with a deep note – blew and the cymbals clashed.

If noise alone could destroy an enemy, Richard thought, then Lodi had already gained the day.

The Mongols stared at them, then slowly withdrew, to join the main body, which now came in sight. This was a strange army, entirely mounted, accompanied by several hundred open wagons drawn by oxen, in which there were more men, and also by a battery of artillery, drawn by mules.

Obviously the Hindus knew nothing of artillery, for they showed no concern, but Lodi and his officers certainly did, judging by their shouts of alarm.

The Mongol army advanced to within a mile of the Delhi position, while the sergeants ranged up and down the Hindu ranks, shouting at their men and preparing them to resist the anticipated assault.

'They are few, we are many,' they bawled. 'We will submerge them as the desert sands submerge those who venture on to it.'

Richard thought they could just be right; there were certainly not more than ten thousand men on the Mongol side.

A group of officers rode out in front of the advanced cavalry, clearly studying the Delhi position. Now was surely the time to launch an all-out attack, Richard thought. But Lodi remained waiting. His strategy was again obvious; he was hoping that the mere size of his army would force the Mongols to withdraw without a fight.

The cavalry did withdraw, but only a few hundred yards. The Delhi soldiers watched as the enemy wagons were brought forward, their mules unharnessed, and then manhandled across the road and to either side, forming a stout wooden barrier; lengths of iron chain were secured from wheel to wheel so that they could not be moved.

Then the cannon were also unlimbered and manhandled forward. There were two dozen of these pieces, and soon their muzzles were protruding in the space between the wagons; they too were chained to the wagon-wheels.

It was very obvious that the Mongols had no intention of retreating.

Now at last the Hindus became aware that they were in the

presence of a new weapon, and the men chattered at each other.

'You!' An officer strode into the midst of Richard's company, cane swinging left and right, pointing. 'The Sultan commands your presence.'

The Hindus stared as Richard was marched off. His spear was taken away, to make sure he was unarmed when he appeared before Lodi, and when he reached the command position, he was thrown to the ground before the Sultan's horse.

'Blunt,' Lodi said, pointing with his tulwar. 'Are you familiar with those weapons?'

'Yes, your excellency,' Richard said, struggling to his knees.

'Must we fear them?'

'Their balls will tear great holes in your people, your excellency. But they take much time to reload.'

'Ha!' Lodi commented. 'Take him away.'

'Your excellency,' Richard cried. 'I would have you know that I have reconsidered my position, and would willingly return to my country on your behalf, and bring my king and his army to your aid against these people.'

'Ha! Of what good would that be to me now? Are you a coward, that you are afraid to fight? If you survive the battle, I may speak with you again. Take him away.'

Richard was returned to the ranks of the spearmen, who had at last been allowed to sit or squat, as the Mongols were making no move. They stared at the muzzles of the cannon, now definitely fearful.

'Will the Sultan not attack them, and destroy them, Blunt Sahib?' asked Prabhankar.

Richard's head turned sharply and he gazed at his erstwhile servant, dressed, like himself, only in a dhoti, and equally armed with a spear.

'By God!' he said. 'I should strangle you with my bare hands.'

'Are we not comrades in distress, Blunt Sahib? Brought to this by our karma. I sought to abscond from you, fell out with a rascal over the price of the horse, was arrested, and imprisoned. You sought the aid of Ghopal Das, and are thus also here. It is clearly the will of fate that we should live and die, shoulder to shoulder.'

Richard supposed he could be right.

'I do not know if the Sultan means to attack or not,' he said. 'But one thing is certain; when he does, we will be in the front rank.'

'To march against the cannon,' Prabhankar said, and shuddered. He had of course learned about cannon from the Portuguese in Goa, and indeed had seen them on board the European ships. 'I think that when the order to advance is given, we are both going to die, Blunt Sahib.' He sighed. 'For a man all of us hate and fear.'

Richard looked at him as an idea began to germinate in his brain. It was late afternoon now, and clearly Lodi did not intend to join battle today. While the Mongols seemed perfectly content to wait for him to make the first move. The conflagration needed a spark to ignite it . . . and could any fate be worse than to be Lodi's captive?

While for the man who might possibly give this Lion the victory, all things might be possible. Besides, he rather liked the concept of a man called the Lion. It suggested nobility, as well as ferocious courage.

'Prabhankar,' he said. 'I think it would be better for us to fight for the Mongol than for Lodi.'

Prabhankar frowned. 'You wish to desert, Blunt Sahib? You would not succeed, and they would hammer a sharp stake up your arse.'

'I would not succeed alone, neither would you, Prabhankar. But what if our entire regiment were to leave. Would the sergeants be able to stop us, or bring us all back?'

'The entire regiment?' Prabhankar picked his nose.

'They are all Hindus. They all hate Lodi. They are here simply because no one has ever told them to do anything different. You speak their language. Go amongst them, as soon as it is dark. Tell them that tomorrow Lodi intends to send us against the cannon. Tell them the cannon will destroy us, every man. Tell them that the army will not move forward until we are all dead, because Lodi believes that will expend all the Mongol shot. Tell them that our only hope is to leave tonight, in a body, and offer our services to the Mongol general.'

Prabhankar considered. 'I have heard it said that the Mongols are Muslims, exactly like Lodi.'

'They cannot be exactly like Lodi, or they would not wish to war on him. And even if they are Muslims, will they not wish to reward us if we seek service with them, against their enemy?'

Prabhankar considered some more. 'It is a great risk,' he pointed out.

'It is less of a risk than waiting here to be blown to pieces, or executed,' Richard retorted. 'Even supposing Lodi wins the day, what do you then suppose will happen to us? Will we not be returned to our cells, and left to die? Only by joining the Mongol have we any hope of surviving.'

Prabhankar was persuaded. After their evening meal of curried rice, they began crawling from group to group of the Hindus, inviting them to desert in a body. There was some resistance to the idea, but that faded as Prabhankar told them of the destructive powers of the cannon, and more, that the Mongol leader, Babur the Lion, was reputed to be a man of great generosity to those who fought for him.

This was the purest supposition, of course, but it was persuasive.

They worked all night, gradually accumulating more and more men to their side, until Richard reckoned they had almost the entire regiment.

'They wish to know when will we act?' Prabhankar asked. 'It will soon be dawn.'

'Why then, we will act now,' Richard said, 'before anyone discovers what we are about. Tell your people to be ready for my signal.'

Prabhankar passed the word, while Richard studied the sergeants who patrolled their bivouac all night. He was aware of a certain light-headedness. Should the Hindus prove faint-hearted and not follow him, he would be stretched across a saddle to die the most horrible and ignominious of deaths. But merely to march to his death because a cowardly tyrant had commanded it was hardly less unthinkable.

Prabhankar crawled up to him. 'The men are ready, Blunt Sahib.'

'Very well, then.' Richard drew a long breath, and stood up, his spear in his hand; how he wished it was his rapier. He found himself a good length of dry wood, went to the nearest camp-fire, and thrust the wood into the flames until it caught. Then he waved it above his head. 'To me!' he shouted. 'Away! To me! Away!'

Then he ran forward, straight at the first of the sergeants. The man gave an exclamation of alarm, but Richard drove the spear through his body before he could defend himself. Richard then seized the man's tulwar, and with the torch in his left hand, continued his forward dash.

Several more sergeants appeared from the darkness to arrest him, but were checked by the huge roar from behind him as the Hindus also ran forward, led by Prabhankar. The officers were overrun in seconds, and then Richard, still waving his flaming torch, was leading his people down the road.

Behind them bugles blew as the army of the Sultan came awake; orders were bellowed and there was a great clanging of arms, but no one was entirely sure what was happening.

From the Mongol ranks there was silence. But Richard had no doubt they were awake, and watching, and ready to blast the force which was approaching them in the darkness.

'Halt!' he shouted, when the crowd of excited Hindus was about half a mile from Lodi's position, and thus just out of range of the Mongol cannon. 'Make them stop, Prabhankar.'

He waved his torch and Prabhankar shouted and ran up and down in front of the mob, at last bringing them to a halt, perilously close to the Mongol position. Now lights could be seen behind the wagon barricade, but still the guns had not fired.

'Make them wait here,' Richard told Prabhankar, and went forward alone, his torch high above his head.

Slowly he approached the chained wagons, heart pounding, aware that at any moment he might be cut down by an arrow or a flying stone ball. And slowly the wagons themselves came into sight.

Richard stopped. 'I seek the Lion!' he called, in Arabic.

There was a brief silence, then someone called back, 'Who comes? What is the meaning of the tumult in the darkness?'

'I am Richard Blunt,' Richard said. 'I have been a prisoner of Lodi Shah. But now I have come to serve the Lion, and I have brought with me a regiment of Hindu spearmen, who wish only to serve with me.'

There was another brief silence, then the man said, 'Advance.'

Richard went forward, right up to the nearest wagon, and was suddenly surrounded, by several Mongols, carrying torches to illuminate him; he could now drop his own, which had all but burned down to his hand.

'Richard Blunt is a strange name, and you are a strange fellow,' said a voice from out of the darkness. 'Where is your home?'

'My home is far away,' Richard said. 'Across the ocean. A place called England.'

He waited.

'Indeed, you have travelled far,' the voice said, suggesting, incredibly, that the speaker had heard of that distant island. 'And have you truly got Hindu spearmen with you out there in the darkness?'

'I have.'

'Tell them to advance, slowly. Remember that my cannon are loaded, and trained on them.'

Richard turned, while relief slowly began to flood through his mind.

'Prabhankar!' he shouted. 'Bring your people forward, but slowly.'

Out of the darkness the Hindus appeared in groups, their spears on their shoulders.

'Are such men of any use to me?' the voice asked.

'I believe they will be,' Richard said. 'But in any event, they are now of no more use to Lodi.'

'Ha, ha,' the voice said. 'Your point is made, Englishman.'

The Mongols parted, and a man came towards Richard. 'You sought the Lion,' the man said. 'You have found him. I am Babur.'

4
THE MOGHUL

Richard found himself looking at a man in his forties, not very tall but very broad of shoulder and hip, suggesting enormous strength; his body also remained lean and hard.

But it was his face which was exceptional. He wore thin moustaches, which drooped beside his mouth, and an equally thin beard. Lips and chin were pronounced and firm, but entirely lacked the suggestion of lurking cruelty that had characterised Lodi Shah's. The nose was somewhat flat, but the forehead was high, and the black eyes peculiarly intelligent and compelling. He wore loose white britches, a long blue tunic, a blue turban, and kid boots. A tulwar with a jewel-encrusted hilt hung at his side, and he carried a horsehair wand with five knots in it.

Babur apparently also liked what he saw.

'I have heard that men from the west of Europe are of exceptional size and strength,' he said.

'There are many bigger than I, my lord,' Richard told him.

'Then I must be grateful that Lodi possessed only one of you. Yet I find it hard to admire a deserter.'

'I owe Lodi no loyalty,' Richard told him. 'He is a mean and cowardly jackal who has murdered my friends. That he kept me alive was merely because he felt I could be of service to him.'

'And now you have fled to me, with this rabble.'

'This rabble, your excellency, represents a good proportion of the Sultan's army. They hate him as much as I, because they are Hindus, and he is a Muslim.'

'Then why should they fight for me? I am a Muslim.'

'You have but to deal fairly with them, and you will secure their loyalty.'

Babur studied him for several moments, then nodded. 'Perhaps you are right. Feed those men, and bid them rest,' he told his officers. 'Place them on the left of the encampment. You, Englishman, come with me.'

Richard instructed Prabhankar to obey the Mongols, and then, surrounded by several of the Mongol captains – presumably to make sure he intended no treachery towards their general – followed Babur into the camp, gazing at the well-accoutred men, the loaded cannon, the restless horses. Every man was awake and watching.

Babur led the way to a tent set at the rear of the camp. It was actually more of a canvas house than a mere bivouac, for it extended over a considerable area and contained several chambers, separated by drapes or goatskin walls. Around it were a group of smaller versions, and there were armed guards at its door.

Babur went inside, and Richard followed him. Lanterns glowed, and he was taken aback by the luxury of the cushions and carpet.

Only five of his escort entered with him. One was a man of about Babur's own age, taller and thinner, with very aquiline features. A second was considerably older, and was clearly related to the first. The other three were hardly more than boys, and looked very like their father.

'My counsellors, Dawlat Khan Lodi and Abbas Khan Lodi,' Babur said, indicating the older men.

Richard bowed, but his expression betrayed his bewilderment.

'Yes, they are related to the Badshah,' Babur said. 'Dawlat Khan is his cousin, and is Governor of Lahore. Abbas Khan is the Badshah's uncle. They have reasons for quarrelling with the Badshah, and are my advisers. And this is my *tavachi*, Kamran.' He smiled. 'He is also my son.'

The young aide-de-camp – Richard soon learned that he was only sixteen – gazed at the big Englishman with very deep black eyes.

'Askari and Hindal are also my sons,' Babur said. 'They are very young, but will soon learn the art of war. Be seated.' He set an example by sitting cross-legged on the carpet. Dawlat, Abbas and the three princes sat to either side. Richard took his place opposite.

Young women came in to serve them coffee, and Richard

observed with surprise that they were not veiled. But they were certainly not Hindus, and in fact he decided they were Mongols themselves, from their features. In their embroidered blouses and baggy pantaloons they made most attractive pictures, while the coffee was sweeter than any Richard had ever tasted.

'It contains a substance called sugar, which is obtained from a species of bamboo,' Babur explained. 'Do you not know of it?'

'I have seen it since coming to India. It is unknown in England.'

'Do you not seek such sweetness in England?'

'We use honey for that purpose. But then, coffee is also unknown in England.'

'Ah.' Babur studied him. 'An Englishman. I have heard much of them, and of the French and the Spaniards. Do you know of these people?'

'I have campaigned in Spain, your excellency. Under the flag of the Emperor.'

'You have the look of a man used to command,' Babur said quietly. 'We must find you some adequate clothing to wear.'

Food was brought, and Babur gestured Richard to eat. He took little himself, but both the Lodis and the young men ate heartily.

As he ate Richard wondered at this man, described by the Sultan as a mere Tatar bandit, who yet knew so much of the world, and had heard about England. There was a mystery here, but, like his people, a strangely attractive mystery.

'Have you heard of us, Englishman?' Babur asked.

'All Europe has heard of the Ottomans.' Richard was fishing for information.

Babur's eyes flashed. 'We are not Turks. We are Mongols. We have fought the Turks often enough in the past, and will surely do so again.' Then his voice softened. 'But the Turks are a mighty people, to be sure, and for the moment we are friends; I am employing Turkish gunners, because they alone understand the art of artillery. Have you heard of Timur, called the Lame?'

'I have heard a legend,' Richard ventured.

'I am his direct descendant,' Babur said, with simple pride.

Once again Richard sat corrected. And this time abashed. The name of Timur was indeed a legend in Europe, but nothing more. That he had erupted out of Central Asia like a tornado, as confirmed by Ghopal Das, was all that was known about him.

And this man was his descendant.

Such a man would surely know of Prester John.

But his instincts told him he must be very patient here. He could again have fallen on his feet when all had seemed lost ... but was this only because of the dangerous situation in which Babur at this moment found himself?

Thus it might be to his advantage to prove his worth before seeking more.

'Will you attack Lodi Shah?' he asked, as saliva flooded his mouth; this lamb was the first meat he had tasted in more than a week, and what lamb, highly spiced and delicious.

'We shall slaughter him,' Kamran declared, eyes glowing.

'What is the strength of Lodi's army?' asked his father.

'Now ... I would put it at more than thirty thousand men.'

Babur glanced at Dawlat.

'I would say that is accurate,' Dawlat agreed.

'And he has the elephants as well,' Babur pointed out. 'I think it would be unwise for me to attack him. And besides, it is no longer necessary to do so.'

'But I am sure that a great many more of his men are ready to desert. If you were to attack ...'

'They might very well fight for him instead. No, no, Englishman, our position is the stronger defensively. We will wait for Lodi to attack us.'

'Suppose he does not?'

'He will. He must, now that several thousand of his people have abandoned him. He will have in mind that if he delays much longer some more may come over to me. He will attack. I would say he will attack today.'

Richard was amazed at the Mongol general's calm confidence. But Babur was proved absolutely correct.

The hubbub in the Delhi camp continued all night, but quietened with daylight. Watching with Babur from behind the wagon barricade, and now clad in a steel helmet and a leather jerkin – no mail surcoat had been found big enough to fit him – Richard could make out the opposing army breakfasting.

The Mongols had already breakfasted, and Babur now gave his orders; the Hindus were formed up on the left of his position, where they had bivouaced during the night. There they were exposed, but Babur placed two regiments of cavalry in reserve of them.

'Who is their commander?' he asked Richard.

'I am their commander.'

Babur frowned. 'They will follow you?'

'Yes, sire.'

'Then lead them. Stand fast, but watch me, and when I raise my wand, lead your men in the direction I will point.'

Richard saluted. He had been given the use of a horse, and mounted he made a conspicuous figure at the head of his people.

'Tell them,' he instructed Prabhankar, 'that today we make an end of Lodi Shah, and his tyranny. Tell them that this Babur the Lion is our friend, and will rule as our friend when Lodi has been defeated. Tell them that we have but to prove ourselves loyal to him, and we will benefit greatly.'

Prabhankar nodded and made a speech to the Hindus, which seemed to please them. They stamped their feet and raised their spears in the air.

'And you will remember how well I have served you, Blunt Sahib,' Prabhankar said.

'Yes,' Richard agreed, 'I will remember that.'

With a great clashing of cymbals the Delhi army advanced. The Rajput cavalry moved on the left – the Mongol right – in a vast clink of harness and arms. As yet they walked their horses, and there was little dust.

The centre and right were composed of Hindu pikemen, with their Muslim officers. There were a very great number of them, but Richard still felt they were Lodi's greatest weakness.

Behind the pikemen came the elephants, moving slowly forward, great feet thumping the ground. Their red and gold accoutrements, and the brilliantly-clad men in their howdahs, made them an arresting spectacle.

Behind the elephants, and clearly designed to give the *coup de grâce* to a defeated foe, were the Sultan's household troops, all Muslims, wearing their blue and silver uniforms and turbans.

Lodi himself and his staff brought up the rear.

The slowness of the advance was punctuated by the enormous noise, for to the cymbals were added the blare of bugles and the shouts of the men.

By contrast, the Mongol army was absolutely silent; indeed, apart from the Hindus massed on its left, very little of it was visible behind the barricades.

The army of Delhi advanced to within half a mile of the Mongols. Then it halted, and the sergeants ranged up and down the Hindu pikemen. Richard could see their whips flailing as they beat the men into ranks.

The noise had not ceased, and now it actually increased in volume. Then with a huge roar the pikemen surged forward.

The tactics were plain enough; the pikemen were to be used to soften up the Mongol defensive position, then the elephants would be launched to trample down the shaken foe, and the cavalry and disciplined infantry would hopefully complete the rout. But Lodi had in fact made a fatal tactical error, due to his lack of knowledge of the usage of artillery, and especially, how long it took to recharge the pieces.

Babur, who had accurately discerned his opponent's plan, held his fire until the pikemen were hardly more than a hundred yards from the chained wagons. Then the artillery pieces exploded. They had been loaded with scraps of stone and iron rather than with the round stone balls which was their normal ammunition, and at this close range they struck the infantry like a hailstorm, only travelling horizontally and at a much greater force. Men tumbled to and fro, spears were burled into the air, blood cascaded along the roadway.

Richard's men moved restlessly. Those were their own comrades being cut to pieces. They wanted to have it done.

But Richard, watching Babur all the time, received no signal. Instead he saw the Mongols feverishly reloading their guns.

The pikemen, still something like a hundred yards from the Mongols, were rallied by their officers, those of them that remained mounted, and once again surged forward, leaving the dark humps of the fallen behind them on the road.

But now they were met by a new hailstorm of arrows. The dismounted Mongol cavalry stepped in front of their wagons, in two vast ranks, the first rank kneeling, the second standing, and discharged their bows into the advancing mass. It seemed that almost every shaft struck home; they could hardly miss at so close a range. The Hindu infantry screamed their terror, threw away their spears, and began to disintegrate. As the Mongols had carefully aimed at the Muslim officers, there were no longer sufficient of these to rally their men, and they began to flee back towards the elephants.

These now took up the attack. Lodi must have realised that his initial plan had failed; the Mongol position was as strong as ever. But the elephants were his truly decisive weapon. If they could once get amongst the wagons and the cannon, the enemy would surely fall apart.

On came the huge beasts, marching straight through the retreating pikemen. Men screamed as they could not avoid the huge feet descending on them, and the wounded stared in horror at the fate which approached them step by step.

Then the elephants were through, and approaching the barricade.

The decision to keep the Hindu pikemen in the field for a second charge now told against the Sultan, however; Babur's gunners had had time to reload their pieces. The bowmen returned to shelter behind the wagons, and the cannon, waiting as before until the ponderous, earthshaking advance was within a hundred yards, exploded.

Now they had been loaded with solid lumps of stone, and these tore into the elephants. Only two or three were actually hit by the flying missiles, but that was sufficient to throw the whole line into disarray. One of the huge beasts fell down, and struck another to his left. One of the others that had been wounded began a violent trumpeting and charged into his neighbour.

And the bowmen were back as the cannon were again being reloaded, sending arrow after arrow into the mountains of flesh in front of them, driving more and more of the beasts wild with fear and pain.

Still Babur gave no signal to the pikemen, but he had been watching the entire field, and was the first to see the Rajput horse preparing to charge. Instantly his own mounted reserve was called out. Some five thousand of the Mongol cavalry had hitherto passively sat their horses behind the barricades. Now they emerged to gallop against the approaching Rajputs.

Richard caught his breath. The Mongols were outnumbered, and more, they were obviously outclassed, the Rajputs being bigger men and mounted on far larger horses. They couched their lances and uttered shrill cries as they increased their speed to a canter.

But here again the Delhi army was in for an unpleasant surprise. The Mongol cavalry advanced as if to meet their foes in a true cavalry charge, and then suddenly wheeled their horses away. As they did so, every man unslung his bow, controlling his galloping mount only with knees and heels, fitted an arrow, and loosed the shaft at the approaching mass. Their accuracy was as amazing as their horsemanship, and mounts and riders came tumbling down. The charge was checked, and before the Rajputs could regroup, they were assailed by another hail of arrows. Following which, the Mongols slung their bows again, seized their lances, and this time did deliver a charge, into the shaken horsemen; within a few more moments even the proud Rajputs were being driven from the field.

The elephants were meanwhile having a contest of their own, many dashing round and round in circles, while their riders clung to the howdahs and shrieked their terror, others already killed by their mahouts driving iron spikes into their brains, so that they thudded heavily to the ground.

Richard cast a hasty glance at Babur, and saw Kamran leave his father's side and gallop towards him.

'Babur tells you this, Blunt Amir,' the boy panted. 'Lodi must now commit his main body. You march your pikemen parallel with the road, and wheel them in behind the Delhi men the moment they are sufficiently advanced. Do you understand this order?'

'I understand,' Richard said. He drew his tulwar and waved it above his head. The Hindus gave a shout and moved forward, to the left of the elephants as they looked at them.

The last of the conscript pikemen had now fled the field, and the way was clear, once they were past the tragedy of the elephants. Lodi ignored the flank manoeuvre, and stood up in his stirrups to shriek orders at his men, who advanced with disciplined tread towards the Mongol barricade. They made a splendid sight in their bright uniforms and in the discipline of their movements. Richard realised that the battle was by no means a certain victory, but he need not have worried. Babur had all his men under control, and although some thousands of his horsemen were engaged in turning the Rajput retreat into a rout, several thousand more – including a part of those hitherto dismounted to defend the wagon barricade – were now being remounted and sent against Lodi's last defence.

The household troops were in turn struck down by the arrow storm, and Richard judged the moment had come to deliver his attack. This was one of the most bitter battles in which he had ever found himself, for the two sides hated each other. Just before the encounter he dismounted and led his men on foot, tulwar in hand. He was in the midst of the Muslims before he had properly regained his balance, calling on his troops to follow, brushing aside a spear thrust before swinging his tulwar to catch his assailant a frightful blow which seemed to open up the entire side of his head, bringing the sword back again to slash at someone else on his other side, panting and slipping to the ground and being helped up again by Prabhankar, surging onwards, always aware that on his right the Mongol cavalry had also delivered a charge.

The household troops broke, and began streaming from the field. Lodi stared at them in dismay. To his credit, he was not a coward, and he spurred his horse forward to try to rally his men. Richard was only a few feet away from him when an arrow struck the Sultan and he fell from his horse. He hit the ground heavily, and before he could recover, Richard stood over him.

The Sultan had been wounded in the chest and was clearly dying. He gazed at Richard with hate-filled eyes.

'You!' he spat, blood flying from his mouth. 'I curse you to your grave.'

'We had best see if we can get him to Babur,' Richard said.

Prabhankar was beside him. 'The Moghul will be interested only in his head,' he said using the Indian form of the word Mongol. He had obtained a tulwar for himself at some time in the battle. This he now brought over in a complete arc, and with a single stroke severed Sultan Ibrahim Lodi Shah's head from his body.

* * *

As the Mongols took no prisoners, but systematically beheaded all the enemy wounded, fifteen thousand of Lodi's men lay dead upon the field of battle – very nearly half of his entire force. The Mongol losses were infinitesimal.

Richard had never been present at a battle fought with such savagery, and without a thought of quarter.

Babur told his Hindu allies that they could loot the dead, and they fell to the task with enthusiasm, while he rode his horse through the ranks of corpses. He did not seem over-elated by the magnitude of his victory.

'My great ancestor,' he commented, 'would have built all of these skulls into a tower, to remind the world that he had passed this way. I shall leave them here to rot. Let us eat.'

The day was well advanced, and Richard was very hungry, yet it was hard to enjoy his food, as the stench of death lay heavily over the field.

'Have you won many such victories as this, sire?' he asked.

Babur smiled. 'Not enough, or I would be a greater monarch, would I not? No, I would agree this has been a triumph. In part due to you. Thus I honour you. Now tell me straight, what brings you to India? Had you ever heard of Lodi Shah, or of me, for that matter?'

'No, I had not. I had heard of a great king known as Prester John, and so carried credentials as an ambassador from my king to this Prester John. Unfortunately I was robbed of my goods by Lodi Shah.'

'Prester John,' Babur mused. 'You sought a legend.' He smiled again. 'And this really is a legend.'

Richard swallowed his meat with difficulty. 'Are you certain, sire?'

'Certain. Yes. I have heard the legend. I have met other men who sought this fabled king. But I have also ranged the length and breadth of Asia, and have known men who have been even further than I, and not one has ever discovered such a man. Were he of any substance, someone would have information about him.'

Richard sighed. He had persisted in hoping, against all the evidence. Now his dreams were definitely proved to be ... dreams.

For which his cousin and several other good men had been sacrificed. And for which he would probably also die; he saw little possibility of ever returning to England.

Babur had been watching him closely. Now he asked, 'What now, Englishman? My army will soon begin its return march to Kabul, my capital in the mountains of Afghanistan. Will you accompany me, or do you feel it your duty to stay with your soldiers?'

Richard frowned at him in disbelief. 'You will return to Afghanistan?'

'Well, of course. That is my home. My kingdom.' He gave a wry smile. 'At least for the time being.'

'But, with respect ... why did you invade Delhi at all, if you mean merely to retreat?'

'I make these raids for money and women for my men,' Babur explained. 'I was first encouraged to do so by Dawlat, who has great enmity for Lodi: although they are distant cousins, Lodi robbed Dawlat of everything he possessed. But now he is avenged, and I have secured a sufficient quantity of both women and riches. My baggage train is some twenty miles back upon the road. I had already intended to begin my retreat when I was informed that Lodi had mobilised against me. I could not risk a retreat with him on my heels, so I determined to give battle first. Besides ...' he smiled. 'This also pleased my men.'

'And now you will go home, to please your men.' Richard's brain was seething. There was no Prester John. But he had been told that the Kingdom of Delhi was the most powerful in India, and now the Kingdom of Delhi was no more, until someone else seized it. That man could well make himself in turn the most powerful ruler in this vast land. A man well worth having as an ally against the Ottoman Turks.

Of course, Babur was a Muslim. And had accepted Turkish aid for this campaign. But he had said enough to indicate that he had no love for them.

And he was a refined, learned man – even if he and his people did fight like devils from hell. In any event, he was the only hope of salvaging anything of value from this disastrous expedition.

'My lord,' he said, 'is not Delhi a greater kingdom than Afghanistan?'

Babur glanced at him. 'You would have me sack the city? Dawlat tells me it is nothing but a ruin.'

Richard drew a long breath. 'I do not speak of the city of Delhi, sire. I would have you take the city of Agra, Lodi's capital, and claim the *Kingdom* of Delhi.'

'With fifteen thousand men?'

'Sire, at this moment, Delhi is yours. Lodi is dead, his army scattered. The majority of the people of Delhi hated him. These men of mine have fought for you and been rewarded. You have dealt fairly with them. Send them ahead of your army into Agra, to rouse the people in your support. The city will be yours in an hour.'

Babur smiled. 'You are bold, Englishman. But then your every action indicates this. And you may very well be right. At this moment the Kingdom of Delhi is like a headless monster. But it will recover. The Rajputs will recover, and raise another army. There are Muslim princes in the south and east who will prefer another Lodi to a Mongol like me. I have not the men to fight them all, or the means to raise a greater army. My life has been filled with mistakes, made by attempting to grasp what I cannot hold.'

'My lord,' Richard said, 'inside the palace of Lodi Shah there is the richest treasure in the world. Have you never heard of the "Mountain of Light"?'

Babur frowned at him. 'I have heard of a legend.'

'Like Timur, this is no legend, my lord. This is the greatest diamond ever known. I have heard it said that it would provide two and a half days' food for the entire world.'

'You have seen this thing?'

'Yes, my lord,' Richard lied. 'And much more besides. With the wealth of Lodi Shah at your disposal you could raise an army the size of his . . . and of better quality troops, too.'

'The Kingdom of Delhi,' Babur breathed. 'Well, why not? We can always take this Koh-i-noor away with us if the going becomes too difficult.'

Richard could only pray that Ghopal Das had been telling the truth.

But, at any rate, he and his daughters had been avenged.

Ghopal had certainly not been lying about the ease with which

Babur would take Agra. After his pikemen had been sent in, a few days following the battle to give his men time to rest, he followed with his main armament, having spent some of the intervening time examining the ruins of Delhi. He was clearly impressed, even if he was equally clearly shocked by the eroticism of the Hindu religious statuary, much of which he commanded to be destroyed.

'These people are obsessed by the flesh,' he muttered. 'We will have to teach them a lesson,' and gave orders for a garden of remembrance, the Ram Bagh, to be laid out by the banks of the River Jumna in honour of his victory.

'This will be my capital,' he announced. 'It will rise again like the phoenix. But, first, Agra.'

Only scattered groups of Muslims offered resistance as the Mongols marched south, and these were quickly cut down. Most of Lodi's supporters had already fled to the east, led by his brother Mahmud.

Richard was at Babur's side as they strode into that so well-remembered palace. But now there was no one to bar them. The hateful Vizier had fallen on the field.

They looked at the peacocks, and then invaded the inner chambers, and came to the throne room. 'Where is the treasure house?' Babur demanded.

It was located easily enough, in a vault beneath the throne room. Richard gazed in amazement at the ingots of solid gold, the chests of precious stones. And then at the Koh-i-noor, an immense incandescent lump. It occurred to him that this must be the richest country in the whole world.

And he had just made a present of it to a descendant of Timur and Genghis Khan!

As Babur recognised. He picked up the huge diamond, and turned it to and fro. 'A marvel,' he commented. 'I shall give this as a present to my son. My eldest son, Humayun,' he added. 'Who will deeply regret not being at my side to enjoy this triumph. But you also must be rewarded, Englishman. Will you remain here, and ride at my right hand?'

Richard did not hesitate. Plans for a return to England could wait, until he had siphoned off some of this wealth for himself. And discussed an alliance with Babur.

'Willingly,' he said.

'Well, then,' Babur said. 'Let us see what else this palace has to offer.'

He led the way to the harem.

No one in Agra yet knew for sure what had happened to Lodi Shah; he had last been seen fighting in the midst of the Mongol ranks, and could well have been taken prisoner – Babur had made no announcement.

Thus the women of the harem had not known what to do. Lodi's death might have impelled his wives to indulge in a jauhur, or holocaust, whereby the entire harem self-immolated itself; this was a Hindu ceremony, akin to suttee, but many of Lodi's concubines were Hindus.

As it was, they stood in groups behind their latticework walls, around their bathing pools, muttering at their eunuchs, listening to the noises in the city about them, anticipating a hundred fates. And gathering together in terror as they heard the tramp of masculine feet in the corridors where only Lodi had ever ventured before.

The eunuchs made no effort to stop Babur and his officers. They bowed to the floor. Their only intention was to save their own lives.

Babur brushed them aside. He was a man of the mountains and the steppes. If he believed that women were the rightful prize of the conqueror, he employed no eunuchs of his own; a Tatar's wife was supposed to ride in the open beside her husband, and if necessary, fight beside him too.

Now he looked at the huddled figures, clad in transparent silk. Most left their breasts exposed, as was the Indian custom, all were elegantly lovely, save that a good deal of the elegance had dissipated into fear.

'Lodi Shah is dead,' he announced.

There was a moment's silence, and then a great wail of misery.

'Why so sad?' Babur inquired, and the sobbing slowly ceased. 'Are you not pleased to be rid of such a tyrant? You will be given to my men, and learn how to be women again. But first, I shall choose from amongst you myself.'

The women seemed to huddle closer together.

Babur walked through their midst, looking from girl to girl.

At the very back of the courtyard there was a small group of seven people. Three of them were women of at least thirty; one was clearly much older than that. The other four consisted of two girls and two boys. The boys were very young, certainly not yet at puberty. The girls were older, and were remarkably attractive. Clearly they came from different mothers; one was dark and the other was quite fair – they were related to the two younger women behind them.

Babur stood before them, and they faced him with some boldness, although they trembled.

'Your husband is dead,' Babur announced again, deducing who they had to be.

They had wailed as loudly as anyone at the first announcement. Now they received the news more stoically.

'Then must we die also,' said the older woman.

'That will not be necessary,' Babur said. 'You will be given a house in which to live, and an allowance.'

'Our children?' asked the fairer-skinned of the two younger wives.

Babur looked at her. 'You are Persian?'

He had recognised the accent.

'I am the daughter of Shah Ismail,' she said proudly. 'Given in marriage to Lodi Shah.'

Babur nodded. 'I had heard the Shah had taken a Persian princess to wife. You may keep your sons, at least for the next year.'

'Our daughters?' asked the darker woman.

Babur studied her in turn, then gazed at the two girls, who moved closer, their hands locked together.

'They are as comely as their mothers. And are clearly of the age to make a man happy. I will take this one to my bed.'

He touched the dark girl on the shoulder, and she shrank against her half-sister.

Her mother bowed her head, hands clasped in front of her face. She could have hoped for nothing better.

'As for the other ...' Babur looked at her again, and she visibly held her breath. 'Blunt Amir, come forward.'

Richard went to the conqueror's side. Suddenly his knees felt weak as he gazed at the girl. Her skin was indeed pale, paler than his own – almost ivory white. She wore a deep blue sari trimmed with gold stitching at the hem; it was well wrapped round her, but yet indicated that she was fully mature – he put her age at perhaps sixteen – and had a splendid figure. A jewelled headband encircled her black hair, which lay absolutely straight and fine to beneath her shoulders.

Her face was small, but the features were regular; pointed chin, thin mouth, straight nose, and high forehead fitted perfectly together, and were controlled by the wideset dark eyes, which returned his gaze in an expression of mingled contempt and apprehension.

She was Lodi's daughter. In her veins flowed the blood of the man who had murdered Shana and Ghona, and put their father to the most shameful of deaths. Almost the lust he had immediately felt for her was submerged in hatred.

'I give you this girl as a reward for your services, Blunt Amir,' Babur said.

'I am grateful, sire,' Richard said. He scarce recognised his own voice.

'My lord,' said the Persian woman, 'is this man of noble birth?'

'He comes from far away,' Babur said. 'Where noble birth is not relevant,' he added somewhat naively. 'He rides at my right hand, which is far more important. Come, Blunt Amir, shall we not enjoy our new wives? I feel a great lust for this little girl.'

He stepped forward, seized the Indian girl's wrist, pulled her towards him, and at the same time lowered his shoulder and drove it into her stomach. She gave a little gasp, and was lifted from the ground.

Babur turned to look at Richard.

Blunt followed his new master's example. He seized the girl's wrist, put his shoulder into her midriff, and lifted her easily. She was very light. Shrouded in her perfume, he now became terribly aware of her; his cheek rested against her buttocks, and he held her thighs against his chest. Her chin bumped on his back.

She had uttered no sound.

Babur turned to his officers. 'Choose your women,' he commanded. He gestured to the guards on the harem door. 'Admit no one without my orders,' he said.

Not a soul had spoken. They knew this was a normal act of

conquest: the taking of the dead ruler's wives and concubines. The three wives could only be happy that they themselves had not been selected for rape; the concubines could only pray that they might be selected by an officer rather than thrown to the common soldiers.

Now there was a great rustle as the Mongols stepped amongst them, stripping away the saris the better to assist their choice.

Richard's lust grew. He had been present at many a sack, and in the heat of passion had raped as willingly as any other soldier. But he had never experienced anything like this ordered destruction of the Sultan's harem. It was also too long since he had enjoyed a woman – and this was a beautiful girl.

Babur had already stepped into one of the adjoining cubicles.

Richard parted the curtain of another, and laid the girl on the divan within. Still she made no movement, but lay supine gazing up at him. The hostility never left her eyes, and clearly she knew what was about to happen to her – had no doubt known it ever since news of her father's defeat had reached the palace.

Here then was the sweetest of all revenges upon Lodi?

Standing above her, he pulled off her circlet. Then he thrust his hand inside her sari to find her breasts.

'I would not tear this fine material,' he said. 'Take it off.'

He stood back from her, and slowly she sat up, swinging her legs to the floor with a practised grace which still managed to convey contempt for him. She stood up and removed her tunic.

Richard gazed at the white flesh, the surprisingly large breasts. His clothes seemed confining, and he was on the point of bursting. He stripped them off.

As the girl stared at him, her expression changed to one of dismay. He understood that she would never have seen an uncircumcised man before. Muslim men all had the foreskin removed when they reached puberty.

But could she have seen an adult member in any event? Yes, he realised; she would have seen naked slaves being driven along the street.

'The rest,' he commanded.

The girl unwound the sari from round her waist, and let the silk float to the floor.

Her slender legs and thighs were even more compelling than her breasts. Her belly was flat, but she possessed a delightfully silky triangle, and no doubt it was as fragrant as the rest of her.

They gazed at each other. He knew he could beat and hurt her while shouting out the name of Shana. Indeed, he was almost tempted. But it was not in his nature to hurt a defenceless creature. Instead he took her in his arms. Clearly she did not know what he intended, so he put his finger beneath her chin to lift her face for his first kiss. She gasped into his mouth, but he found her tongue while clasping her tight against him, feeling every curve of her body.

When he held her away from him again, he discovered at last a touch of colour in her cheeks. He had another sudden urge to hurt her, so as to break down that reserve which was like a suit of armour about her – her determination to suffer in silence. He could not bring himself to tarnish such beauty, such innocence. Yet he would probably hurt her anyway.

While she stood absolutely still, he caressed her breasts and then her buttocks. But her breathing was more rapid, and her cheeks were now bright pink.

He gestured to the bed, and she climbed on to it, on her hands and knees. He slapped her buttocks and she turned her head, hair swinging.

'Lie down,' he commanded.

She fell on her face, so he gripped her shoulder and rolled her on to her back. Now she gazed at him with new alarm. This was not something she had been warned to expect.

He parted her long legs and knelt between, then gathered them up, one under each arm. She panted heavily, her flat belly rising and falling. A tear trickled out of the corner of one eye.

She was to be used in the heathen manner!

Her legs thus parted, and her buttocks raised clear of the divan, she was now utterly exposed to him. He made the entry as carefully as possible, watching her closely as he did so. Her mouth sagged open and she uttered a little moan. Then he could not stop himself.

But he was quick.

Afterwards he remained kneeling, releasing her slowly so that her buttocks slipped down his thighs to rest on the bed. She still breathed deeply, her eyes glazed.

'What is your name?' he asked her finally.

'My name is Gila,' she replied softly.

The news of the overthrow and death of Lodi Shah spread through India like the ripples of a large stone being thrown into a pool of still water. All the Muslim rulers to the south were of Arab or Persian descent; their histories were mainly composed of legendary battles fought by their ancestors against the Mongols of Genghis Khan and the Tatars of Timur. The men from the steppes of Asia were their hereditary foes; and since those earlier battles had invariably been lost, these horse-archers from the north were regarded with a good deal of superstitious fear.

Now here was one who trumpeted his descent from Timur actually setting himself up as the most powerful ruler in India.

They could not help but wonder what else he had in mind.

Babur was aware that his recent conquest was far from secure, and he wasted little time with his new concubine or in exploring the wonders of his new palace. A great deal of Lodi's vast wealth was immediately expended on increasing the size of Babur's army.

Warriors were summoned down from Afghanistan; leading them was the new Badshah's elder son, Nasim-ud-din Muhammed, known as Humayun, a boy of eighteen, who had been left to command Kabul in his father's absence.

In many ways Humayun resembled his father, but he was perhaps an even more complex character. Better educated than Richard Blunt himself, he was yet as brilliant a horse-archer as any of the men he led, but he had a careless wildness in his eye and in his spirit which could be disconcerting.

'He is a true Mongol,' Babur said, with some pride, as he approached.

Kamran watched his father and brother embracing, with smouldering eyes, and Richard felt a pang of apprehension for the future. Because Kamran also watched Blunt with obvious jealousy at his rapid elevation to intimacy with the Lion.

It was an intimacy which Babur sought, not just because of his insatiable desire for knowledge, but because he could share so little with his own people. Richard Blunt was like an alien from another planet, and he had so much to offer in his knowledge of the world beyond India.

Zahir-ud-din Muhammed had been born on 15 February 1483 – in so far as Richard could translate the Muslim calendar into Western terms – into the Barlas clan of the Chatagai tribe of Mongols, and was therefore, as he claimed, a direct descendant of Timur who had led the Barlas family to greatness a century before. Perhaps even more important, on his mother's side he was a thirteenth-generation descendant of the great Genghis Khan himself.

His father, Umar Shaikh Mirza, had ruled the small principality of Ferghana, north of the Hindu Kush. Babur was therefore no mere robber chieftain, however it might please him so to describe himself.

Being a Timurid and a prince, Umar Shaikh could lay claim to all the vast dominions once ruled by his great ancestor. Unfortunately there were a large number of other Timurid princes with the same ambition, and Zahir-ud-din had from the age of puberty been engaged in constant wars at his father's side, it being Umar Shaikh's determination to regain for his family the old Timurid capital city of Samarkand. The city was indeed occupied twice, but each time was lost again.

And then the death of Umar Shaikh had brought Babur – as he had already been nicknamed for his daring in battle – to disaster. At Sar-e-pol the army he had just inherited was shattered by that of his distant cousin, Muhammad Shaybani Khan, ruler of the Uzbeks from beyond the Jaxartes River – another descendant of Genghis Khan. Not only was Samarkand lost for the second and last time, but Babur's own patrimony of Ferghana also fell to the conqueror.

The Lion, aged only eighteen, had thus become a fugitive, but yet he was as experienced and resourceful and loved, a commander as any in Asia. He fled into the mountains to the south, and by a *coup-de-main* seized the Afghan capital of Kabul, and established himself there.

Still his dreams were of Samarkand, and for some fifteen years he had launched campaign after campaign to the north, always to be repulsed. Such failure could have wrecked many a man, but Babur bore his continuous defeats with total equanimity, always learning further the art of warfare. Yet even he finally had to give up this impossible quest and turn his attention elsewhere.

As expansion to the north had thus proved impossible, it obviously had to be concentrated on the south. The Mongols knew nothing but fullscale warfare – for centuries they had lived by raiding their close neighbours.

Babur's first incursion into India had occurred in 1519, and this had been nothing more than a raid. In 1522, however, just four years previous to his conquest of Delhi, and encouraged by the renegade Dawlat Khan, he had seized the town of Kandahar which lay on the traditional trading route from central Asia to Sind and north-western India.

Each year after that he had raided regularly into Badshah Lodi's territory, but never with the slightest aim of attempting its full conquest.

Now the entire kingdom, with its glittering wealth, had fallen into his hands. He gave thanks to Allah for his success. But he also gave thanks to a man who had helped make this conquest possible, by appointing Richard one of his viziers.

5
THE EMPIRE

Neither Babur nor Richard Blunt could be under the slightest misapprehension as to the immensity of the task confronting them. Indeed, the first crisis arose only a few weeks after the Moghul entry into the city.

The Battle of Panipat had been fought on 20 April, by European reckoning. For a while the weather had remained reasonably cool. But by mid-May the summer heat had arrived, followed in July by the monsoon, later here than on the west coast of the peninsula. The Mongols, used to a much more temperate climate, sweltered and sweated – and complained. The treasures of Agra having been thoroughly looted, they wished to return home to Afghanistan and conditions they were more accustomed to. Babur needed all of his skills of eloquence and persuasion to convince them that their future lay in this fertile, over-heated valley.

'I must keep them occupied by leading them again to war,' he explained. 'It is the only life they know.'

For the first time Richard Blunt was forced to come to terms with the business of true leadership. He knew enough history to understand that, two hundred years before, the English kings had been *primus inter pares* among their great nobles, most of whom were related to them by blood. But this uncertain situation was ended by the slaughter in the Wars of the Roses, from which Henry VII had emerged undisputed master of the realm – a mastery confirmed and increased by his son Henry VIII. Equally, on the Continent no one could doubt that Francis of France and, more so, Charles of Spain need merely point and their people followed.

Even more despotic, from what he had heard, were the Ottoman sultans, and certainly it had not seemed there was any check on the rule of Lodi, or of Begarha of Gujarat, who had recently died, to be succeeded by his son Bahadur.

Yet in Babur here was a man who, Richard was certain, had more talent and ability than all the others put together, and yet he was now reduced to cajoling his fierce Mongol warriors. Richard could not determine whether this refusal to be totally subservient to an hereditary prince might be a source of strength or of weakness.

Babur accepted his situation as a matter of fact, for he had never known anything different. He was therefore not overly concerned to realise that his occupation of Agra was merely the first step in a campaign that would take some time to complete. But he could not help but be anxious when he added up the forces which were against him.

In Kabul he had maintained himself in the midst of a group of robber chieftains only slightly less successful than himself. And his raids into Delhi and the Punjab had only slowly become important enough to rouse Lodi into action.

Now that his main strength was concentrated to the south, his Afghan rivals took the field against him. In addition, word was received that the Rajputs were mobilising a fresh army, commanded by Rana Sanga, Lord of Chitor; while, to the east, Ibrahim Lodi's brother Mahmud Lodi was rallying the survivors of Panipat and raising a new force.

'I have disturbed a hornet's nest, Blunt Amir,' Babur complained. 'And now I am completely surrounded. What use is it to possess all the riches in the world when one is virtually a prisoner?' He brooded into his wine cup – he was more a man of the steppes than a zealous Muslim. 'I have overreached myself.'

'Will the Afghans fight for Mahmud Lodi, my lord?' Richard countered.

'Never.'

'Will they fight for Rana Sanga?'

'They are hereditary enemies of the Rajputs.'

'Well, then, will the Rajputs and Mahmud Lodi combine?'

'I would have thought that extremely likely,' Babur said, 'seeing as how they did so before.'

'But, sire, our information is that the Rajput army lies to the west, and Mahmud's army to the east.'

'Thus we are caught in the middle,' Babur grumbled.

'It is a point of view,' Richard pointed out. 'Since we are in the middle, are we not able to attack them each in turn, before they can combine? In European warfare this is known as operating on interior lines.'

Babur frowned at him; obviously a lifetime spent leading great cavalry raids in and out of Asia had not taught him a great deal about strategy, however brilliant his tactical skill.

'What is necessary is an order of priority,' Richard told him. 'So, my lord, will the Afghan barons seek to attack you in Delhi?'

'No, no,' Babur said. 'They will wait for me to be defeated here in India, and seek to fall upon me when I endeavour to return to Kabul.'

'Well, then, it is the Rajputs and Mahmud Lodi who are your principal enemies. Which of these is the most dangerous?'

'Rana Sanga, without question. Mahmud is a true brother of Ibrahim. He is making no move towards us, merely recruits men and issues threats. I would say that he too is waiting in the hope that I will fall to the Rajputs.'

'Then it is the Rajputs with whom we must first deal.'

'By Allah, but you may well be right,' Babur said. 'But we will let them come to us. I have not the men to assault walled cities. On the open field, now, that is a different matter.' He called for Dawlat Khan. 'When will Rana Sanga move against me?' he inquired.

'He will wait until after the monsoon, my lord,' Dawlat Khan replied.

'Well, then,' Babur said. 'We have some months to prepare.'

For the rain clouds were already beginning to gather.

The Mongol leader now had a target at which to aim his amirs and his bahaturs, or valiant knights – for the Mongol knighthood could only be earned by valour on the field of battle, and ranked far higher than its Western equivalent. Nor did he waste his time during the wet months. He continued to enlarge his army, aided by the contents of Ibrahim Lodi's treasury. He taught his new recruits the Mongol way of fighting, and he improved the fortifications of the city itself.

But it was easy to see he had no faith in fortified cities. His triumph would be won in the field.

Richard worked as hard as anyone during the following months. Indeed he had as much to learn as any of the recruits, to adapt his experience to the Moghul concept of tactics.

In European warfare, at least as devolved by Spain's great general, Gonzalo de Córdoba, who even ten years after his death remained the accepted tutor of every soldier, the cavalry charge as part of winning a battle was a thing of the past. The concept had been destroyed, as much as anything, by the English longbows wielded at Crécy, Poitiers and Agincourt, and its death-knell had been sounded by the Swiss pikemen.

Together with the Swiss, the Spanish *tercio*, or brigade of about three thousand men – known as infantry because each was commanded, at least nominally, by an *infante* or royal prince – had become the arbiter of the battlefield. Manoeuvring in a massive square, composed in the main of pikemen but with a platoon of arquebusiers at each corner, the *tercio* was impervious to cavalry assault, and irresistible by any infantry less highly trained and disciplined than itself – which meant any infantry in the world.

Cavalry was used for scouting, and for pursuit when the enemy had broken and was fleeing the field.

Babur certainly understood the use of disciplined infantry; he had seen what the famous Janissaries of the Ottomans could accomplish. But he had never possessed any of his own. The Mongols – or Moghuls, as their name was universally pronounced by the Indians – were horsemen from the steppes of Asia, and they could only fight as they had always done: mounted and using the bow to clear the way for a decisive cavalry charge.

Babur had observed the success of Richard's pikemen at Panipat, however, and agreed that if such a mob could be sent into battle, a disciplined division might well be of immense value. He gave Richard permission to raise such a force, with the rank of tuman-bashi, or commander of ten thousand men, and Richard set to work with a will, recruiting from amongst the Hindus, giving them a rudimentary uniform of a red tunic to wear over their dhotis, arming them with a small leather buckler as well as their spears – which he lengthened to make them more like true pikes – and above all drilling them to advance, or stand shoulder to shoulder, regardless of what was hurled against them.

Babur watched his manoeuvres with an indulgent eye, but it was clear that he still thought little of their chances against the Rajput cavalry.

The arrival of the really heavy rains put an end to troop drilling for several weeks. Richard was quite pleased, as it enabled him to spend more time at home. He was also impressed by the ferocity of the weather, which made the rainstorm they had experienced on their way to Surat seem like a summer shower. He began to understand why all campaigning, and even most trading, ceased during the monsoon. Prabhankar informed him that it was much more severe in the south and on the coast.

He had been presented with the palace which had once belonged to Ghopal Das – Babur had no use for it, and there were many grander houses, previously owned by Lodi's nobles, to distribute to his Muslim officers.

Here Richard could feel at home, and he felt too that the palace and its surviving servants were glad to be in friendly hands. Better still, he found his goods untouched. He could again wear his rapier, and could now reveal to Babur the secrets of the arquebus.

Babur was not impressed. 'I have heard that the Janissaries are armed with these weapons,' he said. 'They make a lot of noise, but are still not as efficient as the bow.'

Richard had to admit that he was right.

As for the rapier, the Moghul was more impressed with the workmanship of the Toledo steel than with the weapon itself, until Richard gave a demonstration of fighting with sword and dagger. Then Babur looked thoughtful.

Prince Humayun, who had also witnessed the exhibition, stroked the sword.

'It is a work of art,' he commented, and grinned at Richard. 'Handled by an artist.'

In Ghopal's house, Richard installed Gila, her mother and her brother.

Babur was amused by this bizarre exhibition of European domesticity.

'A man must always be master in his own house, Blunt Amir,' he pointed out. His shrewd brain had discerned that Richard's attitude to women was not a Moghul one.

If Gila had not resisted him, it had been because doing so would have been pointless, and may have resulted in severe physical harm. She had not known then that he was not a Moghul, and tales of Mongol mistreatment of women were common in North India.

Indeed she had been astonished that he had wished to caress her, explore her ... and then kiss her. She had gazed at him with enormous eyes, suspecting he might be intending to bite off her tongue. But her contempt had remained. She had been given over to a barbarian; contempt for everything about him was her only defence.

Her mother, the Princess Mujhaba, had regarded him with even less esteem. She was still a relatively young woman, in her middle thirties, and had clearly once been even lovelier than her daughter. But, as she never tired of reminding anyone who would listen, she was also a daughter of the late Safavid ruler, Ismail I, given in marriage to Lodi to secure the alliance of Delhi in Persia's endless wars with the Ottomans. Thus she counted herself as much royal as any other princess in the world; it followed that she now considered herself and her daughter to have been shamefully enslaved to a barbarian general entirely lacking in either manners or money – save what his Moghul master allowed him.

Placing her in the same house as her daughter seemed clearly a mistake – or it would have been for any man but Richard. Politely but firmly, he informed the two women that he intended they should live in *his* style, not theirs.

The problem began with the concept of harem because there was none in Ghopal Das's Hindu establishment.

Mujhaba was shocked, and then complained loudly that she was being treated like a servant. Richard ignored her, and she forbade her daughter to go to his bed. When Richard sent for Gila, the maidservant returned to announce that the princesses had locked themselves in their apartment. Richard thereupon summoned several of his men and broke down the door, removing the screaming Gila by force.

On this occasion it was most certainly rape, as she fought him as best she could. But, less than half his size, she was forced to submit in the end, and this time he took her as a Mongol would, from behind while they both knelt.

Mujhaba had screamed as loudly as anyone.

Richard was never resisted again. Though well aware that the two women sat together devolving wild plots against him, he knew they were not to be feared. He was Babur's favourite, and his murder would be followed by instant impalement of the guilty.

His triumph was complete when Gila became pregnant. But he was scoring in another direction. Gila's brother, Tahmasp, a sturdy seven-year-old, was fascinated by his huge brother-in-law, and soon Richard had him drilling with the Hindus, to his mother's disgust.

I am becoming a total Mongol, Richard thought, as he surveyed the Hindu girls Prabhankar had lined up for him, to choose a concubine to serve him during Gila's confinement. And he wondered what his cousin Lizzie would think? Poor widowed Lizzie not even aware as yet that she was widowed. Would he ever see her again?

That depended upon the outcome of the approaching campaign. If Babur won, all things might be possible. Amongst the bric-à-brac found by the inquisitive Mongols, as they hunted through Lodi's palace, had been the cabinet into which Thomas Blunt's wallet had been carelessly thrown. Thus Richard was once again in possession of King Henry's commission – and the constant nagging memory of why he was here at all. But he knew it was crucially important to choose his moment. After a victory, yes. But if the Moghul were to lose, it would hardly matter. Richard could have no illusions as to his fate were he dragged, a Rajput captive, before his outraged wife and her mother.

Even as Sultan of the Kingdom of Delhi, Babur remained the same thoughtful, essentially good-humoured, confident man Richard had first discerned. This although the Moghul prince had a great deal on his mind.

He was as aware as anyone that his fate, and that of all his people, would have to be decided in the spring; and thus he made certain contingency plans for a withdrawal to Afghanistan, following a possible defeat. Yet he had begun to find in Agra a beauty and a promise which had been lacking in Kabul – perhaps even in Samarkand. Despite his cares, he sought to improve the city. But he was even more interested in recreating the city of Delhi as his new capital.

Indian records showed there had existed a city on the site of Delhi for nearly three thousand years, for it was mentioned in the epic poem *Mahabharata* under the name of Indraprastha. Like most Indian cities, it had had its ups and downs as the tides of war and empire swept to and fro; but certainly only four hundred years previously it had been the capital of the famous Indian king Prithviraja. It was Prithviraja who had lost Delhi to the Muslims; and in the following century the slave King Qutb-ud-Din Aybak had erected the tower called the Qutb Minar, which still stood.

One of Qutb-ud-Din's successors, Ala-ud-Din Khalji, had built a new city some three miles away, and yet a third city had been erected by Khalji's successor, Ghiyas-ud-Din Tughluk, and was called Tughlukabad. But this had to be abandoned because of lack of sufficient water, and a return made to the original site, which Tughluk's son Muhammad ibn Tughluk had greatly strengthened with walls and towers. However, Muhammed's successor, Firuz Shah Tughluk, had determined on yet a fifth city, going north again to build Firuzabad, very close to the site of the original Indraprastha.

All of these cities, so close as almost to meld into one, had been torn apart by Timur and his Tartars in 1389, and left desolate. It was how to amalgamate the best out of the five old cities, and make them into a homogeneous whole, that now taxed the brains of Babur and his architects. It never ceased to amaze Richard that someone who in England would be dismissed as a savage bandit could have such an interest in architecture and street planning. But, then, Babur also wrote poetry, and was better read than any man Richard had ever met. Perhaps here was the true Prester John!

But Babur also had severe domestic problems. He had removed his entire family from Kabul to enjoy the beauty of Agra. As he did not maintain a traditional closed harem, although he had the four wives permitted him by the Koran as well as several concubines, these splendid ladies were to be seen out on the streets and in the marketplace, or making their first acquaintance with elephants, squealing with laughter as they were hoisted up to sit in the howdah. They were a lively and happy family, with a single exception. But this was the most important exception of all – Nasim-ud-Din Muhammad Humayun.

Of all of the children Babur had fathered, Humayun was the eldest son, and therefore the obvious heir to both his conquests and his army. Indeed Humayun was very obviously Babur's son: well educated, interested in poetry and literature, and yet a soldier of considerable talent. That he was Babur's favourite was proved by the gift of the priceless 'Mountain of Light' diamond – the Koh-i-Noor. But Humayun found the climate of Agra enervating, and often he would be overtaken by bouts of shivering, when he was rendered incapable of sitting a saddle or attending to serious business.

Babur consulted the best medical opinion in the city, but they could only tell him that this shaking sickness was fairly common even amongst the Indians, and that there was no known cure for it.

When, in the spring, news was brought of the Rajput advance, and Babur marched his army out to meet his enemies, Humayun was once again left behind.

The battle against the Rajputs was fought on 16 March 1527 at Khanua, some forty miles west of Agra.

Even with the augmentations of strength Babur had busily made during the wet season, he still commanded no more than twenty thousand men, as he had to leave adequate garrisons of trustworthy troops both in Agra and along his communication routes with Kabul. His force therefore was evenly divided between Moghul horsemen and Hindu pikemen, the latter commanded by Richard.

But he also had his artillery and his wagons.

The Rajputs appeared as an immense host, a kaleidoscope of flags and banners, of beating drums and clashing cymbals. Richard estimated them as perhaps a hundred thousand strong. Every man was mounted, every man magnificently accoutred. The sun reflected from the burnished helmets, the chain mail surcoats, the swords and lances, the hardly less splendid horse trappings. There were also five hundred elephants.

The Hindu infantry moved restlessly as they observed the great mass approaching them.

'But stand firm,' Richard told them, 'with your pikes presented, and they cannot defeat you.'

The Rajputs still possessed no cannon.

Babur made exactly the same dispositions as before, linking his wagons together, and placing his cannon between them. The infantry were again placed on his left, his assault cavalry on his right.

'Let us see if these proud fellows have learned anything,' he remarked.

But even his Mongols were apprehensive of the coming encounter at such odds. Now Babur revealed his personal qualities as a leader, addressed his entire army with a stirring account of their past victories and the glories they now enjoyed, and then, looking at his Muslim elite cavalry, solemnly swore that from this day forth he would be the most sincere of them all, and broke his drinking cup and a bottle of wine to seal his oath, pouring the wine down a well.

This was stirring stuff, and brought forth an enormous cheer from the Moghul ranks, but clearly there was also going to have to be a tactical change – and Richard guessed what it would have to be, because it was a manoeuvre he had been instructed to practise often enough during the winter.

The first division of the Rajput cavalry delivered the charge. The cannon exploded, and the horsemen were driven back in disarray.

Instantly Babur's wand was pointed, and Richard marched his infantry out before the chained wagons. Here they formed a solid mass to resist the second charge, being assisted by dismounted Moghul archers, who fired over their heads into the approaching foe.

The arrows annoyed but did not disconcert the Rajputs, who clearly discounted the presence of a mass of unarmoured infantry, and rode at the gallop right up to the spears. But they had never encountered pikes before either. Knowing he would be fighting a static battle and that he would not be opposed by firearms, Richard had formed his men into a perfect replica of a Macedonian phalanx – or a Swiss one, for that matter – and against the twelve-foot-long iron-tipped poles the gallant horses hurled themselves in vain. The first two ranks were indeed driven back by the sheer weight of the assault, but those behind stood firm, and the mail-clad riders came tumbling to the ground, to be instantly despatched.

When they fell back, the phalanx was hastily retired and re-formed, while the cannon took on the next charge. Hitherto the elephants had not been used. But now they were sent forward to meet the same fate as at Panipat, thrown into disorder by the flying shot.

Meanwhile Babur had been holding his cavalry in check, but when he judged the moment right he launched them in a sweep to the Rajput left. Again the Rajputs seemed to have learned nothing from Panipat, were surprised and disconcerted by the arrow storm, and then found themselves no match for the Moghul charge.

When Rana Sanga himself went down, the battle was over. The Rajput prince was dragged back into his saddle, badly wounded, and escorted from the field. His men followed immediately, a long trail of dispirited and crushed horsemen.

While the Moghuls beheaded the wounded and the dead, Babur rode amongst his men, congratulating them.

'Where now, great Prince?' Richard asked him, leaning on his bloodstained sword.

'Now we can start to think about Mahmud Lodi,' Babur told him.

Richard would have preferred to go after the Rajputs and utterly destroy them, and then perhaps march south, on Gujarat.

He said so, but Babur shook his head. 'I would rather become friends with the Rajputs than trample them into the dust,' he said. 'They are very fine horsemen. Properly led, they would greatly increase my strength. Besides, now it is time to deal with Lodi.'

Richard had once again to be patient. But, soon after the Battle of Khanua, Gila gave birth to a son.

As Richard entered the apartment, she lay on her couch as watchful as ever, her mother standing by her head. One of her ladies held out the babe to him.

'He will be tall and strong like his father,' she said conventionally.

Richard gazed at the wizened face, the tiny curling fingers, and allowed the child to clutch one of his own.

'His grip is that of a bahatur,' the nurse said.

Richard eased his finger free and stood above the couch.

'Are you well?' he asked.

'I am well, my lord,' Gila said.

It was the first time she had ever so addressed him.

'And are you pleased?'

'Are *you* pleased, my lord?' she countered.

'Yes,' he said. 'Yes, I am very pleased.'

'Then am I also pleased, my lord.'

It was the first acknowledgement that she now accepted him as her husband. Mujabha scowled as ever, but Richard was delighted.

'What will you name him?' he asked.

She looked uncertain. 'Will *you* not name him?'

'I would prefer you to choose.'

She licked her lips, unsure whether he was playing some game with her.

'I would call him Zaid,' she said. 'After my brother.'

'Zaid,' Richard agreed.

Zaid Blunt, he thought. There was a name to present one day at King Harry's court.

By Muslim custom a woman was unclean while she nursed, but for this very reason Gila only gave the boy her own breast for three months, and then a wetnurse was found. Three months later she was pregnant again.

Babur seemed in no hurry to move against Mahmud Lodi, who was certainly making no move to the west.

There were sound strategic reasons for delaying a final settlement with Lodi until affairs in Rajputana were settled. To this end, Babur exchanged ambassadors with the princes of the Rajput confederacy, and endeavoured to form an alliance with them, as they had once been allied with Lodi. Religious differences had at that time been surmounted, and the Moghul chieftain saw no reason why they should not be overcome now.

But additionally, as Richard observed with some disquiet, Babur was more and more revelling in the delights of his new conquest. Though the Moghul had been educated to appreciate the finer things in life, that life had been spent almost entirely in the saddle, waging perpetual war against enemies of himself or his father. No one could argue his mastery of warfare, yet he had remained always a dreamer, and here at least was one of his dreams come true. He seemed to find ever more pleasure in walking beside the fountains and artificial lakes he laid out in his palace grounds in Agra, in discussing the layout of flowerbeds with his gardeners, than in planning his next military campaign.

His bahaturs could only watch this transformation with dismay.

Of more concern to Richard Blunt were the obvious signs of age besetting the Moghul. Babur was no more than forty-four years old in the summer of 1527, yet he moved like a man some twenty years older, his joints aching from so many weary years of fighting. And, significantly, he fathered no more children by the lovely Indian girl he had taken to his bed.

This premature ageing did not seem to disturb him much.

'I have lived a full life, Blunt Amir,' he said. 'A man cannot exceed his allotted span. Once Mahmud Lodi is destroyed . . .'

'When will that be, sire?' Richard asked.

Babur smiled.

'You are impatient, like all my officers. They all have spurs to win. It will happen, as soon as my treaty with the Rajput princes is concluded. Nor am I being entirely idle. I have emissaries working in the eastern cities, telling the people there how great I am, and how feeble Lodi is in comparison. Battles are won in the mind more often than on the field. Do you not study this in Europe?'

Richard had to admit that they did not.

'It is always possible to undermine an opponent's will to fight and win,' Babur continued. 'It is said these tactics were used by Genghis Khan and Timur to secure their great victories.'

'I can see that our European kings have a great deal to learn, my lord,' Richard agreed, and decided that the time might be ripe to open a campaign of his own – the mission which he had still not accomplished. 'How splendid it would be if an alliance could be forged between the Moghuls and the English.'

'Between a Muslim and a Christian?'

'Well, sire, *I* am a Christian, and I am serving with you. And now you are seeking an alliance with the Hindu Rajputs. Does your religion actually forbid you to ally yourself with Christians?'

Babur smiled. 'As a matter of fact it does. Which is not to say that a man may not occasionally bend his conscience in pursuit of a laudable aim. But of what benefit would an alliance with England be to me?'

'Have you ships, my lord?'

'Ships?' Babur frowned.

'Do you know anything of the ocean?'

'I have never seen the ocean, Blunt Amir. My knowledge of it comes entirely from others. But of what use is the ocean to me?'

'As you expand your kingdom, you will come eventually to the sea. When you do that, you will understand the value of overseas trade – and of a navy to protect your ships. My country could supply those ships.'

Babur stroked his beard.

'And of what value to me would be an alliance with your King?'

'The value would lie in trade, of course. My country produces the finest woollen goods in the world. Well-made garments to keep you warm in the winters.'

'Have we not our own sheep and cattle to provide us with garments?'

'Woven clothes are more comfortable, sire,' Richard argued.

'Hm. And what could we offer your King in exchange?'

'This country is rich in gold and precious stones. Those would be most welcome in the West.'

'Gold exchanged for woollen garments?' Babur mused.

'We English also know a great deal about cannon and their usage.'

'I obtain my cannon from the Ottomans.'

'They are surely uncertain neighbours, sire.'

Babur smiled again. 'Now at last you are approaching the point, Blunt Amir. Your people in Europe fear the Ottomans – and with good reason. I have learned that this new Sultan,

Suleiman, is marching on Vienna.'

'Should you not also fear such power, my lord?'

Babur considered.

'I would serve as your ambassador to the West,' Richard added eagerly.

Babur glanced at him sharply.

'I prefer to have you here, Blunt Amir. It is with your arrival that my fortunes seem to have taken an upwards turn. Perhaps I am being fanciful, but it is certain that none of my other captains understand foot soldiering as do you.' He saw the disappointment crossing Richard's face, and rested his hand on the younger man's arm. 'We will speak of this again – when I have settled with Lodi.' He smiled. 'And when we have learned how Suleiman has dealt with Vienna. Or Vienna with Suleiman.'

Obviously he feared Ottoman might more than he would admit, and preferred to play a waiting game in the hopes that Suleiman might overreach himself. However, he had other matters on his mind, which he considered of equal importance, so complex was his character.

During the next monsoon, he began to dictate his memoirs to his secretaries.

Richard was astounded. Henry VIII was considered one of the wonders of his age because he could read with ease and compose poetry. But the concept of the king of any European country sparing the time from the business of ruling – and in the middle of an unresolved conflict – to write his life story, was staggering.

Babur found nothing unusual in it.

'I am growing old, as you can see, Blunt Amir,' he pointed out. 'Should I not set down what I have seen and learned and experienced, for the benefit of my descendants? Besides, it will while away the weary months while we wait for events to favour us.'

Gila gave birth to a daughter, Iskanda, in the spring of 1528. She was now entirely reconciled to her fate, and was even, Richard felt, able to relish her distinctly unusual husband.

Only her mother Mujhaba continued to regard him with attitudes varying from the contemptuous to the venomous. Richard had no doubt she made her daughter's life a misery, but Gila seemed able to cope with the conflicting loyalties.

But there was little time left for domesticity. With the ending of the monsoon, Babur commanded his army to march towards the east. A peace had been agreed with the Rajputs, and although Babur knew that the Hindu princes would merely wait for the outcome of his struggle with Lodi, he still felt sure that his rear was temporarily secured.

The Moghul army was now twenty-five thousand strong, and Babur even employed some elephants, though these were to act as roadmakers rather than weapons of war. His main strength remained, as always, in his light horsemen and his cannon; although he regarded his division of Hindu pikemen with some satisfaction.

On this campaign Muhammad Humayun was able to accompany his father for the first time; Dawlat Khan was now considered sufficiently loyal to be left in command at Agra. Kamran also accompanied the army, as usual being his father's tavachi, or aide-de-camp. So did Prince Askari, but Hindal remained in Agra.

Humayun took command of the right-wing cavalry division, Babur's knockout punch, but he spent a great deal of time riding with Richard, talking about England and Europe, and studying the unfamiliar manoeuvres of the pikemen.

'How would *we* fare, do you suppose, Blunt Amir,' he asked, 'against an entire army on foot, as you describe in Spain?'

'I am bound to say that I think a well armed and disciplined infantry *tercio* would always defeat cavalry, sire,' Richard told him.

'Would our arrow storms not destroy that discipline?'

'Perhaps, could they be delivered. But do not forget that our tercios would each have a contingent of arquebuses to keep your horsemen at a distance.'

Humayun had of course examined the handguns belonging to Richard, and had even fired one. He had not been impressed then, and he did not look impressed now.

But his interest in the West was encouraging and Richard still had every hope of persuading Babur to let him return home as an ambassador . . .

* * *

Any hope of the campaign against Lodi being over in short order had soon to be abandoned. The Sultan – as he called himself – clearly avoided a pitched battle, retiring before the Moghul army and waiting for the monsoon to return to his aid.

This indeed happened after Babur had marched down the valley of the Jumna to the ancient Hindu holy city of Prayag, where the river Jumna joined the Ganga to form the Ganges. Up to this point there had been little resistance, except from the occasionally fanatical tribe of Hindus who were opposed equally to Lodi and to the Moghul, for both were Muslims. The discovery of a large body of Hindus serving with the Moghul army, however, did much to dispel local fears which had been inspired by Lodi's propaganda tales of wholesale massacres.

It was from the inhabitants of Prayag that Babur learned that the Ganges continued east for several hundred more miles before entering the sea.

He summoned Richard. 'Can this be true?'

'I should think it is very likely, my lord.'

'And this sea they speak of, will it be the ocean?'

'I would think so, sire.'

He had actually no idea.

'Perhaps a thousand miles, and then the ocean. This we must do, Blunt Amir. To die without looking upon this sea would be unworthy of me.' He paused for thought. 'Do you suppose Timur ever saw the ocean?'

They had spent many an hour discussing Timur's campaigns, which had carried him from central Asia into Russia, Persia, Turkey, India – only as far as Delhi – and thence towards China, where he had died.

'From what you have told me, I would say no. He may have looked upon the Mediterranean, but that is only an inland sea . . .'

'Then here at least I can do more than he,' Babur said with quiet satisfaction.

Richard began to sense that the notion of looking upon the ocean was looming larger in Babur's ever-inquisitive mind than his final settling with Lodi. In any event their advance had proceeded no farther than the Hindu holy city of Benares when the rains began. Lodi no doubt hoped that Babur would have returned to Agra before then, but the Moghul merely went into camp around Benares.

'I have never known such a climate,' he confessed. 'We have very cold winters in Turkestan, but it is yet possible to campaign in the snow – in some cases simpler, as the rivers are frozen. But this rain turns everything into a swamp ... it is a curse.' As ever, he grinned. 'But we must make the best of it. Not one of us will again set foot in Agra until Mahmud Lodi is dead.'

Women were found for his officers and his men, and they settled down to make themselves as comfortable as they could while the rain teemed down, far heavier here than it had ever fallen in Agra.

Needless to say, Babur rapidly interested himself in the city, founded nearly a thousand years before by Ashoka, the great Buddhist emperor; one of whose famous pillars still stood. Following the decline of Buddhism in India, Benares had become a centre of Hindu worship and Hindu learning.

Unfortunately, it had been conquered by the Muslim rulers of Delhi, in 1194 by Christian reckoning, who systematically looted it of both treasures and brains. All who could had fled; those who remained had mostly perished. Now great areas of the city lay in ruins, and the few who scratched an uncertain living from the area seemed to accept the arrival of this new Muslim army as just another disaster.

Babur sent messengers out into the surrounding country, inviting the savants to return, and to Richard's surprise some of them did.

'This is a mammoth country,' Babur said, 'and not only in size. Central Asia is a huge area but it is empty. This land teems with people, cattle and crops. It could be the greatest country in the world. It shall be my duty to make it so.'

With the ending of the rain, Babur wished to resume his march south-east. He planned to follow the river valley down to the sea, before which it divided into several tributaries.

However, word was then received that Mahmud Lodi was encamped with a vast army around the ruined city of Patali-putra, which had been Ashoka's actual capital.

'We must settle with Lodi first,' Babur decided. He directed his army to march upon Pataliputra, about a hundred and fifty miles to the north-east, where yet another river, the Gogra, flowed into the mighty Ganges. 'Once we have finished with Lodi, we will continue following the Holy River to the sea,' Babur pointed out.

The army was happy to be on the march again. Five months in such insalubrious surroundings had been very nearly too long. There had been a considerable amount of sickness and deaths.

Richard discovered Humayun riding beside him, and was aghast at what he saw. The young Prince's face was yellow, and he trembled ceaselessly.

'It is an ague,' he sighed.

'You should be in bed,' Richard told him.

'How can I be in bed when my father marches to a decisive battle?' Humayun demanded.

Richard shrugged. He could understand Humayun's determination. Besides, as he had observed on his journey from Goa with poor Thomas, when attacked by one of these agues, going to bed did not really make much difference. One either recovered or one did not.

Mahmud Lodi's army was not found at Pataliputra. So Babur instead gazed at the ruins of another once great city.

'This too must be rebuilt,' he said. 'As should Payrag and Benares. There is so much I wish to do, Blunt Amir. A man could occupy himself with this land for two lifetimes. But Lodi still comes first!'

News came in that the Sultan had now retreated up the Gogra. The Moghul army was set in motion once more and, a week after leaving Pataliputra, Lodi's outposts were at last encountered.

He had cunningly crossed the river again, seeking always to keep the water as a barrier between himself and his pursuer. And now his men controlled the only ford. Babur emplaced his artillery on the bank and began a bombardment of the enemy position. But the range was too far, and in the jungle the cannon lost much of its effectiveness, as the stone shot splintered against great trees.

Babur tugged his beard in annoyance as he stared across the fast-flowing water.

'This rascal seeks to wear me out,' he growled. 'What is to be done, Blunt Amir?'

But for once even Richard had no answer. So the army encamped while its generals considered the situation.

'He can play hide-and-seek with us forever,' Kamran muttered.

Humayun made no comment. Though he had recovered from his ague, he still looked very weak.

'A ming-bashi would speak with you, my lord,' one of the tuman-bashis announced to Babur. 'He says he knows of another ford.'

'Indeed? Well, show him in.'

The ming-bashi, or commander of a thousand men, was a small man, roughly the same age as Babur himself, and with the clear gaze and pale complexion of a mountain man.

'I know you,' Babur said. 'You are Farid Khan, the Afghan.'

Farid bowed.

'And you know of an unguarded ford?'

'My regiment forms part of the rearguard, sire. Some of my men sought to snare a buffalo, but the animal made off into the river, hardly swimming, yet wading to the far side. My men would have followed him, but I prevented them and, instead, marked the place.'

'By Allah!' Babur crowed. 'You will be rewarded, Farid Khan. Where a buffalo may go, so may a man. Or a thousand men. Or ten thousand men. Yet must it be done quickly and quietly. Blunt Amir, your pikemen will cross and seize the ford. You will leave tonight clandestinely, while I occupy the enemy's attention at this point. You will hold the ford until I can bring my main armament over. You understand that once my army abandons this position, Mahmud Lodi will seek to discover why, so may well attack you with his entire strength?'

'I understand, my lord.'

'I will guide you, Blunt Amir,' said Farid the Afghan.

Richard and his pikemen stealthily withdrew from the Moghul camp, and made their way back to the place marked by Farid. The existence of a ford was certainly not obvious; only the slightest ripples on the brown water indicated a shoal patch – and there was no indication of how shallow.

'As soon as it is dark,' Farid Khan said, 'you and I will cross together, eh?'

Richard gave Prabhankar his orders: to follow with the men as soon as it was seen that Farid and he had reached the far side safely. Then he accompanied the Afghan into the water. Farid certainly appeared to have no fear, but walked steadily ahead. The water was quite deep – and at one point came up to the little man's chin. Still only chest deep, Richard stretched out a hand to steady him, but Farid merely grinned and went on. A few minutes later he was scrambling up the far bank. Blunt looked back at the long snake of dark men following Prabhankar, and felt a glow of satisfaction.

Richard relayed a message back to Babur . . . and then waited. He had expected Farid to return to the rest of the army, but instead the Afghan preferred to bring his regiment across to fight beside the Hindus.

That afternoon, Lodi, alerted by the withdrawal southward of the Moghul army, moved himself south. As soon as his scouts discovered the Hindus, he realised what was happening. Instantly he launched a fierce assault, and the Hindus received their first true baptism of fire, unsupported by either cavalry or artillery. Fortunately Lodi had little effective cavalry, and of course no guns, and they were able to hold on until nightfall.

Next day Babur attempted to cross with his main army, but Lodi once more attacked fiercely, and it was again left to the pikemen to defend their bridgehead. It was not until evening that Babur had manoeuvred all his men, horses and artillery across. This last was in itself a vast feat of engineering as he had floated the guns on rafts, with men at each bank straining on the ropes to prevent them from being swept away.

Thus on the third day he was ready. The battle was fought against the usual Moghul pattern, Babur being determined to take the fight to the enemy, lest he escape again. Now the Hindus, on whom he was relying more and more, formed a spearhead, marching against Lodi's already shaken force, while the Moghul cavalry manoeuvred on their flanks. The artillery boomed away, while Richard and his men 'fixed' the enemy front, and the Moghuls galloped at his flanks, delivering volley after volley of arrows before charging home when Lodi's men began to waver.

The enemy retreat turned into rout, and soon the Indian army was swept from the field.

'Truly are you worthy of reward,' Babur yelled to Farid. 'As of this moment you are known as "Sher Khan" – "the Mighty Warrior".'

Farid bowed his head in gratitude.

'As for you, Blunt Amir,' Babur said, 'once again you have proved your worth. Now you are bahatur – one of my own chosen knights.'

Lodi was dragged a prisoner, before Babur.

He fell to his knees. 'All hail, mighty Moghul warrior,' he said. 'You are ordained by heaven to rule this land. Fool that I was to attempt to oppose you.'

Babur studied him, but made no reply.

'Spare my life, great Prince,' Lodi continued, 'and I will be the most faithful of your servants.'

'You are not fit to be a servant,' Babur told him, 'much less a king. Yes, you were a fool to oppose me, as was your brother. He at least died a warrior's death. Impale him,' he commanded. 'And all his officers. Behead their men.'

Lodi uttered a shriek of terror as he was dragged towards the stake.

Babur had every right to be proud, since he had now secured the entire vast Kingdom of Delhi which, along with his Kabul kingdom, stretched some two thousand miles from north-west to south-east. Spread over a map of Europe, it would extend from London to Buda, not even the Holy Roman Emperor laid claim to such a continuous area.

Babur remained a frighteningly complex character. That very evening he dictated slowly a new chapter of his memoirs, recalling the events of the battle while they were still fresh in his mind.

Next morning he was summoned to Humayun's bedside. The young man had fought as hard as anyone in the battle, but was now scarcely able to move.

'Will he die?' Babur asked the surgeon, perturbed.

'In this climate, my lord, it is certainly possible.'

Babur scowled.

'Then we must march for Agra with all haste,' he decided. 'I will return another time to follow the river to the ocean.

Babur was more concerned for the young man than he pretended. He knew there was more at stake than merely the life of an eldest son. Humayun was his only practical heir; for Kamran had thus far revealed no ability at administration or generalship, while Askari was too wild, and Hindal was still too young.

The army marched back to Agra as fast as it could. Babur, now acknowledged master of all of the kingdom of Delhi, left garrisons in the key cities. He also sent ambassadors into Bihar and Bengal, countries which had formerly acknowledged Ibrahim Lodi's supremacy, calling for submission. His brain never ceased to roam over all the problems which might face him in the future. But, in fact, the news of Mahmud Lodi's defeat so terrified the Sultan Nasir ed-din Nasrat Shah of Bengal that he acknowledged Babur as his master without hesitation.

Sher Khan, promoted tuman-bashi and amir, was one of those left to govern in the east. But only Humayun really mattered. Agra was regained by the forced march. Accompanying them were Babur and the litter bearing the ailing Prince. Richard Blunt followed with the remainder of the army. Since they did not reach the city until the end of the year, Richard fully expected to find the Moghul court in mourning. But Humayun had clung to life, however desperately.

Richard was now a fully-fledged Moghul general, or *tuman-bashi*, even if regarded as an infidel by his fellow officers. Yet of his prowess as a soldier no man could doubt, nor of the esteem in which he was held by the great Moghul himself.

His reputation had spread before him; when he entered his house the servants vied in their endeavours to bow low before him. Gila stood waiting, with Zaid at her side and Iskanda in her arms. The boy was now three, the babe not quite a year old, her colouring amazing, for although she was black-haired and white-skinned like her mother, she had bright blue eyes.

'My lord.' Gila bowed.

He gathered Iskanda from her arms. The baby stared at him with wide eyes, but did not utter a cry.

'She recognises you,' Gila said.

'She shall, indeed, in the course of time.' He handed her to a waiting nurse, and turned to Zaid. 'And you, little soldier, do you know who I am?'

'You are Blunt Bahatur, the great warrior, my father,' the boy replied.

Richard laughed at the boy's grave response, and swung him into the air. 'One day we will ride together into battle side by side, Zaid Blunt. Now go, for I would speak with your mother.'

He set Zaid on the floor, and dismissed the nurses. They hurried from the room, whispering amongst themselves.

'Your mother is well?' Richard asked.

'Yes, my lord,' Gila replied. She was trembling somewhat.

'I will see her presently. And your brother Tahmasp?'

'He wishes only to march at your side.'

'That certainly cannot be long delayed.'

She wore a sari of translucent pale green, and a tunic of darker colour. There was a circlet of beads round her forehead, and golden bangles on each arm and around each ankle. But none through her nose: she was a slave to no man!

He thought her as beautiful a woman as he had ever seen; she must now be about nineteen years old. He unfastened her tunic and let it fall to the floor. Her figure had matured during his absence. Her breasts filled his hand. Slowly he unwound her sari.

'Was my lord lonely upon his campaign?' she asked softly.

'Very lonely,' he told her, and swept her naked body from the floor and on to their couch.

Never before had she responded so fully and so warmly. If destiny has truly sent me to this land, he thought, then could I be happy here.

What Babur would plan next depended upon the health of Humayun.

'I do not understand it,' the Moghul complained, walking the covered pathways of the palace gardens and watching the rain drip down.

'He is healthy for a week, even a fortnight, then there is

another attack, and he all but dies. Then he rallies again. But all the time his strength is dwindling.'

'I have seen this illness in Spain,' Richard agreed. 'It can last for years, where it does not kill.'

'Leaving my son an invalid,' Babur said. 'How can the Prince of the Moghuls be an invalid? What can I do, Blunt Bahatur? None of these so-called surgeons can help my son.'

'I do not know what you can do, my lord, save pray.'

Babur gazed at him for some seconds, then he nodded. 'Then, as you have brought me much good fortune on the field of battle, we will pray together for the life and health of my son.'

He took Richard into the mosque, despite the mutterings of the imams, holy men, and the mufti, lawyers, and together they knelt before the mehrib, the Mecca-facing doorway. Here Babur prayed silently, but then he summoned his leading imams and led them to the room where Humayun lay, pale and weak and shivering.

Again Babur knelt, and this time he prayed aloud. 'Allah Akhbar, Allah Akhbar.' His voice reverberated round the chamber. 'Oh, most merciful Mohammed, who sits upon the right hand of God, look down upon this poor sinner, and have mercy upon my son. You have given me greatness, but of what use is earthly fame and fortune where my son is sick unto death, and cannot recover? Grant him health, I pray of you. In return, do with me as you will. Strike me down in his place. Kill me or lay me low with the most terrible of diseases. These things will I accept with a smile, O Prophet, if my son can but regain his health.'

His voice faded, but he remained in an attitude of prayer for some minutes longer, then rose and walked seven times round the bed to guarantee his oath.

Again Richard marvelled. It was difficult to imagine Henry VIII or Charles of Spain, or indeed Suleiman of Turkey offering up his own life, while still enjoying its prime, for that of his son.

This man, he thought, deserves to rule India. Indeed, he deserves to rule Asia. For is he not the wisest and most magnanimous monarch in the world?

To Blunt's surprise, Humayun's recovery began almost from

that very day. The young Prince had suffered a vicious attack of the ague which afflicted him, and it was possible to anticipate only a week or a fortnight before another bout overtook him. But a fortnight passed, and there was no further ague. A month later, when the rains had ceased and the sun's heat dried up stagnant water and dispersed the mosquitoes, Humayun was beginning to put on weight . . .

'You have worked a miracle, my lord,' Richard remarked.

'It is a miracle certainly,' Babur agreed. 'Now am I a happy man once more.'

'Then we must start thinking of new worlds to conquer,' Richard suggested.

'Indeed. Next year we shall again march to the east, and this time shall follow the Ganges all the way down to the sea.'

'That is some thousand miles, sire,' Richard pointed out. 'There is a quicker route to the ocean.'

'Tell me of it,' Babur said.

'If you were to march to the south-west, to the Kingdom of Gujarat, it is a distance of not more than seven hundred miles to the sea. And through rich country.'

'So tell me of Gujarat,' Babur commanded.

Richard did so, and told him also of the Portuguese trading concessions on the coast.

'I see,' Babur commented. 'And you would replace these Portuguese with English.'

'There is room for both, my lord. But England is the greater country.'

Babur smiled indulgently. 'Your idea interests me. Where is the point in marching through lands I have already conquered? We will march upon Gujarat after the next monsoon.'

'What do you think of that, Prabhankar?' Richard asked. 'You will be going home next year as a ming-bashi of Babur the Great.'

'My family will be slain,' Prabhankar said ruefully.

'Surely not? Not when they are known to be your family.'

'I meant they will already have been slain, since I have now been gone for five years.'

Was it really five years? That meant it was six years since Richard had left England. Six years since he had last seen his family. Lizzie would be nearly thirty, as he himself was that age. Was she still waiting for her husband to return, or had she long given him up as dead, and married again?

Then what of Master Bottomley and the *Bonaventure*? She had surely long sailed for home, with a report of how the Blunts had vanished into the Indian jungle.

And what of Elena? She would be twenty-two, and undoubtedly married. Did she ever remember the tall Englishman with whom she had flirted so dangerously? Did she blame her treacherous father for his death?

To return to Goa, as a tuman-bashi in the mighty Moghul army, would be a pleasurable experience, he thought.

But then he realised this would not happen. For, as mysteriously as Humayun recovered his health, Babur began to ail, as the next monsoon drew on.

No one knew what was the cause. It was certainly not the ague. Rather was it a sudden immense weariness which seemed to creep over him. The onset was insidious, beginning after a long July day in the saddle reviewing his troops, when suddenly he all but fell from his horse.

But the surgeons could find nothing wrong with him, and within twenty-four hours Babur seemed again as filled with energy as ever.

Until there was another attack. After the third, Babur himself realised there was something seriously the matter.

'I had better make haste to complete my memoirs,' he confided to Blunt with a grim smile, 'or they will not be completed at all.'

'You are not yet fifty,' Richard pointed out. 'You are in the very prime of life, my lord.'

'A man's age is a mathematical computation agreed by other men,' Babur pointed out. 'It has nothing to do with what is going on inside his own brain, his own body. Some men are young at sixty or even seventy. Some are old at forty. I am one of the unlucky ones. And then, perhaps, not so unlucky. I may be but forty-six years old, but have I not lived life to the hilt for the past thirty-five?'

And are perhaps now paying the penalty, Richard thought sombrely.

As the year wore on, the Moghul visibly weakened. He still issued orders for a campaign into Gujarat the following spring, but his tuman-bashis realised that there could be no campaign, unless it was led by Humayun – and the Prince was rather an unknown quantity as an army commander. When the rains began again, the preparations for war were quietly abandoned. The soldiers waited for their Lion to return to health.

Babur spent his time dictating his memoirs, his voice often hoarse as he sought to complete this personal record of his achievements for posterity. Sometimes he railed against his Kismet, which had led him along so many strange pathways. He seemed to consider India the strangest of them all. 'Why did I come here?' he asked. 'Hindustan offers nothing. There is no beauty here, no learning, no science ... they do not even have proper baths. It was an evil day when I followed your advice and marched on Agra, Blunt Bahatur.'

Richard bowed his head and waited for this storm to pass, as he knew it would. As long as the Moghul was reliving the past, he would not die, and he prayed for him to continue.

But at last the work was finished. Babur lay back on his divan and smiled at his viziers and tuman-bashis.

'There,' he said. 'My life's work is complete. Blunt Bahatur, come sit with me and tell me again of the lands beyond the sea.'

Richard talked far into the night, while Babur listened, breathing quietly, his eyes occasionally drooping shut.

Then suddenly they opened wide, and he sat up. 'Send for Muhammed Humayun,' he said. 'Send for Kamran. Send for my sons.'

Messengers were despatched, and the young men came hurrying into their father's bedchamber. The women came too, and assembled at the foot of the divan, some already weeping.

Babur held Humayun's hand.

'Care for your brothers,' he said.

And he died.

As was the Muslim custom, Babur had long ago built his own mausoleum in Kabul, and it was necessary for him to be removed there for burial. This involved a 750-mile journey which took some two months to complete, and it would be made in the dead of winter. Blunt calculated that Babur had died on 26 December 1530.

The route lay first up the valley of the Jumna to Delhi, then across the hills, before descending again into the great valley watered by huge rivers such as the Sutlej and the Indus, thence north, steadily climbing now, until Peshawar was reached, beneath the immense mountains of the Hindu Kush; thence through the mountain passes, often dragging the wagon on which the Moghul's embalmed body lay through waist-deep snow, until finally the fortress city was reached.

Kabul lacked the beauty of Agra, but possessed a rugged grandeur because of its situation in a shallow valley surrounded by mountains. Also it had history, for nearly all the invaders of India, beginning with the immortal Mahmud of Ghazni in the eleventh Christian century, had first possessed themselves of Kabul.

Unfortunately there was little time for exploration or contemplation. During these months the Moghul empire lay stagnant, awaiting the firm grasp of a new ruler. Richard might have expected the Rajputs to take advantage of this situation, but they honoured their treaty with the dead hero.

He was personally much saddened. He had come to India looking for a legend – and had found a living legend. Had Babur lived only another ten years, he would surely have conquered that entire vast land south of the mountains, and truly made himself monarch of the greatest empire the world would see since that of his famous ancestor. Now all was in jeopardy. And the future was Humayun's.

It was late spring before Humayun regained Agra. He had sent his most trusted bahaturs on ahead, including Blunt. No sooner was he reinstalled in his palace than he summoned Richard to his presence, and waved his viziers away. He was twenty-two years old. At that age Babur was already known as the Lion, the undisputed leader of his people. But Humayun had led too sheltered a life, and seemed almost frightened of the immense task which had descended to him.

'You were my father's confidante in many things, Blunt bahatur,' he said. 'You knew his mind. So where would he first have had me turn my attention?'

'The army awaits the order to march on Gujarat, my lord.'

Humayun nodded. 'And you will march with them. You know the country, and the people?'

'I have passed through that land,' Richard said cautiously. If ever he was going to leave Agra, it had to be now. 'But Gujarat itself is of little importance; its coastline was what mattered to your father.'

Humayun muttered, 'It was my father's dream to behold the ocean. What is so fabulous about this ocean?'

'Its lure is the ability men have to cross it in ships – with so much greater ease than they can cross deserts and mountains.'

'As you have done yourself,' Humayun said.

'As I would do again, my lord, to bring the wealth of Europe to your aid. This was your father's wish.'

Humayun glanced at him. 'He wished to send you away?'

'He wished to send me on a mission to my own people, to bring our nations together.'

'Then he was in error,' Humayun said. 'I will not send you anywhere, Blunt Bahatur. You will ride at my side, now and always. And you will bring me fortune, as you did for my father.'

Richard's heart sank.

BOOK THE SECOND

The Phoenix

'The world's great age begins anew,
The golden years return,
The earth doth like a snake renew,
Her winter weeds outworn:
Heaven smiles, and faiths and empires gleam,
Like wrecks of a dissolving dream.'

Percy Bysshe Shelley
Hellas.

6
THE FUGITIVE

Like a weary snake wriggling its way along the banks of the river, undulating over shallow rises, disappearing into green forest only to reappear again more exhausted than ever, the Moghul army retreated from Bihar.

It had been defeated.

Humayun rode at the head of his men, Kamran to one side, and Richard Blunt on the other.

'Sher Khan,' the Moghul muttered. 'Who is this Sher Khan?'

'You met him, once, just before the Battle of the Gogra, sire,' Richard reminded him. 'He showed us the ford.'

'Would I had decapitated him there and then,' Humayun growled. 'But in those days, you brought our arms fortune, not disaster, Blunt Bahatur.'

Richard had known such a reproach was inevitable. It was only surprising that it had taken so long to be made.

It was the spring of 1540, and in the nine and a half years since Babur's death the Moghuls had stumbled from one disaster to the next.

Yet Humayun's reign had begun well enough.

Richard had swallowed his disappointment at the Moghuls' decision not to allow him to return to England, and with his invariable optimism reflected that it might well be a different story once Gujarat had been conquered. Certainly he had had no choice but to make the campaign against Bahadur Shah a success.

As it had been, initially. The Moghul cavalry with their artillery and their Hindu infantry had routed the forces of Gujarat as easily as those of the Rajputs or the Lodis. Bahadur Shah had fled from the field. But too many of his soldiers had also escaped, to be rallied, and in the thick jungle of the south the Moghuls were less effective. Nor did Humayun have the military genius of his father to devise a way of coping with the situation. Richard had implored him to give the Hindus a free hand. They were men who understood the jungle and could penetrate it; the Moghuls, for all their do-or-die courage in battle, gazed fearfully at the dark thickets and recoiled from the rustling lizards.

Humayun had refused to allow his English *condottiere* to operate on his own – no doubt he feared Richard might desert to the other side, or just take himself off. He had concentrated upon capturing every town he could, and on pursuing his hobby of exploring ancient temples, examining ancient books, and where possible, appropriating them. He remained a gallant soldier, and an interesting and often fascinating companion, but where Babur had followed his hobbies when free from the responsibilities of command, Humayun too often let the command wait upon the accumulation of a rare text.

Kamran remained a brooding accompaniment to his brother's careless gaiety.

The cities of Mundu and Champanir had duly fallen. But Bahadur Shah had again not been brought to battle, and all the while the Gujarat sultan had been reorganising his armies. Yet after campaigning for several years Humayun had declared that Gujarat was annexed to the empire, and rode off to Delhi where he wanted to complete his father's work and build a new city, Din Panah, close by the old.

Kamran was left in command in Gujarat, with Richard Blunt as his aide, but Kamran would accept no advice, and as Babur had foreseen, proved himself a totally incompetent general. When, after six weary years, Bahadur Shah had taken the offensive himself, the Moghuls, riddled with fever and discontent, with their leader unable to rally them, had been driven from the country.

It was the first defeat suffered by Moghul arms since Panipat; only the veterans could recall the ups and downs of Babur's early years – the majority remembered nothing but victory.

This especially applied to the Hindus, who had never suffered defeat under Moghul leadership.

'We are fallen upon evil times, Blunt Sahib,' Prabhankar grumbled, because for all his pessimism he had hoped to return to Goa in triumph, as much as Richard.

That was a dream which would never now be realised, Richard knew. He had been so close, and yet had failed to reach his goal. He had turned his back on his own kind forever.

There were compensations enough at home. He had left Gila pregnant for the third time when he had ridden away in 1530. Now he held a five-year-old son, Mahmud, gazing with terrified eyes for the first time at his father.

Zaid was a strong nine-year-old, taller than any of his contemporaries, and Iskanda already a beautiful eight-year-old.

'Soon it will be time to find her a husband, sire,' Gila remarked.

'Soon,' Richard agreed. It was not something to consider. For domestic bliss had been over almost before it had begun. News had arrived of a revolt in the eastern provinces of the empire.

At least, when the army marched down the valley of the Jumna, Tahmasp was at Richard's side, his devoted tavachi.

Babur had left the administration of the Eastern provinces in the hands of various amirs, but he had also left them in no doubt that he would be keeping an eye on their governments, and more, that he intended to return himself in the very near future for a personal inspection.

His death had left them adrift, and it had soon been evident that his successor had no interest in administration. Richard knew little of it himself, but even he could gather from the reports which came in that Bihar was being sadly mismanaged, that tyranny and inefficiency were walking hand in hand through that fertile land. In this sense he had not been overly sorry to have had the Gujarat campaign terminated, even if by defeat. If that had meant the end of a personal dream, he had come to realise that the safety and prosperity of the empire Babur had so rapidly carved out of northern India was more important than his own ambitions; he had elected to serve the Moghuls, and he stood or fell with the dynasty.

He had indeed all but persuaded Humayun to march to the east when news arrived of Sher Khan's revolt.

Farid! He had to be approaching sixty. Yet there had never been any doubt of his courage or ability. And this he had proved again by the rapidity with which he had overrun Bihar and Bengal, defeating the Moghul garrisons by a mixture of cunning and skill.

So Humayun had to march east, to chastise this insolent old man.

At first it had seemed as if the campaign was going to be merely a repeat of Babur's in 1529. The rebels avoided battle, and Humayun recaptured city after city, always following his enemies.

Richard had been the first to notice the difference between the two campaigns – and what a catastrophic difference it had been. When Babur had advanced in 1528, it had been behind an army of agents and informers, men who penetrated the rebel encampments and spoke of the greatness of Babur, the impossibility of defeating him – while at the same time Babur had stretched out the hand of friendship to the Hindus.

Humayun had no time for the Hindus. He understood they were part of his nation, and he also understood their value in battle, but they did not interest him as a people, other than as an historical curiosity.

While spies now began to be discovered in the Moghul encampment, preaching the weaknesses of the Moghul rulers and the greatness of Sher Khan. When they were caught, they were tortured before being impaled, but they cried the greatness of Sher Khan to the end.

Desertions began, and not only amongst the common soldiers. Tuk-bashis disappeared with their entire companies. Even more disquieting had been the news that the local Moghul amirs, who, however incompetent their rule, had been utterly faithful to Babur, were also now declaring for Sher Khan.

Richard had then counselled retreat and consolidation, but Humayun would not hear of it.

'To retreat would be to concede this country to that Afghan scoundrel. Are you afraid of the numbers he claims able to place in the field? What are numbers? Did not my father defeat Lodi when outnumbered by more than two to one? Did he not defeat the Rajputs at odds of four to one? You were there, Blunt Amir. Are these things not true?'

Richard had to agree that they were.

'And am I a lesser man than my father?'

There was no truthful answer to that, and Richard decided

against reminding the Moghul that on this occasion the outnumbering army would itself contain a large element of Moghuls; Babur had never had to cope with that situation.

Despite his problems, Humayun had then settled down to besiege the fortress of Chimar, mainly because this enabled him to establish his headquarters in Benares. He spent several months here, investigating the ancient city's archaeological treasures, while his army dwindled, until at last Sher Khan had decided the time was right.

The battle was fought 26 June 1539 at Chausar, a time and place of Sher Khan's choosing, when he felt he had gained sufficient strength. Humayun, on the defensive, used classical Moghul tactics ... but this time he was opposed by men who understood those tactics. When Humayun had thrown his infantry forward to break up a rebel cavalry charge, they were suddenly assailed from the flank by a hail of arrows, delivered by a force of horse-archers which had approached unseen through the forest.

Humayun had discounted the forest as unsuitable for mounted tactics. He was right in terms of the charge, but the forest could be penetrated by men on horseback, and this sudden onslaught was like a bolt from the blue. Richard, himself wounded by an arrow, tried to wheel a portion of his force to meet this unexpected enemy, but the very formation of the phalanx, so powerful when opposed to a frontal assault, did not permit battlefield evolutions. The Hindus' solidity disappeared, they became groups of disconcerted men, and fled the field.

They had carried Richard with them, but he had managed to rally them, and lead most of them back. By then the battle had been lost, and the Moghul was in retreat.

Sher Khan had celebrated his victory by formally taking the royal title of Farid-ud-din Sher Shah, thus proclaiming himself to be Lodi's successor – the thirteen years that Babur and his son had ruled north India were to be regarded as an interregnum.

'By Allah, but I shall have him crawl at my feet before I drive a stake up his arse,' Humayun growled angrily when he heard the news.

But that day was clearly going to be some time in the future. Now it was Humayun's army that was in retreat, harried by the ever-increasing and totally confident rebels. Strongpoint after strongpoint fell. Yet Humayun would not cut his losses and retreat with all speed to Agra, where Askari commanded and where at least he would be able to recruit fresh troops, as yet uncontaminated by Sher Shah's propaganda.

He counted on the monsoon to give him breathing space.

The monsoon certainly brought campaigning to an end, but yet his force continued to dwindle.

And now the monsoon was over, and he was being forced steadily back, his army tramping along the banks of the Ganges, men already defeated in their minds.

'What is to be done?' Humayun asked his tuman-bashis.

'We must stand and fight,' said Kamran. 'Are we cowards, that we always retreat? Let us die like men who are worthy of our father.'

Humayun looked at Richard.

'I would say let us continue the retreat, my lord. Farid is in pursuit. He has gained a victory. On these things is his reputation founded. He cannot abandon the chase now. Let us lead him back to Agra and the centre of our strength. His force will dwindle, ours will increase.'

'To know what to do,' Humayun muttered.

'The Englishman is afraid,' Kamran sneered. 'He wishes to hide behind stone walls.'

'My record gives the lie to those words, sire,' Richard answered quietly.

'Nevertheless, I think my brother is right. We must stand and fight,' Humayun decided. 'At Kanauj.'

It was the next town on their route, but Richard could not understand Humayun's reasoning; Kanauj was only just over a hundred miles from Agra.

Yet the orders were given, and the Moghul army tramped into the town.

Kanauj was a place famous in history as the site of the last *swayamvara*, or public choice of a husband for a Hindu princess ever held, because it had turned out disastrously. This had been in 1175, and while Jayachandra, Gaharwar of Kanauj, had been looking over the suitors for his daughter, his cousin the famous Prithviraja Chauhan of Delhi had simply carried her off. Jayachandra had been outraged, and the resulting war between the two neighbouring states was generally held to have created that weakness in the Hindus which had left them open to the conquest of Muhammad Ghor and his Muslims.

But that had been a long time ago, and Kanauj was hardly more than a ruined village now. Like so many once-important cities in India it had been fought over and sacked too often.

Babur, Richard recalled, had been intending to rebuild all of these ruined cities and restore them to their greatness. Humayun merely looted them of whatever archaeological remains he could discover.

There were, indeed, many of these to be found in Kanauj. Humayun left the disposition of his army to Kamran while he went exploring.

Kamran slavishly followed the dispositions of his father, and Richard could not help but recall Babur's words, that his younger son would never make a general; incredibly, he refused to make use of the river as an anchor for his left flank, and withdrew short of a mile, establishing his position in front of the town itself. What innovations he did make were, to Richard's mind, equally weakening, particularly when he split the Hindu pikemen into two divisions, giving command of one to Prabhankar, which was sound enough, but the other to a man named Hemu, a small, squat, dark-complexioned Indian who was a courageous enough fighting man – Richard had recently promoted him to ming-bashi in command of a regiment – but had no experience whatsoever of manoeuvring a division.

Kamran explained that he felt the Hindus had become too static in their tactics, and that in two separate divisions there would be less chance of the sort of panic which had overtaken them at Chausar recurring, and he left Richard in overall command, but the Prince was not above jibing at his Englishman. 'Mind you stand and fight this time, Blunt Amir,' he said.

'We will fight,' Richard promised him. If Farid was not at least held this time, there was little hope for any of them.

But there was not in any event. The Moghuls' morale was

ruined, and they muttered amongst themselves as they listened to the cymbals and bugles announcing the approach of Farid's army.

Humayun heard the noise too, and hurried up to gaze at the enormous host of the rebels as they flooded across the plain from the river before pausing themselves in wonderment at the Moghul army drawn up before them in such an unpromising position.

Instantly, great bodies of cavalry debouched to left and right, while the infantry came on in the centre. Humayun's artillery thundered and gaps were torn in the rebel ranks, but these men understood all about the length of time it took to reload and pressed steadily onwards.

Richard's infantry was ordered forward to meet them, and the two forces clashed before the town and the Moghul encampment. Since the disaster at Chausar, Richard had worked hard with his men, managing, despite the continuous retreating, to instil in them again a belief in themselves, that man for man they were as good as any infantry in India. Now, to his great relief, they held the superior force sent against them, the phalanx once more proving its point as the division advanced behind their pikes.

In order to command his two divisions and see what was going on, Richard had remained mounted with several aides, to the rear of the phalanx. Now he realised that the rebel right wing cavalry, which, after Chausar, he most feared, had been sent in an enormous wheeling movement, far too extended, and were for the moment more than a mile removed from the field.

Immediately he despatched Tahmasp back to Humayun, asking for the Moghul left wing cavalry, which was commanded by Kamran, to deliver a charge into the flank of the rebel infantry, a manoeuvre which he was sure would win the day.

His men fought on grimly, but the pressure against them was great, and one or two heads began to turn.

Richard himself was looking over his shoulder. Ten minutes had passed since his request, and no cavalry had arrived, although there was a great deal of dust arising from behind the encampment.

Then he saw Tahmasp galloping back.

'All is lost, Blunt Bahatur. All is lost. Prince Kamran has taken his men from the field.'

Richard stared at him in consternation. Then looked at his men.

He had been with Hemu's division when Tahmasp had come up, and the Hindu had heard what the boy had said.

Instantly he moved away from Richard's side, and called on his buglers to sound the withdrawal, but instead of then going to the rear, as might have been expected, he moved out on the flank, waving his tulwar and shouting to his men to follow him.

Richard understood his intention immediately.

'He means to desert,' he snapped, and urged his horse forward. But one of Hemu's men swung a spear and caught him across the back, tumbling him all but senseless from the saddle.

'I will fetch him back, Blunt Amir,' Tahmasp shouted, and kicked his horse forward, while Richard regained his feet, shaking his head. He still retained his rapier, and the man who had felled him, and who could have killed him, gazed at him for a second with a mixture of consternation and fear at what he had done, and then ran off behind his fellows.

Richard was tempted to run behind them and attempt to rally them, but he knew he would not, and there was still the battle to be fought. He looked for his horse, and saw Prabhankar stumbling towards him, while the other division, having watched itself abandoned, also began to crumble, although most of the men still faced the enemy as they fell back.

'They are finished.' Prabhankar was covered in blood and sweat.

'We must stop them.'

Desperately Richard mounted and rode amongst them, beating them with the flat of his sword. One of them thrust at him with his lance, and, avoiding the blow, he cut the man down.

But all was indeed lost. The second Hindu division pulled out to the right and shouldered their arms to show that they were no longer fighting, while the first had broken and was streaming from the field, throwing away their pikes and tearing off their red jackets in the hopes of being spared. Richard cast a hasty glance back at the camp and Humayun's personal standard, but that was being carried to the rear. Humayun was also fleeing.

For a moment Richard was irresolute. He could have no doubts that this was the end of the short-lived Moghul empire in India. He felt a surge of savage anger and despair. But he could not abandon the Moghuls now – his wife and family waited for him in Agra. He had to go to them, and as he no longer had any men to command he must necessarily behave like the most cowardly prince and run away himself.

'Save yourselves,' he told those few staff officers who had remained with him. Then he turned his horse. But the delay had been too great. The rebel pikemen were upon him.

He cut one pike away and thrust a man down, and was then struck a blow on the back which for the second time that morning knocked him from the saddle. He lost his footing and went down into the midst of a glaring, shrieking horde of men. He lay on his back and looked up at the pikes, a dozen of them seeming about to be thrust into his body.

But then they were waved away by an officer.

'Blunt Amir!' the tuk-bashi said. 'The Great Khan will wish to see your death.'

Richard was dragged to his feet, and pulled through the rows of dead and dying men. One or two called out for him, but their cries were soon silenced by the knives of their executioners.

Above the field there hung the stench of blood and death; the vultures were already gathering.

Farid sat his horse, surrounded by his staff. Before him there knelt several Moghul commanders, amongst them Richard saw Prabhankar.

And at Farid's side was Hemu, who had done to Richard what Richard had once done to Lodi. At least he could not meet Richard's eyes; but that his desertion, at the most crucial point of the battle, had long been planned, and perhaps even known to Farid, was certain.

Farid smiled when he saw Richard being thrown to the earth at his feet.

'Blunt Amir!"' he said. 'I had feared you killed in the fight.'

Richard struggled to his knees. His throat was parched, his stomach light. He knew that he was within a few minutes of that most humiliating and horrible of deaths.

'You at least fought like a man to the last,' Farid remarked. 'I am told both Humayun and his wretched brother have fled.'

'They fled when they saw that you had suborned one of my tuman-bashis,' Richard said, glaring at Hemu.

'But are not those the tactics pursued by Babur himself, on more than one occasion?'

Richard had no answer to that, because it was perfectly true.

'As for the princes, they are hardly worthy sons of Babur. But I will seek them out. Fetch a horse,' he told an aide, 'for Blunt Amir. He will ride beside me.'

Hemu turned to face his new master in dismay, and looked as if he would protest, but thought better of it.

Richard could not believe his ears. 'Am I not to be executed?'

'That would be a waste. Have we not fought shoulder to shoulder, and gained great distinction? You are a fine soldier, Blunt Amir. I think one of the best I have seen. And you are not a Moghul. Will you not fight for me, as the Moghuls are no more?'

Richard tried to lick his lips and found that he could not. 'I will serve you, if you wish it.'

'I do so wish it.' Farid smiled. 'When I am defeated, you may change sides again, if you can. Impale these others,' he said. 'But on high poles, as do the Turks. I wish them to remain a monument to my victory, and their defeat.'

'My lord!' Richard reached his feet. 'Will these men not serve you as well as I?'

'No,' Farid said. 'They are Moghuls. Their loyalty will always be torn between their own people and myself. You are an individual, with no friend in this land save he who employs you. Had Babur lived, I would not have attempted to suborn you.' Another grim smile. 'But had Babur lived, I would not have gained this victory. I would not even have attempted this revolt. But Humayun ... how can you have any hesitation in turning your back on such a cur?'

Every word he spoke was the absolute truth, of course, about the Moghuls.

'But I do have a friend, my lord,' Richard said. 'That man ...' he pointed at Prabhankar, 'has been my comrade now for fifteen years. Where I have gone, he has gone. Whoever I have served, he has served. He will be as faithful to you as I. And he is not a Moghul either.'

Farid looked at the Hindu, and Prabhankar attempted a smile.

'Impale the scoundrel,' Hemu spat.

'I think not,' Farid said. 'He may continue to serve you, Blunt Amir. Fetch him also a horse,' he commanded.

'There is also my brother-in-law, sire.'

'The cur is dead,' Hemu said.

'You killed him?'

'I saw him fall. He was a son of Lodi Shah. He deserved to die.'

'I am sorry about your brother-in-law, Blunt Bahatur,' Farid said. 'At least he died with distinction. Now, let us make haste, so we may overtake Humayun and his brother.'

'You have saved my life, Blunt Sahib,' Prabhankar said. 'I was already feeling the stake in my bowels.'

'I think that makes us about even,' Richard agreed.

He was brooding upon how he was going to break the news of Tahmasp's death to Gila and her mother.

'Perhaps. What is your plan, sahib?'

They rode together, a little to one side of Farid's party.

'Plan?'

'You cannot mean to serve this robber chieftain.'

'Prabhankar,' Richard said sternly. 'Babur was nothing more than a robber chieftain when we first met him.'

'And now Humayun, if he survives, is again reduced to that,' Prabhankar said.

'We will serve Farid, faithfully,' Richard warned him.

Prabhankar grinned. 'Until something better turns up.'

Farid Khan never did catch up with Humayun and Kamran. The Moghul and his brothers disappeared into the mountains. Some said he had fled to Persia, others that he had taken himself back to his father's old stronghold of Kabul.

Others said that he was dead, murdered by the Pathans.

Whatever the truth, he had vanished from the Kingdom of Delhi.

7
THE TRAVELLER

Farid Khan, or Sher Shah of Sur, as he now liked to call himself, sat his horse and gazed at the half-finished new city of Din Panah, Humayun's masterpiece.

'Raze it to the ground,' he commanded. 'And commence building a new city. This will be the Sher Shahi. It will be the last city of Delhi.'

He was undoubtedly enjoying his new-found power. But for all his outward show of arrogance, he did not let it affect his essential commonsense – or his gluttony for work of all kind.

He had hardly properly grasped his kingdom when he was sending for a complete return of all taxes paid, and commanding his fakihs to analyse the figures and those of all crop returns as well as the yields of gold and precious stones from the mines close to the city; from these analyses he laid down precise guidelines for the future, how much would be paid, by whom, and when.

At the same time he was regulating the beggars, reforming the prostitutes, increasing and drilling his army, and negotiating peace treaties with the Rajputs, Gujarat and the lands to the south.

'I wish nothing of them,' he said, jovially and sincerely. 'The Kingdom of Delhi is sufficient for my needs.'

His acts of vengeance were again mostly to impress his power on his people, rather than because of any viciousness in his own character. Those amirs who had been raised to their positions by Humayun – and had not had the sense to flee with him – were duly impaled, their wives, concubines and daughters given to the soldiery.

Humayun had fled in such haste he had not even stopped in Agra long enough to pick up any of his wives or any of his books – Richard rather felt these might be the greater loss to the fleeing Moghul – but he had taken his 'Mountain of Light'. Richard wondered if the great diamond was not perhaps an unlucky talisman, and reflected on the uncertainties of inheritance. Had Humayun been a younger son, able to devote himself entirely to study and learning, he would have been a much happier man.

But would Kamran or Askari have proved a better heir to Babur? Richard doubted that.

In any event, Sher Shah bore no ill will towards Humayun's women. His taking of Humayun's favourite Indian wife to his bed was again purely a symbolic act of conquest; he was growing a little old for rape. The rest he sent off to Kabul.

He gazed at Humayun's vast library with something akin to awe.

'Much of this is infidel matter, or else obscene,' he said, opening one of the Hindu texts and looking at the engravings: he could not read.

'Can the printed word ever be obscene, sire, so long as it imparts the smallest iota of knowledge to future generations?' Richard asked. 'And this is a famous library. Its preservation will add lustre to your name.'

Sher Shah glanced at him, then gave a shout of laughter.

'You are right, Blunt Bahatur. The library will be preserved. But I will not let my sons, much less my daughters, loose in here.'

For Richard, the return to Agra and his house was a mixed blessing.

Everyone of course knew of Humayun's flight, and the destruction of his army. But little further information had reached the city, and Gila gazed at him with enormous eyes.

'My lord?' she asked in wonder.

'I am real,' he assured her, and kissed her to prove it.

Zaid and Iskanda seemed equally amazed. Only little Mahmud took his reappearance for granted.

'I had supposed you dead, or flown, with the Moghul,' Gila said.

'Instead I have changed sides.'

'You fight for Farid Khan? I had thought you loyal to the Moghul cause.'

'It was serve Sher Shah, or die,' Richard told her. 'Do you

condemn me? Have you any affinity for the Moghuls, other than that they are Muslims? So is Sher Shah.'

'Sunnites,' Gila said contemptuously.

Religion was not something they had often discussed, for they were too far apart. But he understood that Gila's mother, as a Persian princess, would have educated her in the minority Shi'ite Muslim faith, which originated in Persia, and was the principal cause of the unending war between Persia and the Ottoman Empire.

'Well, then?' he asked.

She sighed, and shrugged.

'You may serve whom you please, my lord. I am only happy to see you alive.'

But she was cold; she still regarded him as having betrayed Humayun.

Worse was to follow, as he now had to break the news of Tahmasp's death. There was a great noise of wailing and beating of breasts throughout the house, led by Mujhaba, who glared at Richard as though he was responsible. Well, he supposed, he was, by leading the boy to war.

For the first time he began to consider taking a second wife.

But Zaid seemed to understand, and he was old enough now to be a companion. He was already a good polo-player, and Richard began to teach him chess and falconry, and to talk to him of England. For the rest, he decided to wait for Gila to get over her grief, much of which he was in any event certain was assumed.

To Richard's surprise, now that he was totally established in the confidence of the Shah, even Hemu seemed to wish to be friends. Until he understood why.

'You must know, Blunt Bahatur,' the Hindu said, 'that my decision to turn from Humayun to our lord was not taken lightly. But you must also know that the Moghul was quite unfitted to rule this land.'

'No doubt,' Richard agreed, unwilling to risk speaking treason.

'And it has all turned out for the best,' Hemu pointed out. 'Here am I, confirmed as tuman-bashi of the Hindu division ... replacing you.'

'Yes,' Richard agreed coldly.

'To free you for greater things, I have no doubt,' Hemu went on. 'Therefore it seems to me that we have a mutual cause for celebration. Have we not snatched prosperity from the depths of despair?'

Richard studied him, waiting.

'And so,' Hemu went on, 'it occurs to me, as our master is well aware of our common success, that it would please him even more were we to unite our blood.'

'I have a wife,' Richard said. 'And so have you.'

'Which is not to say we should not have another. I understand that this is not your custom. However, that does not apply to me. You have a most beautiful daughter.'

'Who is but twelve-years-old.'

'An eminently marriageable age. I know it would please our master.'

Richard gazed into his eyes. 'Hemu,' he said. 'If you were the last man living on this earth, I would not give my daughter in marriage to you, were she a virgin of a hundred.'

For a moment Hemu's eyes sparked fire, then he bowed his head.

'I must be patient,' he said.

Gila was appalled when Richard told her of the proposal.

'That little rat!' she snapped.

Richard stroked her hair.

'It will never happen, my sweet. But ... we must think about finding Iskanda a husband.'

Except in his dislike for literature, Sher Shah seemed to Richard a vision of what Babur himself might have been like, had he lived to be sixty. Like the Moghul, his ambitions lay in building, and in safeguarding the huge empire he had conquered. To this last end he would talk long into the night with Richard.

'You have travelled through these lands,' he said, when, after two years of frenetic activity, he seemed to regard his kingdom as under control. 'You know these people. Tell me where my greatest danger lies.'

'Immediately, from the Rajput Confederacy.'

'They have agreed a treaty of peace.'

'Their present leader has agreed this treaty, sire. But they are a people to whom war is the only acceptable way of life. It but needs this man to die, and be succeeded by a younger prince eager to win his spurs, and you will have them at your throat.'

Sher Shah looked thoughtful.

'You discount any attempt by Humayun to regain his throne?'

'I doubt he has the will for that, and in any event he would need allies. He will not find them amongst the Rajputs.'

'But there are others. Why do you suppose he is now in Sind? Is it not in a search for support? I have heard he has sent messengers to Persia, and even to Constantinople. Will these peoples aid him?'

'Providing the Sultan is not otherwise engaged, my lord, he may well find some support from the Ottomans. His father Babur dealt with them.'

'And they are the mightiest people on earth,' Sher Shah said, somewhat disconsolately.

Richard couldn't dispute that. 'It will take time for Humayun to secure Ottoman support,' he said, reassuringly. 'If only because he is also seeking aid from Persia. The Ottomans and the Persians hate each other.'

'Because of their religious differences,' Sher Shah agreed. 'Still, when I look to the north, and the mountains, and think of the great warriors who have emerged from the steppes beyond, Genghis Khan, Timur ... Babur himself. Who knows how soon there will be another like those? And if the peoples to the south of me are not to be trusted ... I need allies, Blunt Bahatur. But where am I to find them?'

For a moment Richard could hardly believe his ears, that he was being given the opportunity denied him by both Babur and his son. Perhaps.

'I know of a people who would gladly ally themselves with so great a power as your own,' he said. 'If only because they are themselves sworn enemies of the Ottomans.'

'Tell me of these people,' Sher Shah said.

Richard did so.

'Men like yourself,' Sher Shah mused. 'Military skill. Cannon. Handguns. And ships. These are wonders of which my people know little or nothing. Can you really supply them, Blunt Bahatur?'

'Willingly,' Richard promised. 'If I am allowed to return to my home.'

'How long might such a journey take?'

'Two years, perhaps three.'

Richard's heart was pounding.

'How will you go? Will your ship still be waiting for you in this place Goa?'

'After seventeen years? No, that will not be possible.'

'Perhaps there will be another ship.'

Richard considered. But in the seventeen years since he had left Goa he had heard nothing of European affairs at all. He had no idea of what wars might have broken out, what alliances might have been forged, and what enmities formed. And therefore, what attitude Dom Jaime Alvarado – or more likely, his successor as governor – would adopt towards an itinerant Englishman.

'It would be best were I to travel overland, sire.'

'Can this be done? You would have to pass through the lands of my enemies.'

'Only Humayun is at this moment your enemy, and we know he is in Sind,' Richard pointed out. 'If I were to travel as your ambassador, announcing to the world your conquest of Delhi, and your desire to be friends with all men, I think I would be well received. I would use the opportunity to extol your greatness and your power. In this way I may well be able to counteract whatever Humayun is up to. As for when I reach Europe, I have still the commission given to my cousin by King Henry of England. This will see me safely home.'

He hoped so. But was not this what he had dreamed of, for seventeen years?

'What route will you take?'

'I would travel north, through the Hindu Kush, and join one of the Asiatic caravan routes.'

'To reach them you must pass through Afghanistan. The road to Samarkand goes by way of Kabul. That is Humayun's territory.'

'I have travelled the road, my lord. I know it well. I will not go as Blunt Bahatur, but as a simple merchant. I will use the name Balchi. No one will trouble me. Besides, Humayun himself is not there.'

Sher Shah stroked his beard.

'Let me think about what you propose,' he said.

Richard felt sure he would receive the necessary permission, and made his preparations.

His first decision had to be about his family. But he felt this journey was the answer to all his problems. He genuinely loved Gila and his children. To separate them from Mujhaba for two or three years, with only him to turn to, would effectively end her influence over them, and hopefully reconcile Gila and himself.

'You will love England,' he assured her.

Gila was sceptical, but at the same time both anticipatory and ambitious. 'We will take my mother?'

'Ah . . . no.'

She pouted, and then asked. 'But will we not visit Persia on the way?'

'I fear not,' he had to tell her. 'Our way lies through Constantinople.'

'The Ottomans!' She gave a little shudder. 'They are a hateful people.'

'We shall but be passing through,' he promised her.

His second decision had to be the merchandise he would need both to play his role and to trade along the way. He had always been fascinated by the various herbs cultivated by the Indians, which produced drugs such as the hemp given to Thomas which had so alleviated his pain when he had been dying. This was fairly common throughout central Asia, but grown in the fields north-west of Delhi was another plant with a bright red flower, the seeds of which, when crushed, produced a fine white powder which when inhaled, he was told, not only removed pain but induced all manner of delightful sensations.

He sampled a little, and discovered this to be true. He felt quite odd for some hours, as strong and powerful as ever in his life, clear-visioned and confident, eager for sex with Gila. . .

He suspected that the nomads of the steppes might also enjoy this potent alternative to bhang, and ordered a large amount to be prepared.

* * *

'You will remain as second-in-command of the division,' he told Prabhankar. 'Are you not proud?'

'Under Hemu! I would prefer to accompany you, Blunt Bahatur,' Prabhankar said. 'Did we not begin our journeying together? It would be best for us to end it together, too.'

'You speak as if I am never going to return, old friend. Of course I am going to return. In three years time. Then we will recommence our journeying together.'

'But who will accompany you?'

'I will take Ramdas. He is a good man, and faithful.'

Prabhankar was not reassured. Ramdas came from the mountains to the north-east, from a land called Nepal which did not even acknowledge Sher Shah's authority. He was a little man, whose only weapon was a large, oddly curved knife which he called a kukri.

Prabhankar did not trust him.

It was now the autumn of 1542, too late in the year to start; the mountain passes to the north would soon be blocked with snow. But Richard made every preparation to depart in the following spring. Never had he felt so ebullient, so confident. He was forty-two years old, in the very prime of his health and vigour. He had campaigned for so long, experienced such vicissitudes of fortune, always to triumph in the end, that he could imagine no other result of his embassy but total success.

And he was delighted at the prospect of showing Gila and his children something of the world.

His happiness was evident to everyone. Too evident. Three days before he was due to leave, when the caravan was already loaded and the muleteers assembled, Sher Shah summoned him.

'My heart grieves to see you go, Blunt Bahatur,' he said.

'My heart grieves to leave you. But I hope to bring you great prosperity on my return.'

'And when will that be?'

'Why, as soon as it can be done. I have said, I do not anticipate being away more than three years.'

'Three years,' Sher Shah mused. 'It is a long time when one has reached my age. I would have you return before I die.'

'You will not die in three years, my lord.'

'If it is but three years. Blunt Bahatur, I have considered this matter, and I have decided that it would be best if you were to leave your wife and family here.'

'Sire?' Richard was totally taken aback.

'A journey such as you propose will surely be too arduous for them,' Sher Shah said, his eyes opaque. 'And if, as you say, you will only be gone three years, why ... that is no more than a campaign.'

Richard opened his mouth to protest, and then decided against it; the Shah might just cancel the entire embassy.

Clearly the old rascal feared he did not intend to return at all. Or that he might be considering deserting back to Humayun. Well ... now there would at least be no temptation to do either of those things.

'Then I must place my family in your care.'

'They are already, Blunt Bahatur.'

'My lord, I would not have my daughter married, under any circumstances, until my return.'

'How may a man's daughter be married in his absence?' Sher Shah asked. 'Besides, the girl is very young. She will await your return. You have the word of Sher Shah.'

Gila appeared heartbroken. She wept and clung to him. 'Three years, my lord. Three years.'

'We were separated for longer than that during the war with Gujarat,' he reminded her.

'But then I knew where you were,' she wailed.

'Surely I can accompany you, Father,' said Zaid. 'I am fifteen years of age. I can be your tavachi.'

'You have a more important duty,' Richard told him. 'Looking after your mother and sister, and teaching Mahmud to be a great warrior. I give you these things as your charge.'

Three days later he rode out of Delhi, to the north.

Granted all the money and facilities he required by Sher Shah, Richard had made his plans very carefully, for he well understood the dangers of his journey. Thus he had compiled a caravan of fifty mule-drawn wagons, which indicated that he was a very wealthy merchant indeed. With his drivers and guards and their women, he commanded some three hundred people – he took no women for himself.

Wearing the turban and the silk robes of a Muslim, and having allowed his beard to grow, he felt sure he could penetrate Afghanistan without discovery, and join one of the great caravans which he knew made their way to and fro across Asia, out of China and into Europe, which were welcomed in every land through which they passed, regardless of nationality or religion.

But to reach Kabul, the very earliest stage of his journey, he had to penetrate the great mountains which seemed almost to touch the sky, through the tortuous passes controlled by the Pathans. For this part of the journey, indeed, Sher Shah offered Richard a strong contingent of cavalry as an escort. Richard declined. He did not wish to draw attention to himself, and the arrival of a division of Delhi troops on their doorstep might well be taken by the Moghuls as an invasion.

He took the same route as with Babur's coffin, leaving Kashmir and the Sikhs well to his right hand. From the Agra river valley, the caravan climbed back to the plateau across which Richard and Prabhankar had crawled their way so many years before, and then descended into the plain, heading steadily north west. This was still all Moghul territory, conquered by Babur, and now accepting Sher Shah as their ruler. When last Richard had passed this way it had been dead of winter, and he, and everyone else, had been in haste. Now in the spring he was able to appreciate the fertility of the country, mainly under wheat, and the industry of its people, as he watched carpets being woven with great speed and skill by teenage girls.

The caravan of the great Blunt Amir, by now well known throughout northern India, at least by name, was gazed at in wonder.

Sher Shah's dominions, as inherited from Babur, stretched right up to the city of Peshawar, at the foot of the mountains. Here again, twelve years before this land had been covered in snow, and Richard was amazed to discover himself in the midst of fields of sugar cane, the tropical fruit basking in the warmth induced by the fierce sun and cloudless skies.

Immediately beyond Peshawar was the Khyber Pass, the gateway to Afghanistan.

* * *

It was in the Khyber Pass that the caravan was attacked for the first time, by men who rolled rocks down on them and advanced in deadly silence, supported by their womenfolk.

'What manner of creatures are these?' growled Ramdas.

The assault was repulsed easily enough, but a few days later three men wandered away from the encampment and were taken prisoner. Richard called out his fighting men, tracked the maurauders, and charged home; the Pathans fled, but when the captured men were found, they had been stripped and castrated, their eyelids cut away and their ears and noses also gone.

They had been alive when they had been mutilated.

Three of the Pathans had been taken prisoner in the attack, two men and a woman. These the angry muleteers burned alive.

Richard did not interfere.

Richard had no choice but to go to Kabul, as the only road from the Khyber through Afghanistan to Balkh on the borders of Transoxania – where he hoped to pick up a westbound caravan – passed through the city. But it was early summer before he approached the high valley ... to be taken aback to learn that Humayun was actually there, in front of him. The Moghul had apparently given up his attempts to secure aid from Sind, or Persia, and had returned to his ancient capital, which still held out for him.

'He will execute us all,' said Dermat Ali, the wagon-master.

'Only if he discovers our presence,' Richard pointed out.

'How may he not do that, Blunt Amir?'

'By not addressing me thus, for a start. I am Balchi the merchant, from Bijapur. Bijapur has never been at war with the Moghuls. In any event, we must make our way through the city as quickly as possible.'

Richard's plan appeared to work. The caravan was allowed to enter Kabul without anyone seeming to notice any resemblance between this very tall merchant and Blunt Bahatur. Richard prudently maintained a fold of his cloak half over his face whenever anyone approached him.

They spent two days in the caravanserai, resting their animals and restocking their supplies.

'All is ready to depart tomorrow,' Dermat Ali said. 'I will tell you frankly, I will not breathe freely until Kabul is a hundred miles behind us.'

'It soon will be,' Richard said, as he heard the clash of steel.

He, Dermat and Ramdas were on their feet in an instant, gazing at the gate of the caravanserai, through which there now marched a tuk-bashi and his hundred armed men.

'Where is the caravan from the south?' he demanded. 'Belonging to the man Balchi?'

'We have been betrayed,' Dermat Ali muttered, his hand dropping to the hilt of his tulwar.

'Do not draw,' Richard told him. 'We cannot fight our way out of this.'

'Then are we dead men,' Dermat said.

'We shall see.' Richard stepped forward. 'We are the men from the south.'

The ming-bashi peered into his face. 'Your name is not Balchi. You are Blunt Amir. I have fought beside you.'

Richard remembered him as well. He was actually a Pathan himself, by name Bairam, who had fought under both Babur and Humayun.

'Very well,' he agreed. 'I was Blunt Amir. I am he no longer. I am a merchant taking goods to Balkh for sale. You may examine my caravan.'

'I am ordered to take you before the Moghul, sire. I hope you will not attempt to resist me. Give me your sword.'

Richard hesitated. So much for his hopes. Nor could he doubt that Humayun knew he now served Sher Shah.

He handed over his tulwar.

'And my people?'

Ramdas was shivering.

'They are welcome to remain here until it is time for them to depart.'

Richard and Dermat looked at one another.

'If I do not return to you by tomorrow morning,' Richard muttered. 'You had best go back to Agra and tell the Shah what has happened.'

'I will do that, chelebi. But ... return to us, I beg of you.'

His brain was racing as he was escorted through the curious

crowds towards Humayun's palace, which was more like a fortress than the magnificent house the Moghul had occupied in Agra. He was not yet a prisoner; although surrounded by armed guards his arms had not been pinioned – requiring the surrender of his sword had been merely an act of prudence on the part of the ming-bashi. It was very necessary to determine on his approach to the coming interview.

'The Moghul is well?' he asked.

'Very well,' Bairam replied. 'He will soon march again on Agra, and avenge himself.'

That did not sound quite so good. But now the time for speculation was past; it was time for concentrated thought.

He was ushered past armed guards and waiting men, many of whom he recognised – and who recognised him in turn. But there were no greetings as he was taken into the reception chamber where Humayun sat on his carpet, his brothers Kamrun and Askari beside him; the viziers stood grouped behind them.

'The traitor has come to visit us, brother,' Kamran observed with a sour smile.

Richard made the obeisance to Humayun. 'Greetings, Great Moghul.'

'You can say that to me, Blunt Bahatur, when you have chosen to serve my enemy?' Humayun spoke mildly enough, but his eyes glinted.

'I did not choose to serve your enemy, my lord,' Richard told him. 'Unlike some . . .' he allowed his gaze to drift to Kamran. 'At Kanauj I and my Hindus fought virtually to the last man. That my life was spared was because Farid Kahn – he knew it would be unwise to use Farid's adopted title here – remembered fighting beside me against Mahmud Lodi, under your great father, and he valued my services.'

'Which you gave to him without hesitation.'

'My wife and children were hostages to my obedience.'

'And what of my wives and children?' Humayun snapped. But he did not look so angry as might have been expected. 'And so for three years you have served the usurper, without casting a thought to me, thy rightful lord.'

Richard took a deep breath. 'Why else do you suppose I am here, my lord.'

Both princes stared at him, then Kamran gave a brief laugh. 'You have decided to abandon your family, after all, Blunt Bahatur?'

'Alas, sire, my plans were suspected by Farid. I had secured his permission to undertake an embassy to the West under the guise of a merchant, in order to secure him allies. I was to take my family with me. This was something I had been working towards throughout those three years. My intention, of course, was to come straight away here and join you, but almost the day before I was due to leave Agra, Farid told me I must leave my family behind as hostages.'

'Do you really suppose we will believe that?' Kamran asked.

'You may ask the members of my caravan, sire. They know nothing of my true purpose – only that I was to undertake a mission for Farid.'

Once again the brothers gazed hard at him.

'And now you are here,' Humayun said at last. 'Is that not an omen, brother?'

'Bah!' Kamran commented.

'Did this man not appear to our father just before the Battle of Panipat, and give the great Babur a victory?'

'Our father would have defeated Lodi whether this man was there or not,' Kamran insisted.

'Perhaps. And then, perhaps not,' Humayun said. 'Be seated, Blunt Bahatur.'

Richard sat down cross-legged on the carpet before them. He could only wait and hope to turn Humayun's mood to his advantage.

Sweetmeats were served.

'It is now three years since I was driven from Agra,' Humayun said. 'Three years in which I have sought allies in order to regain my birthright, and found none, save in Persia. And the Shah would have me foreswear my religion for his, before he will send me help. They have been three long and bitter years.'

'This I know,' Richard said. 'My heart has bled for you.'

'And yet . . . how may a man know what Fate has in store for him? I will tell you frankly, Blunt Bahatur, six months ago I had all but despaired. I was reduced to nothing more than my patrimony, with enemies all around, and not a single ally to be found. The Turks will not cease warring in Europe, the Persians will fight no one but the Turks. Where was I to turn – and I was growing old, with no heir from my wives. Do you know that has been what has most troubled me?'

'I do, sire.' Richard could not resist a quick glance at Kamran, whose face was expressionless.

'And then, last November, a miracle happened,' Humayun said. 'There was I, a man of thirty-four. I took my first wife when I was sixteen. Eighteen years, Blunt Bahatur, and I have been unable to father a legitimate son. But last November a true son was born to me.'

'My most hearty felicitations.'

'All that the Shah of Persia would grant me was one of his daughters as a wife. There was I, the Moghul, with a single wife,' Humayun said. 'And she has given me a son. Is that not a miracle?'

'Indeed, sire.' Richard agreed, wondering how he and Humayun were now related by marriage. Certainly his sons Zaid and Mahmud and this new prince would be cousins, however distant.

'I have called him Abu-ul-Fath Jalal-ud-Din Muhammad Akbar,' Humayun said proudly.

Richard gulped. The name virtually meant "Here is the greatest of all the descendants of the Prophet".

'He will be the greatest ruler the world has ever known,' Humayun declared.

'I have no doubt of it,' Richard agreed, casting another hasty glance at Kamran, whose face continued expressionless.

'Thus, for him, I must recapture Agra and rebuild Delhi, that he may inherit a kingdom worthy of his name,' Humayun said. 'I have studied nothing else this past six-month, and I have found no answer to my problem – until today.'

'You will not trust this dog?' Askari was incredulous.

'I have said his appearance, so strangely, and at such a time, is an omen. And is he not also the best soldier we have? Blunt Bahatur, together we will march into Delhi, as you did with my father seventeen years ago.'

Richard needed to think more quickly than ever. Unlike Humayun, he did not believe in omens ... but he did believe that for him to cross the border with a Moghul army would mean the immediate execution of his wife and family, probably by the horror of impalement.

Somehow he had to buy time, and perhaps also gain some strength of his own.

'With respect, my lord, the task will not be an easy one.'

'No worthwhile task ever is. But together we will conquer. I know this.'

'Undoubtedly,' Richard agreed. 'But may I remind you that when I appeared before your father at Panipat, I did not come alone. I had six thousand men at my back.'

'And now you have a caravan,' Kamran sneered.

Richard ignored him, but continued to Humayun. 'Farid despatched me on this mission, to return to Europe and obtain for him the help of my King and his army. This is a measure I have long recommended to you. If you had permitted me to do so ten years ago, Farid could never had defeated you.'

'Is your King's army then composed of demigods?' Askari inquired.

'It is composed of men such as I,' Richard said, looking him in the eye. 'Armed with weapons such as no one in India has ever seen.'

Kamran snorted, but Humayun was attentive.

'These men I will bring – but to your aid, not that of Farid. Then indeed will we enter Delhi in triumph.'

'How long will you require?'

'Two years,' Richard said. What mattered if he was being wildly optimistic, if only he could be allowed to proceed on his journey.

Time enough to decide which of the rivals he was going to support when he regained India – with a thousand Englishmen at his back.

'Two years,' Humayun said. 'And then you promise to return here with your men?'

'If you believe that, brother, you are a fool,' Kamran said.

'I cannot return here, my lord,' Richard said. 'To march an army across Europe would mean a war with every country through which we passed. I will bring my army by sea, in a vast fleet of ships. We will destroy Gujarat, and march north towards you. I will send word in good time for you to move south to meet us. Together we may conquer all India.'

He almost believed it, himself.

'By Allah,' Humayun muttered. 'If that could be so . . .'

'It will be so,' Richard said. 'I swear it, by the Beard of the Prophet.'

He could only remind himself that he was not a Muslim.

'Truly, Blunt Amir,' Ramdas commented as the caravan followed the north road out of Kabul. 'You are a man who works miracles. I had thought us all dead by now.'

'It was but a matter of straight talking,' Richard told him. 'Now all we need is haste.'

This was easier said than done. From Kabul it was two hundred miles to Balkh, and as they were mostly descending from the precipices of the Hindu Kush, and as it was now almost summer, the going was much easier, so that they were there in ten days. But then there was a tedious wait for the arrival of the next caravan from the east.

With Samarkand lying only another two hundred miles to the north, Richard was very tempted to visit this city of which he had heard so much, and for possession of which Babur had wasted so many years of his life, but he dared not take the risk of missing the caravan. Balkh itself, although always an important rendezvous on the caravan route, had never recovered from its sack by Genghis Khan three hundred years previously, and was a place of ruins.

The caravan finally arrived after a fortnight's wait, and, after a few more days of buying and selling, moved on again: three hundred and fifty miles to Herat, in Khorasan.

The route fringed the mountains, but the well-armed caravan kept a careful watch for brigands who might at any moment descend from the hills to the south; to the north was the high steppe.

The caravan made an immense sight as it wound its way along the age-old road. There were perhaps twenty different groups within the whole, each a miniscule world drawing from and giving to the rest. Here were merchants with weird inventions from China, machines which could tell the time, scrolls which could tell the future, as well as bales of silk, and of course, Chinese girls for sale. Here too were merchants from the south-east with spices, and from the south with gold and diamonds and rubies. Richard's opium seemed of little value, but when he let some of the other merchants inhale a sample of the strangely sweet powder, they seemed very impressed.

So much so that he tried it again himself, for the second time, and once more found himself reeling into a world of the strangest fantasies, some of them good, some of them terrifying...

He regained full consciousness to find himself lying in his tent with a naked yellow-skinned girl in his arms, and a very anxious Ramdas hovering above him.

'By God!' He sat up, looked down at the girl, who gave him an anxious smile.

'You purchased her, sire,' Ramdas explained, 'two days ago, and have mounted her ever since.'

'The caravan!'

'It moves, and so do you. Do you not remember these things?'

'Only as in a dream.' Again he looked at the girl.

'Ting-lu,' she explained.

'She does not speak our language,' Ramdas said. 'But she speaks the language of love.'

He rolled his eyes.

No doubt, Richard thought, the faithful wretch has sampled her during my drunkenness. And probably me too.

But he had lived long enough in Asia to know that she could not be returned. And she was certainly a pretty little thing, if small of both breast and buttock.

'Dress yourself,' he told her, holding out her garments.

'Truly, the opium is a powerful thing,' Ramdas remarked as the caravan got moving. 'With enough of it, a man might conquer the world.' He grinned. 'Supposing he remembered not to take it himself.'

Something to think about.

Herat was an ancient city, having been founded by Alexander the Great – traces of the citadel he had built could still be seen. Like every other place of any size in the region, it had been devastated by Genghis Kahn, but unlike most of them, Herat had been refounded by Timur in the course of his equally whirlwind conquest of the Asiatic world. Timur had recognised its value as a marketing centre, and now it was a busy, thriving metropolis.

Richard did a fine trade with his powdered poppies. And why not? he asked himself. These people were no friends of his.

From Herat the road led to Nishapur, Rai, Hamadan and Kermanshah in Iraq.

To reach Nishapur it was necessary once again to climb, for the city lay at a height of four thousand feet above sea level, and yet was the centre of a large cotton- and cereal-growing area. Its principal claim to fame was that it contained the tomb of the twelfth century Persian philosopher-poet Omar Khayyam.

It lay just over two hundred miles from Herat – another three weeks of hard slogging – then four hundred and fifty miles, some six weeks, to Rai.

Rai was even more of a ruin than Balkh, having entirely been destroyed by the Mongols, but even the ruins justified its description as having once been the most beautiful city in Asia; the buildings had all been faced with blue faience, or glazed brick, and its reputation for exquisite ceramic art was upheld by the few people who still lived there, eager to trade with the caravan.

But Rai was also deep in Persian territory; Teheran lay only a few miles away, and most of the trading was done with merchants from the city. Richard instructed his people to keep a low profile.

He was also concerned about the length of time it was taking to travel across this vast land – and he was only seeing a fraction of it. He had left Agra in the middle of March, and reached Kabul in mid May. It was now the end of June, and he had not yet approached the boundaries of the Ottoman Empire!

Hamadan, reached ten days after leaving Rai, was another highly situated city, some six thousand feet above sea-level, while behind it rose the twelve-thousand foot height of Mount Alvand.

Arriving as it did virtually in midsummer, the caravan found itself in a most delightful area, abundant with fruits which to

Richard at least were strange, and with a climate which was perfection itself. He learned that it had in fact been a summer resort for the kings of Persia for many hundreds of years – it had been built upon the ruins of the ancient Ecbatana – but now it was a ruin itself, torn to pieces by Timur because it had resisted him.

Kermanshah, however, only just over a hundred miles to the south-west, had escaped the Mongols, and was thus even more attractive than the northern town; while the caravan was there, the weather was deliciously hot and clear, and they were again surrounded by fruit and vegetables of every description sprouting out of the fertile soil.

Kermanshah was the centre of the Persian carpetmaking industry, and here too the caravan did a busy trade, the merchants endeavouring to buy the carpets at the lowest possible prices for sale further west, the manufacturers wailing that the very food was being sucked from the mouths of themselves and their families. Yet all seemed quite pleased with the price which was eventually agreed.

Richard, having little skill at the oriental art of bargaining, sent Ramdas to act as his agent, preferring to remain in his tent with Ting-lu, of whom he was becoming inordinately fond.

She was a most delightful companion, even if they had made little progress towards learning each other's languages.

Ting-lu would sing to him, in a thin, high-pitched, but not untuneful voice; she attended to all of his darning, and took at least an equal share with Ramdas in the cooking, producing meals which, if highly spiced, were a welcome change from the inevitable curry. And whenever she felt he was bored, she would look meaningfully towards their mutual couch.

In that she was insatiable.

He wondered how she would be received in England. And even more, how she would get on with Gila, when he took her back to Agra.

Ramdas returned with two splendid carpets, for which he proudly claimed to have paid less than half the original asking price.

At Kermanshah, the caravan divided, some of the merchants making north for Tabriz and the easterly regions of Anatolia.

Richard preferred to remain with the main body, which was travelling the hundred and fifty miles to Baghdad. This decision was taken from more than a desire to visit one of the great cities of antiquity; it also promised the easier route for the next few hundred miles.

In the event, the descent from the mountains to the below sea level atmosphere of the Tigris, in July, was startling. Pleasant days and cool nights were replaced by days too hot to venture out of doors between ten and four, and nights so close that one lay awake and sweated.

Baghdad itself, the home of the Abbasid caliphs for so many years, where Harun-al-Raschid had raised Muslim culture to perhaps its apogee, was another half-ruined provincial town in 1543. Genghis Khan had never come this far, but his son Hulagu did. Hulagu had stormed the walls and, it was said, killed eight hundred thousand of the city's inhabitants in a single day.

It was difficult to believe any had survived.

Baghdad was a pestilential place, and Richard could not wait to be rid of it. But it was necessary to remain here for some weeks, for Baghdad was where the caravans entirely split up and then reformed. Some of the merchants made south-east for Basra and the Persian Gulf. Some made due south for the Arabian Desert, and from thence Mecca and Jedda. Some made west for Syria, from whence they would go south into Palestine, Egypt and North Africa. The caravan Richard wanted would head north-west for Anatolia.

But there was the invariable fortnight's delay while the components were gathered together, guards were arranged, disputes settled, and during this time Ting-lu fell sick. In India the rest of them had some experience of this tremendous heat, but Ting-lu, from northern China, had none. She became hot to the touch, and shook constantly. She began to remind Richard of Humayun at his worst, and he knew then there was no hope for her.

But he inhaled some of his own opium and then took to his bed for two days after Ting-lu was buried, and afterwards he set out for Turkey in the grimmest of moods.

* * *

Mosul lay just over two hundred miles north of Baghdad, and was reached by following the Tigris. This was necessary, for to either side, once beyond the narrow boundaries of the irrigation canals supplied by the great river, lay nothing but desert.

Here was a new experience for Richard, and one which made even the tortures of the Indian jungle in the midst of the monsoon seem pleasant. The sun scorched down out of a relentlessly blue sky, and even the water of the river, so providentially close, was warm to drink.

But here at last he was entering Ottoman territory, for the Turks had extended their empire this far south some ten years previously, and in Mosul he had his first glimpse of the famous Janissaries, the foot soldiers who had conquered half Europe. They were all born Christians, he was told, but taken from their homes when still small boys to be brought up as Muslims, and as military monks, too, owning allegiance only to the Sultan. Fiercely moustachioed and bearded, they paid little attention to the merchants as they swaggered the streets of the city in their gaudy blue and red uniforms, their helmets adorned with white horsehair plumes.

It was thought-provoking to consider that if all his plans went right, he might one day command an English tercio against those fine fellows.

He had no doubt of the outcome.

The way now led to the west: to Aleppo, Antioch, Konia and Constantinople.

Richard had come to regard Constantinople as the beginning of the end of his journey, but to his consternation he now learned that he still had eleven hundred miles to go.

'We will not reach the great city until there is snow on the high ground,' said the caravan master, Hildis Abbas.

And there would remain all of Europe to cross.

Richard's realisation that it was going to take him not less than three years to make the journey, supposing there were no delays, led him to lose some of his interest in the intensely interesting and historically exciting country through which he was passing.

Aleppo, another city ravaged by Timur, had been restored by

the Ottomans and become one of the great markets of western Asia: a bustling place, situated on a mound some four hundred feet above a fertile valley. It was protected by massive walls. These walls had been built in the thirteenth century, and had not kept out the Mongols, but the Ottomans had strengthened them and now, with their watchtowers dominating the huge, smooth glacis beneath, they looked impregnable.

Richard discovered that he was now indeed in the land of castles, far greater and more numerous than any he had known in England, or even in Spain. This was the land over which the Crusaders had fought, and for a time had held, some three hundred years before; and they had built the most massive fortifications also at Antioch, another great marketplace where merchants from all over the Middle East were gathered.

It was in Antioch that Richard made the decision to disband what remained of his caravan. Truth to tell it had not seemed quite the same since Ting-lu's death, but more importantly, he had by now sold all of his opium, at a considerable profit, many of his people had died or simply deserted to find a new way of life, and he was down to twenty mules and a hundred men.

He placed Dermat in charge of this small remnant, with orders to take it back to Agra, and tell Sher Shah – and Humayun as well, if his presence in Kabul was discovered – that his master was continuing alone, with just Ramdas as a servant.

They remained with the main body, travelling with only their horses and four pack mules; the sale of the opium had left Richard a very wealthy man.

But now, more than ever, he took on the name of Balchi: the Muslim merchant who was visiting Constantinople to see the greatest city in the world. This became very necessary as the caravan reached Konia, the Iconium of the Romans, which was the centre of the most fundamental Islamic faith – as indicated by the Whirling Dervish Sect which had originated here. In Konia it was necessary for both Richard and Ramdas to assume the role of devout Muslims, and visit the mosque and pray to Allah, or their very lives would have been in jeopardy.

As Richard had been warned, the last leg, over the high plateau of central Anatolia, was almost the most difficult part of the entire journey, with summer now behind them and the weather proving distinctly changeable, the nights especially being quite cool.

Richard had kept his ears open since leaving Mosul, learning everything he could about the manners and customs of the Turks. From what he had been told, those in cosmopolitan places like Constantinople were entirely tolerant, so long as the non-believers paid suitable taxes and did not attempt to interfere with the Muslims. When he and Ramdas crossed the Bosphorus, therefore, gazing in wonder at the huge fortifications which surrounded the city and, within, at the magnificent mosques to be seen everywhere, he declared himself to be a Christian Englishman, and his servant a Hindu.

That he had apparently walked his way home from India – after his ship had been wrecked, he claimed – attracted attention, and he was taken before the Grand Vizier, Ibrahim Pasha, a very grand person indeed, although suprisingly young.

Richard presented his credentials from Sher Shah, and Ibrahim questioned him closely about the power of the Kingdom of Delhi. He seemed quite relieved to be told that the Moghuls were no longer a threat to anyone.

Richard discovered that he had been very fortunate, arriving as he did in Constantinople in the midst of a five-year truce between Suleiman and the Holy Roman Emperor's brother Ferdinand, who ruled Austria and against whom a desultory war had been going on for years. Not that the Ottomans were at peace; they were still warring against the Spaniards and the Genoese in the Mediterranean, but at least there was no actual fighting in central Europe.

In Constantinople, Richard found a European tailor, who made clothes for both Ramdas and himself, while now he unpacked his rapier and belted it at his side. It felt quite strange, after so many years, to be wearing a brown velvet jerkin and base over a blue silk doublet – slashed on chest and sleeves to reveal his white shirt. Also brown hose and slashed shoes, with a brown velvet cap, his beard trimmed to just an inch, and the whole set off by a brown velvet gown.

Ramdas, in a white doublet and hose, as befitted a servant, was hardly less resplendent; he could not stop looking at himself in every reflective surface they passed.

Richard gained but one glimpse of the great Suleiman, known as the Magnificent, on his way to the mosque that bore his name, but the Sultan was so surrounded by courtiers and guards wearing the gaudiest of costumes, that he could not even see his face.

Constantinople was a never-ending delight, even if only boys were ever offered for their creature comforts, and it was a temptation to remain there until the weather improved, for it was now becoming very cold and wet. Time was however the commodity of which Richard had the least, and he pushed on as soon as their new clothes were ready.

There was no man-made difficulty in reaching the Austrian border, the journey for several hundred miles being entirely through Ottoman-controlled territory; the Turks had stamped out even the brigands in the hills.

Or perhaps the brigands were simply too cold. The temperature seemed to drop every day, and even in fur coats, which Richard bought in Belgrade, the travellers were shivering; Ramdas, who had never experienced such weather even in the Nepalese mountains as a boy, was particularly affected. Often enough, too, the road was blocked with snow, which caused lengthy delays. But Richard always pushed on; with the end of his long journey coming ever closer, his confidence grew with every step.

Crossing the border into Austria, however, he received a considerable shock. He had heard in Constantinople, and even more in Buda, of various religious upheavals in the West, but the Turks were naturally not much interested in such matters. Now he was required to prove himself an honest Catholic, for it appeared that not very long after he and Thomas had departed for the East, a German priest named Luther had stirred up a great debate by denouncing indulgences – the sale of pardons for various crimes – and had then extended his denunciation to the entire structure of the Church.

Obviously he had been excommunicated, and like others before him such as Savaronola, could have ended his life at the stake. But he had found powerful protectors in the German princes, with the result that almost all of north Germany had declared themselves 'Lutherans' and had broken away from the Pope.

Whatever the eventual hellfire to which they must be doomed, Richard saw in the movement a political rather than religious motivation, and, like the Turks, he was not disposed to take the event too seriously. Until he inquired as to what was happening in England.

'England!' shouted the innkeeper with whom he was discussing the matter – he was one of the very few Austrians who understood Spanish. 'There is the worst of all. That apostate King has declared himself the head of all religion, and do you know why? Not for any sacred purpose, you may be sure. This King wished only to put aside his wife and take another.'

'And for that reason he broke with Rome?' Richard was astonished.

'Well, what would you? The Queen was an aunt of the Emperor himself. So Henry's request for a divorce – on the grounds that she had previously been betrothed to his brother – was refused. It was then that he broke with the Church. And commenced marrying. Why, he has just beheaded his fifth wife and taken a sixth. He is worse than the Turk: Suleiman at least keeps all his wives alive.'

'And the English people have accepted all of this?'

'They have had no choice. Anyone who refuses to take the oath to Henry as supreme head of the Church goes to the block forthwith.'

Richard scratched his head.

'So you will have to think again, my friend,' advised his informant.

'Indeed I shall,' Richard agreed.

At least western Europe was at peace. Richard guessed that the Pope would very much have liked to launch a crusade against the Lutherans, but found it impossible while the Turks continued to lie in such strength along his eastern and southern borders. So for the time being the great Christian powers maintained an uneasy status quo amongst themselves.

Nor was the name of an Englishman as abhorrent as the Vienna innkeeper had suggested. Richard gained the impression, certainly in France, that people were more amused than shocked by King Henry's antics, and were waiting with interest to observe the eventual outcome of Britain's declaration of religious independence – there was no question, apparently, of the country adhering to Lutheranism; the separation from Rome was one of personalities, not doctrine – while at the same time making wagers on how long this sixth marriage of the King would last.

On the other hand, it was necessary to decide his own position regarding the new system. For twenty years he had had little to do with his own religion, a hurried prayer in a moment of stress being the nearest he had come to worship. Certainly he had not set foot in a Christian church throughout that time. Nor had he travelled halfway across the world to lose his head in some quarrel inspired by a king's lust.

'As we were good Muslims in Konia, Ramdas,' he said. 'We will be good English Christians in England.'

'Of course, sahib,' Ramdas agreed.

The first thing they did on landing at Dover in January – Richard having celebrated his first Christmas for twenty years in Paris – was to buy fresh horses and make for London.

'Blunt you say?' asked the secretary, peering at the tall man in front of him, well dressed to be sure, but with a skin nearly as dark as that of his servant. 'Sir Thomas Blunt and his crew were lost at sea, oh, many years ago. You will be branded as an imposter, sir.'

'You mean the *Bonaventure* and Master Bottomley never returned?' Richard asked.

'The ship was never heard of again after leaving Plymouth.'

Richard gave him the Commission. 'Handle it with care; it is twenty years old.'

The secretary unfolded the tattered parchment. 'By our lady,' he commented, and then gulped. 'You are Sir Thomas Blunt?'

'Sir Thomas died in India,' Richard said. 'I am his cousin. I do not know what happened to Master Bottomley and his people, but it is a fact that he reached India, and that Sir Thomas and I penetrated far into the interior. Now I am returned with great tidings for his grace.'

'Of all the strange things,' the secretary commented. 'Well, we will have to see what can be done. But mark me well, Master Blunt: the King would have himself known as Majesty. I make this point in view of your absence from this land for some years.'

Richard nodded his understanding, even if he found it strange, and somewhat ominously indicative of an overwhelming arrogance – no previous English king had ever been called anything but 'Your Grace'.

'There is another point,' the secretary continued. 'His Majesty is not in the best of health. He is sorely afflicted with ulcers on his leg and other parts of his body. His temper is sometimes short. It would pay you to remember this.'

It was necessary for Richard to take lodgings as close as possible to Whitehall and wait several days. The secretary, a Mr Walsingham, told him to be at Court every morning. There he joined a throng of men, and women too, all hoping for a word with the King, and all, equally, casting sidelong glances at the strange dark-skinned man waiting by himself.

King Henry did not appear at all the first two days. On the third he stamped through the hall in apparent bad humour, shouting at the attendants who scurried around him, ignoring the throng who either curtseyed or made a leg before him.

Richard was astounded. He had seen the King before his departure for the East, and remembered a huge, broad-shouldered, muscular body, a head of flaming hair and an equally ruddy face, young and strong, the smallness of the eyes relieved by the ready laughter of the mouth.

Now he looked at a limping wreck of a man, the shoulders hunched, the muscles dissolved into an enormous paunch; the hair peeping out from beneath his cap was thin and streaked with grey. The face was a mottled and angry mask, now dominated by eyes which glowed like little coals in the midst of bulging red cheeks and jowls. When he compared this evil-looking hulk of a man with someone like Babur or Sher Shah ... and the King was only fifty-two, less than ten years older than himself, and at least ten years younger than the Sur.

His heart sank. But he was here, and must do the best he could.

* * *

It was two days later that the King stopped opposite Richard, who hastily made a leg.

'Blunt? Blunt, you say?' shouted the King. 'Where is Thomas, then? He was a good man. Where is Thomas?'

'Alas, sire, Sir Thomas is dead.'

'Dead, eh?'

'Yes, sire, he was murdered by brigands. In India.'

'India?'

'You sent Sir Thomas to India, to find Prester John, Your Majesty.'

'Prester John! Ha! Now I suppose you'll tell me he does not exist either.'

'If I might speak with Your Majesty in private ...' Richard ventured, as people crowded closer to hear this strange conversation.

'Private, sir? Why should you speak with me in private? Have you treason to utter?'

Richard kept his temper with difficulty. After the honoured treatment and ready welcome he had received from men like Babur ... and this was his own King!

'Then, sire, I must tell you that Prester John is indeed a legend.'

The King scowled at him.

'But I have discovered a truly great king, who lives in the north of India, with whom it would be much to our advantage to trade – and to support against the Ottomans. As to Prester John, I have spoken with men who have travelled the length and breadth of Asia, and found no trace of him.'

'Ha! Does that mean he does not exist? What is the name of this fabled monarch of yours?'

'His name is Farid, Your Majesty, but his title is Sher Shah of Sur.'

'What is this, some rhyming game?' Henry looked from right to left, and the Court obediently tittered.

'That is his title, Your Majesty. He rules over a land some four times the size of England.'

Henry glared at him.

'You are a fable teller, sir. That would be larger than France and Spain together.'

Richard would not lower his eyes. 'I speak the truth, sire. I have travelled this land.'

'And this odd fellow is a Christian?'

'No, sire. He is a Muslim. But he hates and fears the Turks, as do we all. He is prepared to make an alliance with us.'

'The Turks? What have I to do with the Turks? They fight against the Emperor. Well, should not every true Englishman also fight against the Emperor?' He paused to allow another dutiful titter of laughter to ripple through his sycophants. 'This king of yours wishes to trade with us, you say? In return for what?'

'He seeks modern weapons, sire. And the men to use them. A thousand men, armed with arquebuses, a dozen cannon ...'

'An army, by God! And no doubt a fleet to convey it. What does he offer us in return?'

'Gold and silver and precious stones, in which his country abounds.'

Henry's eyes narrowed to the extent they all but disappeared. Then he suddenly flung out his hand, pointing.

'I know you for a rascal, Master Blunt. You dream of being an English Cortes or Pizarro. You would conquer some Indian principality for the enhancement of your own fame and wealth. India, bah – it is half a legend itself. And you would have me ally myself with a heathen Muslim? Begone with you, sir. Out of my sight. You are a rascal. Begone with you.'

He marched on, leaving Richard floundering before such an unexpected verbal assault. When he recovered, he made to follow, but was checked by the same secretary he had first spoken with.

'Would you lose your head, man?' Walsingham whispered.

'But he does not understand.'

'He understands well enough what he wishes to understand. I would leave Court, if I were you, Master Blunt. You have offended His Majesty. Leave Court and seek your fortune elsewhere.'

Richard stared at him, then looked at the courtiers, who were beginning to leave the hall. Some whispered amongst themselves, smiling as they glanced at him.

Oh, he thought, to have some of these upstart fops facing a Rajput cavalry charge.

'Withdraw,' Master Blunt,' Walsingham repeated. 'You are young enough to put your faith in time. Two, three years ... who knows what may then be obtained.'

He was obviously considering the King's poor health.

'Time, sir, I do not possess,' Richard told him, and left the room.

Richard and Ramdas rode through the snow to the Hampshire village he had once called home. This was a familial duty to be carried out, and one he had been looking forward to, even if he knew he must bring grief to the lovely Lizzie.

But he also had to take some time out to think. Except that his thoughts seemed to go round and round in circles. Once he had even supposed that, if the King would not support him, he could raise an army of his own and sail to Goa in triumph. That, he now had to recognise, was impossible. He could not attempt to recruit men here without it becoming known, and in this new England, ruled by such an unstable temper, he would doubtless immediately be charged with treason.

But short of that, his mission had failed entirely.

Yet, return to Delhi he must. All that he loved, all that he valued, was there.

And surely Sher Shah – the most even-tempered of men – would not hold this failure against him. Unless he had heard of Richard's prevarication with Humayun. Even so, that was a risk he had to take.

Besides, he would have had no desire to remain in this new England, even had Gila and his children not been ten thousand miles away. This was not the land he remembered from his youth.

Richard walked his horse up that so well-remembered drive. The manor house did not seem to have changed at all, save to accumulate more ivy than he recalled. But the servants who came out to greet him, the grooms and a footman, were all strange to him.

'Your business, sir?' inquired the footman.

'I seek Lady Blunt,' Richard told him.

The footman stared past him, at Ramdas.

'You are not known here, sir.'

'Why, I am indeed, fellow. My servant is not. Is that important?'

'It was but a question, sir. Lady Blunt ... why sir, I assumed you a total stranger in these parts.'

'She's not dead, I pray?'

'Indeed not, sir. But for the past twelve years she has been Mistress Plummer ...'

'Who is it, Buller?'

Richard turned his head, and saw, emerging from a side door, a tall but rather stout lady, well wrapped up, but easily recognisable for all that.

'Lizzie?' he asked.

She stared at him.

'Richard? Oh, my God ...'

She appeared about to faint, and both Richard and the footman ran forward to catch her, then carry her into the house.

'You'll leave us now,' Richard said.

'Why, sir, with my lady in such a state?'

'I am her own kin, man,' Richard told him.

Buller continued to hesitate, but now Elizabeth made a recovery.

'This is indeed my cousin, Buller. Please leave us.'

'See to my man, and to my horses,' Richard urged.

Buller bowed and left the room.

Richard walked over to the fire to take off his gloves and slap his hands together.

'I did not mean to shock you so.'

His cousin Elizabeth was fanning herself, although even with the fire the room was by no means warm. A large new casement opened on to the rose garden but was obviously not entirely suited to winter weather.

'Is Thomas with you?'

'Thomas is dead.'

She gave a little sigh, clearly of relief.

'No one could blame you for marrying again, Lizzie,' Richard told her.

'Richard ...' she held out her hands, and he took them, lifted her up, and embraced her. 'Oh, Richard ... I mourned Thomas. Really I did. I mourned him for eight years.'

'Which is a year longer than required by law.'

She pulled her head back from his shoulder.

'You *do* blame me. What was I to do? There was no word, of you, or of the ship. Therefore it was presumed all on board were also lost.' She frowned at him. 'What did happen?'

'Sit down, and I will tell you all.'

She listened to his tale with growing wonderment.

'So many adventures,' she said, when he was finished. 'And Thomas ... poor Thomas. To have come so close ...'

'Close to nothing, Lizzie. It was all a wildgoose chase. And yet, there is great promise in India. But ... King Henry will do nothing. I must return empty-handed.'

'Return? Why must you return? Stay here, Richard. Mr Plummer is presently away, but I know he will give you employment. He is a man of wealth.'

'Lizzie, have you not been listening to me? I have a wife and children. And a home.'

'Wife and children. Some dark-skinned heathen?'

'She is a princess, Lizzie. Her blood is as good as any in Henry's veins.'

'Hush!' She looked anxiously at the door. 'You speak treason.'

'Which is another reason I must leave this land as quickly as I can. Were I to remain here I doubt not I would speak treason every day of the week.'

She gazed at him, still holding his hands.

'Do you not wish to see the boy?' she asked.

'The boy?'

'My son. Thomas's son. He is here now, on vacation from Cambridge.'

'Why, I would like very much to see Thomas's son,' Richard said.

To find the boy, it was necessary first of all to encounter three bouncing girls, aged respectively eight, six and four, and very obviously the apples of their mother's eye. Their surname, of course, was Plummer.

Elizabeth looked on her son with less favour, and not only because his name remained Blunt.

Richard could understand this. Peter Blunt was nineteen years old. He had the family height, but was painfully thin, and even at his youthful age his eyes seemed weak, from the way he constantly blinked. He was the perfect picture of a scholar. But there again, Richard reminded himself, what had he expected?

And there could be no cavilling at Peter's enthusiasm for Richard's story, which had to be told again, this time over dinner.

'How I would have loved to stand at Father's side against these Marathas,' Peter said, his eyes glowing.

I doubt you would have done us much good, Richard thought. But he smiled, and said, 'We could have done with you, I can tell you.'

'Take me with you when you return, Cousin Richard. I beg of you.'

'Peter!' Lizzie cried.

'Well, Mother, am I not Father's son?' He looked at the three girls, who were gazing from face to face in wonder. 'I am nothing here in this new household – a stepson. Should I not endeavour to enhance my father's name?'

Lizzie looked at Richard.

He pulled his nose.

'This is no mere adventure we undertake, boy,' he said. 'It is a journey to the other side of the earth.'

That only made Peter more enthusiastic.

Richard tried another tack.

'There is also the matter that we are only acceptable to the Muslims as soldiers, or for some other important purpose.'

'Are there not also poets and scholars in this land, cousin? Will it not be possible for me to teach them some of our English verse, our English philosophies . . . even our English religion?'

'The last definitely not,' Richard said. 'The one thing one must never do is tamper with a Muslim's faith. To attempt to suborn it would be fatal. As for the others, I doubt Sher Shah would have much use for your poems. No, I . . . are you a swordsman?'

Peter shook his head.

'You understand the arquebus?'

'No, cousin.'

'Well, then, I am afraid . . .'

'I understand the bow.'

Richard frowned at him.

'It is still required practice to be adept with the bow,' Peter informed him.

'And you are adept?'

The eldest girl, Margaret, clapped her hands.

'Peter is the best shot in the world!' she cried.

Richard looked at Lizzie.

'He is that,' she agreed. 'He practises for hours every day.'

'Then you will have to show me your skill,' Richard smiled.

8

THE HOMECOMING

'There,' said Richard Blunt, pointing at the line of green trees emerging out of the ocean. 'Goa! At last.'

At last, indeed. Was it possible it had taken him more than three years to return?

Well, it had needed six months to find a sea captain willing to take the risk of such a journey; this time there was no king's commission to enable him to command. Indeed he had only succeeded in the end by offering to purchase half of the vessel and fund her cargo, using nearly all his remaining money to do so.

Then the voyage itself had been close to a disaster. They had encountered a violent storm on the African coast, been embayed and driven ashore. That the ship had survived at all was a miracle. As it was, several timbers had been stoved in, and it had been necessary to cut and shape trees to replace them.

They had at least been fortunate in that the black men they had encountered, small and bearded, had been friendly, even if destitute of anything which could be called civilised. In return for the gift of an arquebus and some powder and shot, they had willingly helped the stranded mariners. Even so, it had been another six months before the ship was again ready for sea.

Then there had been a mutiny. The crew had suffered enough hardship, and wanted to sail for home. Richard had refused, and there had been a confrontation, ended by the whirr of an arrow, which had struck the ringleader in the throat and stretched him dead upon the sand.

Richard had in fact learned to appreciate his youthful cousin well before that day.

He had had to admire the persistence with which the boy had pursued his goal over the tears and entreaties of his mother. Of course, Richard knew he should have refused point blank to take Peter on such an adventure. But he had been able to sense the fact that the boy was at odds with his stepfather, and he had had every sympathy with anyone who wished to abandon the England of Henry VIII.

So he had promised to send him back safe and sound, and as rich as Croesus. It was not the first time he had made a promise he knew he would hardly be able to fulfil. But he had also gained for himself a hopefully faithful companion.

The two Englishmen were very different in character. Peter seemed far more interested in books than in women. Perhaps this was his age, although Richard remembered that he himself had first had to flee a lady's bedchamber when he had only been seventeen.

Equally had their lives taken different paths. When he had been nineteen Richard had already been an experienced soldier; Peter had everything to learn in that direction. But he was very willing to learn, and he certainly knew how to handle a bow. As he had now proved.

Richard had wondered if the boy would ever have the nerve to kill a man. Now he was entirely reassured.

'I am right glad to have you along, cousin,' he said, and recalled that Thomas had once used these same words to him.

Thus had history repeated itself, for he was now just about old Thomas's age when they had begun that first voyage, with a young man at his side. The difference was that, unlike poor Thomas, he knew what he was about; he had no intention of dying before he regained Delhi.

Or even then.

The ship was finally made as seaworthy as possible, and the crew returned to their duties, even if grumbling. Then the voyage had proceeded in fits and starts, for they had lacked proper caulking, and time and again the hull had started to open, requiring another beaching and careening.

The grumbling grew, and no doubt another mutiny was planned. But by now Richard had been able to assure his men that they were over halfway, and thus safer to continue than to think of turning back, and that all the riches in the world awaited them in Goa, and that there the ship would be properly repaired for the voyage home.

He felt that the last, at least, was true.

In any event, no one argued any longer as they watched the two Blunts patrolling the poop, Richard always with his sword at his side, Peter with his bow handy, and Ramdas equally always a faithful shadow.

Richard whiled away the long hours on watch as Thomas had done, so many years ago, and taught Peter the languages he would require, Hindustani and Persian as well as Portuguese. He also told him as much as he could about the country they were approaching, although he realised that mere words could never convey the immensity of it, and everything in it.

While he watched, the boy was almost daily filling out, as he spent most of his time in the open air instead of a study; he climbed the rigging and hauled on ropes with the crew. He had always been stronger than he looked, at least in the arms – from his hours of archery practice. Now his legs filled out as well, and his eyes grew clear; he became a worthy Blunt.

And so at last, they reached the Arabian Sea, and not a hostile dhow in sight.

'We used up all of our ill fortune at the start of the voyage,' Richard said jovially.

Yet his good spirits were tinged with apprehension. He had almost no money left, and no idea what sort of reception he was going to receive in Goa. Certainly he was not returning there in any triumph.

Equally, after four years' absence, a full twelve-month longer than he had anticipated, he had no idea what he would find in Delhi.

But at least they had now arrived.

'Richard Blunt?' the woman asked. 'Can it truly be?'

He was having almost the same effect upon the Portuguese *dona* as he had had upon Lizzie. But it was he who should be asking, can it truly be?

'Elena?' he asked.

The mountain of flesh in front of him gave such a shriek of laughter that her very obvious moustache quivered.

'You have forgotten me, you rogue,' she shouted.

'How could I ever do that,' he protested. 'But ...' he glanced at the man at her side, who was not looking at all so amused.

'This is my husband, Dom Duarte d'Escantara.'

'You have the advantage of me, senhor,' Dom Duarte said. 'You seem to have some acquaintance with my wife.'

'Well ...'

Richard looked at Elena, then at the crowd which had gathered on the Goa waterfront to welcome the Englishmen as they rowed ashore. The settlement itself had grown in the number of houses and warehouses to be seen, while a large church had been built and the population seemed to have at least doubled, but it had certainly not increased in beauty.

Yet there was beauty near at hand – in the girl standing behind d'Escantara and his wife. Clearly she was their daughter: the girl had soft, lovely features, and a much fuller figure than her mother at that age, while the red streaks in her hair were dramatic: clearly inherited from her father.

'But you did not die after all,' Elena said.

Richard realised that her brain had become as addled as her body.

'Well, no,' he said. 'Or I would not be standing here.'

'But how did you survive? Not a word of you ever came back.'

'Not a word?' He was astonished when he remembered the drivers deserting. Well, serve them right – and Barnes, who must also have been swallowed up by that great continent. 'Well, it is a long story. But if I can have a word with your Governor about my ship and other matters ...'

Elena gave another shriek of laughter. 'But you are speaking with the Governor, my dear Richard.'

Richard stared at d'Escantara.

'He succeeded Papa,' Elena said. Her eyes indicated, why else do you suppose I married him? 'Of course we will repair your ship, dear Richard, and make whatever other arrangements you consider necessary. But first, tonight, you will dine with us, and tell me of these fabulous adventures of yours.' She turned her smile on Peter. 'And bring your handsome young friend with you.'

'Oh, Richard,' Elena said. 'To think, that twenty-two years ago you sat at this very table, and toyed with my hand while breaking bread. We flirted,' she explained to her husband. 'I wished to get him alone then.'

'Indeed, senhora?'

But Richard had begun to discount d'Escantara, who was clearly very much ruled by his wife.

As he himself might have been.

'I wished to explain to him that my father was sending him and his cousin to their deaths. I did warn you, didn't I, Richard?'

'Oh, indeed you did.'

'But you went anyway.'

'Well, my cousin was so determined . . .'

'To go to his death.' She waved at a waiting Indian servant, and wine was served. 'Now tell us everything that happened.'

'I shall. But first, is your father well?'

'My father is dead. As is my mother and my sister. I am the last survivor of the Alvarado family – at least in Goa. And sweet Juana here, of course.'

'Of course,' Richard said. 'My heart bleeds for you. Well, shall I begin?'

He smiled at the young girl and gave Peter a quick glance, but the boy seemed too interested in everything else around him, from the whining bugs to the chatter of the cicadas outside the house, to the softly bare-footed serving boys to the odd vegetables and fruits they had been offered for supper, to be interested in the girl.

Or perhaps he just was not interested in girls, Richard thought sadly.

He talked for an hour, choosing his omissions with great care, but leaving even d'Escantara listening intently as he spoke of Agra and Kabul, Baghdad and Constantinople, as well as of Babur and Farid.

'Heavens, what an epic!' Elena exclaimed when he had finished, while Juana clapped her hands in excitement.

'So now you have gone full circle, as it were,' d'Escantara commented. 'What is the purpose of your new expedition?'

'Why, to return to Delhi.'

'To Delhi?' Elena was incredulous. 'Why do you wish to risk your life again?'

'I have explained, I have a wife and children there.'

'Bah!' Her reaction was the same as Lizzie's.

'So you will need equipping,' d'Escantara suggested.

'Indeed,' Richard said.

'Hm. And you have, of course, money to pay for what you need?'

'I have not. However, I have a half share in the ship, and I own its cargo. My hold is filled with powder and shot, and the latest in arquebuses. These, less a few I will need for my journey, and the ship I will sell to you, in exchange for what I need.'

'That floating wreck?'

'She will be repaired, and her crew will sail her back to Europe for you. You may not care for King Henry's new religion, but his silver coins are still of value. I think that is a fair bargain, providing you promise to deal honestly with my people.'

D'Escantara stroked his beard.

'I think that is an excellent bargain,' Elena said.

'Cousin,' Peter commented that night, as they lay in the dark and listened to the buzz of the insects. 'I am beginning to suspect that you are very much of a rogue.'

'A rogue? I?'

'You are very free with your promises. As for telling Dom Duarte that we have a good and faithful crew . . .'

'I learned a long time ago that it is survival that matters in this world, boy. Provided Dom Duarte does not learn the truth of those mutinous dogs until after we are safely on our way, then the problem is his.'

Richard assembled the crew the next day, and had them careen the ship with the aid of the Portuguese and Indians. Then he explained that he had sold his half-share in both ship and cargo to the Governor, who had undertaken to pay them and see them on their way back to England.

'You spoke of gold and diamonds,' said the mate.

'So I did, Master Cutler. I assure you that they are all around. You have but to dig for them. But the ship must be repaired first.'

They had to accept that, outnumbered as they were, and as none of them spoke either Portuguese or Hindustani it would be some time before they learned the truth.

Richard felt no pity for them. Indeed, he was treating them better than they deserved, considering the mutiny. If they did not rebel against d'Escantara, they would regain their homes, and hopefully with money in their pockets. If they did rebel, they would get exactly what was coming to them, he did not doubt.

As for hoodwinking d'Escantara, he was doing nothing more than Alvarado had done to him . . .

His visit to Goa was turning out better than he could have hoped. His sole aim now was to begin the journey north.

Arranging a caravan was however not so easily done, this time. D'Escantara was helpful, but lacked the ebullient drive of his late father-in-law. The Goan Indians looked askance at Ramdas who hailed from so far away; and where the original expedition had been touted as being only as far as Gujarat, this one had no intention of going anywhere near Bahadur Shah's dominions – he would certainly recognise Blunt.

It therefore became a matter of painful negotiation with each man, lying to them as well about the riches they would undoubtedly accumulate on such a march, and not mentioning other matters such as the murderous Marathas at all.

While his cousin negotiated, bullied, cajoled, and organised, Peter explored the settlement. He relished the idea of being alone after so long cooped up on board a small vessel, and with such rebellious companions.

The voyage, in fact, had not been at all as he had expected. But, then, he had not really known what to expect. He had lived all his life in the shadow of a father he had never seen. No one spoke ill of Sir Thomas Blunt. He was remembered as a perfect knight, a friend of the King's, as both an adventurer and a scholar . . . and a man who had gallantly gone to his death at the command of his sovereign.

That had proved too heady an inheritance for a young man who had inherited nothing else. Sir Thomas had left his widow reasonably well provided for, but not enough for substance. She had done the best she could, but things had gradually got worse, until her husband had been gone for seven years and she could legitimately accept suitors for her still beautiful hand.

Peter could remember little of those early years; he had been too young, and he had been ill too much of the time, so much so that his life had been despaired of. He could remember, however, his mother speaking often of his father, and of his gentleness and ability.

She had even, from time to time, spoken of the fierce young cousin who had accompanied him on that final expedition.

Peter's new father had also spoken of the past, but somehow to his disparagement. Not even Martin Plummer would dare traduce Sir Thomas Blunt. He had obtained his pleasure from pointing out that his son would never equal him either physically or intellectually.

Peter had believed him. He had asked no permission to seek a place at Court, had turned away from languages, had accepted that he was to be a second-rate citizen for all of his life. Even archery, in which he had found so much pleasure as soon as he began to gain in strength and discovered a real skill at the sport, was, after all, only a sport. Civilised armies no longer used the bow.

Thus he felt he had been born a hundred years too late. Everyone had learning nowadays, and everyone who would be a gentleman knew the use of the sword. But he could still dream, and one of his dreams had been of Father not dead but returning from the East in triumph.

Instead of his father there had come his reincarnation, this dark-visaged man, tall and powerful and confident, with enough adventures under his belt to satisfy ten men, but yet still determined to return to his dusky bride and his fierce shahs and sultans.

As he had listened to that legend unfolding, Peter had known that *this* was his only chance even to play at emulating his father. He had thought nothing of the risks involved. Risks were only important when there was something to lose, and he had nothing. Even his mother doted more on her three girls than on him. He did not resent her for that, but he reckoned it absolved him of any great responsibility towards her.

And so the voyage, in the course of which he had killed a man; not some savage Indian but an Englishman like himself. He had proved himself, at least in Cousin Richard's eyes. But what of his own? He had stepped into a world stranger than he had supposed to exist. And it was the only world he was going to know from now on.

Suddenly he felt very lonely for England. But as this was his fate, chosen by himself, he must make the best of it.

He knew that Richard regarded Goa with contempt, but Peter thought it fascinating. He found the people and the vegetation unendingly interesting, and tried his hand at sketching one or two of the Indian girls, to their great pleasure; their continuous state of near nudity made him remember all the girls he had known in England, with never a thought as to what might lie beneath their skirts and blouses. Now, when these little child-women crept up behind him and leaned over his shoulder to see what he was doing, it required the greatest effort not to seize hold of that temptingly bare flesh, to what purpose he had no clear idea. Cousin Richard had apparently mated with one of them, though a Persian who was very well born.

In the event, he never did touch any of the girls. He was simply too afraid of their possible reaction. Or that of their brothers and fathers.

His favourite occupation was walking the beach and staring into the translucently shallow waters, in which fish could clearly be seen, some small and brightly coloured, others large and sinister, especially the rays with their dark bodies and whip-like tails.

He enjoyed the heat, to which he had become accustomed during the voyage, but he envied the Indian boys who plunged into the water without hesitation, leaving their dhoties on the sand and diving and swimming and wrestling with one another in the gentle surf, in apparent total innocence.

The temptation to do the same grew with every day until, finding himself on a lonely stretch of beach with no one in sight, he succumbed, removing his shirt and breeches, and entered the water.

It was the most heavenly experience he had ever known, as the water seeped up his body with every step. The sea was perfectly calm, and this and its warmth as different as could be imagined from the tumbling millstream in which he had learned to swim.

He waded out up to his neck, and stood still. Suddenly he heard voices. Looking back to the beach he saw, emerging from the trees, the girl Juana and her duenna. They were together looking at a book as they walked, deep in discussion.

Peter stood absolutely still. In a few minutes they would have passed on, surely without noticing him.

He had been struck by Juana from their first meeting. With her red-black hair, dark eyes and sallow skin, she also had been part of the strangeness of this place. She was certainly worth looking at now, as she clearly wore very little in the way of undergarments, and the sun revealed her slim legs through the thin cotton of her skirt.

Suddenly she pointed at the discarded clothes.

'Where is the rascal?' demanded Doña Philippa, her voice carrying clearly out to sea.

Peter thought of ducking under the surface, but decided against it. Anyway, it was already too late.

'Why, Senhor Blunt,' Juana cried. 'You are a very long way out.'

'Come along, Juana,' Doña Philippa urged.

'But Senhor Blunt ... do you not see the shark?' Her voice was suddenly shrill.

Peter cast a hasty glance over his shoulder. Indeed, there was a triangular fin not very far away. And he had seen enough evidence of the voraciousness of sharks in the Arabian Sea going after the slops dropped overboard from the ship.

He threw himself forward, swimming vigorously as he could – and only checked when he reached waist-deep water.

'Hurry, senhor, hurry,' Juana cried, running down to the water's edge in her anxiety.

Doña Philippa was also shouting in agitation.

He stumbled forward, and emerged dripping.

Juana clapped her hands.

'Juana!' Doña Philippa bustled down the beach to seize her charge's arm. 'Cover yourself, senhor. You are indecent.'

Peter seized up his shirt and wrapped it around himself, his cheeks burning. Juana stopped staring at him, and instead gazed out to sea.

'It was only a dolphin, after all,' she said.

Peter turned to look as well, watching the creature diving

lazily in and out of the shallow waves. Juana had been born and bred on this coast; surely she would know the difference between a dolphin and a shark at a glance.

She smiled at him.

'I shall keep our little secret, Senhor Blunt. As will Doña Philippa. Because it is quite a big secret, is it not?'

She gave a burst of laughter and followed the duenna along the beach.

Peter only hoped she would. He could not imagine what her father or mother would say if they learned of what had happened. But that night at supper, taken with the d'Escantaras, he could not stop himself glancing at her. And she spent most of the meal looking at him, and every so often her tongue would protrude and slowly circle her lips.

The wretched girl was remembering his nudity!

'I would say we are all but ready,' Richard announced. 'Two more days, and we shall depart.'

'You have worked so hard,' Elena gushed. 'But only two more days? We have so enjoyed your company.'

Her husband cleared his throat. 'You would not wish Senhor Blunt to be caught in the monsoon,' he pointed out.

'Bah, that is at least three months away. And this is the hottest part of the year.'

'We shall be in the jungle, and shaded,' Richard reminded her. 'And moving north all the time. But as it is a three-months journey to Delhi, we are cutting it pretty fine already.'

'It is so warm, Mama,' Juana said suddenly. 'Could I be permitted to walk in the garden?' She looked at Peter. 'Perhaps Senhor Peter would escort me.'

Elena burst into a tremendous peal of laughter, and clapped her hands.

'Of course he will accompany you!' she shrieked. 'Doña Philippa! Doña Philippa!' She raised her finger. 'But mind you remain in sight of Doña Philippa every moment.'

Juana was on her feet.

'Will you not come, Senhor Peter?' she invited.

Peter cast his cousin a helpless glance, stammered his excuses, and followed the girl into the garden. Doña Philippa lumbered behind them.

The night was very warm, only marginally cooler than the day in fact, and the garden was filled with the hum of insects. Juana idly fanned them away from her face as she strolled between the bushes lining the path.

'Have you enjoyed your stay in Goa, Peter?' she asked.

'Oh, very much. Senhorita, I do apologise for this afternoon ...'

'What nonsense,' she said. 'I provoked it. Am I not a very wicked girl?'

'Well ...'

'Papa would whip me if he knew of it. Perhaps you should whip me, as you know of it.'

'Senhorita,' he said uneasily.

'Doña Philippa, wherever are you?' Juana demanded.

'Here child, here. But you walk so fast.'

They were now well out of sight of the house.

'I know,' Juana said sympathetically. 'But I have a present for you.'

'A present?' The older woman sounded wary.

'You'll pardon me, Peter.'

Juana turned half away from him and, before he had grasped what she was doing, had lifted her skirts about her waist, and from beneath them produced a bottle.

He caught no more than a glimpse of white, unstockinged leg.

'It is a trifle warm, I am afraid,' Juana said, and held out the bottle.

'Oh, you wicked child,' Philippa exclaimed without conviction, taking it.

'Now, I wish you to sit on this bench and drink to your heart's content. Promise not to move until I return.'

'But Juana, your mother ...'

'Will know nothing of it, my dearest Philippa – lest she also learns of your little weakness. We shall not be long.'

She linked her arm through Peter's and led him off into the darkness.

'You seem to have things well arranged,' he commented, more uneasy than ever, but terribly conscious of the feel of her close against him.

'Doña Philippa and I reached an understanding some time

ago,' Juana explained. 'And where is the harm in it? She is doing what she enjoys most … and I am hoping to find something I enjoy, too.'

She was at least a little breathless at her own temerity.

Peter licked his lips. 'I really feel …'

They had turned a corner of the path, and were entirely alone.

'That as I have the advantage of you, you should also have the advantage of me?' she asked.

He stared at her, quite unable to believe his ears.

'Save that in the dark you would observe very little of interest,' she pointed out. 'But there is a possible substitute.'

She put her arms round his neck and kissed him on the mouth. To do this she had to raise herself first of all on tiptoe, and then virtually lift herself from the ground. Insensibly he found himself holding her waist, and as she began to slip, clutching her buttocks through the thin gown to keep her up and against him, while their tongues seemed to wrap around each other.

'Oh, Peter,' she whispered, slowly subsiding down his chest. 'I do adore you so.'

Peter's brain was tumbling. He had no idea what to do with this marvellous creature who had just literally hurled herself at him.

'Will you not possess me?' she whispered, as she guided him towards another bench.

Richard surveyed his caravan with some satisfaction. But then, unlike cousin Thomas twenty-two years before, he knew plenty about caravans.

There were four wagons, containing every possible supply of food, arms, and ammunition. There were, in addition, six mules. He had recruited twenty drivers, and these he had placed under the command of Ramdas. He had accepted no volunteers from the ship; if Barnes and his friends had proved so disappointing, he could expect nothing from a pack of mutineers; he had no doubt that he, Peter and Ramdas could deal with any emergency which might arise, especially as he was taking a safer route, at a safer time of year.

He thought that he could wish Peter a little less agitated now that the moment for starting the expedition had arrived; the boy was like a cat on hot coals. But he would undoubtedly settle down once they were on their way.

'How splendid it all looks,' Doña Elena said. 'How I wish I was coming with you, Richard. And how I hope to have you return before another twenty years.'

'I shall do my best,' Richard lied with his usual gallantry. 'Well, we had best be off.' He looked around at the watching natives and the half dozen Portuguese who had assembled to see them depart. Dom Duarte was not amongst them. 'You'll give my best regards to your husband, and thank him most sincerely for all his help.'

'I apologise for his absence. He is so busy ...'

'And your charming daughter.'

Elena sighed.

'She is probably sulking. I am afraid all is not well with my sweet Juana.'

'I have seldom seen a happier or healthier child.'

'She is not a child, Richard. And she, alas, must suffer the same fate as myself. Indeed, Duarte has already picked a husband. You have met him, Captain Niñez?'

Richard raised his eyebrows. He remembered the captain as a short, stout, black-bearded man of at least forty.

'Is he not a trifle old for your daughter?'

'Well, what would you do? The girl must marry, and Niñez is the only possible choice.'

'You say she is actually betrothed?'

'No, not yet. On her next birthday. But she is aware of it. Thus she sulks from time to time, and for the rest hides her annoyance under a guise of perpetual gaiety.'

Richard said thoughtfully, 'Elena, that being the case, you really should not have permitted her to walk out at night with young Peter. It could clearly have caused a very awkward situation.'

'Oh, nonsense. this boy, unlike you, my dear Richard, is an absolute innocent. You can tell that by looking at him. But nevertheless I suspect that Juana is sulking in her room from sheer frustration. Peter is quite a handsome boy.'

Richard remarked, 'I think the sooner I get Peter out of here, the better for both of us. So, I will bid you adieu.'

'Will you not kiss me goodbye, sweet Richard?'

'Most happily, Elena.' He kissed her on the mouth, and a huge shudder of satisfaction went down her body. '*Até à vista*,' he said, and hurried to join his waiting people.

The track, as Richard remembered it, had greatly improved in twenty-two years, and could now almost be called a road. The caravan made excellent time, and arrived at the first village in the middle of the afternoon. Despite the heat, Richard decided to carry on; an hour or so gained each day would mean a day gained every fortnight, and his sole aim now was to reach Agra.

He was pleased with the way things were going, and especially the new energy revealed by his cousin. The boy spent his entire time ranging up and down the length of the caravan, making sure all was well with the wagons, encouraging the rear-guard ... perhaps it was a result of his recent nervousness, Richard thought.

'There is naught to concern yourself with here,' Richard assured him. 'In the hill country, now, we may encounter some brigands, but I think we are a strong enough party to deter them.'

'I have no doubt of it,' Peter agreed, but then resumed his perambulations all over again.

It was dusk when Richard called a halt. He used the Moghul methods and had the wagons dragged into a rough square, within which the animals and men could sleep in fair safety, providing a good watch was kept.

'The three of us will have to take a watch each,' he informed Peter and Ramdas. 'We will have two of the drivers with us, but they are not to be trusted on their own.'

'How far have we come?' Peter asked.

'A good way. Not less than twenty-five miles. It is a splendid start.'

'Then there is no risk of anyone from the settlement coming after us?' Peter suggested.

'There never was.' Richard was puzzled.

'Ah, well, then, cousin, I have a confession to make.'

Richard raised his eyebrows.

'I ...' Peter was crimson in the face. 'I had best show you. The poor girl must be half dead.'

Richard sprang to his feet as Peter hurried off towards the wagon in which he had shown most interest all day. He heaved down what Richard had supposed to be a sack of powder.

The Indians burst into a stream of chatter as Peter untied the neck of the sack and a very flushed and overheated Juana emerged. She wore only a cotton shift, but was dripping sweat.

'You'll excuse me,' she said, and without further ado dashed into the bushes.

'Are you mad?' Richard demanded angrily. 'Is *she* mad?'

'If being in love is madness, cousin, well, then, yes, we are mad.'

'Love? How can you be in love? How long have you known this girl?'

'Three weeks.'

Juana returned from the bushes. 'Dearest Peter, I am so very thirsty.'

'Of course, my love.' Hastily he poured her a beaker of water.

Richard gazed hard at the girl; the shift really concealed almost nothing.

'Had you not better put on some clothes?' he inquired.

'There are some in the wagon,' she explained. 'But I would rather cool off first.'

Richard looked at Peter, and Peter looked back, his expression indicating that this was a young woman who knew her own mind.

In every possible way, Richard thought grimly.

'I should put you both in irons,' he growled.

'Why so?' Juana was drinking her second mug of water. 'We are married.'

'What?'

'Before God, if not before man.'

Richard stared at his young cousin.

'It just happened,' Peter explained lamely.

'On that walk.' Despite his anger, Richard had a sudden urge to laugh. Both he and Elena had dismissed the boy as an innocent ... but he had stepped in where the two of them had held back twenty-two years ago.

'You understand that I know your situation, senhorita?' he asked. 'Your mother explained it to me. Well, Peter, this woman has taken this foolhardy action in order to rid herself of an unwanted husband.'

'Is that a crime?' Juana demanded. 'I have always hated Niñez. And he is not my husband. He is not even my betrothed. I merely took action before he could become so. Having,' she hastily added, 'found the only man I could truly love.'

She slid her arm round Peter's waist.

'You believe her?' Richard asked.

'Why, yes, sir. I do. I love her.'

'And just what do you propose to do now? Return to Goa on your own?'

'We intend to accompany you,' Peter said.

'You mean to take this young girl through a thousand miles of jungle, to the strangest land you ever saw?'

'I am looking forward to it, dearest cousin,' Juana said.

'And what do I say when your father sends men after you?'

'He will not send behind me,' Juana said confidently. 'I prepared my departure with great care, took some clothes down to a lonely beach, and there left them with a note to say that I was drowning myself rather than marry Niñez.'

'You could do that, to your own parents?' Richard was aghast.

'It was necessary,' she pointed out. 'And will they not be the happier when they learn that I am alive?'

No doubt, Richard reflected, she considered that the sending of news from Agra to Goa was a weekly affair. Peter had certainly picked a disturbing young woman to carry off. But his secondary reaction was amusement. How Elena, just like her father, schemed and planned ... and how all of those schemes and plans had been set at naught by the determination of a young girl.

'Well, then,' he said. 'Have you not a kiss for your cousin, Juana?'

'Why, willingly, sir,' she said, and went to him.

9
THE RETURN OF THE MOGHUL

It was Richard's intention to avoid the territories of both Gujarat and the Rajput Confederacy, and so he took a new route, more to the east.

Here the land had begun to rise within a few days of leaving Goa, but as it was now the height of the dry season it was possible to follow the valley of the river Krishna, right across Bijapur. He travelled as an ambassador from the Court of Sher Shah, and this worked very well, as he had brought along sufficient arquebuses to make presents to the local hakims, or governors.

Compared with the miseries of his earlier journey, this was a most pleasant expedition. The weather was good, the caravan's progress was excellent, and the one thing which he had feared might handicap them, the presence of Juana, turned out to be a delight. She approached every obstacle with vigorous enthusiasm, whether it was wading a stream with her skirts held high or washing her clothes in the Indian fashion, by beating them with a flat stick against a rock. Inevitably both her complexion and her toilette suffered, as well as the clothes themselves, and she soon had to discard her ringlets, or indeed any attempt at dressing her hair, but she continued to smile.

As did Peter. Their affection for each other could not be denied, and if Richard found it difficult to accept that they genuinely loved each other – Juana being too scheming and Peter too young, in his opinion – they certainly loved each other's bodies. He allowed them to construct a tent for themselves, rather than bivouacing as did the rest of the caravan, and he grew quite envious as they nightly retired into the privacy of their embraces.

But every day brought him closer to his beloved Gila.

Both Peter and Juana were fascinated by the jungle, the density of the trees, the ever present undergrowth, the rustle of the lizards, the seething of the cicadas, the teeming ants' nests, the birds and monkeys which flocked in the trees above their heads, and the lion-tailed macaques, or wanderoos, black-furred, baboon-like creatures which seemed equally at home swinging from branch to branch or scampering over the ground.

There was a good deal of larger wildlife to be seen as well. Since it was so dry, the river was low, and crocodiles could often be observed basking on the mud-flats or waddling into the water with an amazingly gentle splash. Pythons, too, were much in evidence, and there were tigers all around, but being a relatively large party they apprehended little danger from the beasts, although Peter, who kept his trusty longbow ever on his shoulder, was with difficulty dissuaded from taking a shot at one yellow and black monster which came sniffing close around the encampment one evening.

'If we attack him, he will attack us,' Richard explained.

'But do you not suppose I can lay him down with a single shaft, cousin?'

'I doubt even you could do that,' Richard countered, remembering his midnight encounter so long ago.

Raichur, on the borders of Golconda, was reached after little more than a week. Raichur was actually the capital of Bijapur, and it was necessary for Richard to present his credentials to the Sultan and remain there for some days while he was entertained, and gave what news he could.

Yusuf Adil was interested to learn what was happening in Goa, which was at the other end of his wide domain; it was not a place he had ever visited himself, the lease having been granted to the Portuguese by his father. But he was a placid little man who seemed contented enough with the situation.

It was the news he had to give Richard that was devastating: Sher Shah of Sur was dead.

Farid had actually died two years previously. Nor, as might have been expected, was it the result of either illness or old age, but a concomitant of the way he had always lived – at war. While he had been besieging the city of Kaninjar, a powder wagon had exploded and blown him to pieces.

'Then what is now happening in Delhi?' Richard asked in dismay.

'The Sur was succeeded by his son, Islam Shah,' the Sultan told him. 'But the real power is held by the army commander, a man called Hemu.'

Hemu, Richard thought. Of all the ill fortune! But he remembered Islam Shah as an honest man and enthusiastic soldier. If he could gain Delhi before Hemu implemented whatever plans he had in mind...

Yusef Adil had observed his expression. 'Is this bad news for you, Blunt Amir?'

'That I cannot say until I reach Delhi,' Richard said. 'But the sooner I do so the better.'

What of Gila and the children? he wondered, sick with worry. Sher Shah had promised to protect them ... but he had died unexpectedly. Would he have told his son of that promise?

'Will you turn back?' Peter asked, when he learned the situation.

'No, we must press on with ever greater haste.'

Juana watched the two men with anxious eyes; these were all the family she now possessed, and what affected them affected her in equal degree.

'Let us at least hope we do not have to fight our way into Delhi,' Peter said with a smile.

He knew nothing of the true dangers underlying the situation.

From Raichur Richard headed north, some four hundred and fifty miles, to cross the great river Narmada at the borders of Kandesh and Gondwana.

This took some three weeks of hard slogging over the hill country, with mountains towering to either side. But again Richard's passport as an emissary of the Sultanate of Delhi, no matter that it was signed by a dead man, carried them safely through all obstacles. It seemed that Farid's reputation was such that he was feared even in death.

The Narmada, wide and deep, was their biggest problem so

far. But eventually, with much shouting and yelling, with assistance from the locals, and peals of laughter from a soaking wet Juana, the caravan reached the other side and could resume its journey.

Now they had passed the halfway mark and, if for the next two hundred miles they were crossing high land, the weather remained warm. By the time they descended into the valley of the Jumna, a fortnight after leaving the river Narmada, heavy black clouds were building away to the south-east, but now they were nearly home.

They reached Agra a week later, and Richard was surprised, but relieved, to discover that the governor in command of the city was none other than Prabhankar.

Prabhankar, now very grand, dressed in a pale blue tunic over white breeches with a ruby-studded turban and a jewelled sword hilt, was totally astonished to see him.

'Blunt Bahatur!' he exclaimed. 'We had given you up for dead.'

'I've had that greeting everywhere I've been,' Richard told him.

'You have heard of the death of the Sur?'

Richard nodded.

'But now you have come with the English army. How far away is it?'

'About ten thousand miles,' Richard said. 'There is no English army. My King was not interested.'

'Ah. But you have come anyway.'

'Agra is my home,' Richard reminded him. 'Are my family well?'

'You have not been to see them?'

'I was brought straight before you, old friend.'

'When I last heard, your family were well,' Prabhankar said cautiously.

Richard frowned at him. 'Are they not here in Agra?'

Prabhankar could not meet his gaze.

'They have gone to Delhi, Blunt Bahatur. Everyone has gone to Delhi. This was Islam Shah's wish.'

'I see.' That was not unreasonable, he supposed, if the new city was now truly the capital.

But he sensed that Prabhankar was holding something back.

'Then tell me of our new master.'

'I think you had best find out about him for yourself,' Prabhankar suggested. 'I know he will be anxious to see you.'

That was not altogether reassuring. Richard considered the matter, and then took Peter and Juana to Ghopal Das's house. Juana was in ecstacy when she gazed at the size and the space of it, the exquisite workmanship, and particularly when she was greeted by so many bowing servants.

But even the servants were reluctant to talk about Gila and the children, save to repeat that they had removed themselves to Delhi.

'There is some mystery here,' Richard told Peter. 'I think, in the circumstances, it would be best for me to go on to Delhi by myself to begin with. I will send for you as soon as I am sure of a welcome. Should I not send within a fortnight, or should you hear that something grievous has happened to me, then you must take the caravan and return to Goa, make what accommodation you can with your wife's parents, and thence find your way home to England.'

Peter looked extremely distressed. 'If you are going into danger, cousin, should I not be at your side?'

'And if we both fell, who would look after Juana? I do not really believe I am going into danger. I am just endeavouring to take care of every eventuality.'

The boy was not happy, but he could only obey the older man. Prabhankar willingly supplied Richard with Indian clothes and armour and a horse, and an escort suitable for an amir, and he set out the next day. Ramdas stayed behind with Peter, as he alone, Richard judged, was capable of taking the young couple back to the coast if that became necessary.

Richard covered the hundred miles in three days, stopping only when the horses needed resting. His haste was not only out of his impatience to be reunited with his family: he wanted to be the first to bring the news of his return to Hemu.

Delhi had grown out of recognition in the four years he had been absent. Humayun's abortive city had been razed, as Farid had wished, and in its place had risen glistening white buildings and white walls, beautiful gardens and pleasant artificial lakes, above which the old Qutb Minar tower still rose like a beacon.

Richard rode straight for the palace, and had himself announced. Heads turned and people stared; many even hurried forward to greet him, to his surprise. And without delay he was escorted in to see the new Sultan.

No carpet here. Islam Shah sat on an elaborate throne, wearing a high headdress which seemed to be cloth-of-gold stretched over a basketwork frame; his tunic was also cloth-of-gold, and his fingers sparkled with rings, as did the hilt of his tulwar with jewels.

To either side stood viziers and generals, but, unlike the easy custom of the Mongols, there were no women to be seen.

In front of all the other officers, there stood Hemu, as richly dressed as his master.

'Blunt Bahatur! But this is fortune,' Islam Shah said.

Richard bowed, then advanced. The Sultan stood up and came forward to embrace him. When he sat down again, Hemu also came forward to greet him, while the court rustled, apparently with amazement.

'We had thought you dead,' Hemu said. 'Not your wife, however. My dear mother has never doubted your return.'

Richard frowned at him. 'Your mother?'

'Well, she is that, as you are my father,' Hemu said, smiling.

A huge lump seemed to form in Richard's belly.

'As you are also a grandfather,' Hemu went on.

In total consternation, Richard stared at the Sultan.

'I acted for you, Blunt Bahatur,' Islam Shah explained, 'because we thought you dead. But I could conceive of no greater honour for your family than to unite it with that of my Grand Vizier. Now come, and sit at my right hand, and tell me of your adventures . . . and what you have brought back to me.'

Hemu was smiling at him. Richard restrained his rage with an effort. He could have strangled the little man there and then. Iskanda, taken to the bed of this monster! And already a mother. Because he himself had not been there to protect her.

'I have brought you nothing, sire,' he said at last. 'My King had other uses for his soldiers.'

Islam Shah's eyes narrowed for a moment, then he smiled again.

'But you have brought me yourself. What more could I wish?

You are dismissed. I know your wife awaits you. But I will send for you presently.'

Richard held Gila's shoulders to look at her. She was thirty-seven years of age, and had been his wife for more than twenty of those years. And he still thought her the most beautiful woman in the world.

Even with sorrow-ravaged features, and streaks of grey in his midnight-black hair.

'I have seen Hemu.'

She sighed. 'While Farid lived, I was treated with honour. But with his death ... Hemu virtually appropriated our family. Islam Shah did nothing to help us. He is Hemu's creature in all things. Hemu wished Iskanda, of course. But he made a great show of seeking the best for all of us.'

'Where are they?' Richard asked.

'Zaid is with the army, in the east. He is a tuk-bashi, and I hear glowing reports of him. But I do not see him.'

'And Mahmud?'

'Mahmud is with the training camp, north of the city.'

'He is only sixteen!'

'He is being trained. It is the will of the Sultan.'

'And your mother?'

Her lips twisted. 'My mother is dead. It was not Hemu's doing, directly. But the thought of being at the mercy of a low-caste Hindu ate into her mind, her spirit, her heart.'

'I am sorry – for you. But now you are a grandmother.'

'As you are a grandfather. He is a sturdy boy. But ... he is Hemu's son.' She gazed at him. 'What will you do?'

'There is little I can do now.' He sat down beside her. 'My leaving here was a catastrophe. And, worse, I have brought my young cousin and his bride back with me, expecting great things.'

Gila held his arm. 'There will be great things, my lord. Islam Shah has need of men like you, if only to counteract the power of Hemu. And Hemu is no administrator. Your cousin and his wife will prosper here. I am sure of it. But, Richard, it has been so long ...'

He kissed her on the mouth.

However much Richard felt that Hemu's dislike of him persisted, and that his taking over of his family was almost an act of revenge, in that he seemed to be playing with them all until he was ready to destroy them, he had to accept the fact that he had been welcomed in style. Nor could he fault the house which had been given to Gila – it quite compared with the house in Agra – or the style in which she was allowed to live.

While Islam Shah was kindness himself. If he was disappointed that Richard had not returned with an army, he never revealed it. Hemu, of course, was delighted. His position rested upon those divisions of Hindu pikemen which now formed the major part of the Delhi army ... a force which he had himself first raised, Richard thought ruefully.

Hemu, indeed, could not have been more amiable. Within twenty-four hours he invited Richard to his house and they dined together.

'A young cousin! A second Blunt!' he exclaimed. 'Truly would I rather have two Blunts than a whole army. Is this boy as distinguished a soldier as yourself, my father?'

'Not quite so, as yet,' Richard temporised.

'But we must have him here. I will send an escort for them immediately.'

'You are too kind.'

'I am doing only what is necessary, Blunt Amir. To have you back ... my relief stretches beyond words. I will be straight with you, my father. Since Sher Shah has died, the kingdom has had troubles. Sher Shah waged war almost continuously, and he paid for his wars with the taxes he raised. Since his death, there have been problems with these taxes. Our governors are failing us in collecting them, and I have had no one to send to chastise them. Nor could I go myself, for the Sultan conceives himself as surrounded by the enmity of the Rajputs in the south and Humayun in the north. You know that the treacherous Mongol still holds Kabul?'

'I had heard this.'

'I have sent to negotiate with him, and he has ignored my ambassadors – sent them home emptyhanded.'

'His father would have taken their heads.'

'Ha-ha, you are right. Humayun is not the man Babur was.

For which we must be thankful. Yet he lies across the main trade route to central Asia, choking us to death and ready to descend upon us at the first sign of any weakness. These things must be ended, Blunt Bahatur, now that you are back ... yes, they must be ended. I know that the Sultan will wish to discuss these matters with you; his mind is at one with mine in public affairs.' He gave a sly smile. 'Well, in most affairs. You will first of all return our tax-gatherers to their allegiance. Be harsh if you need be, Blunt Bahatur. Our treasury is all but empty. And then, when we are again wealthy, we will see about this Humayun. Together you and I, my father, will smoke out that viper, and bring greatness to ourselves. And to our lord the Sultan, of course.'

It was a great temptation to believe everything Hemu said. If it could only be true, Richard realised he might have fallen entirely on his feet, as father-in-law of the Grand Vizier, commander of the army ... But he could not bring himself to trust the little man.

He remembered too clearly Kanauj and its aftermath.

And his anger still burned at the thought of his daughter Iskanda sharing Hemu's bed.

He sought permission to see the girl, but this was refused; Hemu had encouraged Islam Shah entirely to reinstate Lodi's harem system, as if deliberately turning his back on everything connected with the Mongol culture ... or the Hindu, for that matter.

This did not prevent the Sultan from having Juana brought before him when she and Peter finally arrived in Delhi. Richard could hardly object, as it was well known that his own wife Gila appeared unveiled in public.

And Islam Shah clearly liked what he saw, as did Hemu. Prabhankar's wife had attended to Juana in Agra, and she arrived in all the splendour of an agha, wearing a pale green sari with a matching tunic, her hair coiled on her head and secured there with a golden band. Gold bangles sparkled on her wrists, and her complexion had been at least partly restored by the liberal use of asses' milk during the week she and Peter had waited for the summons from Delhi.

She was certainly different to any woman the Sultan would

ever have seen before; with the reddish streaks in her hair, the pink of her cheeks peeping through the sunburn, and the voluptuousness in one so young.

Islam Shah stroked his beard. 'Are all the women in the West as luscious as this?' The Sultan had hardly even looked at Peter. Now he gave him a quick glance. 'You are blessed, young Blunt. We will speak again.'

'What dreadful men,' Juana confessed when they gained the safety of their new home.

'They are our masters – for the time being at least,' Richard reminded her. 'And now, I would have you meet Gila.'

Juana had clearly thought deeply about this, as she did about most things, and had mapped out her plan of campaign. The moment Gila entered the room, Juana dropped to her knees, her head bowed. This elaborate play-acting did not register on the Princess, however, who took it as her due. She raised the girl from the floor to embrace her.

'You are doubly welcome, child,' she said. 'Not only because you have come with my husband's kinsman, but because you will replace the daughter I have lost.'

It was good to be home, even to a strange home. And it very rapidly became familiar.

Young Peter seemed intrigued and delighted by everything about Delhi, even by the rains which soon commenced, and which came flooding down day after day.

'I can now understand your anxiety not to be caught on the road, cousin,' he told Richard.

Richard spent much of these monsoon months at the palace, going over the tax returns with Hemu's viziers, and also studying Hemu himself.

The little man scarcely seemed to understand what he had achieved in rising so far. He lived in as much pomp as the Sultan himself, always accompanied by a dozen guards with drawn tulwars, ensconced in the brilliance with which Farid had surrounded himself, without apparently having any ideas of how to augment it.

Even Humayun's famous library, spoken of as the greatest collection of books in India, remained absolutely intact. And, as

Hemu could not read Turkish, Arabic, Persian or Sanskrit, and, indeed, Hindustani only with difficulty, the books merely gathered dust.

Islam Shah, hardly better educated than Hemu, paid no attention to his surroundings at all. He was a soldier who liked nothing better than inspecting his household troops, yet at the same time feared to go to war.

Hemu lived even more in continual dread, inspired, Richard assumed, by his low caste. For he was in fact an Untouchable, a member, they said, of the original dark-skinned inhabitants of the sub-continent who had been overrun and enslaved by the first invaders from the north.

However interesting he found them, Richard had never paid much attention to Hindu customs and social divisions; he had originally entered a Muslim-dominated world in which even high-caste Indians like Ghopal Das had been considered inferior beings. But he understood that the class distinctions were perhaps more rigid that anywhere else in the world – and that for those at the bottom of the dungheap social advancement was next to impossible – save in times of warfare and revolution.

As a good soldier, Hemu had been given a command by Humayun. Farid in turn had honoured him. And now he had seized his opportunity on Farid's death. But he was still well aware that Muslim and Hindu alike regarded him as an usurper, a man they would not even speak with on the street, were he not the Sultan's favourite. For Hemu the remedy for this insecurity was money.

The revenue system inaugurated by Sher Shah had been too thorough to be destroyed by two years of neglect, but there was obviously a great deal owing to the government which had either not been paid or had been syphoned into someone else's coffers.

That winter also revealed to Richard the very shaky nature of Islam Shah's rule. The Sultan's relations with the Rajputs were uncertain. They had observed a healthy respect for his formidable father, but the son had never proved himself. Apart from the Rajput threat, the governor of the Punjab, Sikundar Sher, who was a nephew of Farid, had virtually declared independence. He had paid no taxes for over a year, claiming that all the money he raised was needed to defend his viceroyalty against the incursions of the Mongols from Kabul. And in the east there were still more relatives of Farid who were claiming a right to the throne.

This situation left Richard Blunt in something of a quandary. He loathed and mistrusted Hemu, yet the man was married to his daughter, and he held the rest of the family pretty much in the palm of his hand. Nor could he be sure that Sikundar Sher or Farid's other nephews would make better sultans than Islam Shah; from what he had seen of them he doubted that.

The thought of Humayun lurking across the frontier, a man he could both respect and trust, loomed large in his mind. But after Farid's death Humayun had made no move against Delhi. No doubt he was still preoccupied with collecting books and antiques.

For Blunt to flee from Delhi would mean abandoning everything he possessed, including his children, to the mercy of Hemu – unless he could somehow take them all with him. That did not stop him making a few plans of his own – for the time when Hemu stopped smiling at him. For now, however, he could think of nothing better than to serve the upstart and his ineffective master with as much loyalty as he could muster.

So it was that, when the rains began to slacken and Hemu asked him where he would begin his reformation of the administration, he said, 'I can do no better than follow the example of the great Babur. We must decide our order of priorities. Sikundar may dream of an independent Punjab, but he fears the Mongols, and for the time being is totally preoccupied with them. At the same time he is a fine general and has a powerful army; we will need all our resources to crush him. The Rajputs are now too busy quarrelling amongst themselves to coalesce against you. But again, when we decide to march against them, we will need all our resources. Therefore it is my opinion that we should deal with the eastern provinces first, where everything is in disarray, and where most of our taxes are in arrears.'

'Then this trust I place in your hands, Blunt Amir,' Hemu said, and smiled his crooked smile. 'Bring me money – and the heads of those who have tried to withhold it.'

Richard decided to take his cousin with him, to give the boy some actual experience of Indian life in the raw. Peter was tremendously excited at the prospect, and only regretful at leaving Juana, who was pregnant.

'How many times have I nursed a swollen belly in the absence of my lord?' Gila scoffed at him. 'Your wife will be safe here with me. Go and earn your spurs, that you may become an amir like your cousin.'

Juana, though, wept bitterly.

Richard was given a force of five hundred cavalry: large for tax gathering, small for putting down a rebellion . . . or starting one.

He proceeded first of all to Agra. According to his lists, Prabhankar had been honest enough in his returns.

'Blunt Bahatur,' Prabhankar said, 'it is good to see you looking strong and well, and with five hundred men at your back.'

'You mean that you had not expected to see me again?'

'All things are possible.'

'But you would not help me?'

'I would help you whenever it is possible, Blunt Amir. Are we not the oldest of friends, and comrades in arms? But what would you? I have five thousand men here who are loyal to me. Most of them are veterans or the sons of veterans of our campaigns, so I believe they would be loyal to you as well. But Hemu commands many times that.'

'Are these men of yours also loyal to the memory of the Moghul?'

Prabhankar gazed at him. 'You speak treason, Blunt Bahatur.'

'I speak of what may be. Of what may have to be, old friend. Will you arrest me?'

'I, arrest you? That would be an impossibility.'

'Well, then, will you ride with me again.' He raised his finger. 'If it should become necessary.'

Prabhankar sighed. 'I have wives and a family, and I am a wealthy man. It is true that Sher Shah gave me these things, but Islam Shah, or rather Hemu, has confirmed me in their possession, because he needs honest men around him. I know he is a treacherous dog, who would have had me impaled after Kanauj. I know he is not worthy of his position. But now he has given me wealth and power. I do not wish to lose my wealth, and my wives and my sons. Do you, Blunt Bahatur?'

Richard sighed in turn. 'I can respect that determination, Prabhankar Hakim.'

He rose from the carpet to leave, but Prabhankar held up his hand.

'Tell me, should the day arise when you have quarrelled with Hemu and you have a sufficient army to march against him, and I will come to you with my five thousand men.'

Richard's heart gave a great leap of joy.

'Can I count on that, Prabhankar Hakim?'

'You have my word, Blunt Amir.'

Richard had found an ally.

But for the time being he must carry out Hemu's orders. He rode first to Kanauj, where the governor, Sandal Khan, had sent in very reduced taxes during the past year. Richard led his men up to the palace, and left them still mounted in the courtyard, while with a dozen picked soldiers he marched inside.

'Greetings. I had heard of your return, Blunt Bahatur,' Sandal said. 'Truly the sun is shining more brightly this year ...'

'I am here to arrest you,' Richard interrupted.

Sandal goggled as the soldiers seized his arms. His viziers looked at one another, one or two touching the hilts of their tulwars, but they did not truly understand what was happening. The five hundred men in the courtyard might be only the advance guard of a great army – and, in any event, five hundred men led by Blunt Bahatur were more than sufficient to destroy Sandal Khan's bodyguard.

Richard quickly led his men into the recesses of the palace; they scattered screaming concubines and terrified eunuchs as they sought out the treasure chamber. 'All of this must be packed up for removal to Delhi,' he told Ramdas. 'Sandal will accompany us, tied backwards on a mule so that all may witness his humiliation.'

Peter stared at his cousin with a mixture of admiration and dismay; he had not known this Richard Blunt before.

For the next four years Richard carried out a further series of tax-gathering campaigns. After Kanauj he dealt with Payrag and Benares, and then Bihar. Everywhere he either arrested or rewarded, according to his documented list, and at each place he recruited additional men for his army, which he used for garrisoning these various cities. In 1551, when he rode into Bihar, he now commanded several thousand men. Best of all, in Bihar he found his son Zaid, now a grown man of twenty-four, and a ming-bashi in the local army.

Zaid had heard of his coming, and awaited him with evident pleasure. While Richard embraced his son, he could hardly believe that this tall and powerful young man was the fruit of his own loins.

Tax payments were as far behind in Bihar as anywhere else, but the army was happy to see the governor returned to Delhi in disgrace.

Zaid and Peter warily sized each other up, then appeared to like what they saw.

Richard promoted Zaid to tuman-bashi, and entrusted him with half of his command; though he had no evidence as yet of the boy's ability, he could at least totally rely on his loyalty.

Two years later, when Blunt reached the delta of the Ganges, he commanded twenty thousand men.

For each previous monsoon season he had returned to Delhi, both to account to Hemu and the Sultan and to be reunited with his wife. Peter was just as anxious to regain the arms of Juana. Their first son, Thomas, had been born towards the end of 1548; a second, William, had appeared in 1550, and their daughter Isabella in 1552. He was indeed a happy man.

And gradually even Richard's apprehensions began to be lulled, perhaps because he saw little of the Sultan's court.

Bengal, however, was too far from Delhi for an easy return journey, and Richard determined to sit out the monsoon where he was, and to complete his expedition in the spring. He retired to Pataliputra to wait for the weather to change.

'How far do we go?' Peter wanted to know. This would be the first time he had been separated from Juana for a whole year.

'When the rains stop we will follow the river through Bengal and down to where it enters the sea,' Richard told him. 'This is the march that Babur once dreamed of making, but he died before achieving it. Now I will look on the sea for him.'

'You really respected that man, didn't you?' Peter asked.

The boy was now as tall and broad as his cousin Zaid. He had learned the use of the tulwar if not of the rapier, and had become as skilful a horseman as any Mongol. But he still travelled with his English longbow, and delighted in showing off his skill to the amazement of the soldiers, who were used to the short, many-sectioned bone bow and small arrows of the steppes. They pointed out disparagingly that Peter's bow was a foot soldier's weapon, as it could never be discharged accurately from the back of a galloping horse. Peter did not argue with this point.

'Yes,' Richard said. 'He was the greatest man I have ever met.'

'There are none like him today, my father,' Zaid agreed, 'Save perhaps one.'

He looked at Richard, who laughed.

'You would have me now play the usurper?'

'You have an army at your back, father, and you are a far superior soldier to Hemu.'

'Maybe. But it is not a very large army, and I am neither Muslim nor Hindu. I'm afraid my career would be very short.'

The rains in the south-east were much heavier than in other parts of the country, and for four months it was a matter of keeping as dry as possible when every corner of every house dripped with damp.

While they waited for the clouds finally to lift, Richard passed the time by improving Peter's grasp of Hindustani and Arabic, and playing chess with Zaid. It was a tremendous pleasure for him to get to know his son all over again, after such an absence. In 1543 he had left behind an enthusiastic teenager; now he possessed a serious-minded adult who was fully aware of everything that was going on throughout the kingdom.

Gradually the weather improved. Richard was making the preparations to resume his march when he was surprised to receive a messenger from Delhi. The ming-bashi, named Miran Bahatur, was a famous warrior, and commander of Hemu's personal bodyguard – and he had ridden through the worst of the weather to reach the eastern army.

'Grave news, Blunt Bahatur,' he said. 'There has been catastrophe. The Sultan is dead, and his son has been murdered.'

Richard gazed at him in consternation, unable for a moment to grasp what he had been told.

'Who did this?' Peter demanded.

'Well, as you know, Prince Firuz was but twelve years old. He was proclaimed Sultan, under the regency of his uncle Mubariz Khan. But only a month later Mubariz announced the death of his ward, and assumed the sultanate himself – as Muhammad Adil Shah Sur.'

'Then you do not know that the Prince was murdered?' Zaid interrupted.

'There can be no doubt of it,' Miran insisted.

'What part has Hemu played in this?' Richard asked.

'He favours legitimacy, Blunt Bahatur. There are many princes of the House of Sur with a better claim than this Mubariz. Thus Hemu has denounced the new Sultan as an usurper and has seized control of Delhi. Mubariz has fled to the south, but there is no doubt that there will be civil war. You are directed to return to Delhi immediately.'

Presumably, Richard thought, it was the fact that this bahatur was a creature of Hemu's that made it impossible for him to look a man straight in the eye. But in this crisis, at least, he and Hemu were on the same side. 'My army will move within the week.'

'It is you yourself that General Hemu desires at his side, Blunt Bahatur. No doubt your army will prove very useful when it arrives, but he counts your presence as worth more than an army.'

The flattery was blatant, but the man's urgency was evident – and it was a direct order from Hemu.

Zaid was suspicious. 'Do not go without your men, my father,' he warned.

'Then I would be considered in rebellion,' Richard pointed out. 'And your mother and Peter's wife would be in Hemu's hands. I do not think even Iskanda would be safe. I must go, therefore, but I will take an adequate escort – and you bring the army behind me just as quickly as you can. That way we will be obeying every order we have been given, while yet preparing ourselves against treachery.'

Because he had been a soldier all of his life, Zaid did not argue. Peter was not so easily persuaded.

'I will certainly accompany you,' he insisted. 'After all, am I not your tavachi?'

Miran Bahatur did not object; nor did he object when Richard selected ten of his best men as his escort.

Ramdas naturally also accompanied his master.

They departed the next day. The rain had all but ceased now, but the rivers were bursting their banks, and many of the tracks had been washed away. Progress was therefore slow but, surprisingly, once they had left the army and were on their way, Miran seemed less agitated, and less in a hurry as well.

'I do not trust this fellow,' Peter confided, 'any more than I liked his master.'

'Who is also our master,' Richard reminded him. But he nevertheless began to probe.

'Which of Prince Firuz's cousins does Hemu have in mind for the succession?' he asked Miran.

'That is the matter he wishes to discuss with you most urgently, Blunt Bahatur,' Miran explained. 'Perhaps Sikundar Shah would be best . . . Who can tell?'

Sikundar Shah? Richard wondered. Sikundar was not the man to submit to being dominated by a low-caste Hindu – and Hemu would know that. Definitely something was up. It was impossible to believe that Hemu could be contemplating seizing the throne for himself; undoubtedly he would be thinking of some babe-in-arms as a titular sultan. Therefore Blunt was going to be invited, or commanded, to take part in another usurpation – yet he could do nothing but hurry to Hemu's side, at least until he had ensured the safety of the women of his household.

A month after leaving the army, they were within a day's march of Kanauj. By now the weather had greatly improved, and the roads were drying out.

They pitched their tents and, as usual, Peter joined Richard for a talk before dinner, which Ramdas was busy preparing outside.

It was Richard, with his trained ears, who first picked up the clink of weapons surrounding the tent. He leapt to his feet and moved towards his sword, but before he could reach it Miran had entered the doorway with two men at his back.

'You are under arrest,' he snarled.

Peter stared at him open-mouthed.

'And you will die immediately,' Miran continued.

'What is my crime?'

Miran smiled. 'Your crime is being what you are, Blunt Bahatur. You are too successful a man. Our master has no further use for you.'

'And there *is* no civil war?' Richard remarked.

'Oh, there may be,' Miran said. 'But our master suspects you would not support him in his move to regain control of Delhi for the Hindu nation.'

'With himself as sultan?'

'No, no. General Hemu will be Rajah, not Sultan.'

'He is mad to suppose he can succeed.'

'Those are words he thought you might use. However, since you are our master's father-in-law, you will die by beheading rather than the stake.'

Richard glanced at Peter, who still seemed totally in shock by it all.

'And my cousin?'

'Oh, he will be beheaded, too,' Miran said with a smile. 'As his wife has found favour with the Rajah.'

'My wife?' Peter was now on his feet.

'How may the Rajah covet another man's wife?' Richard asked, desperately trying to think of a way out of the situation.

Miran's grin widened. 'That would be illegal, I agree. But it is possible for the Rajah to take another man's widow, if he so chooses. Outside, now . . .'

He never finished, but instead uttered a shriek and fell forward, blood gushing from his mouth.

Ramdas stood in the door, blood dripping from the strangely shaped knife which he always kept at his side.

With a curse one of Miran's men slashed at him with his sword. Ramdas attempted to parry the blow, but the tulwar blade skidded off the kukri, and struck into his neck.

Yet his sacrifice had given Richard time to reach his sword, and now he thrust it clean through Ramdas's murderer. The other soldier swung at him – but encountered Peter's blade and died a moment later.

As Richard dropped to his knees beside his faithful servant, Peter glimpsed out of the door-flap.

'Perhaps thirty men,' he muttered, 'and our own are at a disadvantage.' He reached for his bow.

'Then we are lost,' Richard said, slowly laying Ramdas' head back on the carpet, despising himself for having walked so easily into the trap.

'Ha,' Peter chuckled, stepping out of the doorway, the longbow in his hand.

The remainder of the assassination squad had dismounted and were busy on the far side of the camp, disarming Blunt's escort, who were totally bewildered. But alerted by Miran's shriek, several had turned towards the command tent, and the first of these now received a clothyard shaft in the throat, which sent him lifeless to the ground.

Before the others could recover their wits, a second man lay dead, and then a third. The rest soon took to their heels, confounded by the deadly speed and accuracy of the shooting.

Richard stood beside his cousin.

'My God, that was well done.'

Peter lowered the bow. The animation gradually drained from his face. 'What did he mean about Juana, cousin?'

'That we must find out,' Richard told him. 'At least we now know where we stand as regards Hemu.'

But Richard understood that his situation had certainly not changed for the better. Hemu, the would-be Rajah, still held Gila and Juana, and any sign that Richard meant to lead his army in revolt would mean their execution. But if Hemu should assume he was dead? If he could only reach the city ahead of Miran's failed assassination squad, then it might be possible to get the women out and escape ... but to where? Back to Goa, as penniless fugitives?

Or to Kabul? That was where he needed to go: so as to avenge himself on Hemu with Humayun's help. Supposing he could reach *there...*

They mounted as soon as they had buried Ramdas and the

other dead, and rode on as hard as they could, having sent a messenger back to Zaid to tell him what had happened.

Fortunately they were reassured in Kanauj that none of the survivors from Miran's party had yet reached the city; having failed so completely in their assassination attempt, they were obviously reluctant to reappear in front of Hemu.

That gave the Blunts a head start, and with their small escort they kept going day and night, requisitioning fresh horses whenever necessary. Neither man spoke much now. Their lazy evenings waiting for Ramdas' cuisine were things of the past.

Then, a week after leaving Kanauj, they walked their horses into Delhi itself.

The guards on the city gates made no effort to stop them, which confirmed Richard's belief that the assassination attempt had been a secret plan devolved by Hemu.

Straight away they proceeded to Gila's house. It was dark by now, and that was a blessing; although the streets were thronged, few people recognised Blunt Bahatur and his cousin. The tuk-bashi on the gate would of course make his report as to all who had entered the city, but that report would hardly reach the palace before morning.

As Richard and Peter hurried into the building, the gates of the courtyard closed behind them.

Firdat, the majordomo, was amazed, and dumbstruck.

'The Princess? The Portuguese agha?'

'They are here, sire. But . . .' The fellow looked most distressed.

Peter was already running into the house, unslinging his bow as if he expected to confront an enemy.

Together they encountered Gila.

'Richard? Oh, Richard!' She threw herself into his arms.

He hugged her and kissed her, then held her away from himself.

She wore a white sari of mourning.

'Where is Juana?'

His cousin had already vanished into the inner apartments.

'Hemu sent for her . . .' Gila faltered.

Suddenly Peter re-emerged, carrying his wife in his arms. Juana had some dark bruises on her face, and when Peter set her on her feet she appeared unsteady.

'She has been raped,' Peter said in bitter shock.

'Tell me what happened,' Richard urged her.

Juana took a long breath.

'That man, the regent, he sent for me, and told me that you both were dead, killed by rebels in the east. He told me he would take me into his harem, but first he must see ... what I had to offer. I fought him, Cousin Richard. I fought him and his eunuchs, who held me down to him ...'

'But you escaped?'

'When finally he was spent, they released me and I attacked him. I scratched his face. He had me whipped, and then he sent me home. He said he would call for me again when I had learned some sense.'

'He then sent for me,' Gila broke in.

'Were you also raped?' Richard asked in horror.

Gila smiled. 'Not even Hemu would rape his own mother-in-law. No, he told me to beat some sense into Juana; that if I made the girl more agreeable to him, he would allow me to remain in this house and would raise my sons to high command. I could do nothing but ask for time. Time for what? I did not know, until now.'

'I will kill him,' Peter swore.

'Indeed,' Richard agreed, 'but not right this moment. That would be to commit suicide. We must leave immediately, and seek aid in our revenge.'

'From Persia?' Gila cried.

Richard shook his head. 'From Kabul. I have already sent Zaid there.'

Her face had fallen. Now it fell further.

'And Iskanda?'

Richard sighed. 'We can do nothing about her, at the moment. We can only pray that not even Hemu would execute the mother of his son.'

'We are running away,' Peter said bitterly. 'I had never thought to hear you contemplate such a thing, cousin.'

'We are running to fight another day. This Hemu is not capable of holding the throne of Delhi. Hemu will fall, and we will bring him down.'

* * *

They left within the hour: Richard and Gila, Peter, Juana and their three children, their nurses and Firdat. It was done stealthily, and none of the other servants were informed.

They walked their horses through the North Gate, and then urged them to the gallop, heading for the military training camp where Mahmud was assigned.

Here, with little trouble, Richard was able to summon the young tavachi to his side, and they continued on their way, north-west now – into the Punjab and the land of Sikundar Shah.

For there was no other way to reach Kabul.

Richard and Sikundar had fought together often enough in years past, but Richard knew the Afghan to be an honest if mercurial man.

For his part, Sikundar regarded somewhat sceptically the man now universally known as Hemu's tax-gatherer.

'Have you come to pierce me with a stake, Blunt Bahatur?' he asked. 'And without an army?'

'I have abandoned Hemu,' Richard told him. 'Or, rather, he has abandoned me.'

Sikundar raised his eyebrows.

'He would reverse history, and call himself Rajah.'

'And you wish to defend the House of Sur?' Sikundar looked even more surprised. 'Have you come to offer me a throne?'

'I have come to warn you to look to yourself, Sikundar Shah. I know that Hemu intends to march on you as soon as he has mobilised his army and disposed of Mubariz Khan.'

Sikundar stroked his beard pensively.

'Have you not already heard this from your spies?'

'I have heard so,' Sikundar agreed. 'But I have already asked you: have you come here to fight for me, Blunt Bahatur?'

'I do not believe you can defeat Hemu by yourself, Sikundar Shah. No, I am on my way to Kabul.'

'You would bring the Moghuls down upon me? That I cannot permit.'

'Listen to me, Sikundar. Our enemy is Hemu more than Humayun. Once Hemu falls, Humayun may indeed again assume the throne of Delhi, but if you aid him, he will surely confirm you as ruler of the Punjab. Can you ask for more?'

Once again Sikundar's fingers tugged at his beard.

'Should I not aspire to the Kingdom of Delhi for myself?'

'Do you?'

Sikundar smiled. 'No, as you well know, it is too much for one man to grasp.' He brooded for a few moments. 'This man at least. I am an Afghan, and here in these mountains are my people. I have always considered my uncle to be over-ambitious. I have no wish to rule an alien nation.'

'Yet even here your rule is precarious, surrounded by hostile powers. You have the Moghuls to the north, the Sikhs to the east, the Rajputs to the south-west, and Hemu to the south-east. Even those of your family that remain are not to be trusted. Do you suppose Mubariz Khan would not seek to destroy you, should he regain power? How can you hope to maintain yourself indefinitely against so much hostility? Would it not be better to ally yourself with the one man you can trust?'

Not for the first time in his life, Richard was gambling on a series of half-truths, playing on men's avarice and their desire to survive and to hold what they had.

It would be so easy for Sikundar to send his severed head back to Hemu as a peace offering.

Sikundar gazed at him for several seconds, then he nodded. 'Go to the Moghul.' He looked past Richard at the women. 'Your wife and daughter and your son will remain here until you return with Humayun's words.' He raised his finger as Richard was about to protest. 'They will come to no harm, I swear by the Prophet.' He smiled. 'Unless you betray me.'

Peter was aghast.

'And suppose we are not welcomed by this Humayun?' he demanded.

'Then we must return here and fight for Sikundar.'

'Tell me, cousin,' Peter remarked, 'is all of life in the East lived at this uncertain level?'

'All life everywhere is lived thus when one would rub shoulders with kings and princes,' Richard told him. 'Can you honestly pretend our own King Harry does not whip off heads at a moment's displeasure? And, remember, you wished to come.'

Peter glared at him, and then grinned. 'Why, so I did, and up to a month ago I thought to have prospered.'

Then it was into the Khyber, hurrying to reach Kabul before the first snows.

They travelled under the protection of Sikundar Shah as far as the Moghul border, but he thought it best for them to discard their tarnished finery and dress themselves as Pathans, to avoid any trouble with the hill tribesmen over whom even Sikundar held only a shadowy authority.

In this they were fortunate, but there were many delays, and the snow began earlier than usual. Thus it was mid-December before they stood before the Moghul.

'Blunt Bahatur!' Humayun seemed pleased to see Richard. He himself had aged little; indeed his health had obviously improved, for he had grown stout. Richard remembered that he was over forty.

There was no sign of Humayun's brothers, but standing beside him was a very obvious son. For a moment Richard wondered if this was the boy given the wonderful name of Akbar, and then realised it could not be. Akbar had only just been born when he was last in Kabul but seven years before. This boy looked about fifteen.

'This is my son,' Humayun acknowledged, seeing Richard's interest. 'His name is Mirza Mohammed.'

Richard understood: this boy was the son of a mere concubine.

'You are blessed,' he said. 'And the Lord Kamran?'

Humayun scowled. 'Do not speak to me of that scoundrel. He rebelled against me and sought to seize my throne. Now he is a fugitive somewhere in the mountains. If he returns, I will have his head. But you, Blunt Bahatur, first I hear that you are dead, then I learn that you have returned without an army, then I hear that you are Islam Shah's tax-gatherer ... and now you stand before me like a Pathan bandit. How do you explain all these things?'

Richard told him all that he had already told Sikundar, only presenting a different side of the coin.

'I have heard that Hemu has a very powerful army,' the Moghul said at last. 'And now he has cannon as well, and will be backed by the Rajputs?'

'The Rajputs would regard him as an usurper. But they might well support him against you, because they fear you more than him.'

'Well, then, what have you to offer me? You have no army.'

'To you I bring three things of greater value, sire. The first is my knowledge of Hemu. He is a frightened man, unable fully to comprehend what he has had the temerity to grasp. He is not the man to stand against determined attack, any more than was Mahmud Lodi.'

'A man's courage is a nebulous quality, Blunt Bahatur. When faced with catastrophe, he may well fight like a cornered rat. What are the other things you bring to me?'

'They are more tangible, certainly. Firstly, the offer of an alliance with Sikundar Sher.'

'That bandit? Do his Pathans not raid far into my country, looting and burning?'

'It is the Pathan way of life, sire. That ferocity but needs directing. Sikundar is willing to direct it against his true enemy, and yours: Hemu.'

'And what does he ask in return?'

'The viceroyalty of the Punjab, which he already possesses. There will be no one better. Only Sikundar can control those wild people.'

Humayun snorted. 'And the third?'

'The most important of all. I bring you the governor of Agra and his army.'

Humayun frowned. 'Prabhankar?'

Clearly he was well informed as to what was going on inside the Kingdom of Delhi.

'He is faithful to me, not to Hemu. Give me time to send him a messenger. Then, once you have invaded the sultanate, and Hemu is committed to repulsing you, Prabhankar will raise the standard of revolt in his rear.'

'By Allah, a fanciful plan.'

'One which would have appealed to your father.'

'Why, yes, I think you are right. But to embark on war ...' Humayun got up and strode to the window to look out at the snow which came clouding down.

How Babur must be turning in his grave, Richard thought.

'To regain Delhi, sire. Is that not the entire purpose of your life?'

For several minutes Humayun did not answer. Then he asked casually, 'Is that city still as beautiful as I left it?'

'It is more beautiful, sire.'

'The palace?'

'There is a new palace.'

'And what of my library? Is it burned, destroyed, scattered to the winds?'

'Your library still exists intact. It is the envy of all Hindustan.'

Humayun turned. 'It survives?'

'Exactly as you left it.'

'By Allah, now there is a wonderful thing. Send your messenger to Agra, Blunt Bahatur, and prepare yourself to ride at my side. We will march on Delhi in the spring.'

Richard's plan now worked to perfection. Before the winter was over, Humayun and Sikundar has signed a treaty to recover the Kingdom of Delhi. By then, too, Richard had received an answer from Prabhankar. In April the Moghul army once more set out for the south; Mirza was left in command in Kabul, exactly as Babur had left Humayun a quarter of a century before; Kamran had not returned to make peace with his brother, and Humayun preferred to keep Askari and Hindal at his side. In Peshawar they were joined by Sikundar and his Pathans; Richard and Peter were reunited with their wives.

The only sadness now was the absence of any word from Zaid. But that only increased the desire for vengeance.

Mahmud now went to war, as his father's tavachi.

The army moved south, following that so well remembered road. Word came that Hemu was concentrating against them, and had even obtained the aid of a contingent of Rajput cavalry.

'Now all depends on Prabhankar,' Humayun muttered.

Richard could only pray that the Hindu had not changed his mind.

A week later there was a great disorder in Hemu's camp. Then a deserter informed the Moghul that the city of Agra had declared for him.

Hastily, Hemu abandoned his camp and marched south, and the Moghuls and Pathans followed. Yet Hemu kept the field for two whole years without being brought to battle – before he fled to the Rajputs for shelter.

'I wanted his head,' Richard said.

'I doubt he will survive long,' Humayun reassured him.

Next day he entered Delhi to the cheers of the crowd.

There was the usual ceremonial destruction of Hemu's abandoned harem. Richard was only interested in regaining Iskanda and her son. Her tearful but joyful reunion with her family atoned in a little way for the death of Zaid, who was now known to have been caught and slain by Hemu's agents.

The Moghul victory seemed complete. The Rajputs were in disarray, and the sultanate had suffered enough of Hemu and his tax-gatherers. Even those who remembered Richard as the chief of these, also remembered that he had dealt justly with them. While to Humayun he appeared the architect of a victory of which he had dreamed for ten years – and been too indolent to make happen. Richard was immediately sent on another campaign throughout the country, to re-imprint the Moghul rule. This time he actually did reach the Bay of Bengal.

Prabhankar was named Bahatur and restored to the governorship of Agra.

Sikundar was the one disappointment, declaring the independence of the Punjab almost the moment Delhi had been recaptured; he claimed this was part of the bargain he had struck with the Moghul. Humayun had Blunt recalled to mobilise his army and march against him. The Pathans were defeated, and Sikundar fled into the mountains of Afghanistan.

'I do not understand him,' Richard confessed. 'The time for revolt would have been when you faced Hemu.'

'He has become a Pathan, and all Pathans are mad,' Humayun said, as usual jovial now the victory was complete. 'But we shall bring them to heel.'

He announced that his son Akbar would be the new hakim of the Punjab, under the tutelage of Bairam Kham, Humayun's favourite tuman-bashi, who although an Afghan himself, had no love for the Sur family.

'Be sure you make them into worthy subjects of the Kingdom of Delhi,' Humayun said, looking at Bairam rather than the boy, who was only thirteen.

Both bowed, but it was Akbar who replied.

'It shall be done, my father.'

This was the first time that Richard had met the boy; he had hitherto been in the care of his Persian mother. But now he was being thrust into a man's role at a very tender age – although Bairam would be the actual hakim.

Richard wished he could feel happy about that – he did not altogether trust Bairam, perhaps because he had come to distrust all Afghans – but he was impressed with the quiet calm and certainty of one so young. There was a great deal of promise there for the distant future, although he was disturbed to discover that the young Prince could neither read nor write; this seemed incredible for a son of Humayun, whose greatest pleasure was the written word.

But the present was happy enough. As Gila had wanted, they seemed to have reached a quiet old age. They had lost a son, but they had regained their daughter, and their grandson – a handsome little fellow called Iskander. Hemu had been hoping for a reincarnation of Alexander the Great.

And they had the company of Peter and his young family. The youth had well proved himself, although, thanks to Hemu's tactics, he had not yet fought in a battle.

'But I am content that it should be so,' he assured Richard.

'And, having adventured, will you now return to England, and your mother, to show them your wife and children?'

'It is on my mind,' Peter admitted. 'But I would rather stay in this fabulous land a while longer. Besides, my children are far too young to contemplate such a journey.'

A while longer! The Moghul had only been back in possession of the Sultanate little more than a year when, engaged in indexing his beloved library, he fell from the top of a ladder and cracked his skull.

10
AKBAR

Richard was summoned immediately, but by the time he arrived Humayun was already dead. The whole of Agra had been shaken by a slight earth tremor, but little damage was done save inside the royal palace. Years later it would be learned that on this same day had occurred the greatest earthquake known to history in the province of Shensi in China, where the earth had convulsed for two hours and eight hundred and thirty thousand people had been killed.

Only one had died in Agra, so many thousands of miles away. But that one was the great Moghul.

Richard eyed the body in consternation. Humayan was only forty-seven years old – exactly the same age as Babur when he had died. Was that some terminal point for these brilliant people?

The situation now was far more serious than at Babur's death. Then there had been two adults ready to assume the throne; no matter that they had quarrelled so angrily later, the transition of power had occurred with no dissenting voices.

But Humayun's heir was a boy of fourteen – and he was in the power of Bairam Khan. Bairam had so far proved a loyal supporter of the Moghuls ... he now held the kingdom in the palm of his hand.

Meanwhile Hemu and the Rajputs brooded to the south-west; they would learn of the new situation soon enough.

'What will we do?' Prabhankar asked.

'We have only one course: we must send to Lahore for Prince Akbar,' Richard decided.

Prabankhar gazed at him. 'I would have said there is an alternative,' he remarked. 'It would be to call Prince Mirza from

Kabul. Better a grown man, than turn to a fourteen-year-old-boy?'

Peter Blunt nodded in agreement.

'I cannot agree to that,' Richard said, 'for I do not believe it would work. It would almost certainly lead to civil war among the Moghuls. Akbar is the rightful heir. No one imagined he would need to rule so soon but, with his father dead, they will now expect him to do so. Some indeed may support Mirza, but it would never be all of them. No, as I have said, there is but one course open to us. We must send for Prince Akbar just as quickly as we can. Once he is here ... well, it is up to us to influence him for our own good – and his, too. Meanwhile we must prepare to defend ourselves against Hemu when he marches upon Delhi, because we can be certain that he will do so the moment he learns of Humayun's death.'

'What are your orders then, Blunt Amir?' Prabhankar asked.

'Peter, you must ride with all despatch for Lahore, inform Prince Akbar of the death of his father, and request his presence in Delhi as rapidly as possible. Take this. It is the Koh-i-noor diamond. I removed it from round Humayun's neck. Give it to Akbar as a token of our loyalty, and proof of his father's death. I shall keep that death a secret as long as possible. When I can no longer do so, I shall tell the people that Akbar is already on his way, and I shall mobilise the army against any threat from the Rajputs. Prabhankar, you must do the same in Agra. I need hardly remind you of the fate that awaits us should Hemu regain power in this land. So, haste, for God's sake. Haste.'

'I will go with you,' Juana declared.

'I am to ride day and night,' Peter warned her.

'Then I will ride day and night at your side. As will the children, too.'

'Now I know you are mad,' Gila cried. 'Take three little ones on such a journey.'

'They must come with us,' Juana insisted.

Peter chewed his lip in indecision. However much he adored her, he well knew his wife to be a woman who constantly calculated and deliberated the best course of action for herself – and, he assumed, for himself and their children.

He wished he could decide what real motive she had now, for on the surface it did seem a ridiculous plan.

'Tell me why you wish to do this. Are you afraid?'

She gazed at him for some seconds.

'Yes,' she said at last. 'I am afraid.' She grasped his arm. 'Do you not see, my dear love? Can your cousin really have the power to defend this city against Hemu and his entire army?'

'Then should he and his family not flee with us?'

'Of course they should. But they will not. Your cousin is obsessed with his sense of duty.'

Peter knew she was right, yet he felt he must try, so he returned to Richard in the palace.

'Still here?' the older man demanded. 'I assumed you had already left.'

Peter told him of Juana's forebodings.

'She may be right about my safety,' Richard agreed. 'She is certainly right about my duty. Ride, Peter, ride. The only way you can help me is to bring Akbar to Delhi before Hemu appears before me.'

Peter departed that evening with an escort of ten men, but also with Juana and two of her women, and the three infants, each with a nurse.

By taking the most direct route, skirting close to the lands of the Sikhs, the journey from Delhi to Lahore would be just on three hundred miles, and he intended to accomplish it in no more than a week.

In the beginning the women thought it was a great adventure. The month was January, the monsoon was behind them, and in the valleys the air was crisp and cool and dry. But they were already exhausted after only two days, and by then they were approaching the hill country; and in front of them lay snow and icy winds sweeping out of the Hindu Kush.

They changed horses at every relay station, Peter using both his official rank as Blunt Amir's tavachi and the liberal amount of coin with which Richard had supplied him. He told no one of Humayun's death; the news would be spread soon enough by rumour, by which time hopefully Akbar would be nearly back in the city.

Akbar! As Richard had told him, rubbing shoulders with the great is always a hazardous business. Now he was sent to summon a sultan: a fourteen-year-old boy of whom he knew nothing. What ambitions, what fears, what lusts and what hatreds lay already buried in that still unformed mind, waiting to spill forth one day and set mankind by the ears? More important, what strengths and what weaknesses?

Peter had taken a dislike to Bairam Khan from the moment of their first meeting, and Bairam had now had control of the young sultan's mind for two years.

It was Bairam himself who received him when, six days after leaving Delhi, he rode into Lahore.

Peter and three members of his escort were by then proceeding alone. The women had simply been unable to keep up as the road deteriorated, and the weather too. They had wailed that he was killing them with the hardship of it.

Juana alone had made no comment, aware that it was her insistence which had created this situation. But as he had looked on her exhausted face, he realised he was indeed killing her – and perhaps the children, who cried constantly.

'This was madness,' he said. 'You should be back in Delhi in warmth and comfort.'

'I wish to be in Lahore and safe,' she said fiercely.

'Well, you are safe now – only a few days from Lahore. But I must press on. You will join me as soon as you can.'

She had accepted that.

'So,' Bairam Khan remarked slyly, 'Blunt Amir has remained behind in Delhi.'

'To defend the Sultanate against Hemu and the Rajputs.'

'Of course,' Bairam said smoothly.

Peter began to feel annoyed.

'I have ridden like the wind to come to you, sire. Will you not at the least acquaint the Sultan with his father's death?' He held out the 'Mountain of Light'.

'I will do so, young Blunt.' Bairam took the diamond.

Peter had to kick his heels for the next few hours, worrying about Juana and the children, worrying about his cousins, ever worrying ... Then a majordomo escorted him into a chamber where the boy Akbar sat on a carpet amidst richly stitched cushions. He had been playing at chess, and the pieces lay scattered beside him. The Koh-i-noor had been carelessly thrown amongst them.

Even for fourteen, he appeared as somewhat small, with tight features. And if his tunic was richly decorated, his feet were bare. There was a huge brazier close by which gave off a tremendous heat.

He did not appear overly distressed by what he had just learned; but, then, he had spent very little of his life in his father's company.

Peter bowed low.

'Tell me how my father died,' Akbar commanded, his voice high and clear.

Peter glanced at Bairam. Had he not done so?

'There was an earth tremor and he fell from some steps in his library, and struck his head, my lord.'

'Can a prince die thus?'

Peter felt a start of alarm. Just what had Bairam been telling the new Sultan?

'Unhappily, your father did. Did you not feel the tremor here in Lahore?'

Akbar gazed at him. For all his youth, his eyes were penetrating and cold.

'There was a tremor,' he conceded at last, and then fell silent for a few minutes before remarking, 'And now Blunt Bahatur wishes me in Delhi.'

'He wishes you to take your rightful place, sire, to show the world that Delhi still has a Sultan.'

'You mean he would obtain possession of the Sultan's person,' Bairam interjected.

Peter's head jerked back. Had that been in Richard's mind? His cousin was always a devious fellow ...

'Have you no answer, young Blunt?' Akbar inquired.

'I ... my cousin seeks only your greatness, my lord. If I did not believe this, would I have come through the snow to you, risking my wife and family?'

'They are here?' asked Akbar in surprise.

'I left them some miles away in my haste to bring you these

important tidings. They will be here within the week.'

Akbar glanced at Bairam.

'I still say it could be a trap to gain possession of your person, sire,' he insisted.

'And you could be right,' Akbar acknowledged. 'But, if so, it is a trap of which this man is ignorant. I shall come to Delhi, young Blunt, as your cousin desires, to take hold of my inheritance. But I shall come at the head of an army. Meanwhile, you will remain here at my side, to help me raise this army. And your family will remain in Lahore until I am installed as Badshah.'

Peter could only reflect that this was not the first time Juana had spent a season as a hostage. But it was his business to encourage the Sultan to make haste.

The messenger was covered in sweat.

'It is a huge army, Blunt Amir: a hundred thousand men. All the Rajput strength, and Hemu rides at their head. He now claims all Delhi for the Hindus; and he calls himself the Rajah Bikramajit. My master, Prabhankar Amir, wishes to know your intentions – and quickly.'

Richard glanced at Mahmud, who was the only other man present.

'You need rest,' he told Prabhankar's tavachi. 'My reply will be ready for you tomorrow.'

The young officer bowed, and left the room.

'A hundred thousand men,' Mahmud muttered. 'But you have defeated larger armies than that, eh, Father?'

Richard pulled his nose. I have not, he thought. But Babur has. He was suddenly assailed by uncertainty. Though he had had no doubt that Hemu would seek to seize the throne the moment he learned of Humayun's death, he had still not expected the Hindus to mobilise so very quickly.

The only word he had received from Lahore was that Peter had reached there safely, and that the Sultan Akbar would come to Delhi as soon as certain preparations had been made.

What preparations? He needed Akbar here, now.

'What answer must I give to my master, Blunt Bahatur?' asked the tavachi the next morning.

Richard had made his decision – the only possible one.

'Tell your master it is our business to hold our own main cities until the Sultan arrives from the Punjab. Tell Prabhankar Hakim that Agra is his responsibility, and that he must defend it to the end. Remind him that the Rajputs are horsemen, and that horses cannot take walled cities. Tell him that if he can hold Agra, and I hold Delhi, then the usurper is doomed to failure.'

The messenger bowed, and left.

'You mean to withstand a siege, Father?' Mahmud was frowning.

'I have no choice, boy. I do not have sufficient men – and I am not sure enough of the loyalty of those I do have, to take the field.'

He mustered twenty thousand men. Of these, some four thousand were veterans of his old pike division, and these he felt he could trust. Then there were some three thousand Muslim cavalry. These he harangued with the promise of the coming of Akbar; then he dismounted them and sent them, too, to the walls.

The rest were recruits whom Humayun had intended him train into soldiers. They were enthusiastic but excitable; most were Hindus, and he did not really know whether they would support a fourteen-year-old sultan as opposed to a rajah who was of their own blood and religion.

'I wish you had gone with Peter,' he confessed to Gila. 'It is not too late for you to leave now.'

'Should I not stay with my husband to the end? If it is our Kismet to have reached the end.'

How long ago was it that he had carried her into that cubicle at Agra?

'Can Hemu really defeat us, Father?' Iskanda asked.

'Why, yes, he can. But we shall make it difficult for him.'

'If he defeats you, Father, I shall kill myself,' she said.

She was a grown woman now, twenty-eight years old, and if she had inherited much of her mother's beauty, she had also inherited her father's build, and was tall for a female.

'And your boy?'

Little Iskander was eight.

'Him too.'

'He is Hemu's son, and you are his mother. He will preserve

your life. Iskanda, it is a foolish thing to die unnecessarily.'
'There are worse things than death, my father,' she said.

A week later a Rajput patrol was reported south of the city. By then Richard was as ready as he ever could be to stand a siege. All livestock and fodder from the surrounding countryside had been gathered within the walls; as it was spring, the wheatfields lay fallow. Every man had been armed and given a task; so far they seemed willing and confident.

But Richard intended to conduct an aggressive defence, if possible, and now he took a regiment of cavalry out through the gates. The Rajputs were surprised and driven off, with the loss of several men.

Morale within the walls grew.

Richard hastily despatched yet another messenger to Lahore, informing the Sultan that a siege was about to commence, and imploring him to make haste.

But in fact no further Rajputs were seen near Delhi for the next two weeks. Richard then sent out patrols himself – who returned with the news that Hemu was besieging Agra.

'Well, that is good news,' Richard said. 'Every day that Prabhankar holds out is another day saved for Akbar. If he can hold out until the monsoon, then are we saved for sure.'

But only three days later his scouts told him that Agra had surrendered.

'After only a fortnight?' Richard was aghast. 'Was the city carried by storm?'

'No, Blunt Bahatur. The Rajah Bikramajit himself demanded its surrender and, after some discussion, Prabhankar Hakim conceded.'

'He has betrayed us,' Mahmud said.

There seemed no other explanation. And if Prabhankar had abandoned him ...

There was no way he could keep this news from penetrating the city. People gathered in the market place.

'There is yet time for you to flee,' Richard told Gila.

'I have nowhere to go,' she reminded him.

He looked then at Iskanda, but she was obviously determined to stay with her mother.

* * *

A week later the Rajput forces began to gather outside the walls of Delhi. As strong detachments were sent round to the north side of the city as well, any thought of flight was now out of the question. Or any prospect of sending further messengers to Lahore.

Perhaps even my cousin Peter has abandoned me, Richard thought bitterly.

He was standing on the wall above the main gate when the sound of karrouns announced at last the arrival of Hemu.

The Hindu rode on an elephant, alone in the howdah. Other elephants followed behind, but Hemu's was surrounded by glittering cavalrymen.

In front of him there walked a mule. Mounted on the mule, facing backwards, was the naked figure of Prabhankar. His ankles were tied beneath the animal's belly, so tightly that he could not move, and his hands were bound behind his back. His head drooped as if from exhaustion, and there were red weals on his shoulders where he had been whipped.

If, as seemed certain, he had betrayed Agra, he in turn had been betrayed by Hemu.

He should have known better, Richard thought grimly.

The procession stopped and a herald advanced, beating his nakara, or kettledrum, as he did so.

'Hear me!' he shouted up at the walls. 'These are the words of His Highness the Rajah Bikramajit, ruler of the Kingdom of Delhi. Open your gates and receive your master.'

Richard looked down on him. 'Tell your master to open the gates himself,' he said. 'If he can.'

His men, to either side, roared their approval, and the shout was taken up right round the city.

The herald stood his ground.

'My master would warn you of the fate which awaits those who oppose him.'

'Did not Prabhankar Hakim surrender Agra?' Richard demanded. 'Yet I see him there, bound as if for execution.'

'He is bound for execution as being a lifelong enemy of His Highness the Rajah Bikramajit,' the herald announced.

'Tell your master that I am an older enemy of his than

Prabhankar Hakim,' Richard said. 'To execute me, he must first storm these walls.'

The herald turned and rode back to the Rajput ranks.

Richard turned to Mahmud, standing at his side.

'Prepare to receive the assault,' he said.

But, first, Prabhankar had to die, in full view of the defenders.

It was to be a Turkish-style impalement. The stake was some fifteen feet long, slender at one end, thick at the other, so that it would stand upright more easily.

Foot soldiers dug a pit immediately before the main gate. Then Prabhankar was taken from his mule, and the thin end of the stake forced into him. He was stoical up till the entry, but could not prevent himself from shrieking his pain as he died. Then the stake, with his supported body on it, the end protruding through his breast, was set upright and the hole filled in, so that the ghastly monument would remain on view throughout the siege.

Richard glanced at Mahmud. The impalement of criminals was an everyday occurrence in Delhi, but it had never assumed such a personal inference before. Now neither of them could doubt their fate, were they captured alive.

'We shall conquer or die, father,' the boy said fiercely.

The first cannon of the besieging army exploded.

How slowly the army assembled. Bairam Khan seemed determined to leave nothing to chance, and Akbar was content to leave the ordering of military matters to his advisers.

They had a great deal to consider, for Peter soon discovered that he was not the only one to distrust Bairam. Both Akbar's Persian mother, Hamida Banu Baygam, and his erstwhile nurse, Maham Anaga, in whose company the young Sultan chose to spend a great deal of time, clearly regarded the Vizier with some suspicion. Peter felt these ladies had to be considered potential allies for himself, but as they seldom appeared in public, for the moment he could not determine how to make their common ground known.

When away from his womenfolk, Akbar himself would spend time talking with young Blunt about that outside world from which he had been so largely excluded by his father's neglect.

The Sultan showed as lively a curiosity as both Babur and Humayun had revealed, but, to Peter's astonishment, he discovered that the boy could neither read nor write.

Peter regarded him as a very uncertain entity. Having been separated from his father for so much of his brief life, Humuyan's neglect of him was in the starkest contrast to the interest and love shown by Babur for his first legitimate son. Akbar had been brought up entirely by women, save in political and military matters where Bairam had been his tutor. The Afghan had brought to his task the suspicious and limited political vision of the true mountain-dweller. Akbar seemed to accept his preceptor's mastery in everything to do with government, yet every so often his own determination and his own decisions crept through. But was this his own character asserting itself, or was it the urging of his mother and nurse, behind the scenes?

As to who was actually going to rule the Sultanate of Delhi, that was the biggest imponderable of all. Of one thing Peter was certain; Richard would have to be rid of Bairam just as quickly as possible.

But for the time being Bairam was needed to lead the army to the succour of Delhi.

Supposing there was ever going to be an army. The Pathans themselves were not the most disciplined of troops. Bairam therefore sent messengers to Kabul, requesting aid from Prince Mirza; but Mirza replied that he was threatened from the north and could spare none.

'Your brother is playing a double game,' Bairam growled. 'He wishes you to stand or fall by your own endeavours, my lord. If you stand, he will no doubt call himself faithful. If you fall, he will seek to take your place.'

'Well, I cannot fight both my brother and Hemu,' Akbar pointed out. 'And I have no wish to fight my brother, in any event. Let us move with what men we have.'

'They are not sufficient, sire,' Bairam insisted. 'In these circumstances, it would be best for you to send to Delhi and command Blunt Bahatur to abandon the city and join us here with all the men he can muster. Whoever heard of Moghuls defending a walled city? Moghuls fight in the open – and it is in the open that we will defeat Hemu.'

Akbar looked at Peter Blunt, who was often invited to attend these councils of war.

'With respect, Bairam Khan,' Peter said, 'my cousin commands few Mongols. He has no more than three thousand cavalry; the rest are foot soldiers. He has no choice but to fight the Rajput cavalry from behind stone walls.'

'But yet he would be a valuable force if united with my Pathans,' Bairam argued.

'I agree,' Akbar said gravely. 'I will send a messenger instructing Blunt Bahatur to abandon the city and join me here.'

Peter wanted to protest. He had the feeling that if the boy Sultan once pulled out of Delhi he would never be anything more than a Pathan chieftain. But it was Richard himself who must convince him that the Sultanate was worth fighting for.

And, in his heart, he wanted Richard and Gila here in the safety of Lahore.

The messengers returned within a week, to say that they had encountered Rajput patrols far to the north of Delhi; the city was invested. And Agra had fallen.

'We must march, now,' Peter implored them.

Akbar looked to Bairam.

'We have not the men as yet, my lord,' Bairam insisted. 'Blunt Bahatur will hold the city. If he can do so until the monsoon, Hemu will have to raise the siege. By the end of the year our forces will have grown to a size sufficient to guarantee us victory.'

Akbar gazed at him, and then turned back to Peter.

'We must put our trust in Blunt Bahatur.'

'Then let me go to him,' Peter begged. 'I will tell him the situation – tell him what we want of him.'

'You would never reach him,' Bairam pointed out.

'And that would surely be a waste,' Akbar said. 'Besides, Blunt Bahatur is a veteran soldier. He will realise what we want of him.'

The next month seemed the longest of Peter's life. He spent hours staring to the south, looking for the rainclouds to gather, or for a messenger. The children came to know their father as a grim and angry man, so unlike what they had known before. Even Juana was afraid to interfere with his thoughts.

Akbar had Peter attend him every day. The youthful Sultan had been more distressed by his father's premature death than he had allowed anyone to know. As soon as his grief had dwindled, his nature, naturally sensitive and curious and controlled by a deep intelligence, had begun to consider not only his present situation but what he would inherit when he had dealt with Hemu, supposing he could.

He was keenly aware of his neglected upbringing, when he compared himself with the intellectual brilliance of his father and grandfather. He understood that it was now too late to catch up as regard to literacy, but he still wanted to learn, and during this time of waiting he set aside several hours a day for long discussions, and not only with his Muslim favourites, chiefly the two brothers Shekh Feizi and Abul Fazl who debated matters of Muslim law, and with Peter Blunt to compare these with the European systems, but also with certain Hindus and Parsees, Jains and Buddhists, seeking to understand why they were all so different.

'We Muslims do not eat pork because anyone can see that a pig is unclean,' he pointed out. 'Yet a cow is a relatively clean animal.'

'The Hindus believe that to eat the meat of a cow will lose them caste,' Abul Fazl explained.

'How so?'

Abul Fazl had no answer to that.

Slowly storm clouds gathered to the south. But they were not quite yet blanketing the sky when a messenger and his horse staggered into Lahore.

The man had been wounded in several places, his clothes were in rags and he was half starved, but Peter recognised him immediately as Abdul Nissar, one of his cousins' tavachis.

Nissar was fed and given water, and then taken before the Sultan.

'Tell me of Blunt Bahatur,' Akbar commanded.

'Blunt Bahatur is dead, Majesty.'

The room was silent as the viziers looked around at each

other, and Akbar stared at Peter, watched the knuckles whitening around his clenched fist.

'Tell me of his death,' Akbar said at last.

Nissar drew a long breath. 'Know then, Majesty,' he began, 'that Rajah Bikramajit and the Rajputs first besieged Agra and took it by treachery. Prabhankar Hakim was most savagely executed before the walls of Delhi. Then the Rajput army invested Delhi itself. There were more than a hundred thousand of them, Majesty, with elephants and cannon.'

'Had Blunt Bahatur no cannon?' Akbar inquired.

'Blunt Bahatur had cannon, but not enough. Nonetheless we fired our cannon, and held our walls, and repaired the breaches where they were made, and repulsed the Rajput assaults. And every day Blunt Bahatur would look to the north.'

It was as near to a reproach as he dared utter.

'Tell me how the bahatur died,' Akbar said again.

'Food ran short, Majesty, and the Rajputs dammed off the water. We would have fought on, but there was no more powder for our cannon. Many men were killed, and the rest were faint-hearted. The Hindus in our army believed they could make their peace with the Rajah. So they presented an ultimatum to Blunt Bahatur, telling him that they would fight no longer, and that he must surrender the city.'

'My cousin surrendered?' Peter was aghast.

'Not so, young Blunt. When he realised that all was lost, Blunt Bahatur gathered up his Muslims, opened the gate, and made a sortie. He fell upon the Rajputs with such ferocity he all but put them to flight. But there were too many of them even for Blunt Bahatur and his men. They were cut to pieces.'

'He died? You are sure of this?'

The thought of Richard alive in the hands of Hemu was unbearable.

'I saw him fall, young Blunt.'

'But *you* did not fall,' Akbar remarked. 'Tell me of this.'

Nissar swallowed. 'I wished to accompany Blunt Bahatur into his last battle, Majesty, but he refused me permission, and also his son Mahmud. We two were ordered to remain on the walls. If by some miracle he survived and cut his way through the Rajputs, we were to hurry to his house and attempt to rescue Blunt Agha and Iskanda Agha. If he fell, we were again to go to his house and await the aghas' bidding. This we did – after we knew Blunt Bahatur to be dead.'

'What did the aghas determine?'

'The Iskanda Agha killed herself, and also her son.'

'And Blunt Agha?'

'I do not know, Majesty. She commanded Mahmud and myself to escape from the city if we could, and to come to Lahore to tell you what had happened.'

'You mean she may have remained there to face Hemu?' Peter asked.

'I do not know, sir. I only know that she was still there when we left.'

'Blunt Mahmud abandoned his mother?' Akbar pondered.

'In the beginning, yes. We made our escape from the city, but were pursued by some Rajputs. We had not ridden far when Blunt Mahmud reined his horse. 'I have just played the coward,' he told me. 'You must take the news to the Badshah.' And, with that, he turned and rode into the ranks of the Rajputs, swinging his sword.' His voice broke, and he seemed to sob. 'I should have done the same, Majesty ... but there was no one else to bring you the news.'

'You obeyed your orders,' Akbar said. 'That is always noble and courageous. You will be rewarded. Now rest.'

Nissar stumbled from the room.

'My family is destroyed,' Peter whispered.

Akbar looked at Bairam.

'It would have been suicide to march before we are ready,' the Khan protested.

'But we will march *now*,' Akbar said.

'That would be equally foolish, my lord. The rains will commence any day now.'

'You will wait, and wait – and wait,' Peter cried. 'Do you mean to ever confront Hemu?'

'How may a youth of no standing thus address me?' Bairam complained.

'Because he has lost his entire family,' Akbar said quietly. 'But Bairam Khan is right, young Blunt: we cannot campaign in the monsoon. We shall wait. But you have my word: your cousin will be avenged when the rains stop.' He gave a grim smile. 'And I will recapture my birthright.'

* * *

In some ways knowing that Richard was killed in action came as a relief. Peter had dreaded the thought of his cousin being dragged before Hemu to face abject humiliation and impalement: he knew how much Richard had secretly feared such a fate. But he had died as he had lived: fighting. Perhaps fifty-six was too young, but no one could say he had wasted a moment of his life. Was there any other man on earth who had both sailed around the Cape of Good Hope *and* travelled overland from Delhi to London?

But Richard's death left himself and his young family utterly alone in this seething, frightening turmoil that was India. Richard had also been alone when he had stumbled into Delhi, but without the burden of a wife and children, and he had very rapidly gained the patronage of the Moghul.

Peter was painfully aware that he had no real affinity with any Indian, or any Mongol either. Nor was it possible to presume on the favour of a fourteen-year-old boy. For all his flashes of independence, Akbar remained under the influence of Bairam Khan – and of Bairam's dislike for himself, Peter had no doubt. The Afghan knew he would never forgive the procrastination which had caused the death of his cousin.

The temptation was enormous to abandon this forlorn cause and take his family back to Goa – and there attempt to make a new life for himself.

Juana no doubt held the same fears, but she kept them to herself. Suddenly what had seemed a huge adventure, guided and controlled by Blunt Bahatur, had blown up in her face. She was as frightened of the future as her husband was.

The rain teemed down, and the army fretted. It was growing very slowly, but it now had a nucleus of good fighting men. Had Mirza been prepared to send his Mongols south, it might have proved invincible.

Akbar was a man who kept his word. With the first sign of an improvement in the weather, he despatched his tavachis to every encampment, summoning his ming-bashis to bring their regiments together. Bairam Khan frowned, and complained that it was too soon.

'Our best hope, Khan Babu,' the Sultan said, using a term of endearment which meant Father of the King, 'is to be ready and marching upon Delhi before Hemu can mobilise his people.'

In October the Moghul army streamed across the Sutlej, and began its march.

It numbered some forty thousand men, of whom only a quarter were Mongol cavalry, thoroughly loyal to the legitimate heir. Another ten thousand were Pathans; these marched, and would fight, on foot but they were essentially guerillas, and Peter had his doubts as to how they would stand up to a set-piece battle. The same could be said about the other recruits who had come in: a sizable division of Afghans; groups of various other hill tribes; and even a body of Sikhs, members of the fiercely independent religious sect that had its home to the north-east of the Delhi Sultanate, and with whom even Babur had not been inclined to trifle. Now they wished to fight against the Hindus, whom they regarded as far more their mortal enemies than the Muslims.

The army took the time-honoured road down from the hills. Along the well-worn tracks rumbled Akbar's small contingent of artillery, only four batteries, and his elephants – although, like his grandfather, he had no intention of using these huge, uncertain beasts in battle.

The Mongol cavalry formed the advance guard, and the fierce hillmen covered the flanks of the army, terrifying the peace-loving people of the plain, and only with difficulty restrained from plundering them.

Peter Blunt had been appointed one of Akbar's personal tavachis, and he rode behind the Sultan.

The army had left all its women behind; it was here to fight. But Hemu's spies had not been inactive. He waited for the would-be Sultan at Panipat with his Rajput allies.

Akbar's scouts rode back to warn that there was at least a hundred thousand of the enemy. This figure had been trotted out so often before that Peter now realised it merely represented a very large number of men – significantly more than in the Moghul army.

But the scouts also reported an enormous number of elephants, more than a thousand, and this had to be taken seriously.

'Now is the time we could really use the knowledge of Blunt Bahatur,' Akbar remarked.

'Are there none others here who have fought along with Babur?' Bairam demanded. 'I was but a tavachi then, but I remember the action well.'

'Then make your dispositions,' Akbar suggested.

Bairam did indeed remember the first battle of Panipat, and he could think of nothing better than to attempt to repeat it, despite the fact that circumstances were totally different. For now both sides possessed artillery – the Rajputs having the advantage there, as they did in sheer numbers. They also had many more elephants than Lodi had ever commanded, if reports were true – as indeed they were. The Moghul army started in consternation at the array of huge beasts.

Furthermore, Hemu had most certainly learned from his years of campaigning at the shoulder of Richard Blunt. Instead of useless charges, he advanced his cannon to within range, and began a steady bombardment of the Moghul position. The encampment afforded some protection, but the wagons were slowly battered to pieces.

The Moghul guns replied, and hopefully also did some damage, but there was little evidence of it.

Akbar, seated on a white stallion behind the wagon wall, began to look impatient.

'We must draw them out from their position, Khan Babu,' he said.

Bairam pulled his beard. He clearly had no idea of how to do so.

'A flanking movement, my lord,' Peter suggested. He had not spent years listening to cousin Richard's tales of campaigning for nothing.

'On an open plain? Will they not see what we are about to do?' Bairam demanded scornfully.

'Yet they will have to attend to it.'

'And then?'

Peter bowed in the saddle. 'I will leave that to your superior understanding of warfare, sire.'

Bairam glared at him, but Akbar clapped his hands.

'It will at least break up their front. You, young Blunt, ride to Shuja Khan and tell him to take his Pathans on a flank march at the enemy position.'

Bairam was horrified.

'You would send foot soldiers against the Rajput cavalry?'

'They are mountain men,' Akbar said. 'They can run as fast as any horse.'

'On a mountainside,' Bairam grumbled.

'I would beg your permission to stay and fight with them, my lord,' Peter pleaded.

Akbar grinned. 'You have it. But return to me afterwards.'

Peter kicked his horse and rode off to where Shuja Khan's hillmen waited, surging restlessly to and fro as the shot flew.

'It is the Sultan's command that you move your division to the right, and then forward,' Peter told him.

Shuja snorted. 'How far forward?'

'It is to induce their cavalry to charge, tuman-bashi.'

'At us,' Shuja observed. And then gave a throaty laugh. 'But did we not come here to fight?'

He issued his orders and the hillmen shouted their pleasure. As their general had said, they had come here to fight.

Peter dismounted to be with them as they tramped over the uneven grass, away from the wagon-circle, for perhaps a hundred yards, and then forward.

The Hindus gave a great shout as they saw the movement, yet it contained an element of doubt. It was difficult for their commanders to determine what the Moghuls had in mind.

But there could be no doubt what the Rajputs had in mind. Their cavalry had been milling about, but now several thousand of them came into line and couched their lances.

'Form line. Spread out,' Shuja Khan ordered his men. 'And remember, it is the horses that matter. Evade the lances and bring down the horses.'

Peter slung his favoured longbow and drew his tulwar. He had never hamstrung a horse in his life, but now it was kill or be killed.

Uttering mighty yells, urged on by the beating of their nakaras, the Rajputs charged in *hazaras*, or squadrons. They were disciplined men, mounted and beautifully armoured. Richard had told his cousin of this, and the splendour of their movements – but Richard had played his part in defeating them more than once, with pikemen and Mongol cavalry. There were none of the former here today, and not enough of the latter.

The cavalry advanced screaming at the hillmen, who stood their ground in extended order, ready to leap to one side or the other. Peter watched the dull blue steel of the corselets careering towards him, pennons flying from the lances as they were couched. He drew a deep breath and, as the first rank of horsemen reached him, he leapt to one side, swinging his tulwar as he did so.

He missed his target, and was struck on the shoulder by the knee of the next horseman, who had aimed his spear at a Pathan. This was doubly fortunate for Peter; he was tumbled sprawling on the ground, and was thus missed by the rider behind as well.

But there were yet more to come. Still on his knees, he twisted aside to avoid another lance thrust, and swung his tulwar again. This time it connected with bone and muscle, in a jarring shock that nearly lost him his weapon. Horse and rider fell heavily to the ground, but Blunt had no time for his assailant, since he had to face yet another careering beast which all but trampled him underfoot.

Then the Rajputs were through, streaming in disorder towards the open country beyond. Most of them – but quite a few had been brought down, and these were hastily despatched. The rider Peter had felled was already dead, killed by Shuja Khan himself.

The Pathan chieftain was smiling broadly.

'That was good work. But they will come again.'

About half a mile away, the Rajputs were rallying their blown horses, wheeling them again to confront their foe. But a glance at the battlefield was alarming for Peter. The Rajput cavalry had charged on the right as well, and dispersed the Sikhs opposed to them. Now the entire Hindu army was advancing before their drums and bugles, shrieking their confidence in their victory. Blunt had a surge of anxiety; he had intended something like this, but not a general advance.

The Moghul artillery fired a last time, and then was engulfed in the great mass of the enemy. The morning became a shrieking maelstrom of savage men. Shuja Khan hastily rallied his Pathans and led them back towards the main body, but on their way they had to contend with another cavalry charge. This was more easily handled, as the enemy horses were still exhausted. Yet it engaged the Pathans in a savage mêlée.

Killing one of the Rajputs with a sword thrust, Peter seized the horse's bridle and swung himself into the saddle. He could do nothing further here, and he wished to return to Akbar's side . . . if that was possible.

Everywhere the Moghul forces were being driven back by sheer weight of numbers. And now Hemu was himself coming forward with his elephants, bugles blowing to warn the troops in front of him. His soldiers turned to cheer him, waving their swords and lances in the air. Of their loyalty to him there could be no doubt.

That the arrival of the elephants in the shaken Moghul ranks would be a decisive factor was also certain.

Blunt found himself and his captured horse for the moment free of antagonists as the Pathan–Rajput conflict swayed to one side. The Hindus were up to the wagon-circle now, tearing the wagons apart. The Moghul cavalry had been given no time for a charge, and he could see them milling about aimlessly, and Akbar trying to rally them. But the day was lost. Only a miracle could save the Moghul now – and avenge Richard.

Only a miracle! Peter wheeled his horse to gaze at the advancing Hindus. They were redoubling their efforts to destroy the Moghul wagons, seeking Akbar himself. Thus their vast array, apart from the Rajput cavalry engaged with the Pathans, was concentrated on a relatively narrow front – not more than a quarter of a mile across.

In the centre of this mass, as it moved forward with the ponderous force of the Hindu juggernaut, Hemu stood upright in the howdah of his elephant, waving his sword to urge his men forward.

The effective range of a longbow was usually two hundred yards. By practice Peter had increased this by some thirty yards – but only at a fixed target, and never in the confusion of a battle.

But this was his last chance.

He kicked the horse forward, riding straight at the Hindu ranks. Men turned to stare at him in consternation, assuming that he was committing suicide. A squad was even detached to deal with this lone horseman. But when he was within some thirty yards of them, he drew rein, leapt from the saddle – the horse was panting too hard and would have shaken his aim – snatched the bow from his shoulder and an arrow from his quiver in one movement, strung it, sighted, and loosed the shaft. Then another.

The approaching Hindus stopped in amazement, giving him time to send another shaft after the first. Before they could recover, he turned his attention to them, and loosed two more shafts. At pointblank range he could not miss, and two men fell. Then he was in the saddle again galloping off, pausing moments later to look back towards the cries of dismay.

He saw Hemu's elephant on its knees, roaring and waving its trunk; his second arrow had struck it immediately behind the ear. And, in the howdah, Hemu had fallen over and was vainly trying to pull the first arrow from his neck.

'Foolish boy,' Bairam Khan grumbled. 'Your rash move all but cost us the victory.'

'On the contrary, Khan Babu,' Akbar argued, gazing intently at Hemu's head. The would-be rajah had been dragged, dying, before his conqueror, and there beheaded. 'Young Blunt's brave manoeuvre was the only way we could win against such odds. I have never seen a shot like that, at such a distance. Truly you are a man amongst men, young Blunt.'

'All Englishmen can shoot an arrow with that range and accuracy, my lord,' Peter told him.

Akbar looked thoughtful, and then he stared over the field. Peter wondered if the first field of Panipat had looked like this, with dead and dying in every direction. The fall of their leader had sent the Hindus fleeing, and the Mongol cavalry, led into the charge by Akbar himself, had nothing to do but cut them down.

The boy's arm was stained with blood, but he had fought like a true grandson of Babur.

Now he smiled. 'Then yours is a blessed race,' he remarked. 'You are a worthy successor to Blunt Bahatur, and I give you that title now. Blunt Bahatur! You will ride at my side forever.'

Bairam Khan tugged his beard.

BOOK THE THIRD
The Emperor

'Come out, come out, thou bloody man, thou son of Belial.'

The Book of Samuel
Chapter 16, Verse 7

11

SHAH OF SHAHS

'We are old men,' Akbar said, 'but we have a great deal to remember.'

He looked affectionately at Peter Blunt as he spoke, for Peter, now aged seventy-five in the Christian year of 1600, was by far the oldest of his associates.

Yet the others seated around the Moghul were no less beloved by their master. They were an odd assembly, unique in the annals of the world, for their religious and racial backgrounds were so utterly different.

There was the pink-complexioned English Christian. There were the equally fair-skinned Muslim brothers, Abul Fazl and Shekh Feizi. There was the dark and aquiline-featured Raja Birbal, the Brahmin. And there was the equally dark Todar Mal, the Hindu soldier.

A great deal to remember, Peter thought. Sometimes he wondered how much of it was real. Yet all he had to do was look around him, to read a tax return, or to stand at the Badshah's side to watch a review of his troops.

For forty years the continuing success of the Moghul had been unchecked.

It had not been so in the beginning. Defeating Hemu may have given Akbar the keys to Delhi, but the fourteen-year-old boy then had still been surrounded by a sea of enemies, not least those closest to him.

Not that Bairam Khan, Khan of Khans as he liked to call himself, or Khan Babu as Akbar called him – and which title he valued most – would ever have considered himself an enemy. His whole being was concerned only with the power and glory of the Moghul. But that was to be power and glory as devised by the Khan – and controlled by him.

For four years further Akbar had accepted this continued tutelage, and Peter had all but despaired, aware that his own life hung by a thread, for Bairam had no time for the infidel foreigner. Only Akbar's continued interest in Europe – and his very real gratitude to Peter Blunt for that fortunate arrow shot – kept him safe.

Perhaps there was also Akbar's feeling of guilt at his failure to relieve Richard Blunt in time. A guilt compounded when he had learned of the Agha Gila, who had refused to consider suicide and had walked straight into Hemu's camp with a long-bladed knife concealed in her sari.

She had been allowed to go up to the Rajah, as she was his mother-in-law, but there she had been stopped before she could avenge her family. Then Hemu gave Gila to his soldiers.

They said it was beneath the sixty-eighth man that she had died.

These things preyed on Akbar's mind, for Gila had been a distant cousin of his own mother.

He himself had no taste for lechery. He had been brought up to use women as he needed them, and to discard them as he chose; his concubines were summoned because of physical need rather than any overweening lust. He had never been allowed to know love, other than for Hamida Banu Bayram, and perhaps he never would – even as regards his son Murad, born to one of his Pathan concubines. Yet there was a complete absence of viciousness in his character. What he did, he did without anger, and equally without fear.

He had thus foregone the right of conquest over Hemu's women, and sent them back to their families.

And then, after four years during which his grip on Delhi and the Punjab – but little else – had slowly been strengthened through Bairam, the chief minister had been dismissed.

There were several reasons for this. Bairam's manner had become unbearably arrogant. He had begun to insist that every member of the Shah's entourage address him as Khan Babu, as if he was father of them all; in this he had insulted Hamida, and undoubtedly she and Maham Anaga, who remained the intimates of Akbar's private apartments, had worked on the young man's mind. Equally Bairam's policy of consolidation rather than expansion had become irritating to the Badshah. But perhaps the main incentive had been an eighteen-year-old boy's urge to fend for himself.

Bairam had not taken dismissal kindly. He had stormed with rage and then departed into the Punjab to raise the standard of revolt. It had been necessary for the Badshah and his faithful supporters to take the field. Bairam had calmly accepted defeat, then had spoken of undertaking a pilgrimage to Mecca in atonement. But he had been assassinated by an old rival before he could leave.

It was already accepted that Akbar had learned the true art of government, and when it was necessary he was capable of acting swiftly and ruthlessly.

Or at least his mother was.

No doubt Akbar occasionally mourned his Khan Babu, who had been far more of a father to him than ever Humayun was; but for the moment his affairs had been taken over entirely by the harem party, headed by Maham Anaga's son Adham Khan.

For Peter Blunt this seemed hardly an improvement. But he persuaded Akbar to choose his own Grand Vizier, Atgah Khan, and with the latter set to work to coax the Emperor away from his womenfolk.

It was a slow and dangerous business. Atgah Khan had been in office only a year when he was murdered, and no one could doubt that Maham Anaga's son had been behind the deed. Akbar summoned Blunt and his other intimates to ask what must be done.

'Maham Anaga and her family must be put aside, my lord,' said Abul Fazl.

'And your mother,' Shekh Feizi added. 'There is no need to harm them, sire, but *you* must rule.'

Miserably, Akbar looked at Peter, who understood well enough what thoughts must be going through the boy's mind. It was bad enough contemplating the overturn of that cocoon in which he had been wrapped throughout his life – but to face up to the responsibilities which must follow . . .

They were disturbed by a furious banging on the doors, which were thrown open by the guards, to admit Adham Khan.

'My lord,' he cried, kneeling at Akbar's feet, 'I understand your concern. But Atgah Khan was conspiring against you.'

'I believe there must be many who conspire against me,' Akbar said mildly.

'And you are right.' Adham Khan was gaining in confidence, and now rose to his feet. 'Some of them are in your closest circle.' He glared towards Peter. 'It is not right for the Sultan of Delhi to entertain an infidel in his private apartments.'

Akbar looked around at them.

'They mean to rid you of us all, my lord,' Abul said.

'Then I must choose, now,' Akbar replied. 'Blunt Bahatur, this man is your enemy – and mine. Will you not deal with the matter?'

Taken by surprise at the suddenness of this decision, Peter hesitated for a moment, then drew his sword.

'Do not shed his blood here,' Akbar commanded.

Adham Khan was equally surprised by his unexpected condemnation. He did not move while Peter sheathed his sword and stepped towards him; then he tried to draw his own weapon, but Peter, the much larger man, swept him from the floor, and then carried him out on to the balcony. Adham Khan screamed and struggled, but could do nothing against such superior strength. Peter looked back at his master – and received a quick nod. He held Adham Khan over the balustrade, then dropped him. He listened for the crunch as the Khan struck the ground, fifty feet below.

Hamida Banu Baygam and Maham Anaga were to be confined in honourable imprisonment for the rest of their lives. In fact they both died quickly, of shame it was said.

Far from being overwhelmed by what he had done, the final rejection of these women seemed to release in Akbar a surge of energy Blunt had never seen equalled. A new Grand Vizier, Mun'im Khan, was immediately appointed – and then for forty years, almost without cessation, the Badshah had campaigned. His aim was to conquer all India – and he had very nearly succeeded.

A man who at eighteen was able to grasp simple strategic principles that had eluded even Babur, he had surprised everyone by launching his first campaign south from Agra, into the district known as Malwa. This was the land Richard Blunt and Prabhankar had crossed thirty-five years earlier, to be struck by the fertility of its black cotton soil. But Akbar also sought immediately defensible frontiers. He drove his army through the surprised and disunited petty kingdoms as far as the Narmada, and there called a halt. The campaign had been concluded in six months, and he had secured for himself and his people a virtual breadbasket for all time.

By moving south, he had left the Rajput lands untouched, and the Rajputs themselves had been as surprised as anyone by this sudden eruption of a force they had considered dormant. They had been slowly regaining their strength and their courage, following their defeat at Panipat, and there was no doubt that they would soon be ready to challenge the youth who wore the Koh-i-noor.

Akbar beat them to it, and no sooner was Malwa secure than he turned on these most ancient enemies of his house. This was much more serious stuff, and the campaigns took six years of the bloodiest and most fanatical conflict Peter was ever to know.

But Akbar was inexorable. His military genius was the first of the outstanding facets of his personality to be revealed to the world. It was as if the verve of Genghis Khan, the ruthlessness of Timur, and the tactical eye of Babur had all come together within a single brain. Still not yet twenty, only five feet seven inches tall, and with virtually no formal training, Akbar yet encompassed every aspect of the military art.

In his army he combined every asset he could find or hear of. He constantly sought to increase his artillery, he cast his own cannon, and kept his gunners in perpetual training. He recreated the corps of pikemen founded by Richard Blunt, arming many of them with muskets in the European fashion; and to them he added, as light troops, his wild Pathans. The foot soldiers were placed under the command of Todar Mal, while all India looked askance that a Muslim should entrust a Hindu with such responsibility.

But Akbar knew where the core of his military power lay, and more than any other arm he concentrated on his cavalry, riding with them himself. As usual, he incorporated the best of every civilisation with which he had come into contact, and side-by-side with his division of Mongol mounted archers there rode the lances of the men he had trained in the Rajput style.

Thus for organisation. But tactically he was even more outstanding. He could deduce at a glance the weaknesses in an enemy position, and he disdained ever to fight on the defensive, which had been the Moghul tradition. His armies always surged forward, probing in the right direction, and the Rajputs were shattered time and again.

Yet they resisted with exemplary courage and desperation – and not just their men. After six years of defeats, the last remnants of those who defied him, the Sisodhias, retreated to the stronghold of Chitor, where the town lay beneath a formidable fortress hill. In doing so they declared to the world their determination to prevail or die. For Chitor had twice before been assaulted by Muslim troops: in 1303 under the leadership of Ala-ud-Din Khalji, and as recently as 1535 by Bahadur Shah of Gujarat. On both occasions the Rajputs, with their women and their children, had committed suicide rather than surrender.

So it was again in 1568. The Moghul army deployed in all its magnificent strength beneath the beautiful Jaina towers of Fortune and Victory, erected many years before in more prosperous times. Promptly the Prince of Chitor appeared on the battlements to shout his defiance. Akbar himself seized the musket and fired the shot which left the Prince wounded and reeling. He then made his escape, but the remaining defenders for this third occasion chose jauhur. Flames accompanied screams from the fortress as every man, woman and child was consumed in the holocaust.

It was said thirty thousand people perished in Chitor.

After the capture of Chitor, even the surviving Rajput princes sued for peace. Again they were taken by surprise: instead of wholesale confiscations and executions, Akbar confirmed each prince as master of his own land, subject to the overall rule of Delhi.

Furthermore, he then passed laws to negate the age-old assumed superiority of Muslim over Hindu, cancelled the jizya tax on the supposed inferior race, and gave every man equal rights within his empire.

More, still, where his predecessors had occasionally taken Hindu women as concubines, Akbar married a Rajput princess, the daughter of Raja Bihari Mal of Amber, as his principal wife.

Most remarkably, for a man who had never truly loved, it

turned out to be a love match. Jodha Bai of Amber was undoubtedly a most beautiful woman, and a most natural one too; being a Hindu she would not accept the concept of purdah, and went openly amongst her people. Akbar's pride in her was obvious to all, and his delight knew no bounds when Jodha Bai became pregnant at the end of 1568.

So anxious was the Moghul about her health, that he took time off from his wars to visit the famous Muslim saint, Salim Chisti, in his home of Sikri. To his enormous relief, Chisti told him that the Begum would give him three sons.

'Then here is where she shall live,' Akbar announced, and the city of Fatehpur – or 'Victorious' – Sikri was immediately commenced.

Sikri was a hilltop village in the valley of the Jumna, some twenty miles west of Agra. Close by was Khanua, the site of Babur's great victory over the Rajputs in 1527. Now it became one of the wonders of the Indian world, as first of all the palace of the Begum was erected, followed by the Jami Masjid, or Great Mosque, the southern gateway of which, the Buland Darwaza or Victory Gate, was to remain for all time one of India's greatest architectural works.

Inside the mosque a tomb was built for Chisti, who died soon after his famous prophecy.

This was immediately realised when Jodha Bai, on 31 August 1569, gave birth to a son whom Akbar named Nur-ud-din Salim, thus announcing to all that this half-Mongol half-Rajput with Persian blood would be the next Sultan of Delhi. Northern India gaped in wonder, but from the deserts of Baluchistan – where the last Rajput prince, Rana Pratap Singh, still defied the Moghul until 1597 – to the foothills of the Himalayas, it acknowledged Akbar as its lord.

He was still only twenty-five, an age when Timur and Temujin had been less than tribal chieftains, and Babur had been tumbling in and out of Samarkand.

While Akbar was preoccupied with the Rajputs, Prince Mirza had come down from the Hindu Kush to challenge this younger brother who was travelling so far so fast. Peter Blunt had been despatched with a force to check him, and Mirza had retired in discomfort.

* * *

There had followed six years of peace, as Akbar had consolidated his enormous gains, enjoyed his wife – Jodha Bai gave birth to the other two prophesied sons, Murad and Daniyal – and indulged his family's passion for building.

From one end of the empire to the next, work was carried out on a scale India had never before seen, and the dreams that Babur had once indulged in now became reality.

In the east, Pataliputra had already been refounded as Patna by Sher Shah, but Akbar redoubled the size of the city. Benares was another city which he enlarged and beautified. More important, his extreme liberality in religious matters restored it as one of the prime centres of the Hindu faith; scholars came to Benares from all over India, and much of the greatness of the past was restored.

He paid even more attention to Payrag, because of Ashoka's pillar. He built a fortress to protect it, and renamed it the City of God: Allahabad.

In the north-west, Lahore of course remained his favourite residence, and indeed he was wont to return there every year during the stifling heat of the monsoon season. But places like Multan and Jodhpur also witnessed the imperial will to expand; Jodhpur especially attracted him because of the immense fortress which dominated the city from its rocky crag – and Jodhpur had never been taken by assault.

It was to Jodhpur that Akbar rode two hundred and twenty miles in two days to prevent the Rajah from forcing his son's widow to commit suttee – the ghastly Hindu practice by which a widow was burned alive on her husband's funeral pyre.

Delhi was not neglected, but Akbar had little love for the city which had seen the death of his father, and so many other tragic events.

The true capital of the empire was once again Agra. Although more and more of the imperial decisions emanated from Fatehpur Sikri, Agra remained the centre of business. And Akbar extended his golden touch here as well. To construct a fortress was conventional enough; it was a beautiful building of gleaming red sandstone. But inside the fort he had erected a mosque in white marble, its minarets crowned by the onion domes invented by the Arabs, which were becoming popular throughout the Muslim world. Timur had beautified Samarkand with these domes, and now Akbar adopted them.

This architectural marvel was called The Pearl Mosque.

Those were happy years.

Akbar basked in the love of his wife, and his growing family. For, having fulfilled the prophecy, Jodha Bai now presented him with several daughters. In the cause of unifying his empire, the Moghul had taken several other Hindu wives and concubines, as well as Muslims. But only one woman mattered to him. The mutual affection of Emperor and Empress was plain for all to see, and was enjoyed by all their people. Jodha Bai never sought to interfere in affairs of state; although that she did have opinions and was not afraid to air them in the privacy of the imperial bedroom was obvious from many of Akbar's decisions.

No less attractive was Akbar's delight in his sons, and particularly the eldest, Salim. He himself taught the boy falconry, and he watched carefully as the Prince exercised with sword and lance and bow, on horseback and off.

'This will be a great warrior,' he declared. 'A veritable Jahangir, World Conqueror!'

Akbar himself continued to present a startling picture of mental and physical energy, and unflinching courage.

However exhausting a day he had spent, he would mount his horse and command his amirs and tavachis to follow him to the hunt, and he was never happier than when confronted with a rampant tiger.

Wherever he was, every morning at dawn he stood in the window of his current residence so that his people could see and know their master.

He took the best of everything with which he came into contact, refusing at any time to be constricted by customs or traditions which could not be proved to have retained their value. Thus the Koh-i-noor was seldom seen; Akbar had no use for such ostentation. Neither did he sit on a carpet, as his father and grandfather had done; he was too far separated from his ancestry on the steppes of central Asia. Instead he held court in a comfortable chair, and when the weather was warm he often discarded boots and Mongol trousers, and would sit in a dhoti and tunic, barefooted like any ancient Hindu rajah.

His people loved him for it.

And Fatehpur Sikri grew in beauty and size every day.

For Peter Blunt these years were like a dream come true. He was appointed tuman-bashi of Akbar's personal guard: ten thousand of the finest troops in the empire. Only here did any trace of religious intolerance enter the Badshah's scheme; every man, save for their commander, was a Muslim. This was simply because every man of the bodyguard had to be absolutely trustworthy. Competition for selection was fierce, and in their gold-coloured tunics and red breeches, with their burnished helmets and gleaming lances and tulwars, they presented a splendid sight.

At home he could have asked for nothing more. He was rich, he was famous, and he was happy. Juana basked in her husband's prosperity, and herself supervised the building and decoration of their house in Fatehpur. It was close by the Begum's palace; for she and Jodha Bai had become fast friends.

If there was any regret in Juana's life at this time, it was her inability to make contact with her parents, both to let them know she was alive and to let them see how she had risen in the world. But all of India not ruled by the Moghul regarded Akbar as a potential enemy; and Goa was separated from Delhi by several hostile states.

But one day, she promised herself.

Meanwhile, Peter could teach his sons the arts of hunting with the hawk, as well as horsemanship and swordsmanship, the pleasures of chess and the delights of poetry. For Akbar, with his Persian blood, relished the great Iranian writers and had their works, as well as the most important Sanskrit texts – translated by Feizi who was a famous scholar – published throughout the empire. His favourite poet was Tulsi Das, who often recited to the Emperor and his friends.

Peter's greatest joy of all however, was Juana herself. That same young girl who had laid her plans so carefully, who had schemed and lied to attain what she desired, had never changed in the years since. Only now she planned and schemed for their joint happiness.

Living, as he did, in Akbar's shadow, she counted every

night that Peter came home to her; particularly his safe return from any campaign launched by the Moghul was a special blessing. Presumably she had also made plans in case of his death, but these were never discussed. She certainly would not lack for money: Akbar's beneficence had made his Guard Commander a wealthy man. Nor could she ever be in personal danger, enjoying as she did the friendship of Jodha Bai.

Thus they laughed, and loved. They pleased each other. And they were both delighted, if amazed, when in 1573, at the age of forty-two, Juana became pregnant again.

It was in this year of 1573 that Akbar had resumed his campaigning. He had struck south again, from Rajputana and Malwa, and into Gujarat. Peter well remembered how this had always been Richard's dream. Now it was accomplished. After Gujarat attempted to revoke its treaty accepting Moghul supremacy, Akbar rode with three thousand horsemen over four hundred and fifty miles in eleven days to catch the Gujarati army napping. The Sultan fled, and the Moghul forces tramped through the streets of Surat.

After the conquest of Gujarat, Akbar called a halt; and he began seriously to consider making the Pilgrimage to Mecca, which it was the duty of every true Muslim to undertake once during his life. Fortunately he was distracted and forced to turn his attention to the east, to Bihar and Bengal which were as usual simmering with discontent. Completely pacified in two years, the provinces were placed under the rule of Raja Man Singh Kachwaka of Amber, brother of Jodha Bai, who thus achieved the highest position ever attained by a Hindu in Muslim service. No sooner was this completed than another army was sent across the river Narmada to seize the Deccan.

Command of this was given to Prince Murad, Akbar's second son; but he, alas, had not the military skill of his father, and for the first time since 1556 the Moghuls were defeated.

Akbar could not immediately avenge this disgrace, because yet again Prince Mirza – now calling himself Mohammed Hakim – invaded northern India.

The Emperor now determined to put an end to Mirza's

intrusions. So he concentrated all his forces against his half-brother's mountaineers, and chased them into the mountains. He captured Kabul, and annexed all Afghanistan to his empire. Mirza thus became an outlaw, never to be seen again.

Being in the north, Akbar had decided to extend his power up to the mountains themselves, and a nine-year campaign followed, in which Kashmir, Sind, Orissa and Baluchistan all fell.

Kashmir was ruled by an Afghan chieftain, Prince Yusuf, who was defeated easily enough. More importantly it was the home of the Sikhs, an offshoot of the Hindu religion developed by the famous teacher Ramanuja some five hundred years before the coming of the Moghuls. They had abandoned the extreme ritualistic forms of Hinduism in favour of the simple repetition of God's name, the singing of hymns and of meditation under the guidance of a saint, or guru, who later became their political as well as spiritual leader.

Like the Buddhists, the Sikhs vehemently denied the pre-eminence of the Brahmin class. They had soon needed to defend themselves, and their faith, and this they had done in their inaccessible land, against Hindu and Muslim alike, for some time. In the meantime, through the works of the poet Kabir, they had incorporated some of the tenets of Islamic mysticism into their own beliefs. Their first ruling Guru, Nanak, had been educated in both Hindu and Muslim lore. Nanak was the man who truly organised the Sikh religion, had in fact coined their name *sikh* or 'disciple', had built the first exclusively Sikh temple, and boldly declared that 'there is neither Hindu nor Musselman'.

After Nanak's death in 1539 there had been four gurus in succession, and it was the fourth of these, Ram Das Sodji, who finally had submitted to Akbar with the fullest guarantees of freedom to pursue their beliefs for himself and his people. As a result, the guru-ship became hereditary in the Sodji family for several generations.

Kashmir was a beautiful country. Sind and Baluchistan were the opposite, however, comprising a vast desert save where irrigated by the river Indus. But this terrain was a natural frontier for an Indian empire, as it stretched right up to the mountains separating the subcontinent from Persia.

When the last of these lands had submitted, Akbar could truly claim to be the ruler of all Hindustan north of the Narmada.

But these triumphant campaigns were ended when news was received of the illness of Jodha Bai. Akbar hurried back to Fatehpur Sikri, to find his beloved wife already dead.

After he had buried her, he turned his back on Fatehpur Sikri forever. The beautiful city was abandoned, and he began a peripatetic existence, using Agra as his capital in the winter, and Lahore in the summer.

He also built himself his own mosque, to contain his tomb. But this was in none of his great cities; instead he chose the little village of Sikandra, a few miles north of Agra on the road to Delhi.

'Here I shall lie in peace, far from the bustle of business,' he said, 'and yet keep an eye on the affairs of my descendants.'

In the year that Jodha Bai died, Peter Blunt's youngest child, named Elena after her grandmother, was twelve years old.

His mourning completed, Akbar at last felt able to deal with the south. Taking command himself, over the next few years he annexed Khandesh, and Berar, and Ahmadnagar.

It was in the siege of Ahmadnagar that the legendary Princess Chand Bibi, sister of Sultan Burhanu'l Mulk, herself donned armour and led a sortie through the breach to repel the Moghuls. She had been forced to surrender in the end, and was dragged before her conqueror, spitting defiance to the last, as she supposed.

Akbar merely handed back her sword, and told her to go home to her husband.

Sadly, when acting as regent for her nephew after her brother's death, Chand Bibi was the following year murdered by her own troops.

South of Ahmadnagar, too, Akbar explored the famous caves of Ajanta. Here the early Buddhists had carved some thirty temples and monasteries out of granite cliffs on the inner side of a seventy-foot-high ravine in the Wagurna river valley.

The caves themselves were remarkable achievements, but in addition were magnificently decorated with wall paintings and frescoes depicting the life of Asoka's India with breathtaking energy and vitality.

Akbar was now, due to the speed with which he moved and fought, within a few day's march of Goa, but instead he decided to call a halt and return to Agra, whence he had received news of domestic discord. Peter was a little disappointed that the Moghul empire was not extended to take in Goa. But they had come into contact with Portuguese at Diu, a port the Europeans had secured on the coast of Gujarat, and from the factors there he learned that Juana's mother and father were long dead.

But by then, in this spring of 1600, Juana herself was dead. Even to Peter there seemed little point in heading further south.

Akbar's problems lay with Salim. Now thirty-one years old, the Prince had been left in command at home, and in his father's absence had revealed some disturbing traits.

These traits had been evident ever since his mother's death. No one had ever doubted the young man's talent. Akbar had been very careful to make sure that Salim, besides learning the art of war, had also been taught to write and to read the classics. But Jodha Bai's death had cast the young man adrift – he had been her favourite son. Though married at sixteen to a princess of Amber, a cousin of his mother's, who had already presented him with a son called Khusraw, he had soon taken advantage of the free and easy ways of the Indian court to desire a Persian girl named Mehr on-Nesa. The match would have been quite impossible, for, if very lovely, Mehr was only the daughter of a Teheran official whose fortune had sunk so low he had offered his daughter on the street. She was lucky enough to have been bought by a wealthy Moghul merchant several times her age, who sought a daughter rather than a concubine. Given the best of educations, her natural talents, added to her beauty, had soon made her a popular member of Akbar's court, where Salim had fallen hopelessly in love with her. But as he would never agree to his heir marrying a commoner, and Salim was too infatuated to consider Mehr a mere concubine, Akbar had promptly found the girl a husband:

a Persian tuman-bashi with the army. This had left the Prince embittered and indiscreet. Bold talk of what he would do when he became emperor was not unusual in an eldest son. More disturbing was his weakness for wine, and it was said that he also indulged in opium when the mood took him.

But Akbar's unexpected return soon had Salim kneeling to beg forgiveness for his failings – and forgiveness was one of Akbar's most pleasing characteristics. He, too, remembered that Salim had been his mother's favourite.

So now the Moghul sat with his three oldest friends, and remembered.

It was a special occasion because Abul Fazl had at last completed a work on which he had laboured for a very long time, the *Ain-i-Akbari*, a record of the Moghul's life. This he now presented to his master.

Akbar turned the pages. He still could not read with any ease, but the very size of the volume was impressive.

He smiled at them. 'Have I then done so much?'

It was a rhetorical question.

In his forty years of power his achievements had been breathtaking. All India, save only for the southern states of Bijapur, Mysore, Golconda and Orissa, and the northern mountain kingdom of Nepal, bowed to his personal rule. Far more important, however, this vast land, some two and a half million square miles – more than half the area of all Europe, including European Russia – thought with one mind, and spoke with one voice . . . and was content. Because, although so much of those forty years had been spent in campaigning, Akbar had equally tirelessly recast the entire administration of his huge empire.

He had begun by declaring the reversion to the crown of all lands hitherto held by various tax-gathering officials. Now all were administered by governors, *jagidars*, who with their deputies, *mansabdars*, were appointed from Agra, thus preventing any hereditary governorships being set up.

These governors were all officers in the army, but trained to carry out civil duties, the most important being the administration of local justice and the collection of taxes, of course. They were also required to supply soldiers, horse and foot, to the army when required.

But justice itself rested ultimately not on the Emperor but on the appointed Supreme Judge, Mir-i-adl, whose decision in all legal matters was final – even binding on Akbar himself. Though Mir had been appointed by the great Moghul in the first place, this was the first known separation of executive and judiciary in the history of the world.

And so the empire prospered. Peter Blunt estimated that it must be the richest country in the world.

From Bengal there came rice, lacquer and textiles; from Bihar mangoes; from Oudh opium and indigo; from Kashmir wine; from Multan salt, calico and wheat; from Sind and Gujarat salt and precious stones; from Kandesh salt and spices; from Malwa an inexhaustible supply of wheat; and from Delhi itself came carpets, opium, textiles ... and silver to pay Akbar's troops.

Yet despite all this activity, Akbar still found time, every Thursday evening, no matter where, for a conversation with his friends. His eagerness for knowledge was insatiable.

He continued to seek a deeper understanding of religion, and would invite those of every persuasion to stand before him and discuss their beliefs. Now that he had encountered the Portuguese, he invited some of their priests to debate before him. Unfortunately the governor of Diu sent two of the newly formed Company of Jesus. These Jesuits, Antonio Monserrate and Rodolfo Acquaviva, by their arrogance and their deprecation of every other form of worship, brought the Emperor as close to irritation as Peter had ever seen him.

These Jesuits, however objectionable, were able to bring Peter up to date with events in Europe.

They told him how Henry VIII has been followed by a short-lived son and then by two women, the first two queens ever to sit undisputed on the English throne, and of the great war between Spain and England which had resulted in the destruction of the Spanish fleet by a great storm – which the Jesuits clearly regarded as an act of the devil, defending his own. They told him, too, of civil wars in France ... of the death of Suleiman the Magnificent ... and of the defeat of the Ottoman fleet by Christian allies at Lepanto.

The news of Suleiman's death had, of course, already been received in Agra. It had occurred in 1566, while Akbar was still engaged in his war with the Rajputs; and, although clearly a momentous event, it had seemed but an incident in the long Ottoman march through history. Now what the Jesuits told Blunt cast things in a different light: Lepanto was fought five years after Suleiman's death, and there now seemed little doubt that the Ottoman Empire was already in decline.

Was not Akbar now the greatest monarch in the world?

But what of the man who had for those forty years ridden at the side of the Moghul? He had prospered beyond his wildest dreams.

Akbar had early selected Peter Blunt as the commander of his personal bodyguard. He had determined with his ready insight that he would give him undivided loyalty – particularly since the Emperor was his sole opportunity of wealth and power. Both had followed in ample proportion, and Akbar had heaped favours on his Guard Commander, and also on his beautiful Portuguese wife. Constant campaigning had kept Peter and Juana apart more often than he would have liked – yet they had between them produced four children.

Sadly, one of the penalties of living to a ripe age is to watch other members of one's family die. Both Juana and Peter were forced to experience this; those six years of utter happiness had ended far too soon. Thomas had been the first, killed in a skirmish during Murad's abortive invasion of the Deccan – and only just after Thomas's Rajput wife had given birth to a son, dying in the process.

Isabella had perished from one of the fevers which racked Agra every monsoon; she had then been the wife of a tumanbashi. The younger son, William, had fallen from his pony and broken his neck while playing at polo.

Of the four of them, only Elena survived. She possessed her mother's red-streaked dark hair, and her fine looks as well, but she had chosen never to marry. Instead she remained at Juana's side, assisting her with Thomas's young son William. But then Juana herself had died.

Had she truly enjoyed a happy life, after her reckless choice? There had certainly been times, Peter knew, when she had bitterly regretted deceiving her parents. But those had been in the early days, when fear had ridden at her shoulder. Since Akbar's seizure of power in 1562, she had not known a moment's doubt.

Watching her children die had been her most bitter disappointment.

She had devoted herself ever more to her grandson, the last Blunt. And she had passed on that task of care and devotion to her daughter.

Though grieved by these domestic tragedies, Peter Blunt had stepped from triumph to triumph in the eyes of the world. Few men, he supposed, could have led a more successful life. He had earned himself fame as well as wealth; his name was known throughout the subcontinent. If he had a single regret, it was that it was not known in England. How he would have wished that his mother could have learned of his triumph. But she had no doubt died, long supposing him a mouldering corpse in some Indian jungle.

And now he was content to spend his last years in the company of his daughter Elena. She was twenty-six now. Did she never regret not having known a man's embrace? If she did, she never allowed any sign of it. But, like him, she must look to the future. And the future was only William.

William Blunt was no longer a boy, but a man of twenty-four. He possessed all the family height and strength, although his Rajput mother had left him with a dark complexion. She had also left him with a face far more handsome than that of either his father or grandfather. Brought up to soldiering, he was a tuk-bashi in the Emperor's guard, serving under the watchful eye of his grandfather.

But as he was the last Blunt, it was certainly time he was married and became a father; most of his contemporaries had been given their first wife at the age of sixteen.

William understood that he was different from his companions; all of the children had been taught to think of England as their home, even if they had never seen it. But for a grown man not to have a wife was an insult to his manhood, no matter how many concubines were meanwhile provided for his use.

He had even been tempted to marry the boy to his aunt, and did not suppose the idea would receive any opposition from Akbar. But incest remained a Christian abhorrence, and, besides, Elena loved her nephew as a mother; she would have been appalled at the idea of becoming his wife.

It was Akbar, of course, who provided the solution. 'Why do you not send to Goa or Diu for a wife for your grandson?'

Blunt was taken by surprise; he had not known the Moghul to be the least interested in his domestic affairs.

Akbar had smiled. 'Am I not the father of my people? So should I not understand a man's desire to preserve the purity of his blood? My son is a mongrel. He has Mongol, Persian and Rajput blood in his veins. The mixture seems to bubble, not always to good purpose. Find a Portuguese wife for your grandson.'

Peter had taken his master's advice, and sent a letter to the Governor of Diu, chosen instead of Goa because of any ill-will possibly lingering there.

In his position, as Amir and Commander of the Guard, and one of the richest men in India, and also a Christian, such a request would hardly be dismissed out of hand – especially from Diu, where the Portuguese were aware that they continued there entirely by courtesy of the Moghul.

But would there be a suitable young woman in the little colony? He awaited the return of Taulat Khan, the tavachi to whom he had entrusted this embassy, with some excitement. And too much excitement was bad for a man of seventy-five. Elena rested her hand on his arm to calm him as Taulat approached them across the great hall of their house in Agra.

'There is indeed one, sire, who is recommended by the Governor as eminently suitable to be the wife of your grandson,' said Taulat.

'Have you seen this girl?' Elena demanded.

'I have, agha,' Taulat said, disapprovingly. 'For she goes abroad unveiled, and accompanied by a single servant. But I understand that would not disturb you.'

Peter intervened. 'Is she comely?'

'She is beautiful, Blunt Bahatur.'

'Do you speak poetry or the truth, Taulat?' Peter pressed him.

'I speak the truth, sire. Hair like a raven's wing, eyes like the shallow ocean, nose like a Mongol princess, chin smoothly rounded, lips red as the finest ruby, complexion clear.'

'Go on,' Elena prodded, smiling at his imagery.

'As for the rest, agha, she is tall, but not too tall, and slender, but not too slender. She is fully endowed with the necessities of motherhood, and she moves with grace hardly matched by a cat.'

'I believe you *are* a poet,' Elena laughed.

'Has this paragon a name?' Peter asked.

'Her name is Isabel Dominguez,' Taulat said.

Peter frowned. 'Surely that is a Spanish name?'

'That is so, Blunt Bahatur. Her father is a wealthy Spanish factor.'

'Living in Diu?'

Peter realised that was not so very odd; the Jesuits had informed him that Spain had recently conquered her smaller neighbour. But Spain was currently at war with England.

On the other hand, Spain was not at war with the Moghul Empire.

'And her age?'

'I understood her to be sixteen. I know that is old, Blunt Bahatur, and it may raise a question in your mind as to why she has not already been wed . . .'

'No,' Peter said. 'In the Christian world, sixteen is a good age to wed. Did you present my credentials?'

'I did.' Taulat looked slightly apprehensive.

'And what was Señor Dominguez' reply?'

'He replied, Blunt Bahatur, that words could not express his gratitude that one so esteemed as yourself should ask for the hand of his daughter . . .' he paused.

'Go on,' Peter urged.

'But he said he could never permit his daughter to marry someone whose face he had not seen. The man is clearly a fool,' Taulat added.

'That is no insuperable obstacle,' Peter said. 'William shall go to Diu. We shall all go to Diu. Would you not like that, Elena?'

'If it pleases you, Papa,' she said uncertainly.

'Well then . . .' Peter stood up. 'You have done well, Taulat Khan.'

'I would sooner have brought you the girl, Blunt Bahatur. I was tempted to seize her and carry her off.'

'I am glad you did not,' Peter said, remembering his own courtship. 'I would have this thing done in a civilised fashion. Now let us give William the good news.'

He strode along a corridor, Elena bustling at his heels.

'Papa,' she protested. 'You know you should not exert yourself so. The surgeon . . .'

'The devil with the surgeon.' Blunt reached the balcony and looked down on the courtyard, where William and one of his fellow captains were engaged in swordplay. For some seconds he watched them, then clapped his hands. 'Enough,' he called. 'Your skill is evident. I have news for you.'

William looked up, his dark, aquiline face relieved by his sudden smile.

'We are to campaign again?'

'Ha ha,' Peter laughed. 'Indeed we are. But not with the army. You and your aunt and I. That will be our army. Come up here and learn of it.'

Oddly, he thought, he had suddenly lost his breath.

'Papa!' Elena caught his arm. She shouted, 'Simki! Someone . . .'

William himself ran up the stairs, just as a servant emerged from the inner corridor, to see Elena sink to the floor beneath the weight of the man who had suddenly collapsed on her.

'Grandfather?' William took Peter's arm and pulled him gently upright.

'It is nothing,' Peter gasped. 'Boy, I have found you a wife. I have . . .'

The pain was back. He stared at his grandson in consternation.

He had not expected it to be like this.

12
THE BRIDE

Akbar himself came to look upon Peter Blunt's body.

'Has he no temple in which to be buried?' he inquired. 'How is that?'

'A simple cross is all he will require, Badshah,' Elena explained tearfully.

'A simple cross!' Akbar thundered. 'For my most faithful bahatur? I will erect such a cross as all India will marvel at. But tell me what brought on the seizure.'

'Excitement, Badshah.' Elena related the news from Diu.

'Well, then,' Akbar said. 'At least he died happy. But now the boy must carry out his father's wishes, and marry this girl. It is my wish as well. You will accompany him, Elena Agha.'

She bowed her head.

Peter Blunt, the great Blunt Bahatur, was buried with fullest honours. The entire Guard was turned out in gold and red uniforms, their steel corselets and helmets gleaming in the sun. The coffin was carried by William and five other tuk-bashis of the Guard, and the Emperor himself walked immediately behind, with Abul Fazl. They were followed by Elena, wearing a white sari.

Already workmen were laying the foundations for the mausoleum which would rise over his grave on the outskirts of Fatephur Sikri.

'He will be remembered, always,' Akbar announced sadly.

Now it was time to prepare for the journey to Diu.

Elena felt less grief over her father's death than apprehension at the prospect of this journey. By far the youngest of Peter Blunt's children, since the death of her mother she had been braced for the inevitable, and was only happy that it had happened so peacefully.

She had no fears for herself. As female head of the Blunt household she was unassailable; she knew her father to have been a very wealthy man, and she had her own circle of Muslim women friends with whom she drank coffee and ate sweetmeats and gossiped, and she had William to love and to indulge, almost as if he had been her own son.

These were the comfortable facets of her existence to which she had been born and from which she had never been separated.

Her woman friends had, by custom, been married within a year of reaching puberty, and could not understand her contentment. 'How may a woman live without the love of a man?' they wondered. 'There is no fulfilment save beneath a man,' they insisted.

That thought repelled her.

'I am content to be my father's housekeeper,' she would reply. 'As I was born in Fatehpur Sikri, so will I die here, and in my father's house.'

She had certainly never considered leaving Agra, save to go to Delhi.

But now she had been commanded to go far away . . . and to Diu of all places, a Portuguese city.

Elena had never come into contact with any of her mother's countrymen before, though Juana had taught her Portuguese as her first language. But she had no idea what to expect as to manners or customs or dress, or even morals; her mother's memory embraced the Goa of fifty-three years before.

She fussed and fretted over her wardrobe, but finally decided she would do best to stick to her saris. She had worn them all her life, and they suited her.

William watched these preparations with equally mixed emotions. He had campaigned far into the south, but he had never been to Diu itself.

Now he was going to claim the bride picked for him by his grandfather and the Emperor. But no Indian maiden this, eager to please, to submit, to revere him.

'She will have to be wooed,' Elena warned. 'These European

women are not servile, as here in India.'

William had no idea how to begin to 'woo' a woman nor was he sure that he wanted to. Elena and his grandmother were the only two women he had ever accepted as being in any way his equals. Of course, one bowed to the floor when one of Akbar's wives passed by, or any other great agha of the Muslim heirarchy, but, as Elena had never tired of telling him, his own mother had been a Rajput princess, so he was as high-born as any man in the land.

As for social relations, throughout his life these had been male-oriented. A tuk-bashi in the Guard was not expected to have dealings with women outside of his own home. When he wished sex, he merely summoned one of his four concubines. These were attractive Indian girls, who giggled and chattered but said nothing of the least importance, and whose sole duty in life was to please their lord – and they knew it.

He was far more seriously affected by his grandfather's death than was his aunt. William had been only nineteen when Peter reached seventy, apparently as vigorous as ever. It had not seemed possible for all of that power so suddenly to dwindle. Grandfather had looked as strong as ever before he died.

Now William felt a tremendous sense of loneliness at the unexpected removal of a man he had practically worshipped. It was an awareness that he had inherited the Blunt isolation. No doubt Peter himself had felt this way when he learned of Richard Blunt's death; and Richard Blunt when Sir Thomas had died in his arms. It was a successive misfortune which overtook every generation.

The fault was their own determination to preserve their separate social identity. They were servants of the Moghul, and none other. Despite William's Indian blood, it had never been allowed to interfere with either his upbringing or his education. As he had never known his mother, she had exerted no influence upon him. And since she had come from the far west of Rajputana, he had never known his mother's family either. No doubt he had close cousins galore, but he would not recognise them if they entered the room.

So his upbringing had been largely that of a Christian gentleman, who knelt and prayed every night even if he had never entered a church. Yet his dark skin was a constant reminder of his Indian heritage, and to some extent he feared it. He suspected it lurked deep in his heart and his brain and his belly, and would one day rise up to overwhelm him.

How simple it now was to travel about the Empire since Akbar had commanded the building of proper roads to link his most important centres. Grandfather had told William how Richard Blunt had struggled for several months just to get from Surat to Agra. Nowadays the journey from the capital to the coast took one month only, since the caravan Akbar had fitted out for him could travel at a steady twenty miles a day.

With William's own company as escort, it was in every way an Imperial caravan: a glitter of gold and red, piled with gifts of every conceivable description including jewels of exceptional value, and, to add to this display, four elephants. In the first howdah sat William himself and Elena, accepting the salutations of every village through which they passed.

'I feel like a queen,' Elena confessed.

Diu occupied an island in the Gulf of Cambay of the Arabian Sea, just off the coast of Gujarat. As there were no boats large enough to carry them, the elephants had to be left behind on the mainland, along with the main part of their entourage. William took only six of his guards, including his havildar Talas Ali; and Elena was tended by her four women.

It was a very small island, only some fifteen square miles in area, and the settlement seemed hardly more than a village. But it was dominated by a remarkably beautiful cathedral, while its entire setting was one of peace and tranquillity, surrounded by superb beaches.

Their approach had been noticed, and on the landing stage to greet them as they disembarked was the Governor, Dom Enrique Portalado, with his wife Doña Luisa and several other officials. Also Don Miguel Dominguez himself.

The Spaniard was a fine-looking man with a pointed beard and handsome features. He bowed over Elena's hand, taking in her sari-clad form with great interest – but looked less pleased as he regarded William.

'Welcome Senhor Blunt, welcome Senhorita. You do us great honour,' gushed the Governor. 'I was greatly saddened to learn of the death of the great bahatur.'

'You are most kind, your excellency,' Elena said.

Dominguez looked somewhat contemptuous of these effusions.

'You will of course stay at my residence,' Portalado continued. 'All the arrangements have been made. And . . .'

'You will dine with me, if you will,' Dominguez intervened, looking at Elena rather than her nephew.

'I do not think he likes me,' William whispered to Elena, in English.

'But he will like what you have to offer,' she replied.

William was quite prepared to dislike Dominguez in turn, and even his wife, a large woman named Margharita who sweated profusely – but things were different when he met Isabel. To his surprise, the girl was every bit as beautiful as she had been described by Taulat.

Of medium height, she had a quite lovely face in which the handsome features inherited from her father were delightfully softened by a small nose and rounded chin. Her eyes were indeed green, and glinted like emeralds. Her hair was black; her complexion was flawless. Her decolletage revealed smoothly rounded breasts to complement her trim stomach.

As she was only sixteen, the thought did cross his mind that in thirty years time she might resemble her mother, but he immediately dismissed such a reflection as unworthy. He thought he might even have fallen in love with her at first sight.

Unfortunately she clearly did not reciprocate his feelings and, having stared at him with an expression of dismay, she gave a toss of her head and withdrew the hand he was holding.

Her mother contrived to look even more disapproving.

'They do not like me either,' he told Elena.

'But the girl is a pretty little thing.'

'I think she is the most beautiful creature I have ever seen.'

Elena smiled at his enthusiasm.

'Then you shall have her.'

William wished he could feel so confident.

That first dinner with the Dominguez family proved a small affair, but the following night there was held a reception at

Government House, to which everyone holding the rank of captain or higher as well as all the leading factors and their wives were invited.

It was much the largest gathering of Europeans William had ever seen. He soon realised that he was the only guest present with Indian blood in his veins, for even if the Portuguese maintained Indian concubines, these were not accepted socially.

There were only some score of women present, representing all the ladies of any social distinction in the small settlement, and these were therefore in great demand.

After a sumptuous banquet, the lute players struck up.

Both Elena and William were astounded as men bowed over the nearest available woman's hand, raised her from her seat, and escorted her into the middle of the floor, where they commenced to dance.

At the court of Akbar, or indeed anywhere else in India, dancing was something performed only by nautch girls for the amusement of their employers. But here were dignified Portuguese ladies and gentlemen dressed in all the splendour of hooped skirt and high ruffed collar, embroidered partlet and patterned underskirt, trunk hose and silk jerkin, clasping hands and strutting about, bowing beneath arches formed by the joined arms of other dancers, all the while smiling and chattering to each other in a most unseemly manner seeing that not one of the men was dancing with his wife.

No one had asked Isabel to dance, and she sat alone, gazing fixedly in front of her. The Governor, Dom Enrique, bustled across to William.

'The young lady is waiting for you, *Senhor*,' he explained.

'For what?'

'Why, to ask her to dance.'

'I have no idea how to set about it,' William confessed.

Dom Enrique swallowed, and looked at Elena.

'I am afraid I have never indulged in such a pastime either,' Elena confessed. 'But I am willing to try.'

William was shocked as he watched his aunt, to the great delight of the other guests, performing the slow gyrations in the centre of the room. It had clearly not occurred to Elena that under her sari she wore only the scantiest underskirt and a thin blouse, and as she made the unusual movements to which she was encouraged by her partner, the silk would constantly draw tight against breast or buttock or crotch, leaving very little to the imagination.

Whatever William's feelings, Elena had never enjoyed such a good time before in her life. She was in great demand and, the first dance over, she was invited again and again. At last, with the evening well advanced and everyone very merry because of the amount of wine that had been drunk – with the exception of William and Isabella who continued to stare in front of themselves, at opposite ends of the room – Don Pedro Dominguez himself invited Elena on to the floor.

'I hope your nephew does not mean to insult my daughter,' he remarked coldly.

'Insult her?'

'No man may ask her to dance until he has done so, since they are the two guests of honour. Yet he makes no move.'

'Ah. I fear that William has not asked, simply because he has no idea how to go about it. Such practice is not followed in Hindustan.'

It was Don Pedro's turn to say, 'Ah.' Then he added. 'But you have never danced either, I understand.'

'That is quite true. But my nephew is very shy, whereas I am not.'

Don Pedro considered what she had said, with both interest and pleasure. 'I understand that you have never wed, senhorita,' he said at last, gazing into her eyes. 'How can that be, in so beautiful a woman?'

'It amuses you to flatter me, senhor.'

'I would not dream of doing so. I am merely stating the truth.'

Elena gazed back. 'But you, senhor, are married.'

'Indeed, but we are civilised people, are we not?'

The thought had obviously crossed his mind that she might not be.

'I would hope so, senhor.'

'Then can we not arrange to meet in private, for a discussion?'

Elena decided to let him hang himself.

'That would please me very much, senhor. The sooner the better.'

'Well ... I take a walk on the beach in the mornings. It is quiet there, and private. And very beautiful. Just before sunrise; it is coolest then.'

'I fear that is too early for me, senhor. Could I not come to your office later?'

'My office?' He raised his eyebrows. 'Would you be so bold, senhora?'

'Why not? As we do have matters to discuss.' She smiled at him. 'My nephew will accompany me, of course.'

He frowned. 'You misunderstand me, senhora.'

'On the contrary, senhor. I understand you very well. But I came to Diu to find a wife for my nephew, not to engage myself in adultery.'

Don Pedro's face flushed with anger.

'So,' Elena continued. 'We shall attend your office at eleven tomorrow to discuss the requirements of this coming marriage. And now, senhor, I shall bid you goodnight.'

She left him standing in the middle of the floor, gazing after her in fury.

'There are difficulties,' Don Pedro Dominguez began next morning, as Elena and William sat in the factor's office. 'Some of them are of a somewhat delicate nature.'

'You mean you do not approve of my nephew's Indian blood,' Elena said bluntly.

'Well ...' Dominguez looked embarrassed. 'As you have raised the matter, senhorita ... dismiss me as an indulgent father, but I could never force my daughter to marry a man whom ... well ...'

'She finds repulsive?' Elena suggested, glancing at William whose face was rigid with anger.

'I did not say that, senhorita. It is simply that your nephew is not to Isabel's taste. And, naturally, she is insulted by your nephew's lack of attention at a public assembly.'

'I explained that,' Elena said curtly, while William looked bewildered.

'To my satisfaction perhaps, senhorita – though hardly to hers. But there are other difficulties, more important,' he hurried on. 'There is the question of nationality. Your nephew is English, and England and Spain are presently at war. I know this seems to matter little to our Portuguese friends here, but it is of some importance to me.'

'My nephew has never even seen England,' Elena protested. 'And he has as much Portuguese blood in his veins as English.'

'And then there is the question of religion. Does your nephew have a faith, senhorita?'

'Christianity has no roots in India,' Elena said coldly. 'Although it certainly exists in our hearts. My nephew is a Christian.'

Dominguez smiled sceptically. 'There are so many nowadays calling themselves Christians who are really heretics.'

'So, you have brought us here to tell us that there can be no marriage between my nephew and your daughter.'

'Senhorita, regretful as I am to have caused you so long a journey for nothing . . .'

'Indeed! The Emperor will be most displeased,' Elena remarked.

Dominguez's eyes widened. 'The Emperor is involved in this?'

'Naturally. My son wishes to marry your daughter only because of the Moghul's express command.'

For the first time in the conversation, Dominguez looked nervous.

'There was some suggestion of giving Spain a factory of her own,' Elena continued. 'Now I wonder if the Badshah will even permit the continuance of this settlement at Diu.'

Dominguez had gone quite pale.

'Then there are the gifts we have brought for you and the senhorita. Why don't you see some of them?'

Dominguez appeared tongue-tied, so Elena clapped her hands. The servants brought in a box and laid it on the floor. Elena opened it.

'Your wife might have liked this,' she said, placing a four-carat emerald on the desk before the astounded Spaniard. 'And for the senorita, of course, this diamond . . .' It was twice the size of the other stone.

Dominguez gasped.

'Well.' Elena placed the gems back in the box and signalled a servant to remove it. 'We shall now take our leave of you, Don Pedro.'

Dominguez also stood up.

'Permit me to have further discussion of your proposal with my daughter? Perhaps her first reaction was a hasty one.'

'I will expect your answer by this evening, Senhor Dominguez,' Elena remarked. 'Otherwise my nephew will leave Diu tomorrow morning. Good day to you.'

As they returned to the Governor's house, Elena turned to William. 'Tell me, do you still wish a girl who scorns you as a coloured man?'

'I desire her more than ever,' William sighed.

Elena rested her hand on his arm.

'Use her with care, William. Promise me that. Or you will destroy her – and that would be a sad waste.'

'There are certain requirements which I feel to be obligatory,' Dominguez said that evening, as they sat on the veranda of Government House. Portalado and his wife had discreetly withdrawn.

'Tell me of them,' Elena invited.

'Firstly, my daughter must be accompanied by her confessor, Father Tomas. Secondly, she will also be accompanied by four of her personal maids. Thirdly, she will be permitted to visit us here in Diu at least every six-month. And fourthly, any issue of this marriage must be brought up in the Roman faith.'

'I am afraid we cannot agree to the first three,' Elena said calmly.

Dominguez's head jerked.

'Firstly, Christian priests are an abhorrence to the Emperor, and he would never permit one to reside within his city. Secondly, my nephew's wife will be attended by my own ladies, and no others. Thirdly, it would be impossible for my nephew's wife to undertake a journey such as this twice in every year. Once in every second year, perhaps. However – she gave him a bright smile – 'I am sure my nephew will have no objection to his daughters being educated in the Roman faith. His sons, of course, will be his own decision.'

Dominguez frowned. 'You drive a hard bargain, senhorita. Yet you wish me to allow my daughter to be carried off into the wilds of India . . .'

'Tush, senhor. Your daughter is going to the most civilised

place on earth. And she will be married to a man you should be proud of.'

'Señorita Isabel.' William bowed over the girl's hand and brushed it with his lips. 'This is the happiest day of my life.'

As he straightened, she stared coldly at him.

'It is the most horrible of mine,' she said. 'Although I have no doubt there will be many more horrors to come.'

William kept his face impassive.

'Why, señorita,' he said, 'then I shall certainly do my best to oblige you.'

'Now she really does hate me,' he grumbled to Elena.

'And she will hate you even more – for a season. But her hate will turn to love.'

'How can you be sure?'

'It is human nature. Father often told me about the courtship of the great Richard for the Indian Princess, Gila Lodi. That began as violation, and ended with them dying for each other.'

The ceremony took place in the Cathedral of St Matriz, and was attended, it seemed, by every European in Diu: the biggest social event almost anyone could remember. All looked askance at the tall dark-skinned young man in the cloth-of-gold tunic and scarlet breeches, the soft kid boots, and the jewel-hilted tulwar hanging at his side, the gleaming ruby in his cloth-of-gold turban. Elena thought him the most handsome man she had ever seen.

The bride looked no less elegant in white silk, but her face was completely veiled until the priest proclaimed them man and wife. Then William threw back the veil to reveal tear-stained cheeks. When he kissed her on the mouth she remained absolutely rigid, her lips tightly closed.

At Government House there was a great deal of wine to be drunk, food to be eaten and speeches to be heard. Through it all Isabel sat white-faced and tight-lipped, staring in front of her; while William was aware that he was being eyed by everyone in the throng, but most of all by Pedro Dominguez and the other Spaniards. How they would love to run me through, he thought.

At last the speeches came to an end, and Isabel was led away to be prepared for bed. William also was escorted upstairs to be stripped of his uniform and draped in a nightshirt. He took all the attendant ribaldry in good part, smiling and laughing with the throng as he was marched along the corridor towards the bridal chamber.

Here Isabel was already in bed, wearing a white cotton night-gown which rose to her throat. Her mother stood to one side, Elena to the other. The girl's face remained impassive, and even Elena scented possible disaster.

The crowd pressed into the room behind William and his escort, shouting ribaldry which was close to being obscene. William suspected he was going to have a difficult time.

'You will leave us, now,' he shouted, and the hubbub died a little.

'Leave you?' asked one drunken gentleman. 'We are here to see the consummation.'

'You are to see nothing,' William growled. 'Leave us.' He glared from face to face. 'All of you.'

Elena hurried from the bedside to shoo people through the door. Slowly they filed out, grumbling.

'You also, señor,' William added.

Don Pedro frowned at him. 'The consummation must be witnessed.'

'There will be proof of it, I have no doubt. Now leave me. And you, too, señora.'

Dominguez and his wife stared at each other, and then at their daughter.

'It would be best.' Isabel spoke for the first time.

Dominguez hesitated for a moment, then beckoned his wife. 'I leave my daughter in your care,' he told William.

'You leave me with my wife, señor,' William reminded him.

Elena remained in the doorway.

'You too, Aunt.'

'Remember,' she said, and stepped through the door.

William went to turn the key before looking back at the bed.

'I thank you, señor,' Isabel said.

'For excluding that mob? Such supervision of the marriage bed is not an Indian custom.'

'For that, too, am I grateful,' Isabel said. 'But most of all that our ... marriage may commence in a decorous fashion.'

'I doubt that will be entirely possible,' he said. 'I must confess to an enormous desire for you. But, first ... shall we not say our prayers?'

He knelt, and waited. Isabel had no choice other than follow his example. Carefully she slipped out of the bed, on the opposite side, so that he caught no more than a glimpse of her bare feet emerging briefly from beneath the covers, and she knelt with her elbows on the mattress.

William had no idea what to say, so he said nothing. Neither did the girl, although her eyes closed, and he assumed she was communing with someone.

Her eyes opened. 'That also was most courteous of you, señor,' she said. 'Now, if you will just turn away so that I may regain the bed ...'

'Turn away? Dearest Isabel, I am coming to look at you, most closely.' He stood up, took off his nightshirt and dropped it on the floor.

'Señor!' she cried. 'You are indecent.' She cast a hasty glance at his erection, and then closed her eyes again. 'Please put on your shirt.'

'That is the first time I have ever been dressed for bed,' William told her. 'And it shall be the last.'

He stood above her, and she opened her eyes again, still kneeling, with her hands clasped, carefully looking only at his face. 'What do you want of me?'

'Why, your maidenhead, to be sure. But first, I wish to look at you. Take off your nightgown.'

'I will not!' Isabella raised her hands to her throat. 'You are indecent, señor. I had supposed you possessed the manners of a gentleman, but now I see you are indeed a savage.'

She then began to weep.

But William was too sexually aroused for pity. He seized the collar of her nightdress, meaning to raise her up, but she rose of her own accord and threw herself forward on to the bed, while the nightdress ripped in his hand.

Realising what had happened, Isabel gave a shriek and scrambled right across the bed. At the far side, she gained her feet, holding the remnants of the nightdress against her stomach.

William vaulted the bed and threw his arms round her. As she gasped and kicked, he merely laughed, sweeping her from the floor and dumping her back on the bed. She spat at him as they fought for the flimsy material, but he tore it from her grasp and threw it across the room.

She gave another shriek and tried to dive beneath the bedclothes, but he removed these too, entirely stripping the bed in four great tugs, so that the girl sprawled naked on the exposed mattress. Then he threw away the pillows.

Isabel lay there panting, a miracle of white flesh. He grasped her thigh to turn her over. She really was quite the most delicious sight he had ever seen: and she had the most perfect, translucently white skin.

For the moment she was too exhausted to move, but stared back at him with all the venom she could summon.

'You are a monster,' she panted.

'Some say that is the best way, the first time,' he said, and straddled her thighs.

She gasped as he touched her intimately, and tried to suck her stomach in. He leaned forward to kiss her mouth, and she snapped her teeth at him.

'Very well, then,' he said. 'I will find some other lips to kiss,' and grabbed her legs.

She then uttered the loudest shriek of all, sat up, and tore at his back with her nails. The pain made him rear up and, without thinking, he swung his fist. The blow struck her on the jaw and she rolled over twice before falling to the floor with a thump.

There were also bangings at the door.

'Open this door or I shall break it down.' It was Dominguez.

'Open that door, Don Pedro, and you are a dead man,' William warned him.

He got off the bed and stood over the girl. She was not unconscious, but was certainly shaken.

'Get up,' he snarled.

Slowly she pushed herself up and reached her feet, trembling. There was blood on her chin from where she had bitten her lip, and already a bruise was forming on the white flesh beside her mouth.

'I am sorry for the blow,' he said.

'You are obscene,' she hissed.

'I suppose I am, in your eyes,' he agreed. 'It is my Indian blood. Now it is time to put an end to this farce. Lie down – or must I hit you again?'

She stared at him for several seconds, then lay down on the bed. William gathered up two of the pillows and placed one on top of the other beside her. Then he rolled her over, lifting her middle to place her groin on the pillows, and leave her body arched.

'Oh God,' she said. 'Oh, God, save me from this torture.'

William parted her legs, and knelt between, his hands resting on her buttocks.

'You, sir, are a scoundrel,' Don Pedro announced. 'Had I my way, I would see you hanged from the highest tree on this island.'

William gave him a brief bow.

'Good day to you, señor.'

Don Pedro stared at him, and then at Elena, and then at his daughter, who was huddled against the head of the bed. Before the entry of her father, William had allowed her to wrap herself in an undressing gown, but the fact that she had endured a sleepless and energetic night was revealed by the tousled hair, the heavy eyes – and the bruise on her face.

Now she scrambled from the bed and ran to her father, whispering in Spanish.

'What does she say?' William asked, able to understand only the few words close to Portuguese.

'She begs me not to leave her here with you. Nor can I.'

'She is my wife,' William pointed to the bloodstains on the mattress. 'Our marriage has been both consecrated and consummated. You will take your leave, señor, alone, or I will have you charged with abduction.'

Dominguez hesitated, chewing his lip, while Isabel still clinging to his arm, again spoke in Spanish.

Elena went to stand beside the girl.

'Don Pedro, I think you had better leave. My nephew is within his rights.'

Still Dominguez hesitated, then suddenly he took Isabel in his arms and kissed her forehead. He spoke a few words to her in Spanish, then pushed her away and left the room.

'No!' Isabel screamed. 'No, Papa . . .' She ran to the door, but William stood in front of it.

'Do not touch me,' she hissed.

'You need rest now.' He opened the door and called in two of Elena's maids. 'Stay here with Blunt Agha,' he said. 'Make up the bed and put her in it. Then let her sleep. Under no circumstances is she to be left alone.' He glared at Isabel coldly.

As he went outside, Elena followed him.

'Was it really as bad as it sounded?' she asked.

'She fought me savagely, yes. But we are now man and wife.'

'So I observed. But I suspect that you did not remember my advice.'

'My dear Aunt, what was I supposed to do? The marriage had to be consummated, or that scoundrel Dominguez would be within his rights to call for an annulment.'

'So now she does hate you. I shall go back to her.' She glanced at him. 'With your permission.'

He bowed, and proceeded to the front door.

It was morning, bright and clear and breezy, a very lovely day. The first day of my married life, William thought bitterly; it seemed that the entire colony had heard Isabel's shrieking.

He had not meant to hurt the girl in any way. But the sight of her, the knowledge that she was his, had aroused a dormant lust in him which had proved irresistible.

'Women are always difficult in the beginning,' Portalado encouraged. 'My wife tried to kill me on my wedding night . . .'

'You are very reassuring, senhor. I am sure my wife *would* have killed me, had she possessed a weapon.'

'You see, they behave thus in the beginning, but they always change in the end.'

William had no wish to pursue the matter. Walking down the front steps he headed towards the harbour to look at the ships.

He had supposed she would be unable to resist his love-making. Well, she had not resisted him physically, after the first blow. But she had been so tense he had to hurt her again to make an entry, and she had wept and whimpered with pain. When, to arouse himself a second time, he had caressed her breasts and buttocks, she had merely shuddered, her eyes tight closed. And when he rolled her on her back, she had screamed again.

Could anyone who appeared to suffer so much, and to hate so much, ever eventually feel love? Yet he wanted to earn her love. She was indeed a woman to have and to hold ... and to cherish.

Suddenly he felt miserable, and gazed at the ships with longing eyes. They were the first ocean-going carracks he had ever seen – quite different from the Arab dhows in Surat. One of those ships could one day carry Isabel and himself back to England; there was even one from whose staff hung the huge white flag with the red cross.

But did he really want to go to England? And there was no reason Isabel would wish to journey to what she would consider a heathen country. And what could England possibly hold for him? His life and his future was here in India, serving Akbar, as had his forebears.

Boots crunched on the sand. He turned his head to observe a man he had not seen before. He was tall but very thin, with a hatchet face not in the least relieved by his full beard, and wearing clothes which were hardly elegant, although a sword hung by his side.

'Master Blunt?' the man inquired in English, to William's surprise. 'I must ask you to forgive this intrusion. I could hardly believe my good fortune when I was informed that one of the Moghul Emperor's most trusted aides was visiting Diu. But then, as I understood the reason for your visit, I felt I could not approach you until the matter of your nuptials was completed. But now I am told you intend to leave again – and shortly.'

'Tomorrow,' William said. 'But you have the advantage of me, sir.'

'My name is John Mildenhall.'

'And you are from England?'

'I am, sir.'

'Then I shall shake your hand, sir,' William said. 'You are the first Englishman I have ever met, saving only my grandfather. Did you know of him?'

'Ah, no. You will be interested in the purpose of my visit to India.'

William bowed his head politely.

'I represent a consortium of London merchants, Mr Blunt, who are desirous of trading with the East. We regard it as iniquitous that the Portuguese, and now their masters the Spanish, should have a monopoly of the spice trade and the silk trade, and all the other valuable items that come from these lands.'

'Oh, entirely,' William said. He was feeling rather anti-Spanish this morning.

'The Spaniards and Portuguese also lay claim to the entire continent of America ... and you may know that any of our own ships found in those waters are treated as pirates?'

'I did not, sir.'

'Well, it is true. But America is a savage land, with no native ruler to whom a man may apply for a licence to trade. Here in India, things are different.'

He paused, hopefully.

'There is certainly such a ruler here,' William agreed.

'Whose fiat, once granted, may not be challenged by either Spaniard or Portuguese,' Mildenhall said eagerly.

'You would have me put your case to the Emperor?'

'I would accompany you back to Agra, sir, and put my case myself.'

'I doubt that would be worth your while, Mr Mildenhall,' he said. 'Are you aware that my cousin returned to England half a century ago with offers not merely of trading rights, but of a treaty of alliance between the Moghuls and England, and he was utterly rejected?'

'I have heard of that,' Mildenhall said. 'But those were different times, sir, and different men.'

'The Emperor was alive then, and I have no doubt remembers them. It were best you remain here and await word from me.'

Mildenhall was obviously disappointed, but he bowed in acquiescence. William turned to stroll along the beach, then checked as three men stepped from the bushes.

He recognised them from the wedding reception. Employees of Pedro Dominguez!

Mildenhall had seen them also.

'Do you require assistance, sir?' he asked.

'No,' William replied.

He could feel the blood surging through his veins in anticipation of the coming challenge; he could not have wished a better remedy for his mood.

Mildenhall waited nervously as William approached the three men, who were spread out across a distance of some thirty feet, staring at him grimly.

'Good morning to you,' he remarked.

'Tell me, señor,' asked one of them, 'is your heart as black as your skin?'

'I have heard that your aunt is the biggest whore in India, señor,' another said. 'Is that true? But then, no doubt you have sampled her yourself.'

William drew his tulwar. But the three men had rapiers, which they all drew together.

'Enough!' Mildenhall ran up the beach. He had drawn his own weapon, a long, straight English sword. 'You gentlemen mean murder.'

'I intend to fight them,' William said.

'Of course, sir. But only one at a time.'

'This is not your business, Englishman,' one of the Spaniards said.

'But I have made it my business, señor.'

The three men exchanged glances. It had been no part of their plan to fight William man to man; they knew him to be a professional soldier and, for all his youth, a veteran soldier. But this Englishman was an unknown quality, and they were now three to two.

'Then have at you,' they shouted, and charged together.

William stepped towards them, his tulwar dancing to and fro to parry the first two thrusts. As he did so he swung his foot as well, and one of the Spaniards went sprawling in the sand. William stepped past the pair, cast a hasty glance to his left to make sure that Mildenhall was coping with the third assailant.

William knew nothing of duelling. He had been trained to kill as quickly and safely as possible.

The second Spaniard had turned back to face him, shouting in his native tongue, no doubt encouraging his companion to get up. William ran at the man as he rose to his knees, swung his tulwar, and struck him a deadly blow where the shoulder meets the neck. The razor-sharp blade bit down to the bone, and blood gushed. The man uttered a shriek, and fell to the sand again.

The suddenness and completeness of his annihilation caused

even Mildenhall and his opponent to lower their swords for a moment – while William's remaining antagonist clearly wished nothing else than to flee. But he could not make up his mind to do so.

His momentary hesitation cost him his life. William snatched up the discarded rapier, tested it for balance, and then threw it as he had been taught to throw a spear. The Spaniard received the point in his belly, and sank to his knees, hands clasping the red stain on his doublet.

William was on him in a moment, and another swing of his tulwar sent the man's head rolling across the sand.

William turned towards the third Spaniard.

'Now you, señor,' he said.

The man stared at him, then at Mildenhall, and then dropped his sword and ran for the trees as fast as he could.

'My thanks,' William said.

'I doubt you needed me,' Mildenhall confessed. 'I have never seen such ruthless destruction. Do all of Akbar's soldiers fight like that?'

'They are trained to do so. And whether I needed assistance or not, you gave it. I retract my refusal to help you. You are welcome to accompany me to Agra. But I have changed my mind about when we leave. Be at the landing stage in two hours from now.'

He strode across to the first man he had felled. William swung his tulwar and cut off his head, too. He cleaned his blade on the dead man's clothes, sheathed it, and picked up a head in each hand by the hair.

Mildenhall could not speak for a moment; he seemed to have difficulty swallowing. 'May I ask what you intend doing with those heads?' he managed at last.

'I am taking them where they belong,' William told him, and walked away.

People crowded the doorways and windows as William Blunt proceeded up the street, a head still dripping blood in each hand. They whispered loudly to each other, but none seemed ready to interfere with a tuk-bashi in the Emperor's Guard. Just to make sure, Talas Ali called out his men.

'You should not walk alone, Blunt sahib,' he warned.

'I had company,' William told him.

He moved on to the Dominguez warehouse, where the Spaniard himself stood in the doorway. William threw the heads at his father-in-law's feet.

'Your servants' bodies await burial,' he said. 'You will find them on the beach.'

Elena stood anxiously on the porch of Government House.

'You are hurt!' She ran to him as she saw the brown stains on his tunic.

'It is not my blood, Aunt.'

'What can I say?' Portalado wailed. 'I had no knowledge that Señor Dominguez would plan such a thing. That I swear.'

The very use of the Spaniard's name betrayed him, but William had no desire to quarrel further.

'We shall leave this place now,' he said. 'Talas, summon the boats. And make room for an Englishman who will be accompanying us.'

William hurried upstairs and opened the bedroom door. Isabel, wearing a nightgown, was in bed. The two maids bowed to their master.

'Get yourself dressed,' William ordered. 'We are leaving now for Agra.'

'Murderer!' Isabel spat at him. 'You come to me with blood on your hands.'

William stared at her. The exultation of conflict still surged through his arteries.

'I have changed my mind,' he told the maids, who were already preparing Isabel's clothes. 'Return here in fifteen minutes.'

They glanced at each other, burst into a fit of giggles, and hurried from the room.

William released his sword belt and let it fall to the floor.

'Oh, God!' Isabel cried. 'Señor, I implore you, have mercy on me.'

'You are my wife, and the sight of you arouses me.'

He removed his clothes. She knelt, her hands pressed together.

'I am in pain, señor ... I am in pain.'

He stood above her, and she fell on her face.

'Have you no pity at all?' she moaned.

Pity, he thought. It was not an emotion he had ever much considered before. For it was not an emotion the Moghuls relished.

He grasped Isbael's shoulders and raised her up. She gazed at him, muscles tensed against the coming minutes.

'I will send your maids to you,' he said, and kissed her on the forehead.

The elephants and the escort were waiting for them on the shore.

William sat in the first howdah with his aunt. Isabel sat in the second with her two maids. Mildenhall occupied the third.

'She seems much calmer now,' Elena murmured.

William grinned. 'I have started to woo her.'

He was politeness itself when they camped for that night.

'You may sleep alone,' he told his wife, 'as I have no doubt you are very tired.'

For a while he talked with Mildenhall and Elena, then went to his own tent. Again he had instructed two of the maids to watch his wife throughout the night.

Next day Isabel was actually seen to smile at the antics of a troop of monkeys swinging from branch to branch. That afternoon William sat with her in the howdah, and the maids were dismissed.

He had almost decided to sleep with her that night, but as the camp was being pitched they heard the drumming of hooves. A few minutes later a tavachi and four troopers galloped up.

'Blunt Sahib,' the tavachi cried. 'Thanks be to Allah that I have found you.'

'What is the matter?' William frowned at the men, as his own people gathered round.

'You are to return to Agra with all haste, Blunt sahib. This is the command of the Badshah.'

'Me alone?'

Was he being arrested?

'You and all the men you can muster, Blunt Sahib.'

'You will tell me why?'

'Prince Salim has raised the standard of revolt against his

father, Blunt sahib. The Badshah requires every man that can be raised.'

'My God!' William said.

'What will you do?' Elena asked.

'Ride to Akbar's side with eighty of my men. Talas Ali will command here, and bring you to safety.'

'And your bride?'

William looked to where Isabel waited, open-mouthed at the crisis.

'I put her in your charge, Aunt. Until we meet again.'

13
THE REBEL

By riding virtually day and night, William regained Agra in under three weeks.

The whole way there his brain was spinning with uncertainty, never knowing when he and his company might be assailed – though they never were – and not understanding why Akbar should have summoned him, a mere 24-year-old tuk-bashi in the Guard, in such haste.

Agra was one vast armed camp, but there were no delays for Blunt Sahib. He was hurried straight into the presence of the Badshah. Akbar looked tired – and older than William remembered – but there was no abatement in that constant flow of energy.

'Young Blunt!' he shouted, as William entered his presence.

'Blunt Amir!' he added. 'As of this moment you are Blunt Amir.'

William straightened up, dazzled by his good fortune.

But it was true. Around the Emperor, from the lowest tavachi to Abul Fazl, all were smiling.

'Come closer, Blunt Amir,' Akbar continued. 'You know what has happened?'

'I have been told, my Lord. But not the details.'

'Why, that cur of a son, who would call himself Jahangir, "the World Conquerer", has fled to the Punjab and is raising an army. And from there he calls upon me to abdicate my throne, saying I have lived beyond the allotted span of Moghul Emperors.' Akbar smiled. 'As if such a wretched cur could ever be Jahangir. He would make no move while your grandfather lived, because he feared his strength. But now he has suborned too many of my people, amongst them Taulat, your grandfather's personal tavachi, and Ibrahim Hildas, whom I appointed to replace Blunt Bahatur as Commander of the Guard. Can you believe such ingratitude? And, yet, such foolishness? As I have said, Ibrahim Hildas was his, and often I lay on my bed with only a girl for company, confident in the presence of my Guard. Would not a Babur, intent upon so criminal a purpose, have had me murdered? Instead this Jahangir flees my capital and calls upon me to abdicate from afar.'

The Emperor brooded for a while.

'I shall deal with him most severely, and any traitors who support him', he said at last. 'My army mobilises, but my Guard is unhappy, because Blunt Bahatur is dead, and Ibrahim has fled to the rebel. So I will give them a new commander – with a name they can follow.'

Once again William could not believe his ears.

'So, Blunt Amir,' Akbar said. 'Now you are here, we shall march upon this Jahangir.' His voice was heavy with contempt.

Akbar was impatient for action, and so the army moved out immediately, even though the monsoon was due. Seeking the rebels, they tramped to the north-west, behind a screen of Mongol horsemen, while the Emperor sent spies and emissaries ahead, in the best Mongol tradition, suborning and warning, offering rewards for loyalty and threatening the most dire punishment for any adherence to the rebel Prince.

Word was brought back that Salim had indeed raised an army, supported by the mountain men and the disaffected of Afghanistan, and he was holding the line of the Sutlej. Akbar promptly directed his march towards the great river. They came in sight of it on the very day the rain began to fall.

Akbar and his generals walked their horses to the river bank, and gazed at the rebel array on the other side, hardly visible through the teeming downpour. But clearly it was a large force, with several batteries of artillery covering the ford.

'The guns are useless in this weather,' declared Todar Mal.

'That is true,' Akbar agreed. 'But nonetheless he controls the ford. What would Blunt Bahatur have done?'

William had no idea. He had not been trained as a general. But he remembered what his grandfather had told him of previous campaigns.

'In the war with Mahmud Lodi, sire, the army of the great

Babur sought and found another ford, and made their crossing there.'

'That is true. But this is the Sutlej. There is no other ford for many miles. We must cross here, and we must do it while it rains, so my son's powder will be useless. But we will give it a few more days, to soak properly.'

The army pitched camp and settled down to wait, while the rain flooded the ground and seeped under the tents. It was thoroughly uncomfortable even for those who had brought some of their women with them. William's concubines had been delighted to see him back in Agra sooner than expected – and especially without his new wife. But he had decided against bringing any of them, even Jalna the prettiest, on such a campaign in the wet. Now he regretted that. As some compensation he dined with Akbar every night. Seated with them would be Fazl and Birbal, also Prince Daniyal, the Moghul's youngest – and last – legitimate son. Prince Murad had died the previous year of dropsy, but Akbar had not mourned him greatly. Now Prince Daniyal was always at his father's side. Because, after the revolt of Salim, surely he was the next Badshah.

'My son will be wondering what I am about,' the Emperor reflected, 'sitting here in the rain. But his own people will be wondering what they are doing, too. Tomorrow, Blunt Amir, I would have you earn the title bahatur, like your grandfather. Tomorrow you will cross the Sutlej.'

'I, my Lord?'

Akbar smiled. 'Oh, you will have the army solidly behind you, because they will follow the name of Blunt. Are you fearful?'

William swallowed, realising he had been commanded to go to his death if he could not take and hold the ford.

'I am not afraid where you command me, sire,' he said.

Akbar slapped him on the shoulder.

'Forgive me, my lord,' Fazl said, 'but this is no light thing you do – to destroy a favourite son.'

'He is now my enemy,' Akbar growled.

'He is no doubt misled, and he still grieves his mother . . .'

'What would you have me do? Abdicate?'

'My brother is a traitor,' Daniyal said fiercely. 'He must lose his head.'

'He is still your brother,' Fazl said sternly, and turned to Akbar. 'I beg of you, sire, let me cross the river under a flag of truce and speak with the Prince, so as to return him to his allegiance.'

'Do you suppose he will listen to you?' Akbar asked.

'I can but try. If the Prince will not listen, then you may destroy him with an easy conscience.'

Akbar gazed at him for some seconds, then said, 'You are a good and faithful friend, Abul Fazl. Go to my son, and make him listen. Bring him back across the river with you in submission. Or tell him to prepare to die.'

William Blunt had been allowed a reprieve.

Next day Abul Fazl entered the river alone, carrying a flag of truce. The entire Moghul army assembled to watch him go, Akbar sitting his horse by the water's edge.

Abul was not fired upon. After his horse had struggled through the mud to gain the far bank, the watchers saw him being escorted through the trees towards the tents of the rebel generals.

Akbar then rode back to his own tent, and sat down to play chess with Daniyal, while William watched.

The hours drifted by, then the Moghul ate with his son and his Guard Commander. The meal was not yet finished when they heard a great noise: the clashing of shields and cymbals from the soldiers on the bank.

Akbar went to join them, and gazed across the river. The rain had slackened to a drizzle, so it was possible to see the lance with the bleeding head on it, shouting, jeering men holding it aloft.

Akbar gazed without speaking.

'Now my brother must die,' Daniyal said.

'Tomorrow you cross the river, Blunt Amir,' Akbar said. He went back to his tent. 'Now leave me,' he told them all. 'I am to mourn a friend.'

The plan for the assault was made with Akbar's invariable attention to detail. There were the usual bugle calls and drumbeats at dawn as the camp came to life, but these gave no warning to the unseen enemy behind the rain curtain that any attack was planned for this day. The drizzle continued, the leaden clouds giving no indication of a break in the weather, and the usual dawn mist lay over both encampments.

Akbar again walked his horses to the river bank, and he peered into the murk.

'It is time, Blunt Amir,' he said quietly.

When volunteers had been called for, virtually the entire army had stepped forward. Akbar had picked the first thousand himself, men noted for their size and strength and fighting ability. These now moved quietly to the water's edge. All firearms were abandoned; they would have been of no use anyway. This was a matter for spear and sword.

They had also abandoned their horses, and they entered the river on foot. The rain had already raised the level, and even at the ford it came up to their shoulders. They clasped hands to form a human chain, but William was at the head of the chain.

Heart pounding, muscles tensed he slid down the bank. He had been in sufficient actions before, but this was the first time he had led the encounter. Equally it was the first time he had been required to lead what seemed a forlorn hope. Most important of all, with Isabel daily approaching Agra he suddenly realised he had too much else to live for. All depended upon this day.

The swirling water threatened to pluck him from his feet, at the same time as the heavy rain pounded on his helmet, but he slowly made his way across, his men snaking behind him. Luckily the rain continued to provide concealment, and he was two-thirds of the way over before the pickets on the north bank realised what was happening. Instantly there sounded a bugle call, and he could hear the sound of shouting. It was still a struggle against the water, but after a few more steps the current slackened, and now he was only waist deep.

Watching him from the bank were some twenty men; now they loosed their arrows at him. But their bowstrings were sodden, and there was no real power in the shafts. He threw up his buckler and they clanged harmlessly against the metal.

Now he released the hand of the man behind him, and drew his tulwar.

'Ul-ul-ul Akbar!' he shouted at the top of his voice, and the cry was taken up not only by his men in the water but by the entire army behind him.

Then he was only ankle-deep in water, and splashing for the bank. Four men came down against him, armed with spears, but slipping and sliding in the mud. He caught the first thrust on his shield, skilfully ducked the second, and received the third in the ribs – but it was turned aside by his corslet. He swung his tulwar at the fourth man, to send him rolling down the bank.

'Akbar!' he screamed again, then he was into the midst of the rebels, swinging and receiving, cutting and thrusting. For a long moment he seemed all alone. He knew he had been wounded in several places, although scarcely felt the pain, and then he became aware that some of the men were at his shoulder, swinging their swords, and that more were coming ashore with every minute.

The battle was over quickly. As Akbar had truly said, the rebels had no stomach for it. Soon they were running for their lives, despite all efforts by their officers to halt them. These same officers who were now taken prisoner.

Salim, would be 'Jahangir', sought to escape into the mountains, but was soon overtaken by Akbar's cavalry and dragged before his father. Amongst those of his people who had been taken alive were Taulat and Ibrahim Hildas. They stood before the Emperor with heads bowed, knowing that only one fate awaited them. Salim stood among them, expecting the worst.

They waited, in the rain, while Akbar embraced his captains, particularly William.

'As I prophesied, you are a true stem of a sturdy tree. Would that I could say the same of mine. But go and have those wounds dressed.'

He glared at the captives. 'Foul things,' he raged. 'Have I not always dealt fairly with ye? Surely you deserve to suffer. But when you do, it will be clear to all the world. Bind them,' he ordered his tavachis. 'Strip them naked and secure them man to man, that all may know their disgrace – then march them with the army.'

The prisoners made a doleful procession, dragged at the rear of the Moghul army as Akbar rode home in triumph. Blunt realised the Emperor was very angry, his temper compounded by his age and his disappointment in his son – and the murder of Abul Fazl. But did he really mean to execute his heir?

All Agra turned out to watch the return of the army and to stare at the prisoners, their backs bloody from the whips of the Mongols. They were herded into a group, and left there for the night to await their sentence.

William found time to return to his house and to welcome his caravan, which had arrived the previous week.

Elena embraced him. 'You have won a great victory. But these bandages . . .'

'Merely scratches. I hardly feel them.' He gazed hard at Isabel, who gave a little bow. 'Are you pleased to see me?'

'You are my husband, señor,' she said softly.

He perceived no evidence of love, but a little less of hate.

Being Commander of the Guard, William was required to spend much of his time close to the Emperor. He slept in an ante-chamber close to the imperial couch. If he was lucky, he might spend one day a week at home.

He stood at Akbar's shoulder when Prince Salim was dragged before his father.

'Jahangir!' Akbar said contemptuously. 'That is a title to be awarded, not claimed for no reason.'

Salim fell to his knees.

'I erred, my father. I beg your forgiveness, and swear to serve you faithfully for the rest of my life.'

'And what of the murder of Abul Fazl? For that deed alone I should have you impaled.'

'It was not I, my father, I swear it. The deed was done by a wild Pathan. Abul Fazl angered my officers. This man drew his tulwar and cut Fazl down. It was done before I could move. I was considering how best to make amends for the wrong I have done you – but when Fazl was struck down I knew I had to fight. My heart was heavy.'

Akbar studied him.

'Can I believe you?'

'I am your son,' Salim cried. 'I swear the allegiance demanded by my blood – now and always.'

'Then where is this murderous Pathan?'

'He died in the battle, my father.'

He is a liar as well as a would-be parricide, William reflected.

But Akbar reached forward to touch the Prince on his shoulder.

'Yes,' he said. 'Indeed you are my blood: my own beloved son. You could not kill me when you had the chance, therefore I will not rob you of life – though I have reason. Therefore I do forgive thee. Rise up, Prince Salim Jahangir.' He snapped his fingers. 'Bring robes for the Prince, and wine for him to drink.'

William watched this reconciliation with the gravest misgivings.

The anger returned to Akbar's face.

'As for your men, they will die. Yet, as they followed you so blindly, I shall be merciful: they will be beheaded rather than impaled.'

The Emperor appeared to regain his humour, and two days later Blunt found himself required to attend the traditional Thursday symposium. He raised the subject of John Mildenhall.

'A strange name,' Akbar commented. 'How different to Blunt. That is one of the strangest things about your people, the great difference in their names. Why, bring him before me, so that I may meet another Englishman.'

Mildenhall appeared before Akbar in all the splendour of embroidered red silk jerkin over a doublet of black velvet; he had white ruffs at neck and wrist, and a jewelled collar and pendant; his trunk hose contained embroidered panels, and beneath them he wore hose, garters and leather shoes. There was a feather in his black velvet hat, and a rapier hung at his side.

He cut a splendid figure, though William decided he must be damnably hot. Mildenhall bowed low before Akbar.

Salim Jahangir and Daniyal stood close by their father, while William on this occasion performed the duties of introduction.

Mildenhall spoke Persian.

'I know of your country,' Akbar told him, 'because of the Blunts, who have served me well. Now Blunt Bahatur says you also would serve me.'

Mildenhall gave William a hasty glance, uncertain how to take this remark. William had to leave him to make his own decision.

'Why, yes, sire,' Mildenhall agreed, 'it will be my great pleasure to serve you – but I must also serve my sovereign lady.'

'A queen,' Akbar mused. 'Is she a mighty warrior?' He was thinking of Chand Bibi.

'She commands mighty warriors who are happy to fight for her.'

Akbar nodded, and William noted that the Moghul was not looking particularly pleased.

'Tell me how you will serve us both,' he said.

Mildenhall gave William another glance, and this was apprehensive; he also could understand that the interview was not going well.

'I would serve you both by bringing our two nations together.'

'We are many thousands of miles apart. How can this be done?'

'By trade, sire, and by exchange of ideas ...'

'What will you trade?'

William had already warned the Englishman not to make the mistake of offering cloth in any form.

'Fine weapons, sire. Swords like this ...' He drew his rapier and presented it, hilt first.

Akbar made no effort to take it.

'The first Blunt Bahatur had such a sword,' he remarked. 'It served him well, but it is not suited to my people.'

'We will also trade you fine guns, and powder and shot. Hand guns with which to arm your infantry.'

'My infantry already have guns. But of what great use are guns in India?' Akbar demanded. 'When it rains, they are useless. And what ideas would you bring from this country to ours.'

'Well, sire, ideas of philosophy, of religion ...'

'The Jesuits tell me that all Englishmen are heretics in religion.'

'In the opinion of a Jesuit, sire, even you are a heretic,' Mildenhall pointed out.

Akbar's eyes narrowed, and William feared an explosion. Then the Moghul smiled.

'You have a quick tongue, Englishman. You would do well to curb it. Indeed the Jesuits do think I am a heathen.'

Mildenhall drew a long breath.

'Yet I think England has more to offer Your Majesty than does Portugal, sire. I am sure Blunt Bahatur would agree with me.'

'Blunt Bahatur has never been to England,' Akbar pointed out. 'The first Blunt Bahatur believed as you do, and returned there to seek a partnership but was spurned.'

'That was many years ago, sire. Queen Elizabeth and her people are anxious to trade with all the world.'

'So you would have me evict the Portuguese and install you in their place,' Akbar mused. 'I cannot believe that would be wise. The Portuguese have never harmed me – and they already bring us handguns and fine swords, which we do not use. I think to encourage trade with Europe would be harmful to my people, nor do I believe that the introduction of European ideas will be of benefit to them. Yet I have respect for Englishmen because I have respect for the name of Blunt. Stay here and serve me, and you will prosper, but I will give no further licences for Europeans to establish factories in my dominions.'

Mildenhall swallowed. 'I … I must return to my sponsors, and my family, my Lord.'

Akbar nodded. 'Then go. You will have safe conduct to Diu.'

Mildenhall realised that he had been dismissed. He bowed again, and backed from the Moghul's presence.

Mildenhall was utterly despondent.

'I warned you of his long memory,' William pointed out. 'And sadly you came at a bad time. Do you know what my advice would be?'

'To leave this place with all haste,' Mildenhall muttered.

'Why, yes. That to be sure. But more, that it might pay yourself and your London merchants to reapply in five years time. Prince Salim's rebellion will be all but forgotten then, and the Badshah will have regained his customary humour.'

Mildenhall sighed. 'It is a very long way to travel just for a rejection.'

William smiled and clapped him on the shoulder. 'Why,

then, when you return, bring your wife and family, and do as Akbar suggested: take service under him. I do promise you there is a better life to be found here than in England.'

Mildenhall returned the smile.

'I might just take your advice, Blunt Bahatur. And now I must thank you for your assistance, however unsuccessful.'

'You saved my life,' William reminded him.

Gradually, as the crisis of rebellion faded, the Kingdom of Delhi returned to normal.

Work on the mausoleum above Blunt Bahatur's tomb was completed, the white and red stone rising magnificently above the plain outside the city. For William it was a period of increasing happiness.

Since Agra was now Akbar's principal residence, the Blunt family had returned to the Ghopal Das house which had been their home for so long. When at last William was free to visit them there, he took Isabel on a tour of its many galleries and inner courtyards, and reminded her that here Richard Blunt had brought his princess bride.

Elena agreed that it was good for the girl to understand how the Blunts were part of the history of this land. She was now concerned with ensuring that William's marriage should be a success. She had used every opportunity to win the friendship of the troubled girl on their journey from Diu. This had been easy enough, because they had both been anxious as to what was happening to the north; even if Isabel loathed her current situation. But the business of making her a true wife remained to be overcome.

'My nephew is not a bad man,' she had assured Isabel. 'There is much good in him, as well as courage. He means well towards you – I know he adores you.'

'If he adores anything about me, it is merely my body,' Isabel had countered.

'That is probably true. But all relationships between men and women begin with physical attraction. He will learn to love you for yourself, if only you can accept him. My dear Isabel, you have no choice in the matter. William is now your husband. Can you not see that to resist him will bring you nothing but unhappiness.'

'He will wish to . . . possess me again.' Isabel had shuddered.

'I am much afraid that he will – because he is a man. But I have been told there can be pleasure in it for the woman as well.'

'A pleasure you have never sought to experience,' Isabel countered, bitterly.

Elena had no reply to that: she could only count her blessings that she had never had to accept a forced marriage.

On his first night home, William appeared in a fine good humour, and regaled them with gossip from the imperial court, ever smiling at his wife. Later he walked along the corridor to their apartment. To sleep in his own bed after so long – and with what company!

His four concubines waited outside his door, their heads bowed. He had not summoned any of them for several months.

'We wish our master happiness,' said Jalna.

'I will attend to you in due course,' he promised, and opened the bedroom door.

Here too the maids bowed to him, but he had eyes only for Isabel, who sat up on the divan, cushions behind her back, and the sheet folded across her breasts. She wore no nightgown.

William waved his hand and the girls hurried out, simpering.

Slowly he crossed the room to stand over her.

'They said you would wish this best, sire,' Isabel said.

'And they were right.'

He picked up the hem of the sheet very gently, and pulled it down to expose her. Isabel sat absolutely still, her legs straight out in front of her – but she trembled from her toes to the top of her head, more beautiful than he even remembered.

'There is nothing to fear,' he assured her. 'Tonight I will not hurt you.'

He sat down beside her and took her into his arms. Her body was rigid, but she made no attempt to resist him. He kissed her mouth, but she would not open it for him. And when he fondled her breasts she gave an enormous shudder.

Despite his resolve, he began to feel anger rising in his mind. Had he really married a piece of stone?

Releasing her, he stood up and began to undress.

'Would it please you if I had died in battle?' he asked.

'I would wish for no man's death,' she said.

'You are fortunate that I am not a Hindu, I might risk myself out of sheer spite, for the sake of knowing you would be bound on my funeral pyre.'

Naked, he stood over her again. Her eyes were tight shut, her body rigid with tension. For a moment the anger flowed through him. He wanted to drive his fingers into her hair and drag her from the bed, to squeeze her breasts until she screamed, and then put her across his knee and beat her until she bled ... but then they would be back to the beginning again. At least at this moment she was not struggling with him.

'Very well, señora,' he said at last. 'You abhor me, but I must have a woman this night. As it cannot be you ...' he went to the door and opened it. 'Jalna!' he called. 'Come in here.'

A moment later the Hindu girl was in the room, casting a bewildered glance at Isabel, who remained sitting naked on the bed, her eyes still closed; she had made no attempt to retrieve the sheet.

'I would lie with you this night, Jalna,' William said.

'Yes, master.'

Jalna bowed her head, and she turned towards the door.

'In here, now,' William added.

Jalna gave him a surprised glance. Isabel's eyes had now opened.

Jalna's sari seemed to slide from her body as she took a tentative step towards the bed.

Isabel hastily stepped out of it, and hurried across the room for her nightgown.

'What are you doing?' William demanded.

She hesitated. 'Giving you the privacy you require.'

'I do not require privacy from my own wife,' William growled. 'Get back into bed.'

Isabel stared at the divan. Jalna had crawled on to it, and was sitting cross-legged amidst the cushions.

'You cannot mean me to stay,' Isabel protested.

'Yes, I wish you to stay – and to keep your eyes open. I wish you to learn that when a man and a woman couple it can be a joyous thing. Now get back into bed.'

Isabel hesitated a last moment, then obeyed him. As her

shoulder touched Jalna's, she gave a shudder and moved further towards the edge.

William gazed at them lustfully: two perfect naked women as different from each other as it was possible to be.

'I am a most fortunate man,' he said as he joined them on the cushions.

Jalna excelled herself both in giving and receiving. And William, after so long, was able to renew his passion time and again. When at last he lay still, utterly spent, holding Jalna in the crook of his arm, Isabel piped up, 'May I leave now?'

'No,' he told her sharply. 'You are my wife, and this is where you sleep.'

He slept heavily, Jalna in his arms, Isabel's back unwillingly against his, and he awoke with a tremendous feeling of well-being.

A caress of Jalna's breast and her eyes opened as well.

'Leave us,' he whispered into her ear.

Jalna picked up her sari and tip-toed to the door. She would have a great deal to tell her fellow concubines.

William rolled over to gaze at the black hair scattered on the cushions, the expanse of white flesh. Isabel had pulled the sheet over her during the night. This he gently eased down.

'Are you not sated, señor?' she asked softly.

'With you, no. Nor do I suppose that will ever be possible.'

He slid one arm under her, and with a quick heave rolled her over so that she lay on top of him. She gave a startled exclamation, and attempted to keep moving but he restrained her. After a few seconds she subsided on his chest, her face flushed, panting.

'You are an animal,' she said. Tears trickled down her cheeks.

'For loving you?'

'Love ...' her face twisted as he began to rise between her legs. Hastily she brought them together, and then parted them again; he was between.

He slid his hands up her back, to her neck, and brought her face down to be kissed.

'I love you,' he said. 'I wish to love you more. And you are mine. Give yourself to me, Isabel, and I will promise you great happiness.'

She stared at him, their noses almost touching, their breaths mingling. She had stopped sobbing, although tear stains remained on her cheeks.

Slowly he felt her legs moving on his, coming back together, and then her mouth came down on his.

Three months later Elena could announce that Isabel was pregnant.

That first surrender was hardly more than momentary. She yielded to him because, he suspected, she had despite herself been aroused by watching Jalna and himself. But even that was something else to hold against him, and by the next evening her coldness had returned. Since he was now required to return to duty at the palace, he was not sure he had made a great deal of progress. Jalna at least was delighted.

His anger increased on the occasion he brought his wife a present of flowers and sweetmeats, only to have his gift accepted with cold indifference.

'She despises me, and that is the end of it,' he declared to his aunt. 'So why do I not use her as it pleases me, and beat or rape her as I choose. Is it right for a wife to torment a husband in this way?'

'It is a matter of values,' Elena would reply, quietly. 'Of course you may mistreat her, if that is really all you wish from a woman. But if you wish true companionship, true happiness, then you must be patient. It is all a matter of values, William. If you wish to have something of great value, then you must treat it as of value, nurture it and praise it. Have you ever praised Isabel in any way?'

'Do men praise women, except for their beauty? I have most certainly praised her beauty.'

'There are more important things than beauty,' Elena told him. 'That is, after all, a transient quality.'

Then the pregnancy.

Isabel gazed at Elena in horror when she confirmed the fact. Then she fell on her bed, weeping.

'You should be happy.' Elena was stern. 'This will bind you

more closely to your husband.'

When Isabel raised her head, her eyes looked more stricken than ever.

Then William sat with her, and stroked her hair.

'You have made me the happiest man in the world. Isabel, can we not attempt to count our blessings? If you will but give me a small part of your heart, be sure that I will give you all of mine.'

There remained only tears in her eyes.

Richard Blunt the Younger was born in 1603, and his sister Laura a year after. William even persuaded himself that Isabel was at last accepting him as a husband.

All the while, the empire was at peace.

'Now you have no more worlds to conquer, my lord,' William suggested to the Moghul.

Akbar smiled. 'No man can say so until he is dead. Yet there are other tasks I should attempt. Indeed, I am learning to read. Is that not an admission at my age? Now that I have more leisure, it should be put to good use, and there are all those books collected by my father, waiting ... I will enjoy my old age, Blunt Bahatur. Who knows, I may become a sage.'

For all the Emperor's apparent tranquillity in this the evening of his life, however, he remained concerned about the future of his empire and his family.

Salim Jahangir had indeed made his peace with his father, and was now apparently the most loyal of sons. Yet he remained addicted to alcohol, and by report was drinking more heavily than ever – and using opium more frequently as well. Rumours spread that he was savagely violent towards his servants – and to his sons now growing to manhood. Certainly the eldest, Khusraw, seldom appeared in public without a frown of tension on his face.

All these factors distressed the ageing Emperor. Although he was unfailingly polite to Salim, William could sense that he again held doubts as to his eldest son's ability to succeed. Yet there was scarcely any other choice, for Daniyal drank just as heavily as his elder brother.

'I am cursed,' Akbar would sometimes growl. 'A Muslim plagued by drunkards!'

Drink was certainly the biggest curse the House of Babur had to bear, which was amazing in view of Akbar's own abstinence. But Akbar could consider none of his younger sons as a successor in place of Jahangir or Daniyal . . . for none of them was the son of Jodha Bai, and he counted all his other wives and concubines as nothing.

Akbar mused: 'Perhaps Khusraw – he is a man of spirit, and he does not drink.' He looked at Raja Birbal. 'What does the law say of bypassing the son in favour of the grandson?'

'The law does not enter into it, my lord,' Birbal replied. 'The succession is yours alone to determine. But should you decide in favour of Prince Khusraw, then Prince Jahangir cannot be left alive when you die.'

Akbar stroked his beard.

'My son,' he muttered. 'My dear wife's son. Is he not all that is left to me from her?' He looked from face to face. 'I will give him a year to reform his ways. A year, and then a decision must be taken.' A quick glance around the faces of his viziers. 'Should he not be warned of this?'

It was clear he had not the heart to do this himself, so it was now a question of who would take the risk of issuing a warning to the prince. No one was eager, but William only hesitated briefly. Like all of Akbar's intimates, his future depended on what arrangements the Moghul made for after his death. But he was also the youngest, and had to think of Isabel and the children, to secure their futures as well.

If Salim refused to listen to him, then it would be necessary to pay court to the younger princes.

William chose his opportunity one day when he accompanied Salim out hunting. Salim prided himself on his birds: he used only falcons, that is, females, all of which were passagers: birds caught wild and then trained. He was never happier than watching the graceful haggards, adult birds, swooping through the air. William had inherited his grandfather's birds; these were all eyas, fledglings taken from the nest, and whose training had begun before they could even fly. There was a continuing dispute among falconers as to which system produced the better hunters. Blunt himself believed in the eyas, who were certainly more loyal, and more gentle when not in flight. But on this occasion he had intentionally brought with him only his favourite tiercel, a male, two-thirds as large as the average female. He had him secretly fed before taking him out, so that he should seem sluggish compared with the Prince's falcon.

'Ha ha,' Salim cried out. 'Your bird is useless, Blunt Bahatur. The day is undoubtedly mine.'

'I admit defeat, sire.'

'Then come with me and have a glass of wine.'

The two men dismounted to sit in the shade, while their attendants served them. With them sat Salim's favourite tavachi, a Hindu named Spartu. Spartu was in fact the grandson of Hemu, but his father had been only a child when the would-be Rajah Bikramajit had died, so had been absolved in the general amnesty announced by Akbar following his victory at Panipat. The young man had early attached himself to Salim. He was always unfailingly polite, but William felt uneasy in his company. Yet he could not allow Spartu's presence to alter his purpose here.

As Salim raised his glass to his lips, William checked him. Salim raised his eyebrows.

'Have you the power, sire, to upturn that goblet and empty the wine upon the ground?' William asked.

Salim frowned at him for a moment, then, with a turn of his wrist, he did so.

'What is difficult about that?' he asked, holding out his glass for a refill.

'And now the whole bottle?'

Salim's frown deepened. 'Are you sent to lecture me?'

'To warn you, sire. It grieves me to do so.'

Spartu made as if to rise, but was checked by a glance from his master.

'Hear me out,' William pleaded, as Salim stared at him. 'Your father loves you above all other men,' Blunt continued. 'He loves you as your mother's son, and he wishes you to inherit his empire. But he would even sacrifice a son to prevent that empire from falling into unworthy hands.'

Salim was staring at him coldly. The servant hovered with the wine flask, but eventually the Prince waved it away.

'My father sent you to tell me this?' he asked.

'In effect, yes, my lord.'

'You are a faithful servant of the Badshah.'

'I shall be his faithful servant to the end of his days, sire. But, then, I would equally prove myself the faithful servant of his successor.'

'Words I shall remember, Blunt Bahatur.' Salim stood up. 'Then let us return to Agra, and let me commence being a dutiful son.'

From that day, Salim seemed a reformed man. He abjured wine and drugs entirely, was to be seen playing polo jovially with his sons, and he smiled on the people of Agra when he rode abroad. But much of his time he spent with his father. The two men walked the palace gardens together, deep in conversation. They discussed endlessly the military and financial state of the Empire, the worthiness and unworthiness of its various officials.

They even played chess by the hour, for Akbar delighted in fighting mock battles. He did not, however, play with ivory pieces on a conventional board. Instead he had a huge chequer-board laid out in the garden of his palace, and his chessmen were thirty-two pretty slave girls dressed in elaborate costumes to indicate the pieces they represented. Thrones were placed at each end of the board, and the moves as decided were called out to these girls by a vizier. Such games sometimes lasted for days, the positions being carefully recorded each night.

This new intimacy between father and son was a relief to watch; and the death of Prince Daniyal, in April 1604 of dropsy, seemed hardly to concern Akbar at all.

William discerned that the ageing Moghul was enjoying perhaps the happiest period of his life since the death of his beloved Jodha Bai. He had a career of such magnificent success to look back upon, and now he had the son he wanted as well.

In his pleasure, Akbar became munificent. On the occasion of his birthday, he commanded chests filled with gold coin and precious stones to be placed in front of him, and invited each of his commanders in turn to take away as much treasure as could be contained in his arms.

But William could hardly admire Salim less for the way in which he had entirely turned his back upon his vices – almost at the snap of a finger. Perhaps, after all, he would make a successful Emperor.

But he was content for himself and his family as well. Isabel now behaved as a wife in more than just name, and his children were strong and healthy. It was a happy time ...

Until, at the beginning of October 1605, Akbar fell ill.

It seemed merely some debilitation at first; the Badshah complained of stomach upsets and general weakness. The physicians were called in, but could find nothing amiss. They dosed him with various medicines, but none seemed to help.

Agra soon became a hive of worried officials, heads close together as they pondered whether the greatest man any of them had ever known was likely to recover.

None seemed more concerned than Prince Salim. There were occasions when he would remain with his father late into the night. At these times they were completely alone, since William would withdraw to an outer chamber with Akbar's personal servants. More often, though, he would hand over the guard duty to one of his tukbashis, and go home to his wife.

On the night of 25 October, however, he remained on duty. Having bidden the ailing Moghul and his son goodnight, he retired to his couch in a corner of the antechamber. He was still awake when Salim also said goodnight to his father, somewhat loudly, and he observed the Prince leave the room and the palace. Then Blunt went to sleep – to be awakened at dawn by a servant so terror-stricken he could hardly speak.

William was on his feet in an instant, running into the Moghul's sleeping chamber to gaze at the body of his master.

Akbar lay on his side, his eyes open and staring, his mouth open too. His face was blackened, though he had not been strangled.

He had been dead for at least six hours.

14
THE PARRICIDE

There could be no doubt at all that Akbar had been poisoned. Equally, there could be no doubt who was the murderer. For a few seconds William's brain could not grasp the implications of the deed.

He had supposed Salim to be a man of immense willpower, so easily to have given up his favourite pastimes. Well, no doubt he *was* a man of tremendous willpower, because it needed willpower to kill a father who was also the most powerful man in the land. But that meant everything since their conversation on that hawking trip had been a sham. The Prince must have determined on the death of his father then and there.

And then he had carried out his plan with utter ruthlessness, pretending to all the world how completely he and Akbar were reconciled, while slowly killing the Badshah – because there could be no doubt that for the past three weeks the Prince had been feeding Akbar poison ...

He looked down at the servant, who had fallen to his knees, and was staring at the dead Moghul, shivering with fear.

The servant feared blame because it was he who had found the body. It could easily be assumed he had administered the poison.

Or, William himself, he realised. Salim would deny the crime, would claim he left his father alive and well – hence the loud farewell – in the care of Blunt Bahatur and the servants. And Salim was now the Moghul – Blunt Bahatur merely the Commander of the Guard.

William suddenly felt cold. If the reconciliation had been false, then Salim would not have forgotten how Blunt Bahatur had seized the ford and caused his defeat, how Blunt Bahatur had been publicly rewarded by the Moghul while the Prince had knelt naked and humiliated, how Blunt Bahatur had stood at

Akbar's side while the Prince begged his father for mercy . . .

The cold realisation grew: Salim had none of his father's capacity for mercy.

The slave raised his head. 'What is to be done, Amir?'

William forced himself to think. He had perhaps two hours of life left, whether he reported the crime or did nothing. Because Salim would have to wait for someone else to find the body; he could not allow any hint that he already knew his father was dead; only the murderer could know that in advance of the servants.

But if Blunt could put those two hours to good use . . . Two hours!

If he wanted to live he must be as ruthless as Salim. But if he died, then Isabel and Elena and the children would also die.

'Amir?' asked the servant.

The man was going to die anyway, and probably by impalement. William drew his tulwar and despatched him with a single stroke. The dead body sprawled at the side of the bed. Now had he, no doubt, confirmed his guilt in the eyes of the world.

He cleaned the blade, sheathed his sword, and stepped out of the chamber.

The other two servants gazed at him.

'The Badshah is again unwell,' William said. 'He is not to be disturbed. I go to fetch a surgeon. Let no one into the Moghul's chamber until I return. Bojay will remain with him. Is that understood?'

'Yes, Blunt Bahatur.' They bowed.

He strode from the room and summoned Talas. Then he mounted, Talas beside him. They walked their horses through the slowly awakening streets, and gained his house.

'Saddle horses for my wife, my aunt, and my children's ayahs,' William told Talas. 'And for Jalna,' he added. She remained his favourite concubine. 'Do not disturb the grooms, so do it yourself. And take a further seven remounts.'

'We are leaving Agra?'

William nodded. 'Is there anyone you would take with us?' He knew Talas was unmarried.

The tavachi shook his head.

'I ride where you ride, Blunt Bahatur,' he said, obviously bewildered.

'I will explain later,' William said. 'Now prepare the horses.'

By the time his family was assembled and informed of the situation, Talas had saddled the horses. But the household was awake; the night watchman had seen to that. William now addressed the servants.

'I am sent on a secret mission for the Emperor,' he told them. 'There must be no noise. Go back to your beds. When people come to inquire after me, swear that you do not know where I am.'

'Are you not leaving them to their deaths?' Elena asked, as they walked their horses out of the yard.

'Not if they do exactly as I have commanded,' he said.

They left Agra by the north gate, and rode north-west for the hills, and then the valley beyond.

'Where can we go?' Elena asked. 'To Diu?'

'I doubt we will receive a welcome in Diu, and in any event that is the first place Salim will look for us. His people can be only hours behind us. If we were not able to find a ship there within twenty-four hours we would be arrested.'

'Then where can we go?'

'Lahore.'

'There is safety in Lahore?'

'Prince Khusraw is in Lahore. He is our only hope.' He smiled at her. 'This is not the first time our family has sought refuge in the Punjab . . . and returned in triumph.'

Elena shuddered. She felt totally bemused, cut adrift from everything she had valued. Though she knew the family history, the wild deeds of her father and Richard Blunt had happened many many years ago – they were ancient history. Her own life had always followed such an even path, shrouded in such security. Of course she had known that Akbar must die some day. But like William, like everyone else in Hindustan, she had assumed that his beloved son, now reconciled, would continue in his father's ways – and with his father's ministers and his father's Commander of the Guard.

To be fleeing now like a thief, with Akbar lying poisoned, had all the appearance of a nightmare.

They rode eighteen hours a day. The nurses grumbled, Isabel

and Elena drooped in the saddle, the children wailed their exhaustion and their anguish. Only Jalna retained her laughing energy.

Talas and William constantly looked over their shoulders; even if Diu might be Salim's first choice he would certainly also be sending messengers to Lahore to inform Khusraw of Akbar's death – and on the first day those messengers would learn who had ridden this road before them. William estimated they had little more than four hours start.

They changed horses twice a day, and even so had to abandon six on the second day. The remainder were dropping with exhaustion when, on the fifth morning, they rode into Lahore, three hundred and fifty miles from Delhi.

Prince Khusraw was in his early twenties now. He had three wives and several sons and, as the eldest of his generation of princes, a glittering future. Save that he had always hated his father, Salim.

Khusraw had been named after a famous Persian warrior king, and he had already distinguished himself as a fighting soldier with the armies of Akbar. Indeed, he worshipped his grandfather, and sought only to emulate him. William remembered his own grandfather telling him how he had ridden like the wind to this very city to bring the news to Akbar of his succession to the throne – and what great things had stemmed from that. If Khusraw could prove worthy of that heritage, then was the future assured.

Khusraw received Blunt in private, and listened carefully to what he had to say, his fingers tangling themselves in his beard.

'My father killed him?' he asked.

'There can be no doubt of it.'

Khusraw muttered, 'Was not Akbar the greatest man who ever lived?'

'History will judge him highly, my lord. Will you avenge his death?'

Khusraw brooded. 'I cannot kill my own father – as he killed his. But I will avenge Akbar's murder, Blunt Bahatur.'

'Then we both shall avenge his murder, sire. Akbar was more than my master. He was my friend and my guide.'

'We shall ride together,' Khusraw confirmed.

The army was mobilised, and frontier detachments called in from Peshawar and Amritsar. But they had not yet concentrated when a cavalry regiment arrived from Agra.

'We seek the traitor known as Blunt,' the ming-bashi told Prince Khusraw.

'Blunt Bahatur is here,' Khusru confirmed, and gestured William forward.

'We had heard he rode this way, my lord. Do you know of the death of the Moghul?'

'Blunt Bahatur has told me of it.'

The ming-bashi frowned. 'And he stands freely beside you, sire?'

'He has told me the truth of it,' Khusraw growled. 'It is my own father who should be arrested for this foul crime. As indeed he will be.'

The ming-bashi looked astounded.

'Return to my father,' Khusraw commanded, 'and tell him I know him for a parricide. Tell him I am assembling my people to march upon him – to exact vengance for the death of my most beloved grandfather. Tell him his best course is to surrender to me now. Tell him I declare myself to be the Moghul, for he is unfitted for such an honour.'

The ming-bashi swallowed, but answered boldly. 'The Moghul's wrath will be felt by you and yours, sire.'

'It is my wrath you have to fear,' Khusraw warned him.

Khusraw spoke like a king and looked like a king. He sat his horse like a king, and rode before his men like a king.

'We go to war with a parricide,' he declared. 'Is that not the most heinous of crimes?'

The Pathans and Sikhs, discontented Rajputs and Baluchis who had rallied to his horsetail standard, all raised their swords and spears in loud acclaim.

The Guru Arjun blest Khusraw's enterprise.

'What then do you intend for Salim, when you have won?' William asked.

'Perpetual imprisonment,' Khusraw said firmly. 'For a man cannot kill his own father.'

* * *

Once again the river Sutlej divided the two armies, but when, on William's advice, Khusraw sent a strong body of horsemen to the river, they found the ford open.

Instantly infantry were despatched behind them – it was only fifty miles from Lahore – to seize and fortify the far bank. William began to feel more optimistic, remembering how Salim had shown no great stomach for a fight four years before.

'What would you have us do,' Elena asked, as the army prepared to march out.

'Why, remain here,' William told her, 'until I return.'

'And if your army is defeated?'

'There is a bag of silver brought from Agra. I also leave you Talas Ali, who is utterly faithful and reliable. At the first news of any disaster, take the money, Isabel and the children, Talas and an escort, and ride for Diu. Do this also if you receive a message from me which says simply '*Ride*'. Then leave immediately. Promise me you will do this, Aunt.'

She gazed long into his eyes, then hugged him.

Isabel was also at hand to say farewell. He kissed the babies, then took her aside.

'Our life has scarce begun together,' he told her, 'and now this interruption. But when Prince Khusraw is triumphant I shall stand at his right hand, as I did for Akbar, and we will have great happiness.'

'I am sure of it,' she said.

Jalna wept.

Isabel stood on the battlements with a crowd of others, to watch the army march out, the sun reflecting from burnished helmets and shields and corslets, dust rising above the rumbling artillery caissons.

But even during her brief sojourn within the Moghul Empire, she had seen far larger armies on the march, and far more cannon too.

She hugged herself, then went to Elena.

'I would have you perform a great favour for me.'

'You have but to ask it,' Elena replied.

'I would have you take the children and their nurses, and go to Diu.'

Elena frowned at her. 'While you do what?'

'I shall remain here, as I must, to await the return of my husband.'

'But you wish me to take the babies away now?'

'I wish you to leave, Elena – tomorrow.'

'Then you do not believe that William will return victoriously?'

Isabel would not meet her eyes. 'I know nothing of warfare. I am afraid.'

'Then you should come with us.'

'William would never forgive me.' She grasped Elena's hands. 'If … if I were to learn of his fall, I would come fast behind you. This I promise.'

Elena was in a quandary. She knew nothing of wars and battles either. She only knew that her father had always been victorious, and that William seemed to inherit the Blunt military acumen. Now Isabel's lack of confidence suddenly raised doubts in her own mind. Of course Isabel was a young girl of twenty-two, and rightly her first thought was for the safety of her children.

But what of herself, Elena wondered? William was her entire life: now she was being asked to abandon him, and to seek safety while he was fighting for his life.

Yet what else could she do? Isabel was right: if either of them had to stay, it should be the wife.

'The moment word of a victory is received, you will send behind me,' she insisted.

'The very moment,' Isabel promised, and kissed her. 'Give my love to my parents, and tell them how happy I am.'

Next day Elena and the children rode out of Lahore, with a small escort commanded by Talas, heading south-west for Gujarat and Diu.

Jalna chose to remain in Lahore, and Isabel did not object. The two women had perforce become almost friends, and she was glad of the company.

Khusraw's army crossed the Sutlej without hindrance, the far bank still being securely held.

The tuman-bashi in command had sent his scouts far to the south-east, and these had now returned.

'The Badshah has mobilised his army, my lord,' he reported.

'But it remains encamped outside Agra. He is not yet ready to go to war.' The man suppressed a grin. 'The Badshah is to be married.'

'At this moment?' Khusraw was incredulous. 'Who is his bride?'

'The Agha Nur on-Mesa, sire.'

'But she is the wife of another,' William protested.

'That was so, my lord. But her husband has recently died, cut down by a man who had made advances to the agha.'

Khusraw and Blunt stared at each other.

'Can my father have done this as well?' Khusraw asked. 'Is there no end to his vices?'

'The agha has been renamed, my lord,' the tuman-bashi continued. 'She is to be called Nur Mahal, "Light of the World!". Just as the Moghul is now to be known as Jahangir, "World Conqueror".'

'My father has gone mad,' Khusraw commented. 'How big an army does he command?'

'It is a great army – many times our numbers.'

Khusraw looked at William. 'Why does he not advance?'

'Because he knows you must defeat him, sire,' William said. 'He is the Moghul. Until you win the victory, you are no more than a rebel.'

'But I must have more men,' Khusraw said. 'We shall remain here while we recruit.'

Blunt had to be doubtful about that.

'My lord,' he argued. 'You must attack your father now. At this minute his authority remains uncertain. Akbar has been murdered. I may have been accused of the crime, but there will be many who remember how Jahangir quarrelled with his father, indeed rebelled against him, only five years ago. Now there seems little doubt that Nur on-Mesa's husband has been murdered to satisfy the Moghul's lust. If you go boldly forward now and declare that you know your father to be a parricide and a murderer and a wife-stealer, these men will fight you with even less resolution. But with every day that Salim is in possession of the throne, so every day will more and more men come to accept him as their master, no matter what crimes he may have committed.'

Khusraw listened in silence, but William realised with a

sinking heart that the young Prince was not prepared to take his advice.

'What you say may be true, Blunt Bahatur,' Khusraw replied at last. 'But to engage in battle at odds of two to one would be suicide. We will increase the strength of our army.'

William then realised that Khusraw was not, after all, destined to be a reincarnation of Akbar. And also that the situation was lost.

The army encampment on the banks of the Sutlej soon assumed a certain permanency, while tavachis were sent far and wide to rouse the hill people to fight for their Prince. Inevitably women and tradesmen accumulated round the camp, a bazaar came into being, and soon it became difficult to differentiate between soldiers and civilians.

William was in a quandary. He could see catastrophe staring them all in the face, but lacked the experience or authority to do anything about it.

Khusraw seemed happy enough. He held frequent military reviews and drew up elaborate tactical plans for their eventual advance, deploying imaginary troops he did not yet have. But even he became alarmed when it was reported that an entire regiment had stolen away in the night.

The ming-bashi was dragged before him.

'How could this be?' the Prince demanded.

'They were suborned, my lord,' the colonel protested. 'Men came amongst them assumed to be merchants, but they were agents sent by the Moghul to speak with my soldiers.' He gave William an anxious glance. 'These men say the Moghul wishes no war with his son, only to arrest the murderer of his father.'

Khusraw frowned at him. 'The so-called Moghul is the real murderer of Akbar.'

The ming-bashi gave Blunt another glance.

'The Moghul denies this, my lord. He says that his father was alive when he left him on the fatal night. He says that the murderer is Blunt Bahatur, who then fled Agra, spreading false rumour as he did so.'

William felt his muscles tense as he looked at the Prince.

'Did you lie to me, Blunt Bahatur?' Khusraw asked.

'I have never lied in my life, my lord,' William said.

Khusraw looked at the colonel.

'Your men believed this tale?'

'Alas, that is what happened.'

'So they have deserted to my father. Others will follow if this goes unchecked. Blunt Bahatur, it is your responsibility to seek out these suborners of my people and destroy them – as they are also your accusers. Make haste!'

William saluted and went about his business, but with a growing sense of despair. For every man that he found and executed there would be two others, and more would be arriving every day. Jahangir was fighting in the true Mongol fashion, letting his spies do the main part of his work for him.

William sent one of his own tavachis back to Lahore.

'Seek out Blunt Agha,' he told the man. 'Tell her I send a message. It is one word: 'Ride'. Now haste.'

Over the next few days several thousand more men deserted, and it was obvious that the war was over. That Jahangir was well informed of what was happening was confirmed by reports from scouts that the Moghul army was beginning to advance. No doubt the Moghul had finished honeymooning.

'What are we to do?' Khusraw asked plaintively, all his bravado and spirit gone.

'Retreat on Lahore, sire,' suggested one of the tuman-bashis. 'Make the Moghul come to us there.'

'Can we hold the city? We have never been successful at holding cities. And my father will continue to suborn my soldiers.'

William sighed. 'There is only one thing you can do, my lord: hand me over to your father and make your peace with him.'

'Have you any idea what he would do to you, Blunt Bahatur?'

'It is your only hope.'

Khusraw pondered long. For all his failings as a military commander, he remained an honourable man.

'You have been a good and faithful follower, Blunt Bahatur – too good for me to send you to a miserable death. Yet if my men will not fight for me, I have no course open but to make my peace with my father. Here is what we shall do. I shall place you under arrest, and send an emissary to the Moghul to announce this. Once the emissary has departed, you will be allowed to make your escape. I must not know where you intend to go, therefore I cannot reveal that to my father. I can only wish you godspeed.'

William bowed his head, but his heart leapt. He was being given another chance at life.

15

THE EXECUTIONER

It gave William an uneasy feeling to hand over his sword and allow himself to be marched off to his tent, and there be surrounded by armed guards in full view of the encampment. It would be so easy for Khusraw still to change his mind.

The Prince was a man of his word, however. That night a tavachi released the prisoner, restored to him his weapon, and gave him a horse.

'Ride like the wind, Blunt Bahatur,' he urged. 'Be sure the Moghul will send behind you.'

William clasped the man's hand, and swung into the saddle. A few minutes later he was clear of the camp.

Blunt had to assume that Isabel had received his message, and would now be on her way to Diu with the children. He therefore rode to the west, seeking to put a good distance between himself and any pursuers, before turning more to the south. It was necessary to pace himself, as he had only the one horse. As his flight was as yet unknown, he might have requisitioned other mounts, but the country was gleaned almost clear of good horses by the army.

He made steady progress, certain that he had at least forty-eight hours in hand.

Two days after leaving the camp, he entered a village in quest of food and drink, and found there one of the ming-bashis Khusraw had earlier sent out recruiting.

'Blunt Bahatur!' Semih Ali cried. 'What brings you here?'

'Why, the same thing as yourself,' William lied. 'Our master grows impatient for more men, and wonders why you have not yet returned.'

'For the reason you see, sir: I have been unable to raise recruits. I have even been to Lahore in the hopes of finding some worthwhile men, but to no purpose.'

'Lahore,' William said. 'And what is the word from there?'

'They are fearful,' Semih told him. 'They crowd the walls day and night, seeking news of the army, of a victory ... and fearing to hear of a defeat. Even your wife was among them. I saw her on the walls, staring to the south-east.'

William frowned. 'When was this?'

'Why, but yesterday. I came down here today and mean to rejoin the army tomorrow. Why do you not ride with me?'

'Yesterday!' William cried in surprise.

His messenger had been despatched a week ago. He must surely have reached Lahore at least four days ago. And Isabel was still there?

For a moment he had no idea what to do. To break his journey and return to Lahore would be highly dangerous. But to abandon Isabel and the children to the wrath of Jahangir was unthinkable.

Why had they remained there?

'Blunt Bahatur?' inquired Semih, observing his expression.

'You ride back to the army,' William told him. 'I will follow. But first I will visit my wife.'

Semih grinned.

'I understand your feelings, sir. The Blunt Agha is a pearl amongst women.'

William changed horses and departed that same night. He had some sixty miles to cover, and rode as hard as he could – entering the city at dawn. The captain of the guard seemed surprised to see him, but opened the gate without demur.

The horse was exhausted, so William abandoned it and proceeded on foot, reaching his house half an hour later. The dozing watchman started up in consternation at the sight of his master.

'Where is Blunt Agha?' William demanded impatiently.

'She sleeps, sire.'

'And my children?'

The man rolled his eyes. 'They departed a month ago, sire.'

Bursting into the house, William ran to Isabel's room.

She leapt from beneath the covers to be in his arms – and then held him away from her. 'There has been catastrophe?'

'Yes. That you are still here.'

'What has happened?'

'I am accused of the murder of Akbar, and am now a fugitive. I had thought you safe by now. Did you not get my message?'

'Message?'

'But you sent Elena and the children away.'

'That was several weeks ago. I could not contemplate the thought of them being here if you were defeated.'

'But you stayed, yourself?'

'I could not bear the thought of running away from you.'

He hugged her again. 'Then let us run together.'

William aroused the startled Jalna, and bade her prepare herself. Three fresh horses waited in the stables, which they mounted. He intended taking no one else – speed was all that mattered now.

The servants gathered to watch them go, but these were hired servants only interested in pay. William gave them some money; he could do no more for them.

By mid-morning they were again on the road, riding south-west. Again the guard captain opened the gate for them without question, but that he was sorely puzzled was obvious.

They stopped for the night at a village, where they were made welcome by the headman. It was a sleepless night as they wrestled with the fleas, and with each other, in fearful happiness.

William reckoned he needed only a few more days to reach safety, but while they breakfasted the next morning, they heard the sound of approaching hooves. William stepped outside to gaze at the troop of cavalry nearing the village, apparently having ridden all night.

The villagers clustered on the single street, anxiously wondering whether the soldiers came for forage or for taxes; either way their visit would be unwelcome.

'Quickly!' Blunt yelled.

They ran for the horses, but were impeded by the crowd. William gave Isabel a leg up, and she appeared to have settled in the saddle. But, as he mounted himself, several arrows were fired, and one of these struck Isabel's horse. It reared, and with a scream she slipped from the saddle, landing on her feet but unable to regain her mount.

Blunt swung his own horse round to snatch her up, but before he could reach her she was already surrounded by the soldiers. He drew his sword, but the ming-bashi dismounted and held his knife to Isabel's throat, his arm thrown round her waist.

It was Jahangir's aide, Spartu.

'Surrender,' he said, 'or the agha dies.'

William hesitated, but threw down the tulwar. Instantly he was surrounded and dragged from the saddle.

Jalna had mounted securely, and had ridden some distance off. Now she drew rein as well.

'Ride!' William shouted to her. 'Save yourself.'

But Jalna hesitated, then turned her horse back to them. Instantly she too was seized by soldiers.

'The Moghul will be pleased,' Spartu gloated. 'He is most anxious to behold you standing bound before him. Strip him naked.'

William's armour and clothes were torn off, while he gazed sadly at Isabel. She had caused his capture . . . and undoubtedly his death.

But what of hers?

And Jalna. Faithful Jalna. They were going to die, together.

His wrists were bound in front of him, and then attached to a longer rope. He was to be forced to walk – or be dragged – to Jahangir's presence.

'What of the women?' inquired the sergeant, grinning lasciviously at Isabel, who seemed to shrink in her captor's arms. 'Can we not have them?'

'Our master will wish to try the infidel first, perhaps,' Spartu said. 'But his orders were to bring Blunt Amir, and all found with him, naked before him. Therefore we shall obey our orders.'

He gave Isabel and Jalna to his men to be stripped, which they did with great gusto. Jalna suffered in silence, but Isabel could not forego a moan of horror as they handled her body. Her wrists were also bound and attached to ropes; these were then made fast to the saddles of the three horsemen, and the dreadful journey began.

It took four days to reach Jahangir's camp. By then the three captives were covered with lacerations on their legs and bellies and chests, where they had fallen and been dragged, and more on their backs caused by the whips of their captors. They had been spared not the slightest indignity throughout the march, and never released from their bonds, so their wrists were swollen as much as their feet. They were forced to sleep at the horses' tails when they stopped for the night, and to perform their necessaries as they stumbled along. They were fed only a few crusts of bread, which were thrust unceremoniously into their mouths – as were the spouts of water canteens.

'What is going to happen to us?' Isabel whimpered on the first day of torment.

'We are going to die,' William told her. 'And I fear most painfully.'

'I wish you to know that I love you,' Isabel said on the second day, after again being manhandled by soldiers during their brief overnight stop. Bleeding and filthy as she now was, they yet found her a source of pleasure to grope.

'Will the children escape, do you suppose?' she continued later.

'If anyone can save them, it will be Elena,' he promised her.

'Tell me I did the right thing in sending them away.'

'You did the right thing,' William assured her.

By the fourth day they did not speak at all. They were too exhausted as they reached the end.

Jahangir sat on a high chair and looking down at his prisoners from a raised dais. Seated beside him was the Nur Jahan.

She was undoubtedly a most beautiful woman, who looked totally accustomed to her new role, with no hint of mourning for her murdered husband. Indeed, the arrogance of her expression outdid that of the Moghul himself.

Standing behind the Empress was a man who was evidently her brother, and a young girl of an exquisite beauty which even outshone Nur Jahan's. Even through his pain and humiliation,

William could see that she was the other man's daughter, and thus Nur Jahan's niece.

There were three hundred prisoners: the principal officers of the rebel army, all naked and bound.

Prince Khusraw stood beside his father, his fingers twisting nervously. He did not seem to have been maltreated in any way.

On the Begum's left was the younger brother, Prince Khurram, a boy of fourteen. Like his half-brother, Khurram was the son of a Rajput princess, Manamati, and his complexion was the darkest of them all. He was also clearly of a gentler disposition, looking genuinely distressed to see the misery in front of him.

Around them were drawn up the troops of the Guard, and beyond them the rest of the army. It was a splendid martial array.

The Moghul smiled as the last two captives were brought before him.

'Blunt Bahatur,' he said. 'The assassin!'

William summoned all of his remaining strength.

'You know that to be a lie, sire', he said. 'It is my word to use of you.'

Jahangir's eyes glowed.

'No doubt you will shriek it as you die.' He looked towards Isabel. 'Such beauty,' he remarked. 'But tarnished.'

'My people will attend to her,' the Nur Jahan said softly. She summoned one of her ladies. 'Take the woman and have her bathed.'

'Then bring her back naked,' Jahangir added. 'Such beauty should be revealed to the world.'

'And the slave girl?'

Jahangir stared at Jalna.

'What have I to do with slave girls?' he asked. 'Strike off her head.'

Jalna died without a word. She had not spoken since their capture. Her mind had died at that moment.

They sat, Jahangir, his new wife and the princes, munching fruit while the humiliated prisoners still knelt before them.

Isabel was led back half an hour later, her hair still damp, but her body washed clean and perfumed. The cuts and bruises now showed more vividly, but her pale beauty remained for all to see.

'Let her be mounted on a mule,' Jahangir commanded. 'For now we shall return to Agra.'

Another terrible march at the heels of the cavalry awaited the prisoners. People lined the roads to cheer the Moghul and his victory, and to jeer at the prisoners, shouting obscene suggestions at the naked woman. Blunt could only be grateful that Isabel was spared the ordeal of having to walk – although he suspected a far greater one might await her. They had no opportunity to speak again.

There was nothing to do but think, and compose himself for death. It was easy to blame the past, his ancestry, the ambitions of his forebears. Richard Blunt the Elder had tied his fortunes, and those of his descendants, to the Moghuls. He had achieved great wealth, great distinction ... but he and all of his family had perished tragically.

Peter Blunt had allowed his ambitions to guide him in the footsteps of his cousin, and risen even higher. He and his wife had been fortunate to die in the fullness of their years ... but every one of their children, save Elena, had perished before their time, the men violently.

Now he, the very last Blunt, must die the same way.

Like his predecessors, he had supposed nothing but fame and fortune lay ahead. What a fool he had been. Now he must pay the penalty for that folly. The very name of Blunt would disappear from history.

Spartu tormented William as they marched, prodding him with sticks, abusing him, spitting in his face.

'The Moghul promised the command of his Guard to the man who brought you back,' he gloated. 'That post is now mine. But first I have asked for another, and the Moghul has granted me that too.' He grinned. 'I am going to watch you die, Blunt Amir – because I myself am going to kill you. And the Moghul has appointed me to deal with all the other prisoners.' He glanced at Isabel. 'That will prove great sport.'

When Agra was finally reached, Jahangir perpetrated the final act of his vengeance. Before that, on the last day of the march, he had his army make a detour to pass by the deserted city of Fatehpur Sikri. There William was taken to watch the workmen demolishing Peter Blunt's tomb.

'Not a stone will be left,' the Moghul had declared. 'There will be no memory of the name of Blunt in all Hindustan.'

In Agra itself Jahangir had Khusraw brought before him first of all.

'Well, traitor?' Jahangir demanded. 'Have you nothing to say?'

Khusraw was rendered speechless; he had thought himself forgiven.

'You have ever been a thorn in my side,' Jahangir continued. 'You are as hateful to me as you have become to your mother – but she has begged me to spare your life. How may a husband go against the entreaties of his wife? Yet punished you must be. Fetch the hot irons,' he ordered his tavachis.

Khusraw gasped in horror, and fell to his knees.

'Spare me, my father,' he implored. 'As the great Akbar once spared you.'

'Akbar was a fool,' Jahangir pointed out. 'But I *am* sparing you. Why, I intend to leave you one eye, so that you may still look upon the world, and particularly upon the sight I have prepared for you, before you are incarcerated forever. Then it will be so dark that you will not even need that one eye.'

He signalled Spartu. Khusraw's arms were bound and he was held tightly by four men, while the Hindu thrust the iron into the brazier and waited for it to glow white hot. Then Khusraw screamed in agony as his eye was burned out.

His mother wept ... while Nur Jahan smiled, and Prince Khurram's mouth twisted.

'When will he recover his senses?' Jahangir asked.

'In a few days, my lord.'

'Then we shall wait a few days.' Jahangir smiled at the assembled prisoners. 'We shall all wait for a few days.'

While he waited, Jahangir had the arena prepared. It was situated immediately outside the palace walls, and on the wall itself he erected a canopied throne for himself, another for Nur Jahan, and one for Khurram, now designated his heir. The youthful princess was also present with her father. Before them, three hundred holes were dug in the ground.

Prince Khusraw was led out, and mounted on an elephant, carefully guarded by two other men. William Blunt was then brought out, his wrists bound behind him.

Isabel was already there, bound and waiting for death. They gazed at each other, and then her head drooped.

Then the three hundred other naked prisoners were marched forward, to stand before their nemesis.

When a bugle was blown, the impalements began. These were Turkish-style impalements. The long stakes were driven up into each man's rectum, and then each stake in turn was lowered into a hole and embedded upright. All morning the dreadful work went on; the air was rent with the screams and moans of the dying rebels.

At last a forest of three hundred stakes, each with its hideous burden, rose from the ground before the Moghul.

'Let Prince Khusraw bid farewell to his allies,' Jahangir commanded.

The Prince's elephant was brought forward, and carefully led through the rows of dead and dying, so close that they could be touched. Khusraw blanched, and wept from his one good eye.

When he had been brought face to face with the very last of his accomplices, Khusraw was brought back before the Moghul.

'Now we shall dine,' Jahangir announced. 'And there will be further sport after our meal.'

This time there was no welcome for Elena at Government House in Diu. Dom Enrique had of course received Jahangir's messengers, and had no doubt that what they had told him was true, as regards both William's part in Akbar's murder and the certainty that Khusraw's rebellion would quickly be put down. His manner towards her was cool.

'Do you intend to send us back to Agra?' Elena demanded.

'Of course I shall not do that,' he protested. 'But the sooner you are away from here the better.'

'I must stay here until my nephew or niece arrive – or until I receive a message from them,' Elena insisted.

Dom Enrique raised his eyes to heaven: he was in a difficult position. If he forced Elena to leave, and then Khusraw *did* triumph, leaving Blunt once again the Moghul's Guard Commander . . .

'Let us hope that it is soon resolved,' he grumbled.

Don Pedro Dominguez regarded Elena with obvious distaste, and the two children even less pleasantly. Richard was now three years old, and had his father's black hair. While his complexion was much lighter than William's, he revealed the handsomely acquiline features of his Rajput grandmother.

Laura was more her mother's child. Indeed she promised much of Isabel's beauty – but she too was swarthy.

'So now you are a fugitive,' Don Pedro sneered. 'After all your fine words.'

'Are you not pleased to see your grandchildren?' Elena hissed.

He regarded the children again. 'Where is my daughter?'

'She is on her way.'

'A fugitive, too?'

'Not so, Don Pedro. The Moghul is dead, murdered by his own son. My nephew is now employed by Prince Khusraw to avenge Akbar. He wished his children removed to a place of safety meanwhile. You should honour him for that.'

'And if he is defeated?'

'Should that happen, he and your daughter will join us here, and we shall all take ship for England.'

'England!' Dominguez said as contemptously.

'I was informed that Spain and England are now at peace.'

'Yes, señora, peace has been made.' Dominguez did not seem to relish this thought.

'Then we have naught to quarrel about. But as I do not appear welcome in your house, I shall take myself elsewhere.'

Dominguez scowled thoughtfully.

'You are welcome to stay with us, señora, pending the arrival of my daughter.'

Elena decided to accept his ungracious hospitality. Although she was well supplied with money, she had no idea how far it would have to take her. She had no intention of selling any of her jewellery here in Diu.

Then it was just a matter of waiting. Elena kept to herself as much as possible, sitting on the beach while the children played, brooding on what the future might hold for her. Her life had been turned upside-down in the months since Akbar's death. To that moment, she had never known personal fear, or much anxiety.

Now all was gone. She knew in her bones that William would not be returning to her. She could only pray that Isabel managed to reach safety.

Meanwhile she had to deal with the Dominguez household; she could not spend all of her time alone. She had understood they were going to prove difficult. Neither Dona Margharita nor Don Pedro could forgive her for the fact that Isabel was now in deadly danger.

But Dona Margharita was also a woman, and a grandmother. If she worried for her daughter, and hated and blamed the brutal Hindu – as she considered William – she could not resist the appeal of her two grandchildren.

Don Pedro was a different matter. When he looked at his grandchildren he saw only William's Rajput blood. When he looked upon their guardian, he saw only the woman who had once contemptuously refused him.

'Well, Señorita Blunt,' he remarked, finding her alone on the verandah of his house one day, gazing towards the passage which separated the island from the mainland, and the ferry plying back and forth. 'Things are different to the last time you were in Diu.'

Elena looked from left to right.

'I see very little change, Don Pedro.'

He stamped his foot in anger. 'I meant with your situation. Your nephew is disgraced, and probably dead by now.'

'That I take leave to doubt,' Elena snapped.

'We shall see. But if that is so, and supposing my daughter has died with him, you understand I would have the right to take my grandchildren away from you.'

She could not suppress a sudden intake of breath.

'As you so obviously detest them, that would be a crime as heinous as only the new Moghul might undertake,' she said.

'What is a crime, and what is not a crime is all in the mind, señorita.' He smiled as he spoke. 'I might consider it a crime that a woman as lovely as yourself has never shared a man's bed.'

'You are unworthy of your wife, señor,' Elena told him.

'But worthy of you, my dear Elena.' He seized her hands. 'I want you. I have never wanted a woman more. Though it is not something I seek to understand.'

Elena discovered she was panting.

'Six years ago I rejected you, señor.'

'Six years ago you were in a position to do so, for the power of Akbar stood at your shoulder. Now there is nothing.' He leaned forward. 'I will have you, Elena. Or I will have the children, and send you back, naked and bound, to the vengeance of the Moghul. He will be grateful to have Blunt's daughter in his power, will he not?'

The thought of that made her blood run cold. As did the thought of him.

'And if I surrender to you?'

'Then you may take the children wherever you wish, so long as I do not have to look upon them again. They are an abomination to me.'

Elena gazed at him miserably. She was about to lose the very last of her possessions – herself. And she did not even know if she could trust his promise.

He could read the acquiescence in her expression. But he had weaknesses of his own.

'I should not like Doña Margharita to know of it,' he said.

'And should Blunt Amir learn of this coercion, you are a dead man,' she retorted.

He scowled. 'Blunt Amir is dead.'

'Perhaps,' Elena said. 'Nonetheless, you must swear on a sacred oath that you will make no attempt to take the children from me, no matter what the news from Agra or Lahore.'

Don Pedro drew a long breath.

'And having done so, you will come willingly to my bed?'

Elena gave him a cold smile.

'It would be safer if you came to mine, señor.'

Thus she sacrificed herself for the sake of her beloved children. She could not doubt their fate were they to be left in the charge of a man who hated them. But there was more involved.

Perhaps, as her life had been turned so upside-down, this last act of abnegation provided a strange satisfaction, a devilish self-punishment. Perhaps she even enjoyed it: for, smiling as he straddled her, he watched her naked body twist in a mixture of agony and ecstacy.

Elena had been waiting in Diu for six weeks when the news came.

The Dominguez family were summoned to Government House. There they found Dom Enrique shaking with fear.

'A messenger has arrived from the Moghul,' he announced, 'demanding the surrender of the children.'

'You mean the rebellion has proved a failure?' Don Pedro asked.

Elena could say nothing. The news was overwhelming.

'A failure indeed,' Dom Enrique replied. 'And, my God, Jahangir is a man of wrath.'

Elena spoke at last. 'Tell me what happened, I beg of you.'

'Why, the Prince's army melted away, and his principal accomplices were taken prisoner. I hardly know how to speak of it.'

'Tell me more,' Elena said.

Dom Enrique sighed. 'The Prince's eye was put out. Just one eye, so that he could see what was happening to his followers. It is said he will be imprisoned for life, but I have no doubt he has already been strangled. Then the Moghul caused three hundred of his officers to be impaled.'

Doña Margharita clasped both hands to her throat.

'And William ...?' Elena could scarcely utter the name.

'Blunt was reserved for a different fate.'

'Oh, my God,' Elena muttered.

'My daughter?' Dominguez demanded.

Dom Enrique sighed. 'I cannot speak of it.'

'I insist that you do.'

'She, too, was impaled, before the assembled populace.'

They stared at him. Impalement of a woman was virtually unknown.

'Was William then alive?' Elena asked.

'Yes, señora, he was alive – and forced to witness the dreadful act.'

Elena fell silent. What mental agonies he must have suffered.

'He himself was then executed as the assassin of the Badshah,' Dom Enrique continued. 'Torn apart by four horses.'

Doña Margharita gave a shriek, but Elena was still unable to speak. From being the favourite of an emperor to such a horrible death in just four months.

But Isabel … somehow the thought of that beautiful girl writhing in agony on a stake was the most horrible of all.

'You and your nephew have brought destruction upon us,' Don Pedro spat at her.

'William was innocent of any crime other than loyalty to Akbar,' Elena said fiercely. She turned to the Governor. 'What else did the messenger tell you?'

'The Moghul wishes Blunt's children returned to him. And you yourself.' Dom Enrique sighed.

'We cannot resist the Moghul,' Don Pedro said.

'You cannot send the babies back!' his wife screamed. 'You cannot let them …'

Don Pedro hunched his shoulders and stared at the table.

Dom Enrique sighed again. 'Doña Elena, you must leave this place, and quickly. I told Jahangir's messenger I did not know your whereabouts but that I would find you. He is returning tomorrow to escort you away. Today, this very hour, you must board a ship for Europe.'

'You would defy the Moghul?' Don Pedro demanded. 'That would be suicide for all of us.'

'Would you condemn your own grandchildren to death?' Dom Enrique inquired. 'No, a ship will be made ready now. She can make down the coast to Goa, and take on water and provisions there.'

'This will mean the deaths of all of us,' Don Pedro argued. 'Why do you not give the Moghul the woman? Perhaps that will satisfy him.'

Elena stared at him.

'Señor, you appal me,' Dom Enrique declared. 'This lady is Portuguese, and as such entitled to my protection. In any event, it is hardly she the Moghul wants. It is the last male Blunt: the boy – your grandchild. No, no, when the messenger returns tomorrow, I shall tell him that, unknown to me, Señorita Blunt and the children had already secured a passage and are now at sea. I do not see how we can be blamed for that.'

Don Pedro sighed, and gave up the fight.

'I thank you, Your Excellency,' Elena said. 'I thank you from the bottom of my heart.'

'Where will you go?' Margharita asked her.

Elena considered. 'In the first instance, Lisbon.'

'I shall accompany you,' Margharita announced. 'I shall go with my grandchildren.'

'You?' Don Pedro cried.

'Why not? You have been promising me a visit home to my family for years now. I shall take Doña Elena and the children to Toledo, where they will be safe. And where I will be safe as well.'

Don Pedro looked questioningly at Dom Enrique, who immediately understood what was in the Spanish factor's mind.

The Governor shrugged. 'Oh, you may leave as well, Don Pedro. But you had best all make haste.'

Elena stood on the poop to watch the lights of Diu disappear into the night.

Doña Margharita and her hateful husband were still below, finishing supper. Elena did not know if Margharita suspected the midnight visits her husband had paid to their guest's room. She did know that she no longer had to submit to that indignity. That small part of her life was over – a very small part, she hoped.

Although she had never travelled on a seagoing ship before, much less contemplated an ocean voyage, she did not feel the least afraid. The ocean could hold no terrors to compare with those she was leaving behind.

Her family had indeed been destroyed. Now she remembered the legends which had grown up about them, of Richard Blunt and his Hindu pikemen, his beautiful Persian wife, his remarkable travels and adventures ... how he had died fighting for the Moghul with sword in hand ... but there had always been another Blunt waiting to carry on the family traditions.

Now there was no one save a three-year-old-boy. Surely the Blunt glory had come to an end.

Or had it? She was clutching the taffrail so tightly her fingers hurt. Only yesterday she had wondered what she could do with the rest of her life. Now she knew.

Doña Margharita stood beside her.

'You will never see this land again,' she said. 'None of us will, God willing.'

Elena turned her head. 'Why not?'

'You cannot possibly contemplate returning here – to this dreadful place?'

'It is my home,' Elena said. 'As it is little Richard's. Some day, we will return.'

BOOK THE FOURTH
The Great Moghul

'With Nature's pride, and richest furniture,
His looks do menace heaven, and dare the Gods.'

Conquests of Tamburlaine
Christopher Marlowe

16

THE PRODIGAL

'Alter course a point to starboard, Mr Aitken,' commanded Francis Day.

The mate gave the order; the helm was put across. In the middle of the afternoon the easterly breeze was onshore, and propelling the galleon forward at several knots, for all the weed which undoubtedly clung to her bottom after her voyage from England. Indeed, anxious glances were being cast at the poop, and at the captain; as the ship entered the shallow bay, the land was less than a mile away. It was, to the English seamen, a startling sight: the white sand beach fronted a collection of native huts backed by a considerable cleared area, and then a seemingly solid mass of green jungle which extended north and south for as far as the eye could see. In the distance the peaks of high hills could be made out in the heat haze, shimmering against the cloudless blue sky, but it was the rapidly approaching beach which concerned the sailors.

'Do you remember nothing of it?' Day asked the man standing beside him, indeed towering above him.

'Perhaps as in a dream,' Richard Blunt the Younger replied. 'I was but a small child when I left this land, and in any event it was from a town called Diu, on the other side of the peninsula. But you clearly remember this coast very well. After twelve years?'

'Well, it is not an experience one forgets. We landed at this very place, Madraspatnam. I will show you where we built our factory.'

'But it was destroyed.'

Day shrugged. 'The Emperor Jahangir gave Mildenhall permission for the Company to trade, but not to build a factory to compete with the Portuguese in Diu. We had to look elsewhere, and, having found our way beyond Ceylon, we discovered this bay. The people seemed friendly, and those fields contain rice, a very staple diet. It seemed ideal. We did not think it necessary to journey to Hyderabad on that occasion, to obtain permission from the Sultan of Golconda. We were wrong: the Sultan took offence. So, yes, the factory was destroyed and we were forced to evacuate in some haste.'

'By the Mark Seven,' came the call from forward, where the leadsman was busy.

'Shorten sail, Mr Aitken,' said Day. 'And prepare to anchor.'

'Aye-aye,' the mate acknowledged.

There were people on the beach now, waving their arms as the ship approached.

Day turned round to study the empty sea behind him; he wished it to remain empty. Here on the east side of the peninsula there was little risk of attacks by the native Indians; unlike the Arabs, neither the Moghuls nor their subjects were seafaring people. But he had been warned that there were ships enough in these waters nowadays. The Portuguese, despite the catastrophe that had overtaken their attempt to build a factory on the Hooghli, at the mouth of the Ganges River, only a few years before – it had been attacked by the Moghuls and some four hundred men carried off to slavery – were determined to defend their privileges; and they regarded any other European flag as hostile. An additional complication was now provided by the Dutch who, since gaining their independence from Spain, had sent their ships into every ocean of the world – and they too were inclined to shoot first and ask questions afterwards.

'So now you hope for better fortune,' Richard Blunt observed. 'I have told you that I know nothing of Golconda.'

'But you speak their language. And this time we will do it properly, and visit Hyderabad. It is obvious that Qutb Ali was a man of uncertain temper, as indeed was the Emperor Jahangir ...' Day hesitated, aware that this man's father had been murdered by the late Moghul. When Richard made no reply, he continued. 'But since they are both now dead, why should we not prosper? I wish we had come sooner.'

For, in this year of 1639, Jahangir had been dead a dozen years. After the dismal fate of their first expedition, the Governors of the so-called East India Company had taken a good deal of lengthy persuading before agreeing to try their fortunes in India again.

'But with your assistance, Sir Richard, yes, I would indeed hope to be more successful this time.'

Again he waited for a response, but Richard Blunt was a man of few words. He seemed, indeed, a man of deep and dark thoughts – with every reason.

There was no one the least interested in the Far East who did not know Richard Blunt's story, or the saga of his famous ancestors at the Moghul court, and how his great-grandfather had been the confidant of the Great Akbar and assisted his immortal patron in the conquest of most of this huge land.

Out of the civil war following Akbar's death had come the execution of this man's father. That had been more than thirty years ago. But Francis Day would give a great deal to know just what hatreds and ambitions Elena Blunt had instilled in the mind beside him. Certainly she had created a soldier. Lacking English wars, as King James I and his successor wrangled unendingly with Parliament over money, Richard Blunt had followed the example of his ancestors and sought his fortune in foreign conflicts. He had fought against the Holy Roman Emperor, choosing to serve with Gustavus Adolphus of Sweden. Under that famous general he had taken part in the battles of Breitenfeld and Lützen, which had displayed to the world Gustavus's genius. It was on the field of Breitenfeld that Richard Blunt had been knighted by the King himself, for gallantry.

But Gustavus had been killed at Lützen, at the moment of victory, and during the following years the war raging the length and breadth of Germany, Austria, and Bohemia had degenerated into one huge guerilla campaign. Unable to find another star to follow, Richard Blunt had returned home – to find his aunt dead and his sister married. He was a veteran soldier, a hero and a knight, but a man without purpose – until he had heard of the new expedition being fitted out for India.

Without hesitation he had offered his services, though he was thirty-five years old.

'It is in my blood,' he explained. 'For my father's mother was a Rajput.'

Well, he was certainly swarthy, Day had noticed.

'In addition, I speak Hindustani, Arabic and Persian, all taught me by my aunt.'

'But you are an enemy of the Moghul,' Day had pointed out. 'Even with your talents, you would be a hindrance.'

'My father rebelled against the Moghul Jahangir,' Richard said carefully. 'But Jahangir is himself now dead. And did not the new emperor, Shah Jahan, once rebel against his father as well? There is no cause for the present Moghul to hate me.'

'You consider Jahangir a hateful and cowardly parricide,' Day commented. 'But it is not an opinion widely shared. Have you met John Mildenhall?'

'He once came to visit my aunt, many years ago.'

'Then you will know that he travelled to seek an audience with the Emperor Akbar, requesting trading privileges for the Company – and was refused.'

'It was a bad time. Akbar was faced by Jahangir's rebellion.'

'Perhaps so. But when Mildenhall returned to Delhi, several years later, he was granted what he sought, by this same Jahangir.'

It was Mildenhall, returning after his second and more successful visit to the Moghul court, who had confirmed to Elena the details of how William and Isabel Blunt had died – and had burned the hated name of Spartu into her brain.

Richard Blunt could hardly remember Mildenhall, being only five when the merchant had visited Elena. But Mildenhall's tales had been repeated to him often enough by his aunt.

So he said, 'It is good that he well considered the benefits of trade with England. But did not Mr Mildenhall also relate how, when Jahangir's general Mahabat Khan married off one of his daughters without the Badshah's permission, the Emperor had the young couple stripped and whipped publicly with thorns? Surely that is the measure of the man.'

'No doubt he was provoked to do so. Have you met Sir Thomas Roe – or read his report? He was three years ambassador at Jahangir's Court? Three years in which he was well received. True, he criticised much of what he saw there, and in particular the venality and licentiousness of the Emperor's court ... and he was shocked by the habitual drunkenness of the Moghul himself. But Roe also tells how the Emperor was a great patron of the arts, of literature and painting ...'

'The Nur Jahan was apparently even more vicious than her husband,' Richard interrupted.

'Sir Thomas Roe did not find her so,' Day pointed out. 'Then what of her niece, Arjumand, whom they call Mumtaz Mahal, "the Light of the Harem?" Sir Thomas describes her as even more beautiful than her aunt – and she is the present Empress.'

'These are but names to me, Mr Day. I will tell you frankly, my opinions of the Moghuls are of no account. I seek to return to Hindustan, since I regard it as more of my home than England. I am now offering my services to the East India Company. So all I wish from you, sir, is a plain answer. And I know I have more to offer than any other man in England. Now you must determine.'

'Well, as long as you remember, Sir Richard,' Day had said, 'that if I accept your service, it is the Company, and nothing but the Company, that matters from this day forth.'

'By the Deep Four,' came the cry from forward.

'Anchor, Mr Aitken,' said Day.

The land was now very close, but he knew from experience that the more-than-twenty feet of water presently beneath them carried almost to the steep-shelving beach, and there was little tide.

Again he glanced at Richard Blunt, who was staring at the land with parted lips, his eyes half closed. No doubt Blunt had waited all his adult life for this moment. Yet, throughout the voyage, Day's doubts about employing him had deepened. In the several months they had spent in closest intimacy, far from growing to know his strange second-in-command the better, he felt he knew him even less. As the ship had rounded the Cape of Good Hope and entered the Indian Ocean, Blunt had become ever more taciturn – more seemingly wrapped up in his own thoughts. Or perhaps his own fears.

'Will you accompany me ashore, Sir Richard?' he invited.

Aunt Elena had told Richard about the heat, and of the silence of the forest so suddenly broken by stealthy slither, chattering monkey, or swooping bird. Those were not things he proposed to be alarmed by. In his soldier's career he had already faced death in too many forms. Besides, he had perhaps come here to die.

The Indians clustered around them as they rowed ashore. The men and women were obviously poor, and scantily clad – the children were naked but well nourished. In front of their extensive rice paddy, their fishing boats were drawn up on the beach. Some of them recognised Francis Day, and chattered at him in their local dialect, of which Richard could pick up the occasional word. They seemed pleased to see the Englishmen and their ship.

'The weather is now set fair for some four months, by my reckoning, Mr Aitken,' Day told his sailing master. 'You have time to careen and scrub the bottom. There is fresh water from that stream, and the woods abound with game, while these people will sell you rice and fish. You will dismount your cannon and build a stockade, just inland from the beach and north of the rice field. That you will defend, if necessary. With fortune it will not be necessary. You should at all times try to remain on good terms with the natives.' He knew better than to attempt to command that there should be no intercourse with the Indian women.

'Sir Richard and I should return before the monsoon. If we do not, and at the first sign of bad weather, you must leave this anchorage and seek shelter in Ceylon; there are some good protected natural harbours there. You will endeavour to avoid hostilities with either the natives or the Portuguese.'

'And the Dutch, Mr Day?'

'To be sure, the Dutch as well. But be prepared to defend yourself. When the monsoon is over, then you will return here. If we are not waiting for you, or have not appeared within one month of your return, then you will determine us as lost, and make your way back to England. Are all my orders understood?'

'Aye-aye.' But Aitken looked troubled at the weight of responsibility being loaded on his shoulders.

'Well, then ... we shall leave at dawn tomorrow.'

The bay at which the Englishmen had first disembarked was actually some considerable distance south of the boundaries of the Moghul realm, and lay in the Sultanate of Golconda. Golconda was one of the five remaining sultanates south of the river Narmada which had not yet been absorbed by Delhi; and in the south, at least, it was only sparsely inhabited. As Day commanded a strong party of some twenty soldiers and sailors, and was well provided with both silver coin and the latest muskets, which had been lightened so they could be fired without a rest, the English party was welcomed rather than hindered as it made its way to the north.

To their amazement, at more than one village halt, they were given uncut diamonds as presents.

'The richest country in the world – my aunt always said so,' Richard observed.

'What puzzles me,' said Day, 'is why, with all this wealth lying around, the Moghuls have not yet moved down here.'

'It is simply because they have wealth enough in their own dominions,' Richard suggested.

The rank and file could hardly believe their fortune; every man would return to England with wealth in his pockets ... supposing they returned at all.

The river Krishna was crossed a fortnight after leaving Madraspatnam, and a few days later the travellers arrived at Golconda's capital city of Hyderabad. This city had been built less than fifty years before, when the old capital of Golconda, a few miles to the north-west, had been deemed both inadequate and unhealthy. Making the fullest use of the fabulous wealth provided by their apparently inexhaustible diamond mines, the ruling Qutb Shahi sultans had created an architectural wonder of breathtaking beauty.

Even the site had been selected with an eye to beauty: an area of level ground on the eastern bank of the Musi River. Here had been laid out broad straight avenues, splendid residential areas separated from the crowded trading centres, hospitals and a waterworks, and of course royal palaces surrounded and separated by delightful gardens and parks.

'By heaven,' Day commented, 'but this place makes smokey old London look like a slum.'

And they had not yet seen the true wonder of the city: the Charminar, less a palace than an 'architectural composition', built in the Indo-Saracenic style, with four huge arches from each of which rose a minaret one hundred and eighty feet high. The Charminar formed the centre of the city, and had apparently been designed for that purpose, even before the first brick had been laid.

'A land of wonders,' Day remarked.

Day and Richard were soon summoned before the Sultan, who gravely listened to their proposals.

'I have heard that Bijapur has profited greatly from its trade with the Portuguese,' commented Abdullah uh-din Qutb. 'And perhaps we may do the same from trade with the English. My father was not a far-seeing man; and thus he turned you away twelve years ago. Now, alas, I am no longer a free agent. The Moghuls breathe heavily upon us. Four years ago they demanded tribute. When I refused, my armies were defeated. Now I am nothing more than a servile appendage of Shah Jahan.' He held up the musket which had just been presented to him. 'Yet the Moghuls have no handguns as modern as these. Will your people bring me such things? And cannon? The Moghuls possess a great deal of cannon.'

'You wish to fight the Moghuls, Your Excellency?' Day sounded uneasy.

'Must I remain beneath their yoke for all time? Besides, now is the moment. Have you not heard that Shah Jahan is distracted by the death of his wife, and grows daily more grieved.'

'The Mumtaz Mahal is dead?' Day was astonished.

'Some years ago. It was a sad blow to the Moghul. They say he wanders alone through the corridors of his palaces, beating his breast and calling her name. She was a most beautiful woman.'

'So we have heard, sire.'

'Now, it is said, he builds for her a mausoleum in Agra, which the Moghuls claim will be the most beautiful building the world has ever beheld. Ha! They have clearly never been to Hyderabad.'

'But, if the Mumtaz Mahal has been dead for several years, and the Moghul is still mourning her, who conducted the campaign against you?'

'His son Dara Shukoh, who many consider the actual emperor. They are formidable warriors, these Moghuls. Will your people help me fight against them?'

'Well ...' Day hesitated. It was certainly not part of the Company's plan to join in an Indian war.

Richard had not previously spoken, but now he said, 'It is our purpose to visit the Moghul when we leave Hyderabad, Your Excellency.'

Abdullah frowned at him. 'To betray my ambition?'

'Oh, not so,' Day protested, casting Richard an angry look. 'It is the purpose of our Company to trade with every nation in India, and the Moghul Empire is the greatest of these. We seek trading privileges, nothing more.'

'But we may well be able to bring you back information on the Moghul's intentions,' Richard suggested, to make amends.

Abdullah brooded for several minutes, then said, 'Go to Agra and return to me. Tell the Moghul that it is your desire to build a factory in my country – and see what his reaction is. It is best to deal fairly with him, lest he suspect me of treachery and send his sons to torment me again. But mark me well: betray me and I shall seize your ship and all on her.'

'We shall not betray you, Your Excellency,' Day promised.

'When you have received the Moghul's permission, and have built your factory, then we shall speak again of what goods you will import into my country,' the Sultan declared.

'That forthrightness of yours very nearly ended our venture,' Day grumbled, when he and Richard dined later in the apartment given to them, served by richly-dressed young men and entertained by a troupe of nautch dancers, naked save for their gold anklets and wristlets. 'Now we are engaged in some kind of intrigue. That was not my purpose, and if the Directors learn of it ...'

'You were involved in intrigue the moment you dropped your anchor at Madraspatnam,' Richard pointed out. 'All Hindustan is intrigue. In our circumstances, it is best to be honest with these people. The one thing they will never forgive is deceit.'

'Yet they practise it themselves.'

Richard gave a sombre smile. 'Knowing the penalties for failure, certainly.'

Day had a great deal on his mind.

'What do you think of this news that the Empress is dead, and that the Emperor has abandoned business? Will it be to our advantage, or not?'

'That I cannot say until I have met this fellow, Prince Dara – and his brothers,' Richard pointed out. 'My knowledge of Moghul history indicates that the sons of the reigning sultan are nearly always rivals to one another. So it may be that we are visiting Delhi at a moment of flux, which could well be to our advantage.'

'Providing we back the eventual victor,' Day remarked gloomily. 'But what the Directors will say, should we become involved in Indian politics ...' He eyed the girls as the music stopped. They stood in a row before the two men, smiling, their bodies glistening with sweat. 'Tell them that was very good,' he said.

'They know they are very good, and very beautiful. They are now ready for you to make your choice,' Richard said.

'My choice?'

'Which one you will take to your bed. Or you may take more than one. They will not mind.'

Day swallowed. He was clearly very tempted: the girls were extremely pretty.

'Which one will *you* take?' he asked.

'I did not come to Hindustan to bed women,' Richard reproached him, and left the room.

Definitely, a most strange fellow, Day thought, and beckoned towards the girl he found prettiest.

As soon as their provisions had been re-stocked, they resumed their journey. Within another week they were within the Moghul Empire. Although there was no clear boundary, the difference between these realms was immediately noticeable. The people of Golconda might have untold riches literally lying at their feet, and might possess the most beautiful capital city Richard Blunt had ever seen, yet they conveyed an impression of apathetic indifference to bettering their lives. Inside the Moghul dominions all was order and bustle. Now they were in the land of wheat – *malwa* – and could see elaborate irrigation works which brought water down from the hill streams, while each village was protected by its own wall and fortress, however small – despite the apparent peacefulness of the population.

The first hakim before whom they were taken greeted them courteously, and was most impressed with the handgun with which they presented him, for this was the very latest development in firearms: a weapon small enough to be held in one hand, and yet capable of discharging a ball some thirty paces.

'This is called a pistol,' Day explained.

'It is a wondrous thing,' Mansur Ali commented. But he looked grave when they went on to explain that they sought an audience with the Moghul.

'I doubt the Badshah will wish to discuss any business,' he said.

'We have heard, therefore, it might be best to apply to Prince Dara,' Day ventured.

'Certainly most of the government is in the hands of the Prince,' Mansur agreed. 'But he is presently in the north, fighting the Afghans and the Persians.'

'You mean there is war?' Richard inquired.

Mansur shrugged. 'There is always war with the Afghans and the Persians. You will go to Lahore?'

'It is a very long way,' Richard pointed out. 'Is none of the other princes nearer at hand?'

'None of the princes is in Agra, to my knowledge. However, there is another possibility . . .' he fell silent, still fingering the pistol.

Day knew the drill by now.

'That is, of course, but one of a pair,' he explained, and took the other from his satchel. 'It is my wish that you should have them both.'

Mansur balanced the two guns. 'They are admirable weapons. Indeed admirable. It has occurred to me that, if you truly wish to obtain privileges from the Badshah, it might be to your best advantage to visit Agra. When you are there, I suggest you obtain an audience with the Princess Jahan Ara.'

'A princess?' Day was astonished.

'She is the Emperor's eldest daughter – and reputed to be his favourite. She might be able to help you,' he smirked, 'if you please her.'

* * *

'What the devil are we to give a princess as a gift?' Day demanded. 'She will not be interested in muskets or pistols, and she will certainly possess jewellery far more valuable than anything we have to offer. Anyway, a woman? Since when do women have any influence in the Muslim world? I don't much like the sound of this proposal.'

'Women have always had influence,' Richard told him, 'even if it is exercised behind the scenes.'

'Perhaps, but Muslim women do not give audiences to strange men.'

'The Moghul concept of woman's place in society is tempered by local Hindu traditions,' Richard told him. 'Therefore they do not practise the harem, or purdah, except in very orthodox cases. I think this princess represents our very best hope of reaching Shah Jahan – or at least his ear. As for what we should offer her, I have no idea.'

Clearly Day considered their journey doomed to failure, but even his spirits brightened as they approached Agra and beheld the magnificence of the Moghul state. They passed the ruins of Fatehpur Sikri and Richard looked for some relict of his great-grandfather's tomb, but it had been entirely eradicated.

Soon afterwards they spied the walls of Agra in the distance, were amazed at the beauty of the Pearl Mosque, and then gazed in wonder at an edifice rising just outside the city. The Taj Mahal, as it was to be called – *Taj* meaning cap or headdress, in this case 'the Crown of Mahal', the harem. It was a long way from completion, but the gleaming white marble and red sandstone rising from the ornamental courtyard suggested that the Moghul's intention for it to be the most beautiful building in the world might not be so far wrong.

The travellers were escorted before the hakim, who proved totally uncompromising. 'His Highness gives no audiences,' he said flatly. 'He is still in mourning.'

'This we have heard,' Richard said, having taken over the negotiations since he was more fluent in Persian. 'But we have come a long way, and we have a great deal to offer the Moghul. Is it not possible to speak with someone of authority?'

'I am of authority,' Kazim Khan bristled.

'With the greatest respect, Your Excellency, but have you the power to grant trading privileges?'

'Of course not!'

'Well, then ... some member of the Moghul's household, perhaps? We have heard that Her Highness Princess Jahan Ara takes much interest in such affairs ...' He paused.

'You wish an audience with the Princess? That is unheard of. Who told you of her?'

'Mansur Ali, hakim of Jhansi.'

'Mansur Ali.' Kazim Khan frowned.

'Might it not be possible? We have here this Spanish blade which we would dearly like Your Excellency to have ...'

Kazim Khan took the rapier. 'By Allah,' he commented, 'I have seen a weapon like this. It is in the palace museum. It once belonged to the great Blunt Bahatur, who fought for Babur the Lion.'

'Did you know Blunt Bahatur?' Richard asked softly.

'No, no – this is nearly a hundred years ago of which we are speaking. I knew the second Blunt Bahatur, the Commander of the Guard of Akbar the Great. And his son ...' he frowned at Richard.

'And *his* son?' Richard asked.

'By Allah!' Kazim muttered, staring at him in awe.

Day looked from one to the other in alarm, only able to catch a few of the words.

'I seek no more than my birthright,' Richard said.

'A Blunt,' Kazim said, half to himself. 'Returned from the grave.'

'Will you assist us to an audience with the Badshah? Or with the Princess.'

Kazim took the rapier, and scrutinised the fine working on the blade and the haft. He studied it for several seconds, then he said, 'Walk in the palace courtyard tomorrow morning, and I will give you your answer.'

Next morning, as commanded, the pair of them set off for the palace, and were admitted into the courtyard. There were already some thirty men gathered, muttering to each other, all hoping for an audience with the Emperor or his Vizier. Curious glances were directed at the Englishmen, at their big flat hats, their falling ruffs with their fringed edges, their braided doublets and breeches, their leather boots, and at their unusual swords, but no one addressed them.

'We are to promenade,' Richard reminded Day, and they walked slowly up and down, while Richard endeavoured to look around. The courtyard was totally open, and they were overlooked by the guards and various majordomos who guarded the corridors leading into the palace. There was no sign of Kazim Khan.

There were upper floors overlooking the courtyard. That above the gate was undoubtedly occupied by soldiers, as part of the palace defences. But on the lower floors there were no windows, only an intricate trelliswork which could effectively conceal anyone standing behind it. He felt the hair on his neck begin to prickle.

'I suspect we are being surveyed,' he muttered.

Day raised his head. 'Well, it would be reassuring to suppose so,' he complained. 'Or we are entirely wasting our time.'

It certainly seemed so, for they walked for a good half an hour, before they saw Kazim Khan coming towards them from one of the porches.

'Gentlemen, I have good news for you. Blunt Sahib will be received in audience.'

Day expostulated: 'What am I supposed to do?'

'Wait here,' Kazim recommended. 'Perhaps you too will be summoned in due course.'

Richard's heart pounded as he followed Kazim into a corridor hung with rich drapes, and then down a second corridor, leading away from the first.

He had been chosen because his name was Blunt.

'If I may offer you some advice, Blunt Sahib,' Kazim said, 'it is that you be very circumspect in everything you say during this audience.'

'I shall remember that,' Richard agreed.

They eventually reached a huge pair of ornately carved double doors. The two guards before them saluted Kazim Khan, and the doors were flung open.

'You are now in the presence of the Most High,' Kazim whispered.

He led the way forward, bowing low before he reached the

chair in the centre of the room, and performing the salaam. Richard followed his example as best he could. At the same time his soldier's eyes took in the surroundings.

The room was large, high-ceilinged, wide-walled. The floors were covered with most sumptuous carpeting, the walls with matching drapes. The ceiling itself was decorated with human figures at play: men and women. This contravened orthodox Muslim law, so was interesting in itself.

There were several women present in the room, but no men other than Kazim Khan himself. The women were mostly young and attractive, with complexions varying from the pale skin of the Rajput or Persian to the dark of southern India. They wore vari-coloured saris and sparkled with gold jewellery ... but none of them seemed the least relevant when compared with the woman who sat in the chair.

Jahan Ara was about twenty-five years of age, Richard estimated. Even seated, it was possible to discern that she was a small woman, perhaps only an inch over five feet, and slender. She wore a white sari, indicating that she too was still in mourning for her mother, and her bare feet were drawn up beneath her on the cushion. The last fold of the sari covered her head, as was usual, but strands of black hair could be seen. She wore no jewellery, not even a gold bangle. Her complexion was pale and unblemished. But it was her face which compelled. It was, on the one hand, the most softly perfect face Richard had ever seen, heart-shaped, with small features, thin mouth, straight but short nose, wide-set eyes and a high forehead sitting symmetrically above a pointed chin. This beautiful mask was utterly dominated by the eyes: green and compelling. They were young eyes in their brightness and clarity, yet at the same time suggestive of every possible emotion – and every possible experience, too.

'You are the man Blunt?' she asked in Persian. Her voice was as liquid as her eyes, and she spoke in little more than a whisper.

Richard bowed.

'Come closer.'

He advanced to stand before the chair. He felt as if her eyes were caressing him. This woman's grandfather had murdered his own father. He could never forget that.

'Kazim Khan, you may leave us,' the Princess said.

Kazim Khan bowed and left the room. The doors clanged shut. Richard was now alone with the women. He was aware of a strange mixture of apprehension and anticipation.

One of the maids came to his side with a cushion. This she placed on the carpet, indicating that he should sit.

He glanced back at the Princess, and received a faint nod. The cushion was placed very close to the chair, and when he sat he inhaled her perfume.

'It is difficult to sit when wearing a sword,' Ara commented. 'And it is incorrect to wear a sword in the presence of a lady.'

Richard unbuckled his sword-belt, and handed it to a waiting maid.

Another maid was beside him with a goblet, which he took.

'Drink,' Jahan Ara told him.

He hesitated. It could of course be poisoned. But why should the Princess wish to poison him, when she could just as easily have commanded him to be beheaded? He drank, and gave a little shudder.

'It is kumiss,' she said. 'Have you not tasted it before?'

'I think I may have done, as a boy.'

'Tell me of your boyhood.'

Richard had to think, desperately.

'My first years were spent in this very city,' he said. 'When my father served the great Akbar.'

'Before he rebelled against my grandfather.' She gazed at him for several seconds. Then she said, 'Drink some more milk.'

No doubt she had observed that he did not like the taste. But he obeyed because he had no choice. But now the apprehension was outstripping the anticipation. He was absolutely in this woman's power. And he had deliberately placed himself in this position.

'Do you believe Akbar was poisoned?' she asked.

'I do not know, Highness. I was only a child, and I was separated from my father.'

'I was not yet born,' she remarked. 'Your father fought for my uncle, Prince Khusraw. Do you know that my father had Khusraw put to death?'

He sensed she was leading him, surely and certainly, to his

own destruction. Yet he was also sure that survival could depend only upon utter truthfulness. And if she called for the executioners, he might at least have the satisfaction of strangling her first.

'I understood that Prince Khusraw had been condemned to perpetual imprisonment.'

'He was a rival to my father, even in prison. The man for whom your father fought,' she pointed out.

'My father fought against the Emperor Jahangir, Highness, for what he thought was right. I understand your father also did this, at the end.'

Another long stare. 'You are bold,' she said at last. 'But I have heard this of the Blunts. I have heard, too, of their honour, and their skill in fighting. Are you a soldier, Blunt?'

'I am the greatest soldier the Blunts have ever known. My fame resounds throughout Europe.'

Ara raised her eyebrows. 'Then we are surely blessed,' she said, somewhat enigmatically. 'Why have you come back to Hindustan?'

'Hindustan is my true home, Highness. My grandmother was a Rajput princess.'

'But Kazim Khan tells me you have come here as a merchant, seeking concessions from my father.'

'It was the only way I could do so. On behalf of the English company who provided my passage, I seek a renewal of the privileges granted to John Mildenhall by the Emperor Jahangir thirty years ago.'

She continued to gaze at him. Then she said, 'It is customary, when seeking concessions, to offer suitable gifts, Blunt.'

'Alas, Highness, my colleague and I were unaware that our interests would bring us an interview with one such as yourself. We have fine handguns, and swords, but . . .'

'Nothing that might interest a useless woman.'

'You could never be a useless woman.'

Her eyebrows moved again. Perhaps she was unused to such boldness.

'Thus we are unprepared,' he went on, before she could react. 'I can but promise you that, should you assist our cause, you may ask what you wish from what we can obtain in Europe, and we shall provide it for you upon our next voyage.'

'What I wish?' she remarked. 'Is there anything in Europe I might wish, Blunt?'

'I do not know, Highness. We have much to offer.'

They looked at each other, and then her gaze slowly drifted up and down his body.

'Are you hungry?' she asked.

'Highness?'

'I am hungry,' she said. 'I would have you eat with me.'

'I am honoured beyond words, Highness.'

She glanced at her women, and immediately two of them came forward.

'Blunt Sahib and I will dine,' she said.

The girls bowed, and the Princess slowly uncoiled herself. Richard hastily scrambled to his feet, uncertain whether to assist her or not. Her bare toes sank into the carpet as she stood straight. As he had supposed, she was a tiny woman.

She walked away from him towards an inner doorway, leaving her perfume hanging on the air. He hesitated, uncertain whether he was to follow her or not, and received a vigorous nod from one of the girls. Hurrying behind the Princess, he emerged into an inner court, small but exquisite in its carved balustrades and ceilings. Only the very centre was open to the sky, and beneath the opening was a pool of clear water, which yet circulated constantly. A flight of marble steps led into the water.

To one side of the pool there was a divan, and on this the Princess seated herself.

'Come here, beside me,' she said.

Richard obeyed, feeling wholly uneasy. His had been a largely sexless life, at least when it came to proper behaviour towards a woman. The army of Gustavus Adolphus had been, by the King's decree, a most moral one, with women allowed only if they were married to a soldier, and rape after victory absolutely forbidden on penalty of death. For all his thirty-six years, Richard's experience, therefore, was no more than of the occasional prostitute. Yet he knew he was here being seduced by a woman who must necessarily prove irresistible, if only by virtue of her power. Yet he could not determine why she should choose to seduce him ... and how far she might expect such seduction to go. To be either too forward or too hesitant could prove disastrous.

The Princess, as before, curled her legs beneath her, but now she lay back on the cushions. Instantly the girls hurried forward with plates of curry and spiced foods, which, Richard realised, they intended to feed her with, rolling the meat in the rice and conveying it to her mouth.

They were also waiting to do the same for himself. And he was being watched, as always, by the Princess.

Thus far he had appeared entirely as the suppliant, humbly seeking any crumb of generosity she might throw at him. But by inviting him into her private garden, and more, by eating with him – just about the highest honour a Muslim could pay a stranger – he felt sure she was expecting him to reveal what confidence, what forcefulness he possessed.

And why not, no matter where it led? She was about the most exciting woman he had ever beheld.

Thus he held up his hand to check the girl would have placed food in his mouth, then swung his body round, throwing his left leg across the divan so that it straddled it, facing the Princess, and knowing that his trunk hose, exposed beneath his short breeches, was drawn tight.

She gazed at him, her face expressionless.

'Otherwise, I would not be able to look at you,' he explained.

She commenced to eat. He followed her example, and the meal proceeded in silence, the girls feeding them with spiced baked chicken, curried lamb, unleavened bread, and *raita*, a salad of cucumbers and yoghurt. The food was delicious, the company exquisite if silent: the only sound was the gentle bubbling of the water in the pool, as it constantly circulated.

The meal completed, the girls served them with iced sherbets, and patted their lips dry with cotton napkins. A bowl of fruit was then placed beside the divan and, at a nod from the Princess, the girls filed out of the court, through a doorway at the far end.

Richard's confidence had grown throughout the meal. He felt he could cope with whatever this remarkable woman next intended to do ... but he had not anticipated being left entirely alone with her. He swallowed, but found it impossible to stop looking at her, because she never took her eyes from his face, and she seldom even blinked.

'I will have a peach,' she said.

He reached down to the bowl and picked one up. Then it was necessary to bring his leg back over, and stand up to offer it to her.

'Sit,' she said. 'Here.'

He lowered himself to the cushions beside her, his thigh against hers. Again her perfume shrouded him.

'Feed me,' she commanded.

He licked his lips, then lifted the peach to her opened mouth. Her teeth sank into it, and juice trickled down her chin. She stared at him, not actually biting through the fruit, but holding it there. She was telling him something with her eyes, commanding him ... He drew a long breath, leaned forward, and sank his own teeth into that part of the peach which still protruded from her mouth.

Their lips touched, and he placed his hand on hers. He found it difficult to believe this was happening, that he was about to hold a Muslim princess in his arms.

She put up her other hand and took the peach from her mouth, and he moved his head back. She dropped the peach on the ground and took his face between her hands, bringing his mouth against hers, allowing her tongue to flick against his.

He couldn't decide what to do with his hands. But before he could make up his mind, she had pulled her head back.

'Who sent you to me?' she asked.

'Mansur Ali, Hakim of Jhansi.'

'Mansur.' She smiled. 'He is a faithful servant. I think, Blunt, that there may well be something that you could give me as a present. And which you possess, I am sure, here and now.'

He reached for her, but she smiled and stood up. Before he could move she had released her sari, and stepped away from it. In the same movement she reached the steps and descended them into the water, but not before he had had time to observe that her body was as compelling as the rest of her, small rather than voluptuous, but perfectly proportioned. Now she swam away, using a gentle breaststroke, before turning to look at him. Her hair, he noticed, was gathered in an elaborate chignon secured with a golden pin.

'Are you not overheated, Blunt?' she asked.

There was nothing for it, but in any event he could not stop himself. He pulled off his boots and then undressed, expecting at any moment to be seized by her guards and carried off to a horrible death on a charge which could well be sacrilege, and certainly lese-majeste.

And he had told Day that he had not come to India to bed any woman!

She was now on the far side of the pool, her back resting against the mosaic tiled wall, her arms extended along the rim. With every breath her small, perfectly-shaped breasts emerged from the water, then disappeared again.

Richard discovered that the water was only five feet deep as he waded towards her, the ripples drawing away from his chest. She smiled at him.

'You are a fine figure of a man, Blunt,' she said. 'Are you going to make me cry with ecstacy?'

It was impossible to tell whether she wanted that or not. But now he was up to her, standing against her, and she could certainly feel him touch her. Her arms left the edge and went round his neck as she kissed him. And then her legs parted to wrap themselves round his thighs.

He was inside her before he could stop himself. Then she did scream, very loudly, but whether it was agony or ecstacy he could not tell. Certainly there was no way he could withdraw; both her arms and her legs were tight round his body.

'You are a barbarian,' she gasped into his ear. 'A barbarian!'

Then she drew her head back. 'Carry me to the couch.'

He lifted her in his arms, waded to the steps, and carried her up. He hesitated above the divan, as they were both dripping water. But, as this did not seem to concern her, he laid her on the cushions.

'Now,' she said.

'Highness,' gasped one of the maids, appearing from the inner doorway. 'Highness . . .'

Ara sat up. 'You will be whipped,' she snapped, her voice like a whiplash itself.

The girl fell to her knees. 'But Highness . . . the Badshah comes.'

Ara frowned at her for a moment, then turned to Richard. 'You must leave. He is very jealous. Listen, come to me tomorrow. You will have what you seek, but on one condition: that you remain in Agra. Now take your clothes and go with the girl. Hurry!'

17

THE PRINCESS

Richard had to hurry a thoroughly bored and impatient Francis Day back to their lodging before he dared tell him what had transpired, at the same time warning him never to repeat a word of it. The shipmaster gazed at him in consternation.

'You have bedded the Sultan's daughter? In a Muslim country? By God, now we are both for the stake, I have no doubt.'

'Believe me, Francis, I am as confused as yourself,' Richard protested. 'It was certainly not my intention. What I did was at her command. And I will tell you something: for all her pretended threats to me, both her maids and Kazim Khan – and, I suspect, Mansur Ali as well – knew what was going to happen the moment I was invited to meet her.'

'You mean she is some kind of imperial whore.'

'That may be; she is certainly no virgin. Yet I believe she could carry out her promise.'

'And you would be happy to remain here, your neck permanently in a noose?'

'It was my family's home,' Richard said. 'So why should I not then live here? Besides,' he added, 'shall I not be serving the Company?'

But for all his nonchalance, Richard Blunt had a great deal to ponder on. Day was absolutely right: even if the Princess Ara had commanded him, he had just committed the most heinous crime possible in the Muslim world – next to blasphemy against the Prophet. Yet he was clearly not the first man to enjoy the Princess's charms. Perhaps she might be some kind of female monster who mated with men just for the pleasure of having them executed afterwards – it was a story told about Cleopatra of Egypt. But somehow he did not believe that either. She could have merely imprisoned him, to be enjoyed at leisure. Rather she had made his continuing presence in Agra a condition of granting to the Company concessions he sought.

And what of her father? She had said, 'He is very jealous.' A father might, of course, be jealous of his daughter, but Ara had spoken the words as if he was her lover. According to Kazim Khan, this princess was the living image of her dead mother – the woman mourned to distraction by her omnipotent father! Could his suspicion be true? In which case this family was surely hurrying to self-destruction.

And she wanted him to remain in Agra. Well, was that not what he wished in any event? He had yet to do a great many things; amongst them regain his family's fortune. And perhaps even settle a score with Spartu.

Besides, if he was reluctant to admit it, he thrilled at the thought of being alone with this Princess again.

Next morning, for all Francis Day's fears, he too presented himself at the palace beside Richard. On this occasion, after a very short delay, they were both shown into the Princess's reception chamber.

Everything was exactly as before, save that today Ara's sari was pale blue. Her gaze was utterly haughty as it encompassed both men, and it was difficult for Richard to remember that twenty-four hours before he had held her naked in his arms.

'I have presented your petition to the Badshah, my father,' Ara announced. 'And he is pleased to look kindly upon it. He notes that you wish to build a factory for your goods. Where abouts did you have in mind?'

'A place in southern Golconda, Highness,' Day explained. 'A bay where, if we are allowed to construct breakwaters, our ships may lie at anchor in safety. It is called Madraspatnam.'

'Southern Golconda is a long way from Agra. However, so be it. Have you asked permission of the Sultan?'

'We have done so, Highness. The Sultan of Golconda was pleased to grant our request, subject to permission from the Badshah.'

Ara smiled. 'That is as it should be. Now you have the Badshah's permission. However, there is a requirement. The Badshah is of the opinion that your Company should maintain a representative in Agra. I have made this known to Blunt Sahib, and he is agreeable.'

Day bowed, not daring to look at Richard.

'He will be provided with a house and servants, and will act as your agent in all things,' Ara said.

Day bowed again, then hastened to ask, 'Is there no gift my Company could make to Your Highness in gratitude for your help in this matter?'

He straightened to look the Princess in the eye. Ara returned his gaze for several seconds, then smiled.

'You are most kind. However, I already have all I wish ... You are dismissed. Blunt Sahib, remain while I discuss plans for your accommodation.'

Richard bowed in turn, his heart thumping.

Ara was impatient, having been robbed of her prey the previous day. After the maids were dismissed, they coupled on the divan of the inner court. As before, she screamed, but now he realised it was with ecstacy. On the divan he had full opportunity to enjoy her lustrous beauty, which was truly glorious.

Once she was sated, he could not help probing cautiously.

'Will the Badshah come to visit again today?' He caressed her breasts.

Ara's eyes remained closed. 'Not today,' she said. 'He is old for his years.'

This seemed to confirm his suspicions, but he dared ask no more on that subject. Her frankness was amazing.

'You are the most beautiful woman I have ever seen.'

'There are those who say I am even more beautiful than my mother – and she was the most beautiful woman of her time. Did you know of her?'

'I was but a child when I left Hindustan.'

'Her name was Arjumand, and she was the niece of the Nur Jahan, my great-aunt,' Ara said. 'She, too, was very beautiful.'

'What amazes me, Highness, is that one so beautiful as yourself is not married,' Richard ventured.

Ara smiled. 'Oh, I am married, Blunt. But my husband is a frontier hakim, far away from being able to trouble me.'

'But were he to learn about me ...'

'And attempt to avenge his manhood?' Ara's eyes opened.

'He knows he would die.' She smiled. 'So long as you continue to amuse me.'

She sat up suddenly, and his hand fell from her stomach into her lap.

'Later,' she said.

He moved his hand as she rose and went into the pool. 'Join me,' she said over her shoulder.

Her hair was loose today, and trailed in the water. Thus she seemed more beautiful than ever – but he realised he was coupling with probably the most dangerous woman he would ever know.

He followed her into the water, and held her in his arms.

'Why did you come back to Hindustan?' she asked.

'I was born here, Highness.'

'My grandfather executed both your parents,' she said. 'That is well known.'

'That was many years ago.'

'The son of a rebel is always likely to be considered a rebel himself.'

'And the daughter, Highness?'

They stared into each other's eyes, then Ara smiled. 'You know a great deal, Blunt Sahib. Perhaps too much. Yes, my father did rebel against the World Conqueror. He was defeated and forced to live much of his life as an exile. But, unlike Jahangir and his own father, there were women to bring them together again. The Nur Mahal and the Mumtaz Mahal could not bear to be enemies, so my father and Jahangir were reconciled. Thus my father succeeded as Badshah – but now he is a sorely troubled man. Have you heard?'

'Only rumours, Highness.'

'My father loved my mother too dearly. That is a blessing in an ordinary man; it is a dangerous weakness in an emperor. And also like Jahangir, my father has four sons.'

'But they are all loyal to the Badshah,' Richard said. 'So I have heard.'

'At the moment,' Ara agreed. 'Perhaps they lack the wit to be otherwise. Yet a ruler must always be wary of sons. Shall I tell you of them?'

She left the water and clapped her hands. Instantly her maids appeared with towels to wrap them in, and thus ensconced, water dripping from their hair and bodies, they sat on the divan to be fed.

'I am the eldest of Arjumand's children,' Ara began. 'I have several sisters, but they are of no account. My first-born brother, by *my* mother – no child by another mother matters – is named Dara. He is a great warrior, and wishes nothing more from life than to fight our many enemies – as he is doing now. Dara is very unlike my father: he is arrogant and aggressive, and dreams of being another Jahangir.

'My second brother, Shuja, is a born administrator. He is in Delhi at this moment, examining tax returns – a very useful assistant to my father in all such matters. But he is given to drinking to excess, and has an unstable mind.

'My youngest brother, Murad, is not yet twenty, and is of no account. He seems interested only in the pleasures of the flesh.'

She chewed thoughtfully for a while, perhaps contemplating her own pleasures, then continued.

'My third brother is named Mutri ed-din Mohammed, but is called Aurungzib. You know what that means?'

'Ah ... "Ornament of the Throne".'

'How foolish are these nicknames,' Ara mused. 'My grandfather was called Jahangir, "World Conqueror", and he conquered nothing. My father was named Khurram, which means "Joyous", and he is the unhappiest of men. And now my brother ... he is twenty-two years old, and like Dara is a soldier. The Badshah thinks he will be a great soldier, as great perhaps as Babur.'

'My kinsman and namesake served Babur,' Richard reminded her.

'I know of that. But I would not have you serve Aurungzib. He may be a great soldier, but he is also, already, a deep and silent man. He watches, and says nothing. He watches my father, and sees only dwindling strength – but he says nothing. But, unlike my father, he is not tolerant. He spends much time in the mosque, and when he comes out, he looks at the Hindus with hatred – and says nothing. Yet Akbar himself declared that all men here were equal before God, as regards religion.'

'You do not like your brother?' Richard suggested.

'He does not like me,' she corrected. 'When he is here in

Agra, he watches me. And he says nothing, but I can see the anger in his eyes. He does not approve my way of life.'

Richard refrained from commenting that he could think of no brother on earth who would approve.

'If he were ever to become Badshah,' Ara added sombrely, 'it would go hard with all of those to whom I have been kind.'

Richard swallowed as she stared at him.

'Thus they would have to draw their swords in defence not only of myself, but of my father.'

'I understand, Highness,' Richard said, although he thought it would be an odd turn of fortune that he should fight in defence of Jahangir's son. He could not help asking, 'Are there many of us?'

Ara smiled. 'I am sure there is none so mighty a warrior as yourself, Blunt Sahib.'

As soon as his equipment had been refurbished, Day and his party left for the return journey to Golconda – and thence for Madraspatnam. Richard said goodbye in the portico of their lodging house.

'I trust you will still be here when next I send despatches,' Day said gloomily.

Richard grinned. 'And I trust you will still be there should I need to take ship from India in haste.'

Day clasped his hand. 'May that day never come.'

A fortnight later Richard was given his new home; to his amazement it was the old Blunt palace, which had stood almost empty for more than thirty years. He could remember nothing of it, but he walked the corridors and gazed at the fountains, now dry and covered with dust. Workmen were already busy restoring it to its former grandeur. He was escorted by Birkal Abbas, Ara's chamberlain.

'Her Highness has decreed that no expense be spared to make this palace suitable for a famous warrior,' Birkal Abbas said drily.

'It is magnificent,' Richard said truthfully.

'These are your servants.'

Birkal led him into the kitchens, where twelve people were assembled: six men, and six women. Or, rather, Richard realised: one man and one woman. The others were boys and girls, not one over fifteen, and all very comely.

'I chose them myself,' Birkal said. 'Use them as you wish. But remember only that my mistress is also your mistress.'

'I shall remember,' Richard replied.

With the house there went also a suitable income. It was all rather a lot to grasp at first; Richard was aware that he had suddenly become a kept man, whatever his token role of being the representative of the East India Company.

Ara was clearly providing all of this because she was physically attracted to him. Equally he could not doubt he would lose it all once she lost interest in him. Unless she was looking ahead, and considering her position should Shah Jahan die or be deposed, though Richard did not know what he alone could do in her defence when that day came.

Ara had clearly considered this matter, however. Scarcely was he settled into his new home, than she urged him to take up military training with the Palace Guard.

'Show them your skills, Blunt Sahib,' she coaxed.

The sceptical Mongols were soon interested not only in his handling of a rapier, but of his rapid skill with their weapons as well. At the end of one of these training sessions a clap of hands caused him to look up at one of the windows overlooking the courtyard; and he understood he was being summoned to her presence. Climbing the stairs, he found her standing beside a short man of around fifty years of age, he estimated, dressed in simple magnificence but with a huge plumed feather rising from his turban – held in place, Blunt later realised, by the Koh-i-noor diamond made into a clasp.

Understanding that he was in the presence of the Emperor himself, he hastily bowed.

'This is the man of whom I spoke, Badshah,' Ara said. 'The Englishman named Blunt. His family was famous in the history of our people.'

'Blunt,' Shah Jahan said.

Richard stood upright again.

'Your forefathers were indeed famous warriors,' Shah Jahan said.

'I thank you, Badshah.'

'But this is the most famous soldier of them all,' Ara continued. 'He has fought with the King of Sweden, of whom you know, and I have heard you admire. I think such a man could serve us faithfully and well, and make our enemies tremble.'

Shah Jahan's eyes were cool.

'Your father was accused of the murder of my grandfather, Blunt Bahatur,' he said.

'My father was innocent, Badshah.'

'You are a Christian?'

'Yes, Badshah.'

'But I have heard that the name of Blunt was once synonymous with faithfulness. Will you serve me faithfully, Blunt Bahatur?'

'With all my heart, Badshah.'

Princess Ara smiled.

The next day Blunt was given the rank of ming-bashi, and a regiment of the Guard.

'But please my father, and you will become tuman-bashi, and Commander,' Ara advised him.

All things were possible, with Ara's favour. Life, indeed, had never been so good. Suddenly he had greater wealth than ever before, and an utterly luxurious way of life. He wore the finest silks, was waited on hand and foot by servants who appeared utterly devoted, slept in the softest of beds, was fed the best food, owned a stable of magnificent horses, and was required to do nothing more than please the princess. But he recognised the dangers in all of this, and drove himself and his regiment ever harder to achieve military perfection . . . and noted that he was often now watched by the Emperor.

Blunt was also, for the first time in his life, discovering the delights of domesticity.

Ara was less demanding than he had feared – she sent for him no more than twice a week. No doubt some of her time was occupied by her father, and equally Richard did not doubt that she enjoyed other lovers as the mood took her. He was not the slightest bit jealous; she was not a woman he could ever love, however much he could lust after her body. And in the strangest way she had become his passport to fortune, for he quickly realised that his success depended less on pleasing Ara in bed than in proving himself a fit protector against the day she feared.

This was far more reassuring to a man who had depended on his sword for survival throughout his life.

Thus when he was not training, or attending the Princess, there were his horses to be ridden and his falcons to be hunted, his garden to be ordered, and his concubines to be sampled . . .

Every member of his household seemed willing, indeed anxious, to share his bed, but he wished only one: a girl called Bilkis. An Afghan sold into slavery in childhood, she was fifteen when presented to him. Fair-skinned, with tumbling brown hair and splendid dark eyes, Bilkis was vivacious and amusing. She had been a virgin when Richard took her to his couch, but she soon learned all there was to know of the art of love, and her youthful enthusiasm was ever a delight. Early in 1641 she gave birth to a son, whom he called Zaid – after an earlier Blunt. Never having expected to see himself a father, for the first time in his life he was really happy.

As for Shah Jahan, he may have once rebelled against his father, and put his own brothers to death, but now he seemed to have settled into a premature old age – assuaging any still youthful urgings of his spirit through his family. If he needed to conduct a war, he sent his son Dara. When he needed sex, he went to his daughter. When there were financial affairs to decide, he left that to his Vizier. His main concern was the memory of his wife. For her he built on a scale Richard could not believe had ever been attempted elsewhere in the world. The Taj Mahal was intended to be the crowning glory of his reign and of her memory, but the Taj Mahal was still a long way from completion. Meanwhile he built other memorials wherever it occurred to him. He built to such an extent that his reign would become known as the "Shah Jahan period" of architecture. This style was based largely on Persian originals, as first exemplified by the mausoleum of Humayun which Akbar had caused to be erected in Delhi. Here were found the double-dome, the recessed archway inside a rectangular fronton, always within an enclosure of gardens, with pools for additional beauty. His secret was symmetry and delicacy of detail – never seen before in such perfection – and, of course, the use of white marble. Especially this was evident in the Taj Mahal itself, whose opalescent surfaces reflected subtle changes of light from every angle.

But even the Taj Mahal was not his crowning work. Again in memory of his beautiful queen, he created a fantastic concept composed of nothing but gold and silver and precious stones. This was a throne in the huge replica of a peacock with spread tail. Studded with diamonds, rubies, sapphires, emeralds, and lesser stones, it was impossible to estimate its value – although thirty years later the French traveller Tavernier would attempt a valuation, and estimated one hundred and sixty million pounds in 1665. Not that Shah Jahan ever himself sat on this Peacock Throne; once it was completed he lost interest in it, and it remained, like an empire's ransom, gathering dust, in a corner of his palace.

Richard found himself liking the Badshah, even if they were rivals for the arms of the Princess – a fact of which the Emperor of course was blissfully unaware.

But there remained the thought of Spartu. Not even the contentment found in Bilkis's arms could eradicate his desire for vengeance on the man who had personally murdered his parents. Richard's inquiries were very discreet as his circle of acquaintances grew, and one or two became firm friends, – especially Kazim Khan, who regarded the Englishman as something of his protégé.

'There was a man called Spartu,' he ventured one day. 'The son of Hemu, who fought beside my father for Akbar.'

Kazim frowned. 'Yes, there was such a man. He was the executioner of your parents. Did you not know that?' Then he continued, 'In any event, it is of no matter. Spartu has been dead for many years.'

So there was nothing left to hate. Life was here to be enjoyed.

He even enjoyed playing the factor. When Francis Day returned to Agra the following year, to tell him that the factory at Madraspatnam – called Fort St David – was now completed, Blunt was able to entertain his friend in the highest style. Day was delighted with his own progress.

'The ship will be returning soon,' he said. 'Indeed I hope

there will be more than one, as I sent word of our success the moment I regained Madraspatnam. All we now need do is keep on the right side of the Badshah, and our fortunes are made.' He gave Richard a quizzical look.

He still remained uneasy about Richard's relationship with Princess Ara. That was continually on Richard's mind as well. On the one hand she remained utterly compelling sexually, nor did her desire to have him love her dwindle over the next few years. But the peril of what they were doing sometimes kept him awake at night.

Brooding on their blatant adultery, he even went so far as to ask her why she was permitted to live apart from her husband.

'I am the Princess Jahan Ara. I can live in any manner I choose. Let us be content now to love, and enjoy one another.'

'There will be a judgement day.'

'Why? Our future is simple to control. When the time comes, we shall choose one of my brothers to succeed my father – and offer him the support of the Imperial Guard to achieve his aim. You will remain as Guard Commander, and my domestic arrangements are not to be interfered with, of course. Believe me, one of those four will accept our offer. Perhaps Dara.'

'But he is the legitimate heir, surely?' Richard argued.

'There is no such thing as a legitimate heir where four brothers are concerned,' Ara said shrewdly.

Meanwhile Bilkis gave birth to Iskanda in 1642, and Nasir in 1644. Richard then urged her to use contraceptives – in which he knew the Indians were adept. She was now twenty, and he wished to preserve her beauty. Besides, were not children hostages to fortune? Because even Ara could not foresee every eventuality.

Day's ships had now made several voyages from England, and with each arrival he sent a caravan up to Agra bearing gifts for the Badshah and the Princess, in addition to large numbers of items for trade. Ara was delighted with the Venetian glass mirrors as well as the English pottery, the like of which she had not seen before.

For Richard the arrival of one caravan in Agra proved less of a happy event. It brought letters from his sister Laura, bearing troubling news. England was in a state of revolution, and King

Charles had apparently declared war on his own Parliament. '*Everywhere there are battles and sieges, warfare and murder,*' Laura Sutton wrote. '*The Queen has fled to France, whence she came, and where she should have stayed. God knows there is no more loyal supporter of His Majesty than I, but this has been a sadly mismanaged country these past few years. Even my husband and my sons are following Prince Rupert. Where will it end, dear Richard?*'

I should be there, Blunt kept thinking. But offering my sword to whom? What little he had seen of the Court and its government he did not care for. And did he have any responsibility left to England? Could it possibly be considered his home? Surely Agra was his true home.

'You are pensive, my love,' Ara remarked, leaving the water of her pool.

'There is war in England,' he said.

'A trifling matter,' she assured him, as her girls hurried forward with their towels. 'Your King and his soldiers will easily defeat that rabble of clerks.'

'I believe you are right, Highness. Still, it is a worrying situation. My sister lives there.'

'Then send for your sister and bring her here ...' She turned with a frown at an explosion of sound from her reception room, followed by women's screaming.

Richard watched as the outer door to the garden was thrown wide. A man stood there, wearing a red tunic, white breeches, and brown boots. His turban was red silk, and a tulwar hung at his side. He looked every inch the soldier.

Though not tall, he was clearly fit and strong. He was also young, not a great deal more than twenty-five, Richard estimated. That he was Mumtaz Mahal's son was easy to determine: he indeed looked very like his sister, with small, exquisite features, flaring nostrils, the somewhat tight mouth.

'What is the meaning of this?' Ara demanded. 'Are you some bandit that you come breaking into my apartment?'

The Prince closed the door behind him. 'And are you some whore that I find you entertaining an infidel in a towel?'

'Get out!' Ara snapped. 'Before I have you thrown out!'

'Who would perform the deed?' the Prince inquired. 'Your maids, or your paramour?'

Ara turned to Richard, who was conscious more of embarrassment than fear. Here was he, a grizzled professional soldier of more than forty, caught in *flagrante delicto* like some lovesick swain ... What made this situation impossible was that his sword had been left, as usual, in the antechamber.

The Prince continued: 'Be sure that if you send him against me, I will slice off his head.'

Ara bit her lip.

'Very well, Aurungzib, you have the advantage of me. What is it you wish?'

Prince Aurungzib moved a few steps further into the garden, while Richard studied him. That he had the bearing of a warrior was obvious. That he was a man of strong passions was now also clear. And apparently he had at last stopped merely watching, and saying nothing.

'I wished,' Aurungzib said, 'to see the evidence of your licentious folly for my own eyes.'

'So now you have seen it,' Ara sneered. 'What will you do? Proclaim it in the marketplace?'

'As it is already too well known there, I should be wasting my time,' Aurungzib said.

Ara sat down again, curling her feet beneath her as she was wont. Blunt, feeling foolish, still stood beside her, a tightness in his throat.

'They have more sense than to utter it out loud,' Ara remarked.

'No doubt. But I have already spoken with our father.'

'To what purpose? My father knows my needs, and my remedies.'

Richard turned his head sharply, and she smiled at him.

'Of course, my dear Richard. I have spoken to him, and he is pleased at my choice.' She turned back to her brother. 'So you have been wasting your time, Aurungzib.'

'I know it is a waste of time attempting to persuade the Badshah to punish you, sister. Your face is your safeguard against retribution. However, our father is not quite so foolish as you suppose. Having heard of this scandalous liaison of yours, I came to Agra to remonstrate with him, because he now contemplates making this so-called soldier tuman-bashi and commander-in-chief of the household troops.'

'Why not?' Ara demanded, having entirely regained her poise. 'Blunt Sahib is a famous soldier known on every field in Europe, and he is faithful to the House of Babur. There could not be a better choice.'

'Tell me, sister, what proof do you have of this man's ability – out of bed?'

Ara's eyes flashed angrily. 'I have witnessed him marshalling his men, and training in arms.'

'Many a man can wave a sword about, or summon men to follow him, even when they are not going anywhere,' Aurungzib retorted. 'It is coming face to face with the enemy that counts. I have put this point to my father, that he might be entrusting his life to a man who is not competent to defend it.'

Ara frowned. 'Our father has absolute confidence in Blunt Sahib.'

'He will have more faith when Blunt Sahib has campaigned, and won his laurels.'

Her voice rose an octave: 'What campaign?'

'I have been given a command against the Persians, who are again encroaching upon our north-western frontier. I came to Agra to receive the Badshah's orders, and to bid him farewell. Now I have persuaded him to grant me Blunt Sahib as a tavachi on this campaign.'

Richard's head jerked with interest.

Ara's response was more positive. She leapt from the divan, entirely discarding the towel. 'You did what?'

'The Badshah thinks it an excellent idea. When Blunt Sahib returns with honours heavy on his shoulders, only then will he be a fit Commander of the Guard.'

'I cannot permit it!'

'The Badshah has willed it.'

'I will go to him myself.'

'He told me you would do so – and he has commanded you to stay from his presence until Blunt has left the city.'

Ara sat down again. Her expression revealed that she knew she was beaten.

'You mean to murder him,' she muttered bitterly.

'I would not defile my sword with the blood of such a man,' Aurungzib said contemptuously. 'But I swear to you that, should Blunt Sahib die, it will be with weapon in hand, and facing an enemy.'

'You mean to have him struck down from behind.'

'Only if he turns his back upon the foe. So long as he faces the enemy, I swear that his back will be inviolate.'

Ara was panting as if she had run a hundred yards.

'Dress this man,' Aurungzib told the cowering maids. For the first time he turned to look directly at Richard. 'You, report to my headquarters immediately.'

'He will say his farewells to me first,' Ara snapped. 'You have scored your victory, brother. Now leave me. Blunt Sahib will be at your headquarters within the hour.'

Aurungzib hesitated for the briefest moment. 'One hour, then, or he will be posted a deserter and outlaw, and every man's hand will be against him.'

He turned and left the garden.

There was a moment's silence after the door had closed. Then Ara sighed.

'I underestimated the rascal. Now you understand why I hate this brother.'

Richard made no reply. Now his initial consternation was over, he was aware of a strange sense of relief. He, of all men, had allowed himself to be besotted by a chit of a girl. He was a soldier, and for too long he had done no more than practise. Intensely exciting was the thought of campaigning with a Moghul army – as his father and grandfather and great-grandfather had done. But under a man who so clearly held him in contempt? Under a man who would be sure he was given the most dangerous missions to undertake?

'You are struck dumb,' Ara remarked. 'Are you afraid, Blunt Sahib?'

He glanced at her. 'Afraid? No, Highness, I am not afraid.'

'My brother is at least a man of his word. But there will be many dangers . . .' she held his hand. 'You must return to me, Richard. We have much to do, together.'

'If it is our karma to be reunited, Princess, then I will return.'

She stared at him 'You speak so calmly. Are you weary of me?'

'Does a man grow weary of life itself?' But he was conscious of lying. Seven years of being virtually this woman's prisoner was too long.

His answer had pleased her, however. 'Then love me, one last time.'

'When I return, Princess. At this moment I would prove incapable.' He took her in his arms and kissed her. 'When I return . . .'

Blunt wondered if he would ever see her again. The campaign would take at least a year, and in that time she would surely have found a replacement. That was supposing he survived, of course, yet he was in a mood of fine exhilaration as he hurried back to his palace, to bid a hasty farewell to Dhansi his majordomo. There he selected his favourite boy, Bhuti, as his servant, and instructed him to be ready to leave in fifteen minutes.

Bilkis, his concubine, was distraught. 'What will become of us, sire?' she wailed.

'I will send for you, as soon as our headquarters camp is established,' he promised.

Then he gave his weeping girls a last embrace, before hurrying from the door.

He did not look back.

Aurungzib was camped outside the city, not far from the slowly rising monument of the Taj Mahal. It was a small camp, only headquarters staff, but Richard was clearly expected. A guard saluted him and took charge of his horse, then Blunt was escorted to the general's tent. Wearing the gold and red uniform of the Guard, he was treated everywhere with respect. If Aurungzib had learned of his sister's peccadilloes, his men apparently had not – or were not prepared to show it.

Aurungzib sat cross-legged on a prayer mat inside his tent, gazing towards the goatskin doorway. Richard ducked his head to enter, then stood at attention.

'Now you look more like what you pretend to be,' the Prince remarked. 'What is that weapon?'

'It is a Spanish rapier, my lord.'

'Show it to me.'

Richard drew the sword, very carefully reversed it, and presented the hilt.

Aurungzib took the weapon. Still seated, he made a few

passes with it, sufficient to indicate that he knew how to handle a sword.

'And you wear this into battle?'

'I do, my lord.'

Aurungzig returned the sword. 'No doubt you are skilled in it's use. What is my sister to you?'

Richard swallowed. 'A very beautiful woman who first of all assisted me, and then won my heart.'

'You speak Persian like a native of that country.'

'My name is Blunt, sire.'

'I know your name, and the history of your family. Is adultery not a crime in England?'

'It is, sire.'

'But it is yet indulged there – as it is here. Wherever one looks, one is surrounded by veniality and sacrilege and blasphemy.' The Prince brooded for several seconds. Then he raised his head. 'That you are still alive is because I know my sister to be a greater sinner even than you. If you would stay alive, then you must outdo your famous ancestors.' He stared into Richard's eyes. 'We march at dawn to join the army.'

Blunt could do nothing more than live – and survive – from day to day. As Francis Day had so often reminded him, his head was in a noose; and only he could prevent that noose from tightening.

Yet he knew he could easily grow to like and admire Aurungzib. The boy had the aspect of a fighting man, and if he was at heart a puritan, that might merely be lack of experience of men, and women. Besides, being a puritan could not be condemned – so long as it was kept in a proper balance to the business of living.

And ruling? He thought that Ara was probably wise to fear her brother.

The camp was indeed broken at dawn, and they rode north at some speed. Relays of horses were waiting for them, and they reached Delhi within twenty-four hours, despite the fact that Aurungzib halted four times to offer prayers, kneeling towards Mecca accompanied by his entire company. There was no time for Richard to gaze at places made immortal by previous Blunts, for, changing horses again at Delhi, Aurungzib continued to ride to the north-west. He spoke little, and had little need to. His men were superbly disciplined, and every man knew exactly what he was about.

'That is not surprising, Blunt Sahib,' explained Todal Ali, the other personal tavachi. 'We are the Prince's permanent staff. He has trained us since we were boys.'

They seemed hardly more than boys now. Todal Ali himself was in his early twenties, and no one else was older than the Prince – save Richard himself. The young men watched him constantly for signs of fatigue, but even at forty-four he was as hardy as any of them.

'Does your master always ride at this speed?' he inquired.

'Always,' Todal Ali assured him.

Four days after leaving Delhi they reached Lahore, where the main army was encamped. This was a considerable force: some thirty thousand men, Richard estimated, cantoned over a large area outside the city; row upon row of tents, of corralled horses, of stands of muskets, and a considerable artillery park.

All the troops turned out to cheer the arrival of their new commander. Richard gathered that Dara, the previous commander in the north-west, had been sent to the Deccan to deal with the Marathas. The Marathas had ceased behaving as mere brigands, and now tended to coalesce into formidable fighting forces which put even large towns at risk. Fortunately they operated on the west side of the peninsula rather than the east, so Fort St David was as yet unaffected.

Aurungzib returned the salute of his officers, who were both Hindus and Muslims, and summoned them before his headquarters tent.

'We march tomorrow for Peshawar,' he informed them; 'then on to Kandahar. But first, I have a new tavachi to introduce to you. Though an infidel, he bears a famous name: Blunt! Many of you will remember Blunt Bahatur, who perished at the hands of my grandfather – or at least, of his executioner, Spartu the Hindu.'

Richard turned his head in dismay. He had not supposed that would again be brought up.

'Now this last Blunt has returned to us,' Aurungzib said.

'This is his home, he claims. That may well be so. But as he claims to be a famous warrior, must he not also have anger in his heart for the son of the man who killed his father?'

The officers murmured their agreement.

'Then let us have this matter settled now – before we go to war. Hemu the Younger, are you there?'

'I am here, my lord.'

A Hindu stepped from the ranks of the officers. He was a big, well-built man, and his eyes flashed as he stared at Richard.

Aurungzib now turned to Blunt.

'There,' he said. 'There is your enemy. Prove yourself a man.'

Richard realised that he had been led neatly into a trap.

18
THE AVENGER

'Will you not avenge your parents?' Aurungzib asked. 'All the world knows how they died, and how Spartu laughed as he watched them perish under his hands.'

Richard felt a spurt of almost forgotten anger returning. Now Spartu's son stood before him, to be destroyed.

But perhaps Aurungzib had planned this in order to have the infidel executed and still keep his promise to his sister. Blunt would have to be careful; but he had to fight.

'Yes, I will avenge my parents,' he said, drawing his sword.

'Since I have been challenged,' Hemu said, 'I have the choice of weapons.'

This one had been well schooled, Richard thought.

'That is true,' Aurungzib agreed. 'Is that not also the custom in your country, Blunt?'

'It is indeed the custom,' Richard said.

It *had* all been decided in advance.

'I choose spears,' Hemu said.

'Agreed' Aurungzib said. 'The matter is settled. Throw down your sword, Blunt.'

Richard hesitated a moment, then obeyed. Todal Ali swiftly gathered up his sword. As he did so, he muttered, 'Do you know the spear, Blunt?'

'No,' Richard confessed.

'Do not let him close,' Todal said, and withdrew to the side of the ring being formed by the officers eager to view.

Richard realised he might, after all, have one friend among these men anticipating his death.

One of the tuk-bashis brought forward an armful of spears. These he divided into two groups of six each, thrusting one group into the earth behind Richard, and the other behind Hemu. The weapons were made of wood, but with a steel tip, and were about seven feet long. They were unlike any weapon with which Richard had acquaintance. Even if Gustavus Adolphus had restored cavalry to its proper place on the battle-field, to charge the foe, it had been armed with sword and not lance; while his pikemen had used weapons some fifteen feet long, meant for thrusting not throwing. But these weapons could be used either way.

'Commence,' Aurungzib said. A chair had been brought for him, and he sat comfortably to watch.

Richard knew he had to learn fast. 'Do not let him close,' Todal Ali had said. He watched Hemu reach behind him and pluck one of the spears from the earth – and he did likewise. Then he moved slightly forward, balancing on the balls of his feet.

Hemu also took a few steps forward, leaving a gap of thirty feet between them. How close was *too* close, Richard wondered. He studied his opponent, as Hemu appeared to test the weight and balance of his weapon. The Hindu looked confident but serious – with no trace of arrogance. He had come here to kill.

Suddenly, without warning, Hemu hurled his spear. With a flat trajectory, it came much faster than Richard expected. He could not duck, so had to throw himself to his right, landing on his hands and knees. Before he could recover, Hemu had snatched up and thrown a second. Blunt only just had time to twist his body away from the flying javelin. Even so, the steel tip sliced through his tunic and he felt a stab of pain.

The onlookers gave a roar when they spotted drops of his blood on the ground. Aurungzig smiled.

Blunt continued rolling, and reached his knees just as Hemu ran at him, now carrying two spears. When Richard brought up his own weapon to defend himself, Hamu checked about ten feet away, and hurled his third spear.

Again Richard attempted to twist away but this time the steel thudded into his thigh, and he knew real agony as he fell back to his knees.

Now smiling, Hemu moved forward with his fourth spear for the kill. Richard had to drop his own weapon to wrench out the shaft protruding from his thigh, at the same time rolling away from the next thrust. Blood was cascading down his leg, and he felt his strength ebbing.

As Hemu was about to hurl again, Richard swung out with the bloodstained shaft, and the Hindu jumped backwards to avoid it. Blunt reached his feet, staggering forward. Hemu had no time to throw, so he thrust instead. But this was more what Richard understood. 'Do not close,' Todal Ali had said; the advice had been well-meant, Richard was sure, yet it was wrong. He realised his only hope was at close quarters.

Now he brought the spear down as he would a sword, to parry and thrust, before whipping it back towards Hemu's face. Hemu grunted, for the first time under pressure, and again retreated, now hafting the spear to throw. But Richard gave him no time, closing right up to him and delivering a series of thrusts which left the Hindu bewildered. He parried the first three, but could not stop the fourth slicing into his body.

It was not a fatal wound, but he was bleeding and dismayed, his confidence gone. Now he turned to run, desperately seeking to open space between himself and his adversary. He realised Richard was worse hurt than himself, therefore would weaken sooner.

Richard, too, understood that to give chase would drain his remaining strength. Drawing great breaths, he stood firm, and hurled his spear with all the force he could muster. It was a terrible delivery, and to his disgust he saw that, instead of speeding in a flat trajectory, the spear kept turning over in the air. Yet, so much of his fading strength had he put into the throw, that the haft struck Hemu sufficiently hard between the shoulderblades to stretch him on the ground. Blunt then stumbled forward, picking up his first, discarded spear and, as Hemu tried to rise and turn, he drove the point deep into the Hindu's breast.

Richard stood above his fallen adversary with pounding heart, and watched Hemu's blood pumping from his chest. He was soon surrounded by men, amongst them Aurungzib, who had left his chair to join the throng.

'That was well done,' the Prince said. 'And clearly you had never fought with the spear before. Perhaps you are a great warrior after all, Blunt. Bind his wounds and take him to a surgeon,' he told his aides.

Richard was laid on the ground to have his clothes cut away and his wounds bound up. Then he was placed in a litter and carried into Lahore itself, where several medical men fussed about him. Given bhang to chew, he drifted off into a semiconscious daydream, in which the pain of surgery was dulled.

When he regained full consciousness Todal Ali stood beside his couch.

'That was a mighty contest, Blunt,' he said. 'The Prince is well pleased with you. Here he comes, now.'

Richard tried to move, but found he could not. His legs were constricted by bandages.

Aurungzib stood above him.

'It will be some weeks before you can ride,' he said. 'So you will remain here, in the surgeons' care until you are well again. Obey them in all things, Blunt. You are no use to me unless you are fully fit and able to ride as hard as I do myself. When that day comes, come to me. You understand?'

'Yes, my lord.'

'No matter where I am, come to me.' Aurungzib gave a grim smile. 'There will be no more duels, Blunt. From now on you will face only the enemies of the Badshah.'

The army moved out, and Richard was left alone with the surgeons. He had apparently lost a lot of blood, and it was mainly a business of preventing infection from attacking his wound. For a month he did little but sleep and eat. The surgeons brought in a pretty little dark-skinned Indian girl named Hilma to tend him. He had a great deal of time to think – more than at any time in the preceding four years. He was forty-four years old and, after more than twenty years of soldiering and adventuring, he really had nothing to show for it but a severe wound in the leg, and a certain reputation – which was only just beginning to be accepted here in Hindustan. Even the palace in Agra, with its attendant wealth, really belonged to the Princess Ara, and they could be taken away with as much ease as they had been given.

For instance, if he should not return to her.

He had strangely little desire to do so. Returning to India seemed to have reawakened some dormant love for the country, fed perhaps by Elena's stories. This was the richest country in the world, the most exciting – and it was his home.

Therefore, like his ancestors, he must attach himself to a

Moghul star and rise in its service – regardless of the dangers involved. Only his star was more difficult to find than theirs. For sure there could be no glory to be found as Commander of the Guard of an emperor who no longer went to war. That way lay only intrigue, and, he suspected, disaster. But this youthful prince he now served was only third in succession to the title of Badshah, and could scarcely be destined for supreme power.

Blunt had never met any of the other princes. According to Ara, the eldest two were hardly pleasant characters, but she preferred them to Aurungzib because she believed she could manipulate them. Dara seemed to have a great reputation as a soldier; he was the obvious one to follow, since he was also the heir apparent.

At the least, Richard could do nothing more at the moment than obey orders, which meant following Aurungzib. Time enough for further decisions when he returned to Agra – if he ever did.

After four weeks the surgeons pronounced themselves well pleased with his progress; the wound on his thigh had closed, despite an ugly scar, and the gash on his body had all but disappeared.

The following week he was allowed to mount and ride for a short distance. He was given back his sword.

A week later he was finally given permission to follow Prince Aurungzib.

Blunt took only Butji and Hilma with him, since he knew he must travel very fast. He calculated it was the end of October when he set off after the army, riding north now towards the mountains once so graphically described to him by his aunt. The weather was distinctly cool, but as yet there was no snow; he desperately wished to catch up with Aurungzib before the mountains became impassable. But the road on the high plateau was clear, and for a tavachi of the Prince – who carried the Badshah's own seal, and also wore the uniform of the Emperor's guard – it was easy enough.

In Peshawar he reported to the garrison commander, who informed him that the army had indeed passed that way five weeks earlier. There was no snow as yet in Peshawar, but in front of him the mountain tops were white.

'The passes will be clear, but it is best you have an escort,' decided Ranjit Khan, the tuman-bashi. 'There are still brigands in the mountains, and a man travelling alone would be too tempting a prey.'

So Richard rode out at the head of twenty men. They took the Khyber Pass, which was indeed open, even if affected by an icy wind which came whistling down from the north. If there were any Pathan brigands about, they did not see them; those villages they found were happy to offer food and shelter, and to confirm that Prince Aurungzib had indeed passed this way a few weeks before.

And Richard eventually understood why they were so well received everywhere. The men of one village had attempted to steal some of Auringzib's horses, and in punishment its entire population, men, women and children, had been impaled.

They took the road up to Kabul. Despite the deteriorating weather, Richard was exhilarated: he was following in the footsteps of Peter Blunt and the first Richard. All his previous life seemed as nothing in comparison.

He learned that Aurungzib had spent a week in Kabul, to rest and reorganise his men. Then, despite the imminence of heavy snow, he had marched out again. For the Persians had taken the citadel of Ghazni, some seventy-five miles to the south-west, as a defensive bastion for Kandahar, which was a further two hundred miles away, and the Prince intended to recover it back before winter set in.

Blunt was taken before Murad Baksh, youngest of the four princely brothers, who was hakim of Kabul. The Prince had all the beauty of his brother and sister, but at only just twenty there was a softness about him entirely lacking in Aurungzib, as well as a voluptuousness which must surely disgust his brother. Far from following orthodox Muslim practice, he received Richard surrounded by scantily clad boys and girls, whom from time to time he fondled with careless intimacy. Clearly he took after his elder sister.

'Blunt,' he commented. 'I have heard of you.'

'I am honoured, my lord,' said Richard.

'My brother is a headstrong man,' Murad observed. 'To lead an army into the mountains of the Hindu Kush in winter is the best way to lose it. There are several hundred men in hospital here in Kabul now who are suffering from frostbite. You would do well to remain here until the spring thaw, Englishman.'

'I have been commanded to join the army.'

Murad's somewhat sleepy eyes became alert. 'And suppose I ordered you to stay?'

Richard wondered just what this boy had heard about him . . . and from whom.

'My lord, I am a soldier in your brother's army. I must obey him above all others.'

Murad regarded him for some seconds longer, then shrugged. 'Go to your death, Blunt.'

Richard and his people rode out the next day, confident that they were nearly at their goal; for Aurungzib and his army had left Kabul only a fortnight previously, and in these conditions their progress would necessarily be slow. Indeed, they caught up with the rearguard a week later, and joined the main body, when Ghazni was still a march away.

It began to snow heavily soon after Kabul. The horses floundered along mountain tracks, sometimes up to their haunches. At night they huddled together for warmth. Richard, Hilma and Butji shared the same blankets. The two Hindu youngsters were a great comfort to him, being so enthusiastically anxious to anticipate his every wish.

By the time they reached the army, they were several thousand feet up in the mountains, and there thick snow lay everywhere. The army straggled over a considerable distance along the road, the men huddling close as they tramped along. The artillery caissons had to be manhandled through the drifts, as the mules were helpless. Even before he joined them, Richard knew conditions must be grim. He had passed many dead bodies, mostly women and children, frozen stiff and lying by the wayside. One of his own men dropped out and vanished into a snowstorm.

But Aurungzib seemed unchanged. Wrapped up so that only his eyes showed as narrow slits, he welcomed Richard with a grim smile. 'I had almost thought not to see you again, Blunt,' he commented. 'Have you experience of weather like this?'

'Of weather, yes, my lord. But not of campaigning in it. In Europe we campaign in summer.'

'Then it rains,' Aurungzib remarked. 'Your European soldiers must be soft, Blunt. Yet you have ridden through the snow to reach me, so perhaps *you* are hard. Eat with me now.'

Richard understood the honour as he sat with the Prince and his tuman-bashis inside the huge command tent, where there was a fire and all was warmth. Several other tavachis, including Todal Ali, were also present, but it was on Richard that Aurungzib concentrated his attention.

'Tomorrow we will see Ghazni,' he remarked. 'It is a strong place, surrounded by a high wall and protected by a citadel of great strength. We must capture it before the snows start in earnest. Then we shall winter in comfort – and deal with Kandahar in the spring. Ghazni was once the home of Mahmud of Ghazni. You know of him?'

'Only by rumour, my lord.'

'He was a great warrior who invaded Hindustan fifteen times, and each time carried off a vast booty. He could have conquered the land if he wished, but he had no such ambition. He preferred to use it as a depot on which to draw whenever he chose.' He smiled. 'That was every year.' He paused for awhile, chewing on spiced lamb, then said, 'There have been five great Muslim warriors who have ridden out of these mountains to invade India or Persia. Mahmud was the first. Mohammed of Ghor was the second. Genghis Khan was the third – although I do not believe he ever actually became a Muslim. Timur was the fourth. And my ancestor Babur was the fifth. It is now time for a sixth.'

'Would you not rank Akbar the Great with those names, my lord?' Richard asked.

'He was a notable soldier,' Aurungzib said. 'And a notable man in many ways. But, no, I do not rank him with those five. He thought too much of men rather than conquest.' He turned his head to look at Richard. 'It is *now* time for a sixth.'

The next day, the army began its descent from the high ground to the river valley beneath them. And as Aurungzib had promised, the towers of Ghazni came in sight. And it was indeed a strong fortress, Richard estimated; in addition to its high walls there was the Ghazni river in front of it, protecting it from an eastern assault.

'Will the river be frozen?' Aurungzib wondered. 'Test it for me, Todal Ali.'

The tavachi guided his horse down the mountain track, kicking little flurries of snow as he did so. Meanwhile Richard studied the citadel, from whose towers were flying Persian battleflags. But the general in command, if surprised by the appearance of a Moghul army out of the mountains at the onset of winter, had no intention of allowing an investment. Even as the Moghuls watched, men began issuing from the town gates to take up positions on the banks; and cannon too were drawn out, leaving deep tracks in the snow as they were placed opposite the ford.

There was also some musket fire, as Todal walked his horse down to the water's edge, but he ignored it. He dismounted, prodded at the surface with his tulwar, then he rode back to the Prince.

'It is commencing to freeze, my lord, but is not yet firm enough to take horses or guns.'

Aurungzib looked up at the sky; the wind was icy, but the clouds were lowering, and prevented the temperatures from dropping far below zero.

'It will not freeze sufficiently for the next few days,' he observed. 'We shall camp here. Bring up the guns so that the Shi'ites may see that we are in earnest. But I cannot wait for the ice to thicken. I need a ford not overseen by the fortress, so find me one.'

The army slowly arrived on the east bank of the river, and there they pitched their tents. It was snowing almost continuously now, starting to lie heavily even in the valley. The Persians obviously liked this weather even less than did the Moghuls, and, although a presence was maintained to cover the ford, they rotated their troops with great regularity.

'Their men do not like to fight in the cold,' Aurungzib observed with some satisfaction. It did not seem to occur to him that his own men might feel the same way.

Meanwhile patrols were sent out to right and left, under cover of snow flurries, and, after the army had been camped for three days, one returned to say they had found a ford some twelve miles downriver.

'It is guarded by a Persian detachment, my lord,' the tuk-bashi told Aurungzib.

'Have they cannon?'

'We did not see any, but there is a fortification.'

'Can it be approached under cover?'

'Yes, my lord. From this bank. We did so, and were not observed.'

Aurungzib nodded. 'Zahid Khan,' he said, 'you will take two regiments of cavalry and make your way to this ford. Do this under cover. Send word to me when you are in position.'

The tuman-bashi saluted and hurried off.

'Now let us wait,' Aurungzib said.

His self-possession and confidence were amazing in so young a man. He had come here to take Ghazni, regardless of anything the weather or the Persians might do, and this was the only thing that concerned him. That his army suffered terribly as the weather grew steadily colder, so that several men went down with frostbite and more than one died every night, this meant nothing to him at all. Neither apparently did the fact that they had consumed nearly all their provisions, and that were they to fail in taking the city, they would undoubtedly starve to death long before they could regain Kabul – even if such a retreat over the mountains was possible in December.

Aurungzib sat in his tent playing chess with his tavachis, or reading the Koran. He apparently had no need for women, as he never sent for one. Nor did he reveal to anyone what his tactical plan would be. Remembering the tales passed on to him by Elena of the campaigns of Babur and Akbar, Blunt presumed that when the secondary ford was captured, he would mask the Persian position before Ghazni and take his army to the new crossing. But, with every day, that was becoming more and more difficult, as the snow lay deeper on the ground.

Two days after Zahid Khan had set out, even Aurungzib grew impatient; the river was now frozen sufficiently for the foot soldiers to cross. 'Has he got lost?' he demanded, and looked around at his tavachis. 'Blunt,' he said, 'take ten men and find Zahid Khan. Tell him he must seize the ford at dawn tomorrow morning. You will see that he does; I make it your responsibility. When he has taken the ford, he is to make his way up the west bank as quickly as he can. I shall commence to cross the river here two hours after dawn. When he comes in sight of the Persian army, he is to blow his bugles and sound his drums – and then charge. Is that understood?'

'Yes, my lord,' Richard said.

Richard saluted, summoned his small band of men, and rode out of the encampment. Hilma and Butji seemed desolate at being left behind; it was the first time they had been separated from their new master, and they knew that if he died they could be parcelled out to some brutal Moghul. But now was not the time for domestic worries.

Blunt returned along the trail for some way, as Zahid had done, so that his movements would not be overseen from the Persian side of the river. Even here progress was difficult. On leaving the main road they took a side trail leading south; although they were again in a valley watered by a frozen stream, they floundered through thick snow.

'It is too difficult,' gasped the sergeant. 'This will take us days.'

'We have but one day,' Richard reminded him.

He drove them on, mile after weary mile, so it was dark before they saw the glow of a campfire and heard the jingle of harnesses.

'Two days gone, and you are not yet at the ford?' Richard demanded.

'Mind how you speak to me, Englishman,' Zahid said. 'It has been a difficult journey. The ford is now a mile away. I have reconnoitred it.'

'And will the enemy not see your campfires?'

'Not down in this valley,' Zahid asserted. 'My people must keep themselves warm.'

It was actually himself he was keeping warmer than anyone else, and Richard could only hope he was correct about being out of sight of the Persians. When he delivered Aurungzib's orders, Zahid pondered.

'He expects me to fight my way across that ford, and then return to the city, a distance of fourteen miles, in just two hours, when it has taken me three days to get this far?'

'Perhaps you were not moving fast enough,' Blunt suggested.

Zahid glared at him. 'And suppose that when I do reach the city, the Prince has not forced a crossing? My men would be cut to pieces.'

As will you, Richard thought, which was obviously what was more concerning Zahid.

'The Prince *will* cross the river,' he said. 'He but requires you to do your duty.'

'Go back to the Prince and tell him his orders will be carried out, if in any way possible.'

'I shall remain here with you,' Richard said, 'to make sure that his orders are carried out.'

'Hm,' Zahid grunted. 'Well, you had better get some rest. You will share a tent with one of my tavachis.'

'When do you intend to move?'

'At dawn, as ordered.'

'It is my opinion that you should move *before* dawn,' Richard argued. 'Your orders are to carry the ford at first light.'

'Do you not suppose the enemy will hear our approach?' Zahid sneered.

'They will hear it equally in daylight, but in the dark they will not be able to tell either your numbers or your purpose.'

'They may send for assistance,' Zahid grumbled.

'That will be all to the good, as it will draw other men away from facing the Prince.'

Zahid frowned, but he gave the orders for the two regiments to mount the moment the darkness began to fade.

Blunt took a quick meal, then snatched two hours' sleep. Though exhausted, he was buoyed up by the thought of the coming battle; and he was awake as soon as the camp began to stir.

He was at Zahid's side as the tuman-bashi led his advance hazzara down to the water's edge. The wind had dropped, so the horses' jingling harnesses echoed in the stillness. Immediately there came a challenge from the darkness on the far side of the water.

Richard dismounted to test the ice.

'It is thin,' he told Zahid. 'It may crumble beneath our hooves.'

'It will be impossible to cross at any speed,' Zahid complained, scratching his beard.

Slowly the cavalry assembled, while on the far side of the river they could hear considerable agitation. When it became light enough to see the frozen water, they could also make out the shadowy figures of the Persians. They were sheltering behind a palisade of boulders and rocks.

'Will you not give the order to cross?' Richard asked.

Zahid hesitated a last time, then drew his sword and pointed to the far bank. Instantly the buglers sounded the charge and the kettledrums began to play. Zahid walked his horse on to the ice, which immediately cracked beneath its hooves; but there was firm ground beneath, and he began to force his way forward through fragmenting ice.

Richard followed with the other tavachis; then came the ming-bashi in command of the first regiment, leading his men.

The Persians opened fire with their muskets, but in the half-light of the dawn their bullets did little damage.

Steadily Zahid pressed his way forward, until suddenly his horse slid down into deeper water, which now came up to the saddle.

'Back!' Zahid shouted. 'This is no ford. It is a trap. Back!'

The whole of the first regiment was now in the water, in column of fours, and they all drew rein. The horses began to move this way and that, neighing with fear and uncertainty. The men were shouting.

Realising that in a moment the entire Moghul force was going to dissipate in panic, Richard brandished his own sword.

'There *is* a ford!' he bellowed, rising in his stirrups. 'This is but the deepest part. Follow me.'

He urged his horse on past Zahid – and also sank into some five feet of water. But he forced his reluctant mount to swim, and to his relief the ming-bashi managed to rally his men and lead them behind him.

Now the Persian gunfire became more effective, although the range was still great. A musket ball struck Blunt on the arm, but luckily did not penetrate the thick woollen jerkin he wore beneath his tunic. And now the water was definitely shallower again; his horse's hooves found the bottom. He kicked the gasping animal forward, bullets humming about him, and scrambled up the far bank. Men ran towards him waving swords, but he burst through them and rode at the palisade. Muskets were immediately presented, and one appeared to explode in his face, but Blunt was not conscious of any pain. He cut down the man who had fired it, and then another; he evaded a pike thrust from a third, and knocked him over with his horse's shoulder. Then he reached the piled rocks, and the horse was scrambling over. He descended the far side into the midst of a large body of men, but by now the ming-bashi was at his shoulder, followed by his soldiers. Then the second regiment was almost across, bugles blaring and drums thundering into the morning.

The Persians turned and fled.

'That was insubordination, tavachi,' Zahid Khan yelled, arriving on the scene. 'I had ordered a retreat.'

'And the Prince expects us before the walls of Ghazni in two hours' time,' Richard reminded him.

Zahid fumed: 'You are under arrest.'

Richard met his glare. 'No,' he said. 'By the authority granted me by the Prince, *you*, Zahid Khan, are under arrest for failing in your duty.'

Zahid was speechless – so much so that he did not even demand to see the authority which Richard did not possess.

'Bind that man,' Richard ordered the tavachis. 'The rest of you, follow me.'

All depended upon the ming-bashi in command of the first regiment; but the colonel made a quick response. He waved his sword, and his cavalry followed Blunt, who was already cantering along the river bank. Within minutes the entire brigade was behind him, while Zahid Khan found himself ignominiously arrested by his erstwhile aides.

There were still fourteen long miles to be covered before the fortress was reached, and although the ground was certainly easier on the west bank of the river, the snow created unexpected pitfalls, so more than one rider came crashing down.

They were encouraged onwards by the boom of cannon and the din of combat in front of them, and after more than two hours they came within sight of the towers – and of the battle being waged beneath, as Aurungzib sent his army across the river into the face of most determined resistance. Indeed they had seen evidence of the battle long before, as dead bodies drifted slowly through the ice-floes beside them.

Richard then slowed his men to a walk, giving the horses

time to recover. Though he knew he was going to be late for the rendezvous, he also knew that it would be worse than useless to arrive with blown mounts.

When the Persians were finally sighted, the horses were good for one charge, he estimated. He pointed with his sword, and rose in his stirrups.

'Ul-ul-ul Akbar!' he shouted the old Moghul warcry, and kicked his weary mount. Elongating into lines, the cavalry followed him with shouts of their own, bearing down on the flanks of the astonished Persians. Having never commanded a cavalry charge in his life, Blunt had no idea how to use his men to their best advantage; but fortunately the Moghuls were so well trained that they carried out their battlefield manoeuvres without orders. When within a hundred yards of the enemy, they swerved their horses to allow themselves to fire their bows. And then, almost without checking, they resumed the charge.

In any event the Persians had been alarmed by the sudden appearance of such a large force of cavalry on their flank. The arrow storm had them reeling – and the resumption of the charge sent them fleeing back towards the city.

'On!' Richard bellowed. 'On! They must not be allowed to close the gates.'

His exhausted men summoned up one last effort; they reached the gate together with the fleeing soldiers – and just as it was being finally closed. Here the mêlée was fierce, and Richard was unhorsed. But he remained on his feet, swinging his sword.

And now they could hear the bugles of Aurungzib's troops as they too raced forward. The gate was seized, and the Moghuls poured into the city.

'Seek them out!' Aurungzib roared. 'Let no Shi'ite escape.' He dismounted to greet Richard. 'I had thought you were not coming. But where is Zahid Khan?'

Richard told him what had happened.

'The cur,' the Prince said contemptuously. 'I will have him raised on a high pole that all may witness his perfidy. But you, Blunt, you are not even a cavalryman, yet you led these men to victory!'

It was the first time Richard had seen Aurungzib in a good humour.

'Blunt Bahatur is reborn,' the prince shouted. 'Blunt Bahatur is reborn. Let us now make sure of our conquest.'

Aurungzib was as merciless in victory as he was brilliant in the field. The Persians were hunted down and killed, and any Afghan who had collaborated with the enemy was seized and impaled, along with Zahid Khan. A forest of stakes grew beside the river, while the army took over the city as its winter quarters. Here was food and warmth and safety; no Persian army could possibly move against them until the spring thaw.

It was a time to rest and replenish – while their leader, his humour gone as quickly as it had arisen, hunted through the townspeople for any who could not prove they were faithful Sunnite Muslims. When his aides argued that some of these victims might prove useful in the following campaign, Aurungzib merely snorted, 'We do not deal with heretics.'

Richard was bold enough one day to remark, 'Yet you deal with me, my lord.'

Aurungzib smiled. 'But you are not a heretic, Blunt Bahatur. You are an infidel. There is a difference. You are damned in any event, and while you live, you are a mighty warrior and an addition to my strength. But these heretics and false worshippers, these drinkers of wine and idolaters, who would paint forbidden pictures on their walls, they are the scum of the earth. Tell me have you ever heard of Shaykh Ahmad Sirhindi?'

'No, my lord.'

'He is dead now, but I heard him speak once, when I was a boy, and I have read his works. He was known as Mujaddid-e-Alf-e Sant, which means 'Renovator of the Sacred Millennium'. He spoke and preached against the drunkenness and licentiousness of my grandfather's court. For this he was persecuted nigh unto death. Yet was he a great man, and a much needed one, for our people are far sunk into sloth. I do not exclude my own father in this. As for my sister ... you yourself have been exposed to her pernicious immorality. Are you not grateful to me for rescuing you from that pit?'

'Indeed, my lord,' Richard said. And he meant it.

'Perhaps it is my duty to cleanse our land of heresy and filth.'

One thing was certain: there would be troubled times ahead if Aurungzib returned triumphant from this campaign.

* * *

But that was not to be for some time. Kandahar was assaulted in the spring, and there Aurungzib was repulsed. That city, lying at the foot of the mountains but still at a height of more than three thousand feet, had originally been built by Alexander the Great, a corruption of whose name it still bore. Since then it had been refortified at regular intervals. Both Genghis Khan and Timur had taken it – but at the height of their power, when they had commanded armies of more than a hundred thousand men. With the limited resources at his disposal, Aurungzib could not carry the city by assault – and he wisely did not try – nor could he totally invest it. He retired to think about it, and even rode back to Agra to consult with his father and brothers, and ask for more men.

Richard remained in Kabul. So I have definitely found my star, he thought. He could only hope that he had made the correct choice.

The war with Persia dragged on for several years, and still Kandahar did not fall. Aurangzib could obtain little more than replacement troops from his father. Yet for Richard, these were good years. Using Kabul as his headquarters, and Ghazni as the outpost from which he made a descent towards Persia every summer to fight a campaign – the monsoon had little effect in the mountains – Aurungzib took over the governorship of Afghanistan, leaving Murad Baksh nothing more than administrative duties. Thus his men made their homes there, as did his officers.

At the end of the first campaign Richard sent back to Agra for Bilkis and his children, and they arrived before the winter. But when, the following year, he again sent to Agra for some more of his servants, the messengers returned emptyhanded. He was told that the palace no longer belonged to him, and his servants had been given to another.

'You have clearly angered my sister by your failure to return,' Aurungzib said with a smile. 'But you will find better servants here.'

By now Richard had been promoted: first to ming-bashi; and, after the second campaign, to tuman-bashi. Like his forebears, he was Blunt Amir, Bahatur. He lived in a style befitting a general, spent his winters in a comfortable house in Kabul, and was attended by the usual retinue of servants as well as his two wives. For he had decided, since he was now becoming a thorough Muslim, to marry both Bilkis and Hilma. He was equally fond of them both, although Bilkis, being the mother of his children, remained the senior wife.

The two girls got on well together, and even welcomed a third addition to the family: a delightful little Afghan girl named Shaita. Like Bilkis, her complexion was fair; she had copper-coloured hair, and understood that her sole business in life was to please her master.

So Richard discovered that he was again happy, doing what he liked best: campaigning. In doing so he had abdicated all other responsibilities: in Kabul there was no news of the East India Company, and therefore none from England. Though Aurungzib did inform him, as the Prince returned to Afghanistan for the campaign of 1649, that in England the monarchy had been overthrown, and the King was executed. Richard gave a moment's anguished thought to the fate of Laura, but recalled that in England gentlewomen were seldom victimised, even in revolutions.

He served a man he was increasingly to admire, even though he learned to fear his master's moods of savage intolerance – the more so as these were not brought on by drink or drugs, or even lust. Aurungzib indulged in none of those three curses of his house. Elena had told Richard much about Akbar, and it seemed to him that the Prince had all the attributes of the greatest of the Moghuls, save only for tolerance. But he was still a young man, and perhaps tolerance would come with age.

That Aurungzib was jealous and contemptuous of his elder brothers – even of his father and sister – was very obvious. Both Shuja and Dara visited Kabul during the Persian War, to inspect the situation and give their brother advice. Both were handsome men, Dara especially. He rode beyond Ghazni with the army, and considered Aurungzib's dispositions; then he told him how he himself would have arranged matters, pointing out to Aurungzib's officers how inefficient they were. His arrogance was amazing, and Blunt could see it was deeply resented by the tuman-bashis. Aurungzib made no comment, and listened patiently to the harangue. Shuja, by contrast, was interested only in the money being spent on the campaign, and recommended cuts in expenditure. Again Aurungzib would not reply, but in the evenings he would sit in his tent and watch his brother drink bottle after bottle of wine, with a grim expression on his face.

'They live in a world of fantasy,' he commented, when the two Princes finally took their leave.

Richard could only agree with him. Despite his failure to seize the immensely strong fortress of Kandahar – a failure due mostly to lack of resources – Aurungzib every day revealed a genius for war. Whenever he could lure the Persian forces out into the field, his victory was certain. Unlike Akbar, he considered no reorganisation of his small army to suit his needs. He won his victories by his amazing tactical eye, by his willingness to take risks and to lead, and to suffer as many hardships as his men in the quest for victory.

There was at least one sign of his mellowing, however. He, too, married, and brought his wives to live in Kabul. Soon they were pregnant.

In 1653 peace was finally agreed with Persia. Aurungzib was angry at this; he had constantly importuned his father to allow him to mobilise the entire Moghul army, and take Kandahar by assault, regardless of casualties. And thus carry the fight on to the Iranian plateau itself. But Shah Jahan would not agree – partly, Richard was sure, because he feared to put Aurungzib at the head of the size of army Timur or Genghis or Akbar had commanded in their heyday. But also partly because he could not; the Emperor had sufficient problems in other parts of his huge realm. Indeed, the Persian peace was concluded because there was a serious problem in the Deccan, where the Marathas, growing more and more troublesome with every passing year, had united under an able general named Sivaji, and were in open revolt.

This Sivaji was still not yet thirty years old. A Hindu, at the age of sixteen he had become so disgusted with living under Muslim rule that he had resolved to lead a war of independence. It had taken time to unite his people behind him, but now his depredations were becoming alarming; and Shah Jahan needed his field army, and his most able commander to deal with the rebel. For Prince Dara had not been very successful in the Deccan, where he had been governor for the past few years.

'It will make a change, at least, to fight on level ground,' Aurungzib remarked, as he led his people south.

Richard was fifty years old in 1653, and this came as something of a surprise to him. He had now lived in India for fourteen years. His eldest son, Zaid, was twelve, and Iskanda, at eleven, would soon have to be married. Nasir, the youngest, was nine. But Bilkis herself was nearly thirty; even little Hilma was twenty. Blunt himself felt as fit as ever, rode as hard as ever, and remained as much one of Aurungzib's favourites as ever. He had no idea where this particular star would lead him, but he had left himself with no alternative.

The southern campaign was urgent, so the army's wives and families mostly had to be abandoned in Kabul, to follow at their leisure. Like most of the generals, Richard took with him a single woman, Hilma, as the army proceeded south by forced marches, making for Hyderabad.

But when Aurungzib left to ride to Agra, to visit his father, he commanded Blunt to accompany him.

It was with some apprehension that Richard saw the walls of Agra rising in the distance. It was six years since he had departed, having sworn to return as soon as possible. And Ara had since made her feelings of displeasure perfectly clear.

On his journey south Blunt was surprised at how little had changed during his years in the mountains. So it was at Agra, too, save that the Taj Mahal was now completed, and in every way lived up to its promise. White marble and red sandstone gleamed in the sunlight from the four minarets which cornered the main building, and from the huge dome of the mausoleum which loomed between them.

'Do you know how much that has cost to build?' Aurungzib asked as they rode towards the city. 'Forty million rupees. What an expenditure for a grave. Think what I could have done with the army forty million rupees would have bought me.'

'At least the Badshah must now be content, my lord,' Richard ventured.

Aurungzib made no reply. He had seen his father every year;

but it was six years since Richard had last beheld the Emperor, and he was shocked. Then Shah Jahan had appeared strong and vigorous, if abstracted. Now Richard looked at an old man, bent and grey, who muttered to himself constantly.

'Sivaji,' he mumbled. 'Yes, Sivaji. Bring him to me in chains, my son.'

The Princess Ara stood beside him. She had also changed, only slightly; but her face was as beautiful as ever, and as haughty. There was even a new Commander of the Guard, a handsome fellow whose hand ever rested on the hilt of his sword.

'You remember Blunt Bahatur?' Aurungzib inquired of his sister.

Ara stared at Richard. 'Take that man from my sight,' she said.

'He is, as you once claimed, a great soldier,' Aurungzib pointed out.

'Take him from my sight,' Ara said again.

'Should I ever fall in battle, Blunt Bahatur,' Aurungzib said as they rode south to rejoin the army, 'then my advice to you would be to leave Hindustan as rapidly as possible. My sister has a long memory, and she does not know how to forgive.'

'I understand this, my lord. I wonder if the English Company I once represented still trades?'

'Indeed it does. It is spreading in every direction. I have told my father that it should be checked, but he pays no attention to me.'

Richard decided not to pursue the matter.

Another long and bitter contest was beginning. Aurungzib may have been right to assume they had an easier country to campaign over, but this meant it was easier country for their enemies as well – and the Marathas were in their homeland here.

At the first encounter the Moghuls were inclined to dismiss the Hindus as mere bandits, guerillas who knew not how to fight a pitched battle, and lacked the proper equipment as well. This was largely true, but it was also the Maratha strength. Their army was composed entirely of horsemen – as had been the old Moghul army led by Babur – but these men travelled with no equipment save their weapons. They slept on the ground beneath the sky, and lived off the land. Remembering stories told him by his aunt, Richard did not doubt that Babur's Mongols would soon have caught and defeated them, but the Moghul Army of the mid-seventeenth century was too much at the mercy of its baggage trains and its artillery. So the war was largely a matter of skirmishes and ambushes.

The Marathas – who in Elena's stories had appeared as fearsome monsters of destruction – fought with exemplary Hindu chivalry, and seldom killed their prisoners. This courtesy was not reciprocated by Aurungzib, who slaughtered every Maratha he could capture, less because they were the enemy than because they were Hindus.

Richard found this disturbing: in Muslim eyes the Hindus, like himself, were infidels rather than heretics.

Three years of bitter warfare at last brought a partial success. The Maratha army was caught encamped just north of the Musi River, with the towers of Golconda and Hyderabad in the distance. When the Moghuls debouched from the hills to the north, there was pandemonium in the rebel ranks; but with their backs to the river, and Aurungzib's cavalry already ranging to either flank, they knew they would have to fight their way out.

Aurungzib surveyed the situation with satisfaction. 'They will not escape us now,' he said. 'But what do you suppose they are doing here, if they are not receiving assistance from that wretched fellow Abdullah? We shall have to see about it.'

Richard now feared for the Company itself. During the campaign he had received letters from the Factor, and through them he learned that England was again tranquil, although under the stern rule of a Lord Protector named Cromwell – who, indeed, sounded like an English version of Aurungzib, a military genius holding the most ascetic and puritanical view of morality. More important, he learned that Laura and her husband were alive and well, if in poverty. He wished he could send her money, but that must wait on the conclusion of the Maratha War. There could be no doubt that the Company was trading with the rebels, if only to make sure they were left in peace. He wondered if Aurungzib realised that.

Knowing they had to fight, the Marathas charged, as that was the only tactic they knew. Aurungzib had no need for military genius here. He merely directed his tuman-bashis to their best positions, and before a hail of cannonfire and musketry the horsemen were mowed down. Aurungzib then summoned his own cavalry to turn this defeat into a rout. The rebels streamed across the river, leaving some third of their number scattered on the ground or drowned – but Sivaji had escaped.

Aurungzib growled: 'We shall have him yet. Now let us punish this place.'

He turned his army loose on Golconda. It had already declined greatly in importance since the foundation of Hyderabad; but now it was reduced to no more than a ruin as the Moghuls raped and pillaged for a whole day.

The people of nearby Hyderabad watched in silence. They knew only too well that such a fate could overtake them at any moment.

Aurungzib himself rode to the old palace of the sultans, to see what could be found there. Blunt accompanied him, since his men were not to be controlled until they had run their course. The palace itself had been proscribed from plunder until after Aurungzib's visit, and they were greeted by an anxious majordomo who ushered them inside, bowing and scraping. There, Richard was amazed to discover, were several Europeans sheltering from the rampant soldiery.

'As I suspected.' Aurungzib stood with his hands on his hips, to survey the frightened people gathered before him. 'You Englishmen are in alliance with those rascals.'

'With respect, Your Excellency, I am not English,' said one of the men in excellent Persian. In early middle-age, he was stockily built, with a short pointed beard.

'Then what are you?' Aurungzib demanded.

'I am Venetian, Your Excellency. My name is Ortensio Borgis.'

The Italian paused, as if awaiting recognition.

'So what are you doing in Hindustan?' Aurungzib demanded. 'Here in Golconda? With the Marathas?' He rammed each sentence home as a challenge.

'He is a world-famous lapidary, my lord,' muttered the majordomo.

'What, are there no stones worth cutting in Europe?' Aurungzib demanded.

'None so fine as here, Your Excellency,' Borgis said. 'But I was invited here by Sultan Abdullah, specifically to inspect and if possible cut the Great Stone.'

'What Great Stone?'

'Have you not heard, Excellency? Six years ago, in the mines outside the city, there was discovered a diamond weighing seven hundred and ninety-seven carats.'

Aurungzib stared at him, as well he might.

'I hang liars by their genitals,' the Prince growled.

Borgis did not look alarmed. 'I have weighed this stone myself.'

'And have you cut it?'

'Not as yet, sire. I reached Hindustan only a few months ago. Cutting any stone is a matter of careful consideration. There are so many angles, so many possibilities. But this stone . . . to make the slightest error would damn me for all time.'

Aurungzib turned to the majordomo. 'Why was my father the Emperor not informed of this discovery?'

'I . . . I do not know, my lord,' the man stammered. 'It was the will of the Sultan Abdullah.'

'The Sultan Abdullah,' Aurungzib said grimly. 'Well, Venetian, you will show me this stone.'

Borgis bowed.

'As for these others – are they also lapidaries?'

'Three of them are my assistants, who undertook the journey from Venice with me. But this gentleman . . .' Borgis hesitated.

The man stepped forward. He was tall and fair, dressed in European clothes of a kind Richard had not seen before. Instead of a ruff he wore a very wide collar over a jerkin, and breeches instead of hose. He had a jutting chin accentuated by a short beard.

'My name is Roger Trent, Your Excellency. I am factor for the Honourable East India Company of London in Golconda.'

Richard drew a sharp breath. The fellow had an arrogance about him which he knew was likely to annoy Aurungzib.

And so it proved. The Prince stared at him under furrowed brows. 'You have been trading with the Marathas?'

Trent did not lower his gaze. 'Trading is my business.'

'With the enemies of the Moghul Empire. Then you are a traitor.'

'I am an Englishman, sir! I know nothing of empires.'

'For God's sake man, hold your tongue,' Richard urged him in English.

Aurungzib glanced at him. 'What did you say?'

'I told him to be quiet, my lord, lest he anger you.'

'Anger me?' Aurungzib said. 'Yes, he has angered me. Take him out and impale him,' he told his aides. 'Hoist him on a high stick so all may see the penalty for "trading" with the Marathas.'

Trent opened his mouth and stared at Blunt. The guards moved forward to seize his arms.

'If I have offended the gentlemen,' Trent said in English, his voice now trembling, 'I am willing to apologise.'

Richard sighed. 'He did not understand the gravity of his crime, my lord,' he ventured.

'You would save his skin because he is your countryman, but I will not have infidels coming here to Hindustan and dealing with my father's enemies. He will be impaled. Now, lapidary, show me this diamond.'

'My God!' Trent said. His arms were already held fast, and he was actually realising that he was fated to die in such a horrifying manner. He turned his head in panic, and then from the recess of the room came a shriek.

Richard now realised that there were several women in the corner, no doubt trying to remain unnoticed. But one of them ran forward and threw herself to the floor at Aurungzib's feet, before any guard could intercept her.

'Have mercy, Your Excellency. Have mercy!'

Aurungzib stared down at her. She was not a sight he could ever have seen before, for her hair was a pale yellow. She was dressed in European clothes, like her husband's of the simplest variety, in which the wide collar sat above a very plain and shapeless grey gown. With this she wore a flat black hat. Tall for a woman, she also revealed that she had a good figure and a handsome face, somewhat long but with splendid bone structure. But her hair, tumbling out from beneath the hat, was her crowning glory.

'Who is this woman?' Aurungzib demanded in puzzlement.

'She is my wife,' Trent pleaded. 'Do not harm her, I beg of you.'

'Spare him, sir,' the woman begged. 'He has harmed no one.'

'He has angered me,' Aurungzib said. 'He must be impaled. Take her outside to watch her husband die – then give her to the soldiers.'

She uttered another shriek and appeared to faint, while her husband, shouting incoherently, was dragged away.

One of the aides thew a jug of water into her face, and the woman slowly sat up, shaking her soaking head and looking around her in almost animal desperation.

'My lord,' Richard said.

Aurungzib glared at him. 'What is it now? Even Englishmen can die, Bahatur.'

'This I understand, sire.' He knew he could not save Trent. But the woman – it might be more merciful to let her die too. The thought of her being raped time and again by the Moghul soldiery was repulsive; it tugged at some long-forgotten pulse of chivalry which remained from his European ancestors. 'I would ask her for myself,' he continued.

Aurungzib stared at him for some seconds, then he gave a shout of laughter. 'Her?'

'I would take her to wife, my lord. I have but three wives at present.'

'Then take her. I give her to you.' He pointed a finger. 'Mind that you do.'

19
THE COUPLE

Mrs Trent continued to look from right to left as if unwilling to believe any of this was happening.

'Take her,' Aurungzib told him. 'Take her now or I will change my mind. But do not enter her until her husband is dead. I will not have one of my tuman-bashis commit adultery, not even with an infidel ... Now, lapidary, show me this diamond.'

He strode off behind a shocked and trembling Borgis, followed by his aides. Richard stooped and lifted Mrs Trent to her feet. Her knees gave way, and she would have fallen again if he had not caught her round the waist. He felt only pity for her and her husband, strange emotions indeed for a tuman-bashi in the army of Aurungzib the Merciless.

'You must come with me,' he told her.

'To watch my husband die?' she whispered.

'No,' he said, urging her down the steps to where his horse stood. Around them now were rolling columns of smoke, and the shrieks of dying men and women.

'Where are you taking me?'

'Away from this,' he assured her.

He sat her on the saddle. As the skirt would not permit her to swing her leg over, he let her sit side-saddle as he mounted behind her, holding her in place by his arm round her waist. He picked up the reins. The orderlies grinned their appreciation of the tuman-bashi's golden-haired conquest.

They rode through streets teeming with shouting men and barking dogs, screaming women and wailing children. Eventually they left the houses behind and set out into the plain, where dead bodies still lay thick on the ground. The vultures were hard at work, and everywhere was the stench of death.

'My God!' Mrs Trent shuddered.

Behind them a man screamed in a high-pitched, unintelligible gabble as the sharpened stake was forced into his anus. Richard was thankful that the woman did not seem to realise who it was.

Servants were busy dragging dead Marathas away from a site by the river which had been chosen as Aurungzib's camp. Already the huge Moghul tents were being pitched, dominated by the Prince's red and gold. Richard rode on to the quarter allotted to his division, where his own blue command tent had been erected. His soldiers cheered him as he entered their midst with his captive.

The sight of the men seemed to bring Mrs Trent to her senses. 'Why have you brought me here?' she asked. She twisted her neck to look up at him, her features pale with terror.

'You have been given to me,' he explained.

She gasped and twisted away, trying to slip off the horse. He tightened his grip on her waist.

'Or would you rather be given to the common soldiery?' he asked.

'Is there a difference?' she gasped.

When they reached the tent he dismounted, still holding her close.

Butji was there to greet him, bowing low.

'Prepare us food,' Richard ordered.

Mrs Trent ducked her head to step through the tent flap, and stopped in consternation – as much at the luxury within, compared with the savagery without, as at the sight of Hilma kneeling to greet her master.

Richard had to push the Englishwoman aside to enter. 'Water,' he told Hilma.

Hilma slowly straightened, and gave Mrs Trent a long appraising gaze, her lip curling.

'Hurry,' Richard growled.

Hilma tossed her head and left the tent.

'Through here.' Richard opened the flap to the inner chamber.

Mrs Trent went inside, again pausing in consternation at the luxury which surrounded her: the cushions and carpets. She folded her arms, as if to hug herself, looking left and right.

'Sit on the carpet,' he said – and did so himself, throwing his sword belt into the corner.

Slowly she sank to her knees, still hugging herself. For only the second time she looked at him. 'Please, sir ...'

'My master is a harsh man to those he considers his enemies,' he told her. 'There was no other way I could save your life.'

Tears cascaded down her cheeks, and she fell forward on to the carpet. 'My husband!' she screamed 'Oh, my husband!'

She was still sobbing when Hilma entered with a tray containing a jug of water and two cups. She regarded the woman with obvious distaste as she set the tray down.

'She is *old*,' she commented.

'You, too, will be old one day. I wish you to find her some clothes to wear.'

'She is too big,' Hilma remarked contemptuously. 'Are you sure you have not found a man there, sire?'

'Find her some clothes. Then we will see whether she is a man or not.'

Hilma scurried from the tent.

Mrs Trent raised her head, tears still trickling from her eyes, but her cheeks were pink. She understood enough Hindustani to know what Hilma had said.

He held out a cup. 'This is only water. Our Commander will permit nothing else.'

Slowly she pushed herself up, and took the cup. When it was empty, he refilled it.

'What is your name?' he asked.

She took a breath. 'Anne.'

'Anne Trent, when I obtain leave, I shall take you to Fort St David ...'

'Will you?' For a moment her face was almost animated.

'And there we shall be married in a Christian church.'

Slowly her features seemed to collapse. 'You mean to marry me?'

'I have explained that is what I must do to protect you. Your husband is already dead.'

Staring at him, her face began to break up again.

As he waited patiently, Hilma reappeared. 'Your food is ready, sire.' She glanced at Anne Trent.

'Serve it,' he said.

She returned a moment later carrying a laden tray; Butji came behind her with another. These were set on the carpet, then she knelt beside him.

'I shall feed myself today,' he said. 'Bring water for my hands.'

She gave a sniff, but fetched a basin and a towel. He washed his hands, and she dried them for him.

'Leave now,' he told her. 'But leave the bell.'

She placed a little golden bell on the tray, and departed.

Throughout this little ceremony Anne Trent had remained kneeling. Now her sobs were dry: she had no tears left.

'Wash your face,' Richard urged her.

She leaned over the bowl and scooped water on to her face, patting herself dry.

He rolled a piece of the curried lamb into the rice, and held it up to her.

She shook her head.

'You must eat,' he insisted.

She opened her mouth and he pushed the food inside. Then he took some for himself.

'Listen to me,' he said. 'I do not mean to harm you. I regret what has happened to your husband, but I cannot bring him back to life. Now you have been given to me as a wife – and you will have to be my wife. But I shall wait until you are ready.'

She chewed, while staring at him, then asked, 'Why do you serve such a monster, when you are clearly a gentleman?'

'I serve a great soldier, who one day will be ruler of this land. He is cruel, yes, but he has much of greatness in him. More of greatness than any ruler I have known.'

'You are much spoken of in Fort St David,' she ventured.

'What do they say of me?'

'Opinions are divided. There are those who remember you as a gallant soldier . . .'

'So that is one opinion of me. I am flattered. What do the others say?'

'The others know you only as a creature of this Aurungzib.'

'And which opinion did you hold?' he asked.

'I had never met you, so I had none.'

The meal was finished. He rang the bell, and Hilma came to take the tray away.

'There is another room through here.' Richard got up and lifted the flap which gave access to the sleeping chamber.

'I have never seen tents like these,' Anne Trent said.

'They harken back to the days when the Moghuls were nomadic wanderers in the steppes. They knew how to be comfortable. Would you like to lie down?'

She gazed at him.

'Alone,' he said.

She stepped past him into the interior.

'Try to sleep,' he told her.

She turned her head. 'I am inclining to the opinion that you are a gentleman.'

Blunt went out and sat down, trying not to think of the woman who lay beyond the goatskin wall. Anne Trent attracted him strongly – and she *would* be his wife. At fifty-three years of age, he would take another wife! That she could be no more than half his age did not concern him. But an Englishwoman! It was a long time since he had had anything to do with a woman from his own country.

He wondered if she would give him children. An English child, to be brought up in Hindustan! Then he would truly be giving hostages to fortune.

His head jerked at the sound of bugles.

'The Prince comes!'

'Have you ever seen anything like that?' Aurungzib demanded. In his hand he held an enormous piece of white carbon, dull, but giving off little glows as the light caught it.

'I have not, my lord.'

'This poor fool is afraid to cut it,' the Prince said. 'He says it could be the greatest diamond ever known – and if he were to spoil it . . . I have told him he *must* cut it, if he ever wishes to see Venice again. And he will not spoil it either. Eh, Borgis?'

The Venetian looked extremely ill at ease. 'I will do my best, sire.'

'Then go to it.' Aurungzib smiled. 'My father wears the Koh-i-noor, but I shall have a greater one yet. We shall call it the Great Moghul!' He was in a fine good humour at the enormous treasure which had just fallen into his hands. 'Go back and enjoy your fair beauty, Blunt Bahatur. But dine with me later.'

He left the tent, accompanied by his aides. Richard waited a moment, then returned to the bedchamber.

Anne Trent lay exactly as he had left her, save that she had placed a cushion against her stomach.

They stared at each other.

'There will be no more interruptions,' he promised her. 'Sleep.'

The next day the Moghul army proceeded to Hyderabad. There Sultan Abdullah greeted the Prince with bowed head.

'What could I do, my lord?' he asked. 'Those scoundrels were all about – and I have few troops to defend myself. I could do nothing but pray for your arrival.'

'And, in the meanwhile, you traded with Sivaji,' Aurungzib said, 'and gave him succour.'

'What he had from me, he took at sword point, my lord,' Abdullah protested. 'Though some of my people may have traded with him . . .'

'Find them and have them hoisted on stakes. Have it done now.'

'Immediately, my lord, immediately. Sivaji . . . he is dead?'

'He escaped me,' Aurungzig said. 'But we shall catch up with him,' he promised.

'That rascal is in league with the Marathas,' Aurungzib muttered to his generals. 'If he is not careful I shall burn his beautiful city about his ears.' He brooded at the attentive faces in front of him. 'But we shall deal with him in due course. For the time, there is no better place than here to sit out the monsoon.'

The dead were burned, the tents were packed, and the army moved into Hyderabad itself. The people there grumbled, but there was nothing they could do. Aurungzib appropriated half the royal palace, and his officers were given houses commensurate with their rank; the unfortunate house-owners were forced to move in with their servants. He was treating Hyderabad as a conquered city.

Blunt asked for permission to travel south and visit Fort St David.

'In the rains?' Aurungzib inquired.

'It will be a short visit, my lord. I will get there and back before the rains start in earnest.'

Aurungzib pointed. 'If you seek to play the traitor, and leave Hindustan, then know this: I will destroy that fort of yours, and every man, woman and child in it. More, I will put to death every Englishman in the land. And I shall impale your wives, and all of your children.'

Aurungzib's increasing paranoia and mistrust was disturbing, but Richard understood that the Prince was his master – and there was an end to it. He must make the most of life, while serving with all faithfulness.

He returned to his tent, around which there was a huge bustle. Wearing a dark green sari, Anne sat drinking tea with Hilma. Hilma herself had chosen the garment and the colour suited Anne's complexion to perfection, and the sheer material gave tantalising glimpses of what lay beneath.

For forty-eight hours she had been left to herself, and she seemed to have recovered a good deal of her spirits.

'Now is your beauty enhanced,' he told her.

'Hilma has been telling me of your family in Afghanistan,' she said in English. 'I did not know you had another wife – and children.'

Richard threw his arm round Hilma's shoulders. 'I have three wives, and three children,' he said. 'Does that disturb you?'

'It means there can be no true marriage between us,' she said, slightly breathless at her temerity.

'That is English law, not Moghul,' he argued. 'You are my wife. That I wish to have it consecrated in an English church is for your sake.'

'It cannot be consecrated,' she insisted.

They stared at each other, then he smiled. 'We shall not quarrel about it. Have you children?' he asked, gesturing them both to sit.

A shadow passed over her face. 'I had a daughter, but she died of fever two years ago.'

'Yours has been a tragic life.'

'And yours? Lost in this devilish country?'

'It is a great country,' Richard reproved her. 'I was born here, and I have no doubt that I shall die here. You would do well to learn to love it as I do.'

She could not repress a shudder, and he hastened to cheer her.

'We leave for Fort St David tomorrow.'

Her face lit up.

'There we will be married,' he added.

'But I have said ...'

'And I have said that we shall do so.'

She looked as if she might have argued further, then she lowered her eyes. 'You will commit a great sin,' she muttered.

'Am I to go also, sire?' Hilma asked eagerly.

'You will remain here in Hyderabad. We have been allotted a house, and you will put it in order for my return,' Richard told her. 'I will take Butji. But you may visit me this night.'

Hilma could not resist a triumphant glance at her rival.

Anne sat with bowed head. When Hilma had left them, she raised her head and looked at him, tears in her eyes. 'I fear for your everlasting soul.'

'Do you really hate me for this?' he asked.

'How could I do that? You have been good to me.'

'Would you rather I summoned you, tonight?'

She hesitated, then shook her head. 'I would rather wait, if you will permit it. I ... I do not know about love.'

'Yet you were married.'

'I was given in marriage by my father. Mr Trent was an up and coming man, and he had a post with the East India Company. He was good and honest, and we lived together for eight years, as man and wife.'

'But you did not love him.'

'I have said, I do not know what love is.'

'Then perhaps I will be able to teach you,' Richard said.

He travelled with an escort, more for Anne's sake than for his own. All Aurungzib's intelligence reports indicated that the Marathas had fled to the west to recoup their losses – but there was always the chance of stray brigands. So he took twenty men, as well as Bayan Ali and Butji. They made excellent time, and reached Madraspatnam in a week.

Little was said on the journey. Richard could only hope that she was not planning some desperate venture when they reached the English settlement, because that would have to be prevented by force – for the sake of everyone. But so far she had impressed him as being a sensible woman, who would make the best of whatever situation she found herself in.

Together Richard and Bayan Ali gazed at the stockade surrounding Fort St David, with the mouths of cannon peeping through the embrasures, and men patrolling the walls. The fort was small, but looked very well constructed, and was clearly capable of defending itself against any local disturbance. It was surrounded by neat little houses, and Richard thought these too close to it for comfort – they would have to be burned in the event of an attack. But they bespoke prosperity, as did the warehouses down by the beach, where a dock out to deep water had been built. The rice paddies had been extended, and there were sheep grazing in a pasture.

'There have been changes since the last time I was here,' Blunt commented.

He took Anne straight away to see the factor, now called governor; a soldier called Colonel James Reynolds, who wore a red tunic and low-crowned black hat, and looked both self-important and overheated.

'I must congratulate you on the work done here,' Richard said politely. 'Especially the defences.'

'Well, these are troubled times,' Reynolds said. 'No one seems to know who now rules in Golconda. The Sultan says he must do what the Moghul tells him, but the Moghul never tells him anything, it seems. Meanwhile the Marathas run riot. But you, Sir Richard . . . this is a great honour. And Mrs Trent, here . . .?'

'Mrs Trent is here because the Moghuls executed her husband.'

Reynolds stared at her. 'My dear Mrs Trent . . . But why?'

'He was impaled for trading with the Marathas – the Moghul's enemy,' Richard warned.

'Good Lord!'

'Have you traded with them, Colonel Reynolds?'

'Well . . .' the colonel looked embarrassed. 'We do not inquire into the allegiances of everyone who seeks to buy our goods.'

'You have sold them guns?'

'Well, so have the Portuguese. In far greater quantities.'

'Nonetheless, should Prince Aurungzib hear of it, you will have a hard time of it.'

'Will you tell him?'

'That is not my intention. But as I fight beside the Prince, a gun in the hands of a Maratha is as deadly to me as to him. If I were you I would remember this.'

Reynolds pinched his lip, and decided to change the subject. 'Mrs Trent, my poor lady ... there is a ship from England expected any day now. We will arrange you a passage home.'

Anne had not yet spoken, but now she said in a quiet voice, 'I am to stay here.'

'Stay here? But why?'

'I am to marry, sir.'

'Mrs Trent is to marry me,' Richard broke in. 'And we have come here for that purpose. As I intend to be back in Hyderabad before the monsoon, I wish it done immediately.'

'May I ask when your husband died, Mrs Trent? I had a communication from him dated but three weeks ago.'

'He died ten days ago.'

'Ten days – and you wish to wed again already? Is that not unseemly haste?'

Blunt was deciding he did not care for this Colonel Reynolds. 'You do not understand the situation,' he said. 'Mrs Trent has been given to me by my master – who is also your master as long as you are in Hindustan. She is aware that, from her point of view, what she is required to do is against the teaching of her church, especially as I have three wives already. However, it will be. It is merely an act of courtesy I perform in marrying her in a Christian church. Now let us have it done.'

Reynolds bristled. 'I never heard such a thing in all my life. Given to you, sir? An English lady *given* to a man with three heathen wives? Well, I cannot allow that. I have a good mind to place you under arrest.'

'Do that, and Aurungzib will burn your puny little fort and impale every man, woman and child within it.'

'By God, sir, he will not. Will we not defend ourselves?'

'How many men have you? Aurungzib disposes of fifty thousand men and two hundred cannon.'

'Can this business not be completed without quarrel?' Anne interrupted. 'I am prepared to go through a form of marriage ceremony. As General Blunt says, it is the will of the Prince.'

Reynolds turned to Richard. 'Sir, I understood from Master Day that you were a man of sensibility. Suppose I offered you both passages on a ship to England? Your prince could never reach you there.'

'He would then destroy your settlement just as vigorously as if I were imprisoned here,' Richard pointed out.

Reynolds finally gave in. 'It will cause a great scandal,' he muttered.

But that was already happening. The news that the legendary Richard Blunt was visiting the settlement, that he had brought with him the widow Trent, whom he was proposing to marry even though her husband's tortured body was scarcely cold, spread through the settlement like a plague. People had already noticed the sari-clad figure with the golden hair, and were perplexed as well as fascinated. Now every man, woman and child in the fort turned out to gawk. The English themselves were as dowdily dressed as the Governor – as Anne herself had been when Richard had first beheld her – and many were the adverse comments at her Indian garb.

There was also trouble with the parson. A short, squat man dressed all in black, he was quite adamant that the whole affair was ungodly, and that in any event there had to be the three weekly banns before he could perform the ceremony.

'The decision is yours,' Richard snarled at him. 'I leave here tomorrow morning for Hyderabad. Mrs Trent will accompany me – and she will live with me as my wife. I have brought her here that she may be saved the sin of cohabiting out of wedlock. If in your pedantry you refuse to perform the ceremony, then any crime of hers will be on your own head.'

'You rogue . . .' the vicar spluttered.

'I will issue a special licence,' Colonel Reynolds intervened hastily. 'It will be in order, I do assure you.' He was desperate not to give Aurungzib cause to investigate the Company's trading habits.

It was a quick, short ceremony, attended only by Reynolds and his wife as witnesses. Then Reynolds shook Richard's hand. 'I do congratulate you, sir. Your wife is a good woman. You will, ah . . . use her kindly?'

'She is my wife, Colonel,' Richard told him.

She was waiting patiently by the door of the church, outside of which a crowd had gathered.

'Are none of these people your friends?' he asked.

'Some of them were, once.'

'Now they condemn you for marrying again so soon?'

She glanced at him. 'They also know that this was no proper marriage.'

'Yet it is done,' he reminded her.

'I understand that you now possess me, sir. I have said I will try to please you.'

At least she was his wife. Bayan Ali was waiting outside with Richard's horse. He set Anne on the saddle in front of him, saluted the crowd, and walked the horse away from the village to where the small Moghul camp had been pitched. Outside the tent Butji waited, their meal prepared.

Richard dismounted, and lifted Anne down. Holding her under the arms, he brought her close to him.

She gave a little gasp, and threw back her head to look at him defiantly.

'Lady Blunt,' he said.

'I had never thought to rise so high, sir.'

Sarcasm? He kissed her mouth lightly, then took her hand and went inside. His men applauded their commander's bride, and he saluted them.

'I doubt that curry was served at your first wedding breakfast,' he remarked.

'It was roast beef.'

'Roast beef. It is eighteen years since last I tasted that.'

'Eighteen years?'

'It is not done to eat beef in Hindustan. Now, tell me of yourself, your family. Of England.'

'It is an unhappy place, sir, under the Protector. We were honest folk – my father was a farmer. And when the King's taxes became unbearable, we took up arms for the Parliament, believing we could make a better land for ourselves. We did not contemplate the murder of the King, or the rule of the major-generals.'

'Have you brothers and sisters?'

'A brother died at Marston Moor, another at Naseby. One of

my sisters married. The other died young, of smallpox.'

'And your parents still live?'

'When last I heard.'

'You understand that you will never see them again?'

She raised her head. 'Never, sir?'

'It is not possible. You must find whatever happiness you can here, with me.'

'I believe you will use me kindly, sir.'

Richard stood up, and held the inner flap for her. She stepped inside. Butji had spread a carpet for them, and a few cushions.

She stood before him, by the centre pole, her head all but touching the goatskin.

'Undress,' he said, and took off his sword belt.

Anne unwound the sari, let it float to the carpet. Beneath she wore the short skirt and small blouse affected by most Hindu women.

'Those also,' Richard said.

She obeyed.

'Did your first husband also admire your beauty?' He studied her.

'Female beauty is not supposed to be admired in Mr Cromwell's England,' she said. 'What must be must be, but there should be no enjoyment in it.'

'Ah,' he said, beginning to understand certain things. 'But there is endless pleasure in it here in Hindustan. It is a pleasure meant to be enjoyed, and again and again.' He held out his hand. After a moment's hesitation, she took his fingers. He drew her against him and kissed her firmly on the mouth. Her body seemed to ripple beneath his fingers as he let them roam from her shoulders down the sides of her breasts, to her buttocks.

Then he lowered himself, still holding her in his arms. She knelt against him, as his hand slipped between her legs. She gasped into his mouth as he played with her.

She rolled on her side, away from him.

'Are we being very sinful?' he asked.

'Very,' she sighed.

'Then let us be sinful some more,' he said, and lay behind her, pulling her against him.

* * *

The clouds had started to build on the day they left Madraspatnam, and Richard urged his men along at a faster pace. But then the wind began to blow, and the rain started before they rode into Hyderabad. As they hurried into the house allotted to Blunt Bahatur, they were soaked to the skin.

Hilma was ready to greet them with towels and hot tea. She seemed genuinely pleased to see them both, if saddened by their obvious rapport. He had held Anne in his arms every night, and known great happiness.

I have fallen in love, he thought. For the first time – when I am old enough to be a grandfather. His main concern was that Anne should love him too. She denied him nothing, and seemed pleased to be with him ... yet had denied him nothing from their first meeting.

At least he had taught her the joys of physical love. The rest would surely follow.

For day after day, as the rain teemed down, he lay on his divan with all the beauty that was Anne in his arms. It was a monsoon he wished might continue forever. But it had not yet run its normal course when he was summoned to Aurungzib's palace, there to find the other tuman-bashis assembled.

'A messenger has come from Agra,' the Prince announced, looking from face to face. 'It seems father is seriously ill. And my brother Dara has announced himself Badshah.'

20

RETURN OF THE MOGHUL

'My father suffers from uraemia,' Aurungzib told his generals. 'But this disease is not necessarily immediately fatal, so I and my brothers are within our rights to denounce Prince Dara as a usurper. I have already despatched messengers to Prince Shuja to express my concern at Prince Dara's action, and invite his support in dealing with him. For the time being the Marathas must be left to their own devices. Our empire is at stake. We shall march out of Hyderabad as soon as the rains stop. So mobilise your men.'

Aurungzib's eyes gleamed: he was clearly elated. This was the great gamble for which he had been preparing himself throughout his adult life; he was not actually denouncing his brother as a usurper but as a rival. And Blunt did not doubt who would emerge as victor in the coming power struggle.

His new wife, Anne, was horrified.

'A civil war?' she cried. 'My God! Suppose your Prince is defeated?'

'Only the mountains of Afghanistan have ever defeated Aurungzib,' Richard assured her.

'But to think of you going to war . . .'

'It is my profession – and we have another few weeks yet.'

By the time the army marched out of Hyderabad, she was pregnant.

Richard was delighted – but this was no time to dwell on domestic matters. Should Aurungzib be defeated, his life and those of all his family and household would be forfeit. He had no doubt that the Princess Ara's fingers would be dabbling deeply in the fratricidal strife now beginning.

For Aurungzib the news they received as they marched north

was a mixture of good and bad. In anger at his older brother's action, Prince Shuja had shaken off his alcoholic lethargy and mobilised his army; now he was marching from Bengal. He suggested that were Aurungzib to join him, their victory would be certain. But Aurungzib merely smiled; in this direction things were working out exactly as he had intended.

'We shall postpone that decision,' he decided, and went into quarters at Indore.

The news from Agra was more disturbing. For Shah Jahan, recognising his present incapacity to govern, had appointed Dara Shikoh as his regent – in effect legalising his eldest son's claims. Dara's very first act thereupon was to declare Shuja an outlaw.

Aurungzib promptly sent a tavachi to Agra to inquire after his father's health – he carefully did not go there himself, lest he be thought to be attempting a *coup d'état*; that might unite his three brothers against him. Also he assured Shah Jahan of his undying support. And now that Dara and Shuja were locked in war, he decided to send an envoy to Kabul to sound out Prince Murad.

'You are the man for this task, Blunt Bahatur,' he declared.

Naturally Richard wanted to go: there were powerful ties drawing him back to Kabul. Anne was desolate, but there was no way he could take a pregnant woman upon such a journey. She had to resign herself to remaining with Hilma, while Blunt and a small escort, including Bayan Ali and Butji, rode quickly north.

The clouds of winter were already gathering by the time Blunt and his men rode into Kabul. Heading first for his own house, he was relieved to find Bilkis and Shaita and his children all in the best of health.

'How they have grown,' he commented.

'And how they have missed you,' Bilkis replied.

He did not tell her of his new marriage that night, as they made love.

Prince Murad had changed for the worse in the three years since last Richard had seen him: he had grown stouter and even more indolent. At their meeting he lolled on his cushions with two naked girls beside him.

'Dara. Shuja. What is the difference?' he said. 'One of them will be Badshah anyway, when my father dies.'

'Your father will not die for many years, my lord,' Blunt argued. 'Thus, whichever prince emerges victorious from this coming struggle will have little choice but to usurp the throne. Then he will have constantly to look over his shoulder, because a usurper may easily be replaced by another usurper. Therefore he will seek to destroy all those who might have a claim equal to his – and first of those will be his brothers.'

Murad sat up, frowning, and even brushed aside the girl who clung to him.

'The same would apply to Prince Shuja, should he overthrow Dara,' Richard went on. 'Prince Aurungzig would have me say this to you: that you and he should unite your forces and force the surrender of whoever wins between your elder brothers. And that you should jointly swear to support each other to the end of your days, and support your father the Badshah in everything meanwhile.'

Richard had rehearsed this proposal word for word as Aurungzib had given it to him – commanding him to repeat it exactly. Aurungzib would never break an oath, but what he had actually promised needed careful study, so carefully had it been worded. However, it was not written down, and Aurungzib had estimated correctly his brother's apprehensions, and his desire only for a peaceful life.

'Yes,' the Prince now said. 'That is the most sensible, most honourable thing to do. Here is my suggestion, that we send a joint envoy to my elder brothers and inform them of our intention, and warn them to cease from their conspiracy.'

Aurungzib had foreseen this possibility too.

'That would be highly dangerous, my lord,' Blunt pointed out. 'For would it not cause Prince Dara and Prince Shuja to unite their armies against those of yourself and Prince Aurungzib? And this while you are separated by some hundreds of miles? No, no, it is essential that you now mobilise every man you can spare, leaving only garrisons in your most important towns here in Afghanistan, and then march south to join your brother with all haste.'

Murad pinched his lip. He loathed the thought of haste.

'If I withdraw my armies,' he said, 'the Persians will retake Ghazni. They may even march on Kabul.'

'That is a risk we must take, my lord. The entire empire is at stake.'

Murad grumbled some more, but in the end agreed to mobilise.

Blunt could do no more. He gathered up his own household to travel south, riding ahead of them to tell Aurungzib what he had achieved. The Prince was satisfied, as he had also heard from his father in gratitude for his support, and denouncing Shuja for taking up arms against Dara without permission.

'Now we wait,' Aurungzib said.

It was a lengthy wait; for the whole of the year 1657, Dara and Shuja manoeuvered and negotiated. They ignored both their younger brothers, whom they apparently held in contempt. Aurungzib had failed to defeat the Persians, and his victory over Sivaji was regarded as a minor success against a band of rebels. Murad they entirely dismissed as harmless, even when he finally united his army with that of his brother, which did not happen until after the monsoon.

The two older princes also appeared to hold their father in contempt, and neither made any attempt to march on Agra and secure his person. Shah Jahan, for his part, did nothing more than issue pronunciamentos: in support of Dara and against Shuja. In fact there was no other course he could take – he had no soldiers of his own save his Guard. He kept sending messengers to Aurungzib, imploring him to march east and place himself under the command of Dara, in order to destroy Shuja; but Aurungzib always replied that he was unable to move his army at the moment because of unspecified difficulties. Every refusal was accompanied by the promise of unwavering support.

Thus, for a year all India waited in suspense for the eventual clash between the two older brothers. Blunt wondered that Aurungzib was not afraid they might after all negotiate together and join forces. But Aurungzib knew Dara too well for that: he wanted the supreme position of Badshah, and he did not intend to share it.

Neither did Aurungzib.

For Richard this was personally a happy time, whatever the crisis looming over the entire nation. Bilkis, Shaita and the children reached Indore safely, and then he had his entire family united at last. Anne was by now swollen, but she was blissfully pleased to have him home and safe, and she seemed to like Bilkis as much as Hilma, while proving herself a perfect stepmother to the children.

In the summer of 1658 she gave birth to a girl, who was named Penelope. She could see that Richard was disappointed, and promised that she would next give him an English son. 'Or will he be English?' she asked, puzzled.

'Well, let me see.' Richard frowned. 'Great-grandfather Peter was certainly entirely English. He married a Portuguese, so my grandfather Thomas was half-English and half-Portuguese. He married a Rajput princess, so my own father was half Indian, quarter English, and quarter Portuguese. My father then married a Spaniard, so I am half Spanish, one quarter Indian, one-eighth English and one-eighth Portuguese. But you are wholly English, so our son would be nine-sixteenths English, one-sixteenth Portuguese, one quarter Spanish, and one eighth Rajput. He would certainly be of very mixed blood – though English would predominate.'

'Oh,' she said. He could not tell whether she was confused by his mathematics. Or maybe, Richard thought, she did not realise that he had Indian blood.

It was not until the turn of the year that Shuja's army, which had retreated steadily before the advance of the imperial forces, was finally caught by Dara's at Bahadurpure, north of Calcutta. Everyone waited on news of the battle, Aurungzib impatiently striding to and fro. When the news did come, it was as expected; Shuja had been routed, and had fled into the delta of the Ganges. But he was still at large, and in Bengal he had been a popular governor; there seemed every possibility that he would attempt to raise another army.

Aurungzib gazed at his generals. 'Well,' he said, 'this could not have worked out better. As soon as the monsoon is past, we shall seek out Prince Dara.'

Dara now sent messengers to his two younger brothers, commanding them to disband their forces, and to meet him at Agra.

As usual, Aurungzib made a conciliatory reply, and prepared to move.

'Perhaps we should do as he wishes,' Murad fretted. 'Now Shuja is defeated, and knowing that Dara is supported by the Badshah . . .?'

'Dara would depose the Badshah, if he could. He dare not only while we remain in the field,' Aurungzib advised him. 'You would do best to leave the campaign to me, brother.'

So Murad went back to his women.

Aurungzib's first overt act of rebellion was to send an envoy to Agra, denouncing Dara for having carried out a *coup d'etat* and imprisoned their father, and demanding that Dara disband his army and await the arrival of his younger brothers. It was a superb piece of effrontery, based upon Aurungzib's knowledge of his brother's overweaning arrogance and selfconfidence.

Aware that he had acted entirely with his father's authority, Dara reacted as Aurungzib had guessed he would. Furiously angry, he abandoned Agra and marched south-west to deal with his errant brothers. Nor did he even take the Badshah with him. He wished the world to see that Aurungzib's accusation was false.

But in all the world that was India, only Aurungzib's opinion now mattered.

Aurungzib's army had been mobilised for weeks, and commenced its march immediately. With the addition of Murad's forces, the Prince commanded seventy thousand men, which with their camp followers swelled to some hundred and twenty thousand. The army advanced slowly east towards Allahabad, while cavalry scouts were sent ranging to the north for news of Dara.

Once information was received that Dara's army was moving south to meet them, Blunt was summoned.

'I promote you to amir. You will take your infantry division, and also four cavalry regiments. You will march as far west as is necessary to avoid making contact with my brother's army, and then due north to seize Agra in my brother's absence.'

Richard gasped. 'My orders then, sire?'

'Once you seize the city, arrest any of the garrison commanders you consider untrustworthy, and prepare to hold it until my arrival.'

'If the gates are closed to me?'

'Besiege it, and await my coming. But I do not think the gates will be closed to you, if you announce that you have come to safeguard the person of my father. Once inside the city, you will treat the Badshah with the greatest respect; I will provide you with a letter to him explaining my actions.'

'I understand, my lord.'

'Should my brother turn back to recover my father's person, then you must hold the city against him. But you will not have long to wait, for I shall be on his heels.'

'I am honoured to have been chosen for this task.'

'I have chosen you not only because you are my most experienced soldier, but because I know that, as an infidel, you can never hope to usurp the throne for yourself. But there is another reason.' He smiled. 'You will place the Princess Ara under arrest.'

Richard's heart sank. 'Yes, my lord.'

'You will not harm her in any way. I will judge her when I reach Agra.'

'I understand, my lord.'

Aurungzib smiled again. 'You had best take your wives with you, Blunt Bahatur. To preserve you from temptation.'

Richard had every intention of taking his wives with him. It was eighteen years since he had been intimate with the Princess. She was now in her middle forties, and would surely have lost the ability to totally bewitch a man.

He moved north rapidly, and by the beginning of May reached the gates of the city. The hakim was summoned, still his old friend Kazim Khan. Richard was forced to wonder, not for the first time, whether Kazim had ever graced Ara's private garden. But now he was in a difficult position as he listened to what Richard had to say, and received Aurungzib's letter.

'I shall deliver this, Blunt Bahatur, but I must receive the permission of the Badshah before I can open the gate to such a large army,' he said.

And of the Princess, too, presumably. Richard wondered if she would choose to fight, and force him to mount a siege. But, to his surprise and relief, the gates were opened within the hour.

The people of Agra had grown used to watching armies come and armies go over the past couple of years, but they still turned out to watch the hazaras of lancers trotting through their streets, followed by the blue-uniformed veterans of Richard's division. Blunt rode at the head of his men, and he felt that the crowd was impressed. Certainly it was unlikely that Dara's army could be anything like as well disciplined as Aurungzib's.

He wondered what his women, riding in their wagons at the back of the procession, thought of the wonders of this city; for the Taj Mahal was finally completed, its formal gardens and pools laid out in all their precise splendour, its dome gleaming in the sunlight. If Shah Jahan had put as much energy, and money, into ruling his empire as to creating beautiful objects, what a different India this would be.

The Guard was drawn up outside the Moghul's palace, glittering in gold and scarlet. Kazim Khan was again there, as Governor of the City, to welcome Richard.

'Your master's message was well received, Blunt Bahatur,' he said. 'These have been troubled times.'

'Is the Badshah well?'

Kazim nodded. 'As well as can be expected. He awaits you.'

Richard was swiftly ushered into the imperial presence. Shah Jahan actually sat in his Peacock Throne, the huge golden beak drooping above his head. He looked very old and frail, his skin yellowed by his illness.

He was surrounded by his viziers and officers, and Richard was alone save for Bayan Ali at his side. But a glance from the window would remind the Badshah that his palace was surrounded by Aurungzib's men.

'Blunt Bahatur,' the Badshah said. 'My son pays me great respect. Is this sincere?'

'Prince Aurungzib wishes only to worship at your feet, Badshah.'

'That is good,' Shah Jahan said. 'My other sons have not treated me with respect. When will Prince Aurungzib be here?'

'Very soon, Badshah. The very moment he has disarmed the usurper, Prince Dara.'

'I will not have Prince Dara killed,' Shah Jahan spoke querulously. 'He is my appointed heir. True, he has not treated me with a proper respect, but I will not have him killed.'

'I am sure Prince Aurungzib will deal with his brother in an honourable manner, Badshah,' Richard temporised.

'Then it shall be well done,' Shah Jahan said, and waved his hand to terminate the interview.

But the real interview was yet to begin. Kazim Khan was waiting for him.

'The Princess Ara wishes to speak with you.'

'As I must speak with her,' Richard told him. His men had already been given their orders and waited only his signal. Now he nodded to Bayan Ali, standing outside the doors to the Princess's apartments, and the disarming began. Ara's people were too surprised to resist.

Kazim sighed. 'She is still as beautiful as ever. It is said she will never grow old.'

Richard could believe that Aurungzib was not going to permit that, and he was aware of mixed emotions as he was ushered again into that unforgettable garden. His arrival was likely the signature on her death warrant.

Sitting on her couch, surrounded by her maids, she gazed at him with liquid eyes. Yet when last he had seen her, she had spat hatred at him. She was indeed as beautiful as ever, her breasts as high, her legs as slender.

'You come to our rescue, Blunt Bahatur,' she began.

'I came at the bidding of Prince Aurungzib, Highness.'

Ara tossed her head. 'Now you are here, you must take your orders from me. By Allah, but it has been a difficult time for us, with Dara strutting about like a peacock, and so overweening he could hardly be tolerated. But, Blunt, to see you again ...' she clapped her hands, and the maids hurried giggling from the garden, leaving them alone. Now the Princess rose and removed her sari, certain that she could re-establish her physical domination of him. 'I would bathe with you,' she said, 'as we did so long ago.'

Richard gazed at that immaculate body. So long ago, he thought.

'And then we shall eat together, and talk of many things.' She moved to the steps.

'Please dress yourself, Princess.'

She glanced at him, frowning.

'I have been sent here to place you under arrest,' Richard told her.

Ara's face hardened into a mask of anger.

'You dare to speak to *me* thus?' She clapped her hands.

'Dress yourself,' Blunt said again. 'Your girls have already been arrested. My men are about to enter this garden.'

Ara reached for her sari and wrapped it round her. 'I shall have you impaled,' she hissed. 'And I shall hammer the stake into your bowels with my very own hands.'

Richard bowed. 'No violence will be offered to you here, Princess. But you must not leave your apartments.' He turned to the door as it opened to allow his officers to enter. 'Every door will be guarded until the arrival of Prince Aurungzib. I would beg of you to attempt nothing rash, Highness – and no intrigue.'

'You filthy ingrate!' she shrieked, and ran at him. He caught her wrists just before she could open his face with her nails, then wrestled her down on to the divan. There she rubbed her body against his, and clasped her legs round him, regardless of the watching soldiers.

'Admit the maids,' he shouted, and a moment later he was surrounded by the terrified women.

'See to your mistress,' he panted, throwing the still wriggling Princess away from him.

Ara sat up, nostrils flaring, her beautiful features contorted with rage.

'Get out of here,' she screamed. 'Get out. I do not wish to look upon your face again.'

The news of her arrest rumbled through the city like an earthquake.

'What will happen to her?' Anne inquired.

'What will happen to all of us depends now upon the Prince.'

Richard returned to the Blunt house, which had been standing empty for more than ten years. Bilkis remembered it well and was able to take charge of its refurbishment. This gave the women something to do, even though they could not know whether or not it would become their permanent home. Anne was in rhapsodies at its lavish marble, its interior courtyards, the fountains which soon flowed with water again. She had never known anything like it.

'This house has been the possession of my family for one hundred and thirty-two years,' Richard calculated.

She was utterly surprised, having had no idea of the antiquity of the Blunts in this land.

Blunt continued to attend the Badshah at least once every day, not only to flatter the old man but also to keep an eye on things at court – and also on Princess Ara's guards.

'Why is she confined, Blunt Bahatur?' Shah Jahan asked plaintively. 'Was she not a friend of yours?'

'I obey the orders of Prince Aurungzib, Badshah,' Richard replied. 'He suspects the Princess of seditious activities against Your Majesty.'

'I am not a fool,' Shah Jahan snapped, with a sudden reminder that he was still officially the greatest monarch on earth. 'My daughter would never scheme against me. Unlike my sons, my daughter loves me – almost as much as did her mother. Did you know the Mumtaz Mahal? She was the greatest woman of her time.' To Richard's consternation, a tear trickled down that yellow cheek – after twenty-six years. 'I love her still,' Shah Jahan continued. 'Now I wait only to join her. The Princess Ara is innocent of any wish to harm me, Blunt Bahatur. You must make Prince Aurungzib see that. He hates her for her way of life. But that is my fault, for indulging her. She was only sixteen when her mother died . . . The Prince must accept that there are those who look at life differently from himself. You must make him understand.'

Richard bowed. 'I shall do my best, Badshah.'

Once again they could only wait. But in May a battle was fought at Samugarh, and, predictably, Dara was utterly defeated. Like Shuja, he fled.

Aurungzib then marched on Agra, and arrived the following month. Blunt turned out the garrison to meet him, and had every building in the city draped with banners and flags.

Aurungzib clasped his hand. 'You have done well, Blunt Bahatur. Where is my father?'

'He watches you from that balcony, my lord.'

'Let us go to him.'

Followed by his tavachis and by his brother Murad, he strode into the palace and bowed before his father.

'Badshah, it has been granted to me by Providence to defeat your enemies and bring peace to your great realm.'

'You have not harmed your brother?' Shah Jahan asked.

'I have not seen him. He fled the field.'

'Brother should not harm brother,' Shah Jahan mumbled.

Aurungzib bowed. 'And is the Badshah well?'

'I have pain,' Shah Jahan said. 'Much pain.' He looked out towards the Taj Mahal. 'I shall soon join my beloved.'

'You will live for many years yet,' Aurungzib comforted him. 'But to see you oppressed with the endless burdens of ruling so vast a realm ...'

Shah Jahan said, 'How may I avoid that?'

'By delegating others to carry out these duties for you. What is it you desire most in all the world?' he coaxed.

Shah Jahan sighed. 'Why ... simply the peace to sit here and look at her monument, and remember ...'

'Then it is my duty to give you that peace,' Aurungzib said firmly. 'I would not have you ever leave this porch again. Indeed I forbid it, and I shall instruct my men accordingly.'

'Now,' Aurungzib said, 'there is much to be done.' He looked about him.

'You have betrayed your oath,' complained Prince Murad.

Aurungzib raised his eyebrows.

'You swore to me that we would support our father in all things,' Murad said.

'Am I not doing so?' Aurungzib seemed genuinely surprised at this accusation.

'You have just deposed him, even if he does not have the wit to see it.'

'I asked him what he wished most in the world,' Aurungzib said. 'And when he told me, I granted it to him. How may a son do more for his father? Now I will ask you the same question, my brother, in accordance with our sworn alliance. What is it you wish most in the world? Do you wish to ride at my side into battle ... or would you prefer to settle in a quiet palace, relieved of all duties and granted an abundance of everything you hold most dear in life?'

Murad licked his lips nervously.

'Slave girls from Burma,' Aurungzib said, 'from Persia and from China. The most beautiful women in the world to set alongside your own Indian beauties. Is this not what you truly wish?'

Murad licked his lips again, afraid to admit his vices before the assembled officers.

Aurungzib smiled, and embraced his brother. 'These things shall be yours,' he promised, 'in accordance with our pact that we shall support each other in everything. I have what I most wish, the government of the empire. You now have what you most wish. Together we shall do very well.'

'And now,' Aurungzib said, 'I must speak with my sister. Blunt Bahatur, you will accompany me.'

'The Badshah has especially asked that your sister's life be spared, my lord,' Richard warned.

'I doubt my father understands what he is about any longer,' Aurungzib said. 'In any event, he is as guilty as she. You know of their sin, but no one else must. Her women must not be allowed to gossip – nor her executioners. We shall take two slaves.'

Richard had no choice but to obey, yet was aware of violent emotions as he followed the Prince into that unforgettable garden. He had not visited the Princess since her imprisonment, but he had received reports from her guards. Ara was apparently alternating between moods of high confidence, when she was positive that someone would free her from captivity, and deep despair, when she would shriek and scream in paroxysms of fury.

Today she seemed calm and dignified; as she stood and

gazed at her brother when he marched into the garden, followed by Blunt and the two slaves.

'A gathering of the jackals,' she remarked.

Aurungzib wasted no time. 'In the name of the Badshah, I accuse you of adultery and fornication, of incest and blasphemy, and of plots against the throne.'

'Who has accused me?' Ara demanded. 'That creature at your heels?'

'Dismiss your women,' Aurungzib commanded. 'I would speak with you alone.'

Ara hesitated, then clapped her hands. The girls scuttled through the inner doorway, not realising there were soldiers waiting to strangle them on the spot.

'Have you no answer to the charges brought against you?' Aurungzib demanded.

Ara tossed her head. 'I am your elder sister, boy. I do what I choose. I have always done what I choose.'

'You admit your crimes. And your sentence is death.'

The two slaves moved forward. Ara glared at them. 'These are common murderers.'

'They are adequate for the task. Is not bathing your favourite occupation? They are here to bathe you.'

Ara gasped. 'These swine?'

'Go with them,' Aurungzib commanded. 'There is no need to disrobe; your days of indecency are finished.'

Ara looked at Richard. 'Can you let this happen?'

Richard said nothing.

As Aurungzig gave a quick nod, the slaves each seized one of her arms. She screamed and tried to fight free, but they carried her wriggling and kicking to the top of the steps, then down. Still she tried to fight them, her sari slowly unravelling. When they reached the water, they each placed a hand on the Princess's head, and pushed her face beneath the surface. For several minutes still she fought them, the water boiling around her. At last her body went limp.

Aurungzib drew his sword. As already instructed, Richard drew also. In astonishment the executioners turned to face them – and were each thrust through the chest. As the pool became discoloured with blood, their bodies floated beside that of Ara.

'They beheld too much,' Aurungzib said.

'As I have done, my lord.' Richard's voice shook.

They gazed at each other, each with a drawn, blood-stained sword in hand. Then Aurungzib gave a grim smile. 'But I have need of you, Blunt Bahatur.'

It was then that Blunt was appointed Governor of Agra. He was well aware of the uncertainties of his position, which rested entirely on Aurungzib's favour, and even more on his success. He would actually have preferred to remain with the army, and fight or fall at his patron's side. Instead he had to watch from the walls when, after the monsoon, the Prince again took the field, seeking his brothers.

The women were delighted that their husband would remain at home. By the end of 1658, Anne was again pregnant, but Richard sought news only of Aurungzib.

The Prince's progress was entirely triumphant – and ruthless. Both Shuja and Dara had returned to the field, and there was talk of them combining against the true usurper. But Aurungzib boldly marched between them, and then turned east.

In Bengal, he met Shuja and routed him thoroughly. This time there would be no recovery. Shuja escaped the field, but his men were massacred. Shuja fled to Burma, and died there some years later in misery.

Aurungzib now turned back, and at Deorai in April 1659 the final, decisive battle of the civil war was fought, ending in utter defeat for Dara. Like his brother the Prince fled the field; but he was betrayed by one of his own men after Aurungzib had offered a handsome reward. Dragged before the conqueror, Dara was accused of heresy, condemned and executed.

Aurungzib was back in Agra before the monsoon, entering the city with a fanfare of trumpets. He went straightway to visit his father.

'Your enemies are all dead or fled, my father,' he said.

Shah Jahan raised his weary head. He was not so feeble that he did not notice Aurungzib had not used the correct greeting: Badshah.

'Now you may spend the rest of your days in peace,' Aurungzib assured him. 'No more shall you have the burdens of empire thurst upon you. You will abdicate such things to me.'

Shah Jahan said nothing.

* * *

'My grandfather' Aurungzib told Blunt, 'assumed the title Jahangir, "World Conqueror", no doubt to frighten his enemies. He never conquered anything, but I have conquered the world ... all of it that matters. And I shall soon have the rest. My title will therefore be Alamgir: 'Master of the World.' Is that not fitting?'

Soon after the monsoon ended, Anne gave birth to a son, whom they named Peter after the most successful of all the previous Blunts.

It was a time of great prosperity for the Blunts and for the empire. But Aurungzib immediately resumed his campaigns, and drove his armies south into the Deccan and north into Afghanistan. The Persians were defeated – as were the Marathas. Their dealings with Golconda being proven, Hyderabad was then sacked by the imperial armies, although the Charminar was spared. Abdullah's successor, Abul Hassan, was executed.

The Company had had the good sense to refuse further trade with the Marathas, and from Fort St David, or Madras as it was now called – the original name Madraspatnam having been abbreviated by the British – came word of how Aurungzib's fame had been carried to Europe. To those who traded with his vast and wealthy empire, he was known by a single title: The Great Moghul.

As was the huge gem which hung around his neck.

BOOK, THE FIFTH
The Company

'Men are we, and must grieve when even the shade
Of that which once was great is passed away.'

William Wordsworth, on the extinction of the Venetian Republic

21

THE TYRANT

'The Badshah comes!'

The word spread through Delhi, growing from a whisper. People ran from their houses to line the streets and wait to salute the Great Moghul returning from the wars.

First came the advance guard of household cavalry, their cloth-of-gold tunics, scarlet breeches and turbans making a magnificent sight, while the sun glinted from cuirasses and spearheads. They were proud and haughty men, as befitted the finest élite troops in the world.

Peter Blunt's heart swelled as he watched them from the roof of his mother's house. Once his father had ridden at their head. And one day he would also do so; he had no doubt of it.

Anne Blunt could sense what the boy was thinking, and she put an arm round his shoulders, half reassuringly and half protectively. Peter was the very last of Richard's children.

Fourteen years old, Peter could not remember much of his father, for Richard Blunt had been killed fighting for the Badshah against the Marathas in the Deccan, only a few years after Aurungzib had seized the Peacock Throne and made it his own. Peter had been only six when this catastrophe had overtaken the Blunt family, and his father remained only a vague memory of a tall, strong soldier.

The Emperor's favour had been extended to the dead hero's family. When Aurungzib had moved his capital to Delhi – leaving his aging father in solitary splendour in Agra, gazing at the Taj Mahal – the Blunts had gone with him. Richard's wives had been granted large pensions, and given this splendid palace in which to live. Their children were to be groomed for the imperial service, and Peter's elder halfbrothers were already in the army. Zaid was a garrison commander and Nasir rode as a ming-bashi in the Guard. Peter's halfsister Iskanda had been married to a Moghul noble. Even his full sister, Penelope, had three years ago, at the age of fourteen, gone into an amir's harem.

Peter had been only eleven then, yet able to understand his mother's resignation. When her husband died, Anne Blunt had wished to leave Hindustan with her two children, but Aurungzib had refused permission. 'All else is yours,' he had told her. 'But you have a son who will be another Blunt Bahatur, to ride at my side in my old age. You will stay here, and if you wish, I shall find you another husband.'

Anne had not wished – though now, at forty-four, she remained tall and handsome. But to be locked away in a harem was not her pleasure, and if she must continue to live in India, she wished to possess the freedom of the widow – a freedom permitted no other women in this land ruled so sternly by the Badshah. For the universal freedom of the days of Akbar, even of Shah Jahan, was only a memory. But she had her house, and she had her good friends, and the company of Richard Blunt's other widows, Bilkis and Hilma – Shaita having died of fever when hardly more than a girl – and she had her children. Yet she had known all the time that this last happiness was a transitory one. Aurungzib himself had chosen young Penelope's husband, and Peter already spent four hours of every day training with the other boy guardsmen.

She knew she could have afforded none of this ease in England. True, the reports brought up from Madras or the new British factory in Surat claimed that England had again become a happy place since the death of Cromwell, but for her there could be none of the luxury enjoyed by those who basked in the favour of the Great Moghul.

Aurungzib rode behind the advance guard, and in front of the rest of his troops. His horse was a white Arab, his tunic cloth-of-gold. The hilt of his tulwar sparkled with jewels. Fifty-six years old, he seemed in the prime of life and power. His beard might be turning white, but his energy was undiminished. Shah Jahan had been dead some ten years now, so Aurungzib was the undisputed Badshah; and after a lifetime of campaigning no one could question his military genius. He had now just – not for the first time – defeated the Persians to ensure the safety of his north-west frontier, and in all India there was only one force which still dared to oppose him: the same Maratha Confederacy headed by Sivaji.

But even that confrontation had brought Aurungzib fame. Sivaji had taken advantage of the civil war between the sons of Shah Jahan to reorganise his people and virtually conquer Bijapur; he had even raided the East India Company factory at Surat and taken an immense booty. Realising that this robber chieftain – or Hindu patriot, depending upon one's point of view – was becoming too powerful, Aurungzib had despatched his Vizier against him. But Sivaji had won the battle, and further increased his power.

Aurungzib had then sent his best troops commanded by his greatest general, Mirza Raja Rai Singh, against the rebel. It was in this campaign that Richard Blunt, commanding a division of the Guard, had been killed. But Rai Singh's immense army, some hundred thousand men, had forced even Sivaji to sue for peace. Surrendering on terms, he had been required to go to Delhi with his son, and formally swear himself a vassal of the Moghul.

This he had duly done, but soon realised that he and his son Sambaji were actually prisoners – intended for execution as soon as they had been forgotten by their people.

But Sivaji had escaped by means of a remarkable subterfuge. He had pretended to be taken ill, perhaps even to be dying, and as a devout Hindu he had begun to pave his way into his next world by presenting alms to the needy. These alms consisted of huge baskets of fruit, and every day they had been carried into the palace occupied by the Maratha chieftain, to be blessed before being taken out to the poor. One day the baskets were even larger than usual – but the Muslim guards had by then long ceased inspecting them. When they were carried out again, they contained Sivaji and his son Sambaji.

So the Marathas made their escape, and regained the Deccan in triumph – to be hailed as even greater heroes by their people.

It was said that even Aurungzib had smiled at the boldness of the feat, once he got over his rage at having his greatest adversary escape him. But he had neither forgotten nor forgiven, even if Sivaji seemed content to live at peace over the past few years.

Aurungzib's eyes flashed from left to right at the people

thronging the streets and cheering his progress. The crowds were mostly Muslims, for, since Sivaji's coup, the Badshah had slowly but relentlessly been changing the face of Hindustan. The tolerant, inquiring, progressive nation ruled by Akbar had been gradually converted into a fundamentalist Muslim state. Given Aurungzib's character, this might probably have happened anyway, but Sivaji's defiance had quickened the process. Hindu temples had been razed, and their public expressions of worship were forbidden. The *jizya* poll-tax, cancelled by Akbar, had been reinstated for all non-Muslims. Thus the bulk of the populace muttered in fear and discontent . . . but there was no man prepared to raise his hand against the Great Moghul.

The princes rode behind their father. Azam Shah was the eldest, Kham Baksh the second, Bahadur Shah the third, and Akbar the youngest. Akbar was indeed only a few years older than Peter, and this had been his first campaign. Unlike his brothers, who sat on their horses with the pride and some of the arrogance of their father, Akbar seemed to find it difficult to smile, and he seldom glanced at the cheering populace.

Then came the army. The troops were hardly less arrogant than their master. For they were the dominant force in India, and no one could doubt that, if Aurungzib chose, they could be the dominant force in all Asia. As it was, the Badshah's word was law from Baluchistan to Assam, and from Afghanistan to the Malabar and Coromandel coasts. Even the growing number of English and French factories, which had begun to rival the Portuguese, did so only by the grace of the Moghul.

But Aurungzib's immense power consisted of more than the sheer extent of territory he dominated. Hindustan was the richest country in the world, and the evidence of it was there for everyone to see. Apart from the Great Moghul diamond, which hung around the Badshah's neck, and the Koh-i-noor which by tradition was worn by Azam Shah, the Crown Prince, the glory of the Peacock Throne alone would have conveyed godlike splendour upon him, for Aurungzib used the throne whenever he resided in Delhi, where it had been removed to with all the rest of the panoply of state.

It had been Tavernier, following his visit to Agra some ten

years previously, who had made the glory of Aurungzib known to all the world. He had been allowed to inspect the throne, and had placed upon it an amazing valuation in excess of one hundred and sixty million English pounds, which made it the most valuable single object in the world. On his return to England, Tavernier had told the world of the wonders he had seen; and now there was hardly an adventurer who did not dream of carving a fortune from the subcontinent.

Aurungzib watched the young men at swordplay in the palace yard. Nearby were the tuman-bashi of the Guard and several of his ministers. Below them, at the end of the parade ground, huddled the families of those young men who were hoping this day, on their sixteenth birthdays, to be chosen.

First they performed their sword exercises on foot; and then mounted to do the same on horseback, charging each other with swirling tulwars, to meet with a clash of steel, and disengaging to gallop back to their positions.

'They are fine young men,' Aurungzib commented as he proceeded down the stairs, while the waiting men and women bowed. Being in public, all the women wore veils, as the Emperor commanded, but it was easy to discern Blunt Agha from her height.

Aurungzib approached her. 'Young Blunt does well. Today he joins the Guard.' He gazed at the tears in her eyes. 'He will ride at my side, Blunt Agha, as one of my tavachis.'

'I am honoured, Badshah.'

'But yet you are weeping. We must increase your household. Find your son a wife, agha, that she may bear him children for you to raise.'

Anne trembled. 'With respect, Badshah . . .'

'Ask.'

'I would have my son married to one of his own people.'

Aurungzib raised his eyebrows. 'Are none of our Moghul women good enough for you?'

'Not so, Badshah. It is a promise I made his father.'

Aurungzib studied her for several seconds, but Anne did not lower her gaze, even though she had just lied. Then the Emperor nodded. 'So be it. You may seek a wife from one of the English factories.'

'In due course, my lord. My people do not marry as young as yours. But I am grateful for the permission.'

In all the splendour of his gold and scarlet uniform, Peter Blunt made a handsome figure. He was bigger than the average Moghul, or Hindu for that matter, and when he marched at Aurungzib's side he earned the admiration of the crowd. His future seemed assured, and Anne was both relieved and proud of that.

Nor was he entirely lost to her, as he was enabled to return home one night a week. His half brother Nasir, to whose regiment he was attached, often came with him, although he already maintained a separate establishment. Zaid they seldom saw, and of course Iskanda and Penelope were never permitted to leave their harems and return to their own home – especially since it was well known that Blunt Agha conversed freely with men and never wore the yashmak. Both the younger women were now mothers, and so had much to interest them. But all three of them regarded Anne's youngest as the child with the greatest future; Aurungzib's favour was obvious to everyone.

Although Anne had won a victory in obtaining permission for Peter to wed an English girl, she realised he had to be provided with sexual company lest he be sneered at by his fellow officers. So she and Bilkis and Hilma went to the slave market together, for she knew she would have to rely upon the other wives to make a good choice. Butji, now their majordomo, accompanied them with the bag of money.

Anne had never seen a slave market before, and was utterly taken aback by their blatant exposure of men and women, girls and boys, of every age and colour – the only concession being that the women and girls, even if presented naked on the stands, continued to wear the yashmak – and by the crowds of eager men and women examining what was on offer with minute and indelicate care. The news that the three Blunt Aghas were present spread quickly, and soon they were surrounded by touts trying to attract them to this dealer or that.

'Be off with you,' Bilkis shouted. 'We are here to see Asif Khan.'

'I am his man, mistress,' cried one of the boys. 'I shall take you directly to him.'

'Who is Asif Khan?' Anne was perplexed.

'He is the best,' Bilkis assured her.

They were led through the throng, many envious glances being cast at their silk saris and expensive jewellery, and entered the doorway of an establishment which smelt of perfumes and coffee. Here there were young women ready to escort them to chairs in a softly-carpeted reception room, and to present them with cups of coffee. Apparently there was a separate room for each customer, since no one else was present. Nor was there any sign of slaves, although they could hear murmurs of conversation all around them.

A moment later Asif Khan himself came in.

Anne had been quite determined to dislike the slave dealer, as indeed she felt distaste for the entire business. But to her surprise Asif turned out to be a tall, dignified middle-aged man with a manner which was deferential without being ingratiating.

'I am honoured to receive three great aghas at one time,' Asif said. 'Now, explain to me your wishes. Do you seek domestics, or ...?' he paused.

'We seek concubines for our son,' Bilkis said firmly.

'Ah! For the young Blunt who has recently become tavachi to the Badshah. Of course. Have you any nationality in mind?'

'We wish someone gentle and quiet,' Anne put in.

'And obedient,' Hilma added.

'One who is a virgin – but also experienced at making a man happy,' Bilkis said.

'Of course. But every girl I shall show you will be a virgin; and all have been taught the art of making a man happy. They will also all be obedient. Yet some are more vivacious than others ...'

'She must also be beautiful,' Hilma suggested.

'And intelligent,' Anne intervened.

'Of course,' Asif Khan agreed. 'Will the aghas excuse me?'

He left the room, and Hilma clapped her hands. 'I am so excited.'

She and Bilkis had also bought concubines for their sons Zaid and Nasir, but that had been a long time ago. Nasir, the younger, now aged thirty-two, already had three wives and six children.

Anne, of course, had not been involved in those earlier transactions. Now she pressed, 'Do you not find there's something distasteful in dealing in women as if they were animals?'

Hilma was clearly bewildered; she had been dealt with in exactly the same way before being given to Richard Blunt.

Bilkis gave a sad smile. 'Here in Hindustan, and throughout Asia to my knowledge, it is woman's fate ... but also her only hope of happiness.'

'To belong to a caring master,' Anne countered. 'But how many of them are that fortunate?'

'There is no fate worse than never belonging to a man at all.'

Asif Khan was back. 'Some more coffee?' He clapped his hands, and the serving girls returned to refill their cups.

'Are these not for sale?' Anne asked. They certainly seemed completely docile.

'Everything in my establishment is for sale.' Asif smiled. 'Perhaps even myself. But these girls have no intelligence; they are merely servants. You said you wished intelligence. So here now is Serena.'

He held the curtain open, and a girl stepped through. She wore harem costume: pantaloons and bolero, both sheer in pale blue, with a matching pale-blue felt fez. Her black hair was contained in a single heavy plait which trailed down her back. Her complexion was pale, her face quite pretty, with a short nose and chin and wideset dark eyes. Her figure, clearly delineated beneath the thin material, was youthfully nubile.

She bowed before the women.

Asif clapped his hands, and from behind the curtain music began to play. Serena danced for them, daintily and politely. Asif allowed her to continue for two minutes, then clapped his hands again and the music stopped. One of the serving girls then brought out a stool and a sitar, the many-stringed lute-like instrument of north India. Serena sat on the stool, carefully fitted a wire plectrum to her right forefinger, and plucked out a pleasant tune.

'She is also adept at needlework,' Asif Khan said.

'Where is she from?' Bilkis asked.

'From the north-west, Agha. Peshawar.'

'You mean she is Pathan,' Hilma snorted.

'But from an excellent family. Her father fell into debt and was forced to sell his daughters.'

'I think she is perfectly charming,' Anne said, anxious to have done with it. 'What are you asking for her?'

'It is too early for that,' Bilkis objected, and beckoned the girl closer. 'Kneel,' she commanded.

Serena obeyed, and Bilkis commenced to examine her as she might do a horse. The girl's mouth was opened to check her teeth, Bilkis inhaled her breath to make sure it was sweet, then she was made to drop her pantaloons and kneel with her legs apart while Bilkis examined her genitals, joined now by an enthusiastic Hilma. Anne felt quite faint, and could not meet Asif Khan's eye, but the dealer seemed perfectly content. The girl herself made no protest as she was pushed and pulled and prodded.

'Yes,' Bilkis said at last. 'Show us some others.'

Asif Khan bowed and clapped his hands. Serena dressed herself, bowed to each in turn, her cheeks pink, and hurried from the room.

'What is the matter with her?' Anne asked.

'Why, nothing,' Bilkis said. 'But there may be better.'

'And does she have to submit to such treatment by every would-be purchaser?'

'Of course,' Bilkis said. 'And most of those are men.'

'Some men *never* buy,' Hilma said. 'They only visit the slave market to inspect ... and then reject.'

Four more girls were shown in. One of them was an Afghan, even more fair than Serena, but smiling and forceful, as if offering herself to the women. Two were from the south, dark-skinned and doe-eyed. The last was unlike any human being Anne had ever seen before: a tiny person with the daintiest of movements and a yellow-brown complexion.

'She is a Thai,' Asif Khan explained. 'Obtained from beyond the westernmost boundary of the dominions of the Badshah.'

Like the others she played a musical instrument, but this with the oddest collection of discords.

All of them had to undergo a detailed physical examination by Bilkis and Hilma, but Bilkis could tell that Anne was growing impatient.

'They are poor specimens,' she said, when the Thai girl, named Jintna, was sent out. 'But before we go elsewhere, we may as well know their prices?'

'These girls are the best that can be found anywhere,' Asif Khan protested. 'I deal only in top-quality goods.'

'Their price?' Bilkis repeated.

'For the Indian girls, thirty rupees each.'

Having once been a factor's wife, Anne knew this approximated to ten English pounds.

'And the other?'

'Oh, she is most expensive, Agha.'

'Why?' Hilma demanded. 'Her breasts are nothing more than buds.'

'That's because she is very young, Agha. Her breasts will grow. She is expensive not only because she has come from far away, but because Thai girls – why, they are almost Chinese. They know secrets of the arts of love that have never reached us here in Hindustan.'

'How much?' Bilkis asked.

'Forty rupees, Agha.'

'That is a great deal of money for a concubine,' Bilkis said. 'I will pay you twenty-five rupees for the girl Serena.'

'Twenty-five rupees! Great Agha, that will leave me with no profit at all. It might be possible for me to accept twenty-eight . . .'

'Twenty-eight.' Bilkis appeared to muse. 'Sixty rupees – for Serena and Jintna.'

'Two?' Anne protested.

'How may a strong young man be satisfied with but a single girl?' Bilkis asked.

Anne gulped.

'Sixty?' Asif Khan's voice rose an octave. 'Great Agha, would you have me on the street, my wives and children starving? Sixty-five.'

'Sixty-five,' Bilkis said. 'Butji!'

The servant counted out the money, and the two girls were led in again.

'Have they no personal belongings?' Anne asked.

Asif Khan bowed. 'All that you see is yours, great Agha.'

'What would you two pay for me?' Anne asked, as they emerged on to the street. The two girls were now suitably wrapped in haiks and yashmaks, and thus invisible save for their eyes – but apparently quite content to have been purchased.

'Why now ...' Bilkis gave a little shriek of laughter. 'Five rupees, to clean the steps.' Then she grew serious. 'But when you came to our late lord and master, Anne Agha, I would have paid fifty rupees without argument.'

Anne supposed she had just been paid a compliment.

The two girls waited together in Peter Blunt's bedchamber when next he returned home from the barracks.

'What do we do now?' Anne had asked.

She had absolutely no experience of this sort of thing.

'We just leave them together,' Bilkis had told her.

'But ... will he know what to do?'

Bilkis had laughed. 'They will show him.'

'I am Serena, my lord,' Serena said. 'And this is Jintna. She speaks no Hindustani.'

The Thai girl gave an anxious bob.

'I will speak for her,' Serena assured him. 'Will you know us now?'

Peter surveyed them. His three mothers had been in a state of high excitement when he had arrived, and he little guessed what would be waiting for him.

Women had not played a great part in his life sexually. Though he had grown up in a largely female household, from the age of twelve he had been given over to the tutelage of soldiers. The tuk-bashis of the Guard had made the whole relationship between man and woman seem rather alarming when they spoke of the pleasures of ill-treating females, and recounted the great rapes of their careers. Peter felt no great desire to ill-treat or rape anyone. As a result he felt rather uncertain about the thought of concubines – never mind the prospect of a wife.

But here was a girl beckoning him to her bed. And, as she removed her tunic and pantaloons, suddenly he was eager. Revealing a great deal of smooth-skinned beauty, she then came forward to stand against him, virtually forcing him to touch her.

Even more entrancingly, the little Thai girl was soon doing the same on his other side.

'Why, yes,' he gulped. 'It will be my pleasure.'

* * *

The next few years were good ones. Peter was clearly a born soldier, like his father, and very soon was promoted tuk-bashi. He continued to serve under Nasir who, although a faithful supporter of the Badshah, was clearly not going to progress much farther up the chain of command. He was too indolent, and too fond of women – in addition to his wives he maintained a dozen concubines. But he was a good fellow, and very fond of his young halfbrother, to whose interests he was always alive.

For Peter, Serena and Jintna proved quite sufficient. Seeing them only once a week, they never palled, and in their eager sexuality they seemed always to be vying with each other to please him.

Then in 1678 the Marathas went to war again. As with Bijapur, their expansion was to the south, away from the Moghul's dominions, but Aurungzib exploded in anger.

'I have been too kind to these cursed Hindus,' he roared. 'Now they will pay. *Make* them pay.' He glared about him.

The Badshah had spoken, and the persecution of the Hindus was intensified. The Muslim soldiery was encouraged to treat all Indians with the utmost arrogance, to thrust them out of their way on the street, to enter their houses and insult their women, and even to rape them as they chose.

More Hindu temples were looted and destroyed, and Hindustan became an unhappy place. But Aurungzib now went further than ever. The taxes on Hindus were doubled and, instead of merely tearing down their temples, he erected a mosque upon the site of one destroyed shrine devoted to Krishna.

Peter felt distressed by what was happening. In 1678 he celebrated his eighteenth birthday, and the uncertainty yet complacency of youth had already been swept away by the experiences of manhood. He was a father, by Jintna, of a boy named William.

However, he was above all a servant of the Moghul. He had always accepted this – had always understood this was his only path to prosperity and fame – and a safe old age. More than this, he admired Aurungzib wholeheartedly; his great ambition was to campaign under the Badshah's leadership.

Indeed, he had hoped that Aurungzib would mobilise his

army to march after Sivaji. But the Badshah had other things on his mind, so there was nothing to do but carry out the Moghul's commands – and watch the last of the respect his Hindu peoples had held for the Emperor disappear. Peter knew little of statecraft, but he sensed that a monarch hated and feared by more than half of his subjects must anticipate revolt.

This was not something to discuss with his fellow guard officers, who were all Muslims. Even at home he could find little sympathy for treating the Hindus with more respect. Bilkis, Hilma and Serena were also Muslims; Jintna was a Buddhist, and little interested in anything save her master and her son. And even Anne did not leave the Blunt household often enough to appreciate the extent of the oppression, so was inclined to discount his reports as an exaggeration.

But as he had known would be the case, eventually this mistreatment reached the Rajputs. Aurungzib had recently installed his youngest son, Akbar, as hakim of Rajputana. But now word came to Agra that the Rajput Confederacy was on the march – and at their head was the young Prince himself.

Aurungzib listened with an expressionless face to the trembling messenger. Then he asked, 'My own son leads these people? Has he nothing to say to me?'

'He calls for your abdication, Badshah, and promises a reversal of your policies towards the Hindus.'

'And does he himself mean to take my place?' Aurungzib inquired. 'Or has he discussed this matter with his brothers?' He glanced at Kham Baksh – the only one of the four presently in Delhi.

'I know nothing of this, my father,' Kham Baksh protested.

'Then you will mobilise your divisions. Meanwhile send word to Azam Shah and Bahadur Shah to do the same, and to march with their men to join me here with all haste. The Rajputs have been too proud, for too long.'

Blunt's heart began to pound. He was going to war at last – but could only wish it was in a worthier cause.

The revolt spread with alarming speed, and the Rajputs found a military leader named Drugadas whose talents were superior to those of Prince Akbar, although the Prince remained as a figurehead. Soon several of the Muslim garrisons in Rajputana were forced to surrender, and before the Moghul army was ready to move it was apparent that Aurungzib had a major contest on his hands.

To make matters worse, his persecutions had also roused the Sikhs – offshoots of the Hindu religion – and those proud mountain men were also up in arms. So Aurungzib had to detach a separate army to keep them under observation, while he prepared to march west.

Yet the Badshah's confidence, indeed delight, in his prospects never wavered for an instant. War was what he had been born to.

Anne Blunt held Peter's hand tightly as they said goodbye.

'We do not anticipate a long campaign, Mother,' he promised.

'Was there ever a short campaign?' she sighed. 'Make sure you come back to me, Peter.'

Serena and Jintna wept silently.

The imperial army moved with Aurungzib's usual speed, and it was in Rajputana almost before the rebels knew it was fully mobilised. The Rajput leaders, Durgadas and Akbar, were attempting to raise money to sustain their forces; and several small detachments out tax-gathering were rounded up and executed.

'Exterminate every Hindu found with a weapon in his hand.' Such was Auringzib's grim command to his troops.

The army advanced on a broad front; the princes Kham Baksh, Azam Shah and Bahadur Shah each commanded a large body on the wings; the main force under Aurungzib himself formed the centre. But the general orders were to concentrate on whichever command first encountered the Rajputs in force.

Durgadas wisely attempted to refuse battle, hoping that the revolt would spread and that Aurungzib would be forced to split up his Grand Army. It was known that the Rajput leader had sent messengers to Sivaji, but it seemed the Maratha leader was now indeed ill, and that no help could be expected from that quarter currently.

Meanwhile Aurungzib began to systematically devastate Rajputana, burning its villages and even whole towns. That it was part of his own realm he was destroying – and with it some of the finest fighting men – appeared to make no difference to the Moghul. It was to be a war of extermination.

As a tavachi of the Emperor, Blunt had little opportunity to distinguish himself in the fighting; he was forced to sit his horse at Aurungzib's shoulder and gaze helplessly at the horrors commanded by the Badshah. He watched villages surrounded and set on fire, people seized and mutilated as they ran from the conflagration – the men castrated and the women raped before being thrown back into the flames. He watched whole herds of sacred Hindu cattle killed and eaten by the Muslims.

Blunt accompanied his master into towns which had been given over to the sack, and there watched as each house was systematically looted, along with the usual bestial ill-treatment of the inhabitants. Aurungzib surveyed the terror he was spreading with an expressionless gaze; from time to time he even ordered his tavachis to take part in this pillage. 'To become men,' he told them, 'you must learn to kill.'

Thus, at Jodhpur, Peter rode with Nasir's regiment into the town, behind the cavalry, and after Aurungzib's artillery had blown in the gate. People ran screaming from them, seeking any place to hide – for news of the Moghul's anger had preceded the army. The Moghul lancers laughed with delight as they trotted along the streets, spearing the slower inhabitants as if they were pig-sticking.

The halfbrothers drew rein to survey the situation, then Nazir directed his men to sack the houses to either side. They fell to this with great delight, leaping down from their horses to force open the doors and assault the terrified people inside.

'You must return with blood on your sword,' Nazir told Peter. 'So follow me.'

He turned down a side street, and a man swung at them with a pike, but Nazir easily evaded the blow and cut him down.

'There is another. Make him yours.'

A second man ran off down an alley, and Blunt rode his horse behind him. When the man entered a house at the end, Peter dismounted. The door was shut and bolted, but was rotten and flimsy, so a shoulder charge knocked it from its hinges.

Nazir behind him, he pushed into the gloomy interior. Their quarry stood panting before an inner doorway, his pike in his hands, moving it to and fro.

'Together?' Nazir asked.

'No,' Peter told him. He wanted this to be a fair fight.

Nazir stepped aside and Peter advanced, kicking the few pieces of furniture aside.

The man snarled, and thrust at him with the pike. Blunt parried the blow, moving to the side. Again the man swung the pike to thrust, and again Blunt parried it before moving inside the pike's arc to slash with his tulwar. As he did so, he heard movement behind him and a shout from Nazir – but he could pay no attention to what else might be happening.

His opponent brought the pike back a third time, but too late; Blunt had swept his tulwar from left to right, feeling it jar as it encountered bone and muscle. He watched blood spurt over his hand and wrist as the Hindu collapsed on the floor. As he did so, a blow struck Blunt on the back of the head. The helmet saved him from being knocked unconscious, but as he fell to his knees, he heard a scream. Turning his head, hardly able to focus, he saw Nazir holding a girl around the waist, while fighting off another. Both girls were armed with thick sticks; wore only dhotis, and were young and pretty. Although Nazir retained his sword, he seemed reluctant to use it.

'Are you all right, brother?' he panted.

Peter got to his feet, sheathed his bloodstained sword, and moved towards the second girl. As she swung her stick, he caught it and wrenched it from her hands, then twisted her arms behind her back. Relieved of her hostile attentions, Nazir sheathed his sword and clasped the other girl against him, fondling her breasts.

'By Allah, but she is a charmer,' he said. 'That one who struck you, brother.'

Peter stared at her, and she gazed straight back, her dark eyes filled with fire. He held his captive the more tightly as she continued to wriggle against him.

Nazir shrugged. 'It is the Badshah's command that no quarter be given to those with weapons in their hands.'

'Then let us be done with them now.'

Nasir grinned. 'And rob them of the only pleasure they will ever know in this world?'

Peter felt sick – but he knew he could not dissuade his half-brother. Nasir was Bilkis's son, and there was too much of the Afghan in his bloodstream.

'You will have to help me.' Nasir began to pant as the girl in his arms continued to wriggle. 'So bind the one you have.'

Peter looked around for cord.

'Use her dhoti,' Nasir urged.

Blunt looked down at the girl. She was clearly younger than her sister, and less determined in her defiance. He released her and drew his dagger. 'Take off your garment,' he commanded in Hindustani.

She stared at the blade.

'Die!' shouted her sister. 'Die, now.' She knew what was going to happen to them.

Tears trickled from the little girl's eyes – but she did not want to die. She untied her dhoti.

Peter took away the garment, pulled her arms behind her back, and tied her wrists together. Naked, she faced them, unable to do more than strain on her bonds.

'Filth!' hissed the older girl. 'You are the lowest crawling creature in the world.'

'This one is going to be great sport,' Nasir panted. 'Now come, take her arms.'

Peter grasped the girl's arms and pulled them behind her. Nasir moved in front of her, caught her kicking legs, and between them they laid her down on the floor. Nasir stripped the dhoti from her body, then removed his breeches. She tried to keep her legs together, but he laughed as he rolled her over and forced them apart to kneel between, pulling her thighs from the floor.

Despite his disquiet, Peter could not help but be aroused as he watched them. The girl's frantic writhing, the gasps of pain, the feel of her wrists twisting in his hands – were all intensely erotic.

Then Nasir fell back on to his haunches, spent. 'She is good,' he said. 'Now, give me her wrists and take your turn, brother. Then we will have at the other one.'

Peter licked his lips in hesitation.

Nasir raised his eyebrows.

'Give me her wrists,' Nasir repeated, 'and prove yourself a man.'

For the first time in his life Peter felt a sense of total isolation. When they left the house and the ravaged bodies of the two girls, he vomited on the street.

Nasir laughed. 'You are young, brother – but you are growing up.'

Into what, Peter wondered?

Aurungzib was shown the blood on Peter's sword, and was satisfied. 'You showed the devils no mercy?'

'None, Badshah,' Nasir assured him.

The rape of Jodhpur forced the Rajputs' hand, and their army concentrated. Now Aurungzib sat his horse on a hillock and looked down at the vast array below him, every man mounted and armoured. They shimmered in the sunlight.

'History has a way of repeating itself,' he said jovially. 'My great ancestor Babur faced exactly such an army one hundred and fifty-four years ago. First he defeated them, then he befriended them. My great-grandfather Akbar the Great needed to defeat them all over again, but again he befriended them. Today, however, we are going to destroy them. The Rajputs will be no more.'

His tuman-bashis tugged at their beards, but no one dared remind the Badshah that, ever since the days of Akbar, the Rajputs had always formed the main cavalry arm of the Moghul army . . . or that Aurungzib himself had Rajput blood in his veins.

The Moghul made his dispositions: they were, as ever, offensive, and simple in their tactical brilliance. Azam Shah's division formed the right wing, Kham Baksh's the left – but the Princes themselves rode in the centre with Bahadur Shah and their father, leaving the troops to be commanded by tuman-bashis: Aurungzib was taking no chances, and none of his sons could doubt that their lives would be forfeit at the first sign of treachery or desertion.

The wings of this host were then thrown forward, while the Moghul artillery began exchanging bombardments with the Rajputs. Iron balls flew; men and horses were destroyed. Positioned immediately behind Nasir, and only a few feet from Aurungzib himself, Peter Blunt wondered how the Badshah and his officers could so carelessly stand their ground beneath the flying shot – revealing immense courage and confidence, and yet could act with such ruthless cruelty when given the chance. He remembered his own brother holding the girl by the hair while he drove his dagger into her breast – and laughing. For Nasir was laughing now as he gazed at the approaching holocaust. Did he wish to die, Peter wondered? Did he not care about returning to Delhi and the womenfolk? Would they, too, suffer such a fate, should Aurungzib be defeated here today and the city fall to the Rajputs? No one could doubt that theirs would be a terrible retribution.

While the cannonade continued, to left and right the Moghul horsemen slowly advanced towards a position from which they could mount a charge. Aurungzib knew his opponents well, and knew that the Rajputs would never permit their oldest enemies to come too close. And so it was. The Rajputs charged first, and the Moghuls received them in a furious cavalry mêlée.

But behind the horse were the Moghul foot, huge brigades now entirely armed with modern muskets, and their discipline was far superior to that of the Hindus. At a change of note in the continually blasting bugles, the Moghul cavalry disengaged and rode helterskelter back towards their lines. No matter how many times they had fought, and lost, the Rajputs could not resist this oldest of all the ploys practised by the horse archers from the steppes. Yelling their anticipation of victory, the Rajputs urged their blown horses in pursuit – to be faced by infantry squares belching fire. Now they could no longer form for a charge. Men and horses crashed to the ground, and the survivors withdrew.

As they did so, Aurungzib gave a signal for the centre to advance. 'No quarter,' he told his tavachis. 'Be sure every officer understands this.'

The young men galloped off to inform the various commands, Peter Blunt amongst them. The Moghul horse and foot were tramping forward, though still the roundshot tore great swathes through their ranks. But the Rajput gunners were now looking at the rout of their wing cavalry, and the gunfire was diminishing. Only the centre remained; and, lacking infantry, there was only one resource left – another cavalry charge.

This they delivered with the superb élan that was their greatest glory. But their cause was hopeless. Once again they were checked by the musketry of the infantry, while the Moghul cavalry – their horses having recovered their wind – now attacked on the flanks.

Blunt had allowed himself to be carried forward with the infantry, after delivering Aurungzib's last command to their tuman-bashi. He wanted to fight – though unsure whether he was willing to die. Now he urged his horse forward to the front rank, ignoring the shouts of tuk-bashis who would have called him back. The advancing soldiers raised shrill cries, as he charged into the Rajputs, followed by the rampant infantry. Faces loomed around him and he cut and thrust. He felt and heard the clang of blades on his helmet, felt pain as well from somewhere in his body. Then he tumbled senseless from the saddle as his helmet came off and another blow fell on his head.

'A great victory, Badshah,' declared Rai Singh.

That was obvious at a glance. The Rajputs were everywhere fleeing the field, save those who lay dead or dying.

'Mount a pursuit,' Aurungzib commanded. 'No quarter, remember! Now dispose of the wounded.'

Aurungzib stood over the litter on which Peter Blunt lay. The youth had been stripped of armour and uniform, and his wounds were bandaged. Part of his head had been shaved to allow the surgeons to dress the gash in his scalp. Nasir stood beside him, weeping to see his brother so injured.

Aurungzib grasped Peter's hand. 'You were a veritable warrior this afternoon, young Blunt. Did you seek to die?'

Peter licked his lips. He did not know what to reply.

Aurungzib continued, 'You are a fitting wearer of the Blunt name. I award you the title borne by your forefathers: Blunt Bahatur.' He squeezed the fingers, then released them. 'But mark my words: in future, you fight when I tell you to. At no other times.'

He turned to Nasir. 'Care for your brother. He will be the greatest of your family.'

22

THE BETROTHAL

Prince Akbar had fled to Persia before he could be captured, but yet Aurungzib's victory was complete: the Rajput confederacy had been destroyed as a fighting force. Yet this would prove an irreparable blow to the military strength of the Empire in its constant wars against the Persians and the Afghans. Blunt, who had been taught some English history by his mother, likened it to Edward III suddenly destroying his Welsh archers during his long struggle with France. But that did not appear to concern Aurungzib in the least. Although the Badshah was now past sixty, he still had no doubt that he himself had only to appear on a battlefield and victory was his.

On his return to Delhi, following the campaign, he might have expected a period of peace – especially after news of Sivaji's death. But almost immediately the Marathas were up in arms again, this time commanded by Sivaji's son, Sambaji.

'By Allah, I will finish with them once and for all,' Aurungzib swore – and his army marched south.

Still recovering from his wounds, Blunt was unable to accompany them. He was left with instructions to join the Badshah as soon as fully restored to health. Standing on the roof of the Blunt Palace, he watched the army march out, as he had done so often as a boy.

'I pray this campaign may be a short one, and the army return before you are fit to join it,' his mother Anne admitted.

'Yes, so do I,' Peter agreed.

She glanced at him questioningly. It had not escaped her notice that he had returned from the Rajput War a much more serious young man than when he had left – or that he no longer seemed as close to his halfbrother as before. But she dared not let her hopes rise too far: he was a Blunt, and fighting was in his blood.

'I sometimes wonder what the future holds for us,' she murmured.

'Why, to serve the Badshah – for me at least.'

'Have you no desire to visit England?' she asked. 'I would love to take you there.'

'I doubt the Badshah would give us permission.'

'That is true – except, perhaps, if you sought a wife there. The Badshah has granted permission for you to seek an English wife. And if we can find none suitable in Madras, or Surat, or Bombay, we should have to look farther afield.'

'I will not marry,' Peter said curtly, and left the roof.

But the campaign against Sambaji would not be over quickly. The Marathas had clearly been prepared for a long time, and were determined to fight to the last. Thus it was that, after the monsoon of 1680, Peter, now again fully restored to health, set off to join the army. Since he knew that Aurungzib had established a regular headquarters in Hyderabad, he took with him both Butji and Serena. Jintna remained to look after little William.

There were the usual tearful farewells, but he was glad now to be back in the saddle and campaigning. He had found the company of the womenfolk cloying at times – even his mother. Her talk of marriage to an Englishwoman alarmed him. Over the months as he slowly recuperated, he had come to understand that he was committed to being a soldier. And if he would never enjoy the killing and rape as Nasir obviously did, he would still do his duty and obey his master's orders. And take his pleasures, when he needed, from one of his concubines. But to share that violent life with a woman as softly innocent as his own mother was unthinkable.

It would be up to baby William to carry on the line.

So the campaign dragged on, year after year. Each year Aurungzib seemed to have gained the advantage but, every time, the Marathas melted away, seemingly defeated but always ready to re-form elsewhere. Yet the Badshah would never consider granting terms which might accommodate these superb horsemen into his empire and into its armies. His objective seemed nothing less than the extirpation of all Hinduism, and he pursued it with a single minded determination that was frightening.

Peter Blunt grew old over the next seven years. For him the normal traverse from youth to manhood was accomplished sword in hand; the murder of the two girls in Jodhpur became nothing more than a shadow in his memory. He could see himself changing in the eyes of his mother and the womenfolk; on the few occasions he managed to get back to Delhi, they gazed in awe at this tall, gaunt soldier they remembered as once an innocent boy.

But, with every year, he grew in favour with the Badshah, who clearly saw in him a man to be trusted above all others. At twenty-two, Peter was made ming-bashi, colonel in command of a regiment of the Guard. Five years later he became tuman-bashi. As the Guard now consisted of two divisions, he was not yet at the overall pinnacle achieved by his father, yet that he would one day achieve the rank of Amir and be commander of the entire Guard could not be doubted; and he was not yet thirty. Thus he was not in the least disturbed, when, on an autumn day in 1688, as the army reassembled after the monsoon for yet another campaign against the Marathas, he was summoned for a private consultation.

Aurungzib was not in a good humour as he received him.

'These Maratha bandits are now using modern muskets,' he complained. 'Now, where do you suppose they obtain such weapons?'

Peter looked at some of the guns taken from dead rebels. 'From European traders, Badshah?'

'Exactly. But look more closely.'

Peter obeyed, and gasped. 'These were made in England.'

'This has happened before,' Aurungzib growled. 'Mark me well, Blunt Bahatur, I have been generous to these people. Your father came to us as a trader – and stayed to fight with us. Also he brought us weapons like these, therefore I have given the English far-reaching privileges. But these countrymen of yours grow too bold: they will sell their weapons to both sides. That I will not tolerate.'

'With respect, Badshah,' Peter argued, 'we cannot know for sure that the English sold these muskets to the Marathas. It could well have been the Portuguese, or the Dutch.'

'I believe it was the English,' Aurungzib said. 'For they are the boldest, and they grow bolder every day. I have received a report that a fleet of English ships in the Arabian Sea engaged and destroyed a squadron of my own vessels on passage to Mocha. How do you explain that?'

'Perhaps they thought your ships meant them harm, Badshah.'

'It was an act of war,' Aurungzib snarled. 'Be sure I will burn them out root and branch, should they persist in their perfidy. But I will give them one opportunity to reaffirm their loyalty to me. You will go to Bombay as my representative, and there speak with your countrymen to warn them of my anger. Bring me back their contrition, or when I have done with Simbaji I will turn my armies west.' He stared at Blunt. 'You are but eight-and-twenty. But they are your people, and I have faith in you. I now give you the rank of amir. Take a suitable escort – and bring me back a satisfactory reply.'

Nasir and several other officers of the Guard came over to congratulate him, and spend a convivial evening.

Peter felt pleasantly anticipatory: he had never visited any of the English factories. Additionally, that he had been promoted and singled out for such a special duty was a mark of great honour. As for the English themselves, he kept an open mind regarding their supposed perfidy. He was curious to discover how he would find them.

He selected a company of horsemen from his own division – together with their tuk-bashi, Billim Abbas, to act as his tavachi. Although the route to Bombay lay well north of the current fighting, there were always robbers to be considered, so he treated the march as a military campaign. But the journey was luckily uneventful, and also speedy. As one of Aurungzib's officers, he knew no other way to travel except as fast as possible.

Like Diu, Bombay was an island situated off the north-west coast of the peninsula. Originally a Portuguese factory, twenty years ago it had been ceded to Charles II of England as part of the wedding portion of his wife. It was considerably larger than Diu and, shaped rather like a pear dangling southwards, parallel to the coast, it enclosed a considerable area of sheltered water in which several ships lay at anchor, all flying the Cross of St George.

On its far side, white sand beaches faced the Arabian Sea. Much of the jungle between had been cleared, and houses and warehouses built, as well as an oddly roofed building which Peter recognised as a church from his mother's descriptions. And the whole place was full of people, many Indians to be sure, but also a large number of white men. As the ferry carried himself, with Serena and Butji and part of his escort, across from the mainland – not being large enough to take all at once – Blunt was increasingly intrigued. Most of the men on the approaching shore were simply and sensibly dressed, having regard for the climate. Their white shirts, heavy breeches and leather boots were different from the Moghul mode, but only in quality. However, there were two men standing on the dockside who made him want to laugh. These wore scarlet knee-length coats made of silk, open to reveal linings of a deeper shade of red; their cuffs and pockets were trimmed with gold thread. A sword-belt hung across each's shoulders, secured there with ribbon loops; their weapons were thin rapiers, such as had been worn by Peter's own father. Within each scarlet coat was worn another garment, in blue, buttoned tightly up the front and extending from neck to thigh. Their shirts were white, with a peculiar frilled accessory at the necks.

Beneath this finery, pale blue silk breeches extended just below the knee, secured there with red garters. Their calves were encased in white stockings which ended in black leather shoes with high red heels and huge ribbon bows.

Most amazing of all, beneath his broad-brimmed black felt hat, each man had a magnificent head of curly black hair which fell to his shoulders. But as the ferry came alongside, Peter saw one of these men take off his hat, and then his entire head of hair, revealing a close-cropped scalp beneath. This he proceeded to mop with a kerchief before replacing everything, somewhat askew, and resuming his observation of the boat.

Serena had watched this strange manoeuvre as well, and gave a giggle. 'It must be useful to take off one's hair at will.'

The Englishmen for their part were equally interested in the pale-skinned man in the magnificent cloth-of-gold tunic, red breeches and matching turban, with brown kid boots and a very serviceable tulwar hanging at his side. Not to mention the veiled woman standing with him.

As the wooden gangplank was carried ashore, one of the men stepped forward. 'Your business?' he demanded in passable Hindustani. He was about forty, Blunt estimated, well built and with a handsome face, although his complexion was reddened by the sun.

'I am a tuman-bashi in the Guard of His Imperial Highness the Badshah of Hindustan,' Peter told him. 'I am here on official business for my master . . . who is also yours,' he added for good measure.

The two men exchanged glances as Peter strode ashore, beckoning his escort to follow him.

'Send the ferry back for the remainder of our company,' he told Billim Abbas, and turned to the waiting men. 'You'll take me to your governor?' he said, switching to English.

By now a small crowd was gathering to hear what was going on.

'Why, sir, surely I will take you to our governor, Captain Keigwin,' one man offered. 'If you will come this way.'

Peter turned to Serena. 'You must wait here until I return,' he told her in Persian.

Looking disappointed, she squatted down beside the dock, the folds of her sari gathered in her lap.

'My name is Knolles,' said the Englishman as they walked together along the dusty, sunbaked street, followed by the crowd of onlookers at a distance. 'Charles Knolles, Major in the 17th Foot, and officer commanding the garrison of Bombay.'

'Peter Blunt,' Peter replied.

Knolles stopped. 'Then you must be the son of Sir Richard Blunt? So that is why you speak such good English.'

'Did you know my father?'

'I have heard much of him over the years. Your father served the Moghul Emperor.'

'As do I,' Peter told him.

'A most remarkable occurrence that you should have been sent to us here . . .'

'Not at all, sir,' Peter told him. 'As I speak the language, the Badshah considered me the obvious choice.'

'Ah,' Knolles said, and stopped to announce the visitor to the guards at the gate of a quite imposing building situated on the edge of the village. These soldiers also wore red tunics and flat black hats, in a much simpler design. They presented arms with much smartness.

Then there were some male secretaries to approach – and at last, the governor himself.

Richard Keigwin was somewhat short and red-faced. He wore a blue tailcoat and white breeches.

'An envoy from the Emperor, eh?' He frowned at Blunt. 'Well, sir, state your master's business.'

He did not invite Blunt to sit down.

'My master's business is the business of all Hindustan,' Peter replied. 'He is angry that some English ships have attacked and dispersed a Moghul fleet bound for Mocha.'

'That is a lie, sir. A damnable lie.'

Blunt bristled, but Knolles came swiftly to the rescue.

'Possibly the Emperor has confused the action with one we fought some years ago against a fleet of Maratha ships, Mr Blunt. The Emperor will be pleased to know that we destroyed them. Captain Keigwin here was in command.'

The Governor beamed, clearly susceptible to flattery. Blunt later learned that, Bombay then lacking a governor and being officially ruled from the factory at Surat, Keigwin had seized control following his victory and had declared himself Governor. He was still waiting and hoping for recognition from London.

'I am sure the Badshah would be pleased to learn of that,' he said. 'But there can be no doubt that a Moghul fleet was indeed attacked and the survivors claim it was by English ships.'

Keigwin sat down heavily, and at last gestured Peter and Knolles to chairs. 'I can assure you they were not attacked by ships of the East India Company, or of His Majesty's Navy.'

Knolles broke in: 'Is it possible these attackers were free-booters from the West Indies?'

'By God!' Keigwin exclaimed.

'How so?' Peter asked.

'Well, the fact is that the English Government has been at war in the West Indies for some years, firstly with the Spaniards during the so-called Commonwealth, and more recently with the Dutch. Governor Keigwin served in the West Indies,' he added, clearly anxious to bring his superior officer into the conversation.

'And damnable hard work it was, too,' Keigwin commented.

Blunt waited. He could not relate events on the far side of the world to an attack on the Moghul's shipping in the Arabian Sea.

'One offshoot of these wars,' Knolles went on, 'was that a considerable number of English vessels – and French and Dutch, I may say – simply took to attacking Spanish ships without proper orders from their home governments – even during periods of truce.'

'Pirates,' Keigwin muttered.

'Their commander was a fellow called Henry Morgan,' Knolles went on. 'And the menace became so great that at last the late King Charles determined to put an end to it . . .'

'Which he did by making this scoundrel Morgan lieutenant-governor of Jamaica, by God!' Keigwin put in. 'There's diplomacy for you.'

'It has actually worked well,' Knolles explained. 'Perhaps too well. Sir Henry Morgan made his own followers obey the law or become outlaws; and those who became outlaws have been hunted down wherever possible. So I fear quite a few of them sought to make a profit elsewhere than in the West Indies.'

'And you think it was some of these pirates who may have attacked the Moghul's fleet?'

'I am certain of it, sir.'

'Well, then, gentlemen, my advice to you would be to man your own ships and put to sea, to capture these rogues,' Blunt said.

'What, sir? What?' Keigwin demanded. 'In these waters, piracy is no concern of ours, so long as they do not attack our East Indiamen.'

'You mistake the situation,' Peter told him. 'I doubt you will find the word "pirate" in Persian, Urdu or Hindustani. It is certainly unknown to the Badshah. He is simply aware that his ships were attacked by others crewed by Englishmen. That makes them England's responsibility, and you, gentlemen, are England's representatives here in Hindustan. That is not something you can afford to forget.'

'Well . . .' Keigwin looked at Knolles. 'That seems damnably unfair to me, sir.'

'Perhaps it is. But should the Moghul point his sword in the direction of Bombay, you would find your position desperate.'

Keigwin went even redder in the face.

'Now we come to the matter of the muskets,' Blunt went on. 'A month ago the Badshah defeated the Marathas, and amongst their dead were found modern muskets of European make. Some of those were of English manufacture.'

'Good God! Are we now accused of arming the rebels?'

Keigwin looked at Knolles; he seemed ready to explode.

'I do assure you that we have not done so, here in Bombay,' Knolles said. 'As I explained, we have recently fought an action against Maratha ships, which must surely be evidence of our good faith.'

'The Badshah demands an undertaking from you that no more English-manufactured weapons will reach the Marathas,' Blunt interrupted.

'Oh, we shall willingly give that,' Knolles said quickly. 'And now, perhaps, some refreshment?'

He seemed anxious to bring the interview to a close, and Blunt sensed that there were other matters to be discussed, which the soldier preferred to do in private.

'I need quarters for myself and my men,' he told Knolles presently, as they sipped a white liquid he had never tasted before. It had a strong although not unpleasant taste, and made him quite light-headed – alcohol being banned in Aurungzib's army.

'I shall attend to that. Your men will be bedded in the barracks. As for yourself, why I would take it as a great honour if you will lodge with my wife and me.'

'That is very good of you, but I have two servants . . .'

'They will be accommodated as well.'

Feeling distinctly odd from the effects of the liquor, Blunt returned to the dock where Serena and Butji and his escort waited patiently, still watched by a curious crowd. Knolles accompanied him, together with an officer of the garrison.

'We are to stay here in Bombay?' Serena asked in Persian.

'For a few days,' Peter reassured her. 'It is a most pleasant place.'

* * *

He was quite pleased with his reception there. Keigwin was clearly a difficult man, but Charles Knolles seemed to have his measure.

He was also impressed by the smartness of the English garrison, which mustered some three hundred men; and he was determined to board at least one of the ships in the harbour to study their construction.

But first there was the business of being welcomed into the Knolles' household. Lucy Knolles had apparently been warned in advance – indeed all Bombay by now knew of the arrival of an envoy from the Moghul – and she waited with her two daughters to greet him as he entered the curious, single-storied wooden building which was their home. The Knolles's son was an officer in the garrison regiment under his father, and the two girls were introduced as Angelina and Caroline.

Peter Blunt was utterly taken aback at the sight of these women. Caroline, the younger sister – and hardly more than fifteen – was quite modestly dressed with a bodice cut square just below her throat, while the skirt of her voluminous gown sustained by several petticoats, spread from her hips to brush the floor. But Angelina and her mother had bodices which were at once tight-fitting and extremely low; their breasts thus both compressed and exposed seemed ready to leap out at him – the nipples only partially concealed.

He cast Knolles a hasty glance to see his host's reaction to such a shameless display on the part of his womenfolk, but Knolles did not seem concerned at all. Having removed his hat, he now again removed his hair as well, and left it off to allow his shaven scalp to cool. He also took off his outer coat with a great sigh of relief.

So Peter allowed himself to look again. The women made a decidedly attractive trio, very alike each other. They were all somewhat short, with splendid neat features dominated by sparkling green eyes. It was their hair, however, which drew his gaze now, even more than their breasts. His mother's yellow hair had made her a notable figure wherever she went in India, lighter than most around him. But never had he seen red hair before, a glorious deep, almost wine colour which perfectly showed up the pale texture of their skin. This beautiful hair was dressed loose in masses of ringlets trailing past their shoulders.

The ladies curtsied, and revealed even more – and all in the most flawless white and pink.

'Mr Blunt will stay with us for a few days,' Knolles explained, as if they did not already know.

Peter turned to Serena and Butji who waited silently, both equally astonished by the wantonness in front of them. 'My servants,' he said.

Lucy Knolles clapped her hands, and a native Indian appeared. 'You will attend to the sahib's people, Duleep,' she instructed.

'Of course, memsahib,' Duleep agreed. 'If they will follow me, please.'

Serena looked at Peter uncertainly.

'I will send for you later,' he told her in Persian.

Reassured, she followed the butler. So did Butji, carrying their gear.

'You'll sit down and take a glass, Mr Blunt,' Knolles said ushering Peter into a rather over-furnished room. There were only a few cane-matting rugs on the floor, but a number of chairs, to one of which Peter was shown. A glass of the same white liquid was thrust into his hand. 'I'm afraid there is no wine available,' Knolles explained. 'The stuff nearly always spoils before we can transport it out here. But this rumbullion is very palatable, would you not say? We make it from the sugar-cane we grow ourselves.'

Blunt sipped and gave a little shudder. But, to Peter's astonishment, Knolles was pouring drinks for his wife and daughters who, even more astonishingly, had followed the men into the room and were sitting down as if intending to stay. He decided that he had a lot to learn about European custom.

Meanwhile the Knolles family was anxious to learn about the Moghul, and about India's vast interior. They plied him with questions throughout the meal that was soon served, and he answered as extensively and politely as he could, leaving them in no doubt of Aurungzib's power and majesty. But at the same time he told them nothing which might in any way hurt the sensitivities of the women, whose continued presence soon ceased to be embarrassing, even if he found it difficult to prevent himself from staring at those beckoning breasts. It was even more difficult to determine which of the bewildering array of knives and forks in front of him to use.

Towards the end of the meal he began to feel decidedly drunk from the amount of rum he had consumed. It was now that Knolles broached the subject up to which he had been leading for some time.

'I really am very sorry that the Moghul should think our people sold muskets to the Marathas,' he said. 'It is the dearest wish of our directors to remain on good terms with His Majesty.'

'That would certainly be wise of you,' Peter agreed.

'Indeed, our directors would like to expand our trade with India . . .' Knolles paused. As Blunt made no reply, he went on. 'We now have two factories here on the west coast, at Bombay and Surat, and we also have Madras on the east coast of the Peninsula. Now we would like to build a factory in Bengal, at the mouth of the Ganges. Do you think your master would give us permission?'

'The Portuguese who built a factory there were arrested and imprisoned,' Peter warned him.

'With respect, that was some years ago. And I understood that the Portuguese did not trouble to seek permission – as we are doing now.'

'Yet I doubt the Badshah would look kindly upon such an idea. Particularly at this moment when he is displeased with you.'

'But, if you were to explain to him the truth, and if you would also tell him how we defeated Sivaji's fleet for him . . .' another pause. 'We would of course be prepared to make it worth your while, Mr Blunt.'

Peter gazed at him. What does this man suppose he has to offer me, he wondered. In any event, he was by now too fuddled to think straight.

'You must give me time to consider your proposal, Mr Knolles,' he said. 'At this moment, if you will excuse me, I wish only to retire.'

'Of course. You must be exhausted. We have been most remiss in keeping you from your bed. We can talk some more tomorrow.'

Blunt stood up a trifle unsteadily. 'I should like to see something of this island tomorrow. I should also like to see over one of your ships.'

'It will be a pleasure.'

'Let me show you to your room, Mr Blunt,' Angelina Knolles offered, taking a candle from the nearest sconce.

Once again Peter was utterly surprised. The idea that a young virgin, one in any event half naked, should escort a male guest to his bedroom was incredible. Yet neither parent seemed the least perturbed.

The girl stepped past him, and he followed her into the corridor, watching the gown swaying over her hips.

'How old are you?' he asked with a slur.

She stopped, and he could see her ears pinken. 'Why, sir,' she said, 'as you are so interested, I am seventeen.'

He felt that in some way he had offended her, but he could not decide how. Then she was opening a door, and actually entering the bedroom to place the candle in the holder by the bed. Meanwhile Peter looked around him, again totally astonished.

The room was unlike any he had ever seen before. In the first place, it was very small and, like the rest of the house, uncarpeted save for a few cane mats. The furniture consisted of a very dark, heavy upright chest with drawers in it, surmounted by a glass mirror; a single chair of the oddest description, because its legs rested on wooden arcs so that it could rock back and forth when one sat in it; and, strangest of all, a high narrow bed with a pillar of wood at each corner, supporting a kind of tent roof.

'I hope you will be comfortable, sir,' Angelina said.

'I am sure I shall,' he said, without conviction. 'Can you send my servants to me?'

'Both of them?'

'Well, of course,' he said.

She gave a little bob of her hips, and left the room. A few minutes later Serena and Butji came in.

'But this is the strangest place, sire,' Serena remarked. 'And there is no bathing chamber.'

'They will show it to us tomorrow, no doubt.' He stood still while they undressed him. 'Now come to bed. I am perfectly exhausted.'

Serena managed to fall out of bed twice during the night.

And when Peter asked for a bath for them both, she gazed in horror at the small tin tub that had been brought in and placed in the centre of the room. Butji was painstakingly filling it with lukewarm water.

'We must do the best we can,' Peter told her, as they took turns at dousing themselves. Then he dressed himself to join the Knolles family.

That morning Knolles showed Peter over the barracks, turned out the regiment for him to inspect, and then inspected Blunt's company in turn. Knolles then had him rowed out to the largest of the ships in the harbour.

If Peter was astonished by what he saw, this time he was also impressed. The sails were unlike anything he had ever envisaged; he could not fathom how sailors could find their way through the maze of halliards and sheets and miscellaneous lengths of rope, all carefully made fast, and all fulfilling a necessary function. The sails were presently furled, of course, but Blunt needed little imagination to envisage them set and the ship bowling along in the wind.

It was the guns, however, which really fascinated him. The Moghul nowadays disposed of several hundred cannon; but they were all of very light calibre, for manoeuvrability. He had never seen anything like the huge 26-pounders or the even larger 32-pounders on the gun deck; and when Knolles claimed that they could hurl an iron ball of that weight for upwards of a mile, he was almost disbelieving.

'Do you possess many of these ships?' he inquired.

'The English fleet has more than a hundred.'

'And are all armed with guns like these?'

'Most of them. Do you suppose your master would be interested in such guns?'

'Most definitely – if they could be got to him.'

'Well, that is something to be discussed. Have you considered the matter we spoke of, last night?'

Blunt actually had not. He had been too drunk and too busy trying to keep Serena in bed beside him. However, he said, 'I am prepared to put your proposal to the Badshah. As to what he will say, I do not know. But guns like these . . .'

'As you say, we shall have to see what can be done.'

'This matter of Bengal is of great interest to you?' Peter observed.

'Why, yes. I will tell you straight, Mr Blunt: England has become an unhappy place since the death of King Charles. Our present King, James, seems determined to turn back the clock to fifty years ago, when a monarch claimed the divine right of Heaven to rule as he chose.'

'How else should a monarch rule?' Peter asked.

'Well, things are obviously different here in Hindustan. However, sir, I do not believe that true-born Englishmen can long accept such an intolerable state of affairs. My father perished in the Great Rebellion, sir. I have no wish again to become embroiled in such civil strife. Thus I have sought my fortune elsewhere. And since I have elected to make Bombay my home, I naturally wish the Company I serve to be successful. Is that unreasonable?'

As they were rowed back to the shore, Knolles continued. 'There is also the matter of your own remuneration.'

'I have not thought about it,' Blunt said truthfully.

Knolles considered this. Later, as they strolled towards the bungalow for dinner, he asked, 'Forgive me, but does your, ah, female servant, travel with you, everywhere?'

'How may a man travel without his concubine?'

'Oh, quite. Unless, of course, he travelled with his wife.'

'I have no wife.'

'It was my impression that men in Hindustan married very young.'

'That is absolutely true. But my mother wishes me to marry an Englishwoman, like herself. And there are no Englishwomen in Delhi, so in fact the first Englishwomen I have ever met – apart from my mother – are your own wife and daughters.'

'I see,' Knolles said thoughtfully.

On returning to the house, Peter heard shrieks of laughter from his bedroom. He was delighted to find Caroline and Serena together making the bed. Caroline Knolles of course spoke no Persian and very little Hindustani, but they seemed to get on very well. At his appearance, Caroline gave an embarrassed little squeal and ran off.

'She is high-spirited,' Serena remarked. 'And she is English.

Maybe she would make you a good wife.'

'But she is not the eldest,' Peter pointed out. 'Nor is she as good-looking as her sister.'

'She will be better when she is older,' Serena argued. 'Her sister is too stiff.'

'I assumed you did not care for this place – or its people?' He rumpled her hair. 'I did not come to Bombay to marry,' he told her.

But suddenly the idea was more attractive.

At lunch they were joined by Knolles's son and his wife, a rather plain young woman who, nevertheless, also displayed a great deal of breast. She had clearly heard all about her parents-in-law's strange guest, and seemed to expect him at any moment to do something remarkable. After a while Blunt excused himself, as he was again feeling decidedly tipsy, and went out into the garden surrounding the house.

He was also feeling thoroughly relaxed, and sank to the ground beneath a huge mango tree with a sigh of contented relief; the afternoon was delightfully warm and drowsy. Perhaps it was a result of the alcohol but, even if they regarded him as some kind of a freak, he liked these people. He even felt he liked them more than any people he had ever met.... their womenfolk especially. Yet however attractive he found Angelina, he could not help wondering if she was anything like as shameless as her dress suggested.

Caroline would make him a good wife, Serena had said. But Angelina would obviously make a better since she possessed real beauty. He wondered what Knolles would say to the idea that his daughter should marry a Moghul warrior? Yet the Englishman seemed reluctant, or even unable, to return to England. Perhaps he was anxious to establish himself and his family here in Hindustan, and the quickest way to do that was to deal with Blunt, and through him with the Badshah. And the English possessed things the Badshah might be pleased to obtain – particularly those cannon.

Thus Blunt had been invited to act as intermediary. But Knolles had nothing to interest him save perhaps his daughter. Of course, Angelina would have to be taught to dress properly, and change her manners. She could not stay where the men were talking, nor drink strong liquor. But Serena could lick her into shape.

And his mother would be pleased, though no doubt she would rather have had the choice of the girl herself. This would be a purely business transaction. That hair, those breasts – and whatever other treasures lay beneath her gown – in exchange for Blunt's good word with the Badshah. It was certainly something to be considered.

The sooner he returned to Hyderabad with his report, the better ... yet he was strangely reluctant to leave this pleasant place, with the whisper of the sea and the soughing of the wind in the trees. It made Delhi and Hyderabad seem like another, harsher world.

Hearing the rustle of skirts, he sat up suddenly to regard Caroline standing just a few feet away.

'Are you feeling all right, Mr Blunt?' she asked.

He stood up – having observed this was a custom followed by Englishmen whenever their women joined them. 'Perfectly.'

'Then I have interrupted a reverie. I apologise.' She turned as if to re-enter the house.

'By no means,' he said. 'Why do you not sit with me?'

It was not a suggestion he would ever have made to any Muslim girl ... but then he would never have found himself alone in a garden with a Muslim girl either.

As Caroline sank to the grass, they gazed at each other.

'Mama and Papa think you have come in search of a wife,' she said leaving her mouth in an O as if astounded that she should have mentioned this so boldly.

'What a delightful idea,' he agreed. 'Where should I find one, do you think?'

She licked her lips, the pink spots flared in her pale cheeks. 'Angelina says you may wish to marry her.'

'Indeed?'

'But *she* says she could never marry a man who keeps a mistress, much less travels around with her.'

'And would you marry such a man, Miss Caroline?'

Another quick flick at the lips. 'If the man pleased me, perhaps.'

'Well, then, I would say you are wiser than your sister.'

My God, Peter thought. This little girl is *willing* me to ask for her hand! And why not, when she was so agreeable?

'Caro, whatever are you doing?'

Caroline sprang to her feet as Angelina appeared round the mango tree.

'Why, Mr Blunt, I had no idea you were here,' she lied. 'Has my little sister been annoying you?'

'On the contrary, she has been entertaining me greatly.'

'Well, I am sure you have been bored long enough.' Angelina clapped her hands. 'Off you go, Caro.'

The younger sister hesitated, then gave a brief curtsey in Peter's direction and hurried off, colour again flaring in her cheeks.

'I hope she has said nothing indiscreet,' Angelina remarked coyly. 'My sister is a scatterbrained girl, who delights in suggesting the most ridiculous things.'

Indeed she was an *intensely* attractive young woman – especially when clearly agitated, as now. But the decolletage was what truly attracted him; it smacked so much of the brothel. In Hindustan a lady was totally covered at all times, however sheer the silk of her sari. Only courtesans, who relied upon snaring men, would sometimes half reveal themselves – indicating that the rest was available at an agreed price.

But this girl was clearly no prostitute; thus she intrigued him. The whole relationship between Western women and men now intrigued him.

So Angelina actually expected him to ask for her hand – for the pleasure of refusing him? But her father wanted it, he was certain. He wondered if the daughter knew that?

Suddenly his mind was made up: he *would* invite Knolles to trade this girl for his services. But first, she could be investigated . . . as he was in the mood to enjoy this delightful freedom practised by English females.

'Will you not sit with me?' he invited.

'Why, sir, that would be nice.' She sat down on the grass with another great rustle of skirts – though carefully out of reach. 'Are you enjoying your visit to Bombay?'

'Very much – there is much here that is strange to me.'

She turned her head to look at him. 'But you are English, Papa tells me.'

'I have never been there – and your family are the first English I have ever met.'

'Ah!' she remarked, somewhat enigmatically. 'No doubt I would feel the same in Delhi.'

'Were you to visit Delhi, Miss Knolles, you would already have a friend to assist you in understanding the ways of its people.'

'Would I really, Mr Blunt?' As with her sister, little pink spots appeared in her cheeks. 'Then one day perhaps I shall. But cannot you pretend that you have in me an old friend to assist you in understanding our habits here?'

'May I?'

'I should like you to.'

'Some of my questions might be embarrassing.'

'I shall give you my word not to be embarrassed.' She now gazed straight in front of her.

'Well ...' He determined to reconnoitre the ground before attacking. 'This rumbullion you drink ... it seems very strong. Alcohol is forbidden in Hindustan by order of the Badshah.'

'Oh! If I visited Delhi, I would have nothing to drink?'

'Water and sherbets. Do all your people drink rumbullion?'

'In England? Oh, no. We only drink it here because wine will not stand the voyage. In England we drink wine.' She smiled. 'Have you no desire to visit England?'

'One day, certainly. Now may I ask you, at what age do women marry in England?'

'Why ...' Her ears pinkened to match her cheeks. 'At any age from sixteen, perhaps.'

'But you have not done so.'

Her colour deepened further. 'Papa and Mama have not yet found me a suitable husband, sir.' She turned her head. 'Will all your questions be so direct?'

'You told me you would not be embarrassed.'

'I am not embarrassed,' she bridled.

'How often do you bathe?'

Her head swivelled once more. 'Sir?'

'In Hindustan women must bathe every day before attending their lords. Men also, when possible – but women, most certainly.'

Her bosom rose and fell most enticingly. 'Why, sir, Englishwomen bathe as necessary. Nor do they have masters.'

Peter smiled at her. 'You, at the least, do not as yet. But tell me, Miss Knolles, what is the procedure for obtaining a woman in England.'

She had turned away from him again, but now threw him a look. 'Sir?'

'I meant for the purposes of concubinage or marriage? Is it customary to make the father a gift, or is it a matter for other negotiation?'

'Sir, there is no such thing as concubinage in England . . .' she hesitated. 'As for marriage, it is a matter for negotiation between the parents.'

'Unfortunately my mother is a very long way away.'

Angelina frowned at him. 'I do not understand you, sir.'

'I am considering approaching your father with a view to obtaining you for my harem,' he explained.

Her face froze, and she scrambled to her feet. 'You are insulting me, sir.'

'In asking for you? But surely I am paying you a compliment?'

She turned to glare at him, her hands clasped in front of her skirt. 'Do you suppose you can just come here and look at me, and then decide to take me to . . . to . . .'

'To Delhi,' he reminded her. 'It is a beautiful city. But I asked you how an Englishman would go about it, and you gave me no reply save that it would be for negotiation. I am fully prepared to negotiate with your father.'

She stamped her foot. 'You do not understand, Mr Blunt. Negotiation, well . . . it would be between old friends who know each others' worth. And their children would have known each other for several years, perhaps since childhood. Their two families would have mutual interests, perhaps in land, or commerce. Every condition would be entirely different!'

'Why do you not sit down, Miss Knolles?' Peter said equably. 'Or may I call you Angelina?'

'You may not call me so,' she snapped. 'That is reserved for close friends and my family.' Nevertheless she sat down again.

'And are you determined that we shall be enemies? As you say, things are different here in Hindustan, and yet not so very different. You are in a strange land, and have not been here long. Therefore there is little chance of your being given to a family of long acquaintance – while your father and I most certainly have common interests.'

She looked at the ground. 'You even spoke of concubinage.'

'I will marry you.'

She raised her head. 'Just like that? With not a word of love or even affection?'

'How can there be love or even affection before marriage?' he asked reasonably. 'These things grow out of marriage, if they are to grow at all. My mother was given to my father as a chattel. She certainly could not have loved him then.'

Angelina shuddered.

'But a true love grew between them,' Peter continued.

She glanced at him. 'And at this moment you merely lust after me,' she said at last in a low voice.

'You have much worth lusting after.' He smiled.

'And having ... purchased me, you would share me with your servant.'

'I have said, I would marry you. Serena is my concubine, and you would take precedence over her. You would even take precedence over Jintna, who is the mother of my son.'

She gasped. 'You have more than one concubine? And a son?'

'Does any man have only one concubine?' he asked. 'And, yes, I have a son. But you will give me more.'

Angelina looked away. 'Why are you telling me these things if you have already made up your mind to speak with my father?'

'Because you are here,' he said, 'and I wish to go about it the English way.'

She almost managed a smile. 'I doubt that would ever be possible, sir.' She stood up. 'Papa will never agree.' Quickly she went inside.

But now Peter truly wanted her. He had never spent such an unusual and stimulating half-hour. But then he had never spent half an hour alone with two strange women, who were neither related to him nor belonged to him. He was not to know if she would confide the experience to her parents.

Later that afternoon, Knolles suggested they make an inspection of the factory. But Blunt suggested they have a talk instead.

Knolles seemed rather to have expected this. Without hesitation he took Peter to the fort, and ushered him into his little office overlooking the parade ground surrounded by low mud-brick walls.

'I have considered your proposal,' Blunt said, 'and I am prepared to recommend it to the Badshah.'

'That is most kind,' Knolles said watchfully.

'There remains the question of what you will offer in exchange.'

'The Emperor will have his cannon,' Knolles assured him.

'And myself?'

'Well . . . what did you have in mind?'

'Your daughter Angelina,' Blunt said quickly.

Knolles licked his lips.

'As my wife,' Peter added.

'Your wife?' Knolles muttered.

'I am a tuman-bashi in the Imperial Guard,' Peter told him, 'and one day I will command the Guard itself. I am well-favoured by the Badshah, and will undoubtedly rise in his services. My mother is very wealthy, and lives in a palace in Delhi. Your daughter will therefore know nothing but luxury.'

'In your harem,' Knolles pointed out.

'She will live with my mother, and my stepmothers, and my concubines,' Peter said. 'It is the custom of the land. However, her life will not be as restricted as you fear. Just as my mother possesses a great deal of freedom, my wife would also.'

Knolles rose and took a turn around the room. 'Are you a Christian, sir?'

'I have never been baptised, because there are neither churches nor priests in Hindustan,' Peter explained. 'My mother is a true Christian, and has taught me much of her religion. I will endeavour to use your daughter as a Christian should, Major Knolles. I have already spoken with your daughter.'

'The devil you have,' Knolles muttered.

'I trust that was not offensive?'

Knolles waved his hand, as though to indicate it was of little matter. 'And what was her reaction?'

'Surprise, I would say.'

'Quite. I will have to discuss your proposal with my wife.'

'If that is your custom,' Peter said.

'It is indeed, sir, especially in these unusual circumstances. May I ask how old you are, Mr Blunt?'

'I am twenty-eight years old.'

'Young for marriage, perhaps?'

'Old for marriage in Hindustan and I assure you that my mother's consent will not be withheld.' Peter looked him in the eye. 'Major Knolles, I am a soldier, and I believe in straight speaking. If I leave here, and obtain my master's permission for you to establish a factory at the mouth of the Ganges, will you then grant her to me? Yes or no.'

Knolles blinked. 'In all the circumstances, Mr Blunt, though unusual circumstances ... I would have to say that if Angelina is willing. ...'

Peter smiled tightly. 'Well, then, let us go and find out.'

Only the son and his wife were absent from the family group. Angelina sat between her mother and father on the drawing-room settee, with Caroline hovering anxiously at her mother's shoulder, more flustered, it seemed, than any of them.

Knolles had outlined the proposal. 'I hasten to add that Mr Blunt has conducted himself with admirable honesty throughout. He has agreed to accept the decision of Angelina herself.'

'And his domestic arrangements?' asked Lucy Knolles.

Peter raised his eyebrows at her.

'I am speaking, sir, of that woman who appears to travel with you, wherever you go.'

'I am sure your daughter will find Serena a most pleasant companion, Mrs Knolles.'

'Oh!' Lucy Knolles seemed about to throw her hands up in exasperation.

'As will Jintna, no doubt,' Angelina intervened quietly.

'Jintna?' demanded her mother in surprise.

'Mr Blunt's other concubine: the mother of his son.'

For a moment Lucy Knolles appeared truly speechless. Then she said softly, 'I am afraid, Mr Blunt, that in view of the vast difference in customs and manners between us, such a marriage would appear to be out of the question.'

Knolles threw his wife a look of utter dismay – but it was Angelina who came to the rescue.

'Papa has said the decision would be left to me, Mama.' She drew a long breath. 'And I am prepared to accept Mr Blunt's proposal.'

Caroline clapped her hands with delight, however much Peter might suspect she had wished herself to be chosen.

'Angelina, my dear,' Lucy protested. 'Have you really considered . . .'

'Yes, Mama. I have considered most deeply.' She gazed intently at Peter. 'But I would make one request of Mr Blunt. There may be neither church nor priest in Delhi, but there are both here. Will he consent to being baptised now into the Christian Church?'

Everyone stared at him.

'Why, most willingly,' he agreed – knowing it would delight his mother, too.

'Well, then . . .' Knolles was on his feet, wringing Peter's hand. 'I am most heartily pleased, Mr Blunt. Why, the very moment I have the agreement of the Emperor, the banns can be announced.'

'And in the meanwhile?' Peter asked, puzzled.

'Why, you and Angelina are betrothed, to be sure.'

After hesitation Lucy Knolles slowly came forward and, to his amazement, presented her cheek. It took him a few seconds to realise she actually meant him to kiss it. When he did so, she said, 'I welcome you into my family, Mr Blunt,' in a tone with which she might have welcomed a visit of the plague.

Even more alarming was the behaviour of young Caroline, who threw both arms round his neck to kiss him hard upon each cheek. 'I am so happy for you both.' She turned to do the same to her sister.

'Now,' Knolles said, 'when do you propose to begin your return journey?'

'Why, I think the sooner the better, Major Knolles. I shall leave tomorrow morning.'

'Well . . . in that case, you will wish to say your farewells to your betrothed. Come along, Lucy. Come along, Caroline.'

He ushered the two other women from the room and closed

the door, leaving Peter to gaze at Angelina in total confusion.

'Is it customary to leave a young woman alone with a man in England?'

'We are betrothed, Mr Blunt. Is it not also the custom in Hindustan?'

'Indeed it is not. But you will have to explain it all to me. I do sincerely wish to learn your customs, as far as I may .'

Angelina gazed at him for several seconds, her cheeks pink. Then she seemed to come to a resolution, and patted the cushion beside her. 'Will you sit here?'

Peter sat next to her.

'It is customary,' she said, 'when two people have become engaged to be married, for them to kiss each other.'

'But we are not yet married.'

'We are *going* to be married,' she pointed out. 'God willing.'

They stared at each other, and nervously he licked his lips. He was terribly aware of her *décolletage*, her mouth, her eyes and her hair, which combined to make her quite the most desirable creature he had ever known. And she was inviting him . . . he threw his arms round her, pulled her against him, and kissed her mouth. Her lips parted as she gasped at the fury of his assault – and he found her tongue. She put up her hands to push him away, and he slid one of his own round in front to hold her breast. She panted and fought for several seconds, before relaxing limp in his arms.

Instantly he released her, and she fell back on the cushions, entirely disarranged. Her hair was scattered; her breath coming in huge pants.

'I have hurt you?' he inquired anxiously.

Slowly Angelina sat up, straightening her gown.

'Is all your lovemaking that violent, Mr Blunt?'

'I am a passionate man – and you are a beautiful woman. Would you have it otherwise?'

Angelina swallowed. 'No, Mr Blunt,' she said, 'I would not have it otherwise. Shall we not join my parents? I think they will be in the garden.'

'I will become a slave,' Serena said dolefully, as they were ferried across to the mainland for their return journey.

'I do assure you that your new mistress will treat you as a friend,' Peter told her.

'You should marry the young one,' Serena pouted. 'She is my friend.'

'But I am to marry the older one,' he said firmly. He felt like breaking into song. For in a very short space of time he was going to possess all of that magnificent translucent flesh, that sunset-coloured hair.... He had never before thought of women in terms of love, yet he wanted to love Angelina and make her happy, to see her eyes glow with pride as he went about his duties and rose in the Badshah's favour. He wrote to his mother while still on the road, and despatched the letter by Butji.

Meanwhile he hastened on to Hyderabad, where little had changed in the month he had been away. Aurungzib received him promptly, and listened with care to what his envoy had to say. Blunt had obtained from Knolles one of the balls fired by the thirty-two pounders, and this he now presented to the Emperor. Aurungzib had some difficulty in lifting it.

'They really have cannon which can throw this ball for more than a mile?' he asked incredulously.

'That is so, Badshah.'

'Then why do your countrymen not rule the world, Blunt Bahatur?'

'Perhaps one day they will.'

Aurungzib gave him a hard look, then smiled. 'Not if they will give *me* guns like these. And in exchange they wish a trading post in Bengal? Why not so? But I must have these cannon first.'

'Blunt Bahatur tells us these monstrous cannon are mounted in ships,' Rai Singh pointed out. 'We will have great difficulty in transporting them on land. We will need great carriages, and many mules.'

'Those are details I leave to you to work out,' Aurungzib declared. 'The guns we will have. Return to Bombay, Blunt Bahatur, and tell them that.'

Only a week later Butji arrived carrying a letter from Blunt's mother.

My dear Peter,

I am overwhelmed with joy at your news, and thus I write briefly and in haste. My contentment would be complete had I had the opportunity to meet the young lady of whom you speak in such glowing terms. But that she pleases you, and you her, is sufficient. Bilkis and Hilma and I look forward most earnestly to welcoming your bride in Delhi, and our permission for your marriage is most heartily given.

Your loving mother,
Anne Blunt

Peter departed the next day. Again he took his company of Guards, and also Butji, but left Serena behind in Hyderabad. She wept bitterly, but he had realised that her presence was a constant source of concern to the Knolles family, and he had no desire to upset his in-laws in any way, and still less his bride.

Then it was haste, haste to return to Bombay. They made the journey in eight days, and his heart was pounding as if to burst its way from his tunic while the ferry made its slow way across to the far landing. An officer of the garrison waited to greet Peter as he stepped ashore.

'Roger Munro at your service, sir. I am Major Knolles's adjutant. We met the last time you visited Bombay.'

'Indeed we did.' Peter shook hands. 'There is nothing wrong, I hope.'

'Well, sir ...' Munro looked distressed. 'I have been asked to escort you immediately to the Major's residence.'

Peter left Billim Abbas to organise the men, and hurried along beside the captain. Clearly something *was* wrong.

Knolles was there to greet him as he entered the house, and the younger daughter Caroline, who burst into tears at the sight of him.

'She wishes to see you,' Knolles said, as Peter was led along the corridor and into Angelina's bedchamber. There her mother sat with a strange man, who turned out to be a surgeon.

But his dear Angelina! She lay beneath the covers, her magnificent hair spread out on the pillows – and she looked utterly beautiful. But utterly desperate. Her cheeks and throat flamed scarlet; the rest of her face was pale as death. Though she lay still, too weak to move, every few moments the bed would tremble as an enormous shudder racked her body.

'Peter!' Angelina whispered as she opened her eyes. Lucy Knolles stepped aside, and he sat down on the bed. He took up Angelina's hand; it felt as if on fire. 'Peter!' she repeated. 'Are we to be wed?'

'Yes, indeed,' he said. 'As soon as you leave this bed.'

She smiled. 'I will soon be well.'

Blunt presently went outside to discuss with Knolles and the doctor. 'I have seen fever like this many times in Agra and Delhi,' he said. 'It is essential that her temperature be brought down. Angelina must be placed in a bath of cool water and kept there until she herself is cool.'

Dr Pinckney pinched his lip. 'I have never heard of such treatment, sir. You will give the poor girl penumonia.'

'Her fever will come down in twenty-four hours,' Blunt assured him. 'Then she can be put back to bed and well wrapped up. But it is the fever we must deal with first.'

'I do not like this,' Pinckney grumbled.

'Nonetheless, if it is a tested remedy ...' Knolles said anxiously.

'It is, sir,' Blunt confirmed.

'Then we must find a large bath. I shall see to it immediately.'

But even before he left the house, they were summoned back to the bedchamber by Lucy Knolles's cries. They crowded in and gazed down at Angelina, whose entire face was suffused as she gasped for breath, giving a long sigh as each gasp faded away.

'It is the crisis,' Pinckney said.

Blunt found that Caroline was gripping his hand so tightly it almost hurt him.

Then Angelina uttered another sigh – and was quiet. They stared at her in dismay for several seconds, then Lucy Knolles uttered one great sob and fell forward on to her daughter's silent breast.

23
THE OUTRAGE

Peter gazed at the still lovely features, stiff in death. Angelina had been hastily washed and her eyes closed, and was dressed in one of her best gowns. In the Bombay heat it was necessary to bury the dead quickly, and now it was dusk; she had been dead for eight hours.

The coffin was closed. He walked with her family and, it seemed, nearly all the white residents of Bombay, firstly to the church and then on to the cemetery. He understood little of the religious service itself, but he did know that he was in the presence of great grief.

His own feelings were strange to him. He had lived so much of his life in the midst of war and sudden death, but somehow that had all lacked the element of tragedy which now accompanied this beautiful, innocent girl to the grave. He had only known her fleetingly, yet had looked forward to knowing her so much better. Now he found himself gazing sadly across the grave at Caroline – who flushed and stared at the ground.

Was the very thought of that obscene? Or was it the most natural course? He had come to Bombay to find an English wife. Would he return to Hyderabad empty handed? He had no doubt of what Caroline would wish.

When they returned to the house, Lucy Knolles and her daughter promptly disappeared; they had been weeping openly. Knolles poured two tumblers of rumbullon, and handed one to Peter.

'We have not had the time to discuss your business,' he remarked with a sigh.

'It is all as you wish,' Peter said. 'Upon delivery of a battery of those large cannon, the Badshah will grant you permission to build a factory in the delta of the Ganges – or immediately above it, if you prefer.'

'I am deeply gratified and I wish I could express it more coherently at this moment.'

'I also have my mother's approval for my marriage to your daughter.'

Knolles sighed. 'Man proposes, Mr Blunt, and God disposes.'

When Peter said nothing, Knolles raised his head. 'This unhappy event will not mar our relationship, surely?'

Peter turned to stare at Caroline, who had just entered the room. She had washed her face, and now even attempted a smile. 'May I take a glass to Mama? I think it might do her good.'

'Please do,' Knolles murmured. He glanced at her, and then noticed that Peter continued to stare at the girl as she left the room, her cheeks pink. 'My God,' he said aghast. 'Is there no humanity in your character?'

Peter frowned at him. 'If you mean, do I not mourn my betrothed, I do. Less than you do, of course, as I had known her but a short time. But what is done is done. It is to the future that we must look.'

'And for you the future means nothing less than obtaining *one* of my daughters to wife. But Caroline is all that is left to us, and she is only fifteen. In England we regard that too early an age to consummate a marriage.'

'When will she be sixteen?'

'Well . . . in a month's time.'

'Then I will give you my word not to consummate our marriage for that month.'

'Sir, you leave me speechless.'

'I will be good to the girl – as good as I would have been to her sister.'

'That is scarcely the point,' Knolles cried in frustration. 'You cannot just move from one of my daughters to the next. And, at a time when we are overcome with grief, it is unmanly of you, sir. Unmanly.'

'We are not living in England now, Major Knolles,' Peter said coolly. 'There is also one point you may have overlooked. The Badshah himself is expecting me to return to Hyderabad with a bride. Indeed, he has commanded it.'

Knolles's head came up sharply. 'And is it not done in Hindustan to speak of love, and faithfulness, and honour.'

'Why, sir, perhaps we speak of them less than you do, but we believe in them just the same. To remain faithful to a corpse is an absurdity. I will learn to love Caroline as I would have loved Angelina. I will treat her with honour. As to raising this matter in the midst of your grief, I regret the necessity, but my master is campaigning. I shall not be able to return here in the foreseeable future, so whatever must be done, must be done now.'

'And you think the Emperor may renege on his agreement if you do not return with an English bride?'

'I do not believe he would for sure,' Blunt replied truthfully, 'so long as he receives his cannon. But he is a man of uncertain temper, and he would look less happily upon our agreement. He has decreed I must marry.'

Knolles seemed at a loss for words.

Peter watched the door open as Caroline returned. 'However, as with her sister, I will abide by Miss Caroline's decision. Have I your permission to address her? Here, in front of you?'

Caroline looked from face to face, and a slow flush spread up her throat and into her cheeks. She clearly could guess the subject of the conversation.

'You had best sit down, Caroline,' her father suggested.

Caroline sank down opposite Peter, sitting very straight, her knees pressed together, her gown carefully arranged to either side.

For a moment Peter found words difficult as he gazed at her, even more innocent than Angelina had been. 'I have suggested to your father that you should replace Angelina as my wife,' he said softly.

Caroline drew a long, slow breath, and looked to her father.

'I am appalled at this suggestion,' Knolles told her. 'And at such a time. But this scoundrel has intimated that there may be repercussions for us should he not obtain an English bride upon his visit here. I have given him permission to speak with you, but I wish you to know that should you reject him, I will stand by your decision, no matter what may follow.'

Caroline looked back at Peter Blunt.

'I wish you also to know, Caroline,' he said, 'that I extend to you all the promise of wealth, honour and distinction, of kindness and love, which I had promised to your sister. I have also sworn to respect your maidenhead until you reach your sixteenth birthday.'

Caroline licked her lips, and turned to her father again.

'I am sure that not even Mr Blunt will demand an answer just at this moment,' Knolles told her miserably.

'But I am prepared to give one, Papa.' Her voice was composed. 'Is what he proposes legal: to marry a betrothed sister?'

'It does have the sanction of precedent,' Knolles said. 'But I fear that in any event English law counts for nothing in this heathen land.'

Caroline turned back to Peter. 'You do me great honour, sir,' she said. 'And I will be most gratified to become your wife.'

Lucy Knolles was horrified, and was reduced almost to hysterics at the news. Knolles himself was also clearly very unhappy. But Caroline gazed at Peter with almost a smile.

That evening Blunt took his men and himself back to the mainland to pitch camp; he knew he was scarcely a popular person in Bombay.

The next morning, however, he went back across the harbour, ignoring the hostile stares he received from all the Englishmen he passed. Caroline herself answered the door.

'Mr Blunt! Do please come in.'

Peter stepped through the doorway, and closed it behind him. He took her into his arms and kissed her mouth, sweeping her up from the floor. She gave a little gasp, then responded enthusiastically, placing her lips on his and throwing her arms round his neck to support herself. Running out of breath, she pulled her head back. 'Oh, Mr Blunt,' she said. 'I do adore you so.'

There was a strangled sound from the end of the corridor, where Lucy Knolles had just appeared.

After that Blunt called to visit every day. For the first week Lucy insisted on remaining with them, but soon she gave up and allowed them to sit together in the garden, where they could be overseen from the house. Peter found Caroline more and more of a delight. If she did not quite possess her sister's beauty, and if her figure was that two years more youthful, there was enough beneath the high-necked gown to give every promise for the future. Best of all, she confessed unhesitatingly, she had fallen in love with him at first sight.

This troubled her somewhat.

'Am I a very wicked girl?' she asked.

'You are adorable.'

'But poor Angelina . . . do you think she is looking down and uttering curses upon us?'

'I think she is giving us her blessing,' Peter assured her.

Governor Keigwin was equally scandalised at what had happened, and decided to issue a special licence and thus dispense altogether with the business of banns and the three weeks which should elapse.

'If this is to be done,' he told Knolles, 'then let us have it done quickly. The presence of those Moghul fellows make me uneasy. The whole community is disturbed.'

'This whole affair is a catastrophe,' Knolles moaned. 'My God, when I think of it . . .'

'Did you not encourage the fellow in the first place?'

'Well . . . it was a promising situation.'

'And you say the girl has agreed.'

'Oh . . . the little minx is in seventh heaven. She does not have the wit to know what she is going to.'

'There is the licence,' Keigwin said. 'Let's have it done.'

The marriage took place the very next day. The bride wore white. Everybody else wore black, except Blunt, who was in uniform. Lucy Knolles wept throughout the service, and there were also tears in Caroline's eyes – but these, Peter knew, were tears of happiness.

'We shall leave for the mainland immediately,' he told his new father-in-law when the wedding luncheon had ended.

Knolles gazed into his eyes. 'Are you a devil, or a good man, Peter Blunt?'

'I am a man, Major Knolles. I can offer you nothing more than that.'

Knolles looked over to where Caroline stood surrounded by weeping women. 'They think she has been sacrificed to my ambition and to your lust,' he muttered. 'Treat her kindly, I beg of you.'

'I will treat her as kindly as I treat myself.'

Knolles continued to stare at him, then nodded. 'I believe

you. But will I ever see her again?'

'When the Maratha business is finished, I would certainly hope you will visit us in Delhi. I will send for you myself.'

'And we shall come, by God!' Knolles held out his hand. 'I wish you happiness.'

'With your daughter at my side, I think I will find that.'

Lucy Knolles could hardly bring herself to say goodbye to him, but at last it was done, and Blunt set Caroline upon his horse, as was the Moghul custom, and escorted her to the ferry. Whatever the feelings of their English masters, the Indian population gathered to cheer him. His own men were waiting on the farther shore to welcome him.

'We move out immediately,' he told Billim Abbas, and turned to a still very excited Caroline. 'Can you ride astride?'

'Will it not do me an injury?' she gulped.

He had blankets strapped over the saddle to soften the perch, then lifted her up as she swung her leg over, her skirts riding above her knees.

'I am sorry for the discomfort,' he told her. 'Had there been more time I would have brought an elephant for you.'

'I *am* adventuring,' Caroline said with a smile.

Blunt was making haste to regain Aurungzib, as he had been ordered. He kept his people moving until dusk, before pitching camp. Caroline was now clearly very sore, but still she smiled.

Butji already had the evening curry sizzling when Caroline appeared. 'Are you all right?' Peter asked.

'I have never felt better – and I am so hungry. Our first dinner as man and wife, here in the jungle.' She looked up at the trees, listening to the cries of birds and monkeys as the sun set. 'Is it not romantic?'

'It is uncomfortable, to be sure.'

'It is romantic,' she insisted. 'Here, Papa gave me this before I left.'

Peter frowned at the bottle of rumbullion. 'Alcohol is forbidden in the Badshah's army.'

'Can we not pretend we are still in Bombay? This is the first night of our wedded life.'

He summoned Butji, who produced two cups.

Caroline raised hers, and brushed it against his. 'To us.'

'To us,' he repeated.

As they ate, she seemed impatient. 'I have something to show you,' she told him finally. 'A wedding present.'

'You have already given me the richest present in all the world – yourself.'

'This is a part of myself,' she promised him. She held his hand, and led him into the tent. Butji smiled indulgently.

Once inside the tent, the girl showed signs of embarrassment.

'There is nothing to fear,' Peter told her. 'I have promised your father that I will not touch you.'

'That is absurd,' she said. 'Do you not desire me?'

'I desire you more than any other in the world,' he assured her. 'But I have promised.'

'You cannot mean to leave me now,' she cried. 'How can you look upon me and not immediately wish to take me?' She burst into tears, and rolled over on her face.

He gave her bottom a gentle tap, and she raised her head.

'I have given your father my word, and that is an end to the matter. 'Yet, you are right. I cannot look upon you and not desire you.'

She turned back towards him, mollified.

'Do you know anything of assuaging a man's desire?' he asked.

'You will have to instruct me, my lord,' she said.

Was ever a man more fortunate? When Peter thought of the haphazard liaisons of his ancestors ... his own mother tossed over to his father by an angry Badshah ... and here he was married to a girl who revelled in his presence, who sought only to please him like the most perfect concubine. Though Caroline needed to be taught everything about sexual matters, about satisfying a man, yet she was so eager, so delighted to learn, that he found himself every day looking forward to their time alone in their tent.

His men smiled indulgently. Their tuman-bashi was honeymooning. Peter wondered what they would say did they know that his bride remained a virgin – that their lovemaking was entirely a matter of hands and lips.

Oddly, as the days slipped by and they approached Hyderabad, Caroline began to worry about it. 'Suppose we encountered an enemy, and you were killed?' she asked. 'What would become of me – a virgin bride?'

'You would be returned to your father and mother to make a new life for yourself,' he assured her. 'With another man.'

'Never,' she said. 'I would take the veil and live out my life in solitary contemplation.' She gave another wicked little smile. 'I would live on my memories, such as they are.'

When they reached Hyderabad ten days after leaving Bombay, Blunt took his bride before the Badshah.

Caroline possessed only European clothes, so he made her put on her severest gown, although even this exposed her throat. He also had Serena equip her with a yashmak and a haik to cover her head.

Aurungzib seemed intrigued; enough of Caroline's auburn tresses escaped the haik to attract stares from all the men present, and the Badshah clearly liked the way the girl carried herself.

'You have chosen well, Blunt Bahatur,' he said. 'Your bed will prosper.'

That she, for her part, was totally astounded by the wealth of the Moghul court was obvious. But she also seemed equally happy in her new house in Hyderabad, and making the proper acquaintance of Serena. The latter went out of her way to instruct Caroline in the ways of a Muslim housewife. There seemed absolutely no friction between them.

They both explored the beautiful city of Hyderabad and exclaimed over the Charminar ... and awaited Caroline's sixteenth birthday.

But Blunt's honeymoon period was now long over – and by the time the promised birthday arrived, he was far away, campaigning with the Badshah. For the Moghul was determined to launch another drive to destroy Simbaji's forces before the monsoon of 1689. This was again largely unsuccessful: several victories were gained, but still the Marathas kept the field, and still Simbaji eluded capture. Aurungzib's temper deteriorated steadily, and he began to query the non-arrival of the English guns. Not that guns would have made the slightest difference in the jungle warfare presently being waged. But Peter had to use all his arts of diplomacy to convince the Moghul that such things took time.

The true reason was that Charles Knolles's prophecy had been borne out; the English had revolted against James II and expelled him, raising his son-in-law, William of Orange, to the throne in his place.

These events Aurungzib could understand when news of them finally reached India, but he found much to complain about in the character of the man sent out by the East India Company to found their factory at the mouth of the Ganges. Job Charnock was, judging by reports received from the Governor of Bengal, a most arrogant man who antagonized all with whom he came into contact. Peter was even obliged to write critical letters to Bombay.

The rains were imminent when the army at last returned to Hyderabad, frustrated and angry. But now Peter's bride was ready for him. When he entered his house, both Serena and Caroline bowed low before him. Serena had equipped her in a new cloth-of-gold sari; with her auburn hair and bright colouring, it made her appear like a rising sun in the centre of his entrance hall.

'Am I pleasing to you, my lord?' she asked in Persian – for she had been learning that language too.

'You are pleasing to me,' he said, and swept her from the floor, carrying her straightaway to their bedchamber.

Serena came too, and was put out when he sent her away.

'Tomorrow you may join us – even share us,' he promised. 'But this night I will be alone with my bride.'

Serena pouted.

'Now you have offended her,' Caroline said.

'Would you have had her stay?'

Caroline wrinkled her nose. 'I would rather be alone with you, sire.'

Gently he removed the sari, gazing in awe at the translucent skin. 'You know that I must now hurt you.'

'I know only that you are going to make me the happiest woman in the world,' she told him.

* * *

It was indeed a happy time for them. After so long a separation, Anne came down from Delhi for the close season, accompanied by Jintna and William. So he had an almost complete household.

'I must be the first Blunt ever to be truly happy,' Peter told his mother.

'Then set another precedent, I beg of you,' she said. 'Become the first Blunt to die in his bed.'

As soon as the rains stopped, Aurungzib was again campaigning. But Simbaji kept the field for another year before he was at last captured, and his people brought to terms. Though Simbaji attempted to negotiate a surrender, as his father had done over ten years earlier, Aurungzib would have none of it. The Maratha leader was dragged naked before his conqueror, his arms bound behind his back.

'There can be only one fate for one such as you,' growled the grim faced old warlord.

Simbaji made no protest as he was hustled away. Aurungzib commanded that he should die before the assembled army, and their women. Peter remembered Elena's tale of how the élite of Jahangir's court had gathered to watch the execution of his grandfather. Now he stood with the other bahaturs and amirs, behind the Moghul's throne, as Simbaji and his officers were led out. To one side stood the women, Anne's face twisting as she recalled the execution of her first husband, Caroline totally subdued by this sudden intrusion of the horrific where she had hitherto known only happiness.

It was the usual custom to grease the stake, so that entry and death came quickly. Aurungzib commanded that Simbaji's stake be left dry and chipped, so that the Maratha died slowly and screaming his agony.

'He is a monster,' Anne said, when they regained the privacy of Peter's house.

'He is our master,' Peter told her.

That night for the first time Caroline was unresponsive.

But her spirits returned as the army marched north for Agra and thence Delhi; as she gazed at the beauty of the architecture and the teeming population. She was welcomed warmly into the whole family of the Blunts, meeting Nasir's wife and children, and was taken to the new Blunt palace, to exclaim in wonder at the size of her home, the horde of slaves and servants, the splendour of the appointment.

'I feel as if I have entered another world,' she breathed.

Her joy was unbounded when Peter invited her parents to visit them in Delhi. This was a personal triumph for her, as they seemed as impressed by the city as their daughter had been. Caroline took the greatest pride in showing off her wealth and her beautiful home to her mother and father.

With her exceptional colouring and vivacity, Caroline was becoming a great favourite with the imperial family. Aurungzib's wives would invite the Blunt ladies to the royal harem from time to time, and although by custom no whole man – not even the Emperor – was allowed to be present when one harem visited another, Peter had no doubt that the Badshah could see the garden and the unveiled women, from one of the many secret windows overlooking the harem.

Caroline herself found a particular delight in Aurungzib's youngest daughter, Shalina. Only ten when Caroline first reached Delhi, Shalina was already a lovely girl. Her mother was an Afghan, and to the tawny hair and flowing limbs of the mountain people had been added the exquisite features of the Persian-Mongol heritage of the House of Babur. After the age of ten, Peter Blunt never saw her face; having reached puberty, whenever she left the harem she was veiled, but his wife told him that she was quite lovely as she grew to womanhood, with a figure to match her face.

This was apparently a period of great prosperity for the Moghul Empire. Only those at the centre of affairs understood that in fact the magnificent structure erected by Akbar the Great was rotting from within.

Perhaps because he was a foreigner, and was known to belong to none of the cliques at court, Blunt was made the recipient of confidences from every quarter, and from these he was able to draw some very disturbing conclusions.

One of the most alarming of these was the drain of commodities. Blunt had always regarded India as a virtually bottomless pit of gold and precious stones. Perhaps it had been but the spendthrift Moghul nobility, once introduced to the amazing variety of manufactured goods available from Europe and transported into India by the British, the French and the Portuguese, bought them without considering the cost, and paid for them in gold.

Most spendthrift of all was Aurungzib himself. Although he bought no Western luxuries, he ever sought newer, improved equipment for his armies.

Hardly less of a concern was the drain of manpower. This was less due to losses in battle than to sheer alienation. More and more Aurungzib sought to recruit only from among devout Muslims, and there seemed fewer and fewer of these available. He had already ruined his cavalry strength by his destruction of the Rajputs; now he refused to restore it by making an honest peace with the Marathas and turning those magnificent horsemen into a new mounted force. Instead he continued to treat them as bandits, and hunted them down remorselessly. This caused them to take up arms once again, even after Simbaji's execution.

But most disturbing of all was the utter lack of capacity, for either war or government, shown by the royal princes. Mohammed Akbar had died in exile. His brothers all paid lip-service to the Badshah, were given royal governorships – and hastily recalled when they proved incompetent – or given army commands only under the supervision of senior officers. Yet they often discussed with their intimates the death of their father, which in view of his age seemed imminent. There was little doubt that at the first indication of failing health on the part of the Badshah, they would be at each other's throats as viciously as had Aurungzib and his brothers thirty years before ... but this time there was no Aurungzib Alamgir waiting to dominate events.

Aurungzib was aware through his spies of these conclaves, and one after the other the three brothers were imprisoned. He was equally severe with other members of his family who disappointed him. His eldest daughter, Zib-un-Nesa was imprisoned for the suggestion that she might be taking after her Aunt Ara; she was later executed.

None of these domestic discords or public weaknesses had the slightest effect on Aurungzib himself. As he grew older he seemed to become more vigorous, physically at least, and he sought the solution to all problems in war. He marched north-west and fought the Persians and the Afghans; he marched east and fought the Thais; he marched south to fight the Marathas time and again, as those hardy horsemen remained in a state of simmering rebellion. He campaigned from one end of his empire to the next, year after year. He won all his battles; there was no warrior in all Asia who could stand up to Aurungzib Alamgir, his troops were armed with the latest in European weaponry.

Yet he suffered disasters enough, too. And these were brought on him by his own methods – by marching at great speed straight at any enemy, regardless of weather or natural obstacles. Thus, in forcing the crossing of the River Bhuna, despite warnings that unseasonly heavy rainfall in the neighbouring mountains had raised the possibility of flash-floods, he lost twelve thousand men and all his treasure when a torrent of water suddenly surged down on to the plain. Yet the campaign went on.

But, even while campaigning, Aurungzib still ruled his country; he received and dismissed ambassadors, he made and broke alliances, he dictated memoirs – revealing the activity of a man half his age. It was in 1694 that he determined to marry his daughter Shalina, who had just celebrated her sixteenth birthday, to the Ottoman Sultan Ahmed II. For Ahmed had heard tales of the beauty of this girl, and Aurungzib now saw the opportunity for cementing an alliance with the Ottomans against the ever-hostile Persians.

This was tried and trusted international diplomacy, and Blunt had no doubt that the young princess had been coached from birth to accept that she was destined to make a diplomatic marriage in which love could play no part. He was thus taken aback when summoned by the Badshah for a private conversation soon after this marriage alliance was announced.

'I know not what the world is coming to, Blunt Bahatur,' Aurungzib grumbled. 'Young people of today have no understanding of their responsibilities.'

Blunt made sympathetic noises, and waited to learn more.

'My daughter screams and wails that she does not wish to

wed,' Aurungzib continued. 'She has heard some tale that Sultan Ahmed is a monster, and a veritable satyr in his bed. Well, should not a wife expect these things in her husband?' He brooded a moment. 'I am growing old, Blunt Bahatur. Do you know what age I shall be on my next birthday?'

'You will be seventy-seven, Badshah. But never have I seen you looking better.'

'I am growing old,' Aurungzib repeated. 'Were I a young man I would have my daughter thrashed for attempting to defy me. Now ... I even consider her whims. This alliance is important to me, so finally my daughter has consented to wed the Sultan, if only she can be escorted to Istanbul by her dearest friend, your wife.'

'Caroline to travel to Istanbul?' Blunt was astounded. 'Am I to accompany her?' he asked.

'No, you are not,' Aurungzib told him. 'For I need you here.'

'May I ask for how long my wife will be away on this journey?'

'The Princess Shalina will wish the comfort and support of Blunt Agha for up to a month following her wedding. My wives have persuaded her to settle for that period. I am sending the bridal party by sea, so if we suppose the journey takes one month, and the return another, then you must be separated from your wife for three months. Remember that is considerably less time than for a campaign, Blunt Bahatur. And it will please me greatly if you agree to it.'

Caroline herself was ecstatic. 'I have heard so much of Istanbul.'

'It is a decadent place,' Peter growled. But there was nothing he could do about it, so he endeavoured to share her enthusiasm for her great adventure.

'Just be sure you come back to me,' he reminded her.

The preparations for the great event took nearly a year, while envoys travelled back and forth between Istanbul and Delhi, finalising arrangements, and arguing about various points contained in the fine print of the treaty.

The Princess and her fleet would sail from Surat and make for Basra, at the head of the Persian Gulf. There they would disembark and proceed by caravan, under the protection of the Ottomans, via Baghdad, Mosul, Antioch, Konya, Ankara, and thence to Istanbul.

'It will be the journey of a lifetime,' Anne Blunt commented.

'And it is going to take a great deal longer than one month,' Peter grumbled.

In view of the length of time it took to finalise the terms of the princess's marriage, he had some last hopes that if Caroline became pregnant she would need to be left behind. But this seemed impossible to achieve. This was the more annoying since both Serena, for the first time – and after nearly twenty barren years – and Jintna for the second time had recently given birth, Serena to a boy christened Richard, and Jintna to a girl named Elisabeth.

Then, at last, the appointed day arrived.

Caroline considered she was embarking upon the greatest adventure of her life.

Bombay had been exciting, of course, at first. But it had been so small, and the society there so limited, that it had in time become boring. Often she had stood on the landing stage and gazed across Back Bay at the forest and, on a very clear day, the shadowy outline of the mountains in the distance, and she dreamed of one day travelling into the interior of such a vast and fabulous land. That out of that same forest should have come the most handsome man she had ever seen to carry her off, had seemed an enormous adventure – and even more so because of the unexpectedness of it.

She still had to pinch herself sometimes to make herself realise that she had actually now shared Peter's life for seven years, that she lived in a palace with a hundred servants at her beck and call, that she was surrounded by loving and caring women and children, that she regularly drank tea with an empress and her daughters, that she wore jewellery of a value she had hardly knew existed in her girlhood.

Or that, whenever summoned to her husband's bed, she willingly behaved in a manner which no doubt Mama would consider utterly disgusting, immoral and un-Christian, yet which produced an ecstacy she could never have dreamed of.

Mama, with her memory of England, would undoubtedly

consider her position to be servile – but that was the Muslim way. And if she was forced to stand behind her husband and follow him through doorways, and was reminded all the time by those around her that she was his chattel, to be used entirely as he chose, even unto death, yet she knew he would never harm her; and when they were alone together they spoke almost on terms of complete equality.

Besides, her mother-in-law had accepted *her* situation many years before, and yet preserved her integrity; and was indeed the dominant personality in the household, especially after the death of Bilkis, the eldest of Richard Blunt's widows, in 1692. Caroline could think of no better future than to become a second Anne Blunt – although hopefully not to spend over half her life as a widow!

She could not imagine there was a woman more blessed in the entire world. Only in her inability to give him the legitimate heir he sought was she disappointed.

Well, there was going to be no less safety and comfort in voyaging to Istanbul with the imperial entourage. Not only would it be the first adventure she had undertaken without her parents or her husband, but she realised she was virtually going to be in charge. There would be a coterie of elderly royal aunts and female cousins, a bodyguard of eunuchs, and a small army of female attendants, but Princess Shalina regarded Blunt Agha as her mentor in everything, as was made clear even before the caravan departed for Surat, seen off by seemingly every inhabitant of Delhi, and escorted by a regiment of the Imperial Guard.

Caroline had half hoped that Peter could accompany them as far as Surat, but he was required for other duties.

'You will be back in his arms within a few months,' Shalina assured her dolefully. 'Whereas I shall never see Delhi again.'

The two young women – Caroline herself was still only twenty-two – shared a howdah on the lead elephant, and with the curtains closed it was possible for them to remove their yashmaks and make themselves comfortable. Now Caroline put an arm round her friend's shoulders as huge tears welled up from the dark eyes and rolled down the rouged cheeks.

'You go to found a line of sultans,' she reminded her.

Shalina shuddered. 'I go to an old man who is steeped in vice.'

This was not an arguable point – certainly from the point of view of a sixteen-year-old girl. Ahmed was forty-three, and it was well known that he kept a harem of young boys as well as girls.

'It is your karma,' was the best that Caroline could offer.

Shalina's reply was to burst into tears.

But she possessed an ebullient personality, and was soon having Caroline again relate what it was like to be possessed by a man. She would become quite excited at such moments – although she was obviously dreaming of someone young and handsome. Caroline guessed that, once she had become used to being Ahmed's wife, she would probably enjoy it well enough.

Travelling with an imperial princess was even more exciting than travelling with Blunt Bahatur. No wayside encampments for Shalina. Horsemen rode ahead with all the equipment, so by the time they stopped for the night, huge and elaborate tents had been pitched, food had been prepared, and the Princess had nothing more to do but step down from her howdah and retire into the privacy of her apartment. Unless, as happened often enough, they were close to a village or town, when she was required to sit outside, suitably veiled and surrounded by her ladies, and receive deputations and gifts, some of amazing value – carved statuettes, jewellery, occasionally entire flocks of sheep which she despatched back to Delhi – and thank them all from behind her yashmak, like the Sultana she was about to become.

Surat was *en fête*, with every building flying a flag, the entire garrison turned out on parade, the ships in the river dressed overall. There was an English factory in Surat, and Shalina gave Caroline permission to be entertained there by the factors and their wives. Some of these had encountered Colonel and Mrs Knolles, and they received Blunt Agha with considerable awe, gazing in wonder at the diamonds and emeralds and rubies with which her fingers sparkled, and at the gold bangles which she wore on her arms.

There was a large fleet assembled in Surat and waiting in the Rann of Kutch at the river mouth. Most of the ships were of small size, for the Moghuls had never really taken to the sea the way the Arabs had. But the flagship was a good-sized vessel of several hundred tons burthen, built rather more on the lines of an old fashioned carrack than a modern galleon, but very beamy and therefore comfortable, at least when sailing downwind. It contained the most lavish appointments aft for the Princess and her intimates – the entourage was so numerous it had to be divided up between all the twenty ships of the fleet – and also four of the big thirty-two pounder cannon, recently arrived from England, on the main deck to give an impression of enormous strength. Appropriately enough, she was named *The Great Moghul.*

Predictably, Shalina was upset all over again at actually having to board a ship for the first time in her life, and especially when she looked at the seemingly endless ocean which stretched away to the south-west. But again Caroline Blunt was able to reassure her; and, although embarking all the ladies and the trunks and the gifts from Aurungzib to Ahmed took several days, at last they were underway, and making west before a brisk easterly breeze.

'Isn't this splendid?' Caroline asked, as the two women sat together in the stern, a canvas screen having been erected to protect them from the eyes of the crew.

To her own surprise, Shalina was not the least seasick, and had to agree that it was certainly exhilarating.

The next day they sighted a strange sail.

The sail appeared out of the western horizon and rose very rapidly, moving from side to side in front of them. Clearly the strange craft was tacking towards the Moghul fleet – as the wind remained in the east – and at a considerable speed. Soon the hull itself came into sight, long and low, rigged as a brigantine, that is, she was two-masted, with a squaresail on her foremast – pulled as tight as it could go – and a fore and aft mainsail, which together with her three foresails or jibs gave her the extra windward capacity.

'Whatever can she be?' Caroline wondered, she and the ladies having left the shelter of their screened poop to stand on the quarterdeck beside the captain.

'I think she must be an English pirate, Blunt Agha,' the Captain said.

'A pirate?' Shalina shrieked.

Since the arrival of the Europeans in Moghul waters, the word had become familiar.

'English?' Caroline demanded. 'How can you be sure?'

'Because the English are the boldest of these rascals,' the Captain told her. 'But there is nothing to be afraid of. One ship will never dare attack twenty.'

'I feel quite faint,' Shalina remarked, and returned to the poop.

Caroline Blunt remained on the quarterdeck, watching the approaching ship and feeling distinctly nettled, yet also admiring the way the stranger was being handled. The breeze was quite fresh, and on each tack the brigantine was heeling, her starboard gunports clearly revealed – she seemed to have a very large number of guns.

'They are mad,' the Captain grumbled. 'Does he mean to collide with us? Load the guns,' he bellowed. 'Chase that rascal away.'

The guns were loaded, a slow business. Caroline gazed at the pirate. That he intended to sail into the middle of the Moghul fleet now seemed certain. He was close enough now for her to be able to make out his flags; if one was black with some indecipherable device on it, another was certainly the Cross of St George.

She began to feel an urgent desire to wave her arms and shout; go away, you fool, go away!

Instead she remained by the gunwale, her fingers tight on the wood, as the brigantine came about yet again. Now the pirate was up to the foremost dhows, who opened fire upon him. But their guns were light, and did no damage.

The next time he tacked, he was so close that Caroline could make out the men on deck: bearded figures of every complexion from white through several shades of brown to black, stripped to the waist and barefooted, heads bound up in colourful bandannas – and every man with cutlass and pistols thrust through a broad leather belt.

And now, lying well over on his port side, he was making directly for *The Great Moghul.*

'Come about!' the Captain bawled. 'Come about, and fire a broadside into him.'

Men swarmed into the rigging and began pulling on the

sheets. But the Moghuls were not natural seamen, and again the manoeuvre took too much time.

The Captain then remembered his passengers. 'Blunt Agha,' he said, 'take Her Highness below, I beg of you.'

Caroline hesitated, eager to stay on deck and see what would happen. The morning was now a blaze of sound as all the dhows kept popping away, although aiming their guns away from each other and the big carrack, and thus hitting only water. Their crews were raising an enormous cacophony, as if noise alone might drive away the intruder.

While the pirate kept on soundlessly, white water spurting away from the bluff bows. Before Caroline had come to a decision, and at a distance of no more than a hundred yards, the brigantine put in another superbly efficient tack – while *The Great Moghul* was just beginning her turn – and his starboard side burst into flame.

Caroline was suddenly shrouded in a hot wind which blew off her yashmak and sent her sprawling on the deck. She heard screams and shouts, and the crackle of shattered wood and cordage, as the whole carrack seemed to shake from stem to stern.

Dizzily she regained her knees, and stared forward in horror. The entire bow of *The Great Moghul* had been shattered; the bowsprit trailed in the water and the foremast had also gone, lying half over the side beneath a cat's-cradle of ropes, and, from the piteous screams, on top of a good number of men.

Completely out of control, the big ship drifted sideways, while her gunners discharged their broadsides aimlessly, doing more damage to the escorting dhows than to the pirate, who came about for the last time, and in the next few minutes rattled alongside the carrack with another huge jar.

Caroline recovered her senses, scrambled to her feet, and up the ladder to the poop. The canvas screen had been blown away by the blast of the broadside and, although no shot had reached back here, the Princess and her ladies were screaming as they picked themselves up from the deck.

'Highness!' Caroline yelled, pushing through them to grasp Shalina's arm. 'Quickly, you must get below.'

The Princess gasped as she was dragged towards the ladder, but there Caroline halted, sensing that she was too late. The pirates had already swarmed over the bulwarks of their brigantine and into the higher waist of the carrack. The Moghul sailors came hurrying from the guns to repel them, but they never stood a chance before the exploding pistols and the flashing, razor-sharp cutlasses of the invaders. Men screamed, cursed, groaned, and died. The tide of battle had already surged up the ladder to the quarterdeck, and around the companion hatch to the Princess's quarters.

'We are lost,' Caroline moaned. 'We must throw ourselves overboard.'

Shalina shrieked again at such a thought, and tried to fight free. For a moment, the two girls wrestled, and now were indeed lost. They were surrounded by men who forced them apart, laughing. With coarse remarks they pulled the yashmak from Shalina's face, then began tearing away both their saris, while others dragged the rings from their fingers and ripped them from their earlobes. The pain and viciousness of the assault made Caroline scream – but then she was left breathless as someone hit her in the stomach.

'Avast there, ye scum!' shouted someone in English.

Caroline and Shalina were mercifully released, half naked, with blood dribbling down their necks from torn lobes. They hugged each other as they stared at the surprisingly young man, with a scanty beard and glittering blue eyes, who had just thrust a bloodstained cutlass through his belt and now stood in front of them.

'Which one of ye is the Princess?' he demanded in broken Persian.

Shalina managed to pull herself together. For the first time in her adult life her face was exposed to strange men.

'I am the Princess Shalina,' she said softly.

'She's the one I wanted,' the pirate captain said, and his men gave a great yell. Then he looked at Caroline. 'But here's an even better bed warmer,' he remarked, and made a leg. 'John Avery at your service, ladies, and happy I am to make your acquaintance.'

24
THE FURY

'You are a madman, sir,' Caroline addressed Avery, speaking English and endeavouring to hold her torn sari against her breasts, grateful that the clutching fingers had fallen away. All the rings had been snatched from her fingers, and the gold bangles from her arms. 'Do you realise what you have done? This is the daughter of the Great Moghul. He will have every English man, woman and child in India impaled.'

Avery grinned at her. 'D'ye suppose that bothers me, darlin'? Haste, lads, let's away.'

Caroline glanced from left to right. The dhows were endeavouring to close on their flagship, but were moving far too laboriously. Now, before she could think what to do next – even to hurl herself and Shalina over the side, in the hopes of being picked up by a dhow before they drowned – she was seized by two men and bundled down the ladder into the waist.

Here she gasped and retched, for dead bodies lay everywhere, and the pirates were calmly cutting the throats of the Moghul wounded. Blood flowed across the deck and on to her sandals, and she stamped her foot in fear and disgust. Then she was dragged to one side, and thrust over it. Now it was her turn to give a shriek of alarm, as the deck of the brigantine seemed very far away. She was suspended by her arms, trying to get her legs free of the folds of the sari, but only succeeding in kicking off her sandals. Then she was seized from below; men held her ankles and her thighs, once again obscene in their remarks as their fingers slid over her flesh. Hands even encircled her breasts as she was lowered to the deck. She looked up to see Shalina being similarly manhandled, but mercifully the Princess seemed to have fainted.

Behind them were hustled the comeliest of the other ladies. Caroline dared not think what might be happening to the older women – she could hear shrieks of despair, then a series of splashes as, having been stripped of their bangles and jewellery as well as their clothing, they were thrown over the stern in a flail of brown arms and legs.

Caroline was bundled along the deck of the brigantine, through a companion hatch and down a ladder, into a small after-cabin. This was a mere five and a half feet high, and contained four bunks, two end to end along each bulkhead, and between them a table bolted to the floor. A lantern, presently unlit, swung from the centre of the deckhead.

The place smelt of bilge water and stale sweat, alcohol and rancid food. Each bunk contained a horsehair mattress – and nothing else.

Into this cabin Caroline was thrust so violently that she stumbled and fell on to the nearest bunk. Before she could recover her balance, Shalina was hurled on top of her. Desperately she sat up, pulling the Princess against her, expecting more of the girls to be thrown in. But only their captors followed them. She expected instant rape, but instead their wrists were bound behind them, and then tied together, so that they lay on the bunk back to back. A further rope was passed round their waists and secured tightly, to leave them quite incapable of movement, save for their legs, while the rope prevented them from sitting or standing.

All the while, feet were drumming above their heads, cannon exploded, men were shouting, then the ship began to move. Their captors now hurried from the cabin, slamming the door behind them, – and they were alone.

'Highness?' Caroline said. 'Are you hurt?'

Shalina sighed. 'What is happening? I do not understand.'

'We have been seized by pirates.' Her turn to sigh. 'English pirates.'

'My father will be very angry,' Shalina sobbed. 'And to take away my veil! It was indecent. Do they not know who I am?'

'I fear they do.'

'I will have them all lopped for touching me so,' Shalina decided.

Clearly she had no idea that she might be in danger of losing a great deal more than her veil, and Caroline did not know how to tell her. Everything had happened so quickly . . .

The door began to open. Caroline was facing it, and she tensed her muscles. She found herself gazing at a young boy, hardly more than fourteen or fifteen. He wore breeches like the rest of the pirates, but no shirt or shoes, and not even a bandanna. His brown hair hung in greasy tendrils past his ears. His face was not unattractive, but it was utterly wanton.

He stood over the two girls, staring down at them and grinning.

'Will you not cut us free?' Caroline asked hopefully.

'Cap'n wouldn't have that,' the boy said. 'He'd stripe my arse for me, he would. I'm to watch you for 'im. You the princess?'

'No,' Caroline said.

'That one?'

To her consternation he climbed on to the bunk and knelt astride her thighs while he held Shalina's hair and pulled her head up to look at her face.

'Ow!' Shalina shouted. 'I will have you flogged, you dog.'

'What's she saying?' the boy asked.

'She's very angry,' Caroline gasped. He was now sitting on her thigh.

'She has a pretty face,' the boy said. 'But you have bigger tits.'

To Caroline's horror and disgust he pulled the remnants of her sari away and began to fondle her breasts, rather as he might have kneaded dough.

'Cap'n may let me have you, after,' he remarked.

She wanted to curse at him – but that might only make him really hurt her. She had to keep control, to stay alive: the Princess was still her responsibility. 'Does your captain mean to ransom us?' she asked.

'Don' know 'bout that,' the boy said.

To her great relief he stopped playing with her, but then, to her alarm, he reached over to do the same to Shalina.

'Stop it! Stop it!' Shalina screamed. 'I will have you flayed alive!'

'She makes a lot of noise,' the boy said.

The brigantine was heeling now, and the clamour outside was beginning to dwindle, although the cannon still exploded from time to time.

'Listen,' Caroline said. 'The princess is daughter of the

wealthiest and most powerful man in Asia. If you help us, you will be well rewarded. If you ill-treat us, you will be most savagely punished.'

The boy left Shalina to attend to her again, squirming about on her thigh. 'We'll all swing,' he retorted. 'A short life and a merry one, that's the Cap'n's motto.'

He dismounted, and began pulling the sari away from her thighs. Savagely she kicked out at him, but he laughed, and caught her ankle, exerting considerable strength to make her bend her knee, and thus forcing one leg apart from the other. She realised she had made a mistake: bound to Shalina as she was, she couldn't turn sufficiently to use the other leg. The boy, holding her left leg in the air, was advancing so that he stood between her thighs and right against her crotch.

'I could ram you now,' he said. 'I bet Cap'n would never know.'

'Wait,' Caroline said desperately. 'Wait . . .'

The door opened, and she gasped with relief. It was the Captain, the man who had called himself Avery. He carried a canvas bag, obviously of some weight.

'What're ye at, scum,' he said, and struck the boy across the side of the head so hard that the lad gave a shriek, dropped Caroline's leg, and cannoned into the table, then fell to the floor.

'Scum!' Avery shouted again, kicking him. The boy dived still further under the table and burst into tears.

'I said afterwards – maybe,' Avery reminded him, looking down at Caroline, who now had her legs clamped firmly together. 'But you're a right pretty, and that's a fact.' Drawing a knife from his belt, he bent over her. First he cut the rope holding the women together, then he cut the ropes binding their wrists.

'Showed 'em a clean pair o' heels,' he remarked. 'But they're no seamen. Not them.'

Slowly Caroline sat up, massaging her wrists as circulation returned. There didn't seem much point in trying to retrieve her sari.

Shalina continued to lie facing the bulkhead, although she brought her arms in front of her, hugging herself and whimpering as the blood forced its way back into her hands.

'Something the matter wi' her?' Avery poked the Princess in the backside, and Shalina gave a suppressed scream and rose to her knees.

'She is a princess,' Caroline told him. 'Can you not treat her with respect?'

'I allus knew I'd have a princess, one day,' Avery said, and held Shalina's shoulder to turn her round. She did not resist him; instead she gazed at him with huge black eyes from which tears welled to leave furrows in the smudged rouge of her cheeks.

'Oh, she's a charmer,' Avery said. 'And a princess, too ... Ye know something, I reckon this day'll make me the most famous o' them all. What the hell did Morgan ever do, save loot a few cities? I got me a princess. You reckon she'll fight me? Tell her, if she does, I'll bite her nose off, and then fuck her just the same.'

'Please,' Caroline said. 'She is on her way to be wed to the Sultan of Turkey. If you return her unharmed, the Moghul will reward you handsomely.'

'Reward?' He grinned. 'I've got me rewards.' He emptied the bag on to the table; together with their own jewellery there was considerably more taken from the other women.

Avery scooped it all up again, and retied the satchel string. 'And we took a sizable chest o' gold from yer ship. Rich, and famous,' he commented. 'And possessed of the two sweetest charmers in the world. Tell her what I'll do if she fights me, and that when I'm done I'll gi'e her to the crew.' He began to take off his breeches.

Shalina stared at him in horror. As the youngest of Aurungzib's children, she would not even have seen a naked baby brother before.

'He means to possess you,' Caroline told her.

'I understand,' Shalina said. Her tongue circled her lips as she gazed at the enormous uncircumcised member.

'He says that if you fight him, he will bite your nose off and then give you to his crew.'

'Can he not understand that my father will seek him out, no matter where he flees, if he does such a thing?'

'I do not think he cares for that.'

'She got the message?' Avery inquired.

It was going to happen. Caroline did not know what to say or do.

'Tell her to strip,' Avery said. 'Billy, come out from under there.'

Caroline drew a long breath. 'He wishes you to undress.'

Shalina tossed her head. 'My maids undress me.'

'She requires her maids,' Caroline said.

Avery chuckled. 'They're busy – or swimming. You want the boy to do it?'

Billy was on his feet again. He was grinning at them.

'No,' Caroline said. 'I will do it.' She held Shalina's hand. 'I am to undress you, Highness. I beg of you, do not fight this man, or he may hurt you very badly.'

Shalina nodded. 'I understand.'

As Caroline undressed her, all manner of ideas were roaming through her mind, such as choosing her moment when Avery was in the throes of passion to hit him on the head, or to get possession of his cutlass and run him through ... But she could not determine what advantage she would thereby gain, save the doubtful privilege of opening the stern window and throwing Shalina and herself out to drown.

She did not want to die, no matter what was about to happen to her. Life had been so marvellously good these past years; to end it now seemed a terrible waste.

In any event, Avery was not taking the slightest risk. When Shalina at last stood before him naked, he grinned at Caroline.

'Put your wrists behind yer back,' he said.

Caroline hesitated, and her arms were seized by Billy. Her wrists were again tied, and she was made to sit on the farther bunk.

'You just keep an eye on her, Billy,' Avery said. 'And if she tries anything, belt her one.'

'You cannot mean to ... do it in front of the boy,' Caroline protested.

'Why not? He's got to learn.'

'Can I have the big one after?' Billy asked enthusiastically.

'Maybe,' Avery said.

'But I can play wi' her tits the time?'

'Just don't make her squeal.'

Avery was staring hard at Shalina, who was still standing in front of him, her slender body swaying slightly to the movement of the ship.

'Ye're something,' he muttered. 'A real-life princess.'

His fingers traced the outline of her jaw, then down her neck and over her breasts to her stomach, and thence lower to her shaven crotch.

'I like the style,' he said. 'Let's a man see what he's getting.' He took her in his arms, rubbed her body against his, kissed her mouth again and again, then threw her on the bunk, pulled her legs apart, and was on her and in her in a single vast movement. Shalina gasped and moaned, and her head turned backwards, half off the bunk, her long hair brushing the deck.

Caroline watched in helpless horror, hardly noticing the prying fingers of the boy.

Avery surged back and forth a few times, then lay still. Then raised his head to grin at her. 'Don't be jealous, darlin'. Gimme half an hour an' I'll be ready for ye, too.'

Shalina wept in despair.

Aurungzib stared at the terrified messenger. The entire throne room was silent, not a soul daring to breathe. Then the Badshah's head slowly turned. His face was suffused, his white beard seemed to bristle and tremble at the same time. 'Blunt Bahatur,' he said. 'Where is Blunt Bahatur?'

'I am here, Badshah.'

Blunt stood to attention. He could scarce credit the news. That Caroline should have been captured by pirates was sufficient to drive him half out of his mind with rage. That the mighty Badshah's virgin daughter should also submit to such a horrifying ordeal was too much for his mind to grasp.

'The ship was English,' Aurungzib said. 'English!' he screamed. 'Summon my generals. Summon my armies. I wish every Englishman in Hindustan brought before me, that I may hear their screams as they die. You will do this, Blunt Bahatur. They will die!'

'With respect, Badshah ...'

'I wish to hear nothing. I wish them brought before me.'

Blunt held his ground. 'The men who kidnapped your daughter are pirates, Badshah. They are outlaws as much loathed in England as they are by you. But since they are

English they must be punished by Englishmen. Let me go to Bombay and command them to deliver your daughter back to you, together with the pirates who captured her, or else suffer the consequences.'

Aurungzib glared at him.

'Do you not wish your daughter returned, Badshah?'

'She will no longer be my daughter,' Aurungzib growled. 'But fetch her back, yes. With the scoundrel who has taken her. I wish him before me.'

'He has also ravished my wife,' Peter said. 'I would crave your permission to sail with the fleet and find him for myself.'

Aurungzib nodded. 'Yes,' he said. 'Go and find your wife.'

His anger fading, he suddenly looked very old.

The women stared at Peter, unable to speak. They knew how much he had loved his red-haired bride, and they had hardly loved her less themselves for her spirit of fun and laughter, her delight in the pleasure of living.

'You must bring her back,' Anne Blunt said at last.

'I will bring her back,' he vowed.

Charles Knolles shoulders were bowed. 'We had heard of the Princess,' he said. 'But I had no idea my daughter was with her.'

'Who did this?' Blunt asked.

Knolles sighed. 'We believe it was a man called Avery. He is known to be in these waters, and he is a dastardly fellow. There are several English pirates operating east of Africa, but only Avery has the effrontery to commit a crime like this.'

'Where can he be found?'

'We believe he is based on Madasgascar. But Madagascar is a huge island, and there is a considerable colony of pirates there – as well as hostile natives. This is no light undertaking. We shall need a naval squadron.'

'Then send for one.'

Knolles sighed again. 'You know what will have happened to them?'

'Yes.'

'Do you also know it is very probable that after having enjoyed them, Avery will have cut their throats and thrown them to the sharks?'

'We do not know that has happened.'

'And if it has not . . . my daughter, your wife, at the mercy of that brute day in and day out . . . we are the most unfortunate of men.'

'She is my wife, as she is your daughter. We must have her back, Charles. And the princess – for the sake of every Englishman in India.'

Knolles nodded. 'We shall visit Governor Gayor immediately, to make our arrangements. However long it takes, we will have her back.'

Their life was bounded by the beach, the trees, and the sea.

The beach was long and white, and exposed; the sand was hot in the noonday sun, and cold at dawn. Behind the beach was a cleared area of perhaps half a mile square, and in this had been erected several huts. None had the least suggestion of permanency about them; they were somewhere to shelter when it rained, which it did often enough. When it was not raining, the pirates and their women slept on the sand, swatting mosquitoes and sandflies even in their slumber.

Behind the 'town' – as it was called – the trees clustered close together, and the land began to rise; Madagascar was a mountainous island. No one ever ventured into the interior; the native tribes were too warlike. However, the local chieftain tolerated the white men on the beach because they brought him guns and powder, and also a tenth of their booty. He found them a useful source of income and slaves, especially Arab women for his harem. He also knew their power.

Lapping at the beach was the sea, enclosed by a reef some half mile offshore. Within this shelter the pirate fleet could ride securely at anchor, except when the monsoon blew with exceptional force; then the ships had to be careened until the storm was past.

There were never less than three ships at anchor, and usually at least three away, scouring the Indian Ocean and the Arabian Sea for victims. Although there was no admiral, and every captain was a law unto himself, often they hunted together. Madagascar lay athwart the route from the Cape of Good Hope to Bombay and Goa, Madras and Diu, and back again. The pickings were both plentiful and good.

But no other captain had ever equalled Avery's feat of sailing into the midst of a Moghul fleet with a single ship; and then out again with a prize which still made their heads spin. He was certainly first amongst equals.

Thus his women were inviolate, even in his absence, where the other women became communal property when their 'husbands' were away at sea. This was Caroline's and Shalina's sole blessing. Yet even living at the lowest level of humanity can become acceptable when one is determined to survive.

Caroline's thoughts had returned to suicide during the voyage, when she had been raped again and again and in-between times given to the boy Billy 'for his education'. She had known that fighting against them would only amuse them; so it had been a matter of submitting while still hating, and dreaming of vengeance. The Princess was her main worry. Shalina was only a girl, and her mind was far younger than her body because of her utterly sheltered upbringing. No doubt she had listened to harem gossip, and she had learned to accept the thought of a man, and of her destined Ottoman husband particularly, even while she feared him. Now she had discovered that a man, even a drunken, unshaven, filthy monster like John Avery, could also be a source of pleasure. Shalina had been educated to believe that the man who took her maidenhead would be her lord and master for life, and that the only course open to her was to learn to love him. Now she was pregnant, and proud to be so, and waited anxiously for the return of her 'husband', desperate for him to be present at the birth of her child.

Shalina's accepting attitude left Caroline in a total, fearful quandary. She equally had been treated as Avery's 'wife', if only in a secondary capacity; but since the Princess had begun to swell, she had been more in demand, although she understood that she could not compare in Avery's eyes with the very thought of Aurungzib's daughter. For this she was grateful, but the future loomed very dark. Were they to remain on this beach until they died, probably of the fever which was rampant amongst the pirate crews? Or were they to be rescued? Because that might be an even less acceptable prospect.

Caroline stood on the edge of the beach, watching the men dragging a heavy seine net towards the shore. The seine was the simplest method of fishing: two boats were rowed out towards the reef, each carrying one end of the heavy, weighted net. The net was then dropped into the water, and the boats slowly towed the ends back to the beach. Once the shallows were reached other men dashed into the gentle surf to handle the net, while within its rapidly enclosing space all manner of fish leapt and danced, to be hit on the head by the eager pirates and their no less excited native women.

Caroline had even taken part in the ritual once or twice herself, splashing naked amidst the blood and water and frantic, slippery creatures. Today however she merely watched, wearing a shapeless cotton gown and a wide-brimmed straw hat; both of which she had made herself. Her feet were bare, and her complexion, always susceptible to exposure, was now a sunburned mass of freckles. Although she always wore her hat in the sun, even her hair seemed to have faded from dark red to a paler colour, streaked with gold. Shalina, standing beside her, was similarly dressed and similarly sun-tanned, although her smooth white complexion had responded in a more even fashion.

The shouting and yelling increased as the net was drawn right into the shallows, and now the work of killing began as the pirates waded amidst the fish, their knives and clubs flashing. It was the high spot of their week.

For the rest, they lay on the beach and smoked cigars and drank rumbullion, until it was time to go to sea again – which was whenever they began to run out of supplies and needed to trade ... and before trading it was necessary to take a prize to obtain the wherewithal. Often they fought over a woman or some imagined insult, and such fights were usually to the death. An atmosphere of casual violence hung over the encampment like a miasma. Even the women fought with unsuppressed fury, usually egged on by the men, who liked nothing better than to watch two naked females figures rolling about on the sand, scratching and biting, tearing and gouging.

The women were mostly black, traded for muskets and fine cloth from the natives of the interior, but some were Indian or Arabic, taken on raids, and several had once been the Princess's maids. Like her, they were indistinguishable from any of the others save for a certain paleness of their complexions.

Also like her, they had learned to speak the bastard English which was the *lingua franca* of the beach, and had become almost reconciled to their fate and their men, since they could not conceive of ever returning to their old life of perfumed palaces and total seclusion.

'There ye go,' Billy came along the beach, carrying two good sized fishes, with blood dripping from his fingers. 'Dinner for ye.'

Caroline squatted on the sand, her skirt gathered between her legs like any native woman. Shalina knelt beside her; her stomach was too large to allow her to squat. Both drew their knives to gut the fish. Billy knelt between them to help.

Eight months ago, Caroline thought, she would have used this opportunity to drive the knife into Billy's heart. Now the boy was almost like a brother, save that he adored her sexually and could not keep his hands off her in Avery's absence. Avery was well aware of the boy's passion, and was amused by it; so Billy was nowadays left behind to look after the two women – with strict instructions never to touch the Princess.

So they grinned at each other as they worked. Have I also become reconciled to my fate, Caroline wondered: the plaything of a fifteen-year-old boy. She refused to accept that – but she too lacked the capability to hate constantly.

'I'll build the fire,' the boy said, and headed up the beach. Other fires were already lit, and the smell of roasting fish filled the air.

Shalina rubbed her stomach. 'We are hungry,' she said. She usually was, and always referred to herself and the babe as a pair. Now she stood up, and stared out to sea. 'Why doesn't he come?' she asked. 'Oh, say he will come.'

'Of course he will come,' Caroline said – although it was likely that one day he would not. Someone was going to catch up with him eventually. But now she squinted in the glare. 'See, there is a sail.'

Shalina clapped her hands in joy, and the beach around them became excited. Men abandoned their cooking and rowed out to the ships to load their cannon; a strange sail could easily be an enemy. Others hurried to the small fort established on the headland, for there too was a battery. The women gathered on the beach to watch the preparations, and the approaching vessel. But soon enough they could make out the pennants streaming from Avery's masthead.

'He's here!' Shalina shouted. 'He's here.'

Avery's face was grim as he stepped ashore, to be surrounded by his fellows.

'There's trouble,' he told them. 'Seems the Moghul wants his daughter back.' He gazed at Shalina. 'Swollen belly and all ... There's a fleet out of Bombay. We took an Arab trader, who told us the Moghul will execute every English man, woman and child in India if they don't deliver me. So it's up to the John Company to find us and, according to this Arab, before I cut his throat, they know where we are. They've even rounded up some Navy ships.'

'I allus knew that coup of yers would bring us to this,' Captain England growled. 'Well, lads, I'm off. The Indian Ocean is done if the Company *and* the Navy are after us. Next thing they'll be here as well.'

'We'll all have to get out,' Avery said. 'And the sooner it's done the better. We'll find a new ground, lads.' He stamped up the beach, followed by the two women.

'Where will you take us?' Shalina asked.

Avery glanced at her. 'Ye? I'll not take ye anywhere, sweetheart. Ye're the cause o' the trouble.'

Shalina stared at him.

'So ye'll stay here. Make yer peace wi' yer daddy, if ye can. If the darkies ain't had ye for dinner by then.'

'You cannot mean to abandon me?' Shalina cried. 'I am your wife.'

'I'll get me another. Don't worry your pretty head about that.'

'I am carrying your child!' she screamed.

'And right ugly ye are wi' it, too.'

Shalina drew her knife and struck out at him. He caught her wrists easily enough, and Caroline held her shoulders to drag her away.

'Yeah,' Avery said, wresting the knife from Shalina's hand and throwing it on the sand. 'Ye keep her off me, Caro, or I'll kick her in the belly and she can drop the child here and now.'

As he went off, Shalina sank to her knees, tears flooding her cheeks.

'How can he abandon me,' she wailed. 'I am his wife.' She clutched Caroline's hand. 'Make him take us with him.'

'He will not,' Caroline told her, uncertain whether to weep or shout for joy. If Avery and all of the other pirates were fleeing Madagascar, and the Bombay fleet knew where to come ... surely they were going to be rescued. Dared she hope for that? Dared she face Peter again? But the only alternative was death.

She stayed with the sobbing Shalina while the pirates hastily packed up their goods. That did not take them very long, for none had any permanent establishment ashore. None of the women would be taken along, and there was a tremendous wailing and shrieking as this became known.

'What is to become of us?' they screamed.

'Ye'll catch fish,' the pirates told them.

'Or ye can go to the blacks,' said another. 'They'll make a meal out o' ye. One way or other.'

The women stood in a silent group to watch the ships put out. Most of them were still suffering from shock at this sudden upheaval in their lives.

Billy said goodbye with tears in his eyes. 'If I'd been cap'n I'd have taken you wi' me, Caro,' he said. 'To the end of the earth.'

'A short life and a merry one,' she reminded him.

His shoulders hunched as he waded into the shallows and climbed into the waiting boat.

Avery did not even look back.

The beach was very quiet after the men had left. Occasionally there was a scream of maniacal laughter from one of the women; they were drinking up the last of the rumbullion as rapidly as they could. Most, however, seemed to be experiencing a rare sense of freedom just being allowed to sleep as much as they wanted.

'What is to become of us?' Shalina asked.

'There is a fleet coming from Bombay,' Caroline reminded her, cooking the rest of the fish. 'We shall be rescued.'

Shalina shuddered.

The pirate fleet remained hull down on the horizon for some time, as the wind dropped. They would be visible from several parts of the island, however, and the Madagascans could count – at least as high as eight. As soon as the other women had settled down for the night, Caroline touched Shalina on the shoulder. The Princess awoke with a start.

'Has the fleet come?'

'No. But we must leave this place.'

Shalina blinked at her in the darkness.

'The natives will have seen all the ships leave together, and they will come down to the beach. We have nothing to resist them with.'

She held Shalina's hand and they stole away from the others. In the eight months they had been on the island they had explored this stretch of beach thoroughly, and Caroline knew that where it ended, in a large outcrop of rock, there was a small cave, its overhanging lip descending almost to water level, while its entrance was washed by high tide. She led Shalina into this.

'Now we must be very quiet,' she warned.

They even managed to sleep, but were awakened at dawn by the sound of screaming, accompanied by whoops of triumph and the fierce barking of dogs.

'Can't we help them?' Shalina whispered. Although none of the women could be described as a friend, they were at least all companions in misfortune, and some had been her maids.

'No, we cannot,' Caroline told her. 'Do you wish to have your babe cut from your womb?'

'My babe,' Shalina moaned, hugging her stomach. 'My baby.'

Caroline did not venture out until the very last sounds of conflict had died away, then she crawled cautiously from the cave and peered through the rocks. Both the beach and the town were a shambles of destroyed huts, broken utensils, and scattered bodies; several of the women had been slaughtered, the rest had been carried off. Some of the dogs remained, tearing at the corpses, baring their teeth at her as she approached, while the flies were already busy, and the stench was fearful. Caroline returned to the cave.

'I am so hungry,' Shalina complained.

'You will have to wait until dark,' Caroline told her. She did not intend to take any risks.

When it was dark, she ventured out again. Even the dogs had

now abandoned the beach. She took off her gown, waded into the water, and set two of the fishtraps which had been overlooked by the natives. Then she climbed a coconut tree – another art she had learned during her stay on the island – and hacked off some of the fruit, carrying them back to the cave to be split open. The coconut flesh and milk would sustain them for a considerable time, she knew. But the fish would have to be eaten raw, as a fire would most definitely alert the natives to the fact that there were still people living on the beach.

Three days later Shalina gave birth. Caroline had known this was likely to happen soon; but she was still taken by surprise.

As Shalina moaned and screamed, Caroline could only pray that no natives were in the vicinity. She had but the vaguest idea of what needed to be done, but helped as much as she could with the actual delivery, her hands slippery with blood, and then cut the umbilical cord with her knife and tied it off.

She took the baby – it was a boy – down to the stream to bathe him, and then returned and placed him in his mother's arms.

'Give him your breast,' she said.

'But there is nothing,' Shalina wailed.

'There will be. He'll have to go hungry for a few hours.'

She cleaned up the mess, and went to sleep – but was awakened by the barking of dogs and the voices of men. The natives had come back. Fortunately the tide had risen right up to the cave mouth in the night, and the dogs could not follow their scent. But that the Madagascans were aware that they had not secured all of the women seemed obvious.

When Caroline next ventured forth, she found that her fish pots had been emptied and carried away. That left them with only coconuts. Where, oh where was the fleet? She stood on the beach, staring out to sea, and her heart gave a little jump as she thought she saw lights. She closed her eyes very tightly, then opened them again. Yes, there were lights, and coming closer!

She turned with a surge of excitement – straight into the arms of the man who had been creeping up behind her back.

Caroline gasped, but he had enveloped her, and her own arms were pinned to her side. She tried to wrestle herself free, even as she realised that he was alone, and was not even accompanied by a dog.

The man grinned at her, his teeth gleaming white in the darkness, then hooked his right leg round her left, and exerted his weight. Caroline gave a faint shriek and struck the earth heavily ... and became aware of the haft of her knife, thrust into the back of her waistband, pressing into her thigh.

She stopped fighting against him, as he rose to his knees above her and tore at her skirt. She slipped her hand beneath her buttocks and found the haft, while he discarded the loincloth which was all he wore. Still grinning, he pulled her legs apart and knelt between – and she surged upwards, driving the knife at him with all of her strength, aware that if she did not kill him now she was dead herself.

As the knife sank into his chest, he gave a startled exclamation and fell backwards. Caroline was on her knees in a moment, stabbing again and again, her arms and gown soaked in spurting blood. Her attacker moaned, and died.

For several minutes Caroline knelt panting, then she pulled herself together. She grasped the man's ankles and dragged him down to the sea. He was heavy, but once in the water it was easier. She towed him out until the gentle waves came to her shoulders, then let him go.

She washed off as much of the blood as she could, and then returned to the beach and scuffed the sand to remove the marks of the corpse being dragged, although she knew the dogs would sniff out the blood.

'You've been swimming,' Shalina accused, hugging her babe to her breast.

'The fleet is coming,' Caroline told her.

'The fleet has been coming for days.'

'It's coming now. I've seen it. No, don't go outside. It won't be here until tomorrow.'

Oh, pray that the wind holds, and that it does arrive tomorrow, she thought.

Next morning there was a great hullabaloo on the beach as the Madagascans searched for the missing man. His body was found quickly enough in the shallows, and that he had been knifed to death was easy to determine. But by now their attention was distracted by the approaching ships, which were very close to the land, with guns run out and the Cross of St George flying from their mastheads. Boats had already been put down to find a way through the reef. Now one of the cannon roared, and the round shot scattered the natives back into the bush.

Caroline and the Princess crouched by the cave until the boats filled with armed men actually came ashore. Caroline could hardly believe her eyes as she saw her own husband step on to the sand, his sword drawn. Now she felt afraid.

Peter Blunt had come prepared for every eventuality. There were women on board his ship to take charge of the Princess, wrapping her and the babe in blankets, while he led a large armed force into the forest.

Also wrapped in a blanket, Caroline sat in a chair on the poop, and listened to the sounds of gunfire, watching smoke rising beyond the trees. The Company was determined to make an example of somebody, and the Madagascan village was their only possible target.

Blunt himself led the attack. He had embraced her, but there had been no time for further talk. That would come later. And what would she say?

The men returned in triumph three days later. They had slaughtered a good number of the Madasgascans, and even obtained some gold.

By then Caroline had been well fed, bathed, and dressed in a sari. For the first time in nine months she was properly dressed, and she awaited her husband wearing a yashmak, for which she was grateful.

'How long ago did Avery leave?' he asked her.

'Perhaps a fortnight. He was making for the Atlantic.'

'There is a squadron of the King's ships out seeking him there. I doubt he will get very far. At least, we still have to convince the Badshah of this.' Peter's smile was grim. 'Who is the father of her child?'

'John Avery.'

They gazed at each other.

'If you wish to divorce me,' Caroline said, 'I shall raise no objection.'

'Were you also his mistress?'

'He made me so. And another's.'

His nostrils dilated. Under Muslim law he had the right to kill her, for adultery.

'There would have been a third,' she said, 'but I killed him.'

She was desperately trying to discover where she stood.

'But you could not kill them all,' Blunt observed.

'No,' she said, 'I could not kill them all.'

He stood at the rail and looked down into the waters of the bay. 'You may imagine how worried your parents have been.'

'I am grateful for their concern,' Caroline murmured.

He turned, leaning on the rail.

'I also was worried,' he said.

Suddenly she was in his arms.

'Can you forgive me?' she whispered.

'Forgive you? I honour your survival. I nearly went mad with every day's delay, while the fleet was being gathered. Oh, my dearest girl.' He held her close. 'It seems that no Blunt woman ever managed to live a tranquil life. We shall have to do better in the future.'

A great warmth spread over her. But she still felt a responsibility for the Princess.

'And Shalina?'

Peter sighed. 'That depends upon the mood of the Badshah.'

25
THE FLIGHT

Aurungzib surveyed the two veiled women standing before him. It had taken four months for them to return to Delhi. In that time Caroline's spirits had entirely recovered. On the voyage back to Bombay she had realised, perhaps for the first time, how much Peter Blunt truly loved her ... and how much she loved him. The separation of nearly a year might never have been. Yet it should have hovered like a cloud over both their minds as he now bedded her with all the passion of a man separated from his adored wife for so long.

On returning to Bombay, she had spent a marvellously happy week with her parents, while the caravan for Delhi was being prepared. Then she had set out on the road ... and had promptly missed her period, for the first time in her life. As it was then two months since leaving Madagascar, and Avery was absent for a month before that, there could be no doubt that the child was her husband's.

It was as if her experiences on the beach had somehow freed her mind and her body too – which almost made it all worthwhile.

She only wished she could have worked some similar kind of a miracle with Shalina. Caroline herself had by now recovered to a great extent from her physical ordeals. She did not suppose she would ever lose the heavy coating of freckles which had spread over much of her body, but this did not seem to trouble Peter. The important thing was that she had enjoyed his comfort and support, as well as that of her parents. They had never talked about her nine months with Avery. She suspected that her mother would like to discover more ... but had wisely felt that would be to open a Pandora's box. Better that Avery and the others be locked away in her daughter's mind forever. Caroline knew her own strength now.

Shalina lacked any of these things. From the moment she had been rescued she had reverted to being the Badshah's daughter, wrapped in a cocoon of seclusion and protection. She had also withdrawn into herself; she had never truly contemplated having to face her father again.

Caroline had spent much time with her, but found she had even withdrawn from their friendship, hugging her babe as if terrified he would be taken away from her. She was a woman for whom the present had no meaning. She could only remember the past – and fear the future.

And now the future was here.

'Why did you not kill yourself?' the Emperor inquired.

Shalina's yashmak fluttered as she breathed. 'I wished to live, Badshah, to look upon your face again.'

'You are a reproach to your name and your house,' Aurungzib growled. 'And whose child is that?'

The child was carried by a nurse at Shalina's side.

'He is *my* child,' Shalina said trembling. 'And your grandchild, sire. He will grow up to be your strongest support. I will see to that.'

'You are a whore,' Aurungzib told her. 'And that thing is an abomination. Take it from my sight. Have it strangled and feed its carcass to the dogs.'

'No!' she screamed. 'You cannot!'

Soldiers moved forward to take the babe away from the nurse.

'You cannot!' Shalina screamed again, and ran at her father, but was seized by others of the guard before she could reach the throne.

'Foul thing!' she screamed, tearing the yashmak from her face, to a gasp from the assembled courtiers. 'If you kill my child, you must kill me as well. I hate you, you bloated monster. You pile of ordure . . .'

'Take her from my sight,' Aurungzib said. 'Lock her up where no man may ever behold her again. Begone with her.'

Struggling and screaming, Shalina was dragged from his presence.

Aurungzib glared at Peter. 'You have failed me, Blunt Bahatur. Where is the pirate who destroyed my daughter?'

'He had fled, Badshah. And the oceans are vast. But the entire Royal Navy of England is seeking him, and he will be found.'

'Must I exist on promises? I wish his head. That I allow you another chance is merely because I have lost nothing by this fiasco. Ahmed of Turkey is dead. He died before my daughter could even have reached his bed, so in any event all would have come to naught.' He brooded for several minutes, as if considering the whims of Fate. Then continued 'I wish the pirate's head. Bring me that, or suffer my displeasure.'

'He is a mean and vicious and despicable old man,' Caroline cried when she gained the safety of their palace.

'He is the Badshah,' Peter reminded her, 'and his word is law.'

'And you have lost favour because of it all,' she said.

'You are distraught,' he told her. 'I shall regain favour because I am too valuable to the Badshah to be out of favour long.'

'Ha!' she commented.

But she knew that to rail against him was both pointless and unjust. She could only weep for Shalina. . . .

And attempt to pick up the threads of her life. Here again she was assisted by the love and encouragement of her mother-in-law and Hilma, of Jintna and Serena, of Richard and Elisabeth; even of William who, now nineteen, was already a tuk-bashi in the Guard.

And wait to give birth herself, to the English son that Peter so desired.

Blunt himself returned to Bombay.

'It is essential that Avery is caught,' he warned Governor Gayer. 'I cannot say how long the Badshah's patience will last.'

'Then what is to be done?' Gayer asked. 'There is no word as yet, and I very much fear that the rascal has got round the Cape of Good Hope and into the Atlantic. Once there, we are really helpless until he shows his hand again. . . .'

'Do pirates ever cease being pirates?'

'Any of them with any sense – particularly after making a killing such as Avery did,' Knolles intervened.

'Then you think he may escape?'

'The odds are in his favour.'

'In that case we must practise a subterfuge. Is there anyone here in Bombay who knows what Avery looks like?'

'I doubt it.'

Peter looked from face to face. 'We need the head of an Englishman in his mid twenties, I think.'

'My God!' Gayer commented.

'Will not my daughter recognise him?' Knolles asked.

'Undoubtedly. But Caroline will not betray us.'

'And the Princess?'

'The Princess will never again see the light of day,' Peter said.

'This is a serious business,' Knolles said. 'You are asking us to dig up a corpse . . .'

'No,' Peter said.

'Well, to wait then, for some unfortunate to die of disease . . .'

'No,' Peter said again.

They stared at him.

'Do you suppose Aurungzib and his viziers are fools?' Peter asked them. 'This man must have died suddenly by violence, and while in good health.'

'You are proposing murder.'

'I am attempting to save the lives of all the English in Hindustan, and your precious factories.'

'Well . . . I suppose someone may commit a capital crime here before too long,' Gayer suggested.

'That will not do either. Your Indian servants would know of it, and for any suggestion of trickery to reach the ears of the Badshah would mean the deaths of us all. One of your ships must put to sea, manned by an utterly trustworthy crew, and return here some months hence with the head of John Avery. They will have been handed it by the captain of a Navy ship. It would have to be pickled, of course to preserve it.'

Gayer looked anxiously at Knolles.

'As you have suggested,' Peter said, 'I am sure the Navy can lay hands on some scoundrel deserving of death. But it is essential that he is executed privately.'

'We had best see about getting a ship,' the Colonel agreed.

Knolles and Blunt walked together in the garden.

'You and I have trodden a long and winding path together,' the Colonel remarked.

'Which is far from ended, I would hope,' Peter added. 'What is the news from England?'

'What would you expect? Now that King William is firmly on the throne, he thinks of nothing but war on France. I, however, am more interested in our situation here: in what Aurungzib will do next.'

'That is impossible to say. In two years time he will be eighty. And for forty years he has held power of life and death over every living creature in this vast country, with not a soul to say him nay. His ancestors, Shah Jahan and Akbar, and even Jahangir, had wives whom they loved and honoured, and who undoubtedly played a part in their decisions. They also had sons of talent, who rebelled often enough, but could yet be relied upon to exert a certain restraint upon their father. Aurungzib has none of these things. His wives are terrified of him, and certainly he does not love any of them. His surviving sons are no less afraid of him, and they are utterly lacking in talent. He is aware of all this, and it makes his temper uncertain; and there is no one, no one at all, who can impose the slightest restraint upon him. That is why I insist a substitute for Avery be found soonest. It would take but a single explosion of his temper, and all your factories would be in flames.'

'You are painting the picture of a despot,' Knolles remarked. 'Yet you serve him.'

'I have no choice, for all of our sakes.'

'For which you require a head.' Knolles sighed. 'Oh, we will find one for you. There is too much at stake. Tell me how you see the future?'

'It is difficult to be optimistic.'

'You say Aurungzib is on the verge of eighty. Is he still in good health?'

'His health is astonishing, as is his vigour.'

'But all men must die. And he will be succeeded by weaklings, or by civil war if your judgement is correct. We must wait and see. I shall tell you one thing, Peter. The East India Company is not easily going to be driven from India. We are ever improving our forts, and enlarging our armies. We are here to stay.'

'You would defy the Badshah who can ride at the head of a hundred thousand men at the snap of his fingers?'

'I pray that it will not come to that. But I say again, we will not be driven out. And should you ever decide or have cause to leave his service, be sure of a command in the Company, either here in Bombay or in Madras, or in Calcutta. I speak with the authority of the Directors in London.'

Blunt returned to Delhi in a thoughtful frame of mind. Much of what his father-in-law had said was undoubtedly bravado – but, all the same, if the Badshah's fleet could be virtually routed by a single pirate, it would never stand up to a squadron of the Royal Navy. Equally, from the reports received from Europe, one could wonder if even the Moghul hordes would find it easy now to defeat a disciplined European army. It would certainly prove a tremendous conflict.

And on which side would he find himself? Could he abandon the Badshah and go to serve his own people? But were they really his own people? He had never even seen England, and doubted if he thought like an Englishman. It would be an enormous, irrevocable step to have to take. It was a decision he hoped he would never have to make, for he did not see how his family could survive. Too many Blunt generations had already been consumed in the gaping turmoil of Moghul politics; he wanted better for his own.

In the spring of 1697 Caroline presented Peter with a son. They named him Thomas after the first of all the Blunts to visit India. A year later a daughter, Joanna, was born. It was hardly a time to brood on changes.

And by now, too, Aurungzib was again in good humour with the British. The pickled head of John Avery, pirate, had been delivered to Delhi, where Aurungzib gazed at it with great satisfaction. 'Come,' he said to Peter. 'We will show it to the Princess Shalina.'

Blunt was aghast. He had not expected this.

In dread he followed the Badshah and his escort to a very private wing of the palace, separate even from the harem, where the Princess had remained confined in a narrow tower for the past two years. The guards saluted, and, as they entered, two women bowed low. These were the only attendants allowed to the stricken girl.

Princess Shalina stood by the one small window in her reception room, looking out over the city. The window was both narrow and barred, and no one in the streets below could have any idea that she stood there.

She turned at her father's entrance, but made no attempt to bow or greet him. Nor was she apparently the least concerned that she was wearing no yashmak while there were several men at his back.

She had lost weight, but none of her beauty.

'Behold the head of your paramour,' Aurungzib said triumphantly.

Blunt held his breath as the box was opened, but Shalina looked away.

'Look at him,' Aurungzib commanded.

Shalina tossed her head.

'Make her look, Blunt Bahatur,' Aurungzib said.

Peter stopped to draw breath, then went forward. 'Will you not humour your father, Highness?'

'I have no father,' Shalina said.

'Make her look,' Aurungzib repeated in annoyance.

Blunt grasped Shalina's arm and drew her towards the box, wondering if he was thereby signing his own death warrant.

'Hold it up,' Aurungzib ordered.

Two of his guards lifted the box in front of the Princess. Her nostrils dilated as she gazed at the mottled face which was beginning to decompose, even though treated. Then she turned away again.

Slowly, Peter relaxed. Perhaps she had not looked sufficiently closely.

'Now dream of him for the rest of your days,' Aurungzib snarled.

He waved a hand, and the box was taken outside. Then Aurungzib followed, Blunt at his side.

'Murderer!' Shalina shouted after them.

Aurungzib hesitated, and Peter feared an explosion of rage. But then the Badshah proceeded on his way.

He did not tell Caroline of how near they had all come to

disaster. Life at the Blunt palace had again become good. There was William to be married, and the company of the young ones, Richard and Elisabeth, Thomas and Joanna to be enjoyed.

There were sadnesses, too. Zaid died of a heart attack, and Iskanda of fever, but Penelope continued to prosper. So did Nasir, who was now a tuman-bashi.

And still the Badshah campaigned, spending most of his time now in the south, warring endlessly against Sivaji's descendants. Though none had the capabilities of their great ancestor, yet the Marathas kept the field, determined never again to yield to Moghul power. Countless men died, and millions of rupees were squandered, yet the campaign dragged on year after year; and often months went by without Blunt seeing his family. It was as if Aurungzib had set himself this one final task before he died, and nothing else in his empire mattered.

But the empire creaked and groaned, as if waiting for some immense burden to be lifted from its shoulders. The Hindus were still persecuted, and robbed of all they possessed to pay for these wars, but now the Muslims too began to feel the heavy hand of taxation as Aurungzib's financial difficulties grew – and as their sons died in his endless campaigns.

Yet there were no open revolts: the Badshah's ruthlessness was feared by all. Everyone was waiting for his death. Meanwhile those who nibbled at the edge of Hindustan were prospering. After the monsoon of 1706 Blunt visited Bombay to say a last goodbye to Charles and Lucy Knolles, who were retiring to England.

'After twenty years,' Charles said, 'it is hard to believe we are leaving.'

Peter looked out over the settlement, at its myriad buildings, new cathedral, the gun emplacements and red coats who manned them, the dozen ships in the harbour, and thought of the huddled village he had first visited in search of a bride.

'You will not forget my offer,' Knolles continued. 'It remains on the table.'

'I will not forget it, old friend,' Blunt said. 'But I must tell you that my affairs have never been more prosperous, and my relations with the Badshah are amicable.'

'Then long may they continue so,' said his father-in-law.

'I but wish we could have seen Caroline one more time

before we left,' Lucy broke in. 'Will we ever see our daughter again?'

Peter could only squeeze her hand. The possibility was utterly remote.

Before that year was out, Aurungzib was back in Delhi. He had won the usual number of victories, but the Marathas were still in the field, and the old Badshah was worn out: he was now approaching his eighty-ninth birthday.

Peter was now forty-six himself, as Caroline was thirty-one, but beautiful as ever. She listened sadly to his account of her parents' farewell. She also knew she would never see them again. But now it was time to induct Richard, just sixteen, into the Guard, and congratulate William on becoming a ming-bashi at the early age of twenty-nine.

'Will you have to campaign again?' his wife inquired.

'The Badshah is certainly planning a campaign for next year.'

'How I hate that old man.' She spoke in a whisper, even in the privacy of their bedroom.

'Say that again after he is gone,' Peter told her. 'And we see what follows.'

The next day Blunt was summoned to the palace. This was not unusual but, to Peter's surprise, the Badshah was alone. Not even the Vizier was with him.

'Badshah?' He bowed.

Aurungzib's white beard now descended to his waist, and his hands trembled. Yet his face could still grow dark with fury.

'Tell me this,' he said. 'Have I not been good to that she-devil who claims to be my daughter?'

'Indeed, Badshah,' Peter temporised.

'I should have had her strangled the day you returned her to me. Yet because I am an indulgent father I spared her life.'

Peter thought of Mohammed Akbar and Zib-un-Nesa, who had not been so fortunate.

'Now I have just learned that the Princess Shalina is pregnant.'

'But how, my lord?'

'How do you suppose? She has seduced one of her guards. Your father once was required to assist me in a distasteful business: the execution of my own sister. Now I place you in charge of this matter, because it must be done with extreme secrecy. I wish to know the name of my daughter's paramour. Tear it from her throat, if you must. And then dispose of her. I do not wish to look upon her face again. But bring the man before me. You understand?'

'With respect, Badshah, I am a soldier, not a torturer.'

'You are my trusted aide,' Aurungzib snapped back. 'I will send two men with you, experienced in obtaining information. The deed must be done this evening, after dark.'

Blunt longed to reject so terrible an assignment. Yet he could not do so and live. And if he died, then all of those he loved would also die.

'The torturers you must despatch as soon as they have done their task.'

'With respect, Badshah, but may I ask who brought you this news of the Princess's condition?'

'One of her maids is my agent.'

'And does not this maid know the identity of this lover?'

'She says she does not. She says it happened some months ago.'

'And you believe her, my lord?'

Aurungzib frowned. 'You think she would dare lie to me? Very well, put her to the torture as well. And see that she is executed too. She knows too much. Then bring me the name of the man. He and everyone of his blood will suffer for this crime.'

Blunt realised there was nothing for it. He had been turned into a murderer.

Now he wished it done as quickly as possible. He dared not go home, so spent the intervening hours pacing up and down. The moment it was quite dark that evening, with the two executioners appointed by Aurungzib he went directly to the Princess's tower, where he dismissed the night guard standing outside.

He was aware of a very uneasy feeling in his belly as he opened the door, the two torturers at his side; each carried a flaming torch.

By the flickering light he beheld the Princess.

Shalina was now twenty-seven years old. Since he had last

seen her, ten years before, she had put on weight, and was now quite plump, and remarkably healthy looking – though she had also lost the naive innocence of her youth. She regarded Blunt with an unblinkingly hostile stare, then glanced at the two executioners. Only then did a faint tremor trickle down her body.

Her two maids had both bowed low at the entrance of Blunt Bahatur.

Five people, he thought, all of whom must now die.

'Which one of you is named Bibi?' he inquired.

The smaller of the two young maids bowed again.

'It is you who has given information to the Badshah?' Blunt said.

Bibi threw a hasty glance at her mistress, who frowned.

'This woman has informed your father that you are with child, Highness,' Peter told her.

Shalina stared at Bibi.

'The Badshah is my master,' said the maid in a low voice.

'I am your master, now,' Blunt told her. He looked at the Princess. 'Is it true, Highness?'

'You are impertinent,' Shalina snapped.

'She has missed three periods,' Bibi said hurriedly.

'The Badshah wishes to know the name of the father.'

Shalina tossed her head, and turned away.

'You,' Blunt said. 'Bibi. If you know so much, you know this also. Give me his name.'

Bibi faltered. 'I do not know it, sire. It all happened three months ago. I was not on duty then.'

Blunt realised she was telling the truth, but he wanted her punished for her betrayal of Shalina.

'Prepare her for torture,' he ordered one of the waiting men.

The man smiled. He placed his torch in a vacant sconce – as did his companion.

'No!' Bibi shrieked as her arms were seized by one of them, while the other removed her sari. 'The Badshah is my master!'

Peter glanced at Shalina, to see if she would intervene to save her maid, but the Princess was staring out of the window again. The second maid had backed against the wall, panting with fear.

Bibi's wrists were tied together behind her back, then she was thrown to the floor, screaming again and again. Her body twisted to and fro, while one of the men held her legs apart. The other took down one of the torches.

'What will you do to her?' Shalina asked at last.

'We will burn her, Highness.' The man grinned. 'Here and there, where it amuses us.'

'Mercy!' Bibi screamed. 'I did as the Badshah commanded! As Allah is my witness, I did only as the Badshah commanded!' She broke into sobs as the torch was held between her legs and the flames licked against her shaven groin.

Blunt looked at the other girl. If Bibi was telling the truth, then *she* would be the one who knew the name of the guilty man. *Someone* had to say it, before they died. As they all had to die.

Bibi shrieked again in agony as the men rolled her on her face, holding her buttocks apart to send the flames between.

'Enough,' Shalina cried. 'Yes, I am pregnant. Must I spend my time in this tower without the slightest solace?'

'Release the girl,' Blunt ordered.

Reluctantly the torturers abandoned their work. Bibi rolled herself into a ball, moaning and sobbing.

'Your father wishes the name of your lover, Highness.'

'Why, he is your own son, Blunt Bahatur,' Shalina said. 'And could I have chosen better?'

There was a moment's terrible silence in the room. Peter felt his heart pound with shock.

'You have proof of this, Highness?' he growled at last.

'Would you call me a liar?'

'You are speaking of my son William?'

Shalina shrugged. 'He will confess it soon enough, as your torturers go to work on *him*.'

Shalina gazed at him for several seconds, then uttered a little laugh. 'You men are creatures, to be used. And I found one that satisfied me, and who was anxious to do so even though he was standing in as captain of the same guard which confines me.' She turned again to her barred window. 'Perhaps the Badshah will even allow me to leave this tower to watch him die. Will he do that, do you suppose? I should enjoy that. Perhaps I only seduced him for that reason.'

Blunt had come to the tower to kill, yet with repugnance at

the idea of destroying this lovely woman who had shared so much with Caroline. Now he realised that she was no longer a lovely woman. Perhaps she never had been. Perhaps Aurungzib was right about her character. Now Blunt only knew that her lust had destroyed his family. For even had he been willing to sacrifice his son to Aurungzib's terrible vengeance, that vengeance would surely now encompass all of the Blunts – as Aurungzib had sworn.

The dream of several generations all gone to waste through a young man's weakness, and a woman's careless, cruel lust.

He suddenly drew his sword. The torturers gave a startled exclamation, then threw the torches at him and rushed for the door. But Blunt sidestepped the flying flames, and both had died before they could even draw the bolts. Bibi followed a moment later, and the other maid screamed once as she too perished. Blood was spattered across the Princess's white sari. Yet he knew he had been merciful to all of them compared with the fate the Badshah would have decreed.

Wide-eyed, Shalina stared at him. 'Do you seek to save your son?' she asked. 'Do I not have other maids who summoned him to my chamber?'

Peter pondered, inhaling deeply.

'So what will you do?' she jibed.

'What I must,' he told her.

'And I?'

'I have your father's orders for your execution. Will you kneel?'

Shalina hesitated, then slowly gathered her sari from around her calves and knelt on the floor, her head bowed.

'Did you not even love my son in the least?' Blunt asked.

'I hated your son,' Shalina said. 'As I hate all men. You and my father most of all.'

Cleaning his blade on the Princess's sari, he locked the slaughter chamber carefully behind him. He was aware of many emotions, but too jumbled together to be identified.

At the foot of the stairs waited William with the guard squad. He had clearly heard news of what was afoot. Peter beckoned to his son.

'You have destroyed us,' he whispered, 'with your careless lechery.'

William stared wildly at his father.

'Now listen to me very carefully,' Peter continued. 'Tell the sergeant that you have been summoned before the Badshah on an urgent matter. Tell him that no one is to be admitted to the Princess's apartments until you return. I shall wait for you outside.'

William spoke at last. 'What have you done?'

'I have carried out my orders.'

'She would never have betrayed me.'

'You are a fool. To her you were but a plaything. Nor is she the only one knew your identity, so we have but a few hours. If you do not obey me now, we shall both be dangling on stakes within twenty-four hours – with our wives and children beside us. Now make haste!'

William having been sent off to fetch his wives and children, Blunt hastened to his own home, where he summoned all the women and children and told them they must leave within the hour. 'No one will question us before tomorrow.'

'What of Nasir, and Penelope?' Anne asked.

'I can only send them a message.'

Anne shivered, and tightened her cloak around her.

'We have no choice,' Blunt added.

They set out before midnight, a party of some twenty people.

There was also no doubt that the age of many of the party would prove a handicap: Anne was seventy-seven, Hilma and Butji only a few years younger, while Serena and Jintna were both in their late forties. On the other hand sixteen-year-old Richard would clearly be a tower of strength.

But he did not waste his time on such considerations as they rode south.

At dawn it became necessary to rest.

'I wonder you do not leave me behind,' Anne said. 'There is very little even Aurungzib can do to me, now. I'm an old woman.'

'We survive together or we die together,' Blunt told her firmly. But he knew they were not going to succeed. They made only twenty miles that day, and by the next morning their pursuers were in sight.

He stood with William and Peter on a slight rise to watch the cavalry of the Guard approach. Aurungzib had sent an entire regiment behind them.

'We have only two options,' Peter told them. 'Either to kill our women and then ride into our opponents and die like men. Or to surrender, and die like animals – hoping that our women will be spared.'

The two young men stared at him. That was too great a decision for them to make.

Nor could it be put to the women. Blunt gazed from face to face as he returned to their encampment. His mother Anne impassive; Serena a bundle of nerves, constantly tugging at her nose; Jintna as fatalistic as Anne; fourteen-year-old Elisabeth glancing from face to face in anxious fear; nine-year-old Joanna not truly able to grasp what was going on; ten-year-old Thomas full of martial excitement, and too young to understand what might be his fate. And then there was Caroline, her small face full of fight and determination.

There was no possibility of him driving his sword into that fervently beating heart.

'They are too close to us,' he told them. 'We have no choice but to surrender.'

'Surrender?' They were aghast.

'It is my doing,' William said. 'I will surrender.'

His wives burst into tears – not even knowing what it was he had done.

'The Badshah wishes us all,' Peter told him. 'You must remain here,' he told the women.

Caroline clutched his hand. 'Let me go with you.'

'They will come for you soon enough.'

To what was he condemning her? But she had to live to the last possible moment, and pray for a miracle. Aurungzib still depended upon the Company for his new weapons and munitions, so it might still be possible to save the women's lives.

Blunt and his two sons then rode out to meet the approaching horsemen, who were commanded by none other than Billim Abbas himself. At least that meant they would be not be ill treated before they regained Delhi.

Billim looked thoroughly miserable. 'You are under arrest, Blunt Bahatur.'

Peter nodded, and held out his sword.

'You and I have campaigned together too often,' Billim said. 'If you will give me your word not to use it, you may keep your weapon.'

Peter sheathed the tulwar. Richard and William did likewise.

'And our women?' Peter asked.

'They are to accompany you back to Delhi.'

The party was assembled, and moved off. Peter rode beside Billim.

'What news of my brother?'

'Why none, Blunt Bahatur.'

'And my sister?'

'There, too. Yet you understand that the Badshah seeks vengeance,' Billim said. 'On your son, certainly. He is to die most disagreeably.'

Peter nodded. 'And on me?'

'I would say that is also the case, for he is very angry. He regards you as having betrayed his friendship and his trust. It might be after all best to use your swords before you regain Delhi.'

'But ... if William and I do kill ourselves, what will become of our women, our families?'

'As I have told you, he has made no move against your brother or your sister, knowing as he does that they are innocent. Therefore I do not believe the Badshah will punish your women. You have not been in rebellion against him. You carried out his orders – and only fled in an attempt to save your son. I believe he will understand these things.'

That night Peter was allowed to share a tent with his wife.

'What will become of us?' Caroline asked.

'You must be very brave,' he told her. 'I shall endeavour to have you and my mother sent back to Bombay and thus to England. You must return to your parents there, and Thomas and Joanna will accompany you. I think I may even be able to save Richard, although I fear the Badshah will keep him in Hindustan.'

'But you cannot save yourself.'

'I'm afraid that is impossible.'

She was silent for some seconds. 'Will I have to watch?'

'No,' he promised her. 'It shall be done privily.'

Again she wept, but did not seem to understand what he meant.

The next morning Peter sought out William and told him what they must do that same night.

William swallowed. 'Is there no other way?'

'Not if we would save our women and children. This is our best chance of saving them. We must believe that, at least.'

They rode on mostly in silence, and Blunt thought of many things as the day wore on. The past, of course, and the fortunes of the Blunts. He did not suppose it was all about to come to an end. Aurungzib had a powerful belief in the faithfulness of the Blunts, and Peter was sure he *would* wish to keep Richard at hand. Perhaps Thomas as well.

Well, then, the future. He himself was still a young man. He had always supposed he would have some part to play in whatever happened following Aurungzib's death, even if he could not determine which of the heirs would succeed. Even more had he looked forward to watching his sons grow to manhood under his careful eye. But his eye had not been careful enough.

The sun was drooping towards the western horizon when Billim called a halt and camp was pitched. The Blunts sat around their fire to eat an evening meal, watched over by their guards.

Billim sat with them, and spoke of past campaigns. The meal was half finished when they heard the drumming of hooves. A moment later a tavachi galloped into the encampment and leapt from his horse.

Billim was on his feet.

'My lords,' the boy cried, 'we are in the midst of catastrophe.'

They stared at him in astonishment.

'The Badshah is dead. He suffered a seizure – and he died immediately.'

Peter and Billim glanced at each other, then Billim turned back to the messenger.

'What is happening in Delhi?'

'There is turmoil, sire. Messengers were sent off to Prince

Azam Shah in Lahore, but scarcely had they gone then Prince Bahadur Shah announced that *he* would rule. There has been no word as yet from Prince Kham Baksh.'

'Kham Baksh will certainly also take an independent position,' Blunt said.

'Then there will be civil war,' Billim muttered. 'Blunt Bahatur, the orders I was given regarding you ... since they were issued by Aurungzib himself, they no longer obtain.'

Peter and William had been reprieved on the very steps of the scaffold.

'I must return to Delhi with all haste.' Billim continued. 'Will you accompany me? Your sword would prove useful, on one side or the other.'

Blunt hesitated. The temptation was enormous. He knew he might succeed in re-establishing the Blunt fortunes, and thereby set Richard and Thomas on the road to success ...

But he knew there was no Akbar or Aurungzib, much less a Babur, now waiting to seize power. Just as he realised that the entire empire was rotten, waiting to fall apart.

'No, Billim,' he said finally. 'If you will set me free, I will continue on my way, with my family, to Bombay.'

Billim clasped his hand. 'I will certainly set you free, old friend. But you mean to leave Hindustan?'

Blunt smiled. 'I intend to remain here in Hindustan,' he said. 'But from now on I will serve my own people.'

Peter Blunt was correct in his estimate of the situation. Out of the civil war between the sons of Aurungzib, Bahadur Shah emerged victorious, and it was his descendants who ruled in Delhi for the next hundred and fifty years. But not one of them was a worthy successor to their ancestors; the substance of the race was gone.

During the half century following Aurungzib's death, the Persian adventurer Nadir Shah captured Delhi and carried off both the Peacock Throne and the Great Moghul diamond; then the resurgent Marathas fragmented southern India into a series of principalities; and finally the British and the French, through their East India Companies, began to take control of the entire subcontinent.

The victory of Robert Clive over a Franco-Indian army at

Plassey, exactly fifty years after Aurungzib died, left the British East India Company the supreme power in India. When, a century later, after the abortive rising against British rule known as the Indian Mutiny, the British Government deposed the last Moghul Emperor, Bahadur Shah II, they formally brought to an end the 331-year-rule of this most colourful of dynasties.

British rule lasted less than a century after that.